WITH LEGS WIDE SHUT

"You ever done what Special Warfare calls a 'suicide drop'?"

"No," Kendra said, wide-eyed as she pulled a parachute rig from the bulkhead. Another maneuver threw it hard against her. She clutched it and reached for a helmet. Long and repetitive training was all that let her run through the prep, as her brain was numb with fear. Again, she forced her knotting and trembling fingers to steady as they fumbled fasteners.

"Well, at least you've jumped before. You'll be going out the side door. I'll drop into a valley, pull the nose up and yaw left. Inertia will pull you out. 'Chute drogues on the way up, you swing twice and hit the trees. Everything goes right, they'll never see you. Anything goes wrong . . . but it shouldn't."

The door slid and latched open with a cold roar of slipstream, leaving her above a landscape tearing by in a blur.

"One last thing," he warned. "You don't have leg armor, so keep 'em crossed when you hit the trees or you risk tearing your femoral arteries. STAND IN THE DOOR! Or sit, in this case."

She was ripped out the door by the violent rotation, arms trailing. A distant clang of the static line link striking the fuselage was drowned out by the turbines. Deceleration caught her as the 'chute grabbed air. Blue sky turned dizzyingly to bright green trees, to blinding Io, to trees again, and she closed her legs tightly as those trees came up hard.

FREEHOLD

Michael Z. Williamson

FREEHOLD

This is a work of fiction. All the characters and events portrayed in this book are fictional, and any resemblance to real people or incidents is purely coincidental.

A Baen Books Original

Baen Publishing Enterprises
P.O. Box 1403
Riverdale, NY 10471
www.baen.com

ISBN: 0-7434-7179-2

Cover art by David Mattingly

First printing, January 2004

Distributed by Simon & Schuster
1230 Avenue of the Americas
New York, NY 10020

Production by Windhaven Press, Auburn, NH
Printed in the United States of America

To my parents:
We disagree on so many things,
but I am who I am because of you.

FREEHOLD

Chapter 1

"Adversity has the effect of eliciting talents, which
in prosperous circumstances would have lain
dormant."

—Quintus Horatius Flaccus

Sergeant Second Class Kendra Pacelli, UNPF, was
looking forward to finally finishing the admin from her
deployment to Mtali. The entire experience had been
unpleasant, from the tedious, cramped trip there in a
military transport, to the tedious, cramped trip *back*
in a military transport. In between, the stay had been
mostly boring, very aggravating, and exhausting when
it wasn't boring.

She'd been eager at first. The chance to visit another
planet, even one torn by war, she found exciting. Upon
arriving, they'd all been restricted to base, so she saw
nothing of the local culture. They were shipped through
the UN starport, and there were not even vendors of

1

local food to sample. Most of the other UN troops, predominantly from Earth, had insisted on not listening to "that raghead crap" music. She'd heard nothing but Earth pop for the entire six months.

Then the long-term troops had resented her for her trip's duration. They had eighteen-month rotations. It wasn't her fault, and she was there to help the Logistic Support Function, thus freeing someone else to go home early, but that didn't seem to matter. Apparently, they'd rather have stood the extra time than have her take a short tour.

There'd been a couple of missile attacks on the base while she was there. She'd been in an orbital station doing admin during one, and the shuttle simply waited until it was over to land. The other one was over before she realized it wasn't a drill, and the damage was negligible. She understood some areas had been pasted daily and had regular body counts, but she was nowhere near those places. She wasn't complaining, but the end result was that she had no war stories of any kind.

It had been typical logistics work; issuing, returning and accounting for gear and filing docs, except that the days were longer, the facilities nonexistent and the entertainment lacking. She wasn't a big fan of vid and the rec center's supply of books and games was slim. She also found few people who could play table games well. All in all, she might just as well have stayed home and not left her dorm.

She had received additional pay and got a tax incentive, which would mean more records-keeping in exchange to justify the tax return. The rest of the pay came at the cost of, naturally, more admin. Sitting at her carrel, she coded off on her travel itinerary, her waivers for tests and boards missed while deployed and the return of her issued combat equipment. She had been ordered not to open that unless attacked, which she'd found bothersome. The fact that to inspect her gear for safety was deemed wrong because it generated more admin seemed illogical. But then, it *was* the military.

The thing which she wished she'd put off but had waded through first, was the documentation and her personal statement on missing property. Her personal gear was all accounted for, but literal transport loads of gear had gone "missing" on Mtali. She was a stickler for procedure, so she had accounted for the fact that everything *she* issued had gotten where it was supposed to. The first sergeant had relayed to her secondhand that some clown was claiming that her attention to detail proved she was involved. "He's just digging. Relax," she'd been told.

She still felt nervous. Trucks, generators, weapons and tools didn't just walk off by themselves. Most required lift gear to move. A rapidly maturing and increasingly cynical part of her surmised that they were being sold by someone in system. Well, if they checked her bank accounts, they were all as she reported. She just wished they'd hurry up and do so and get done with it.

Her musing was interrupted when her phone rang. Not a military line at her carrel, but her personal phone. She dug it out of her purse, wondering who was calling.

"Pacelli," she answered.

"Hi, dear. Don't mention my name," the caller said. It was Tom Anderson, an old lover who was an MP. "We are getting all kinds of activity. Arrests are expected for Robinson, Bruder, Jacobs, Pacelli and several others. If those people are lucky, they are *off base right now*. They'll be in for a nasty surprise when they return."

"Why? What's up?" she asked, shocked beyond reason.

"Apparently, the government has found the parties responsible for the equipment that went missing during the Mtali mission. All those people are part of the conspiracy."

"I'm not part of any conspiracy," she protested in a whisper. "All I did was document what went walkies. That was at the general's request."

He continued as if he hadn't heard her protest. "What's important is that they are looking for those people. The way things look, they'd be lucky if they were missing, permanently. You know how the Department of Special Investigations can overreact. I just hope they don't come through the gate; I don't need any excitement right now. Anyway, the reason I called: you left some things at my place last night," he said, although she hadn't been there in weeks. "I put them *in the car*. Gotta run, we are about to start a gate exercise. Love you." *Click.*

Kendra hung up the phone, hesitated a half-second, then stood, grabbing a folder. She tried to be casual as she walked down the hall. A quick nervous glance didn't show any suited goons coming for her, but she had no doubt Tom was correct. There were horror stories of people being dragged in for even being "associated" with criminals. But where could she go?

Just before she reached the door, Janie came out of the back office. "Kendra, can you—"

"Sorry," Kendra replied, waving the folder, "I've gotta take care of this for the lieutenant right now." The old trick of looking busy had always seemed rather shallow before. It now had a whole new meaning. She stepped outside, whipped her hat on and tried to walk slowly to her car, as if she were running an errand. Unlocking it, she climbed in and discovered an overnight bag on the passenger seat. As she started the engine, she glanced in. Street clothes, socks, shoes, underwear and some cash cards. Tom must have used a security code to override her dorm room lock. She hoped that wasn't traceable, but he was good at such things. That had made her nervous, when she discovered he could crack codes and bypass records. Now she thanked Tom silently while backing out carefully. A wreck now would really be hell. Could this really be happening? She had to believe him, but it seemed so unreal.

The UN Bureau of Security was not known for its polite inquiries into alleged crimes. If they believed a person was involved with "improper activity" or "activity prejudicial to the public good," they proceeded to investigate thoroughly. The accused was held incommunicado, all assets seized and in-depth interviews conducted with the accused and any family or friends who might be involved. If they suspected any dissemblance, they could always revert to the clauses that gave them authority to hold the accused until they were satisfied. There were also numerous rarely enforced laws they could invoke to continue their efforts. The story was that they only used those tactics against someone they couldn't prosecute any other way, but Kendra had recently come to believe, in part due to vids Tom had shown her, that those tactics were unfair and designed to make the prosecutors look good, not do justice to the accused. She'd been creeped enough by his near-sedition to stop seeing him. There were enough antigovernment activists in America now without having to deal with out-and-out traitors.

It had a whole new feel now, she reflected briefly as she drove out of the logistics zone of the sprawling base. They thought *she* was guilty. Several tens of millions of marks worth of property had gone missing during the Mtali mission. She'd done the file search, at the request of the chain of command, to determine

how much. That was the total extent of her involvement. She knew she was innocent and they couldn't
prove otherwise . . . or could they? "The wicked flee
when no man pursueth" didn't apply when circumstances dictated that both guilty and innocent alike
should wisely flee for their lives. She shivered slightly.
Did she really want to leave? Wouldn't it be better to
trust in her innocence? Where could she go?

She aged ten years in the six blocks to the gate, then
relaxed very slightly when she saw Tom in the booth.
What is he getting himself into? she asked herself. The
traffic control outside the gate signaled a stop and she
aged ten more years. Behind her, she could see the
barricades rising and swallowed hard. That made it
rather permanent, she thought. She picked a route
north into Maryland and kept the car on manual. She
didn't know how long it would be before an override
signal got her. She'd have to lose the car. She had no
idea how, or where to go after that. Off planet, maybe?
The Orbitals were not as strict on ID, but fleeing
criminals were captured regularly. Outsystem? But
where? Ramadan was not friendly to unescorted
women, Novaja Rossia demanded strict qualifications
and background checks, Caledonia was a UN nation . . .

Counting the cash in her bag, she found a thousand
marks in three money cards and cash and a note
scrawled, *"All I can spare. Hate to see you get driven
like this. I disabled your override circuit, so don't use
auto. If you can, lie low for a few months, they may
sort this out. Still care about you."* It was unsigned.
She cried while driving and tried to think of a solution.

Her mind was whirling too hard for thought, but
she knew she'd need cash before they locked her
work and insurance number. Stopping at a rest area,
she picked a remote parking slot and changed,

hunched in the front seat. Wearing her uniform off base would not only be distinctive, it was also an invitation to be mugged and raped, especially for women. Once done, she pulled back onto the highway and found a suburban exit. She pulled into a plaza and used a bank terminal, then found another one a few blocks away. Six different transactions yielded every penny she had in the world, in small enough chunks that no single one would show up at UNRS immediately. As she made the last withdrawal, an idea occurred to her. It was insane, but there was no logical reason why it was impossible. The odds were such that no bookie would take the bet, but better than nothing, which was what she had now.

The Grainne colony had been independent for ten years now and had not only refused to join the UN, but had refused to go along with most of the common standards of ship registry, public health, public standards or even reciprocity of laws. *That* was the crucial bit. If she could make it there, they wouldn't extradite her. It was quite the rogue as nations went. It also reportedly had an excellent standard of living. As with many frontier worlds, there were not enough people for all jobs. A frontier colony was not the nicest environment for an urbanite like herself, but it would be safe until this resolved.

She gave one last searching thought to whether or not she should do it. The millions of marks at stake made her believe that scapegoats, bribes and various irregularities would be the end result of this. She was sophisticated enough to realize that being innocent would not protect her and being poor and of low rank would make her a doormat. This was a chance to wait things out. She reached for her phone, hesitated, then sought a public phone and looked up the address.

❖   ❖   ❖

In a suburb south of where Kendra had made her decision was the embassy of the Freehold of Grainne. It was an old twenty-third-century windowless block, surrounded by a wall and other, less blatant, security measures. In a spacious office on the top floor, an old discussion was being rehashed yet again.

Assistant for Policy Gunter Marx entered the office and informed Citizen Ambassador Janine Maartens of the Freehold of Grainne, "The UN is protesting our declaration of withdrawal again."

"Any new language?" was the bored return. Maartens' desk defied the advantages of electronic data. It was strewn with notes, official copies of documents, flash ram, memory cubes and assorted other items in archeological layers by age in a display that clashed with the spare blond paneling and carpet.

Marx said, "No. All the same as last year. John Abraham requests a meeting with you to discuss the perceived inequalities. He is sure we can find an agreeable solution."

"One that involves taxes, government interference, restrictions of our personal rights 'for the public good,' and a seven-year plan for the future, of course. Tell him I'm dead."

"Ma'am?"

She sat back and ran a hand through her graying waves of hair. "You know what I mean, Gun. My regards to Secretary Abraham and I'll call him at my earliest inconvenience. Right now I am dealing with major industrialists and billions of credits are at stake. I don't want to deal with an issue that should be seven years dead."

"Yes, ma'am," he agreed. He didn't envy her position and wondered again why he'd elected to throw himself into the bureaucratic rat maze. "Also: Warrant Leader McLaren says there is a car across the street, occupied by a young blond woman, that has been there for most of a div. She is watching the gate."

"Great. An obvious decoy. Any sign of the real threat?" the ambassador asked. The UN and several of its member nations loved to play spy games. Observers here, line taps there, always some kind of low-level harassment.

"Not yet. He says his people are ready, though," Marx confirmed. He'd made sure of that himself.

"They always are," she nodded. At least the espionage kept her security people alert. "Keep me informed. I have to smooth out some details between GM North America and GM Freehold. The UN Secretary of External Trade is the problem. Everyone else sees the advantages of the deal."

"Yes, ma'am."

Kendra became attentive as a truck pulled up to the gates. She started the motor and waited. Her plan was to pull through after the delivery of whatever cleared the entrance. Cautiously, she gave the motor a bit of rev to ensure it was working. It was, of course. She gasped her breath out in furious realization of how panicky she was. She hadn't realized she'd been holding it and didn't realize she was holding the next one. Watching the truck, she tried to judge distances and space while keeping an eye on traffic. There'd be an opening in the flow right after that red car in her mirror.

The gates were already sliding shut on their powered rails. She stomped the accelerator while swearing, yanked the wheel hard and pulled right behind the red vehicle while almost crashing into a pillar as she bounced inside the embassy grounds. She immediately had to brake to avoid the truck, which was stopped for inspection.

An armored guard leaped in front of her, pointing one of the brutal-looking weapons that the Grainne military used. He took a step sideways as she locked her car in park and barked orders that were clearly audible inside her little Mazda Jog as several other guards materialized from somewhere.

"Shut the motor off! Place your hands on top of the steering wheel! Reach over with your right hand and open the door!"

She moved her left hand to comply and he bellowed, "*Right* hand! Place it back on the wheel! Eyes front!" She did as he ordered, eyes nervously leaving the gun, guts knotted in fear, and saw movement out of the corner of her left eye. One of the other guards was crawling under the area swept by the door, in case of a boobytrap. He rose next to her, placing the gaping maw of his weapon against her kidney and fastened magnetic shackles firmly around her wrists. Grasping them, he pulled her around and out of her car, his rifle now under her breastbone. About ten meters from the vehicle they stopped. Her escort stepped back and slung his weapon as a woman with an explosion of red hair around her helmet stood in front of her. The woman's face was mostly hidden by a darkened visor, but her mouth was visible and totally emotionless. Her weapon was unwavering.

Kendra heard more orders from the first guard, who was behind her now. "Spread your legs wide. Wider. Place your hands on top of your head." She did so, feeling the shackles bite into her wrists. Her shoulders stretched back awkwardly.

She had expected to be searched by the woman, was surprised that the second male guard was approaching. He started at her head, mussing her hair, crushing the fabric of her collar while looking for small items, slid his hands down her back, over her hips, down each trouser leg and into the tops of her boots. He stood and walked around in front as the other two guards moved to keep him out of line of fire. He resumed his search. He pulled at her lips with gloved hands. He then felt along her sleeves and under her arms in a fashion that might have tickled had she not been so scared. He reached inside her shirt and felt the neckline again, then ran fingers along the contour of her bra and grabbed both her breasts. By the time she realized it was neither an intimate gesture nor an assault, but still part of a very thorough search, he had felt around her waistband and clutched at her crotch. He slid down her legs again and checked the fasteners of her boots. Finished at last, he stepped back.

Kendra said, "I need asylum. My name is—"

"Silence. You may see the ambassador later."

He unslung his weapon and all three guards moved back. She was directed inside, the three standing well clear and keeping their weapons on her. Not a word was spoken to her and Kendra didn't feel like offering anything. She was taken down a service elevator, marched in front of a door and stopped.

The woman approached this time and quickly unfastened every button, snap, zip and rip on Kendra's clothing. She stepped around behind Kendra, grabbed a leg and pulled off a boot and sock. She repeated the procedure from the other leg, then yanked her pants and underwear down together and pulled them off one foot at a time. Reaching up, she uncharged the shackles, whisked them away and pulled Kendra's arms down behind her. Shirt and bra were pulled off, leaving her naked. A wand ran over her, seeking anything dense, metallic or electronic, and while she expected it to be silent, she having nothing concealed, she was reassured that it didn't betray anything. Illogical, but her current situation had her scared beyond reason. "Bend over," she heard, and complied. There was the expected snap of a medical exam glove and cold but surprisingly gentle prodding, which she knew included a camera and another sensor. These people were thorough. She shivered despite herself. A door opened, and she was pushed gently but firmly into what was obviously a cell. The door closed with an ominous heavy click.

Kendra looked around, breathing again, and took stock of her environment. It was adequately warm, well lighted, and contained a stall shower, a toilet, a sink and a futon with a quilt. The whole room measured three meters square.

There was a security camera mounted in one corner. It was not even discreetly hidden. Kendra stared at it as it glared unblinkingly at her. Finally, she made an obscene gesture and ignored it. She needed to use the toilet, and the camera obviously wasn't going to be a gentleman. Or lady. Or polite machine.

Brooding and pacing would be totally unproductive, so she brooded and paced. She had no idea of the passage of time, and was wondering if this attempt at asylum was the right idea. So far, she had been asked no questions, given no opportunity to speak and had no clue what was going on.

Right idea or not, she had to play it out to the end. There was no possible way she could return now and be believed innocent.

After what seemed like hours, the door was opened. The redheaded woman was there alone, without armor. She still carried her rifle/grenade launcher. Her combat uniform, designed to be loose, was close in spots over firm muscles. She motioned slightly with the muzzle and said, "This way. You can see the ambassador now." Her voice was amazingly well modulated and pleasant.

Kendra walked out, still naked, preceding her guard. She was directed when to turn and quickly realized how large the building was. She passed a man in one of the corridors, who nodded disinterestedly. She flushed crimson. The second man they passed swapped greetings with the guard and Kendra wished for a swift end to her ordeal. After several minutes, she was shown into a well-lighted office with large windows. The woman behind the desk stood, nodded briefly at Kendra and said, "Romar, please get a robe for our guest. There's one in my suite." The guard snapped to and left.

Turning back, the ambassador continued, "Please accept my apologies. Well-disciplined guards, but not overly familiar with Earth customs. Our climate encourages casual nudity, but I'm sure you're not used to it. She'll be back momentarily. Coffee?"

"Yes, please," Kendra nodded, shifting her hands around to keep herself covered. While the ambassador poured, the guard knocked, stepped in, handed Kendra a robe and moved unobtrusively into the corner. Donning the garment, Kendra felt much more comfortable.

The ambassador spoke again. "I am Citizen Ambassador Janine Maartens of the Freehold of Grainne. You are Sergeant Second Class Kendra Anne Pacelli of the UN Peace Force, wanted for embezzlement and pictured on all the news loads. I am recording. Please tell me briefly why in the name of God and Goddess you are in our embassy?"

"I need asylum," Kendra began. "I was—"

Maartens interrupted with, "We do not grant asylum to crimin—"

"I DIDN'T DO IT!" Kendra shouted her down. "I knew nothing about it until this morning when the MPs tried to grab me. I have little idea what is going on, but I know they need me as a scapegoat. General Robinson probably has me rigged to take the fall as part of his cutout. My only way out is to get off Earth."

Sitting down, Maartens chewed on a pen. "Tell me the rest of it," she demanded while gesturing at another chair.

Sitting also, Kendra breathed deep and said, "I was assigned to the Forty-Third Logistics Support Function's detachment during the Mtali Mission. The general and Colonel Bruder were very concerned with our operation. Stuff was missing by the truckload on a daily basis and they made us keep track of it. No one knows where the stuff was going, so there had to be inside help. They were probably selling it to the rebels is my guess. This is all deduction in the last four hours. Then, I assumed the problem was being investigated. Eight a.m. today, the MPs were going to drag me off for questioning. I saw where things were going, thanks to a friend of mine. I left the base and drove around until I figured out that of all colony worlds, you could probably help me."

"We are not a colony anymore, Sergeant," Maartens said coldly, then thought hard. Colonel Richard, the Freehold unit commander from the Mtali mission, had made similar deductions regarding the UN forces logistics system. Pacelli's story was probably true. Perhaps the military would be interested in her information. Citizen Maartens would have to decide that on her own. Unlike a national ambassador on Earth, she could not call for advice; advice was thirty-four light years away and any question would take at least two days for a response, to allow a message to be relayed through the jump point on the next ship. If it had to be sent physically to reduce the risk of interception, it would take at least twenty days each way.

The best approach was a firm one, see how the

situation developed, Maartens decided. "I'll have to check all angles of your story. You may stay in the meantime." Her voice was grudging but not hostile.

Heaving a huge sigh and slumping from released tension, Kendra replied, "Thank you, ma'am."

"You're welcome. There are conditions. Number one, if you are a spy, you'll disappear. Two, whether or not you are guilty, if the evidence points that way, you'll be handed over to UNPF. I can't risk an incident without solid substance to back it up. Relationships are critical and delicate right now; they always are. If you check out as legitimate, I'll help you arrange travel to the Freehold. It won't be cheap and you'll have to pay for it. We don't have budgets for such things."

"I have some cash. Not a lot."

"We can acquire any assets that haven't been seized, and make it untraceable. Our technicians will expect a share, however."

"Ma'am?" Kendra asked.

Sighing, Maartens explained, "The Freehold is a completely neutral nation with a tiny government. We don't budget for refugees, publicity, tourism or any of a hundred other things you take for granted. We can't do anything officially, so this will have to be done clandestinely. If our staff are to convert your assets to cash or pull funds from your accounts, they'll be doing it on their own time and with their personal gear at some small but real risk. For that, they expect to be paid."

"I have what I came here with," Kendra said, scared again.

"Then with your permission, we can move your car as parts. This will make it harder to trace you, and gain you some more funds."

Kendra thought for a moment only and agreed.

"Fine. I'm afraid we must keep you under guard for the time being." Maartens waved and the guard approached. "Corporal Romar," she said, "you are to accompany Sergeant Pacelli. She has free access to unrestricted areas, but only under escort. Find her secure quarters in the guest wing tonight. Keep me informed of anything relevant. She is not to leave."

"Yes, ma'am," the young woman replied. Turning to Kendra she said, "Please come with me, Sergeant."

Kendra stepped into the hall. After the door was closed, Romar asked, "Where do you wish to go, Sergeant?"

"I . . . don't know," Kendra replied. "I'd like to get some clothes and some lunch, if possible."

"Certainly. Would you like a shower, too?"

Kendra realized how stressed and exhausted she was. It had been less than six hours since her ordeal started, but seemed like a week. She needed a shower, both to wash away cold, clammy sweat and to relax. "Please," she said. "And call me Kendra."

"Okay. Follow me, Kendra. And you can call me Jelsie, since it doesn't appear I'll have to shoot you anytime soon." There was a disturbing dryness to the joke.

They wound up at what apparently were Romar's quarters. The room was small but well appointed and had a fantastic comm system. "Shower's in there," Kendra was told, as the woman pointed through a door. "I'll be next, so don't take too long."

Kendra gratefully made use of very luxurious facilities, borrowed soap and shampoo and was surprised to find her bag waiting when she got out. All ID had been removed, but her clothes and personal items were intact. She picked casual clothes, dressed and entered the room.

Jelsie was sprawled in a chair, watching a news load.

"You're on vid again," she said. "What evidence are they basing all this on?"

"I belong to the same unit as those responsible. And I deal with logistics," Kendra quipped.

"I can see that. You have a felon's eyes. I'm about to shower. My orders are to keep you secure. You can sit in here and we'll talk through the door while I do, but I have to cuff you to the doorknob. Otherwise, I lock you in a guest room and come back for you. Sorry, but that's as much leeway as I have."

"I guess so," Kendra replied. The Freeholders apparently took security a lot more seriously than the UN forces. Romar ordered her to sit in the corner and to not move without permission. The cuff was firm on her wrist and she said so.

"It'll loosen up with wear," Romar joked with a friendly grin, but loosened it slightly.

Kendra watched as her guard stripped and headed into the bathroom, an action reinforcing that nudity was a casual thing for her. Romar's skin was flawless, hairless except for the flaming waves on her head and matching eyebrows, and rippled with heavy muscles. Kendra asked, and found out that she spent almost three hours a day in the gym. She also recalled that their gravity was a bit more vigorous than Earth's. Remembering a brief encounter with the Freehold 3rd Mobile Assault Regiment's staff on Mtali, Kendra decided she never wanted to fight with them. They seemed to regard their military service as a religious duty. Romar even kept a pistol with her in the shower. "I know you won't try to escape, considering your circumstances," Romar's shout echoed from the tiled room as she lathered her rich red hair, leaning out of the stall to make eye contact. "But I'd look pretty stupid if you got away. It's a rough duty model anyway."

Kendra was shown to a dining hall that was again

small but luxurious. She grabbed some sandwiches and a bowl of soup, which she found too spicy. The sandwiches had a lot of mustard and peppercorns, but she found them manageable. Once she got past the heat, they were actually quite tasty.

Jelsie showed her around briefly. The compound had a gym, small theater and a day room that included a decent-sized pool and a long, rectangular hot tub, which held an older man and an Asian woman and had room for several more. They waved at Romar in passing and resumed talking and drinking. "I'm off duty now," Romar told her, "except for my responsibility regarding you. If you don't mind, I'm suggesting a plunge."

"I don't mind," Kendra said. "I'll just sit and watch vid."

"Why? You're welcome to join us."

"I don't have anything to wear."

"Sorry. That's a problem here, isn't it?" Jelsie said, peeling out of her uniform. "Well, if you change your mind, feel free. Sit on that side," she gestured, "so I have you in plain sight."

Kendra watched vid halfheartedly. More people wandered in and part of her mind deduced it was a shift change of some kind. They looked over and saw the depression emanating from her, but decided not to interfere. She was grateful for their discretion, but made no outward sign. Being properly morose took work.

Ten minutes later, her face was flashed on the screen. At least it wasn't mainstream news, only a specialty channel on political matters. Hopefully her parents wouldn't see this immediately. The announcer gave a fairly accurate description up to the point where he claimed she was armed and dangerous and had overpowered Sergeant Janie Woods, then

attempted to run over Sergeant Tom Anderson as she
fled the base "Just seconds ahead of the Military
Police." Kendra snapped it off viciously and strode
over to the tub, which now held six. She snatched
off her tunic, almost ripping it, and jumped in in her
underwear. The water was scalding, and shocked her
out of her daze.

"You okay?" Jelsie asked, looking concerned.

"No." After a few seconds of silence, Kendra continued, "I'm supposed to have attacked two of my
friends as I left. They're probably being interrogated."

"Goddess. That's a pretty slimy trick to pull."

"This isn't going to work," Kendra said, shaking her
head sadly. "I need to go back. If they have Tom, it
means either they retrieved the phone call or they think
it suspicious that I got out when I did. And Janie didn't
do anything. They might wind up dead because of me."

"You won't change that by going back," an older man
said. Kendra recognized him as one of the two who'd
been here when she and Jelsie arrived. She looked at
him in curiosity.

"Walter Andropolous," he introduced himself. He
was about forty, very lean with near black skin and
had a wire braided through the entire length of his
left ear. "I'm the intelligence analyst here and I used
to be in military intelligence. If they have your
friends, it's to make you come back. You do and
they'll rope them in too. If you stay, they have nothing to go on and might let them go."

"Do you know what they do to people when they
interrogate them?" Kendra asked, teary-eyed.

"In disgusting detail," Andropolous assured her.
"And you won't help them by going back. Your
friend Tom risked his life to cover for you, presumably because he believes you're innocent. Your
coming here took an equal amount of guts. If you

skip, you'll be wasting both of you, because it'll be assumed you're guilty, and I know how your investigators will proceed with that assumption. The best thing for you to do is have a drink," he suggested while handing her a glass, "and display some more of that courage by not wasting your friends' sacrifices."

Kendra gulped at the glass as Jelsie placed a hand on her shoulder.

Three hours later, soddenly drunk, Kendra was helped out of the pool by Andropolous and Romar. They assembled her clothes and half carried her to an elevator. Kendra allowed herself to be led into a small suite. The other two put her on the bed, then took seats across the room.

Kendra woke bleary eyed and glanced at the clock. It gave both Freehold and Earth time, claiming it was 0430. At twenty-five, she was barely old enough to drink and had never had a hangover before. She decided that everything she'd heard about them was hype and propaganda designed to entice people. Her head *hurt*. So did her stomach. Things were spinning very eerily.

Jelsie looked up from the screen she was reading, came over and handed Kendra an effervescent glass of orange stuff. "Drink this," she said.

"Thank you, no," Kendra replied. "I just want to lie here and regret it."

"It wasn't a request," Jelsie insisted, hoisting her upright with one hand. The room spun again and Kendra decided to comply. It tasted okay and did seem to settle her stomach.

"Didn't you sleep?" Kendra asked, her brain finally starting to track.

"No. I didn't want to lock you in and leave you

alone, so I stayed. That requires me to leave my hardware outside and cuff you to the bed or stay awake. I prefer to stay awake."

"You didn't have to do that for me," Kendra said. These people were strange. Compassionate and warmly friendly, but utterly unforgiving in their security.

"I know." Jelsie sat back down and asked, "Feeling better?"

"A little," Kendra agreed. Her memory was starting to fill in some gaps. Remembering some snippets of conversation, she asked, "Was whatsisname interrogating me last night?"

Considering for a moment, Jelsie said, "I don't think it's a security breach to say 'yes.'"

"And what did he find out?" Kendra prodded.

"I have no idea. Obviously he doesn't think you're a spy or you wouldn't have woken up," Jelsie explained.

"That's a pretty cold-blooded trick," Kendra commented.

"Yes," Jelsie nodded. "We could have done what the UN agents do and tied you to a chair, beaten you senseless, injected you with drugs and left you in a flophouse afterwards."

Kendra winced as she thought about Janie and Tom.

"Sorry," Jelsie said, sounding very sincere.

Chapter 2

"All changes, even the most longed for, have their melancholy; for what we leave behind us is a part of ourselves; we must die to one life before we can enter another."

—Anatole France

Kendra was in the embassy ten days, slowly going insane. She played interface games until disoriented from the feedback, found herself unable to concentrate on vid or books and got angry at the tedium of doing nothing. After three days, she spent some money she couldn't spare to have one of the Freehold technicians hook up a phone patch with a shift for her voice. He assured her it was untraceable and she decided it must be; the embassy didn't need the complications it would bring if her presence were discovered.

Her parents' lines had to be monitored, so there was no way to call them. She tried Janie's personal number first. No answer. Her own duty number was answered by Lieutenant Moy. Kendra disconnected without a sound. She called Tom's personal line.

"Hello?" she heard a harsh, unkind voice ask. It was not Tom's voice. She mumbled and disconnected. She realized now that she had, in fact, burned all her bridges.

On the seventh day, Kendra was taken to see Ambassador Maartens again. This time, Jelsie acted more like an escort than a guard. She left Kendra at the door and departed with a smile and nod. Inside the ambassador's office she was invited to sit down and Maartens said, "If you are still serious, we can have you out of here in three days."

"I am," Kendra said. Everything suddenly took on an icy clarity. She realized she wouldn't see Earth again for a long time, if ever.

"Okay. Here's how it looks. One of our less reputable personnel, coincidentally from logistics," Maartens said with an ironic smile, "managed to part out your car for about ten thousand. You have slightly less than a thousand in cash. The staff threatened me with mutiny if I charged you for your stay here, which we ordinarily do, so there's no boarding bill. They also took up a collection of fifteen hundred. I don't know how you feel about charity, but I advise you to take it. Our chief of security was extremely impressed by the courage you displayed and the speed with which you acted. In his opinion, you probably would have been snatched the next time you stopped for any purchase. He passed the hat for you himself. From sources I am not at liberty to discuss, there is a grant of four thousand available. So, you have roughly sixteen-five in assets.

"Now, there's a Freehold registry commercial

transport departing in three days. It's an Earth crew, but the ship is registered out of Station Ceileidh in Freehold space because we have less bureaucracy. The crew doesn't know who you are and might try to turn you in for the reward if they ID you. We'll get you aboard and manage the adminwork.

"After that, you are going to pretend to be sick for twelve days. Your meals will be delivered and you'll stay in your cabin. That's not too unusual; lots of travelers do that, anyway. We'll also give you additional cover. Once in Freehold space, you're safe. You'll be met at Station Ceileidh and transferred insystem.

"Transit fee is fifty thousand. Residency fee for planetside is five hundred. I believe your best chances are in Jefferson. Local residency fee there is one hundred. That's fifty thousand, six hundred total. You need thirty-four-four."

"I don't have it," Kendra said with a grin as a façade.

"Of course not," Maartens agreed. Her expression was not discouraging and it was clear she had an idea. She continued, "So the problem is raising it. Which is no problem at all. Now, let me explain this before you say anything.

"We have a system known as indenturing, but it's not the historical system you may be thinking of. A Citizen will be assigned to your case, and you pay a fee to the government for his service. He will arrange for you to find employment and a payment will be deducted from your wages. You are free to change jobs or make other arrangements for payment. You are responsible for your own lodging and food, so you are not going to be assuming a spiraling debt. I'm sure you'll have no trouble locating work in a city like Jefferson."

It took Kendra a few moments to sort through the

statement. She was only peripherally aware from her schooling that indenturing had existed, but its context was clear. The rest was plain enough after some thought.

"I don't have a lot of other options, do I?" she asked rhetorically.

"No, not really," Maartens said. "But you've come this far. Otherwise, we'll give you your assets and slip you out the gate late tonight. Your presence is potentially very embarrassing to us."

"I'm sorry to be a burden."

"Has anyone complained? Look, lady," Maartens said, her face softening, "You are about to enter a system that's totally out of your experience. It's bound to be a shock. We're trying to be honest and give you as much help as we can. If you're willing, we'll get you to a new home. If not, we need to protect ourselves."

"Well," Kendra said, "I came here to get away, so I suppose I should finish the job."

Nodding, Maartens said, "I'll get to work."

The vertol was sitting on the roof of the main embassy building. Standing near it, Kendra was seeing the suburbs of Washington from a completely different angle. There were still a few details to take care of, so she took the chance to look around. The old city really was pretty, especially when seen through the murky morning haze.

"Hey!" Kendra head the yell subliminally over the howl of the aircraft and turned to see Jelsie come up the stairs. She waved. A few seconds later, the two of them were hunched over, trying to hear over the whipping wind and the roar of turbines.

"You need some candy money," Jelsie said, handing her a palm-sized folder of Freehold currency.

Kendra pushed it away. "Thanks, but I can't take any more. You've been so generous already."

Jelsie grabbed her with powerful arms, stuffed the money into her chest pocket and said, "Then take it as a 'thank you' for not making me shoot you. You've got a great attitude for back home. You'll be fine. I'll be back in about a year and I plan to look you up. Pay me then, if you wish."

Smiling, Kendra said, "I'll do that. Thanks again."

"Sure. You owe me. We have a saying in Freehold Military Forces. 'Friends help you move. Real friends help you move *bodies*.' Next time I have a mysterious corpse, I'll be calling."

Tears leaking, Kendra promised, "I'll be there." She hugged the shorter woman, was almost crushed back, and turned quickly. She climbed in through the vertol's broad hatch and waited. It was a basic transport craft, not a diplomatic courier with appointments, and it was loud and stark.

Two men joined her, personnel rotating home, and the hatch slammed as the craft lifted smoothly and angled toward the south. She spent the flight nervously rubbing the small scar on her hand, where her implant ID had been removed. The chip was used to locate people during emergencies. It was also used to locate criminals. Once out of the embassy's heavy shielding, it would have been an immediate giveaway, as there was an open warrant out for her arrest now and they would be looking for the trace.

The flight was smooth, brief according to her watch no matter how subjectively long it seemed to be and there was no interference after they landed. She was getting away clean, so far. With a hundred kilometers down, she had only thirty-four light years to go until she'd be safe in the Iota Persei system.

✧   ✧   ✧

Kendra and the two embassy personnel simply walked through the scanners at Kennedy Spaceport. She was wearing a hat, had her hair darkened and tucked into her collar and her skin slightly darkened with a nano. She reminded herself to slouch a little. Slouching was very un-Freeholder, but it disguised her height. By Earth standards she was tall; by Freehold standards she towered over people. Taking a cue from the others, she flashed her diplomatic pass at the guard. Unlike the others, she was sweating.

She needn't have worried. The guard gave the brilliantly forged document the most cursory of glances, nodded imperceptibly and turned back to his vid. No one paid much attention to diplomatic personnel, she realized. Certainly not to determine if they might be administrative criminals trying to flee the system. Kendra almost felt insulted on behalf of the specialist who'd doctored the pass. She grinned inwardly at the thought of walking back and *demanding* that the guard examine it in detail. It kept her spirits up as they entered the shuttle and took couches. She had no trouble with the familiar safety harnesses, having done this before only a few months previously. She adjusted the lumbar support, angled the neck pads for comfort and nodded briefly to the attendant, who glanced over to ensure everything was secure and moved on without a word.

By prearranged plan, Kendra was feigning a sore throat, ostensibly from shouting at a concert. She rasped some favorable comments in a whisper. The two men with her did most of the talking, both to her and to each other. They kept a cheerful conversation going, interspersed occasionally with comments about going home, until the final count before lift.

The ride was familiar. Three gees tapered off slowly as they headed into low orbit. Kendra found herself undisturbed by microgravity. She fell asleep, relaxed by the condition, even though she was not out of danger yet. One of her escorts nudged her awake as they docked with the station.

A small, rather ugly tug took them to the *Shamaya*. She wondered about the name. Some person of historical significance? The ship was old but sturdy and smelled adequately clean as she swam through. The three of them were given cabins in the same passage and Kendra relaxed considerably as the klaxon sounded and thrust began with gentle gees, building to slightly more than Earth standard as they headed out. It would be her second and quite possibly last trip out of the Solar System.

As she placed her meager possessions on the lone rack in one outer corner of the pie-shaped cabin, there was a knock at the door. "Yes?" she rasped.

"It's me," Kevin Sanchez said, sticking his head in. The embassy had listed him as a computer technician, but Kendra felt sure he was an electronic spy. He was the most normal looking, by Earth standards, of the personnel she'd met, with short blond hair and brown eyes and no exotic coloring, jewelry or tattoos. "Thought you should know," he said, "that there isn't likely to be any trouble. I've met the crew of this ship before. The captain-owner and his family are most of the crew. They maintain Earth citizenship because it makes smuggling, excuse me, *trading*, much easier. They don't have to worry about some of the bonding fees. They are good mercenary Freeholders at heart, probably haven't seen you on any loads and wouldn't care if they did. The reward would interest them a little, but they wouldn't want the Freehold Military Forces angry with them. Keep in mind, however, that there are at least six crew of unknown loyalties who might jump at it. So don't sweat, but don't flaunt either."

"Got it. Thanks, Kev," she acknowledged, feeling greatly relaxed.

Kendra woke immobilized, stared at the grins on her captors' faces and tugged at her restraints. Nothing moved, and one of the special investigators stepped forward. He pulled his arm back, prepared to deliver a vicious backhand.

Yelping, she woke for real and thrashed, getting tangled in the bedclothes. Her breath was ragged, the sheets soaked with sweat. Eight days of grinding tedium punctuated by eight nights of terror. She rolled out of bed, stood and walked to the lavatory to rinse her mouth. She stared into the mirror at her sunken eyes. *Four more days,* she told herself.

Sleep would be a long time returning, so she sat up and turned on the cabin comm to find something to do. None of the thirty-odd channels she flipped through had any appeal, although she did spend a few minutes listening to the traffic between the *Shamaya*'s bridge crew and engineering, which was interspersed with jibes at each other and at other ships in the queue of tonnage heading for Sol System Jump Point Six, all bound for Grainne, then perhaps elsewhere.

She decided to do a bit more research on what was to be her new home and pulled up the Freehold's Constitution again. It was a bizarrely short document and effectively denied any legislative power to the government. The "Residency fee" she was paying was a head tax, but one so low as to be negligible. None of it made any sense to her. It almost seemed as if there was no government. She wondered again if she really knew what she was doing and switched over to an atlas.

Grainne had one large sprawling continent writhing from southeast to northwest around two-thirds of the planet. There were a couple of continental islands and several archipelagos of smaller masses. The climate was roughly like Earth's, but that "roughly" was deceptive—with smaller oceans, greater solar influx and a longer year, it had seasons that swung the temperate zone from the Minnesota-like winters she was familiar with, to scorching summers akin to those in the American Southwest.

She tackled the business analysis for the nth time and was confused in seconds, as she had been every time before. Nothing about it was comprehensible. It was an absolute anarchy in the economic sense, from her perspective. She sighed and shut everything down, called out the lights and selected some soft dance music to ease her back to sleep. It was some time before her thoughts drifted into the warm comforting blanket of unconsciousness.

The *Shamaya's* klaxon alerted everyone to the impending point jump. Kendra actually relaxed, knowing that most of her ordeal was over. The lights flickered once, her stomach turned upside down and they were in the Freehold system. In less than an hour, they were trimming into an orbit around Station Ceileidh, the roughly cylindrical rock that was the business, industrial and government office for Jump Point One. She was led into an office and someone drew blood from her forearm. They implanted a nano tracer in her thigh, handed her a flash ram bearing a label with her name and directed her toward a gate. She loped in the low centripetal gee of the station and she was shortly aboard an in-system craft bound for Grainne proper. It would be another ten days of boredom before they arrived.

This shuttle, the *Torchy*, was new, built with travelers in mind, and was typical of those run by any large line. She took another small stateroom, strapped down and waited for launch. She was still nervous, but it was a different kind of nervous. The UN authorities couldn't touch her now, but she was still alone and without connections or friends. It felt almost like stage fright.

Chapter 3

"If a man neglects to enforce his rights, he cannot complain if, after a while, the law follows his example."

—Oliver Wendell Holmes

It was amazing how fast things were accomplished in a society run by commercial concerns and not much else. The *Torchy*, which had brought her this far, docked at a tether. They swam through into a shuttle cabin and strapped in. *Torchy* cut loose and they were already headed for the surface, but without thrust. She asked for an explanation.

Kevin replied, "Let me think how to sum it up briefly . . . wow . . . okay, let me try this: It's called a 'skywheel.' It's two tethers extending outward from their mutual center of mass. The whole assemblage cartwheels from high orbit to almost ground level, I think about twenty kilometers. Cargo or shuttles are attached to the ends and release at the far end either near ground, near surface rotation speed of the planet, or in orbit at high velocity to ship out. Where it's released determines the vector outward. Does that make sense?" She nodded and he continued, "We pop things up to the receivers on magnetic launchers or by direct thrust, since we don't have enough launchers yet. It's cheap to operate, minimizes pollution and easy to schedule trips without waiting for launch windows. There are six huge ones throughout the system, rotating in free space. We use them to ship industrial products around the Halo. There aren't any in Sol System, because the UN safety bureaucrats are convinced they're dangerous. They're worried about one breaking and crashing, but we've never had a problem. The theoretical strength is about ten times the actual load usage."

Kendra had heard of the concept, but hadn't realized any were in use. She nodded politely and stared in terrified fascination at the view. Safe, certainly, but what if one *did* crash from accident or malice? How large a footprint would it wipe out on the planet? Several hundred kilometers? At what velocity? Ten thousand kilometers per hour? More?

The starscape moved rapidly up, the planet rose at an appalling rate. After a while, the direction had noticeably changed and the rate appeared to have diminished. There was a clank as the shuttle detached and the rest of the ride was a straightforward touchdown. They rolled out on a long runway bleached white in the Sun—or rather, Iota Persei, she reminded herself—and she squinted against the glare. Shortly, they pulled up to a terminal.

The hatch opened and more glaring daylight streamed in, along with local air. Kendra waited for the crowd to thin and stood, wobbling. She made her way forward, gripping couchbacks for support and squinted

again as she entered the tube. Light from Iota Persei
poured through the clear roof. It was 2.3 times as
bright as the Sun, she recalled, although that was
diminished somewhat by the greater distance Grainne
was from Iota, 1.5AU. It didn't seem that much
brighter, but had a glare at the blue end of the spectrum that hurt her eyes, despite polarization.

At the exit to the terminal, she suddenly felt dizzy.
Grabbing a rail for support, she remembered Kevin
warning her about the atmospheric pressure—about
seventy percent of Earth's, with only eighty percent of
the oxygen. She was hyperventilating, or not getting
enough, or something, and she held her breath for a
moment to regain her equilibrium. Kevin took her arm
to guide her as they walked through the tunnel.

She entered the terminal and looked around. She'd
had no idea what to expect and had been prepared for
rough hardpan dirt or facilities like a second-tier city
would have on a commercial route. Instead, Jefferson
Starport was small, but as modern as anything in an
Earth national or regional capital. All construction was
new, everything was so clean it gleamed, and she was
impressed. Perhaps things would be better than she'd
expected.

The exit was to her left and down a level, according
to glowing signs placed in easy view. She followed Kevin
to a slideway and took it. Several other passengers
merged from other orbital, ballistic and local flights along
with them, and she studied them while Kevin pulled out
a phone and punched a button. "Sergeant Sanchez," he
announced into it. "We're here. Sure. Out."

The travelers' modes of dress didn't appear to follow
any real style. She very carefully kept her eyes averted
from a man in a backless breechcloth and then had to
look away again from a pubescent girl who was topless.
Some wore full-length robes, several light-colored

coveralls and two what she considered normal business dress. The spaceport apparently had tremendous security, as she could see uniforms in every direction. Three people near her were apparently plainclothes officers and were wearing guns.

Then she realized that undercover officers wouldn't display guns. Also, all three people carried different guns, rather than a standard issue type, and the holsters were garishly decorated. She recalled the embassy, where guards and staff walked around armed. Apparently, the whole society was like that. As this thought worked through her brain, she realized that there were other people armed, also.

My God! They let people swing guns around the fucking spaceport!? Sweat broke out all over her and she kept looking around nervously. She calmed a little when she realized that the soldiers present carried the same rifles she'd seen up close a few days before and in use on Mtali and had them loaded. Then she thought about what a firefight inside the terminal would look like and quickened her pace to get outside.

Outside, under a large concrete awning, she found a place near a pillar at Kevin's suggestion, dropped her bag, which felt much more than eighteen percent heavier in the local gee field, and waited. She wanted to sit and rest her feet, which were hurting already, but there wasn't a seat nearby. She watched the traffic, vehicles brighter and more garish than anything on Earth and presently, one of them pulled up next to her. Kevin said, "I think that's your ride."

A man climbed out the driver's door, tall, olive skin tanned almost black, straight black hair with gray at the temples, slender but rippling with muscle like a panther. "Kendra Pacelli?" he asked.

"Uh, yes," Kendra agreed. He motioned and she opened the passenger door and sank into a seat built for fast maneuvers. The driver continued, "Pleased to meet you, Kendra. I'm Citizen Hernandez and I'll be handling your case. How was the trip?"

"Scary. I don't know when I'll feel safe again," she admitted.

"We'll see what we can do. I should warn you that society is very different here. People will be happy to help you, but you must ask. Privacy is very important and you'll be left alone unless you do ask. I have arranged a meeting with Calan Employment, to find you work, and I'm working on housing. I'll point out a few landmarks as we head there. My office is within walking distance of his and I'll see you afterwards." He turned to Kevin and nodded acknowledgment. "Thank you, Sergeant," he said and made a notation in Kevin's comm. Kevin nodded at him, waved at Kendra, turned and left as Hernandez shut her door and eased back into the driver's seat.

They were airborne in seconds, diving into traffic flow, and Hernandez steered manually. They were passed often, as he flew slow enough to give her a tour. He gave her a few details as they flew. Jefferson was what she would call a small town, but with a downtown. Population was only about two million, and this was the third-largest city on the planet, theoretically the capital. That simply meant that the Citizen's Council Building was here, he explained.

"Not that we ever use it, other than on holidays," Hernandez told her. "We hold all conferences by vidlink." The building was pretty, though. It was styled a bit like an Egyptian temple. She couldn't say much for the view, in a sharp bank to her side of the car, with nothing between her and the ground except a few hundred meters of empty air.

She'd had no idea what to expect and had provincially assumed that Earth had a monopoly on modernity. The flight gave lie to that theory. Buildings towered hundreds of meters above their flight level, ranging from straight older towers to modern sculpted designs. They gleamed in ivory, gold, copper and less familiar colors. It was much like an equivalent Earth city. She recalled a joke she'd heard with the punchline, "Grainne? What planet is that on?" It seemed silly in this context.

The skyway was insane, most vehicles apparently on manual, most flown at high speed and with lots of dodging and weaving. They took it on a straight path downtown and braked hard before landing on a ramp. The streets below were nightmarish. While well laid, well paved and logically designed, it appeared that traffic laws were optional. Reckless driving was apparently the norm. Kendra just hoped it was also "wreckless." Hernandez darted in and out of traffic and finally pulled in next to an older and typical office block. Kendra relaxed her white-knuckle grip and was shown up to a second-floor suite.

"I'm Tom Calan," the only person present told her, shaking hands. "Have a seat and let's see what we can find." She took one of two client seats, looked around the spare but neat office and turned back to look at her hosts.

Hernandez nodded a greeting to Calan and left, saying to Kendra, "Call me if there's any trouble. I'll see you later."

Kendra sat at a console and answered the questionnaire displayed, asking Calan for elucidations where necessary. Name: Kendra Anne Pacelli. Address: To Be Determined. Resident Number: TBD. Height: 185 centimeters. Mass: 73 Kilos. Hair: Blond. Eyes: Blue. (Capture pic). Physical

Limitations: 25 Kilos max lifting. Skills and Training: General Bachelors, North America Public Education System. Logistics Specialist, UN Peace Force. Previous occupations, in detail: She listed her work in the 43rd Logistics Support Function.

"That's it," she said when finished.

Calan pulled it to his screen and read. Then he frowned. "There isn't a lot here to work with," he said, doubtfully.

"I realize there may not be anything in inventory or a related area," Kendra acknowledged. "But I can do loading, stocking or whatever, until something administrative shows up."

"The problem is," Calan explained, "that all the light jobs get snatched up by juveniles looking for spending money, veterans get preference for technical positions and unskilled heavy jobs are rare, with the industrial base we have. If you can lift fifty kilos regularly in this climate, I can find a few, but they don't pay well."

"*Fifty?*" She repeated, shocked. "No, not for very long."

"That is the detail. I can recommend a couple of prospects that usually aren't hiring, but will probably make an exception for you. They both offer training. Cavalier Enterprises and Bellefontaine."

"What would I be doing?"

"Cavalier Enterprises is one of the most respected escort services in Jefferson. They offer dancers, modeling, escorts for business or social functions, massage and exotic sex fantasies. The Bellefontaine is a club that offers erotic dancing and they specialize in dancers with rare or off-world looks."

Kendra was silent in amazement. A chill shot down her spine and all the way to her left heel. She opened her mouth twice and finally got out, "No."

"They are both excellent companies," Calan stated simply. "I occasionally visit the Bellefontaine myself."

I'll bet you do, Kendra thought. She wished as hard as she could, but the man refused to fall over dead. Outwardly, she simply shook her head.

"They do provide training," he repeated. "And the pay is excellent, with good benefits, plus tips."

"No!" Kendra said firmly, feeling dizzy. Her breath was ragged and her pulse raced.

Calan shrugged. "I'm afraid I don't have anything else. You have listed no marketable skill."

Kendra took a deep breath. "I want to see Citizen Hernandez," she said.

Shrugging again, Calan said, "We can see him. I don't know what you expect him to do." He stood up and gestured for the door.

Outside, he led her quickly into the bright afternoon Iolight. They strode through an architectural dream that Kendra would have stopped to admire had she noticed. She thought about making a break for it, but she had no assets and she still had a tracer implanted. The few blocks to Hernandez's office seemed an eternity and her pulse had slowed only slightly by the time the Citizen's secretary had ushered them into his office. She was panting from both exertion and fear.

Hernandez bowed briefly and inquired, "I understand there is a problem?"

"Hell, yes!" Kendra exploded, tears streaming. "This . . . individual is trying to tell me that I have a choice of stripper or whore. If that's what's here, then you can send me home and I'll take my chances with prison."

"Going back without a bond is out of the question," Hernandez replied, while looking inquiringly at Calan.

Calan was not paying attention. "The job is safe, well paid and provides free training. No one in a nonservice field is going to pay for unskilled grunt labor—"

"Quiet," Hernandez said softly. Calan obeyed.

Beginning again, Calan said, "I offered her the best that is available. If that doesn't work, I can only suggest a delay-on-credit and wait for something more to her taste."

"Oh, so I can run up a debt and be a company girl—"

"If you—"

They both raised their voices and resumed the argument. Hernandez interrupted at about half their volume, "Calan, sit down!" he turned slightly and continued, "Pacelli, sit down!"

They did as he ordered, Kendra panting with terror.

Hernandez looked from one to the other, stood up and headed for a bar. "Ms Pacelli, before we begin, would you like something to drink?"

"No, thank you," she replied icily, trying to calm herself.

Hernandez shrugged and tapped orders for himself and Calan. He passed a filled tumbler to Calan and took the stack of hard sheets he held.

Hernandez raised his glass and sipped while glancing through the sheet. Finally, he said, "I don't see any problems here," and Kendra nearly fainted before he added, "that we can't resolve. I'm looking for . . . ah, here." He turned the sheet around, indicated a line and said, "We have a misunderstanding of terms. Ms Pacelli, all you have listed as far as skills is your military training for logistics."

"That's the only training I have, sir," she said.

"As far as formal training. While credentials are a plus, they are neither common nor required here.

You should list everything you feel competent to do, even if you do not have formal instruction."

"Oh!" she exclaimed, considering. "I've done some drafting. A bit of bookkeeping. I took mathematics as far as calculus and differential equations. And I have run a few machine tools, but not recently."

Hernandez nodded. "Any gardening?"

"Yes, we used to grow vegetables and flowers, before the city annexed our burb."

"The city has a groundskeeper's slot," he said. "It hasn't even been put up for contract yet, although," he turned to Calan, "if she takes it, we'll credit your fee."

After a moment, Calan nodded. "Fine with me."

"'Groundskeeper,'" Hernandez quoted, "'Mowing, pruning, weeding, trimming, cleaning of park property, repair of pavements and buildings, designing, planning and planting of seasonal decorative displays, plumbing of sanitary facilities and fountains, maintenance of vehicles and equipment, arrangement of seating and tentage for events.' I think you could do most of that and the rest you could pick up on the job. Pay is nineteen thousand eight eighty-seven, which means your buyout is between two and five years, depending on rate. I would suggest doing three point five for now and you can adjust it in a few weeks if you wish. Interested?"

Kendra thought for a few moments, finally asking, "What's the fine print say?"

"The city is buying your contract, obviously. If it decides to sell or close your position, you have the option of transferring or rehiring or buying out. You may buy out at any time on ten days' notice for balance due. You may rehire at any time on ten days' notice if an employer will buy out the balance. There is an escape clause for emergencies, which says that you may be dismissed without notice at no further obligation to you, if the city cannot fund your position—act of war, act of nature type of thing. Standard wording, don't expect that to happen."

She considered briefly. Five years in debt. Actually, that didn't sound too bad. She said, "Okay, I'll take it."

"Excellent," Hernandez smiled, handing her the contract to read and sign. It said, in remarkably simple language, exactly what he had told her. She signed it. Looking up, she said, "Thank you." Turning to Calan, she said, "I'm sorry for losing my temper." She didn't feel very sorry, but she did think it would help to be mannerly. No need to create enemies.

"No apology," he replied, speaking as stiffly as she had. "You were scared and I neglected to consider your background. I don't often deal with immigrants. None of us do, what with the cost involved." He stood, bowed and left.

"And you're a mercenary bastard," Hernandez said to the closed door. "He gets paid on commission," he explained as he turned to Kendra. "Those are excellent-paying jobs, because they require good training, looks to go with it and the right personality. It's hard to find people who are qualified. And I'm surprised they'd take an indent, as they are scrupulous on their ethics. But if you took the job voluntarily, he stood to make about three times what he is getting from this one. To be fair, the lower-paying jobs wouldn't be worth the time you'd put in and his commission would have been even lower, of course. Sorry for putting you through that, but he was next on the rotation. All that said, if I'd thought he'd stoop that low, I would have warned you and I do apologize."

Kendra breathed deeply, nodded and asked, "Could I accept that drink, now? And thank you, sir." She grinned weakly. It would take a while to get through this. She had a sudden mental picture of her being left on the streets to "consider" her position: homeless, without assets, in a strange society where everyone was armed. Or would Calan and his cronies simply have dragged her off, had they known she'd object? She wanted to believe Hernandez, but she vowed to stay alert. This was not a refuge for the meek.

"My pleasure. You will need to arrange for sufficient life insurance to cover your contract. Technically, you should do that before you leave, but I think a day or two to shop around is a decent gesture. Call me with an account number when you've arranged it."

In a few minutes, calls had been made, data exchanged and Hernandez advised Kendra, "I've located some possible apartments for you. The cheapest is two hundred a month, the top is five hundred." He indicated images on three screens. "The cheap one is in a run-down area and is a long walk from the park. The expensive one would be a bit of a squeeze for you but is a very nice place. I recommend this one at three ninety. It's quite close, a decent neighborhood and only six years old. It's a bach, but roomy as bachelors go."

"I'll trust your judgment, if I can have the weekend to change my mind if there is a problem," she said, sipping the wine. It was quite good. She kept herself from tossing it down to steady her nerves.

"Under the circumstances, I think the landlord will agree. A Citizen's request carries weight." He turned again to the phone and secured the landlord's consent.

Finishing the call, he turned back, "All that's left is the Oath of Responsibility. It's a legal requirement," he explained, "and also a rather important occasion to many people. If you wish, you can take it at evening court, publicly and formally or I'll have my exec witness now."

"Can we just do it now? I don't like formal events."

"Certainly," he agreed, pressing a button. "If you change your mind later, you can have a court ceremony anyway."

Hernandez handed Kendra a slip of paper as the receptionist came in. He spoke to her, saying, "Hi, Patty, we need you to witness the Oath of Responsibility." She nodded and agreed and he turned to Kendra, continuing, "You need to stand at attention, and recite the Oath from the card. At the end you may affirm on your honor or make a religious oath of your choice."

"This makes me a Citizen? Resident, I mean."

"It makes you an independent resident, legally an adult. Read it over, it means exactly what it says."

She glanced over the words, nodded, then took a deep breath and stood at attention. She recited from the card, "I, Kendra Anne Pacelli, before witness, declare myself an adult, responsible for my actions, and able to enter contract. I accept my debts and duties as a Resident of the Freehold of Grainne." Shifting slightly, she finished, "So help me God," and crossed herself.

"Done without pomp and speeches. Very well said," Hernandez acknowledged, "and congratulations. Now. Please be aware that if you desert your contract, a bounty can be placed on you. Once brought in, you would be required to pay the bounty and interest and finish your contract with a prisoner's transceiver that won't let you through any 'port security. I don't think you're the type to need that warning, but you should be aware of it." Kendra shuddered at the thought of wearing such a thing while working as an "exotic hostess," or whatever they called the job at the smut club. She still wasn't over that.

Kendra nodded, turned as Patty took her hand and congratulated her before leaving.

"Well, that's it, then," Hernandez told her. "Here's your Residency ID plate, a credchit from First Planetary and a cash advance. If you wish to change accounts, feel free." He handed her items and adminwork. "This is your contract and the code to your apartment. Address is here," he indicated a scrawl on a map, "And this is the park garage. You need to be there Rowanday at three. It's the weekend, so you have three days to look around. This is my home code, if you have an emergency. Your place and the garage are both walking distance, so that'll save you on transport." He handed her another print, saying, "Here's a calendar for the next month, with your schedule marked. Any questions at the moment?"

She hesitated, still amazed at the speed with which things were happening. "No," she replied cautiously, "I think I understand." She was grateful he was such a professional. What a place of contrasts.

"Good," Hernandez smiled. "Do call if there's a problem. Good luck," he finished, bowing briefly.

She returned the gesture as Patty showed her out. She retrieved her bag from the receptionist's office and left.

Chapter 4

"And if a stranger sojourn with thee in your land,
   ye shall not vex him
But the stranger that dwelleth with you shall be
   unto you as one born among you . . ."
                                        —Leviticus 19:33-34

Her height was the first thing Robert McKay
noticed; followed by the fact that she was an offworlder.
Her skin was too pale, she was sweating profusely, and
she lugged frustratedly at a travelbag that couldn't mass
as much as her effort suggested. He quickened his
pace, passed her and asked, "Can I give you a hand
with that?"

The suspicious look in her eyes suggested a home
planet with high crime. She scanned him, obviously
looking for signs of danger. She saw something that
dropped her caution just a tiny bit and replied, "Sure,
thanks," gratefully. Her accent was North American,
he thought.

He scooped up the bag, which was as light as he suspected, slung it over his shoulder and asked, "Where are you heading?"

"Seven Rushton Avenue, number sixteen. But I have no idea where that is, other than this way," she replied, indicating the direction with a forward nod.

A stunning woman, tall and with a sexy drawl, moving in right next door! Definitely a situation to deal cautiously with. "Across this park is faster," he advised her, "I'm in number fifteen. Robert McKay." He offered a hand.

She held hers out and looked confused when he took it in both of his. "Uh . . . Kendra Pacelli."

"Sorry," he said, "Just a normal polite greeting here. I know it's not common on Earth."

"Is it that obvious?" she asked, smiling wryly.

He heard a slight strain to her breathing and slowed his pace a little. It was glaring to his trained eye, but he didn't want to alarm her. Instead, he told her honestly, "I've been there. Military duty." He took a quick, unobtrusive look up and down, trying to memorize every line of her. As far as physical beauty, this was a jackpot of a neighbor—incredibly tall, slim, creamy skin and eyes like the East Sea. He guided her through the small corner lot, lush with flowers and grasses and across Crow Lane to Rushton. "And here we are," he indicated the stairs, then led the way up.

He paused at his door and opened it, reached under his tunic and tossed a holstered gun and a pouch in the direction of the bed, closed the door and turned to hers.

"What do you do?" she asked.

"Operations analyst, currently on contract to the city. And vertol pilot for the reserves."

"Can I ask why everyone is armed to the teeth?" She was obviously bothered by the profusion of hardware she'd seen so far. Well, that fit with Earth's cultural attitude, he thought—ban anything that wasn't mandatory.

"Vicious native animals," he told her. "If you are anywhere out of the downtown area, it's very advisable to carry. We also carry to assert our rights, but don't worry about the philosophy now. It'll take some getting used to. Let me show you around," he suggested, placing her travelbag on the bed and guiding her through the one-room flat.

The kitchen was small, neat and efficient. The bathroom was nicely equipped and more spacious than she expected. A comm was provided, with excellent link capabilities, and he cautioned her that she would be charged for almost all access. The whole was about the size of a nice hotel suite on Earth. Considering her rent as a percentage of her income, it was more than adequate lodging in what seemed to be a fairly nice neighborhood. She was glad not to have taken the cheapest available.

"So, who will you be working for?" he asked.

"City Parks," she replied. "At least until my indent is paid."

"You don't have much other luggage then," he stated.

"None," she agreed.

"Ah," he nodded and moved to her bag. "May I?" he inquired.

She nodded a curious assent and he opened it, neatly laying things out on the bed. He nodded when it was empty and said, "As I thought. We need to take you shopping before you wind up hospitalized."

"Isn't my clothing appropriate?" she asked.

"Not at all. If you don't get shoes quick you'll be crippled by Rowanday. Let me take a quick shower and I'll take you out . . . unless you have other plans?"

"Uh, I really appreciate it, but could we do it tomorrow? I just want to drop from exhaustion."

"You can do that," he agreed with a concerned nod, "but once the food, gravity and air hit you, you'll spend two or three days wishing you were dead. I recommend buying now before you collapse."

"Well, I guess. You are a native guide. And thanks."

"No prob. See you in fifteen segs—I think that's a little less than twenty-five minutes?" He waited for her assent, then politely left.

Kendra had trouble using the shower and scalded herself repeatedly while adjusting it. The controls seemed fine, but the temperature scale was different from the kind she was used to. The tub and shower were one unit to save space, but large enough. They had the latest frictionless sides and seamless bends to prevent bacterial growth. Everything was padded and heated for safety and comfort. It hardly fit her perception of a frontier world, but this was the capital and it had been settled for almost three hundred years, she recalled.

Finishing, she yanked her hair into a quick mane and hoped the style wasn't too far out for Grainne. She slipped into casual jeans and tunic, pulled on her loafers and stepped out.

She knocked on McKay's door and heard a "Come in!" She opened the—unlocked—door, stepped in and froze. McKay was standing naked, halfway into briefs.

He looked up and looked embarrassed. "I *am* sorry," he apologized, quickly grabbing for pants. "We are pretty casual here and I forgot." Kendra realized his distress was on her behalf, not his own. Before she could respond, he was dressed and came over, dragging a different gun—this one polished and decorated—and belted it low on his right hip. He scooped up his pouch and another small bundle on his way.

The gun bothered her, but she realized it was not her place to criticize. Anyway, he was a military officer. Responding, finally, to her earlier surprise, she said, "I think I'm going to be shocked a lot in the next few days."

"Probably. I'll try to ease you into the difficult parts, but it won't be easy to remember most of what I take for granted. If something comes up, just ask."

"I will," she agreed, letting him take her arm and guide her out into Jefferson's late-afternoon madness. People were far more comfortable with physical contact here than on Earth. That of itself would take getting used to.

The stairs, she noticed now, were broad and shallow, likely because of the gravity. The ironwork was real iron, but her eye could tell it had been done en masse, not as individual pieces as she'd originally thought. It still lent a nice, airy touch to the square of buildings and the inner courtyard. She noted with a frown that the complex didn't have a gate to restrict access. Anyone could walk up to the doors. This obviously wasn't one of the better neighborhoods. The central courtyard was pretty, though, with more ironworked grilles and railings. Kids' toys were scattered around unlocked and she puzzled over that. Did the security cameras work that well? Was there a guard she didn't see? Or were the possessions coded for tracing?

They walked several blocks, winding up in an area full of shops. There were a few of the large megastores she was used to, but most of this neighborhood was little specialty shops, apparently family owned and operated.

Kendra spent much of the walk looking up, not at skyscrapers, although they were impressive, but at the heavens. The sky was turning a most amazing orange

with magenta streaks to the west, with Iota brilliant
yellow below it. Slightly higher, the sky maintained a
blinding ultrablue, fading to violet in the east. The air
was becoming breezy as the long dusk descended and
an eager tension was moving through the crowds. There
was a slight tang from the ocean, which was only a few
kilometers away.

The first stop they made was for proper shoes.
Her feet were already starting to hurt and she
eagerly took his advice for a pair plain enough for
work without looking too industrial, so she could
wear them out as well. They had generous support
and additional cushioning for tender feet, such as
those of lower-gravity newcomers. When she asked
about her old pair, he advised her to "Rag 'em.
Unless they have some personal value." After a few
moments consideration, she decided to bag them for
the time being.

He led her to the lingerie section and promised to
return shortly. She began looking through the bra racks.
Little was available for a woman 1.8 meters tall. She
sought the clerk.

The proprietor was a small woman, partly African
in ancestry, her skin really dark in this environment,
who hurried over to give advice.

"I've narrowed it down to this or this," Kendra said,
holding up two styles from the sample rack for her to
view. "What do you think?"

"Do you want these for a date, lady?" the old woman
asked, twirling a lock of frizzy hair. "They'll look great.
But if you want something for work, you'll be much
more comfortable in something like this," she continued, indicating a different style. "Our gravity is higher,
remember."

"Do you have it in a 100/110?" she asked, slightly
unsure.

"Probably, but gravity will compress your spine a bit, so your chest is going to be expanded. Let me measure you. Arms up," she directed, whipping out a measure and walking around Kendra. The ball tickled as it rolled around her and flashed numbers.

Glancing at the readout, the clothier reached up and grabbed a different style from another rack. "Here," she said, handing it over. It was a 102/110. "Try that one and keep in mind that underwire, shelves and lace are for show-only here. You want elastic and lots of shoulder, especially until you build up your muscles. Otherwise, you'll droop, probably painfully."

Kendra nodded and made mental notes. "Okay. Where's the changing room?" she asked.

The woman looked confused. "Chang . . . oh, no such thing. Go ahead, honey, no one minds," she reassured Kendra.

Kendra bit her lip, then shrugged. It was obviously normal here and a fuss wouldn't produce a fitting room. She peeled off her tunic and tried the sample garment, trying not to be self-conscious or look ridiculous. She succeeded at the latter, not the former. The garment fit so she bought five.

Rob came back with a wrapped package and led her across the street to another specialty shop. They were far more common here than on Earth and she asked him about them.

He shrugged. "Just our way. The prices are about the same, but the smaller shops are friendlier. We use the big ones when doing seasonal stock-up and for bulk purchases." He pointed to her left. "Here's our next stop."

He had her buy a cloak, and not a cheap one. "The weather changes in segs," he told her, "and the temperature drops drastically at night. A cheap cloak is just a waste of credit." She had to admit it was a nice piece.

It was a dark blue that set off her skin, thick and warm without being bulky or heavy. There were slits for her arms, buttons down the front and the hood had a drawstring. It looked to be a multipurpose and multiclimate item, and she could tell the workmanship was excellent. The same store furnished her with three tunics and an equal number of loose shorts in local style. From there, they walked across a corner into a huge green area. She counted her remaining funds and was depressed. She might have enough left for food, if she stuck to basics.

"Liberty Park," he announced. "Jefferson's largest, and where you'll probably be working. I thought you might want to look around."

"Great!" She acknowledged while taking his offered hand.

The color of the people was changing, from the soft grays, whites and light colors of daytime, to blacks, metallics and screaming hues in stiffer, tighter clothing, mostly revealing, designed to show off heavy-gravity physiques and high-UV tans. A few people were in various stages of nudity, while some were covered to the neck. Slash-and-puff was popular, along with iridescent pattern shifts. Whatever they had on, the evening clothes were worn to impress. Many were armed with pistols or knives or both, and those items too were embellished and prominent. Jewelry was unlike anything Kendra had seen before, and crime obviously was not a problem, considering the mass of precious stones and metals she could see with every blink. The crowd was boisterously loud and cheerful and an utterly disorganized mob bent on confusion. They moved with a *purpose*, and the purpose was revelry.

They approached a portable teppanyaki stand, where the chef whirled his knives like implements of combat, interrupted by a gout of flaming alcohol that elicited a shriek of delight from one onlooker and bellows of approval from two soldiers in uniform. Kendra stopped to stare.

They were in dress uniform. Off post and in public. Had she done that on Earth, she would have been attacked, beaten and mugged inside of six blocks by some gang or other.

A few steps past the chef, Robert guided her to a food vendor who had the plumpest, healthiest fruits and vegetables she had ever seen. The display looked as perfect as an advertisement. Rob grabbed a small, elongated item and began to haggle.

"So how much for these sickly looking Satan peppers?" he asked in mock disgust.

"Such a deal at five for a cred. But for you, my friend," the bearded vendor returned, grinning, "twenty for five creds."

Rob snorted. "After I saved your life on Mtali? Fine gratitude you show me. Five for fifty cents and I'm being generous." While he said this, several onlookers started giggling at the exchange.

The reply was, "Indeed you are, but I must feed my three wives and seventeen children. I hope you will understand. Seventy-five cents." This elicited more chuckles.

"Okay, fine."

"But only if you take ten."

McKay laid three quarter cred coins down and said, "Not fast enough."

"Thank you." The merchant smiled, clutching the coins greedily, "Now little Johnny can get that operation he needs."

"They're putting in a soul?"

"Taking out his conscience."

The audience responded to the finale with howls of appreciation and moved back in to buy huge quantities of produce. McKay grabbed several other items, slipped them into a paper bag and money swapped palms again.

As they resumed their walk, McKay munching on a "Satan pepper," which did not sound at all like a snack food to Kendra, she commented, "If that shtick happens all the time, I'm surprised he doesn't need an entertainer's license."

McKay blew air and licked his lips. "Whoo, that was a potent one!" he remarked, eyes glazing slightly. He turned and said, "You don't need licenses here. I'll show you the bazaar if we get a chance." He shook out the bundle attached to his pouch, which turned out to be his cloak, and laid it on the ground, gesturing for Kendra to sit. As she did so he sat next to her and pulled three fresh strawberries the size of plums out of the bag. "I don't know how hot you like your food," he resumed, "But Satan's are hotter than anything you'll find on Earth, habaneros included. So I got you these instead."

"Thanks." She smiled, then wrinkled her brow. "No licenses? But how do you keep out bad entertainers and merchandise?"

"Hey, bad ones have to learn somewhere. And shoddy merch gets noticed pretty quickly."

"I can't believe that works as a quality control measure," she said doubtfully.

"Try your strawberries."

She did so and was amazed. Juice dribbled down her chin. Sugar would have been wasted and cream would have masked the flavor. "Okay, they're great," she mumbled around her second bite. "Thank you."

After snacking, he guided her to the restroom so they could wash the juice off their hands. Kendra winced, knowing the condition of public restrooms back home, but walked in anyway, hoping to find an automatic faucet that worked . . . and was stunned.

First, the restroom was for both men and women. And there were private stalls. There was no guard visible. She thought of the possible crimes behind those doors and made a note never to enter a public restroom alone after dark.

Second, the facility was clean. As clean as the one in her new flat. After washing her hands, she wandered around outside admiring the architecture, amazed that a restroom could have architecture, and bumped into McKay again. "I don't get it," she said. "No rules on anything, and this is the cleanest park I've ever seen. How?"

"People care enough to maintain it," he explained as they went outside again, "and any vandalism is gone in less than a day, at the vandal's expense if he's found, so there is a real motivation against damaging things." He was leading her back the way they came as he said this and stopped briefly to retrieve his cloak, which was still on the ground, untouched. She was silent again.

Liberty Park was too huge to be seen all at once in purple duskiness, but they toured the main north-south walkway. All lawn edges were neat, the grass appearing to have been laid like carpet. Occasional flower islands erupted in wild bursts of native and Terran flora. The trees were beautifully pruned and some of the bushes were shaped interestingly. They passed a broad fountain with people wading and playing in it, wandering entertainers and vendors of food, liquor and intoxicants, thousands of cheerful people and several playgrounds occupied by happily screaming mobs of children.

As they neared a darkened area of tall, manicured bushes in a closed design, Kendra pointed and asked, "What's that?"

McKay glanced over and said, "That's the maze."

"Oh, I love mazes. Let's go look," she suggested.

"I don't know that we should," he said, some doubt in his voice.

"Why not?" she inquired back.

His unconscious leer of a grin grew back. "Besides being a maze, it has many little cul-de-sacs. Usually occupied, especially at this time of night," he explained.

"Occupied . . ." she began, then continued, "I think I'm misunderstanding you. You seem to be implying 'occupied' by lovers."

"No implication. Flat statement."

"Ohh!" she exclaimed, then looked doubtful. "You're pranking me, right?" she asked with a sideways grin of her own.

"We could go and see, if you doubt me," he told her.

"Now I know you're bluffing," she said. "Let's go, then."

He pulled on her hand as she neared the entrance and said, "Shall we bet on it?"

"What odds?" she asked doubtfully.

"If I'm wrong, I buy you a drink. If I'm right, it costs you a kiss."

And she knew she'd been had. He led her in and as her eyes adjusted to the darker environs, she could see in the smaller side passages that couples and small groups *were* making love. Creatively, in some cases. Kendra felt like an intruder and kept her eyes averted most of the time. They strolled the passages for a minute or two and McKay said, "Only thing is, I can't find my way out in the dark."

"You better be pranking on that one," she told him, unafraid.

"Maybe if you jog my memory," he said, pulling her closer.

She grabbed his head and locked lips with him, doing her best to shock *him*. He returned in kind and several seconds later they parted breathlessly.

"Oh, yeah. The exit," he said distantly. "And dinner, I think. I'll treat. If you insist on equity you can treat at some future point."

"Okay," she agreed. "Thank you."

They walked out by a circuitous route, then angled across gentle rolling slopes through an area with several small stages full of performers. They found themselves suddenly out of the park on a sidewalk, no fence or other barricade to indicate the boundary. A sign across the crowded thoroughfare proclaimed, STANLEY'S SURF N' TURF. The restaurant had a number of tables scattered across the broad sidewalk and looked to be doing excellent business.

Crossing the street was a game, played by dodging manually controlled traffic one lane at a time, then pausing for another opening. It was exciting and terrifying and Kendra was breathless by the time they arrived at an empty sidewalk table.

McKay dropped his cloak and pouch to his side and peeled off his top to reveal his corded muscles. Kendra looked around, realized that most people were topless, some women wearing halters similar to hers, and took off her tunic. It *was* more comfortable.

A waiter approached and placed a bowl of brightly colored salsa between them, with a basket of freshly baked chips, still steaming and fragrant. "Hi, Rob," the man greeted cheerfully. "Drinks for you and your lady friend?"

"Just a friend, Rupe. Drinks, yes. Amber ale for me. And we should probably have mild salsa this time."

"Certainly," Rupe replied. McKay always ordered hot, but perhaps the lady . . .

"Wine cooler for me, please," Kendra supplied.

"Oh, you're from offworld," Rupe said, taking her hand briefly. "Rupert Stanley, owner and manager. Your drink is free, then, lady."

"Kendra. Thank you. And I think I can manage medium salsa."

"I would recommend the mild also," Stanley suggested. "Rob will not lead you astray knowingly. Not while you're sober, anyway." His grin implied the comment was a joke. He wandered off to greet other patrons, speaking into a comm as he did so. Shortly, another server brought drinks and a less garish bowl of salsa. They ordered prime rib, medium rare, with salad and potatoes and Kendra was amazed at how cheap food was.

"No ID check," she commented, almost used, in her mind, to the virtually nonexistent government on Freehold. "Drinking age on most of Earth is . . ."

"Twenty-five," McKay provided. "And you look about fourteen Freehold, or twenty-one Earth."

"I *am* twenty-five, actually," she corrected. "But thank you. I don't drink much," she admitted.

"A problem easily cured in a town where ninety-six percent of chowdowns brew their own house beverages," he advised. "So be careful. Servers will politely tell you when they think you've had too much, but won't stop you short of bankruptcy or public disaster."

"Uh-huh," she nodded, taking the data in while scooping salsa with a chip. She took a bite, felt the chip melt away and swallowed. It was very fresh and tasty.

Then the bite hit her throat. She grabbed for her drink and downed two gulps. Finishing, she yelped, "That's 'MILD?' "

"Too much?" McKay asked.

"Dealable with," she admitted, "but I'd call that at least medium-hot."

"The original and second settlers had a large minority of Southwestern Americans, Thais and Indonesians. Peppers do very well here and became a hobby, eventually a lifestyle."

"You're telling me," she agreed, recovering at last. She resumed nibbling, but in much more delicate bites than her first. It was delicious, once her tastebuds were seared off.

Changing the subject, she asked, "Were you really on Mtali?"

"Oh, yes," he said, looking quite serious, "Spent three days dodging triple-A, had most of a Hatchet shot out from around me, lost several close friends and spent the rest of the month flying nonstop CAP missions and expending an impressive amount of munitions."

"You arrived just as I left, then," she told him.

He looked surprised. "What were you doing on Mtali?"

She smiled wanly, "Pacelli, Kendra A. Sergeant Second Class, United Nations Peace Force. Service number 6399-270-5978. Logistics and Fuels."

"Okay," he nodded, "now you are indentured to Jefferson City, with almost no personal belongings. I think there's a story here."

"I can't go into it," she told him, shaking her head and looking distressed. "No one should know my background either, but I had to tell someone. You having been on Mtali . . ." she faded off.

"I understand that at least, without explanation."

"Please promise you won't mention it."

"Mention what?" he asked, a mock puzzled look on his face.

"Thank you." She smiled.

The steak and salad arrived and they dug in. The food was fantastic, with subtle flavors that made it unlike anything she'd had before. Garlic was omnipresent here, and pepper, with traces of ginger, horseradish and lemon. Despite the wonderful taste, Kendra was beginning to realize that she would never enjoy the foods she grew up with again. Then she felt the gravity tugging at her breasts, the growing ache in her feet, the thinness of the atmosphere that made breathing a chore for her. She was lost in a strange city full of armed people, unaware of most of the mores and dependent on a chance-met guide for her survival. She didn't notice her glass being refilled and drank more as her spirits sank lower. This society had a system that just didn't *care* about people.

Then she remembered that the system she had barely escaped didn't care about people either, despite its talk.

"You look very unhappy," McKay remarked.

"I know," she said, "and I shouldn't. It's just that every time I think I understand, everything around me changes again. The food is different, the people, all the rules, including the ones I don't realize exist. The only thing that seems similar is the language."

"That is the problem exactly," he told her.

"What?" she asked, confused.

"If we spoke a different language, you would realize that this is an alien culture and that you were an outsider trying to fit in," he explained. "But the similarity of language confuses you, especially since we use some of the same words for entirely different concepts."

"Such as?"

"Ever seen Central Park in New York?"

"Once."

"Does Liberty Park fit your definition of 'park'? Does Jefferson fit the word 'city'? We use the same words, but with completely different images in mind."

"So what can I do?" she asked, understanding but not reassured.

"Pretend we're aliens. And I would suggest putting a hand over your glass, so it doesn't get refilled." She did as he suggested, startled, just as a server came by with a pitcher. She listened as he continued. " 'Drink' here implies refills until done and we sip them, while swallowing lots of water for the heat and dryness. I suggest you drink that full glass."

She did so, forcing herself to swallow. She had never liked drinking water. "Even the water tastes funny," she complained.

"It's low on chemical purifiers, compared to what you're used to," he explained while donning his tunic and cloak. She realized that the air was quickly becoming brisk and followed suit. The cloak did ward off the night air.

McKay paid the check with cash, she saw, rather than a credcard, sliding out bankslips from a folder she wouldn't dare carry openly on Earth. As they left, she said, "I'm sorry to be so depressing a guest. That was a memorable meal, thank you."

"You're welcome. For future reference, if someone offers you dinner, discuss intentions first. On a social basis, it frequently implies sex," he warned.

"Ohh!" she exclaimed. "I didn't know. I'm sorry."

"I knew that, which is why I phrased the offer the way I did. That way, if you were aware of that particular cultural thing, you could graciously decline. If you didn't, you weren't trapped. Although," he tossed his head and looked at her, "I'd be delighted if you accepted."

She smiled back, feeling slightly threatened. How to politely decline? What were the rules here? She decided he knew she was a stranger and to be direct. "I'm flattered, but no, thank you. I'm not ready for sex my first day here."

Nodding, he said, "I didn't think so, but it never hurts to ask. Don't feel obligated to anyone, even if there's a misinterpretation of signals." The advice seemed genuine.

"Is casual sex really as common as it appears to be?" she asked.

"It's not casual," he denied, with a shake of the head. "It's as serious as anything else, but very common. If you recall, the only health concern at Freehold System Entry is venereal and bloodborne pathogens. Everyone, every time, including diplomatic personnel, gets tested. There is no risk of infection here."

"That's . . . amazing," she replied, stunned. Then a thought occurred to her. "What about smugglers?" she asked.

"Who would smuggle when there is no restriction on merchandise and no duties?" he asked rhetorically. "Everyone goes through Orbital because it's cheap and easy."

"*No one* ever tries to skip in unreported?" she asked incredulously.

"Occasionally," he said. "And they wind up as ashes before touchdown. Since there's no reason to blow System, anyone who does is assumed to be an enemy invader and gapped by Defense. I got called to nail one they missed when I was on active duty, just as they hit the swamps in the Hinterlands, but Orbital dropped the bar on them and all I had to do was recon the crater."

That was a startling discovery. Bring in anything you want openly and freely that's fine; try to do it clandestinely and wind up a wisp of vapor. And a planet where all sex was safe.

On Earth, even rapists wore barriers against infection.

They reached their building again, Kendra wobbly from gravity and fatigue and alcohol. She found herself leaning against McKay as they climbed the stairs. She was beyond exhausted; she was drained.

At the top, they were greeted by a large black cat. "Hi, George," McKay replied, reaching down to scratch the creature's ears as it buzzed and bumped his ankles.

"No pet licenses either, I assume," she said, reaching to scratch George's shoulders.

"*Pet licenses?*" McKay exclaimed, shocked at last.

They continued to his door, which was closed but not locked. He walked in, dropped his extraneous gear and escorted her next door.

She unlocked her door and the cat headed inside. "Oh, damn!" she exclaimed.

"Don't worry about it," McKay advised "Unless you're allergic?"

"No."

"I recommend fresh air, despite the chill. You take care and I'll see how you're doing in the morning."

"Okay," she agreed.

He put his arms around her again and stared levelly at her eyes. She stared back. His were a curious sea green with flecks of gold foam. She wondered what his heritage was besides Scottish. He really was attractive. Still, the attention was unnerving. "Look . . . why are you being so nice?" she asked, and was embarrassed by asking.

He withdrew from her space a few centimeters and moved his embrace to a simple light grip on her forearms. "I'm interested in you," he said, honestly. "But you're not obligated for anything. If all you want is advice from a neighbor, that's fine." He looked faintly disappointed at that prospect. "But we do try to help guests, and strangers here, and it never hurts to have friends. I'm sorry if I'm encroaching too much." He cocked his head and looked at her, waiting.

Nodding, she leaned forward and kissed him briefly

and lightly. He broke it before she got too uncomfortable and she felt less intruded upon. She'd have to consider this, among hundreds of other cultural issues.

"Later," he said, stepping back.

"Uh-huh," she agreed, distractedly, and went inside. The whole exchange had felt odd and a bit forced.

She closed and locked the door, felt the heat of the day swat her like that of an oven, and looked for a thermostat. She didn't find one. Verbal commands didn't work. She forced herself to open a window on the wall next to the door slightly. Crime was supposed to be rare.

Her new possessions she hung in the closet then looked around at the comfortable but sterile room. She thought a shower would help her muscles relax, but was too exhausted. Undressing to underwear, she crawled into bed and was asleep in seconds.

Starting, she became aware of an intruder in the room. Then she realized it was that damned cat. Her adrenaline rush gradually lowered and she noted the time: 1:30. Then she tried to convert Freehold's twenty-eight-plus hour day with its decimal clock into a time she could understand, and was unconscious again before she determined the hour.

Chapter 5

"I would say that my position is not too far from
that of Ayn Rand's; that I would like to see
government reduced to no more than internal
police and courts, external armed forces—with the
other matters handled otherwise. I'm sick of the
way the government sticks its nose into everything,
now."

—Robert A. Heinlein, as quoted by J.
Neil Schulman in *The Robert Heinlein
Interview and Other Heinleiniana*

Kendra woke to bright sunlight. It hurt. A lot. Her
legs and feet were a pounding, itching ache, her sinuses
felt like cotton bales and her stomach insisted it was
hungry, but the thought of food was horrible. She lay
there, barely able to breathe, for three hours, more
than a div local time, drifting in and out of consciousness. Iota glared painfully through the window, but she
was too morose to even reach the polarizer.

"Hello," McKay's voice said softly through the window. "May I come in?"

She groaned and said, "Yeah." She heard him try the door, which was locked. "Door unlock," she croaked, then remembered that the latch was manual only. Standing made her head throb, so she crawled and unlocked it.

At her height and mass, she was shocked when, in this gravity field, McKay scooped her up in his arms and put her back in bed. He slipped into the bathroom and returned a moment later with a warm, damp towel. "Breathe through this," he advised and disappeared out the door. He returned shortly with an athletic bottle of clear liquid. "Drink this. It's good for you. Trust me."

"That's what you said last night," she complained as she complied.

It did seem to help and the damp cloth cleared her sinuses of most of the ache. Becoming less fuzzy, she said, "Thank you. Do you have any painkillers?"

"Painkillers are a bad idea. You might strain something worse if it doesn't hurt. You'll feel better in a couple of days and fine in a week," he told her.

A Freehold week was ten twenty-eight-plus-hour days. Not a pleasant thought. "What is wrong with me?" she asked weakly.

"Newcomer's hangover," he said, ticking off points on his fingers, "composed of muscle aches from higher gravity, upper respiratory infection from different viruses than you're used to, compounded with much drier air than you're used to, plus a strange diet. No way around it. The best way through it is to embrace it hard and fight it quick."

It did feel like the one hangover she'd had, but— "The food can't have that much to do with it. I eat hot food back home all the time," she argued.

"And aren't you glad? Or else you'd feel worse. Take it easy today. Stay here this morning, but keep the windows open for fresh air. Don't use cooling, as you need to become acclimated. I advise minimal clothing during the midday, unless you do go out, then wear your cloak also, to protect you from Io. When the temperature drops this evening, bundle up again. In the meantime, this will keep you occupied," he handed her a wrapped package.

She tore off the paper and revealed a book entitled, '*A Cultural Primer for the Freehold of Grainne.*'

"Thank you," she said, surprised. The book was printed on a tough polymer and bound into a heavy cover. Not an expensive process, but requiring more thought and attention than a simple ram or throwaway. She opened it and saw it was inscribed "To Kendra, good luck in your new world, Robert."

Before she could say anything else, he was leaving again. "Got to run," he said. "Things to see and people to do. If you make it to Liberty Park, I'll be there most of the day. If not, I'll stop in this evening to see how you're doing." The door closed and he was gone.

Kendra drifted in and out of sleep for a while longer, finally deciding she was alive enough to rise. She spent several uncomfortable minutes on the toilet before taking a warm shower, sitting on the floor of the stall rather than fight gravity, and felt considerably refreshed. Her sinuses were much clearer, her muscles down to a dull ache, and her feet—

Well, she did feel better, on the whole.

A glance in the refrigerator reminded her that she would need to shop for food. It also added to her minimal resolve to venture outside. Perhaps she would take a look at more of Liberty Park or seek out this "bazaar."

She sat down on the bed and glanced through the book, then became absorbed. It contained a detailed description of the Iota Persei system, including planets, satellites, planetoids, habitats and resources, among other things. She noted again the local time system. It seemed straightforward enough: ten divs per day, ten segs per div, one hundred seconds per seg. A Freehold second was approximately one Earth second, so it wouldn't be too hard to get used to. The kilogram was about eighteen percent heavier here due to gravity, but was still the same mass. Since the measure was based on the mass of a liter of water, that made more sense than adjusting all other measurements to fit. One chapter listed colloquialisms of the dialect of English spoken on Freehold, some of which she'd already picked up from context. There were maps, both geographical and political, for the planet and the "Halo," which was the name given to the space environment. The census figures were estimated, since the government made no effort to account for anyone who did not report their existence. Other than the annual fee she would pay to the Freehold and to the city of Jefferson, there were no taxes of any kind, and that fee was *voluntary*, she read. She used her comm to make pages of notes for later access. She read, engrossed, for about three hours, then realized the time that had passed.

Considering McKay's advice on dressing took five seconds. She wore her pumped-up shoes, a pair of shorts from her travelbag and one of her new halters. A few seconds' inspection revealed how to remove the lining from her cloak and she was ready to go. ID and cash—one ID, little cash. That went into her pouch, along with her useless, until she got paid, credchit. She took it from force of habit.

Before leaving, she ran a staticbrush through her
hair, snapping it up into a horsemane. It had worked
the night before and she wasn't familiar with local
styles. She stepped out into the glaring daylight,
which was reminiscent of the American Southwest
even at the almost 40 degrees latitude Jefferson
occupied.

She found Liberty Park by asking at a charge and fuel
station and confirmed that the bazaar was in the park.
Several minutes' walking brought her to the same
entrance they'd used the night before and made her
realize that she would need some more items, UV shielding among them. Iota Persei was brighter than the Sun
and beat down through the clear, dry air like a hammer
on an anvil. She kept her hood up with a hand shielding her face and still had to squint.

Freeholders seemed to regard a park as *the* place to
hang out. Hundreds of small groups, tens of entertainers
and vendors, pets of all descriptions filled her vision in
every direction. The simple geometric beauty of the
park's architecture fought a fierce battle with chaos and
lost. She found the central fountain, which was even
fuller of bodies than the night before, and took the main
path to the right and west. She shortly located the bazaar.

The previous discordance paled in comparison. Tents,
awnings, parasols, trailers, vehicles and the ever-present
bicycles looked to have been tossed out of a bucket en
masse. She wended her way in slowly, unconsciously
keeping a hand on her pouch, and examined the signs
(of those vendors who had them) and the wares (of those
who didn't).

Several merchants were selling UV-damping contact lenses. She compared prices on them, came back
to the stall that had the best price on a style she
liked, and was reminded to haggle by the actions of
the customer ahead of her.

"Okay," she began to the seller, "I like these, but fourteen just isn't in the budget of a bum like me."

"Well, you get what you pay for," he returned, casually running a hand through his hair. "I've got the best price around and I really can't go much lower without a bulk sale. If you want three or four colors or different-shaped pupils, I'd be glad to drop ten percent," he hinted.

"I'd like to," she agreed wistfully, nodding, "But I just unshipped and can't throw the dough."

"All right," he said, "I'll drop them to thirteen, but only because you have such incredible eyes I'd hate to see them burned."

She bit her lip, considering. It sounded like a good offer, but she really needed to be stingy. She also needed to protect her eyes. She haggled a bit lower, wasn't sure if she got a deal or not, but was satisfied for now. That was another thing to learn about. Task accomplished, she took possession of the contacts and popped them in her eyes. They cut the glare, deepened the blue of her pupils and were plain otherwise—no odd-shaped irises or strange colors or effects. He handed her change, receipt and a business card with a polite scan that told her it wasn't just her eyes he liked. Thanking him, she pushed on.

There was no real style to the crowd, but she did notice hats and scarves being used more than cloak hoods. She found a stand selling light but well-constructed scarves and threw back her hood to try some on.

"Oh, I love the hair!" the woman selling exclaimed. "Where did you pick that up?"

She explained its Earthly origin and the static pin placement that held it up, and was rewarded with a considerable discount on three scarves. The merchant helped her arrange one over her hair and neck and thanked her for the style tips. It seemed the horsemane was just being imported from Earth and she was at the front of the fashion trend. Her morale received a much-needed boost.

She hurried away as soon as was polite. She had been unable to avoid staring at the woman's naked, tattooed breasts and it had seemed very out of place to do so. No one else had given any indication of notice.

She received quite a few looks from passersby and realized many of them weren't for her hair. She mistook them for critical looks and was oblivious to the real cause of the attention: her beauty. A self-assessment indicated that no one was wearing loose, floppy shorts. She sought another clothing display.

She found an elasticized brief akin to those worn by many of the women present and bought three. After the purchase, she found her way out of the bazaar and sought a restroom to change. She headed in the direction she knew would find her such facilities—the park center.

She got lost, reoriented when she saw the fountain erupting over the crowd and walked that way. As she passed the broad, shallow pool, something else surprised her. A woman, expensively dressed in a short blue liquid-sheen dress yelled a friendly obscenity to her friends, then peeled the garment over her head and tossed it onto a grounded cloak.

She wore nothing underneath except subtle tattoos and unsubtle Celtic knotwork tanned into her bronze skin and protected with blocker. Unconcerned, the woman headed for the fountain.

Kendra knew she should be getting used to it by now, but it was still a bit of a shock. Shrugging, she continued, entered the restroom, sought a stall, slid out of her shorts, slid into the stretchy trunks and pulled them on. She looked much closer to the local styles.

She also felt ridiculous and dangerously exposed. Steeling herself, she stepped outside again and sought a new path—Rob had said he'd be in the park, but she had no idea where.

She awoke with blurry vision, confused, and grabbed for her pouch, which someone was removing from her waist.

"Easy, lady," a voice cautioned her. She focused on the young man in military uniform, who continued, "I'm Medic Jaheed. You collapsed a few seconds ago." As he spoke he drew her pouch aside, lifted her head and rolled a cloak under it. Turning, he raised his voice, "I need some water!"

Shortly, a girl ran up with a bottle. He made her drink several swallows, cautioned her, then dumped the rest on her head and chest. She recovered with a gasp, arching her back. As she relaxed again, Jaheed placed his hand in hers and told her, "Grip."

Satisfied with the strength of her response, he nodded. He and a woman bystander helped her to her feet, escorted her to a water fountain and waited while she slowly drank several more mouthfuls of water. Kendra insisted she felt fine and Jaheed insisted just as firmly that she should be escorted home and rest.

"Offworlder, right?" he said.

"Just got here from Earth," she admitted.

"You need rest and you need someone to go with you for safety," he reiterated. Kendra finally relented and was accompanied home by the woman.

"Thank you for helping me," she said to her guide. "I'm Kendra."

"I'm Alexia, professionally. It's no trouble. I have a client in this direction, anyway."

"Oh? What do you do?" Kendra asked, looking her

up and down. She was a bit above average height for Earth, had obvious Asian and Hispanic heritage, coffee-toned skin and a poise that took her from simply "beautiful" to "striking." Her eyes were violet from contacts and her hair was jet with purple flames dyed into it to match the shades of her lipgloss and makeup. Kendra would be some time getting used to casual nudity, she decided. Alexia's outfit was black leather cut away around the breasts, split and laced entirely down both sides, open to the mid back, broad shouldered and collarless. Real leather was illegal on Earth and the outfit itself would get her hassled by punks no end. Then, some nations still had laws against "indecent exposure." Bare breasts were technically legal in North America, but only a fool would exercise the privilege, with the risk of inviting attack it entailed.

"Escort."

Kendra caught on almost immediately and again said, "Oh!"

"Alexia" realized Kendra's assumption and replied, "It's not what you think. I do have sex with some clients, yes. I also dance, hostess, act as tour guide for visitors and anything else someone wants. It's all done on my terms."

"I think I see," Kendra said. "But it's definitely not my thing. They offered me that when I landed and I . . . didn't take the suggestion well," she finished. Yesterday. Had it only been yesterday?

"Well, if you ever change your mind," Alexia fished out a card, "call me."

"Right. Like I have the body for it."

The dark woman whirled, looked stunned. "You don't think you're attractive?"

"Hell, no!" Kendra responded vehemently. "I'm way too light-skinned, too skinny and too tall. You have a market for that?"

"Kendra," Alexia said soothingly, taking her by her arm and guiding her back in the right direction, "I don't know Earth standards, but by normal ratings here, you are incredibly exotic. Besides which, talent is at least equal to looks and I think you could manage just fine. You could retire to the Islands in ten years. Think it over."

Taking a deep breath and then deeper to compensate, Kendra said levelly, "I appreciate the offer. Thanks anyway."

Alexia nodded and responded, "Sorry to offend."

Kendra changed the subject back to safer areas by commenting, "I can't believe how hot it is."

"Yes it is," Alexia agreed, "When summer hits, it'll be unbearable."

Shocked again, Kendra asked, "This isn't summer?"

"Late spring. Summer starts in four weeks and it'll get hotter after that."

"Ouch." Again Kendra felt that alienness that seemed to encroach everywhere. She almost missed her building, but the sight of a convenience store a block away reminded her she needed food. She thanked Alexia and went to grab some staples.

Twenty minutes later, she was realizing that she should have bought a knife. The package of "mild" enchiladas didn't have a pull strip and wouldn't tear. As she fought with it, there was a knock at the door.

She turned around to see Rob at the window and waved him in.

"Are you feeling okay?" he asked as he entered.

"Fine," she replied. Then she realized where the question came from and added, "How did you find out?"

"There can't be many one-eighty-five-centimeter Earth blondes in this city. And if there are, I want their data codes so I can invite them to a screaming orgy," he said, approaching. Upon seeing the wrapper she struggled with, he continued, "That needs a knife."

"I realize that," she said in exasperation.

Rob reached past her with a knife that appeared to be the size of her forearm and sliced the poly open with the whisper of a *really* sharp edge. "You could have borrowed one from my kitchen."

"Huh?" Kendra replied, confused, still focused on the knife. The blade had to be fifteen centimeters.

He slid it back into a sheath at the waist of his trunks while explaining, "Walk next door and grab one from the rack above my sink next time. The door isn't locked."

Again, culture shock hit her. *The door isn't locked. Just go in and borrow whatever you need.* She was silent for a few moments, placing the food on a plate and sliding it in to heat in the microwave. Finally she said, "Thank you. I'll remember."

Her brain started working again and she turned to face him. "Did you come back just to check on me?"

"That and lunch. Bring those next door and I'll whomp up some sides."

A few minutes later, she was sitting at his table, biting into a wonderfully crisp salad to refresh her palate from the enchiladas and Rob's tacos. She could smell a cake baking for dessert. She was amazed at Rob's ability to cook from packages or improvise from scratch. He was amazed that she didn't know how to cook. She asked about the table, which had a rocky, pebbly blue-gray look under the smooth waxed finish. He told her it was "nuggetwood."

After lunch, Kendra insisted on accompanying Rob back to the park. He insisted she bring a water bottle. The conversation continued as they walked along a different route to the east side of the park. This route took them through a wooded area, the somber greens and browns of Earth plants clashing with the riotous blues and yellows of native growth. It was cooler under the trees and they slowed their pace. Rob explained and named the exotic trees. Holding her hand, he pointed out nuggetwood, dragonwood, crazyquilt, pillar and bluemaple.

"What's that bramblelike stuff?" she inquired, indicating an orange tangle set down in a depression. It resembled concertina wire more than anything.

"Firethorns. Stay away from them," he warned. "That clump is one of several carefully maintained bushes kept here. They carry a formic acid sting and are very springy. If you get caught, hold still, because they coil and wrap you up tighter. They spread quickly if allowed and fertilize themselves with dead animals."

Kendra stared in queasy fascination at the large plant. Freehold's equivalent of a Venus flytrap and large enough to eat people. Terrific. Terrifying.

She leaned a little closer as the tour of the glade continued. He listed other trees—tanglewood, forker, smoketree. A long, looping vine called hangman's noose was usually found on the gallows tree. As she stopped to rest, back against a bole and gasping for breath, he pointed out several bushes and flowers—the long, warm summers and harsh winters, both with lots of ultraviolet from Iota, created a tremendous ecological diversity. She nodded, too worn to speak, as several small animals made brief appearances and Rob told her of the larger animals out in the wilds—ninety percent of the planet—that made necessary loaded guns for travelers.

"And that's something you should take care of at your earliest inconvenience," he advised as they entered the open park center again.

"A gun?" she asked, not entirely comprehending.

"The city gets most of its labor in the form of petty criminals. You, as an indent, can expect to be in charge of those work details. And the perimeter park areas sometimes get wild animals, including rippers. You will need a gun."

"Well, if I have to, I have to. But I don't like it," she warned him.

"You'll get used to it."

"I suppose." She shrugged.

The sound of a local band interfered with further conversation and she sat with him to listen for a while. The music was dissonant, loud and odd to her ears and she wondered if Earth music had any following here.

The performance wound down at just about the same time Kendra decided she could take no more heat. She walked with Rob to a vendor selling beverages and selected one.

"Sure that's your taste?" he asked.

"I'll find out."

"Okay," he shrugged. They took their drinks and found some shade near a copse of trees on another artificial hill. Sipping, he explained more about the local lifeforms. There were two rabbit analogs. One was compact and looked a bit like an oversized kangaroo rat. It was known as a bouncer. The other, very leggy and capable of deceptive maneuvers, was called a bugs. Most of the higher animal forms were a variety of mammal analog that took evolution the next step. They had three orifices; one each for reproduction, urine and feces. Their liver functions were served by three different organs. And just about everything had enough extra bones that it slunk like a cat. The ripper was reminiscent of a leopard or a cheetah in movement, but looked more like a badger on steroids, only with long, muscular legs. It maxed out at better than 135 kph—Rob graciously translated, then gave the speed again as 365 kilometers per div. It had retractable claws and fangs and could bring down land prey the size of a rhino unassisted. Kendra agreed it might be an idea to carry a gun and hope she could think faster than an animal like that.

As they stood, Kendra swayed, lights at the edge of her vision. "Woah!" she giggled. Rob helped steady her. She leaned on him and had to use him for support.

"What's happening?" she asked. "Is the heat getting to me again?"

"No, the Sparkle is," he told her, taking more of her weight.

"The what?"

"That drink is an intoxicant and mild hallucinogen. That's why I asked if it was what you wanted."

"I didn't realize it was a drug!" she protested. "Why didn't you tell me?"

"It was on the vendor's sign."

They began walking and Kendra marveled at another sunset. The colors were impressive and the hallucinatory effects were *fantastic*, in the true meaning of the word. She made Rob stop, and stared at the clouds as they writhed.

It took quite a bit longer to get back to Rushton Avenue, Kendra leaning on Rob when the Sparkle kicked in and returning to her own feet as it faded. Apparently, the effect came through in waves. He helped her up the stairs and took her into her room. "You need to lie down," he told her.

It took some time for the effect to wear off and she had the attention span of a goldfish in the interim. Rob left her to float back down—it was essentially a harmless euphoric drug. He checked on her periodically and brought a tray of food in afterward.

While they ate and she vowed again to read signs, she asked, "Tell me about this 'voluntary' tax system."

"Simple. You may pay fees or not. If, however, you are called into a legal action in any capacity, you must be able to document payment for the last three years or pay the amount due plus prevailing interest. That is a generic 'you,' of course, as yours will be deducted automatically until your indent is paid."

"So if you don't do anything wrong and keep your mouth shut you can cruise?"

"In theory. However, the chance of spending a year without going to Citizen's Court is negligible."

"You're joking. Go to court every year?"

"It's a different system than Earth. The Oath requires a court appearance, so does a documented marriage. Registering the birth of any children who will be able to inherit or of your own birth if your parents didn't. Traffic incidents. Use of force in self-defense may, if there are questions. Civil disputes over wages or benefits. The only reliable way to avoid the system is to move so far out in the brush that no one will encounter you. Some do that."

"And the whole government runs on those fees?"

"Citizens pay for the privilege of ruling, getting a small stipend in return and the court fees paid are more generated income. The military and safety patrols charge for any assistance we render on duty and most of the large corporations donate a small percentage to the military as an insurance against our need in industrial accidents. They also use us as testing and advertising for any products we may find useful. Our main exports are industrial and military technology, and our military is better than any media advertising. There is a strong charitable and cooperative tradition here—if people are done with something, they generally hand it down or leave it where it can be salvaged. Taxes aren't needed for welfare or to be wasted on second-rate education or artificial 'pensions.' You buy everything for yourself on an open market of companies that want your business."

"I don't see how that can possibly work fairly," she disagreed, shaking her head.

"Well, it costs less than half as much to educate a student here, who will score much higher on any aptitude test. Literacy is above ninety-six percent, and I believe North America is about eighty-nine percent. And no, it isn't fair. Some schools are better than others. But more depends on the student than the school, and people are not equal. I point out that our standard of living is considerably higher than anywhere on Earth and we accomplish it without taxing people into poverty."

Kendra wasn't convinced, but the system did seem to work. She hadn't seen many homeless people on the street, although she suspected that a lot of them probably starved in short order. Starvation was probably a wonderful motivator. It was also probably a painful killer. Then she considered that millions of people starved on Earth every year and all the politicians could suggest was a higher contribution rate. She decided that somewhere was a solution that would work for everybody, and fell asleep pondering a philosophical issue unresolved for at least three thousand years.

It was odd waking the next morning. Between the Sparkle and the interrupted sleep, she felt bouncy, but remote. She slipped out of bed and headed for the shower, feeling better than the previous day, but still weak and congested. Her legs ached horribly from even the little she'd walked. The steam helped her sinuses and her feet were a bit better. She dressed in the same basic casual garb and stepped into the uniroom. Rob was still asleep in the chair, having dozed off while they'd talked, and she decided to let him rest while she dug into her comm. She had been wondering what the libraries had to offer and now was a good time to look. She began a random search.

Rob woke a few minutes later, brushed his fingers across her shoulder and went into the bathroom. He was out quickly, showered, alert and naked. "I'll get some breakfast," he told her, walking toward the door. She nodded distractedly without interrupting her reading. The library she'd found was amazing.

He returned clothed, with a sandwich, freshly baked and warm, that contained some cut of pork and a strong cheese. She took it and put it down, saying, "Thank you." She turned in her chair, pointed to the screen, and said, "I don't believe this!"

"What?" he asked around a mouthful of breakfast.

"There are books in here on demolition, keypass forgery, manufacture of firearms, vid manuals on sadomasochistic sex, a treatise that claims Caucasians are an inferior species responsible for all rape and warfare and recommending our random murder—"

"That would be Invidi Masul's pathetic inferiority complex. He's done six vids and a series of lectures on that subject and keeps finding idiots to support him, including Caucasians," Rob elaborated.

"They allow him to say things like that?!" Kendra burst out. She was incredulous.

"Which 'they' is going to stop him when there's an obvious market for idiocy?" Rob asked. "You must be reading the Metapanics catalog. They'll publish anything that someone will buy, from Masul's verbal masturbation to an excellent selection of books that were smuggled off Earth when the history books were made 'relevant and nonjudgmental' about a hundred years ago," he helpfully provided.

Kendra was silent for a moment. "He was advocating genocide," she said, trying to make her point. Was everyone on this planet unaware of the risks? "The same listing has detailed instructions and engineering diagrams for nuclear weapons!"

"Colonel Watanabe's *Improved Low-Yield, Reduced Radiation Mining Charges for Populated Areas,*" he agreed. "A text used in most engineering schools. We built one at the secondary school I went to. Basically moved a small mountain three meters to the left."

Kendra was stunned silent again. This society had no restrictions on hallucinogens, sex or weapons-grade nuclear material. She tried again. "It's dangerous to allow people to build bombs. At the least, they might screw up and take out their own subdivision."

"Nukes are necessary for asteroid industry and heavy mining. We've never had a problem," Rob assured her. "And I believe Sydney, Tomsk, and Saint Louis have all had terrorist-built nuclear weapon incidents."

"Well," she returned, offended, "I can guess where they got the stuff."

"Sorry. Sydney and Tomsk were before we started trade with Earth. The Saint Louis material came from Argentina according to my military history training," he said. She looked about to protest and he quickly continued, "Now I want you to consider: any legal adult here can do anything he wishes with the only restriction being that no one else gets hurt. Every few weeks, some idiot blows his kitchen apart while trying to make fireworks for a holiday, and has to pay his neighbors for broken dishes. About five percent of the people in the park yesterday were armed—"

"Including children!" she put in. "There was a girl who couldn't have been more than sixteen Earth years, whatever that is here, toting a pistol."

"Yeah, that really is stupid," he agreed. "What kind of pervert would want to rape a nubile eleven-year-old?"

Catching the sarcasm, and realizing the thrust of the question, Kendra calmed a little, and said, "If there was a decent police force, she wouldn't have to worry."

"Earth has a policer, deputy, armed federal or national agent or soldier for every forty people. How's the crime rate?" he asked rhetorically. "Please believe me; statistically, you are perfectly safe on the streets here. The crime rate is the lowest of any human society on Earth or out here."

Kendra was still in turmoil. She believed his numbers were correct, she also knew in her heart that anarchy caused crime. It wasn't *safe* to let amateurs carry guns or make explosives and it was just plain irresponsible and sick to let people advocate genocide or take photos of a man tied up in positions like that, having things like that done to him.

Not for the first time, she wished she could go home.

They agreed to table the discussion, and Rob told her of local events, sports and customs. He suggested that it was a good time to learn about guns and said he'd loan her one for the time being. She protested loudly, until he called up a picture from a news archive that showed an adult male ripper standing over the body of an Earth elk in Lakeside Park. She agreed with his logic on the only way to negotiate with such a creature and followed him next door to his apartment.

He showed her the basics of weapon safety. He showed her his guns.

"Are you planning on staging a revolt?" she asked.

"No. Why?" he replied.

Pointing at the hardware on the bed, she said, "All of this."

"Well, let's see," he said, reaching for the first and explaining at length. "This is my military issue weapon. It stays here most of the time, unless I'm on an extended trip, in which case it goes with me. The Merrill is my primary sidearm, in public or on duty. The Colt is an antique. The Sig-Remington is for game—"

"You *kill* animals with those things?" Kendra was really getting scared.

"I'm not a sport hunter. I eat what I kill," he said. Kendra was disgusted that he thought that justification.

"It is a truly *sick* society that kills helpless animals," she said.

"Rippers, goddams and slashers are not helpless. And you seemed to enjoy your steak last night."

"It came out of a vatory and you know it," she volleyed back. She stared at him for several seconds before understanding the expression on his face. "My God, that was an animal?"

"Used to be, anyway," Rob said with a nod and a grin that was meant to be mean.

Kendra ran for the bathroom and lay down on the floor. She'd hoped it would be cool, but it was heated for comfort. Right now she didn't care. She was afraid the roiling in her guts was going to turn to vomiting and just as afraid it wouldn't. Nausea washed over her, her pulse thrummed in her temples and she broke into a sweat. Rob was over her in seconds. "I'm sorry about that. I knew you didn't know, but I didn't think it would hit you that hard."

Crying quietly, trying to keep her face taut, Kendra opened her mouth to speak and felt her composure shatter. "I don't belong here. I come from a civilized little town where people live normal, decent lives. And I want to go home," she wept.

Rob pulled her head gently into his lap. "I know it's hard. I've had the same culture shock the other way. The difference being that I knew I was going home. This is a lot to throw on you all at once, but you have to learn it or you won't be able to cope."

Nodding, she forced her breathing to normal. It was some time before her nerves quieted. "I need to go lie down," she told him as she rose carefully. "It's not personal, I . . . I've just had too much input today."

His strong grip helped her to her feet. "Sure," he replied, voice still cheerful, if a bit forced. He walked with her and at the door he said, "Hey—"

She turned to face him. "I'm sorry. I get very intense. Tell me to back off if you need to," he told her.

With a smile that was only half forced, she said, "Okay," before turning to go.

"Here," he said, and thrust a holstered pistol into her hand. "I hope you never need it."

She replied, "Thanks." It felt odd in her hand and she wasn't sure what else to say.

Back in her room, she resumed reading at the comm desk, ate a sandwich and soup for dinner, as that was still about the limits of her pantry, and made notes of other things she'd need. Everything she'd ever taken for granted had to be reassessed and considered. It was frightening in many ways. Everyone wants "freedom," she decided, but the more free one was, the more responsibility one had. She wondered again if she'd made the right choice of new homes.

Periodically, she'd touch the holstered pistol on the corner of the plain polymer desk. Its presence bothered her in many ways, and yet it became more reassuring as she read about what was essentially a frontier planet.

The fact of that reassurance bothered her even more. The gun was a tool, not a talisman. It couldn't solve problems.

Sighing, she dimmed the window and turned off the lights—manually—and crawled into bed for a nap. She twitched restlessly and got little benefit from it.

About dinnertime, Rob knocked on Kendra's door, heard her say, "Come in unlock door goddammit!" as she remembered there was no voice circuit available. She opened the door for him.

He squeezed her shoulder lightly and asked, "What's going?"

"Shopping for insurance," she said sitting down at her comm. "It's outrageously expensive."

"Not compared to paying a bureaucracy and . . . ah," he interrupted his own monologue, looking at her sidescreen of notes. That would make it really expensive. "Like some advice? Systems efficiency is my job. You've fallen for Novice's Trick Number Six," he said.

"Okay," she said. "Can you explain that?"

"Start here," he pointed. "How likely are you to have cancer or cardiovascular trouble in the next five years?"

"Not very," she admitted.

"Then cancel it and don't waste money on it."

"But it's part of the package," she protested.

"That's just a marketing ploy. You can build any policy you like. Your renter's insurance will be cheaper through these people and unless you plan on running a home industry in this shoebox, you don't need much. If you damage the furniture, just work out a payment plan with the owner. Add this, eliminate this. I would spend money for a wrongful death policy—"

"Why? What is that?" she asked.

"In case you mistakenly kill someone thinking it self-defense or accidentally run them over or such, you don't want to have a court find you negligent and fine you their life's earnings."

"They can do that?" she asked, suddenly scared.

"Can and will. You also need investigation insurance; if you are involved in a crime or a victim of it, someone has to pay to dig up evidence for you. Spend money for good vehicle operations coverage and a minimal amount for disability and unemployment. You need to be fed and have a roof, but not much else, since you don't have extraneous assets. If you take that, your total is . . . one zero three twenty a month."

"That's . . . lower than I expected," she agreed.

"Great. Glad to help. My basic service fee is two hundred credits. Cash or account?" Seeing her face he added, "I'm joking. But do keep people's intentions in mind when asking help from strangers. There are some really mercenary people out there."

"Yeah," she agreed, "I met one the other day." She thought unkind thoughts about Tom Calan again. That memory would last a long time.

Kendra woke at 7:30 Monday morning, or 2:75 Rowanday, local figuring, and got ready for her first day at work. She dressed in pants since she expected to crawl a lot, and checked the map before heading for the park garage. She stepped outside and began to walk. The sky was clear, turning that incredible blue again, and she enjoyed the sights. Nearing her destination, she began to realize how chill it was and that she'd forgotten her cloak. She hurried and was out of breath when she arrived. Despite the claims of "walking distance," it was a good twelve hundred-meter blocks to the park.

The personnel door was open and she hurried inside. Squinting at the relative gloom, she saw a short man of obvious Asian heritage, who nodded. "You're Kendra?" he asked.

"Yes," she agreed. He took her hand in the two-handed shake that she was gradually getting used to.

"Hiroki Stewart," he said. Pointing, he continued, "Pot's over there."

She nodded again and walked in the direction indicated and into a large bay. Several people were present and conversation died as they looked her over. She ignored them and headed for the coffee urn.

A box next to it held several tenth cred coins. Deducing their meaning, she reached a tenth out of her pouch and dropped it in. She grabbed a poly cup from a stack and filled it, then couldn't find any sugar. There were several flavored mixes, but no sugar. Shrugging, she tried it straight.

At first she thought it was mocha. Then she realized it was just chocolate. Actually, not *just* chocolate, but chocolate thick enough to stand a spoon in. It was bittersweet and warmed her through. She took it to a table and found a seat. She rapidly found herself standing again, being introduced to fifteen people whose names she knew she would forget by lunch. There was another, larger group off in one corner, who looked more reserved. They were not introduced.

Stewart came out a few moments later. "Simms," he said, reading names off a roster, "take five of the labor and clean up the North End from those concerts yesterday. Pasky, you take ten through the south side of Liberty and the Bazaar. Juma, take five to Riversedge and put up chairs and power for the Rally by the River . . ." He read off several other names and tasks. Finally he called, "Pacelli."

"Yes, sir?"

"I'm told you can run coordinate machines."

"I've done some."

"Good. Come with us."

She followed Stewart and a redheaded woman to a medium flatbed hauler. They all piled into the cab and Stewart drove them into the park. "Kendra, this is my wife Karen. She's my deputy and does most of the administration while I do the designing, although we switch off, sort of. Karen, Kendra is the immigrant from Earth I told you about."

"Great!" Karen smiled, gripping hands. She was in her local late twenties, or mid forties for Earth, younger than Hiroki. She was slightly lined, but very well kept. She smiled a huge, toothy grin. "Glad to have another tech. We've been needing one for several weeks now. Maybe we can be caught up by mid-summer. I'm told you're familiar with several varieties of imported flowers?"

"I've only used industrial CMs," Kendra explained, "not the free operating ones you use for commercial exterior work. I know flowers informally."

"There's only a few quirks that are different on the machines. You'll get it," Karen assured her.

They stopped in an area of the park unfamiliar to Kendra and got out. The two showed her the basics of the machine, made sure she had a passing familiarity with the programming language and handed her a flash chip for the system.

"There's the manual in case you need it. We want a flowerbed laid out like this," he said, indicating a sketch on the screen, "on the south slope of that hill. We'll pick you up in about a div. Here's a radio in case you have any problems."

They watched as Kendra activated the machine and had it walk out of the trailer and up the hill. They then drove off, leaving her nervously flipping through the manual. The device was apparently similar in concept to the computerized tools in her father's force-beam shop. Once set, it would plant the various seeds in the geometric patterns programmed into it. She got to work inputting the data, the code being almost identical to what she was used to with the shop tools. Once that was accomplished, she dug in the included toolbox for a scale and measured off distance from the path. She found the appropriate starting place and let the machine go.

It ambled around, scraping and furrowing the ground, drilling holes and dropping seeds. She watched it for a while and realized there was a problem. Two large trees were very close to the edge of the pattern and might interfere. She paused the program and considered options.

She listened to the radio for a few moments and determined that the traffic was utterly without formal rules or code—it was mere chatter. She waited for a break in conversation and said, "Mister Stewart, this is Pacelli."

"Yes, Kendra?"

"We appear to have two trees in the way of the program. What do you want me to do?"

"Can you work around them?"

"With some reprogramming, yes."

"That's fine."

When Stewart returned, he looked over her modified arrangement with a critical eye and smiled. "Very nice," he said. The machine was walked back onto the hauler and taken to another location. Kendra was given another flash and set to work again. They picked her up at midday, looked around at length and Stewart said, "I think we are very fortunate to have acquired you. You do some excellent work."

"Thank you, Mr. Stewart," she acknowledged, relieved and happy.

"Hiroki, please. Can you design arrangements, too?"

"I'm not very familiar with local flowers," she said apologetically.

"Then you should get familiar with them. I'll give you maps tomorrow, both city and of individual parks. I'd like you to plan some arrangements," he said. Turning, he spoke to his wife, "Karen, give her a ride home and park it."

She spent the days working and the afternoons and evenings exploring. With Rob as guide, she saw the city and suburbs.

Despite its small size, Jefferson was very modern. It had all the expected industry, parks that exceeded anything she'd seen on Earth, stunning architecture and an amazing collection of museums, galleries and theaters. Every venue was constantly packed with activity, and smaller halls and street corners hosted local entertainers. It was the cleanest, prettiest, most impressive city she'd ever seen or heard of. And no one on Earth was aware of it.

The local patterns would be forever strange, she decided. Every so often, she'd run into another glaring difference. Ground traffic was one example. Traffic signals were optional. If there was no cross traffic, people paused then continued, disregarding the old-fashioned lights. One day she came across a broken signal. She'd thought someone was directing traffic, as smooth as it seemed to be moving. Actually, people were acting as if it were still there and functioning, taking turns for several seconds in each direction. Bizarre. She couldn't even fathom how that came about.

One afternoon her second week insystem, she discovered her shower controls had gone bad. There was no control over spray intensity and the temperature was erratic. She called in a message to the building custodian.

Less than a seg later, Rob knocked on her door with a toolbox. "You called?" he said.

She stood confused for a moment. *Rob* was the building custodian? "You?"

"Maintenance, security and resident manager for the owner," he told her as he headed for the bathroom. "I get my apartment for free and a small salary. It doesn't interfere with my regular work and it's easy money."

He ran the shower through its cycles, nodded and stuck a driver in to uncode the latches. He slid out a module, replaced it and a gasket and closed back up. "All done," he said. "No charge, but a gratuity is customary."

She grinned and made a rude gesture. He laughed. "You said you wanted to show me some of your work at the park? Let's go over," he suggested.

He looked impressed at the numerous beds she'd laid out. When she showed him the new riot of color around the main fountain, he looked stunned. "Wow," he said, not moving. "That's incredible."

"You really think so?"

"Ask for more money," he said.

"Uh . . . can I do that?" she asked, unsure.

"Ask for more money," he repeated.

When she mentioned the subject to Hiroki, he sighed. "I'd love to give you a lot more, even double. But it all depends on donations and fees. We won't see that until later in the year. I'm sorry, but the reason we advertised for an indentured contractor was to save money. It's not a deliberate ploy to hurt you. As soon as we can, you'll get it." He looked genuinely embarrassed.

Chapter 6

"Whether a party can have much success without a
woman present I must ask others to decide, but
one thing is certain, no party is any fun unless
seasoned with folly."

—Desiderius Erasmus

The summer was hot and Kendra took to working in shorts, kneepads and a halter. The predomi-
nant local custom of removing body hair now made
sense as a precaution against the reek of sweat and
the rash it caused, and she went along with it. She
wore her contacts and either a hat or scarf and gradually eased off on the blocker to a light protective layer
against the desert-bright Iolight. She was developing
a tan.

She arrived one morning, dreading another day of
sweat pouring down her back, tickling and itching, dust
in her nose and the still heat from all the wind breaks.
She got a reprieve when Hiroki arrived and said,

"Kendra, we need to set up facilities for Solstice this weekend. Take twenty of the labor and get the fences set." He showed her a map and pointed, "And we need courtesy lights along here and the toilet trailers go here. Take the large truck."

She nodded and gulped. The large truck was ten meters long. She grabbed the code, checked it over and very carefully backed out, then pulled in front. Walking back inside, she looked at the labor pool and said, "Okay, let's go, people."

Some came over immediately, a few hesitated until she waved at them. Two older adolescents sat at the table, talking and smoking and ignoring her.

"I said, 'Let's go!'" she repeated, louder. One of them flicked his eyes her way, deliberately looked back and kept talking. She finally walked over and grabbed his shoulder.

He threw her hand off, stood up and loudly said, "You just better back the fuck *off*, indent! When I'm done, then we can go!"

Myrol Jamal, the park mechanic, came over at the commotion. His broad mustache fluttered as he spoke, knotted arms and hands twisting a rag. "And *you* better back off, *criminal*, or you may find yourself in shackles. The lady asked you to do something you've been assigned to, so get to it."

The tall youth looked down at him, up at Kendra and snorted. He swallowed his drink, threw the bulb at the recycle can and jumped into the truck. Kendra gave Myrol a grateful look and jumped into the driver's seat. He nodded slightly. He was a hard man to intimidate and very decent, if normally reticent.

The idiot hung off the side and hooted all the way across the park. Some of the kids thought it very amusing but Kendra steamed. He was going to be trouble.

Most of the crew worked at least adequately diligently at the task. Some were outright industrious. The punk, whose name was Rubens, did nothing but talk and get in the way.

Finally, she said, "Rubens, go home. Come back when you are ready to work. I'm marking you off for the day."

He spun, walked over and pressed his face up to hers. His breath stank. "Who's going to make me, indent? You? I'll take off and stay right here with my friends. And if I don't get credit, there just may be an accident. Get me?"

Kendra swallowed. This was the first hint of violence she'd seen since arriving. Still, if this punk thought she'd be intimidated, he had something to learn. She came from a *big* city, fifteen times the size of this place.

She knocked his arms aside, put a hand on his chest and shoved. "Get the fuck out of my face, get your lazy ass working, unless you aren't adult enough for a job, in which case I'll call your daddy to come get you. And I will write up any report I damn well feel like! Understand me, prisoner?" she shouted. She took two steps toward him.

He stood, not sure if she was going to hit him or not. But he couldn't back off once he'd set a position. He approached.

Two of the others flanked him and grabbed him. "This isn't up, man," one of them said. "She's doing her job. If you start a fight, you'll be shackled and doing shit work."

"Yeah?" he replied. "You afraid of her?"

"No. But I don't want to get dragged into your fight and I don't want to be a witness and I don't think there's any reason to fight. Just do the damn work and we can go, okay?"

Kendra was only too glad to get back at midday and be done with it. She privately thanked the other two, who were paying off petty theft charges. Rubens was being held for assault, which was apparently unusual. She reported all of it to Hiroki.

That evening, Rob quietly read her the riot act. "Lady, you need to be armed! There's a very few idiots, and that was one of them, who only understand brute force. You aren't strong enough to tackle them."

She didn't like that idea. But she did agree he had a point.

She read Earth news that evening, sitting at her desk, and it didn't reassure her about the future. General Robinson and Colonel Bruder were being tried for misappropriation and more people were being dragged in. This was a scandal that kept growing and tied in to illegal arms shipments to several of the plethora of factions on Mtali, a general assemblywoman, military officers . . . and there was still a secondary listing of her as a suspect, with a reward attached. She'd been hoping that it would eventually blow over and she could somehow head home. She realized she'd not thought it through, couldn't go home and would be wanted for life. Sighing in depression, she buried her head in her hands. She was stuck here permanently. She'd known it intellectually, but not in her guts until now.

So, she had to pay off her indent at menial work that wasn't much of a strain on her faculties, some- how create a new life without drawing attention to herself and avoid contact with anyone from Earth who might recognize her. What did it take to change a name here?

She went back to talk to Rob. Then she realized she couldn't give him too many details. Then she decided she had to talk to someone. She told him everything.

He sipped a beer and listened quietly, then replied, "Okay, so what?"

"So *what?*" she replied, storming. "Didn't you listen to me?"

"Yes, now relax," he replied. He waited while her breathing slowed. "We don't have security cameras, we don't have implants for location in emergencies. Who's going to recognize you? Why change your name? The whole point of coming here was that they wouldn't look for you here, right?"

Considering and taking another breath, she replied, "Maybe you're right."

"Of course I am," he assured her, taking another swallow of beer. "Of course, I wouldn't make a big deal of it. There are people who'd take the reward money after all, but even then, it'd be hard to extradite you."

He sounded so relaxed. She'd grown up thinking of the government as omnipotent. The hazy inefficiency in any large bureaucracy wasn't something she'd considered and it didn't apply here anyway. She still wasn't sure within herself.

Rob interrupted her musing by saying, "Now, that UN General Assembly vote condemning us for selling technology to 'nonapproved users' is a bit annoying. But again, they can't do anything about it."

The next day, she was by herself again, the regular work supervisor back from his day off. They dropped her in the far eastern side of the park with two planters, a mower, an edger and a map. She had until 3:75, about 10 a.m., to get things arranged and trimmed, then the labor crew would arrive to lay out chairs. The day heated up quickly and the work was complex and demanding despite the automation. She finished on time, heaving support equipment back aboard the trailer and shortly was taken back to the garage. As Hiroki drove, he asked, "Would you mind working on Berday? There is a bonus."

"Sure, if it's a normal shift. My friends want to show me around."

"That's fine," he nodded. "We'll set up and be done in plenty of time for the party."

"Thanks. I need the money."

Solstice was on Gealday, local Sunday, but the celebration was Berday night, leaving the three-day weekend and Rowanday as a holiday. Kendra had gladly embraced the seven-day workweek and three-day weekend as a better schedule than Earth's. One could actually get things done in three days. The work week was long, but the hours—divs—were not bad. It actually worked out to slightly less than the time she put in on Earth.

Most local businesses gave Berday off, too, just so people could travel. Kendra had laughed in delight at the idea of a five-day weekend and was sorry she couldn't give it a try. The extra money would be welcome though, and she had nowhere particular to go. She helped arrange and organize toilets, seating, barricades, ropes and traffic avenues for the half-million people expected to throng the park that night. There were trash containers to put out, edges to neaten and more vendors of all the usual holiday trinkets and drinks. It was as big an event as the Fourth of July in America or World Federation Day. Not only that, but it was a commercial event that had her bemused. There was so much hype about it that she didn't understand at all.

Crowds were beginning to form even before the crew finished. They were good at taking direction and keeping the avenues clear, but it promised a crush of people later. The cleanup was likely to be staggering, but two others were supervising that and the labor would be all prisoners. She wondered again if there were enough trash bins and toilets, but she knew they handled this every year.

The pyrovisual company doing the main display had brought in floater after floater of launch tubes, banks of lights and lasers, their own generator in case local power was lost and an army of technicians. It was owned by one family who did nothing but travel the planet and some of the habitats doing displays, and they cheerfully dragged out the kilometers of wire and hundreds of transceivers they would use. Long practice gave them seemingly effortless professionalism and the towers and racks seemed almost to fly together from pyschokinetic forces.

As promised, Kendra was released in plenty of time to get home. She arrived close to dinnertime, which was at 6 div, about 2:30 p.m. Most of the other tenants were gathered outside in the quad, burning charcoal and steak, chicken and shellfish and sucking down liquor at a rate that was truly awe inspiring. Virtually everyone was walking today and most of those who weren't were riding the "public" transportation, which was of course all privately owned. Kendra was surprised to find that they had lowered their prices for the holiday to almost nothing.

Rob had several items grilling, including a vat-raised steak for her. She appreciated the gesture, knowing how expensive it was here, and accepted a beery kiss. He'd had a few. As soon as he disentangled, he gripped her arm to indicate she should wait and jumped onto a picnic bench.

"Listen Up!" he bellowed. "That means you, you booze besotted inbreeds!" There were chuckles and a few retorts at that. "All of you know I'm the local maintenance, security and general dogsbody around here." He rode out more insults and raised a hand for quiet. "You may want to reconsider those comments," he grinned. "As of Rowanday, I will officially be the owner of our little slum. Official notification will come down then, but I wanted to confirm it now. Rent is as it was, which I'm sure is your first question, ya deadbeats, and nothing will change much. Except that your payments will go to my account now. That's the only important issue."

There were more jokes, some cheers, some cheerful boos and he stepped down. Kendra asked him, "How did you manage that?"

"Old man Lindeman is expanding on the North Side. He isn't getting as much return on this as he'd like, it's too far from city center to bring a high price and he can't raise the rent much on what's here. So we came to an understanding," he said.

"Still building your little empire, then?" she asked playfully.

"Damn skiffy," he replied.

"And just what would it take to come to an understanding on rent?" she joked.

"Should I categorize by act?" he leered. She howled in mock protest and nudged him, unsure if he was serious or not, deciding she didn't want to pursue that line of thought. "Seriously," he said, "if you ever don't have rent, let me know. But you'll have to prove it. And I'm not cutting deals for friends or lovers. I'd be paying people to *stay* here if I did."

She nudged him again.

They left as soon as they finished eating, Rob dragging a cooler. The streets were crowded with pedestrians, all heading for Liberty Park. Their dress

ranged from utter nudity to garish costumes of lights
and phosphorescence, casual garb and half-removed
businesswear, from the light flowing daytime styles
to the tighter, revealing nighttime outfits.

The park was packed. The crowd was thin near
the edges and osmotically flowed across the streets
to the cafés, pubs, bars and mobile vendors. Nearer
the center, it became tighter and tighter, until it
seemed the throng would crush itself. Rob guided
them toward a hillock on the northeast side. It was
covered with blankets, but there was still room to
squeeze in.

It was nearing dusk, Io low in the west and a slight
breeze blowing from the coast. The heat wasn't too
bad and the swarms of Earth and native insects had
been driven off with pheromone repellent sprayed
across the park. The people were a blaze of color and
style as far as could be seen, over the hills and along
the edges of the walks. Kendra noted gratefully that
they did not trample the flowerbeds and kept the
walks reasonably clear. City Safety officers wandered
through on foot and bike, ensuring traffic was clear,
and they had a cart with water for emergencies. It
was a surprisingly well-behaved event, from Kendra's
viewpoint.

Some people had brought small grills and braziers,
as well as coolers. Food vendors and trinket dealers
wandered around, selling shirts, glowtoys and
mementos. The glee was infectious even to Kendra and
she was totally immersed in segs. Children were galloping through the tangle of legs, carelessly getting
caught and yelling apologies as they played. People lit
small fireworks all around, pops and sparkles adding
another acrid scent to the haze of atmosphere. The
reckless abandon was unlike anything she'd ever seen
on Earth, but seemed to fit here.

Music began to blare from receivers and mounted speakers. There were several bands and orchestras somewhere in the huge park and broadcasts ranging from classical to dance to oddrock and the distinct dissonance of Freehold contemporary tunes. Lights and lasers probed the sky and the cloud generators started pumping a screen upward.

"Test fire!" sounded through the speakers and an explosion rocked the air, snatching Kendra's breath. A cheer and a few whoops rose around her.

The music tapered off, and the crowd became tense with anticipation. It was that electric feeling to the air of a half-million people awaiting amazement and thrills. A slight shiver ran down Kendra's spine. Rob brushed fingers along her hairline and shoulder and she leaned toward him.

Music roared back into being, lights glared across the crowd, who were now shouting and cheering and rising to their feet. She was a bit puzzled as everyone stood still. "National anthem?" she asked Rob.

"Yes," he replied, ramrod straight at attention. She kept quiet and looked around slowly. The safety officers were saluting. She couldn't see any military in uniform.

The bright, powerful theme ended and a roar went up from the crowd. It drowned out the announcer's voice for a few seconds, then Kendra could hear "—ors Freehold and Clash Ale. Facilities by Budreau Activities and the Jefferson City Parks. A celebration of summer, in light and soun—" The last word was cut off by another report.

Kendra would remember little of the next half-div. Concussion shells, actinic explosions, multi-colored bursts of geometric shapes, fireworks that painted animated pictures across the sky, with lasers and spotlights and roaring music, launched from the center, from building tops downtown and from skylifted platforms stunned her into amazement. She simply lay on her back and stared. She was vaguely aware of Rob fondling her left breast and shoulder, but paid no attention. The spectacle was awesome.

A pause, a cheer, then the finale hit. It lasted segs and lit the sky from horizon to horizon, crashing in her ears and dazzling her eyes. She lay still after it finished, feeling her nerves tingle. "Wow," she said simply.

She rose to her feet with Rob's help. The crowd was dazed-looking, elated, and she could smell the alcohol content in the air. More than a few looked to be under the influence of recreational drugs.

She was glad they were walking. It helped clear her head, despite the acrid smoke drifting down from the clouds. She'd drunk a bit too much, too. "That was incredible!" she said to Rob. "They do this every year?"

"Solstice, Landing Day, Heritage Day and Independence Day. We're looking for more holidays to declare, so we can do this every month," he said, half joking.

They wove through the dispersing crowd and Kendra noticed the trash lying around. There was very little, actually. What there was seemed to have dispersed from the filled cans. The civility of these people was just amazing.

She was too exhausted to go out barhopping with Rob, so she kissed him goodnight before retiring to her apartment to collapse.

Chapter 7

"In vino, veritas."

—Pliny the Younger

That local Sunday—Gealday, the need for something familiar had become unbearable. Besides, she hadn't been to church in quite some time and not at all since arriving. There were things she needed to say that she couldn't say elsewhere. She asked Rob to help her find a church and if he'd come along.

"I'll do what I can," he agreed. "But you'll need to pick the church. The few times I go I'm Druidic, not Christian." More strangeness. Druidism had had a resurgence on Earth some centuries back, but had waned again. She'd heard of it, but was unfamiliar with it.

Saint Patrick's Catholic Second Reformed Church was styled as she expected, after the early Twenty-Second-Century Geometric school of architecture. It wa straight, clean lines and simple planes in light earthy colors. Inside, it was well lit through huge expanses of glass, open without being cavernous and warmly styled in more umbers and browns. A peace flowed through her and she felt more at home and relaxed than she had since leaving Earth. It wasn't that she was particularly devout, but it was ritual and pattern she was familiar with. She left Rob in the sanctuary and went to confession. She finally had an opportunity to bare her feelings in safety.

She sought an empty confessional and sat down. A moment to compose her thoughts, a breath, and she intoned, "Bless me, Father, for I have sinned. It's been . . . two months since my last confession . . ." She detailed her departure and her concerns about her friends back on Earth. "I feel like I abandoned Tom after he did so much for me," she said. "And I didn't stay to put things right. I feel cowardly. I didn't know what else to do. And I had an oath to serve . . . I broke that in the process." She poured out her feelings and paused finally. She hadn't realized how much of a burden she'd been carrying.

"Have you prayed for your friend Tom, daughter?" the priest asked.

"Yes, Father. Daily. Almost," she qualified.

"Then God will take care of him and your thoughts will help. He acted from conscience and you have made his sacrifices worthwhile. Somewhere there is a reason for his actions, even if we don't see it."

"Yes, Father," she agreed. People kept telling her that. Maybe it was true.

"It seems to me that your oath was broken by those you swore to, not by you. If they acquit you, will you return?"

"I . . . don't know," she replied. "I'm scared."

"That will be your decision if it happens. That will be the judge of your oath."

"Yes, Father."

She felt better afterward. Rob was waiting and had held a seat for her and held her hand while she recovered her composure. He made no comments and followed the service as if he'd practiced.

"You sing well," she said as they left.

"Right," he snorted.

"Really!" she insisted.

"Must have been good acoustics in there," he said. "Do you feel better?"

"Much," she said. "Thanks for coming." He looked good in a jacket, and her new dress made her feel she was progressing. It was a luxury and she had very few of them yet.

"Sure. Anything for a friend," he said.

She knew he meant it. She also knew he was a bit more than just a friend by now.

She was never quite sure how she'd wound up inviting him into her apartment that night. She needed company, but that wasn't it alone. He had been very undemanding of her, had not mentioned sex since a frustrating attempt the week before. If she needed answers to questions or a friend or neighbor or tour guide, he was quickly available.

But she'd invited him in, he'd brought wine, they'd cooked, then spent the evening sitting watching classic movies. His place would have been more comfortable, being larger and better furnished, but this was her territory and made her feel safer. Touching had led to kissing and she realized that she was unconsciously planning sex. She shrugged inwardly and agreed with herself. It was about time she stopped trying to be a tourist and became a local, and Rob was a very decent guy.

She pulled Rob closer to kiss him. It lingered and she worked her lips along his cheek to whisper, trembling, "I want to make love to you."

He was kissing her neck and spoke gently near her ear, saying simply, "Yes." He drew gently away, slipped an arm around her and ushered her in to her bedroom. He closed the door with his foot and pulled her close again.

Kendra felt his growing urgency as his hands found their way under her tunic and around her breasts. His mouth sought her throat and she gasped. She turned her lips to his shaved temple, caressing the warm skin with the edges of them. He bit into her shoulder and squeezed her harder with his hands, then they quested further. He released both their clothes with practiced hands and coaxed her to the bed with him.

Sex without a barrier was much more intimate and much more frightening. She felt her soul truly bare to him and clutched tightly. She was losing her virginity all over again, it seemed.

This time would be better. With practice in the mechanics, she could concentrate on the torrent of sensations raining over her and shuddered silently in pleasure. The motion of him inside her seemed to go all the way to her center, to collide with a wave emanating from his mouth on hers. She dizzily enjoyed the intense heat of him for a while, then fought her way back around, pulling him on top of her. She locked in a kiss with him, grabbing his buttocks, wrapping her legs behind his knees and screaming muffled against his mouth his seeking tongue feeling him come again deep inside her nails on his back.

They made love twice more that night and she never did get to sleep. She arrived at work quite energized, and did find people still in the park from the holiday weekend when she made a preliminary inspection. She decided they weren't hurting anything and let them sleep. There was an enforceable rule against more than one day's residency, but they weren't in any danger of breaking it. She felt fine until just after five—midday— when the previous night suddenly caught up to her and she had to sit down to rest. The weather was working on becoming oppressively hot, but the low humidity made it pleasant in the shade of a tree. She sipped some water from her bottle, sat on her cloak and looked toward downtown. The gleaming cleanliness of the edifices and the crystal sky behind them was never a boring sight. Even from this distance, they towered above the plain, appearing taller than the mountains behind them.

A skeletal frame protruded above the nearer buildings. As she watched, it rose and halted, then rose again. It had to be the new FreeBank Tower that was being built. She hadn't realized they were starting so soon. As she mused, assembly drones crawled up the supports and began lashing them with cable. That would be mono-molecular boron cable, she recalled, and the struts would be tube-molecular crystal carbon composite. Incredibly strong stuff. The building should be proof against anything short of a direct hit by military explosives.

"Goofing off?" Karen asked from behind her. Kendra hadn't heard her approach.

"Oh, I'm sorry, Karen," she said. "I was taking a break and got distracted."

"That's fine," Karen chuckled, "it's almost quitting time anyway." She grinned her usual toothy grin. Rob had once made an innuendous comment about her slightly prominent teeth and Kendra had poked him for it. He could make comments about anything.

Karen continued, "I love watching them build, too. And you're done with the maze already, so relax. You'll make us look bad by being so industrious."

They sat and watched as the frame rose, joint by joint. Out of sight from them, below the near horizon, heavy machines worked furiously. The vertical pybraces were connected on their pivot points and pushed aloft. As they swung vertical, the trailing ends would be held ready for the loading tractor to attach the next set. It would have been impossible to do without modern lightweight materials and heavy machinery, even in lighter gravity.

"I wonder what they used before boron and carbon?" Karen mused.

"Low-carbon steel," Kendra replied.

"What? You're kidding! The mass would be outrageous!" The redhead was incredulous.

"No, really," Kendra insisted. "Steel truss towers with braces and crossbeams."

"How'd they erect them?"

"Using large cranes with kilometers of steel cable, set on top of gantries built of triangular steel frameworks. Then they'd move the crane onto the frame and build as they went. I studied it in class," she said.

"That had to take weeks," Karen pondered. As she spoke, the building jolted again and passed the two-hundred-meter mark. Aircars buzzed the structure, chased away by security drones.

"Months usually," Kendra agreed. "Then they used prefab modules inside, much like we do now."

Karen was fascinated. "Why so much steel? Didn't they have polymers or titanium? I recall polymers and graphite came out about then."

"They did," Kendra agreed, "and boron whisker, but it was all outrageously expensive. About like using crystal iron or beryllium now."

"Hard to think of steel as cheaper than carbon. And it couldn't be easier to work with," Karen replied, still not convinced.

"They had tools for it, and an industry. Some of them still stand. The shorter ones, anyway, like the Sears Tower in Chicago. They replaced most of the structure in the last hundred years, but it's still steel and it still stands," Kendra said. "I felt nervous in it, but they insist it's still safe."

They watched, rapt, as the scuttling pods fed cables across. The building would widen slightly from its base, then taper toward the pinnacle. Its own mass would hold the shape against the cables, with only a few crossbeams for structural support. Many thinner pieces served as traylike mounts for the modular office sections that would be installed by skycrane.

It bumped up another level and the crews adjusted the cable tension to rein in one corner that was sagging. Since the top was being built first as it rose, it was widening slowly but perceptibly and the upper sections had a tendency to draw slack from the unfixed ones being raised.

Kendra suddenly burst out laughing. "What?" Karen asked.

"It just occurred to me," she explained, still laughing, "that the cabling tractors look like insects. As they link together, they perfectly match the brand name of 'Caterpillar.'"

Karen laughed too.

While they were sitting there, a familiar voice greeted her, "Hi, Kendra."

It was Alexia. She was wearing a short dress in fluorine green that covered much of her but not her breasts, and had a black cloak over it. She was carrying a briefcase.

Kendra indicated for her to sit down, flipping more cloak out. "Hi, Alexia," she returned. "I managed not to pass out this time."

"Good! Go ahead and call me 'Marta.'"

"Okay," she agreed. "Why? And this is Karen, one of my bosses," she added.

Marta spoke to Karen, saying, "Pleased to meet you," then turned to Kendra and said, "Well, 'Marta' is my real name."

"I suppose that's a good reason. What's going?"

"Working," Marta said. "Needed my toys for this one," she explained, casually flipping open her briefcase. Kendra stared in fascination at the most amazing collection of sex toys she had ever seen. The presentation in public in front of Karen made her flush beet red.

Trying not to stare, Kendra said, "You'll have to show me what some of those things are for sometime."

"Ask me at a party sometime, when I can do a demo for advertising."

"Demo on *who*?" Kendra asked, shocked.

"Well, you, of course. It's the best way to find out. Unless you can find someone to volunteer for you."

"All I want is a brief explanation, nothing complicated, nothing public," Kendra told her, flushing again. Karen's snickers didn't help matters.

"I could do that," Marta agreed. "But then I'd have to charge you a consultation fee."

"You're . . . not joking," Kendra said, answering her own question.

"It's the same way I explain to clients. It seems mercenary, but I have to make a living. Information or demos or samples cost, and there's no refund possible."

"I guess that makes sense," Kendra nodded.

Karen interrupted with, "Kendra, we're done today. I'm going to catch a view of the construction. See you in the morning." She stood and walked off.

"Okay, Karen," she replied to the other woman's departing back, still distracted. Turning again to Marta, she asked, "How do you separate your business and social lives?"

"It's business until I book a minimum amount for the day or until I give up and call it quits or until I have a drink. I'm happy to talk about it with you, but details become a service and that's what I charge for."

"I definitely couldn't deal with that," Kendra said, shaking her head. "I wouldn't know when to quit."

"That is a problem in this business. Some people hold to a regular set of divs, usually evenings. Some are nonstop and confused and burn out quickly. I try to split the difference. I get a lot of the daytime business."

"And you don't work for a service," Kendra noted.

"No. There are very few services here, although I belong to a referral co-op. When I'm booked, my code allows a client to reach another and vice versa. The only actual services are clubs, with set divs, which I hate. They are slightly safer, but don't pay as well. I can afford to hire a chaperone when needed and I hold an expert rating in unarmed combat and have combat experience, so I'm not too concerned."

"Is everyone here a veteran?" Kendra asked. "That's all I seem to meet."

"A lot of people in this vicinity are, with Heilbrun Base just out of town. But you met me because I used to be active duty with Jaheed."

Both women got up and headed north through the park. Marta angled west and Kendra followed as they continued this most informative discussion. They wound up dodging traffic—even scarier than in the dark, when you saw the vehicles up close and realized they were all on manual or self-auto, not district control—and were shortly seated at Stanley's. Marta glanced at her phone, adjusted a setting and said, "I can't go off just yet, so I'll stick to soft drinks. Second round can be yours, if you like."

"Uh . . . okay," Kendra agreed. Her rent was paid, she had food, and her indent was an automatic deduction. She didn't need to be stingy, but it would take conscious effort not to be. She had no experience being poor—it was an entirely new state of affairs to her, as was everything else. To shift from the new pattern back to the old was difficult.

Rupe arrived, slid two small bowls of salsa, one hot, one "mild," in front of them, along with fresh baked chips, and greeted them. "Alexia, and Kendra, I believe?"

Kendra agreed and thanked him. Marta said, "Just Marta. I'm on call but not working. Ginger ale, spiced for me. Kendra?" she asked, turning.

"One of those wine coolers would be wonderful right now."

"Right up," he agreed and returned in seconds with their drinks.

Kendra found herself talking about gardening. "Apparently I have a lot of talent and my design skills are becoming useful. And I like the fact that I actually get to work here, rather than just wasting time. It gives me a sense of accomplishment I rarely got back home."

Moments later, they were interrupted by Rob. He bounced up, yelled, "Mar!" and gathered Marta in a close embrace, kissing her in a fashion that made Kendra slightly jealous. He turned then and grabbed Kendra close, kissing her in a way that made her head swim. He plunked down next to them.

"Pardon me for rudely interrupting," he said. "But I just picked up a contract with Jefferson Central Machinery to straighten out their parts files, deposit paid in advance and rather well, thank you. So I'm celebrating. Would either of you object to a drink?"

"Just one," Marta agreed, bending her rules. "And congratulations."

"Congratulations," Kendra echoed. "And I don't object."

"Done. Rupe, line us up four Silver Birches and a jalapeno lime ice for me."

Rob invited Stanley to join them, hence the fourth shot, and toasted, "To windfall profits!"

Kendra downed her Silver Birch. It had the burn of strong liquor, with a smoky sweet bite to it. It warmed her stomach and a glow suffused her. Though she had never liked liquor, this was very interesting.

Stanley went back to his counter and Rob and Marta explained their common background. "We met on Mtali," he told Kendra. "I had some yokel running up to my Hatchet as I landed it in a firefight and she popped out of nowhere and gapped him."

"That was right after he dumped a burst of fifteen millimeter into an armored vehicle bent on turning me into road pizza," Marta added. "We both are from this area, so we meet up occasionally for drinks and soshing."

"Hey," Rob put in, "Should we go down and watch the construction? It isn't every day they put up a seven-hundred-meter building." All agreed, so they wandered that way on foot. It was only a few hundred meters farther.

There was quite a crowd gathering as they approached, with several City Safety officers trying vainly to keep vehicles moving. There was a private security firm using drones and aircars to chase away those flyers who were too inquisitive. As much complaining as could be heard all around, Kendra decided it was no worse than traffic around construction sites on Earth. Most people here weren't foolish enough to get too close. The risk of getting sued and indentured for life if one interfered probably helped dissuade many of them.

The frame bumped above five hundred meters. They graciously accepted an invitation from a parked driver to stand on his car for a better vantage point. That let Kendra see into the cleared area, where the rams were sliding four more pybraces into position. The heavily silenced machines still growled as they thrust the pieces out from the center, to be caught, connected and raised by the lifts.

While the construction process was fairly standard, it wasn't a common sight to see, as quickly as the buildings were erected. The local cafés and street vendors were doing booming business with the gawkers and it was clear that traffic was snarled for the day. Automatic controls would have prevented it, Kendra thought, but these people would scream bloody murder at the suggestion of handing vehicle control over to anyone or anything. The onboard safeties prevented only impacts and did not provide flight planning.

The security cars were chasing away the same three flyers, she decided. That red one was clearly the same one that had been run off a bare seg before. The Freehold had the same idiots as the UN, even if their numbers were fewer. Some things never changed, she thought.

High overhead, the red car tried to dodge around a security drone in a dangerous game. It didn't work. The drone's automatic responses were fast enough to interdict, not fast enough to predict what the human pilot would do. The two objects intersected.

The drone was a bare thirty-five centimeters tall, tubular with steering vanes, strobe and transponder in a small instrument package. The collision speed was not great, but the drone's thrust blew directly down into one of the car's ducts. The vehicle bucked and recovered as the pilot tried to dodge and as it rose it bashed against the drone. The fan blades brushed the damaged housing and tore into shrapnel at 100,000 revs. The pieces punched and ripped holes through both casings and into the car's port-forward fan.

The cars loped crazily toward the building and the pilot steered sharply away. With port control almost gone and a conflict between automatic and manual control he tumbled and fell. The car twisted and spun as it dropped, whipping between buildings it was never supposed to approach. Kendra stared, frozen, and heard Rob mutter, "Oh, shit!" He grabbed her arm and yanked her off the car. They landed hard, stumbled, and he shoved her against the wall.

"Everybody Back!" he bellowed. Other shouts could be heard and people stared upward, trying desperately to predict where the car would land. Many people and drivers were blissfully unaware of the impending crash and Kendra stared horrified as the crippled vehicle descended.

At the last moment, the pilot righted the craft through a combination of skill, panic and blind luck. Emergency override must have kicked in, because the vehicle poured power into its three operational fans and tried to level out. It was moving at too high a velocity and at too low an altitude to accomplish that, but it did slow the inevitable impact. The slamming crunch it made as it hit two vehicles was no louder than at any other accident Kendra had seen. A pedestrian had leapt away barely in time and was swearing in relief.

Marta sprinted across the street through a stunned throng. Rob said, "C'mon," and followed, not waiting to see if Kendra followed. Several others were approaching also and Kendra tagged along, terrified at what she might see.

There was very brief confusion as everyone approached. Rob started shouting orders and was instantly obeyed by everyone. *"If you aren't a medic, get on traffic control. If you can't do traffic control, keep the crowds back ten meters. Everyone else please stay back. You! Call city safty again anyway and keep the band open. You, organize people for tools and find some strong volunteers."* He turned back with the assumption that he would be obeyed.

Marta was reaching in the tangled mess looking for casualties. Fortunately, the material was lightweight and easy to move. The hardest part was pulling out chunks of the foam that had blown into the compartments to provide support and reduce impact. There were three injuries visible: the pilot of the red car and the two in the remains of the vehicle underneath. It had been just lifting to navigate over traffic and had somehow rolled during the accident. Probably one side had dropped on proximity warning and then been hit. It had completed its tumble as it smacked another car underneath.

City Safety vehicles were landing all around and two salvage trucks arrived. An ambulance was trying to find space to land. Rob shouted and his crowd controllers pushed back to give it room. They dragged the third vehicle out of the way to give more space.

"I'm a doctor, but I'll need help," a man said as he pushed through the crowd.

"Great! What do you need?" Marta asked as she applied pressure to a wound. She had blood up to her elbows. "Kendra, I need your shirt as a bandage. Your shirt," she repeated as Kendra hesitated. Right. Nudity was okay and this was an emergency. She slipped out of the cotton garment and handed it over, feeling self-conscious. She felt cold without it, despite the sweltering heat in the air.

The doctor replied to Marta, "Uh, a good trauma medic preferably. I'm an ophthalmologist. But I can handle it while we find one."

Marta grinned as she pulled shears and a knife out of her pouch. She clicked the blade out, handed it to Kendra and said, "Cut it into five see emm strips. You're in luck, Doc. Corporal Hernandez, Third Mobile Assault Regiment combat medic. I'll stabilize, you advise."

The doctor was sufficiently experienced with emergency medicine to exceed his concerns. Marta handed over bandages and dressings and splint material when it arrived, and the two medics did all the work while City Safety and the ambulance kept them supplied with saline carriers and tools. It was a messy procedure.

The flyer was only marginally injured, although he had a slight concussion and was in shock. He kept apologizing as Rob and a safety officer extricated him and had him lie down. Rob had to be forceful when the man wanted to apologize. His victims were not in any shape to talk, nor was he.

The two casualties in the car underneath were young women, the passenger IDed as a college student. She had a severe laceration to her right arm and was unconscious. The other one moaned, but could not be reached yet. "Get that damn crane in here!" Rob shouted. Everyone else had assumed he was in charge and simply did as he said. The salvage truck backed in, extended a boom, and the driver, Rob and two others glued shackles to all four corners of the red car. "Clear so we can lift," he told Marta.

"I have a bleeder here. Get on with it," she replied.

"It isn't safe," he argued.

"Then it can fucking be unsafe, I'm not leaving my patient!" she snapped. Her voice softened and she added, "Sorry. Do it. I'll risk it."

He nodded, realized she couldn't see and said, "Okay. Kendra, grab her arm. If I yell, drag her out of there."

The red wreck lifted with a groan and space opened up underneath. Light streamed in and it was possible to see the extent of the driver's injuries. She was in bad shape, but alive.

As soon as the vehicles separated, Marta carefully turned the passenger and began to ease her through the open window. Rob and two others taped the web-cracked windscreen with emergency tape, then cut around the edge with small, whining saws. They peeled it back to gain access to the driver.

The passenger slipped out and the ambulance crew gently strapped her to a litter. Marta squirmed in and had Kendra reach in to hand her tools. Mar's dress was shredded, she wore nothing underneath and the tight quarters made for a grotesque parody of an intimate encounter.

The doctor went around the other side and between the two of them they determined the extent of the victim's injuries. She had several seeping wounds, a minor vein bleeding and some fractures. Rob and his crew commenced chopping and cutting away the safety cage while the crane kept weight off. He briefly conferred with the rescue technician from the response team, who agreed with his proposal and directed his crew to assist. Mar and the doctor dealt with the bleeding, first with bandages and pressure, then with a pneumatic pressure pad. The victim was still supported in part by the impact foam and they reinforced that with pillows, blankets, rolled cloaks and anything else they could get from volunteers. "She's getting weak," Marta said. "Do we dare try a stimulant?"

The doctor, Devon Perkins was his name, said, "It might cause a reaction, or her to start hemorrhaging if she's hurt internally. We can use a nano for shock, but only a half dose to start with," he advised. Kendra relayed the request to the ambulance crew, who delivered the drug without questions. Marta pinched the capsule, dribbled half of it away and pressed the carrier side against the victim's neck.

She stirred shortly and Marta spoke loudly to her. "Jai, I'm a medic. You've been hurt, but you're going to be okay. If you understand, wiggle your fingers . . . good. Now, we have to cut the car away from you. If you move, it might fall. You have to stay still. Do you understand? Good. Can you feel your toes? Good. Can you feel your left arm? No? Okay. Your shoulder is hurt, but we'll get you out soon. My name is Marta. Just grip my hand if you need anything, okay? Good. I'm going to stay right here. There's a doctor here, too. We are both very experienced and you're going to be fine. Just don't move, because we don't want the car to fall."

There was no risk of that, but she might have a neck injury. There was no sense in risking complications and it wouldn't be reassuring to let her know.

"Thir . . . sty," the girl mumbled. Kendra wiggled back to get her bottle and handed it to Mar. It was stinking and sweaty in the vehicle and sharp bits of frame poked at her. She wondered how the girl had survived.

"You can have a sip only, because you're upside down," Marta advised. She didn't mention possible internal injuries. "If you want, you can spit into this towel. But don't try to swallow."

Rob tugged at Kendra's ankle. "We're ready to lift," he said.

She wiggled her ankle and said, "Okay," and turned back. "They're ready to lift, Rob says," she relayed.

"Do it. Get in here as far as you can and help support her weight," Marta instructed.

Kendra propped her arms under the girl's shoulder and hunched to press against her side. Marta and Perkins gripped her legs and Rob signaled. The crane lifted very carefully, a few centimeters at a time, the metal groaning and shrieking. They gingerly wiggled her feet from within the footwells and were showered in falling chunks of safety foam. It stuck to any bloody or sweaty surface, which was everything.

Once her feet were clear, the crane howled as it pulled the load straight up and swung it aside. Other rescuers reached in to help fasten the woman to the form-fitting splint, then lifted her out and lowered her to the ground. In moments, she was also braced in a litter, still in a sitting position, and was taken away.

"I need your name," one of the safety officers said at Kendra's elbow. He was streaked with foam and oil and reeked of spilled fuel. She gave him her name and address and he moved on. Someone handed her a towel and she wiped off dried blood and grime.

The road was clear again, Kendra had noticed while Marta peeled her dress off. It was destroyed anyway. One of the safety vehicles had a box of decontamination wipes and they used them to wipe all residue away. "There's blood in your hair," Kendra said.

"And yours," Marta agreed. On Earth they would have been hospitalized against contamination, but there were no bloodborne diseases in this system. Kendra was grateful for that fact.

Before they could leave, they and all the others nearby were herded toward a restaurant called The Green Man. Inside, Kendra was thanked by several people including the construction manager, a man from the safety office and a FreeBank representative. They were offered showers in the hotel above and dinner immediately following, and it appeared that "no thanks" was not an answer they would understand.

Kendra wasn't hungry after seeing vehicles mangled and blood splashed around, although she was calmer than she would have expected. She washed down and put her work shorts back on. Marta didn't seem to notice her own utter nudity, nor did anyone mention it, other than an occasional glance and smile. They were stuffed full of salad and seafood and steaks and beer and wine. The alcohol did feel good after all the earlier stress. Her hunger returned and she plowed into the food with gusto. The Green Man was one of the city's five-star eateries and she had to admit it more than lived up to its reputation. They even had vat-grown steak.

She got into a discussion with an insurance agent who had been expressing an opinion of damages. The woman noted Kendra's surprise that unlicensed passersby had done most of the work. On Earth, few would have offered and none would have stayed after the police arrived. There was too much risk of being sued, since it could be claimed that any injuries were the result of negligence.

"How rude!" the woman had objected. "They would actually sue for helping them? And the courts would allow it?"

It was another sign of cultural dissimilarity that Kendra thought she'd never get used to.

The three left fairly late, after drinking a few generously offered rounds. Kendra sipped at hers, not wanting to get too drunk, but finally relented and drank enough to unwind. It had, after all, been a shocking afternoon. The walk back cleared her head slightly and the restaurant had found a shirt for her, with their logo on it. Marta declined clothes. Kendra still wondered how people could casually walk around naked.

At Rob's apartment, Kendra sat down heavily on the bed and said, "After last night and today, I need to rest."

"Go ahead," he agreed, lifting a thin quilt over her.

Kendra lay down and passed out from exhaustion. She woke briefly a while later to sounds. The shower was still on, with the door open, and she could discern heavy breathing and occasional gasps. Vaguely, she was aware that Rob and Marta were making love, but she was too tired to continue the thought. She fell back asleep.

She woke among bodies about ten, according to the clock. Rob was on one side, Marta on the other. The haze in her mind started to clear and she remembered what she'd overheard earlier. It bothered her a little, but she realized that she had no claim on Rob. She tried to turn on her side, but was hemmed in rather tight. As she carefully twisted over, she came face to face with Rob, whose eyes were open. He smiled, took her shoulder and pulled her close to kiss her.

When he drew back, he whispered, "Good evening."

"Hello," she whispered back. "Did you have a good time?"

"Fantastic," he agreed. "Mar was really wound up after that. Are you upset?"

"A little, I guess," she said, trying to shrug. It took effort. What *was* their relationship?

"I didn't want to hurt you, so I tried to be discreet. I'm not sure how you think of us as a couple."

"We don't really have a commitment, do we?" she observed.

"No. Would you like to?" he asked.

Shaking her head, she said, "I'm not sure."

"We'll discuss it later, then," he said and pulled her close again.

He kissed her deeply, then began to caress her neck, rubbing his lips down the side of her throat, over a shoulder. His hands stroked her gently, all down her side. She felt her leg lifted over him and he rubbed up against her.

She enjoyed the sensations, stroked him back and then there was movement behind her. She suddenly realized that she felt too many hands.

Marta was kissing the back of her neck and gliding hands over her back and thighs.

She turned, and Rob caught her body language. So did Marta.

"Should I stop?" Marta asked.

"This feels very weird," Kendra told her.

Rob hinted, "Sexuality is very different on Earth."

Marta said, "Ohh!" and pulled back, comprehending slightly.

"Kendra," Rob said, "We can do whatever you want, by whatever rules. Let us know and we can adjust."

"I don't want to cut you out," she said to Marta apologetically.

Marta placed a calming hand on her. "If you don't swing, it's not a problem. I don't want to cause any tension."

"I don't know," Kendra said awkwardly.

Rob leaned over and said, "On Earth, when I was there, most people were very restrained and although it wasn't mentioned, I got the idea that most don't do much experimenting."

Marta looked slightly askance. "You mean you've never even tried it, to see what it was like?"

"I've never even thought about it," she admitted. "I had two regular lovers and exactly three casual sexual encounters before I got here."

"I didn't mean to impose," Marta said, moving to get out of bed.

"Wait," Kendra told her, then sat awkwardly again

for a moment. "I want you to stay," she said finally. She wasn't sure she did. This was more awkward than any previous cultural variance. "But I don't know how far I'm willing to go."

"Just give me a signal and I can stop whatever you don't enjoy or I can leave. I don't want to cause any trouble at all," Marta promised.

Kendra made love to Rob while Marta played around the edges. It felt strange having an extra pair of hands and an extra mouth in the equation. She enjoyed the attention she got, but was disoriented at times, feeling almost as if she were watching and not participating. Questing hands and kisses across her neck were definitely a case of more being better, but the presence of a third person and her being an attractive woman was a hindrance.

She enjoyed herself, Rob had a great time with double the attention and Marta didn't seem to mind. Kendra tabled the idea of a rematch, deciding to think about this encounter for a while, and sat back to catch her breath. Marta ran hands down her again and she shivered in both enjoyment and tension.

They all wound up showering again then Marta gathered her things to head home. She moved quickly, but stopped at the door to kiss Rob deeply. Turning, she pulled Kendra close.

Kendra expected a hug and was numbed by surprise as she felt lips against her own, a warm, spicy tongue slipping between them. She tried to relax, feeling disconnected again, and kissed back. A few seconds and hurried goodbyes later, Marta was gone.

She was still short of sleep, overloaded on input from what had been the busiest day of her life, and so made her way next door to her own bed with an apology to Rob. She had time for perhaps another div of sleep, if she wasn't too groggy to catch it.

The next morning, there was a knock at her door, just after she woke. She answered it wrapped in a towel and still bleary from waking, and accepted a package from a System Express courier. He was young, and pretended not to stare at her as she signed for it.

She felt amused again that signatures were used and not thumbprints. Very old-fashioned, these people. She opened the envelope, which was from an insurance company, and dumped out the contents. The cover letter was full of the usual greetings, etc. Then she read the part about "Associated Liability wishes to thank you for your assistance in yesterday's accident at the FreeBank Tower construction site. We are informed that you donated labor and materials to assist in extricating our client and that your clothing was damaged on the scene. The enclosed draft is reimbursement for your losses and any inconvenience you may have suffered. If it is insufficient, please contact our office to discuss the matter. Also, we welcome the opportunity to discuss your own insurance needs at any time." It was signed by a company agent and attached was a draft rom. She plugged it into her comm and gasped. Cr1000. That would replace her cloak, shirt, shoes, water bottle and buy her two more outfits besides. Expensive ones.

She woke Rob, who had stayed up to work. He shook his head to wake himself and said, "Sure, it's legit. They'd rather pay you than the professionals. It's great PR and it's the decent thing to do. I got mine a little while ago. Cash it and enjoy." He stumbled back in to sleep and she cleaned up for work. It still felt odd to bathe twice a day, but everyone here did so at least that often.

She had to repeat the story for Myrol, Karen, Hiroki and the others. Oddly, she still wasn't scared. It had just been too shocking to feel real and she hadn't had to do anything but pass bandages and assist. The danger had never really impinged on her, so she hadn't had cause for worry.

It was a long day and brisk. The holiday weekend litter and all the gear had been torn down and piled for removal. She set lawn machines to trim and fluff the worn grass and reseeded a couple of bare spots. She kept notes and photos of the areas she passed, so they could be taken care of later. Sprinklers were dousing the dry growth, trying to revive it from the ordeal. There were still scattered pieces of trash under bushes for her to retrieve. She could see other workers chasing out the occasional leftover drunk, staggering awake and heading home. Apparently, some people celebrated for days afterward.

Children from five to teen by Earth reckoning screamed cheerfully through the park. Few adults were in sight. She was finally getting used to the idea that it was *safe* for kids to do that. No one would abduct them, bullies were rare and the older kids would stop the few there were. Nor would parents sue the park if a child had a minor accident. It was accepted that parents bore sole responsibility for their children.

One of the local gangs came through, music blaring. They wore red bandannas and canine teeth and black cloaks, shades and lipstick. That would be the Masters. She'd been shocked to find gangs here and even more shocked to find they were not feared or hated. They were nothing like the petty thugs in Earth cities.

The Masters claimed as territory an eight-block square north of the park. Their boast was that it was the safest, cleanest urban environment in the system. To that end, they patrolled regularly at all hours, organized community sales and cleaning parties and kept vandalism and petty crime under control. There'd been a minor incident the month before, when a troubled youth had been caught graffitiing a building with bonded polymer spray. Two of the Masters had scuffled with him and he'd tried to resist. He hadn't been seriously hurt, but City Safety had taken him to a hospital for observation. The gang had apologized publicly, but stressed that they would not allow that behavior on their "pave."

The idea of street gangs being a desirable and safe environment for youths and a useful aid to safety in the city was an irony that made Kendra chuckle every time she saw them. They were the politest, most helpful teens she'd ever met, even asking permission before raiding the trash for useful items for sales or for the poor. They'd donated and installed a climbing frame in the north playground a couple of weeks earlier and were talking about adding another slide. They were snagging trash as they walked through, too. A couple of them waved and grinned. She waved back. One of them wandered over. "Hey, lady, how goes?"

"Good. Tired," she said. "That was a great display, huh?"

"It kicked. Hey, Ms. Chang, the mother of that boy you found, says to thank you a lot."

"Oh, sure, she's welcome. Glad he got found," she said. She remembered that vividly, too. The young boy had come running crying to her the week before. He'd gotten separated from his mother and had headed for Kendra as the closest thing to an official. She'd taken him to the garage and asked for help. She had no idea what to do with a lost child and had been scared of the responsibility. City Safety had already had a report and took him home a few segs later. The thought of a lost child in an Earth park made her shiver, but every time she turned around here, the safety of the system was pounded into her yet again.

The Masters wandered on, the music and their intense young energy fading in the distance.

Back at the garage, Kendra and coworkers cleaned and performed preventive maintenance on the big machines. As they worked, Kendra dug for more info. "Hiroki?"

"Yes?"

"How is the park financed?"

"We get a small stipend from the city, quite a bit in donations from civic groups, corporations and wealthy individuals and user fees wherever possible," he explained. "The vendors, concerts, any large meeting or reserved pavilion space generate fees."

"Isn't that rather sporadic? How do you manage cost accounting?"

"Very carefully," he said with an inscrutable grin. "Karen does a lot of juggling to keep things as steady as possible. At the moment, we have a small reserve."

"Ah," she said, understanding. "And who owns it?" was her next question. Most of the outlying parks were clearly private but accessible property. But Liberty Park wasn't, and the Freehold Constitution prohibited the government from owning property.

Hiroki grinned an inscrutable grin. "No one does," he said. "It was always a public area, always maintained, and everything grew up around it."

She said, "But then those people who squat here—"

"Actually could claim in court to own a chunk of land," he finished for her. "It's never come up, isn't likely to and would almost certainly lose in court or by duel."

She pondered that at length. Whenever she thought she had a handle on things, something else odd came up.

Idle thoughts aside, she considered her future. She was finding the work a bit challenging, but only as an intellectual exercise. She didn't *belong* to anything here and it bothered her. She needed more to her life than gardening and plumbing and setting out chairs for concerts. The work wasn't objectionable, wasn't hard, but wasn't giving her anything other than a roof and her meals. She'd been an equally small cog in the UN military, but could look at the news and see things being done that mattered. This was pure fluff and getting on her nerves already.

Her thoughts were interrupted when, several segs before quitting time, a brilliant purple coupe with garish green stripes and what sounded like a huge turbine pulled up across the gate. Marta hopped out, wearing what for her must have been scummy clothes—shorts and tunic. They were bright red and emphasized her figure well. Running up, she spotted Kendra and said, "Hi, dear. Do you have plans tonight?"

"Ah, no," Kendra replied.

"Up for some?"

"Sure, what?"

"Concert at Dante's, over in Delph'. My treat. See you at your place at six-fifty?"

"Okay. Thanks," Kendra nodded, a bit surprised.

"Great! Gotta run—client," Marta explained. She kissed Kendra quickly but hard, turned and vanished. The car screamed off the drive, all four tires leaving compound behind. As soon as there was clearance it lifted into the air.

"Ladyfriend?" Karen asked behind her.

"Ah, no," Kendra said, startled as she turned. "Just a friend." She was really embarrassed at being kissed in public and was blushing hard. She thought her ears must be glowing. She decided to mention it to Marta when they met up.

After work, she hurried home to get ready for the date. Rob was at his comm, working. He apparently hadn't showered or eaten all day. He had to be busy, knowing local customs. She threw a sandwich together and handed it to him. "Thanks," he acknowledged. "Did Mar find you?"

"Yes, and kissed me in public," she told him.

"Hmm. I can see why that would bother you. I also see why she didn't think of it. The two of you could be really good for each other."

"Meaning?" she asked.

His grin grew back. "Never mind. Idle thought. Oh, your comm downed the info you wanted. Next time, let me know. I can find the stuff cheaper than most commercial programs and I get a discount on access."

"Thanks, but you don't need to," she said, smiling back.

"Lady," he said, turning slightly, "I buy my mem a googlebyte at a time. Twenty or thirty yoctobytes is hardly a dent. Not a worry."

"All right then, thanks," she said, acquiescing. "Did Mar invite you?"

"Yeah, but this block has to be ready by two tomorrow. I'll be staying here."

"Get some sleep," Kendra insisted.

"Sleep is for wimps . . ." he began. It was a mantra of his and she'd heard it all weekend long. She joined him for the rest.

" . . . Healthy, happy, well rested wimps; but wimps nonetheless!"

Leaning close, she wrapped arms around his shoulders, licked his earlobe and whispered, "You need sleep so you can make love to me later."

"I'm out," he agreed. "Are we still flying tomorrow?" he asked. He'd offered her a ride aboard a combat vertol and she'd been intrigued.

"Oh, yes!" she agreed. She wasn't going to miss that.

She walked into her apartment, showered and put on clothes from her small selection that was appropriate for evening wear. She chose a shoulderless tunic with a mandarin collar and stretch slacks in gray, with a broad belt for her pouch and holster. Done, she headed for the kitchen alcove and mixed up a soup that would have made Rob scream in disgust—thick with starches and with a paucity of spices—and ate while reading her loads.

The news from Earth was available in the Freehold system, but most of it had little market. There was an interest in trade and industry, although not as much as Kendra expected. Earth was regarded as a backward, slightly industrialized source for second-rate products. She appreciated the irony that the public back home regarded the colonies as rustic and rural agricultural backwaters.

Considerable digging had yielded what she sought. She found the listing on her parents' business, saw it was doing well and wished again she could send them a message. They must think her dead by now and she wondered what they'd done with her personal belongings. Or did the government still have them as "evidence"? That was a common enough occurrence. Still, her vid gear, music, clothes and such wouldn't have done her much good here. There was no word on her brother, either good or bad, but he often didn't post to his site for weeks at a time, with all the fieldwork he was doing in grad school.

The general system news was slightly worrisome, containing many negative references to Freehold, its businesses and politics. The North American regional report listed crime, weather and special events. She had trouble remembering that it was only a day old, that being the minimum time for a message to crawl to a ship in transit, be received before jump and retransmitted immediately after. Most of what she had downed was the same news it always was, but she read intently, enjoying the closeness she perceived from loads written in a language she could understand. When done, she switched to local news.

If Utopia was defined as a lack of news, Freehold was not Utopia. A Citizen had been shot by an offended plaintiff and was hospitalized. The editor of Jefferson Live News announced that it was the seventh shooting of the year. That couldn't be right, she thought. Minneapolis, at fifteen million people, typically had about fifteen hundred by mid-year, and firearms were illegal for all but police, federal officers and a few state and local agents. They had less than seven percent of that total here, per population. It didn't seem possible.

The suspect was in custody and would be tried as soon as the investigators put a case together. Since a Citizen was involved, the government had hired an investigator on contract, having none of its own. There was a side issue of the contractor having previously been owned by another Citizen and hints that favorites had been played. Politics mixed with a murder was so suddenly familiar that she laughed in relief. At least some things never changed.

There was a huge financial row over Resident Service Labs. Since there were no government standards, most manufacturers paid to be rated by one of three large or several smaller rating firms. The firms' integrity was their stock in trade. RSL employees had apparently been caught accepting bribes for ratings. Instantly, all companies rated by them had lost business by concerned customers. The other two large houses were promising to rate them as soon as was practical, but refused to rush the jobs, not wanting their own quality to suffer.

Quality Assessment Specialists had offered a discount to all the injured parties and was likely to move into the top three. RSL seemed destined for bankruptcy. So did the handful of operations that had bribed them, and their senior staff would likely be indentured for life. Simple enough.

The problem was that all the injured businesses, and all the soon to be former employees of RSL, wanted blood, as did the owners and shareholders of RSL against the employees in question; they'd been hurt and needed compensation. Several insurance companies were involved as well. There were suits from clients against the companies that had bribed for ratings, and by more insurance companies, who wanted settlements from both the bribers and RSL. There were more than ten thousand plaintiffs party to the suits already and more seemed certain. Then there were suits by employees against employers. Citizen Hernandez and four others had agreed to referee several mass settlements as soon as the facts of the case could be established and to hear the other cases as quickly as possible after that. Their regular case loads were deferred among several other citizens. The news estimated that the government's cut of the settlement was likely to be close to half a billion credits.

In other news, the Freehold military was conducting an exercise near one of the jump points. An Earth fleet was on the other side and was conducting "safety inspections" of ships entering Earth space from the Freehold. This had happened before, she vaguely recalled. It hadn't seemed important from an Earth-based view, but from a tiny nation like this, she suddenly saw the intimidation it could create. Earth didn't like the lack of cargo manifests made possible by the Freehold's laissez-faire approach to trade, but couldn't do anything until the ships were in their space. Then, however . . .

They were apparently seizing some shipments, if the crew didn't have a good story as to who they were transporting for. Both the carriers and the shippers were outraged and had filed complaints. In response, some in the Assembly were calling for more action against the Freehold.

Had she walked into a war? she wondered. Then she decided she had to be reading too much into it. It was just politics and something she'd never paid much attention to. Not until now, anyway.

She finished digesting the headlines and out of curiosity, dug for info on the Freehold Military Forces. She found a wealth of information and selected some graphs and figures as her first inquiry.

It was tiny! The whole military establishment numbered less than one million on a planet of two hundred eighty million, and thirty million more in the Halo. The Table of Organization & Equipment was actually available to the *public*, and listed tons of hardware—vehicles, aircraft, spacecraft, support equipment and heavy weapons. She was just treeing another search, with a note to Rob as to what she was seeking, when Marta called through the door, "Anyone here?"

"Come in. I'm just about ready," Kendra replied.

Marta walked in and smiled. "You look good, lady. Grab your cloak and let's go."

"Okay," Kendra agreed. She eyed Marta up and down and noted she was wearing a black unitard. It was cut high and low to emphasize her snaky hips and firmly muscled chest. She wore black makeup painted as spiderwebs across her face and her hair was tied straight down in back and left its presumably natural black color.

"That seems a little plainer than usual," Kendra remarked.

"Yeah, well, this is social, not professional. Should I dress up a little more? Does it look all right?"

"It looks great," Kendra assured her. "Let's go."

Marta had left her car running, which shocked Kendra. No, it wouldn't be stolen; she was learning to accept that fact, but didn't they care about pollution? Then she remembered that the fuels here were formulated to minimize it. They were also dirt cheap and the vehicles extremely efficient, if not economical. She climbed in and fastened restraints as Marta nailed the throttle again.

Kendra hung on in terror as Marta wove through traffic and north out of town. Her responses to Marta's cheerful conversation were rather terse, because she kept remembering that there were no traffic laws, only advisories. Her mind kept seeing an advisory that two women were splattered here last month, so please slow down.

Once out of town, the traffic density dropped drastically and she relaxed slightly. It was odd not to be flying, but the view was interesting. Marta explained her plans. " 'Cabhag' is the name of the band. They're very eclectic, so there should be at least some of it that appeals to you, but I think you'll like it all; they're very good performers. We have time for a bite first and I know a great place nearby. You like lamb?"

"Umm, no. Unless it's vat raised," Kendra said apologetically.

"Oh, well. They have some good seafood, or so I'm told, but I hate the stuff so I wouldn't know."

"That'll work," Kendra agreed. She'd decided that marine animals were low enough on the chain that she'd manage to eat them. It still made her feel a bit adventurous.

She looked Marta over again and wondered what was bothering her about her friend. She was energetic, but so was Rob, so that wasn't it. She was a little intimidating, and her career would take some getting used to, but that wasn't it either. She turned back and watched the scenery. The north suburbs were buried in forest that was composed of Earth evergreens and local trees that looked like a cross between ginkgoes and palms. An old style, painted, non-interfaced sign noted, "Delphtonopolisburg 80 km."

"Delphtonopolisburg?" she asked incredulously.

"Yeah. The first settlers had a twisted sense of humor."

"No fake," Kendra agreed.

The trip progressed and Kendra realized that there was little between the two towns. There was the occasional cleared farmstead beside the hardened roadbed and two little charge stations, but not much else. Breaking down out here would be a disaster, and the alienness of it all got to her again. She was glad to have a competent local guide and looked over again at Marta. They were just taking a moderately hard bend and her shoulders rolled as she turned the wheel. It was a movement that was perfectly average, but on Marta it was suggestive and sexy.

Kendra realized what was bothering her and wasn't sure how to handle it. She'd been in an erotic encounter with this woman and Rob last night. Rob had told her that by local custom a date frequently implied sex. Marta might be expecting more than Kendra was prepared for. That was slightly confusing. What was *very* confusing was that she'd just looked at Marta and thought her sexy.

"Travel to the Freehold of Grainne and discover within yourself passion and sexuality you never knew existed." It sounded like a ridiculous concept for a campaign and Kendra decided she'd never see an ad like that. She laughed to herself and tried to relax.

Her mind was playing tricks on her. This was just a friendly outing. She turned her attention back to the road and tried not to stare at Marta.

Delph' broke the rules again. It was a small Gulf State town with East Coast hedonism spilling out of it, transported across space and dropped in a far northern evergreen forest. Bright lights and dark woods clashed within meters and Marta pulled into a dirt parking area. "Lock the door," she said. "There are a lot of idiots around here who might pull a dumb stunt like pass out in back and yack on the upholstery."

If that was the worst risk they faced, Kendra thought it would be a very enjoyable evening. They walked toward a lighted strip and Marta moved closer to her. Shortly, she felt fingertips on her back, drifting idly down to her hips. Adrenaline rippled up her spine, and she was about to speak when Marta drew her hand back. She knew she should still say something, but had no idea what.

The Coracle of Delphi sat on the banks of the river called the Frigid Ditch. Marta requested a table on the edge and they were seated immediately, on a wooden deck with running water below. Kendra ordered a glass of wine and Marta picked a drink called "blog." It was garishly bright and apparently very potent. "Mind if I light up?" she asked Kendra after they ordered.

"No. You smoke tobacco?" Kendra asked back.

"No, this is tingleweed. I don't smoke often, but this has been a busy week and I'm celebrating," she explained. "Like some?" she offered.

"Thanks, no," Kendra said. "Has it been a profitable week?"

"Very," Marta agreed.

The fish was good and Marta paid, as Rob and most others did, in cash, with a generous tip for the server.

The amount of cash she was casually carrying made Kendra flinch. Very well paid indeed. That roll would be dangerous on Earth.

It was getting dark as they left and Marta led Kendra along the river. It was quite gloomy under the tree-lined bank and bright lights were visible ahead. Kendra had good night vision. She stayed close to Marta, however, because instinctively she felt uncomfortable away from the lights.

Fingers slid along her back again, traced a circle over her left hip and tightened around her waist. She felt a bit uncomfortable and shifted slightly. The movement put her shoulders closer to Marta and in a moment they were standing face-to-face, although Kendra wasn't sure how. Hands slid under her cloak and around her neck and lips brushed hers. She was about to protest, but the sensation had caught her by surprise and she hesitated just long enough for Marta to start kissing her.

She kissed back, her brain disconnecting itself. It felt different than any other kiss and it wasn't Marta's intensity or technique. After a few seconds, she pulled back, although Marta was obviously willing to make it last.

"I . . . hm . . . ah," she began.

"Yeah, I liked it, too," Marta said, grinning.

"No . . . I mean . . . I think . . . this is a little confusing," she started again. "I'm a bit overwhelmed by all this. And I'm not comfortable with public touching. Can we keep this nonsexual? Please?"

"Yes! I'm sorry," Marta said, concern in her voice. "Am I making wrong assumptions? It seemed you were getting used to the idea."

"Getting, yes. It's still not comfortable."

"Okay," Marta agreed, turning back to the path. "I didn't mean to be pushy. And I'm sorry if I got the wrong idea."

"I don't know if it's the wrong idea," Kendra said. "I don't know if it's the right idea. I find you very sexy and I don't know how to deal with it, because I never found a woman sexy before."

"I see," Marta said. "After I come down from this buzz, we should talk about it. Right now, let's go enjoy the concert."

The hall was small, situated in a tessellated rectangle of pavement and looked very well designed acoustically. That aside, Kendra didn't like the concert. The hall was clouded with smoke from a variety of substances. The audience screamed and yelled at the tops of their voices. The music was too loud, as well as being dissonant, complicated and in weird scales. The three musicians had an amazing array of instruments, from archaic strung guitars and similar items she couldn't name, to electric and fiber-optic versions of the same, synths, glockenspiels, marimbas, electronic and acoustic drums and ethnic percussion and a dizzying collection of other gear including a hammer dulcimer. She missed the simple, fun melodies of Earth Phillippian and case music or even the mellow classical tones of death metal and swing jazz. Marta was having a great time, apparently. She yelled, laughed, sang along, wrestled with other attendees and even spent several segs in an almost sexual encounter with one man. Ever the businesswoman, she handed him her card as she wiggled away, giving him a final quick but thorough grope. The div-long show seemed to last forever and Kendra's hearing was noticeably reduced as they wandered out afterward.

Marta was laughing and Kendra had to keep her steady as they returned to the car. "You f-fly," Marta suggested.

"I think we should wait until you straighten out," Kendra replied. She wasn't up to driving a strange car on a strange road at night with no traffic laws. Flying with no automatic sounded deadly.

"Tingleweed, pixie dust, three stiff drinks, a stiff cock I almost downed," she broke into laughter again, "and a violet zap. You fly."

"Ohh-kay," Kendra reluctantly agreed. She got the car started and cautiously pulled out of the dirt area onto the hardpan road, which was apocalyptically black. She lifted aloft hesitantly and followed the glow of Jefferson to the south. There was a standard beacon, but only as a guide, no way to slave to it. The only light was stars and the moon Gealach, which was unnerving. She did feel safer airborne, with less to collide with. She spent several segs getting used to the controls and the outrageous amount of dynes escaping from the engine. The impellers were very responsive and she enjoyed it once she was used to it, despite her leeriness. One didn't get to fly often on Earth, and certainly not manually.

She turned on the receiver, sound only, and found a talk show to keep her company as she flew. She couldn't handle most of the music but the talk had sucked her in at once.

"—UN is that they don't grasp the basis of our system, either politically or socially," a speaker said.

"No," argued another. "The problem is that they grasp *exactly* what we stand for and can't allow it to exist. It's a pattern repeated through history. We don't fit with the majority position, are successful despite that, and that creates a threat to their system, because they can't insist to the peasants that they live in the best of all possible worlds when we're doing better than they."

Kendra's thoughts were that most people on Earth—she couldn't speak for Space Nations—had no real idea the Freehold existed in the fashion it did. She snapped back to attention when the second debater said, "—there's going to be a war about it sooner or later."

"I disagree," argued the first. "It's a simple lack of empathy but not critical."

"Car, sound off!" she ordered, and it went silent. She was getting sick of alleged experts about Earth who'd never been there. And talk of war was silly.

As she took them silently back to Jefferson, she was passed by most of the light traffic heading south and was a shaking bundle of nerves as they neared the outskirts. She gratefully landed on a ramp at the ring road, switched from impellers to wheels and took the ground route. Glancing over, she saw that Marta was still asleep, as she had been for most of the trip.

"Hey, you," she said. "Wake up."

"Okay," Marta agreed, stretching. "I'll give you directions."

"How do you feel?" Kendra asked.

A sadistic streak in her was disappointed when Marta replied sincerely, "Wonderful. I really needed that. I'm sorry it wasn't to your liking."

"I thought it was interesting. The food was good. And I was glad to see some more of the planet. Thank you."

"You're welcome. Left at the sig."

Marta directed her through downtown, still hectic even at 8:70, which was really not that late for social activity, Kendra thought. Business was still in full swing, however. The day's heat was gone and people were wrapped in cloaks as protection against the coming chill. The crowd thinned with the buildings and soon Kendra was driving into the wealthy section called Harbor Hills. She was glad to get into quiet streets; manual control in traffic was nerve-wracking.

She parked under the huge house, allowed Marta to lead her inside, then stared around in shock. She'd thought Marta lived with her family, but she was

obviously the only resident. It came to her that Rob
had very simple tastes, reserving his money for his
hoped-for eventual Citizenship, while Marta lived a
more flamboyant life. Well, that fitted her occupation
and personality.

Marta took her cloak, led her into a sunken living area
with a cathedral ceiling, disappeared and returned in
moments with wine and goblets. She poured two tall,
slender glasses of "Violet," and Kendra took one. She
raised the glass to her lips and tasted it.

It was a sweet wine with a powerful bouquet and her
mouth erupted with the taste of fruit and flowers. As she
swallowed, it seemed to evaporate straight into her brain
and the residue created a pleasant warmth as it went
down. She looked around at the decorations; mostly large
starscapes, all signed originals. The furnishings were in
soft earth tones. A few tasteful sculptures sat on low
marble tables and a cut-crystal cabinet contained rare
geologic pieces from several planets and systems. Overhead, a chandelier was hand wrought in iron and bronze.
It was finally hitting Kendra that Marta was really, really,
rich.

"Actually, I have *another* ulterior motive in asking
you here," Marta smiled, removing her jewelry.

"Oh?" Kendra prompted, tearing her eyes away from
the magnificent room.

"I have a weeklong assignment coming up, as guide
and escort to a visiting Earth dignitary. I want to dig
through your brain for further background," she
explained. "If you do me that favor, I'll give you a run-
down on toys and techniques. There's this one thing I
know makes Rob squeal . . . Anyway, we could call it a
fair trade, consultation for consultation."

"So I am a professional advisor on Earth, now?"
Kendra grinned. "I hate to break it to you, but I only
have firsthand experience on one continent, in three

particular areas, and I was a child when we lived in two of them."

"It'll help. And you ought to load up an ad as a consultant. If one customer calls, you've covered the cost. The second one is money in your pocket," Marta advised.

Kendra realized that this young woman with only twenty-two Earth years could probably buy her contract out of petty cash. The advice was worth taking and she let it percolate in the back of her mind. Thinking as she went, she began talking about Earth: Her childhood, schooling, social life, politics, business, cultural jokes and clichés. Some of those Marta understood with adequate explanation, others were apparently lost in translation. Marta asked a lot of questions about social issues, such as music, sports, film, individual entertainment and of course, sex.

Kendra gave a lot of detail and poured out a lot of repressed feelings. She gave Marta an edited story of her departure, wishing she could tell more, and found herself crying, partly in anger, partly out of homesickness. "I can't ever go home again," she wept.

Marta began massaging her head and neck, and it did help. Kendra asked some questions and Marta explained her background. Her military training was in emergency medicine. Her private education included physical therapy, psychology, music, dance and business. Exactly the education a personal escort in a culture like this needed. Kendra wondered why so few societies treated prostitutes as anything more than convenient sex toys. Marta apparently sometimes earned more in a day than Kendra did in a month and no one tried to haggle over her rates. She claimed her reputation as a social companion was known citywide, and indeed, several framed newsprints showed her with various prominent people at major functions. The pictures were obviously taken with consent and the men in question seemed proud of her presence. Kendra was shocked to find that there were schools that actually taught lab courses in sexuality. Marta was a visiting faculty member at one of them several times a year.

"Do you get female clients?" Kendra asked. Marta was massaging her back, having taken her tunic off, and was working lower. She was using oil that tingled gently, warming the skin.

"Rarely. Women don't usually have a problem finding company of either sex. When I do get them, they are usually celebrating something very special and sometimes ask for a male and female couple. Even if it's just me, they spare no expense—food, liquor, intoxicants, neither of which I touch, expensive suites. They're a lot of fun."

"Do you enjoy sex with clients?" Now nude, her thighs and calves were being kneaded. Kendra was very relaxed, but not sleepy. Marta definitely knew what she was doing.

"Usually. Some I have to work at, some I simply blacklist after one encounter—I get about sixty-percent repeat business. And I always have the option of leaving, since my base fee is just to show up. From there I charge all I can get. But only about thirty-five percent are calls for sex. About fifty percent are massage, conversation and some posing or dancing. Fifteen percent are social functions," Marta explained while working on Kendra's feet. She gave some kind of subliminal signal and Kendra turned over. The massage started again.

Kendra felt Marta's skilled fingers on her cheeks and ears. They drifted over her jaw and pulled lightly at the skin of her shoulders while Marta kneeled next to her, staring into her eyes. Kendra stared back briefly, then averted her eyes, looking everywhere except at

Marta, finally closing them and relaxing. She tensed and inhaled as fingers stroked the sides of her breasts.

"Tell me if you're uncomfortable," Marta said.

"It's . . . interesting, but I'm not used to it," Kendra replied.

"Want me to stop?"

"Not yet. What do you want to do?"

"Make love to you," Marta said, staring into her eyes with a smoldering intensity.

Kendra had been expecting a response along those lines and took a deep breath. Calming her racing heart a little, she said, "I don't know how."

"That's fine. Or are you saying 'no'?" Marta asked.

Thinking furiously or trying to, Kendra said, "Why don't you keep doing what you're doing and we'll see how I react." The attention, the drink . . . was this real?

"Okay," Marta agreed and resumed kneading. Her touch became lighter, more caressing, and traced the lines of Kendra's jaw. Her hands moved over Kendra's collar bones and across her shoulders, following the curve of muscles. Eventually, they were trailing along the swell of her breasts again. Kendra tensed at first, then relaxed. It was a pleasant sensation.

Marta was fantastic with her hands and mouth, she decided, and her collection of toys, both automatic and manual, would take some getting used to. She accepted the attention and was able to reciprocate. *The fact that I'm doing this again,* she thought, *means that it's not bad. But it's not something I'm going to get used to quickly.* She shuddered as a wave of pleasure passed through her, triggered by a warm, sensual device riding low between her thighs. It throbbed and pulsed, time changing to match her shaking muscles, and she bit her lip. She closed her eyes, reached out with hands and lips and drew Marta in close, her attention splitting to enjoy the old-fashioned sensation of fingers through her hair.

Moments later, she noticed that Marta was shaking furiously, her breath in gasps. The elegantly kept hands wrapped deep in her hair and pulled her tight between thighs corded with muscle. She felt another tingle, not quite orgasmic, and let her hands drift and tease.

Later, as they sprawled together on a deep, soft divan, Marta reached an arm around her, kissed her gently and said, "You have a marvelously sexy body. And you use it well."

"Thank you," Kendra replied, still nervous about meeting those intense, spearing eyes.

"Thank *you*. You're the most exciting woman I've met in months." Marta stretched out, her compact figure rippling. She reminded Kendra of a cat.

"It was . . . interesting," Kendra agreed. "I don't know when or if I'll do it again."

"Tell me about it," Marta encouraged.

Thinking for a moment, Kendra said, "Sometimes, it almost felt as if I was watching someone else. It felt . . . weird. Not what I expected."

"And what were you expecting?"

"How would I know?" Kendra admitted, "But that wasn't it." They both grinned and kissed again. "But thanks for a very educational evening."

"Sure. Come on, I'll show you upstairs," Marta said with a nod of her head. "My bed's plenty big enough."

Marta's phone woke them before the alarm. "Line three. Line three. Line three . . ."

Groaning, Marta sat up and ordered, "Answer phone voice line three Hernandez."

Kendra heard a vaguely familiar voice say, "Hi, Mar, sorry to wake you. Can you talk?"

"What about, Dad? I have company."

"Sorry, I'll be brief. Your Earth client has cut the Halo tour short. We expect him sometime today or tomorrow."

"Right. I'll get ready and call you back."

"Sounds good. Out."

"Phone off. Curse." She stood and stretched.

Kendra looked her again, noticing features, and the sleep fog left her brain. "Hernandez? As in 'Citizen'?"

Marta nodded, began limbering exercises and said, "My father. You know him?"

Kendra replied, "He's handling my case. Oh, my God."

Marta shrugged in the middle of a bend. "Your business and his, not mine."

"He hires his own daughter for a client?" Kendra was shocked to her roots once again.

"Does it bother you?"

"I . . . I . . ."

Marta walked over, gave her a hand out of bed and put her arms around her. "I keep forgetting that sex is very major to your thinking. Here it's quite expected and a regular topic of conversation. It's my chosen profession and I'm good at it. My father hired the best he could arrange for, who he knew was utterly trustworthy."

"It's still hard for me to come to terms with. It seems . . . *wrong*."

"I'm being paid a chunk."

"That doesn't help me."

"Oh, well." Marta shrugged. "Join me in the shower?"

Marta made another advance in the shower, which Kendra expected, and declined with good humor. "You are an insatiable little thing, aren't you?"

"One of the reasons I love my work," Marta agreed, while lathering her hair. The shampoo was an expensive formula with several chemical treatments and a couple of nanos, too. It *did* do amazing things to Marta's hair, Kendra decided, but Cr50 per bottle was just too much for a normal person to spend on routine items. "Oh, and we have to bare your temples if you're flying with Rob," Mar added, reaching for a trimmer.

"Why? I'm not flying it," Kendra protested.

"He left me a message to do it and I know from experience the helmet is designed for skin contact. Just up here," Marta said, and Kendra felt a tickle. Marta clipped the other side to match. It reminded Kendra of the captail hairdo she'd worn in school one summer.

Chapter 8

"The essence of war is violence. Moderation in war is imbecility."

—Admiral Sir John A. Fisher

Marta hurriedly dropped her off at home, although Kendra was less than thrilled by the delivery. Mar flew her car low and fast around downtown not far from the buildings, swooped through several advisory zones without heeding the warnings and dropped to a quick landing on the grass in the complex's quad. Kendra opened the door and felt a wave of fresh air that stopped the woozy feeling she'd developed. She wobbled toward the steps as Mar lifted off with a beep of acknowledgment. She decided not to mention her wooziness to Rob, and wondered how she'd let herself be talked into a vertol ride over a combat range.

"You look like you had a good time," Rob leered at her. She blushed and shoved him. "Ready?" he asked as he effortlessly blocked her hands.

They drove rather than flew, which gave her time to try to relax. Heilbrun Military Base was northeast of town, and actually had a modern eight-lane road with automatic controls, although Rob didn't use them. It was a sunny, warm morning and promised to be quite nice. They stopped at Pass and ID, which was located outside the gate, Kendra noted with a nod. Security actually appeared to be a concept given more than lip service here.

She was photographed and cleared through with a badge and Rob pointed out the standard facilities of any military installation as they drove. She felt homesick again. Something about a block of warehouses with lift pods and trucks and vertols floating overhead made her remember how much she'd enjoyed her service. She watched soberly as they entered the air facility.

The airfac had vertols scattered about. The UN aligned its craft neatly for easier caretaking. The Freehold spread them to make attacks and sabotage harder. She saw a tail number and remarked, "You have over six thousand of those things?"

"No. The tail numbers are changed regularly for security and do not reflect the actual numbers, which I can't tell you," he replied. They were just parking outside the Operations building.

Rob led her to the Life Support section, kissed her and left her there while he went to get briefed. She was handed over to a very capable corporal who sped her through the emergency training.

"Kendra is it? I'm Rita. First let's get you a flight suit. Go ahead and strip," she said as she turned for equipment.

Kendra removed her shoes and the few items she wore and stepped onto the grid. A quick scan sized her and Rita handed her a flight suit, then explained how to wear it. The lecture and demonstration was a whirlwind tour.

Suit. Connections for environment and oxygen. Waste tubes, if necessary. Medical monitor. Oxygen controls here. Temperature here. Microphone. Attachment points for the seat. How to sit, how to brace, how to relax. Position of the ejection system controls, not to be used without arming them *here* or by voice command, *"Emergency Emergency Emergency."* Not to be used unless the pilot orders, *"Eject Eject Eject."* Head back and eyes closed as the change fires. The strap will pull your head back, but its best to do so ahead of time to avoid neck trama. Emergency kit here, contains transponder and radio, dye marker, smoke marker, surgical kit. Other signal gear, food, shelter section, water, basic weapon and full combat load, brush knife, instruction manuals for various terrains. Map of the range and convenient points to be found if necessary. Avoid these areas and these, as live fire and unexploded munitions may be present. Kendra wondered if she'd remember it all and fervently hoped it wouldn't be necessary.

Bundled up and sweating, Rita stuffed her into a small shuttle and ran her out to the flightline. "Keep your badge visible on your left shoulder at all times," she warned.

Kendra climbed out and took the offered hands of the ground crew. She clambered aboard the vertol in a half-daze. Rob was at the nose of the craft, walking around with a checklist on his comm. The nose art she glimpsed briefly proclaimed the craft—an "Aircraft, Vertol, Attack, Design 12, Variant J, 3rd Generation"—as *The Sword of Damocles*, and had a painting of a cartoonish figure, obviously supposed to be Damocles, gorily beheading four opponents with a single stroke of a sword larger than himself, swung in a very Freudian manner. There were kill markers for missions further back and three battle stars.

Modern close support vertols bore slight resemblance to their paleontological ancestors of helicopters and tilt-rotors. They were blocky, tough aircraft, with lift fans kept inboard and armored in swelling nacelles. The ducts for directional thrust were also behind plate and poked out like fat pig snouts below the lines of the resting craft. Stubby wings, not intended for lift, bristled with munition clusters and blocks, twin rotary cannon protruded in front and every surface was armored.

The ground crew assisted her in, helped her into an environment helmet, slapped it, removed her line badge and closed the cockpit around her. She waited in near silence, listening to the air feed, smelling the disinfectant-and-polymer smell of the hose, noting the almost spherical view she had, the canopy wrapped over, under and around her. Several bumps declared Rob's entry behind her. She tried to turn, but couldn't move far enough to see. A turbine whine began, then another and she straightened back. The noise rose to a howl and his voice sounded in her ears.

"Ladies and men, this is your captain speaking. Hell Airways Flight six-six-six is now departing for the plain of Meggido. Please keep your lunches inside your stomachs. The no-freaking sign is lit, and will remain so for the duration of the flight. If an in-flight emergency occurs, it will be announced by my scream. How you doing, lady?"

She laughed briefly and replied, "Nervous." She felt the craft move slightly around her. Then gravity increased as they lifted with a slight jolt.

"Don't be. Nothing can possibly go wrong, go wrong, go wrong, *Now cut that out!* This is going to be a fun trip. If it gets to you, just do what I do."

"And what's that?"

"I close my eyes."

Before she could retort, the craft rotated, tilted and accelerated upward. In seconds, she had an unobstructed view of everything from the coast to the mountains. Despite the gorgeous view, she felt her gorge rising and swallowed hard. A whimper escaped her lips.

"Want something to hang on to?" he asked, hearing the noise or perhaps anticipating.

"*Yes!*"

"Your controls are dead. Grab away."

She clutched the sticks nearest her hands and jumped as he said, "Not those ones! No, just kidding."

"I am going to kill you when we get back," she promised, while trying to control her breathing.

"Sorry. Pilot humor. Ordinarily, I would tell you to reduce your oxygen level to avoid hyperventilation, but considering your background, I don't see the need. I will explain the controls and I'm toggling your helmet into the combat environment so you can see things my way. If it gets too much, just say 'envi off.'"

The view became very disorienting. Her left eye showed normal field of view, overlaid with instrument readings, while her right looked at an enhanced landscape with symbols indicating buildings and "dense masses." A target reticle followed the motion of her eyes and she could feel little touches rippling over her shaved temples. She had no idea what they meant, but Rob apparently took them as another input. He'd mentioned an implanted signal converter, and she assumed it helped translate the wealth of input into useable form. She could hear his breathing, and then he spoke to flight control as he began a turn. They passed across a chord of the bay in less than a seg, waves flashing below them, over the southern part of the city with a quick swoop near Marta's house and then out across the empty plains. "How do you get used to the double vision?" she asked.

"I have an implant module that enables me to process the stereo image or even tri images. I get feedback from the controls and the seat, which you are probably feeling but can't comprehend as a signal. Weapons locks also are controlled by it, and it helps me maintain control when orientation shifts, which is a fancy way of saying I can fly sideways or upside down without thinking I'm about to crash into the ground or yacking my guts.

"I can designate as many targets as I wish, by sight-aligning a reticle and numbering it verbally or by touch if I want other than sequential priority. It can prioritize for me by mass or distance or I can set up custom systems. It has a fairly fine snap-grid, so it will correct for errors in aiming. Weapons can be selected by voice or touch. Comm is by voice, either private scramble or 'bro' for broadcast. Data comes from ground and vehicle observation, other craft and satellite observation when possible. You'll see all that in your environment when we get to the range in three segs. And it's an interesting exercise today, too."

Kendra was beginning to realize that Rob had different definitions of "interesting" and "fun" than she. *Damocles* angled lower as they flew over sparser and sparser settlements. Far to the south, they headed over foothills, and Rob took them down almost to the ground. It passed in a dizzying blur, as if they were riding an elevated rail.

As the hills grew, radio traffic came on. A woman's voice announced, "Claymore Four, this is Gladius Six and Katana Seven. We have visual and will rendezvous in forty-three seconds."

"Bro—Gladius, Claymore confirms. Exercise commence. I have report of enemy armor in grid seven golf. PARSON reports *Avatar* interceptors at three five mils. Close up and prepare to engage—break—hang on to your delicious ass, Kendra, we are about to be the proverbial fan." He punctuated the statement by heaving *Damocles* into a roll to the left, and accelerating at what her helmet said was five gees. Five *Grainne* gees, she reminded herself, feeling the suit squeeze her lower extremities and forearms as her guts compressed and her vision started to pinpoint. It cleared shortly and she saw two other Hatchets. The other craft slipped out of sight behind, their positions became visible on a side screen of her helmet she could see by glancing to the left. One trailed behind the other, and then everything happened at once.

Rob spoke, in a clipped voice, orders, instructions and observations. "Bro—intel display, estimated, stand by for actual as I break the ridge. Arm weapons and test." A roar shook *Damocles* and twin lances of fire shot out a good ten meters on either side of Kendra. She jerked and gasped as Rob continued, "Bro—Katana will charlie and overwatch. Gladius will follow me, then take the valley from the south. Now." They swung viciously to the right and it appeared they would crash into the hill. Then gees pushed her hard, the suit viselike to compensate, and the contour of the hill was suddenly *down*. She grunted and gasped for breath and felt the oxygen delivery increase to her demands. They cleared the top by scant meters, surging against safety restraints, her stomach in her mouth, as Rob said, "Active scan. Share. Cease scan. Target one, target two, target three, main battle tank, main battle tank, target four, command tank, ammo carrier, seeve"—and everything except the grass disappeared from view. Her stomach dropped back down and out the bottom— "bunker, bunker, position, target five, ayda priority—" "Ayda" had to be ADA, which had to mean the air defense artillery vehicle she recognized from Mtali, and Rob fired a missile—"target six, target seven, target eight." Two more missiles roared off, as Kendra swallowed her stomach and tried to determine what she'd seen. Nine targets, nine designations including the priority, had sorted themselves by color, number and flashing codes in her vision and three of them had winked out, including the "seeve," which she found out later was "CEV": combat engineer vehicle. They headed for blue sky again and pulled back into a loop. Before she could panic, they were aimed straight down under power and the command tank mockup was directly below them, dug into a revetment. The twin cannons belched again and smoke and flame erupted as Rob turned them horizontal and upside down through the cloud, hanging against the harnesses and the seat. As she gritted her teeth and clenched her fists, he rolled upright and launched two more missiles. A sweep right slammed her against the seat, then an opposite maneuver to the left did the same. Another burst of shells took out another vehicle, then the one behind it. Rob took them through a break in the woods and for less than a second, she could see treetops at eye level. She swallowed hard.

Rob spoke again. "Bro—Katana, confirm on command vehicle and my target number three tank and tank retriever for Gladius. Avatars in seven seconds. Suck trees, folks." They flew through a pillar of smoke from another vehicle and Kendra glimpsed the carnage created by the number-two Hatchet. That craft then appeared directly ahead and Kendra gritted her teeth in a grimace as they passed each other at bare meters.

Then the ride became violent and she was thrown in all directions, seeing nothing but trees. Beeps sounded as a trailing interceptor tried to lock onto the rapidly viffing vertol. Rob suddenly yanked them hard left at the bottom of a valley, looped crazily back into an immelman and dropped down to the trees again, all without quite getting above the crest of the hill. "Goddess, I can hear him cuss from here," he joked. Apparently, the trick had lost the faster but less maneuverable interceptor. There were more violent aerobatics, level flight, then Rob announced, "Bro— Exercise terminate. Katana, that was a commendable run. I think you are ready to try a second slot on the next game. We'll check the results in the tank when we get back."

"Claymore, thanks, Warrant," the younger pilot acknowledged, his grin visible though the transmission was voice only.

"Bro—Okay folks, let's go watch the fireworks." As Kendra managed to get her shakes under control, forcing herself not to vomit, Rob sought altitude and headed over the mountains, then north.

A new road was being constructed to the west, an area currently serviced only by aircraft, and the contractors had bought military assistance. Orbital Defense was to utilize one of its older systems in a practice exercise and blast a cut through a hill that was on the route the road would take. Heavy blocks of metal would be decelerated from orbit and drop in a line along the surveyed area, cutting the path in question with kinetic energy. The military would get target practice and a large fraction of the old system's cost back and the builder got a cut through a mountain in segs rather than days.

Prior to that, however, evac and transport vertols would patrol the area to ensure that any persons in the area were well clear. It was unlikely that anyone was in such an area, as they would be over a hundred kilometers from any major settlement, in deep woods. The precaution was taken, however, and would scare most wildlife away, too. The Hatchet pilots were there for fun.

"Kendra, I'm going to slowly increase your control sensitivity. Feel where my positions are, there's a slight detent notch . . . now move slowly. You can fly us for a few segs."

"Is that wise?" she asked.

"You'll be fine. I can lock you out instantly if there is a problem and we have plenty of altitude. Here you go."

Kendra felt the controls stiffen and the craft wobbled a little, until she adjusted to the delicacy that was required. Rob said, "I've made them less sensitive than normal, so you can't maneuver too hard or too fast. Start gently and take it as far as you feel safe. Any questions?"

She discovered that the hands were for two-dimensional steering and vertical lift and tilt. Twisting the wrists was throttle, and it would trigger thrust to the sides when she pushed her elbows in the corresponding direction she wanted to go. Pushing with her feet provided thrust at the nose and pulling them did the same at the rear, apparently for combat maneuvers. The cockpit was almost worn rather than controlled, and the sticks in her hands were basically guides. She looked around and asked, "What are these things with tape over them?"

"What things?" he replied.

"These areas with oh-dee tape over some kind of readout," she said, more precisely.

"I don't know which ones you are referring to."

"This area on my left, in front of the stick," she insisted.

"Sorry."

She concluded that whatever it was was none of her business and dropped the subject. Flying was fun, although she was much more cautious than Rob. She could understand, however, why he enjoyed flying it and why these murderous little craft had so intimidated the warring factions on Mtali. They packed a demonic amount of firepower, could outmaneuver anything in the sky and were flown by pilots utterly fearless and thoroughly insane. The exercise she had witnessed was more impressive than the air combat she'd seen the UN pilots engage in. She turned a few circles, did some swoops and a high-speed run. Slowly lowering the craft, she watched the instruments read "200 meters" and "1900 kpd," which was no better when read as 700 kph.

At a warning from Rob, she felt the controls slip away. He headed in a different direction and joined several assorted other craft in a slow circle.

"Nineteen seconds, off to our left," he advised.

Exactly nineteen seconds later, according to the clock in her environment, tremendous flashes, like an over-enthusiastic string of firecrackers, caused her visor to polarize. The black splotches of impact and diagonal incandescent streaks of the incoming projectiles were surrounded by blue sky that almost instantly darkened with dust.

Close to thirty seconds later, her view almost back to normal, the shock wave from the impact slapped them, sounding louder than any thunder, and rumbled off for what seemed like forever. Rob warned her again and seconds later, another volley tore across the same landscape. As its blast washed over them, there came a third. Kendra found it eerie to be so close to energy equivalent to a medium nuclear weapon.

The fourth cut across their field of view and they were immediately slammed upside down and sideways. Kendra was numb, listened to Rob curse, and realized that something had gone wrong. *Damocles* shook and sounds that could only be warnings were shrieking in her ears.

One by one, the warning sounds ceased. The craft was righted and Rob shouted a combination report and chewing out into his mike. "Kendra! Your vitals look good, are you conscious?" he finished.

"I'm fine. What the fuck happened?" she demanded, surprised at her own vehemence.

"One of the bright boys apparently rounded pi off to three and missed the x. Ground zero was less than five hundred meters from us."

"Trif. Are we okay?"

"Other than almost literally having the shit scared out of me, I'm fine. The craft is unscathed—these bastards are built to take near misses from stuff like that. Great Goddess, that was intense! Missile-lock warnings on my ass have never been that scary!"

He swung back in the direction of the strike zone and swapped relieved jokes with the other pilots. Two others had been affected by the blast and the three of them loudly discussed the intelligence and ancestry of the technician who had plotted the last fire mission. Kendra tried to slow her galloping heart and studied with interest the gash left by the four strings of impacts, now visible through a diminishing haze of dust.

The cut was a perfect line through the hill, surprisingly even at the bottom and close to one hundred meters wide, with trees blown down on either side for another four hundred meters. It was exactly aligned with the distant stretch of road that would connect to it. The entire area had taken on brown hues from the huge amount of ejecta thrown during the operation. Approximately 1,500,000 cubic meters of mountain had been vaporized in less than two segs.

The UN EPA might have objected to the method, but it was a most impressively efficient engineering feat.

And, she thought to herself, a weapon that could do the same to a city for only a few thousand creds. *That* concept she quickly put out of her mind.

Rob took them over the single stray impact. The errant round had blown a crater seventy meters in diameter, with a bull's-eye of trees around it. She stared silently at it as they swung back toward home.

"Rob?" she asked, as their course straightened.

"Yes?"

"That near miss really has me freaked."

"Well, it was a miss, so that's good. Consider the top surface area of this beast relative to the four-hundred-meter radius we were from impact, and consider that as a fraction of the area contained in the ten-thousand-meter safe zone. Then the odds of an error like that happening—apparently it was a defective targeting mechanism. It was an unlucky event, but the odds of it coming close enough to kill are remote."

"I guess." What she didn't say, and wouldn't, was that she was bothered by the mention of "Avatar" interceptors for the exercise. The Avatar was a UN craft . . .

Chapter 9

"Government cannot make man richer, but it can make him poorer."

—Ludwig Von Mises

Pacelli Information Associates
Earth Culturalists
Consultants *Specialty North America*
36651-96908 Jefferson

Kendra stared at the cards. She had an ad on her phone, another in the public nets and these cards to hand out to strangers. She squeezed it again to see the animation flash across the surface.

It was a new concept, again. *Her* business. She'd worried about the publicity of her name, with a search still on for her. "Just use your last name. They won't make the connection," Rob had insisted. "You're thinking a massive bureaucracy is efficient and can think. Won't happen."

Nervously, she'd agreed. Marta and Rob had helped her set up, with surprisingly little money. No fees, licenses, taxes or background checks. No certification or insurance. Print up advertising and *go*. They had advised her on the rate she should charge, which seemed outrageous, but they insisted she should demand it.

"You won't be taken seriously if you are too cheap," Marta had explained. "And the people who need your service will pay without a twitch. You can haggle slightly if someone is desperate or just needs a quick question."

"What about long-term deals? Should I offer a discount?" She couldn't imagine a long-term contract happening, but thought she'd better ask.

"Depends. If they want you to go to their site, demand more."

She'd agreed, even though she didn't entirely understand.

Only a few days later, she arrived home from work to find a message waiting. "Line Two. Line Two. Line Two . . ."

That was her business line, Kendra realized after a moment. She reached for a shirt.

"Answer phone Pacelli," she ordered.

"Returning call," the machine advised. "Dialing. Connecting."

"Yes, I'm Kenneth Chinran," the caller said as he came on screen. "I'd like some information on a consultancy." He was dressed very conservatively, very Commerce Boulevard.

"Okay," she agreed, smiling politely while her mind raced. She decided to stall. "Tell me what you're looking for."

"My company is preparing to send a group to North America and we'd like them to be familiar enough with customs that they can get immediately to the job at hand with few distractions. We'd like them to interact smoothly."

"I see. Where would we be meeting?"

"We would fly you here, to Marrou. We would like to have your services for three days, long divs."

"How long?" she asked.

"Three point five per day."

She nodded while quietly taking a deep breath and said, "My fee is two hundred creds per div. And I'll need transport and lodging."

Chinran nodded back, "Very well. How soon are you available?"

"I can come this weekend if your schedule is tight." *Two grand! For three days of lecturing!*

"It is. We also will require an oath of confidentiality."

"All my clients have confidentiality," she replied smoothly. *Since you're all of them.*

"Very well. We'll have a ticket waiting for you on Eastern Shuttle Service at six on Berday," Chinran advised.

"I need to know how many people and exactly what type of information you want."

"Nineteen people and myself. We'd like background on customs, slang, shopping, dress and accents. Mostly, we simply need to talk at length. We will ask some specific questions and you'll need to fill in whatever you think we may have missed. We'll trans a print for you."

"Sounds good. Berday then."

"Berday. Bye. Off."

"Off," she ordered.

She packed a bag for the weekend trip and commed to confirm her ticket. Rob had agreed to drive her to the 'port and waited almost too late: he was working on something for Freehold Rapid Courier and seemed distracted. He drove fast, and she gripped the seat in fear at some of his maneuvers. Other drivers didn't seem bothered so she tried to relax.

At the airport, the procedure was strange to her. There was no search of her or her luggage, she didn't need fingerprints or retina pics to prove who she was and they had a procedure for weapons safety. She'd forgotten she was wearing her sidearm, as she now wore it out of habit.

"Please clear your weapon, Ms Pacelli," an attendant asked. She blushed and complied, stuffing the magazine and spare round into her pouch. "We'd prefer that you store it in your pouch and in the underseat stowage. You'll still be able to reach it quickly in an emergency, but it eliminates the chance of an accident."

She nodded in response. It made sense. Given the obsession with personal freedom here coupled with the need to avoid accidents, it made sense. A historical scan she'd done the week before indicated there'd never been a successful act of piracy, questionable commandeering or hijacking aboard any Freehold aircraft, transport or registered vessel. Ever. She couldn't conceive of any UN nation ever considering allowing personal weapons, however. It was an alien concept.

She was still nervous as she boarded the ballistic shuttle. The concept of atmospheric flight with the local lack of central control bothered her. The trip was short, at moderate gees by her new standards, which was still fairly brisk. She was glad they had complimentary drinks for the long descent; it had been a rough week. She had three and was cheerfully mellow when they landed.

A cab ride took her to the hotel, which was midrange and quite decent. It had a good café and she grabbed a bite before retiring. She decided to go to review her notes and go to sleep early, since she had a long weekend ahead of her. She was nervous about the presentation.

The next morning, she was picked up by a young driver. He said, "I'm here for Chinran, Ms. Pacelli," and showed her to a car. That was the extent of the conversation, other than very few pleasantries. She decided reticence was not a social skill she would cultivate. He led her inside another hotel to a small conference room and she was introduced to Kenneth Chinran.

"Here is our contract," Chinran said, handing her a sheet. She was still getting used to single-page legal documents. "You agree to answer our questions in detail, make no recordings and make no investigations as to our ID. There are some other points, but those are key."

She read the sheet, noted that basically the meeting was not taking place and signed.

Chinran handed her a copy and led her down a hall to another conference room. Once inside, the door was locked and antieavesdropping equipment activated. A young man, boy really, ran a wand around her, nodded and sat down.

There were twenty people in the room. All young, six of them women. In Earth terms, they ranged from probably sixteen to thirty. They were dressed impeccably, in business style, with no tattoos or jewelry. All had an intense look to them and were in even better physical shape than most Freeholders.

Scanning them, she nodded curtly. Walking over to the front row, she offered her hand. "Ah'm Kendra, who ur you?"

The kid reached for her hand with both of his.

She snatched back, snapping, "Doan be grabbin, minor. Shake with one hand, doan like to take ma arm.

You lookin fer handout? Fuggoff, ya liddle drop." There were a few giggles.

She continued, "Streeter talk ain' educated idiom, but it common to the cities, 'specially to anyone under thirty—that's Earth years—and affected by tough business persons. Ya will need clodes more like mahn, und not quite so neat. Look a little worn."

As she continued, the group made notes. Questions were asked and she answered them, sometimes in a different direction than they expected. She would elucidate on things that were not apparent to them, but obvious to her.

"Doan be so dam helpful," she warned, "und doan smile much. You happy, you draw scopes. You help someone, they sue you for innerference."

As the session progressed, she noticed that their accents were changing rapidly, getting closer to her Great Lakes drawl. Apparently, they had been chosen because they were quick studies. At the end of the div, they took a break.

Chinran approached. "Excellent presentation," he observed. "Text only goes so far, und then ya need practice." He was picking it up, too.

He suggested some topics and they resumed again a few segs later.

She began, "You gurls need to look less likely. You get dragged fer a rape if ya look bright und wide. Hunch a liddle. Be suspicious. Flick yer eyes a bit. Better."

At the end of three divs, she was exhausted. She wound up in the hotel's plunge with a strong drink, letting the steam relax her. She dried, pulled on briefs and went to one of the nearby restaurants for dinner. She had another drink.

By the time she returned to her room, she'd declined advances from three men and a woman. She refused partly out of tiredness, partly because she regarded her relationship with Rob and Marta as complex enough. She had no idea why she was considered so attractive, but was beginning to enjoy the attention.

The second day, the difference between her accent and theirs had all but disappeared. The discussion was mostly on shopping.

"Doan carry things around ya doan need to. Ask for delivery. It's cheap. When in a store, doan pull things off the rack. Ya'll alarm and get hassled by rentas. Don't flash cash, in fac', doan *carry* cash. You won't find veggies of the quality you do here and the server will selec' them for ya, usually from the bottom. Food isn' nearly as spicy . . ."

She answered numerous questions:

"What's the point behind the repetitive double crash in so many schrack songs?"

"How do you handle traffic if you have to cross in the middle of a block? You say they won't stop for you?"

"What recourse do you have if the landlord won't make good on maintenance?"

Almost ten hours of disconnected factoids was incredibly wearing.

On day three, she was blindsided. Thirty segs into the discussion, someone asked, "How hard is it to find false ID chips in North America?"

"I wouldn't know," she replied. "Why?"

"I'd just like to know," the speaker replied.

The group asked detailed questions which she answered, finding within herself answers to questions she'd never considered. The sudden shift in attitude was scary. These people weren't planning "business," she was sure. There was something creepy, predatory about them.

"When could a landlord enter commercial premises without permission from the tenants?"

"How many times can you pay a bill with cash before it gets reported to UNRS?"

"What would be the best way to avoid random vehicle checks on North America Route Ninety-Five?"

"Can you describe a typical Bureau of Industry inspection?" That one she could answer, as her parents' shop underwent them regularly.

She was exhausted by the end, accepted her cash payment, and fell asleep on the shuttle. She realized as she drifted off that she had probably just assisted espionage. Now she had a legitimate reason to leave Earth. A sickly grin crossed her face before unconsciousness hit her. An attendant woke her as they opened the hatches.

Walking through the terminal, she was bemused by irony; here she was, walking through the 'port with a wad of cash and a gun. Three months ago she would have—*had*—freaked out at that concept.

Marta was waiting for her, in Rob's car. She delivered a brief but steamy kiss as Kendra strapped in. "How was it?" Marta asked, whipping into traffic.

"Tiring. Very, very tiring," Kendra replied. She explained a little of the business of her schedule, careful not to mention topics of conversation.

Chapter 10

"Prostitution involves sex and free enterprise.
Which of these are you opposed to?"
                                    —Joseph A. Hauptman

Marta's phone beeped. She whipped it out and answered, "Lady Alexia." Business, of course. Kendra politely ignored it and continued listening to Rob spin out a joke for Rupe.

"One moment while I check," Kendra overheard subliminally. She turned as Marta touched her arm and said, "I hate to ask. Two business gentlemen at Bon Place. I'm set with one, the other wants an exotic woman. They want to hit Bellefontaine, then dancing at Level Three. I can't think of anyone available and I don't want to lose what could be some good money."

"Are you asking *me*?" Kendra blurted. Three months previously—one hundred and fifty days—she'd been politely cold in her answer. Now, she asked, "Is it public only? No sex?"

172

"That's all they've asked for. Those are nice places, too."

"I wouldn't know how to act," she evaded.

"I can coach you. Your call."

Considering for a moment, Kendra replied, "Ohhkay."

Nodding, Marta spoke into her phone. "I have an associate available who's very exotic. One eighty-five tall, about eighty kilos, long blond hair, blue eyes, a sexy drawl, measurements about one-oh-two, seventy, ninety-eight . . . Yes, she's very bright . . . All set, then? Sounds good." she clicked her phone off and said, "Let's go, we have to get you dressed," and stood up.

She followed Marta outside and down Park Street to the clothing district. She'd come here with Rob her first day, but this time she was visiting the more expensive shops. Marta pulled her into a store that dealt in evening wear only.

"White shows you off well," she said and indicated several styles. They were built for Kendra's frame and could be tailored in minutes. She tried several in short order and settled on one she thought very daring.

It wrapped around her throat, crossed in back between her shoulders, in front over her breasts, in the small of her back and then formed a four-piece skirt at both sides, front and back. Every step showed thigh almost all the way to her buttocks and crotch. She felt well covered, but showed almost her entire body. Underwear, of course, was out of the question.

"Very elegant and professional," Marta commented. Kendra still had trouble with local styles. This was not an outfit she would have considered professional.

She winced at the price tag—Cr500. Marta explained, "Your basic fee is going to be a thousand and I'll lay money you wind up over two; social calls are big money."

Kendra bought it and a cloak in the same shimmering white, then matching shoes at Mattias Shoes, which Marta specifically chose. "Your client owns this chain. Never miss a chance to stroke an ego." They used the restroom at the store to apply makeup, including bitter-tasting lip and tongue glitter and temple coloring. Marta did Kendra's hair by hand, then her own. Several layers of lipgloss shaded from rich blue to violet from the edge of her lips in. Once done, Kendra looked very poised and sophisticated. Some borrowed silver jewelry set off the cool blue tones of her pale skin. To complete the look, Marta took her to a salon to have her nails lengthened and scrimshawed.

As they walked to the hotel, Marta gave her a history. "I'm Alexia Urquidez. We should make you sound Scandinavian. Any ideas?"

"No, not really," Kendra replied. She was becoming very nervous.

"Let me think, then." Alexia paused, but kept walking. "Let's call you Stacia Jorgensen." She pronounced it "Stah-see-ah," emphasizing the first syllable. "You're good with gardens, so work with that. Don't be afraid to be technical. You're an immigrant, but with your parents several years ago. You're thirteen"— Kendra figured that as twenty-one Earth years—"and new to escorting and have only been doing this about three months. You're part time."

"Got it," Kendra agreed. "Who are we meeting?"

"You are meeting Joseph Mattias, as in Mattias shoes. He's divorced, thirty-three—fifty Earth years— Very wealthy and quite a nice gentleman."

Marta added a few details as they approached the Bon Place. She drew a half-step ahead and steered Kendra toward two smiling businessmen waiting outside.

"Ryan!" she greeted, hugging one of them warmly and kissing him lightly. "And you must be Joseph," she said, greeting the other. "This is my friend, Stacia Jorgensen. Stacia, this is Ryan McAran and Joseph Mattias."

Mattias took her hands in his and smiled. He leaned forward and kissed her very softly. "Delighted to meet you, Stacia. Alexia said you were exotically beautiful, but she didn't do you justice when she described you." He looked her up and down, obviously pleased with her appearance. Kendra smiled demurely, while blushing.

They climbed into a waiting limousine, Mattias opening the door for the ladies himself and sending the driver up front. He got in last, spoke directions, then asked, "Drinks?"

Alexia said, "Ginger ale, spiced, please." Ryan asked for scotch and "Stacia" took a lime ice. Heeding Alexia's advice, she sipped carefully, so as not to disturb her lip glitter. It was a brand used by professional models and very durable, but not indestructible. She looked around briefly, something she was expert at after seven months trying to adapt to this culture and noted the plush leather interior in soft earth tones. There were two huge seats, an autobar, entertainment system, a comm that made hers look like a toy and a fold-out work desk.

"What are your interests, Stacia?" Mattias asked, reclining. He held her hand in his lap.

"I'm a consultant on Earth culture and I'm a horticultural designer," she returned. Damn, it sounded swank.

"Really. I've always loved well-sculpted gardens. I find them very relaxing. Sometime you must see my home and tell me what you think."

"I'd be thrilled," she lied. Mattias seemed nice enough and was in excellent shape. He was decent looking, and she relaxed a little.

"We should discuss business first, gentlemen," Alexia reminded.

"Of course," Mattias nodded. "Ryan, you located two stunning ladies to accompany us, please allow me." He reached into his jacket, shuffled money, then laid four five-hundred and four one-hundred credit chits on the low table between the seats. The tipping had started already, Kendra saw.

McAran nodded, looking slightly put out. Apparently his host had just made points in some business game they were playing. Kendra watched with interest and kept a surreptitious eye on Alexia for clues. When Alexia placed her drink down, she smoothly retrieved her twelve hundred and slid it into a slot in her pouch, apparently built especially for that purpose. Kendra followed her lead, tucking the money under the flap and down with the hand farthest from the group. She felt very self-conscious taking money like this.

They reached their destination soon enough and Kendra was eager to see the Bellefontaine. After her first offer of employment, she'd heard it mentioned several times, always as somewhere the ordinary person could never afford.

As they entered, a girl took their cloaks. She wore nothing save a thong and some jewelry and not much of that. Kendra figured her for ten local years, which was not unexpected. The girl had a willowy figure that bulged when she moved her shoulders and was obviously maintained by a div of hard exercise every day. Muscles were considered attractive here, whereas the Earth style was for softness.

They were greeted by a marginally older boy in the same dress. His deep brown eyes were piercing but friendly, and he locked eyes with Kendra for just a second, lust flaring in them. Ryan McAran was apparently a known name and they were shown to a large booth. Two other couples were there and introductions were made. McAran was a textile producer, Mattias was in shoes. Jesslyn Niec owned a company that specialized in fabricating machines for clothing, and was accompanied by her boyfriend, Garett Kameha. Andrew Garner and his wife Janie were in molecular fabrics.

The woman who appeared at Kendra's elbow with a menu was in her local early twenties. She wore more in the sense of mass of fabric, but was still effectively naked. Bellefontaine appeared to Kendra to be like the underground adult clubs mentioned in the news back on Earth. Apparently, they were perfectly acceptable here.

Kendra accepted the menu and froze when she saw the prices. Even if she wasn't paying, they were a shock. She waited while Alexia and the two gentlemen ordered drinks and asked for a lemon cooler when it was her turn. She gave her attention back to the menu, smiling at a funny comment from Mattias while trying to decide on food.

Everything looked good and delicious smells emanated from somewhere. Remembering her personal restrictions on food, she hungrily eyed two pictures on the screen, one of a whole lobster, the other a local shellfish called a spiker. As good as they looked, she recalled Alexia's advice not to order the most expensive items available and decided on a grilled orange roughy. That was a fish transplanted from Earth, cheaper here than back home, and very tasty. She closed her menu, sat back and froze.

Calan was seated several tables away, with Citizen Hernandez and two others. She hoped he wouldn't recognize her, but at that moment, he glanced over. He stared for a few moments, then returned to his meal.

Kendra caught Alexia's attention, gave her a prearranged signal, then turned to Mattias. "Would you
excuse me for a moment?" she asked, rising.

"Certainly. Please hurry back," he encouraged.

Kendra went to the restroom, which was spacious,
had private booths with makeup tables and a human
attendant who was young, male and very sexy. She
waited for a few moments. Alexia arrived and asked,
"Problem?"

"Your father and Tom Calan are seated two tables
over."

"I don't recognize the other one," Alexia prompted.

"Tom Calan, the slime who tried to force me to work
here for a bigger commission," Kendra explained
vehemently.

"Ah," Alexia nodded. "Hernandez won't say a word
to anyone. I can take care of the other. And remember not to eat too much, as good as the hors d'oeuvres
are. How are you holding up?"

"Okay, I guess. This place goes beyond opulent."

"That it does. I'll be out in a few. Don't forget to
tip the attendant."

Kendra headed for her seat, smiling at her companions as she neared it. She was doing a lot of smiling
this evening, but didn't feel most of it. She dropped
the expression seconds later when Calan stood and
walked her way. He stood nearby and said, "Things
seem to have improved for you since you arrived here,
Kendra."

Kendra froze again and was saved by Alexia returning and stepping between them. "Well, hello, Mister
Calan," she said agreeably. Her voice was sultry and
enticing.

"Hello, lady," he grinned brightly, slightly taken
aback. "I don't believe I've had the pleasure."

"You haven't," she agreed. "And you aren't going to.

Kendra is with us this evening and you should stay with
my father. Get it?" The vitriolic delivery hadn't budged
the delighted smile from Alexia's face. Anyone watching
would feel sure they were close friends.

"I do. It seems that there is a professional breach
and I have a fee coming. Or should we go to Citizen's
Court?" he returned, staring unkindly at Kendra.

"I'm trying to decide if you're thinking with your
wallet or your balls?" Alexia suggested. She glanced up
and down as if he were a lab specimen and said, "Must
be your wallet." He stared, wide-eyed at her rudeness.
"Kendra is here as a guest, if it's any business of yours,
which it isn't." She returned to polite manners very
smoothly and took his arm, escorting him to his table.
While Kendra resumed her seat, Alexia whispered
something to Hernandez, her arm over his shoulder
in a friendly fashion.

Kendra felt a little better and sipped at her drink
while awaiting Alexia's return. As Alexia sat down, the
server appeared at Kendra's elbow with a folded slip
of paper. She opened it and read, *"Father is explaining free enterprise to the man. He won't bother you
again. Relax and enjoy the show. A note from the staff
always makes you look known and experienced. By
the way, Niec's 'boyfriend' is another professional.
Destroy this note—Mar XX."* Kendra looked up, crum-
pling paper, wondering how Alexia had written the
note and had it delivered from plain sight. She met
her eyes and received a wicked grin and a sexy flick
of tongue to upper lip. No one else had noticed, as
the show was starting. Kendra turned her attention
that way.

The stage was in easy view of all tables, well lit
and had a set based on geometric shapes, with many
straight lines in neon colors. Two dancers came out,
one male, one female, and whipped around athletically.

The music score was dissonant but interesting and drew attention to the performers. Kendra watched so intently she was distracted when the food arrived. She placed a serviette in her lap, took a bite and enjoyed a delicious clash of rich flavors. She remarked on it to Mattias, who offered a bite of his smoked venison in honey wine sauce. In return, she offered him a bite of hers and allowed him to slip an arm around her waist. He wasn't bad company.

She almost choked when she looked back to the stage. The dancers were nude, painted or tattooed with very suggestive marks and fondling each other very sexually. They made another fling across the stage, the woman tumbled back gracefully, slipping her legs over her partner's shoulders and pressing herself vertically on whipcord arms, legs held in aerial splits. He made a great show of licking her from crotch to chin as she slid down, knees folding against her shoulders. She made contact with him and they were so perfectly choreographed that he slid straight into her. Their eyes bored into each other, muscles standing out all over. There were murmurs in the audience, approving of the dancers' skill and poise. Kendra stared in horrid fascination.

The stage darkened to applause, which Kendra joined from politeness, then lit with a different set. The next act was even more graphic, involving a woman and three men. Kendra wasn't sure what purpose the woman served, as she seemed mostly to stand disconsolately in the middle of the stage. Kendra kept most of her attention on her food and client.

After the meal, which McAran paid for, the four waited for an intermission and headed out to the limo again. Mattias held her hand as they rode to the club known as Level Three.

The limousine pulled up to the curb and they climbed out, the men being gallant again. Apparently, the purpose of Alexia and Kendra was to impress the local populace. Kendra had felt a brief moment of panic and an extreme flush of embarrassment earlier when a passerby had remarked to his friend, "You couldn't afford five minutes with the blonde. And if you could, you'd probably die in the process."

"Yeah, but I'd die a happy man," the other promised.

It had taken careful study of the crowd for Kendra to realize that the two of them were held in high esteem as professionals and she still had trouble accepting that by local standards she was regarded as a stunning beauty.

Level Three was three levels under Commerce Court. They took a slideway down, past some of the really expensive shops in Court Mall that Kendra had only heard of and never seen. She hung back for a moment and whispered into Alexia's ear, "What type of dancing are we doing?" She had sudden images of formal dances she'd never seen and being a total embarrassment to the party.

"Oh. Fairly standard stuff in most cultures," Alexia said. Kendra but realized there was a lot to this business and most of it she didn't have a clue about.

She needn't have worried. Club dancing on Freehold was much like on Earth or anywhere else. Kendra had good rhythm, was energetic and even recognized some of the tunes. She'd had dancing in school, including waltz, swing, liquid and meld and most of it came back to her. She enjoyed herself thoroughly and almost neglected Alexia's advice not to sweat too much.

She led Joe back to the booth they were all sharing and took a needed swallow of water. They sat, holding hands above the table. Underneath, he lifted her right thigh over his legs and began caressing it gently. His hand slowly worked higher and made Kendra slightly nervous.

"So, can I persuade you to join me at the Bon Place?" he asked.

Kendra froze. She hadn't expected this or hadn't wanted to, and had no idea how to decline. Or accept. "Well . . . I don't know," she replied, fixing her smile, hoping desperately that Marta would be off the dance floor soon.

"I can manage your fee, I'm sure," he insisted. "If you're interested."

"We'll see," she said neutrally. "I need to ask Alexia what our schedule is."

"Okay," he agreed, tabling the issue. He returned to his drink, occasionally asking more about flowers.

When Alexia returned, Kendra stood, took her arm and guided her to a quiet corner.

"He wants me," she explained.

"Right. That's up to you," Alexia replied. "If you go, ask three hundred. That gets him a massage and another half-div of conversation."

"What if he wants sex?"

"Ask at least another six hundred per half-div. That's my rate. You're not as skilled, but you're better looking."

"*Sure* I am—"

"Don't argue, just take the millionaire's money. If he wants exotic sex, double it. Or tell him you'll let him tip you what he thinks you're worth. His reputation isn't cheap and the name of this business game is to impress people, including us."

"It's working," Kendra admitted.

"Ah, these are big fish in a small pond. Now the board of Lola Aerospace, *those* are some powerful men and women."

They were heading back now, smiling still. As they resumed their seats, Kendra told him, "I have some time, I think."

"Now?" he asked.

"If you like," she replied in what she hoped was an agreeable voice. She rose with him and let him take her arm again. They said goodbye to the others and headed for the door.

Outside in the corridor he asked, "So what do I owe you?"

"Three hundred. We'll see where we go from there." She tried to sound assured.

"Fine," he agreed, drawing cash unobtrusively from a pocket and slipping it into her hand. They walked through several of the Commerce Court buildings, skyscrapers to rival anything on Earth, but descending ninety levels down also.

Bon Place was the poshest hotel Kendra had ever seen. The fittings in the lobby were black marble, malachite and real silver. An attendant called an elevator for them and smiled politely.

The corridor upstairs had similar appointments to the lobby and his suite was fantastic. He took her cloak and asked, "Something to drink?"

"Plain ginger ale, thank you," she replied, gawking while he busied himself at the bar controls. The ceiling was five meters or more, a plunge the size of her bach was on one side and a bed that seemed almost as large on the other.

She accepted the drink and slipped off her heels.

"You're still incredibly tall, even without those," he noted.

"I'm more comfortable like this," she said.

"The shoes? Possibly one of my stores has something more comfortable."

"Actually, these came from one of your stores," she said. *Thanks to great planning on Marta's part.* "They fit fine and I wear them professionally." *All two divs of it.* "It's my height in them that makes a lot of people nervous and therefore me."

"I like tall women," he replied, undressing and hanging his expensive suit. "Even if they do intimidate me."

"Why would we do that?" she asked. Nudity in general was bothering her less, but *his* nudity made her very uncomfortable. She kept her eyes on his.

"An executive in my position isn't used to looking up at people in any fashion," he laughed. She joined him.

"Perhaps I could get a massage?" he suggested, lying down.

"Certainly," she agreed. She retrieved the bottle of oil from her pouch and knelt over his back.

His muscles certainly were tense. She kneaded and caressed and worked knots out for half of the time he'd paid for, working down from his neck and shoulders to his calves, finally his feet. He turned over then and she dealt with his well-developed chest and arms, working down to his thighs. She avoided his erection.

"That's tense for different reasons," he said, catching her staring. "But I wouldn't complain about a massage there, either."

Nodding, Kendra oiled her hands generously and began to caress him. After a few moments he said, "Oh, stop, please, that's almost too much." She lightened her touch considerably, and touched his chest with one hand.

"Our time's almost up," she reminded him, feeling odd. An intimate encounter on a timetable with a near stranger was just bizarre.

"I know," he said. "But I'd like you to stay. What do you charge for sex?"

Here we go. There was a tight knot in her stomach as she tried to sound experienced and confident. "Six hundred."

He slipped more chits to her and she took them to her pouch, then turned, letting the gown slide sinuously off her shoulders. Breathing hard, she stepped out and approached him.

Thirty segs later, they were both dressed, she in her gown, he in a robe, and sat talking for several minutes. Kendra nodded and appeared attentive and made what seemed like appropriate replies. She was feeling very weird, and noted that she was thinking in both Earth and Freehold time. What an odd time to notice that. Mattias rose finally, saying, "Well, I hate to see you go, and I don't want to appear rude but I have adminwork to prepare for tomorrow and I'm sure you'd like to get home."

Kendra nodded, gathered her things and left. She was polite, but totally nonlucid as he said goodbye and slipped her more chits.

She was oblivious to everything as she passed through the lobby and merely nodded when the attendant asked, "Can I get a cab for you, lady?" She carried her cloak and failed to notice the distinct autumn chill as she waited.

Reaching home, she tipped the driver generously, found her way upstairs, opened her door and kicked off her shoes. She hung the gown neatly and walked into the bathroom.

And was violently sick.

Rob knocked at the outside door. She mumbled, "Go away," but it was so quiet he didn't hear. He came in anyway and stroked her hair while she sobbed over the toilet. He spoke for a long time and finally she understood his words. He handed her a glass, which she downed in two gulps, feeling the burn of liquor. She began talking, at last. She poured out the story and he listened silently. When she finished, he helped her into bed, crawled in next to her and held her gently. She was a long time getting to sleep.

❖   ❖   ❖

She woke to voices and realized it was light outside. Marta and Rob were arguing quietly.

"She could have stopped at any time," Marta insisted.

"Sure. Everyone rubbing her financial position in her face, not to mention her ignorance of business principles."

"She doesn't need money that badly," Marta interjected.

"No," Rob agreed, "she doesn't. But she isn't used to wads of cash like that and is not familiar enough with our mores to be able to gracefully decline. She said it just followed a progression and she didn't even realize she'd gone past her limits."

I said that? I don't remember, she thought to herself.

"But money is not that big a deal," Marta protested, "She has all her bills covered and took in a nice piece last week on that consultancy."

"She comes from a planet that pays only lip service to free enterprise. Her family is relatively well-to-do, owning one of the few types of business that has minimal financial regs and a good return. She will never see them again, is wanted for serious crimes she didn't commit, is effectively a refugee and damned near a pauper by the standards she grew up with. She is now in the first truly free society in human history and has no one to tell her when to stop for her own good. Most of what she couldn't morally or legally consider yesterday is de rigueur today. Socially, you need to think of her as an immigrant child, not a seventeen-year-old who has grown up here.

Rob was still talking. "I think it was very unfair to do what you did to her and selfish as well. You didn't want to pass on one millionaire of many, so you urged her into it and let the client do the same, a bit at a time."

"I . . . don't understand her thought processes! You've been on Earth, I haven't. When something isn't right, you speak up. All she had to do was say she wasn't interested!"

"No, *we* speak up. She's from a society where you keep quiet and mind your own business. She can't handle the raw business world at this point. And she can't know whether or not she's interested if it's a new experience."

"I still don't see the problem," Marta said, shaking her head. "She said he wasn't unattractive and she's done much racier things with us."

"It wasn't just the sex that bothered her. It was the act of pretending to be someone she isn't. She said she felt like an appliance."

"Well, sure, it's an act. The clients know it and we know it. We create a fantasy and they pay for that creativity."

"Yeah," Rob nodded. "But that's *your* world, not hers. I don't know how she's going to feel when she wakes up, but—"

"Mar," Kendra said, interrupting. She turned over and sat up. She had a serious hangover, but not from booze.

"Yes, Kendra? I'm sorry for what happened."

"I'll be okay. It wasn't all bad, but some parts were disgusting. I made a lot of money, and it was very hard work, and I respect your talent even more, now, but please," she shook her head, "don't ever ask me to do that again."

"I'm sorry, love. I won't." Marta was teary-eyed.

"Look," Kendra said, shaking her head, "we should talk later, but right now I need a shower and some solitude. Thanks for your help, Rob." She meant it as a hint.

"Sure. I'll check on you in a couple of divs. If you need anything, just yell. I'll be at my comm." He departed, but wearing a frown instead of his usual grin.

Kendra stared at the closed door, conflicting emotions in her. She'd made 3400 credits gross in about three hours of preparation, five hours of feigned socializing and three hours of massage and explicit sex. Minus the cost of her dress and makeup, about 2500 total, for the equivalent of a tiring day's work. More than she'd made in three days of consulting for rich spies.

She'd stick to consulting, she decided. Marta probably wouldn't understand, but creating sexual fantasies was not something she could do on a first date with a random stranger who had no emotional interest in her whatsoever.

Rob's "child" comment had bothered her, but she understood what he was telling Marta. By local standards, she was a child and needed to grow up quickly. "The first truly free society in human history," he'd said. She was learning at breakneck speed that the price of freedom was responsibility. It was impossible to blame anyone else for one's actions.

She went into the shower and spent a long time scrubbing her face, breasts and groin. She felt filthy and knew it was psychological. She washed anyway.

She felt better afterward, and dug into her comm for more info on sex and sociality in this system. She found several fictional and pseudohistorical pieces and a couple of instructional texts that were clinical but graphic. After noon, or five local, she wandered over to Rob's and wrapped him in a hug. "Thanks for looking out for me," she said.

"I'm sorry I couldn't have done something sooner," he replied, patting her arm.

"That's fine. I guess I needed my nose rubbed in something to make me remember that I'm still a stranger here."

"You going okay?" he asked.

"I will be," she said.

❖   ❖   ❖

Calan was in his office early the next morning. It was time to find out what was going on. He didn't like Hernandez. He'd thought Pacelli was a sniveling little good girl and here she was demanding better money than he'd offered and screwing him out of a commission. Good act. He wondered what she charged and just how far she'd go. And as for Hernandez' spoiled bitch of a daughter, he'd see about her, too.

Pacelli came here in an awful hurry, he thought. She had to be running from something . . . and there it was! Hmmm. There might be a lot of money stashed somewhere, waiting for her. Or maybe her boss had cut her out of it. He'd "retired." An odd way to be punished for embezzling. Obviously he'd paid somebody off. The UN was like that. Always sneaking business around under the table. Either way, she was still wanted.

He couldn't just turn her in, though. She was a registered resident and could demand a trial here. Hernandez would certainly take her side. Actually, most Citizens would. A charge elsewhere was worth nothing in the Freehold. And if he tried to push the issue, he'd wind up with a suit for damages. Still, the information could prove useful at some point. He'd hang on to it.

Chapter 11

"There are those who don't understand military rituals. Some even ridicule them. I feel pity for those people."

—Sergeant Mel Butler, US Army

"Military Override Call. Military Override Call . . ." Kendra heard the first alarm while asleep, was waking by the second and snapped totally alert when Rob answered.

"Answer call Warrant Leader Robert McKay," he said, sitting up.

"Hi, Rob," the caller began. He was in his thirties and looked very tired and disoriented. "Sorry to bother you, but you are on the list. Warrant Leader Bjorn Gatons died about a div ago."

"What?" Rob replied, shaking his head. "No, I heard you," he said to the caller's attempt to repeat. "Where? How?"

"Hunting trip in the Dragontooth Range. Massive heart attack."

"Didn't they have a stasis box or a medic? No, I guess they wouldn't on the side of a mountain. Goddess, that's terrible."

"I am to inform you that the funeral is at nightfall tomor—well, today, actually, at Placid Lagoon Memorial Park. His request was that you command the firing party."

"That . . . I'm honored," Rob said, shaking his head again. "I'm sorry, but I'm very short of sleep. May I call you later when I can track?"

"Absolutely. Apologies for disturbing, but, well, you understand. Before you go, do you know where Corporal Hernandez can be reached?"

"Right here," Marta acknowledged, sitting up and pulling the covers off Kendra. The camera swung to focus on her. "I heard," she said preemptively.

Nodding, the caller said, "You are requested to serve on the firing party, also."

"Did you need to ask?"

"Not really, except as a formality. Your father is in command of the Honor Guard."

"Got it. Is it a closed service?"

"Not at all. All family friends and any veterans are invited."

"Understood. Out."

Kendra sat back as Rob and Marta dressed. Except for brief glimpses in the park, she had never seen the Freehold Forces dress uniform and was impressed yet again.

Both wore straight black pants, tucked neatly into boots with gleaming gold-thread laces. Rob explained the laces were for parade only. Kendra didn't care; they looked sharp. The coats they wore were green,

epauletted and high throated. Rob's emphasized his
shoulders and tapered lightly in at the waist. Marta's was
cut to flatter the female figure without looking cute or
sexy. Hats were optional, they told her, but would be
worn for this function. They donned brimmed hats,
green and trimmed in black and pinned up at the side.

Insignia was sparse. Rob had four ribbons, Marta
only two. Kendra had acquired nine in her three years
of service and asked about those she saw. Rob spoke
a few commands and a chart of decorations was displayed on the back wall. Kendra read, then turned back
in shock. Ribbons were almost unobtainable except in
combat, and the first of the four Rob wore was the
Citation for Courage. It was the third-highest award
possible.

"How did you manage that?" she asked.

"First engagement on Mtali. I used my vertol to
draw fire away from the ground units and flew a very
extended support mission. By some mathemagical juggling they credit me with saving better than fifty
lives."

Thinking over comments she'd heard from others
since arriving, she asked the next question. "Those
people who I thought were joking with you about
saving their lives weren't joking, were they?"

"No," Marta supplied. "We all owe this lunatic big
time, especially after he took out a missile battery by
crashing into it."

"*What?*" Kendra demanded.

"Well, my racks were empty and my engines almost
dead. Mass was the only weapon I had left. But it was
a useable weapon," he said with a shrug.

Kendra pondered silently while the two adjusted
their buttons and other accoutrements. She spoke again,
saying, "Those are seriously bright. Gold plated?"

"Gold," Rob corrected.

"*Real gold?*"

"Yeah. Looks better, wears better, has a better psychological feel to it and in an emergency makes good trade goods." As he spoke he completed the look with a side-tied green satin sash and thrust a huge cross-guarded sword into it.

"What is that?" Kendra asked, awed.

"That's a Viking langseax. We may carry just about any blade that suits personal taste for dress. Standard issue for combat is a kataghan," he said, handing her a different one from his closet. It was slightly double curved, had a small round guard and a grip big enough for both hands despite its shorter length. She then looked at Marta's dress blade, which was a smaller, wickedly pointed piece with exotic wood and gold wire fittings.

"Just a poniard," Marta said, "But a *long* poniard."

Finished dressing, the two looked proud, professional and deadly. Kendra was starting to wish she could join the Freehold Forces. They commanded a respect that the UN couldn't, and from professionalism, not fear. But it was a silly thought. She was an outsider and they wouldn't trust her.

Kendra felt out of place as soon as they arrived at the funeral. Most of the hundreds of attendees were in uniform and those who weren't were all acquaintances, judging from their actions. She stood nervously close to Rob and Marta and felt slightly better when she recognized Medic Jaheed approaching.

He greeted his compatriots and turned to her. "Greetings, lady. Have things been well?"

"Excellent. Thanks very much for helping me. And please, call me Kendra. Kendra Pacelli," she insisted.

"And I'm Andrew, Drew to my friends."

"Incidentally," Rob interrupted, handing a package to Kendra.

"Oh! Yes," she nodded and handed it to Drew. "I was going to have Rob deliver this, but since we are here . . . Well, thanks for your help."

"Thank you," he replied, taking the box. He glanced quickly at the contents. "Silver Birch! Thank you indeed. If you feel the need to collapse again, please do, I owe you," he said, laughing.

She laughed with him, then cut short. This was a funeral, after all. But no one had seemed offended and there were other smiles around.

"We have to run," Marta reminded Rob. Turning, she spoke to Drew, "Would you mind keeping Kendra company and explaining the service to her?"

"Delighted," he agreed and offered her his arm.

Rob and Marta headed toward the center of the round field. Drew led her to the edge of a circle of people that was forming spontaneously and stood beside her. In short order, Iota was sinking behind the earth rampart that surrounded the clearing and the service began without preamble.

Three people took position in an equilateral triangle at the perimeter, all nude and bearing items. They began walking slowly in the direction of the planet's rotation, chanting as they moved. The first one, a young girl, passed by a few moments later, swinging a censer and repeating, "With Fire and Air we draw the Circle." Some of the people nearby repeated the invocation.

Many seconds later, the second figure approached. This one was an adult woman, sprinkling water from a bowl with a wand. "With Water and Earth we seal the Circle," she said. Again, some responded.

The last to pass was also a woman and mature if not old. Despite her age, she whipped a short sword around her body in a complicated form that denied any frailty. "With Spirit and Sword we guard the Circle," she called, louder than the others.

Finally all three returned to their starting points, just as the sky was coloring with dusk. The soft roar of waves on the lagoon muted some of what Kendra could hear. Stray beams of Iolight flashed off leaves in crimson, green, scarlet and violet. The air was becoming brisk and she was glad of her cloak. She strained to hear again, through shuffling waves and whispering boughs.

Seeing the expression on her face, Drew leaned closer and spoke quietly, "We can talk. The Circle is a ritual to enclose friends and to ward off evil. The service within is meant mostly for the next of kin and is kept quiet on purpose."

Kendra nodded understanding and watched politely. She noted that Rob had the firing party drawn up facing away from them and toward the bier on which the body lay. The pallbearers formed a triad of pairs around it and the service was being held just to the left, so the body was between the firing party and the lake.

Soon, the speaking ceased and Citizen Hernandez, in uniform although he was retired, turned smartly to Rob and barked, "Firing party! Fire three volleys!" He raised his hand in salute.

Rob returned the salute and snapped, "Firing party, by my command, port arms."

Swish-*Thump* went seven rifles.

"Half-right face."

The party turned as one, as if mounted on a board.

"Ready."

"Aim . . . *Fire!*"

Krack. Kendra started at the noise. She had expected primers only, not full power loads.

"Aim, *Fire!*" *Krack.* "Aim, *Fire!*" *Krack.* Ready, front.

"*Pre*-sent . . . *Arms!*" Rob's arm raised his sword as

all seven rifles pivoted to vertical. Next to her, Drew saluted with his blade, as did most of those around her.

Kendra was expecting the next phase, a bugler playing "Taps," and felt the eerie calm that she'd felt on previous occasions at military farewells. A deeply seated part of her longed to be in uniform so she too, could participate. She blinked at damp eyes. At least it was acceptable here. On Earth she'd seen people sneer at the military rituals, even some who were in service. She didn't understand them.

The bugler trailed off the last note, tucked his instrument under his arm and saluted. The tableau was complete, and stayed that way as the pallbearers retrieved the flag covering the body and proceeded to fold it. The UN flag was always folded with the center of the globe up, the Freehold flag folded until only green showed. The finished piece was handed down the line from one to another, each pallbearer stepping back and saluting as he or she finished. The flag ended up in Hernandez' gloves. He spoke an order and all salutes dropped instantly, all across the field. There was a metallic swish of blades entering sheaths, then silence. Hernandez turned and marched to Gatons' widow.

Reverently handing the flag to the old woman, he spoke loudly enough for all to hear, "Lady, this flag is presented with the thanks of a grateful Freehold, in memory of the service performed by your husband." He raised a salute and lowered it very slowly.

Kendra could see the woman crying and blinked again. Military funerals were always hard to watch, in that respect. She expected that to be the end, but there was more.

Hernandez marched back to the bier, retrieved a case, and returned to face the woman again. "I hold your husband's sword," he said, drawing that item from the case, and laying it in her hands. "With it, he served honorably and so honored we return it."

Taking it in both hands, Ms Gatons gripped it silently for a few moments, then handed it back. "I wish to return it to the Freehold, that it may be of service again," she said through weeps.

A murmur passed through the crowd and Kendra turned to Drew again. "What?" she demanded.

Leaning over, he explained, "Usually, a sword is willed to another soldier or kept as a treasure. To return it is a rare gesture of dedication."

Kendra turned back again, to see Hernandez offer his arm to Ms Gatons. He marched slowly and she walked proudly, her eyes shining. They approached the bier. The murmurs rose again.

"Great Goddess . . ." Drew whispered. "They're going to . . ." Kendra tugged at his arm to no avail.

At the bier, Hernandez held the sheath and Gatons fiercely drew the sword. She passed it expertly over her hands, presented it hilt first to Hernandez and silently mouthed, "Thank you."

With a hand at each end, Hernandez slapped the blade over his knee. It had obviously been pre-stressed, as it snapped cleanly and loudly. He returned the two pieces to her and she placed them on the body as someone started clapping. In seconds, the entire crowd was roaring. Rob shouted above the din and another volley sounded from the firing party. Despite the confusion, it was still a crisp, single crack. Letting out a yell, Jaheed finally noticed Kendra again and said, "Destroying the sword says that for another to touch it would lessen the honor he did by serving. It's very rare to see."

The crowd quieted quickly and Hernandez faced the body, saluting again, as Gatons walked to the central fire. She drew out a brand and held it aloft.

Somewhere behind the rampart, a bagpipe began "Amazing Grace." Gatons walked slowly back to the bier and thrust the flaming limb into the base. The old woman with the sword was at the edge of the water, waving wildly and shouting things unheard by Kendra. The woman made a chopping motion with her sword and stepped back as Ms. Gatons leaned her weight against the huge structure and heaved. In moments, the pallbearers and Hernandez joined her.

The bier slid to the shore on rails and began floating slowly out into the lagoon. Kendra began crying again and noticed others were too. The piper sounded the last bar as the flames licked upward.

Then, with a mighty wail that seemed to shake the earth, came the sound of many pipes, joining the first in another verse. The lead piper crested the berm, followed by others from all sides. The triumphant notes were almost drowned in the noise from the crowd and Kendra was blinded with tears, holding her hands to her face to cover it. She didn't see the pipers converge in the center and form up behind the fire.

She regained her composure in time for the three women to reopen the circle, in almost the same manner it had been closed. She followed Jaheed as he fell into a line with the others. There was a touch at her elbow and Rob and Marta were there.

Gatons was making her way along the line, greeting each person individually. *I can't be here!* Kendra thought to herself, but by then, Jaheed was shaking hands with the woman.

Letting go, Gatons turned to Marta and hugged her close. "Thank you so much for coming!"

Rob held her hands, then hugged her also. "Warrant Leader McKay," she said almost formally, "thanks for leading the firing party."

"You're welcome, lady," he replied. "It was an honor."

Gatons then turned to Kendra. "I don't believe we've met," she said, but there was a friendly twinkle in her eye.

"Kendra Pacelli, ma'am, uh, lady," she stumbled, holding hands.

"Kendra is our ladyfriend," Marta explained, "and is a veteran of the UN Forces on Mtali."

"Interesting!" Gatons smiled, "We are honored by your presence," she assured Kendra.

"It has been a privilege," she replied.

Kendra joined them at the wake and had an enjoyable time. There were toasts and discussions of the happy times in Gatons' life, then food and dancing. When she left with Rob, Marta and Drew were still dancing, along with a few other diehards. She discovered she felt really good and joined Rob in his apartment. Sex was becoming a pleasant pastime and she decided that life in the Freehold was good after all. She just wished she could let people back home know. She cried quietly after they made love and he held her gently until she fell asleep.

Chapter 12

"Great things are done when men and mountains meet."

—William Blake

The next weekend was lovely. It was autumn, brisk and clear, which Kendra had always liked, and it was perfect for a camping excursion Rob had been urging her to accompany him on. She was a bit hesitant, not thrilled at the idea of sleeping in a tent outside, but had agreed. He promised to have her back in time for work. She noted that he didn't promise sleep.

They took his other vehicle, a battered groundtruck that had badly scratched and faded panels, but whose turbine sounded brand new, and tossed in some gear from his warehouse. She asked if it was possible to get a rent discount, since she wasn't using the substantial storage unit that came with the apartment.

"No," he responded reasonably, "but you can rent it to someone else, can't you?"

It had never occurred to her. Sublet it? Well, sure. Not on Earth, of course, but here . . .

They headed west into the mountains. The city ended quickly, commerce giving way to light industry giving way to a few wealthy houses on large lots, to scattered farms, to a quick rise in elevation. There was no autocontrol and no barricade on the edge of the road as they wound up through the trees, and she gripped the arms of the seat. She wondered why aircars weren't more popular.

"Problem?" he asked.

"Scared," she replied.

He nodded and slowed. "Better?"

"A little," she replied, watching the tall pines and maples and local nuggetwood flash past. The air was clean and warm, the view across the seaside plain breathtaking and the dark hills romantic in their mystery. She'd never been into wilderness this untamed.

Shortly, they turned off onto a side road that was unfused dirt. It was narrower, and areas were gullied away by rain. Rob slowed further. They were no longer on the edge of the hill, so Kendra relaxed slightly. The trees thinned a bit and a grassy meadow opened up. It had been mowed recently and there was a fence at the edge of it. A sign detailed ownership, inspection dates and listed a contact number for emergencies. "Here we are," Rob told her. He parked the truck to one side and jumped out.

"Oh, Rob, it's beautiful!" she breathed. The east side tapered off onto the hillside and looked across the plain to the East Sea far beyond. There was the streak of a launching shuttle just visible from the starport. Then she noticed the silence. A few birds, the whispering of twigs and leaves and nothing else. It was eerie. It was very arousing. She grabbed him.

They threw a blanket to the ground and made love immediately. Kendra had had a fantasy of making love in the wilderness ever since she had first discovered her sexuality, and here was the chance. No distractions, no people. It was very erotic, and she orgasmed in a crashing series of waves. They lay still afterward, until a few Earth-born bugs began to get too inquisitive. They redressed and Rob explained the tent as he pitched it. She helped by handing over poles.

It was the same design the Vikings had used 1500 years before: a wedge over a framework of poles at every edge. No ropes, no fuss. Once pitched, they each grabbed a side and moved it to a flatter location. Rob tossed in an air mattress and pulled the tassel to inflate it, then added quilts. The truck contained a small fridge for food, a framework that unfolded as a toilet seat and a couple of chairs. He built and lit a small fire, a tough task in the even thinner atmosphere at this altitude, and dragged dead boughs from the forest to feed it. He showed Kendra how to chop wood with an axe and she gleefully got blisters and a splinter until she remembered the gloves he'd handed her.

They went on a short hike, Rob slinging a heavy rifle over his shoulder and handing her a much lighter one. She made him wait at the gate while she read the owners' sign. Rob's name was one of those listed. "Yours?" she asked, surprised.

"For now it's a retreat that friends and I own. When the city expands more, we'll build it as a campsite and rent it out. That will keep the scenery intact."

"What about the land lower down?" she asked. "Once it's built you won't have a view."

"Most of it is unsuitable for basic construction. That was one of our considerations. It would take expensive methods to construct anything, and we own quite a strip of it anyway. And if and when that type of stuff moves in, we'll sell it as commercial property. Right now, we are paying a local to conduct weekly perimeter patrols in decent weather, just to maintain the claim. And it is registered with Public Records."

They strolled around the western edge, gathering berries and a few edible plants as they walked. They took breaks for her benefit; the air was almost too thin and she yawned often. The trees whispered above them in the thin breeze and Iolight dappled the ground. She saw occasional animals, including Earth squirrels and the local rabbitlike bugses. The animals chittered back at them, curious but not terribly afraid. It was amazingly idyllic. "Give me your gun," Rob interrupted.

She handed it over immediately and silently, wondering what was wrong. "Mine's too big for this," he said as he sighted and fired. The rifle popped and twitched and there was a sound of something crashing through the branches. He went forward at a run and she hurried to catch up.

He'd shot a rabbit-sized animal off a tree limb and it curled in death on the leafy ground. She felt queasy. "What's that?" she asked, knowing part of the answer already.

"A scrambler, and dinner. I brought other stuff if you don't want any."

"Thanks," she acknowledged. No, she would not be eating scrambler.

After smelling it roast on the fire, she agreed to try some. It was utterly delicious, rubbed with local herbs and crisped on the outside. She drank some wine, then a bit more, and had a few bites. Then some more wine and a few more bites of meat. She knew she'd have a philosophical war with herself later, but for now she tabled it. Her ears were roaring.

As dusk grew, the city began to light up, along with
the few ships large enough to be seen from here. The
cityscape turned into a long, twinkling curve below,
tapering off in an arm to the north where the road led
to Delph', curving northeast around the bay, and cut
off on the south in a broad arc that was the delta of
the Drifting River. Rob dragged out a pair of binoculars
and pointed out where they must live. It was at the
edge of the glare of downtown, and she nodded.

The fire died down to embers, leaving a rich smoky
taste to the air. He guided her back from it and, after
their eyes adjusted, he pointed out the constellations,
many of them the same as on Earth, but much easier
to see through the clear air without city glare. It was
stunning. Thousands of stars and the Milky Way were
clearly visible, as opposed to tens within an inhabited
area on Earth or mere hundreds in such preserved
"wilds" as the Boundary Waters. And there was the
Sun, he pointed out to her. It was a barely visible
pinpoint near Sirius.

When they finally went to bed, she clung to him.
For the first time in her life, she felt really insignifi-
cant. Not even space travel had brought that home to
her before.

The next morning was shivery cold, the altitude and
clear, thin air conspiring to drop the apparent temperature. She huddled under the quilts, struggled into
clothes and then dared to rise. Rob began packing gear.

A mist rolled slowly down the meadow's gentle slope
and tumbled over the hill. It wafted below in ghostly
fingers, occasionally tearing into the sky as something
below warmed in the hazy Iolight cutting across in
front. The long turn of seasons here led to an amazing spectrum of colors in the dual plant kingdoms, and
the light through the leaves threw colored shadows
across the hoary grass. She wished for a camera, then

realized no picture could ever capture this moment. Rob came and stood next to her, hand on her shoulder, and said nothing. As the gray tendrils thinned, he squeezed and pulled, urging her to the vehicle.

She had forgotten how cold she was and gratefully soaked in the cab's heat, cupping the proffered mug of chocolate in both hands. They bumped along the rutted path to the road, Rob keeping the speed down to avoid spills.

They headed further west, over the mountains. The range barely topped three thousand meters and was quite old geologically speaking. The road got straighter as the basaltic tops smoothed out to domes, trees giving way to scrub. They were suddenly over the divide and facing the central plains. Kendra gasped.

Woods. Trees. As far as the eye could see, nothing but trees. Millions of hectares of them. No sight like it had been seen anywhere on Earth for five hundred years, and not in "civilized" areas for at least a hundred more. She quivered inside, overcome with emotion, and uttered not a word. Her exhaled breath made an almost inaudible "ohhhhhhhh!"

She finally remembered to breathe in.

"Now," Rob cut into her thoughts, "Why would *anyone* who's seen this *ever* want to live anywhere else?"

"I don't," she replied very quietly, tears blurring her vision. With crystal clarity, she realized the pain she'd been feeling was that of rejection from her old home. Nothing now could pry her from her new home, Grainne.

She wondered why sights like this weren't better advertised? Surely there would be more tourist traffic and better trade? Then she realized that that very traffic would destroy the beauty that brought people.

The Freeholders kept it quiet, not as selfishness, but as a personal work of art to be shared with those who would seek it out or could best appreciate it. She vaguely was aware that the investment to start such a tourist trade would be huge—facilities and infrastructure would have to be built.

The unfolding vista knocked such thoughts from her mind. She forgot her fear of the winding road and stared silently for long segs.

Halfway down the far side, Rob turned off the road onto another packed dirt trail. This was a plateau, not a meadow and there was a trickling stream feeding a small pond. It had been dammed deliberately for the small cabin nearby. "Inside tonight," he promised her.

"Is this yours, too?" she asked.

"Partly," he admitted. "We have to do some upkeep as our share."

"Sure," she agreed.

He parked in front and began unlocking sliding covers over the windows and doors. "To prevent vandalism?" she asked.

"Huh? Nah. Don't want storms or swinging branches to break any windows."

It was cool inside, lit indirectly through the trees and windows. Rob lit a fire inside a stove and pointed to a list of chores.

They spent the morning gathering and chopping firewood, clearing brush from around the road and cabin with machetes, sweeping and doing some touch-up painting. The cabin was built of wood, making Kendra feel like a pioneer in the old American West.

She shrugged and agreed to leftover scrambler, salted and spiced, and they mixed a salad of items brought along. There was crusty bread, cheese and beer. They stretched out for a short nap after the exertion of the morning and Kendra awoke to Rob attempting to make love to her. She feigned sleep a bit longer, then let her legs fall open for him. Finally, unable to restrain herself, she burst out laughing. He joined her.

The cabin had a composting toilet inside and minimal running water filtered from the stream. The best part about modern society was that they could have solar receivers and a small generator on the stream; no long buried or strung cables to disturb the landscape were necessary.

"I'm going to take a walk," she announced. "Want to come with?"

"No, I'm going to tidy up," he said. "I'll catch up shortly. Make sure you take your rifle," he added.

"Okay," she agreed, grabbing it from the rack as she opened the door. It was warm and sunny now and no jacket was needed. She stepped down, closed the door and stood, inhaling the clean air and listening, eyes closed. She opened them and strode off across the plateau.

It was pretty. The trees could be seen to sway gently and a lone cloud scudded across, seeming to be just out of reach. She examined the granite of an outcropping, similar but different from Earth granites, and handled a piece in curiosity. There was a rustle to her left that didn't register for a moment, then triggered some unconscious reflex.

She turned, startled. A fluidly graceful form sprang out of the bushes, bounded off the grassy edge of the clearing and leapt again. She realized its direction, groped for her rifle and swung it, shaking.

She automatically followed the steps Rob had drilled into her; point, squeeze, point again, squeeze. Four shots coughed out of the muzzle, recoil shoving at her shoulder. There was an agonized roar and the creature's next bound ended with a tangible *thump!* on the ground in front of her. She stood, shaking and stared at the long-legged beast sprawled on the grass. Bloody froth oozed from its nostrils.

"I'm behind you," Rob advised, gently reaching around her to grasp her weapon and lead her back a few steps. Drawing his pistol, he walked wide around the animal and fired a round just behind its ear. It twitched once.

"What the hell is that?" she demanded, shaking again.

"That *was* a ripper. Now dead. Well shot, lady," he said, holstering his own gun.

She glanced at the weapon still in her hand, reached down and returned it to its slung position. Her shakes continued. "What?" she asked, not tracking properly.

"It was going to have you for lunch. You were quicker," Rob explained.

"A bare victory for human intelligence," she said with a sickly smile, trying to relax.

"I didn't say smarter, just quicker," he returned. "Never think of these bastards as stupid."

"Yeah," she agreed, nodding vigorously.

Adrenaline from the ripper attack kept her awake the entire way home. The rolled-up skin in the truck bed didn't reassure her. She'd declined to watch the skinning process and felt queasy about it. The remains had been left for scavengers, except for one large steak. "Pretty rank tasting, but not something you get every day," Rob had said.

Pretty as it was, Freehold was no Utopia. Utopia didn't have bloodthirsty predators that hadn't had millions of years to learn to fear hominids.

She didn't even notice the fast drive down the mountains, in the dusk, that would have terrified her two days before. She helped Rob unload in a daze, got back in and was silent as he drove to Marta's. Once inside, she showered at length, luxuriating in modern equipment and safety, then crawled into bed. Rob was already asleep.

She stirred from a bad dream as Marta snuggled in behind her.

"Hi, love," Marta greeted her, kissing her thoroughly. "Is that a ripper skin in my other freezer?"

"Uh, yes. It jumped me this afternoon," she agreed, muzzy-headed.

"Well done! Can we use it as a rug in front of the fireplace? Please? Cash? Barter? Two hours of scorching sex?" Marta teased her.

"Sure, I guess. I hadn't thought about it." She was back asleep before Marta could continue her seduction. She barely was aware of a soft, frustrated curse and didn't hear or feel Marta shifting to get comfortable against her back.

Chapter 13

"You never hear anyone say, 'Yeah, but it's a *dry* cold.'"

—Charles A. Budreau

Kendra's duties at the park changed as the seasons did. First came removal of tons of leaves, and insulated bowls for the more sensitive plants. Flags were planted along walkways to mark them under the snow. She learned how to do basic maintenance on the heating systems at the restrooms. Then the fountains were shut down, to turn into skating rinks. Additional rinks were laid out with timbers, to be filled with water when the temperature reliably dropped below freezing.

The merchants dwindled in number to a few diehards selling souvenirs and the food vendors who never stopped. She inquired, and found out that various halls staged sales of assorted merchandise throughout the winter and some of the entrepreneurs

were strictly seasonal. It seemed like a rather insecure way to make a living, but the overhead and
operating costs were low.

It got cold, and she went shopping for appropriate
clothing. There was an excellent selection of warm gear,
from dirt ugly and cheap to very nice high-end stuff.
Rob was digging into someone's operation, so Marta
went with her. Her first advice was, "Remember
everything I told you about fashion? Ditch it. You're
trying to stay warm."

It was good advice. She got two heavily quilted and
waterproof coveralls and two sets of boots, one for
regular wear, one for temperatures below -20, and
Marta assured her they'd have them. She elected blaze
orange for her parka, just for visibility. Gloves and a
balaclava completed her shopping. There went another
Cr800. She sighed and bundled the stuff home.

The first blizzard hit in early November—unlike the
other time divisions, they'd kept the familiar month
names. Ten months of five local weeks each, with no
July or August. June to September was a change that
would take getting used to, but she was grateful that
the whole calendar hadn't changed. There were too
many things to learn now. Like this blizzard.

She wouldn't have thought that a coastal plain on
the East Coast could have a lot of snow, especially
considering the overall climate. She was stunned when
it hit. She opened her door one morning and there was
thirty centimeters of snow there. Some of it trickled
in, propelled by a chill blast. She exchanged her pants
and tunic for a coverall, her jacket for a parka and her
shoes for boots. Her cloak stayed home.

It took her longer to walk to work. The city did
little snow removal. This was one case where the lack
of state infrastructure *did* hurt. The retailers were
busily shoveling, melting and pressure-throwing snow

off their accessways. Some had coils installed underground and were simply brushing the surface aside as it melted underneath. A few either left it to compact under foot and wheel or didn't open. The larger stores either had or contracted for plows, blowers and melters, which were simply road fusers set on low heat. The city did have a good drainage system at resident expense. It would have been impossible to live without one.

Traffic was heavier than she expected, because there was little automatic control to sequence it. Also, the thick clouds and wind had grounded all the flyers, which increased the traffic density tremendously. She had originally been amazed at the number of flying vehicles in this society and wondered why most people had dedicated ground cars also. Now she knew. The thought of a crash in midair or into a building in heavy snow was enough to make her skin tingle, and the sound of sirens some distance away added to her queasy feeling. She hoped most pilots were smarter than to risk it. Apparently, local streets and small neighborhoods either pooled funds or did without removal, hoping someone would drive by and clear the street in passing.

As soon as she got to the garage, she was sent out to help clear the surrounding streets, the maintenance access road and the main park walkways. Then she was called to plow some nearby housing complexes on contract. This was where City Parks made a substantial chunk of its revenue for the year. Hiroki called her and directed her to plow a few areas near the homes of disabled and elderly people. She found most of them had already been done by neighbors, and was again impressed by the Freeholders' social responsibility. Something about still being in the process of taming the system, she surmised. Her final tasks were the areas

around the smaller, outlying parks, then she headed
back, cold despite the cab heater. Then they had to
clean the vehicles. She'd worked an extra div and
earned the gratitude of Hiroki and Karen.

It was already well toward sunset. It was amazing
how fast the day changed with a 20-degree axial tilt.
She walked through the park, heading north, and
stopped to watch a group of artists. They were piling
and compacting snow and carving it into sculptures.
She could see a castle, a dragon—a whole scene from
high fantasy. A couple were spraying water and fixa-
tive over the finished parts to preserve it for a time.
"Hey, do you work here, lady?" one of them asked,
guessing from her mode of dress.

"Yes?" she replied.

"Where can we find a power hookup? I thought
there was one over here, but . . ." he tapered off,
indicating the snow.

She helped them dig for a connection and watched
as they set up an outdoor lighting kit. They were
prepared to work late, apparently. Another returned
with food and drinks, and several passersby were gathering. The inevitable hat was getting stuffed with chits
and someone brought beer. Kendra finally left, laughing. Any excuse for a party!

The winter was as long as the summer had been.
Wind howled through the artificial canyons of the city,
whipped across the bay and dumped occasional snow.
Rob took her to a Winter Solstice ritual, a relaxed one.
Marta went to one that was a much more frank celebration of fertility. It sounded interesting to see as
an observer, but not the type of thing Kendra would
participate in.

Long divs of work and short daylight was stressful.
She and Rob had a few fights over stupid things and

she spent more social time with Marta. The young woman had an incredible amount of energy, considerable disposable income for entertainment and was very generous. It took Kendra a while to realize that Mar enjoyed blowing money with her friends and was neither trying to show off nor create obligations.

Still, she had only the two friends and a handful of acquaintances. Cabin fever was a drain and the winter was two and a half months long, or a hundred twenty-five dull, gray, dark, blustery local days. Ice storms, blizzards, occasional freezing rain, broken branches, stuck vehicles, all the bad things she knew from home and for almost twice as long. She realized now why these people were such manic partiers in summer. They had plenty of pent-up energy from winter.

She accepted an invitation to dine with Marta's family. Rob would meet her there, but she was traveling with Mar. The family home was on the west side, where development was still continuing, and surprised Kendra at first. She'd assumed from Marta's spread that her family would have a huge mansion or sprawling ranch. Instead, it was a quite typical contemporary villa. It was modern enough, with variable-polarity solar windows, automatic climate control and a huge heat sink to go with the windows and vents and all the nice accessories that made maintenance simple. The house had good land area and would almost certainly appreciate well as the city grew, but was nothing spectacular like, say, Marta's own monstrous digs.

She pondered the apparent modesty while being greeted and it finally came to her. To become a Citizen, Hernandez had had to achieve considerable wealth, then donate virtually all of it to the Freehold. Citizens wielded huge political power. They were not allowed economic means to go with it. That one tenet of society Kendra had never argued with, as it made perfect sense.

She looked at Hernandez again with new respect. Here was a man who had served in the military, independently made a fortune in the millions, then voluntarily gave most of it away to lead. He now had a textbook average middle-class existence and an equivalent income that was dependent upon the good graces of those he ruled. That said more about his integrity than any thousand campaign speeches back on Earth.

Marta's mother was half Asian, half Caucasian, and that blend with her husband's Hispanic looks had created the exotic beauty of their children. Kiki and Umberto, as they insisted on being called, introduced their other children, Kichan and Carlos. He was just now ten local years, tall and lean, and would be moving out shortly to pursue his own fortune. Marta's older sister, Kichan, was an engineer out in a Halo habitat, home on vacation between projects. She was plain only by comparison to Marta. Rob arrived shortly, looking very good in a kilt in Kendra's opinion. He'd brought wine and mead. Kendra had almost forgotten the local custom of gifts for every occasion and had remembered just in time to stop by a store for some imported Swiss chocolate. It was received enthusiastically.

The meal was good, being a cross between Thai and Southwest. It was something resembling quesadillas and burritos, but with plenty of meat and vegetables and not much in the way of beans or rice. She'd been told it was vat-raised meat and was quite grateful for that and for the fact that the spices were served as sides. The salsa was fresh and corrosive, the beer was Umberto's own brew, crisp and refreshing. To make it even more pleasant, the company was cheerful and highly intelligent. That made sense.

There were no stupid genes in this family. Kendra felt very welcome as the conversation swung from space to weather to business to politics, and to a comparison between the Freehold and the UN. Kendra discovered that the group was quite educated as to Earth, far more so than she was to the Freehold, even after more than a year of residency.

Somehow, crime came up. She knew that crime was far lower here, by several orders of magnitude, but the attitude about Earth, from people who had never been there, offended her. She politely said so.

Kichan was quite vocal. "I wasn't trying to offend you personally, Kendra, but don't you admit to being much safer here?"

"Yes," she agreed. "But the mindset on Earth is different. We aren't as bothered by most petty crimes."

"'Petty crime'?" Kichan asked, a tone of irony in her voice. "I'm guessing you mean shoplifting or larceny? I suppose I see that, if you're used to it as a common occurrence. It's just hard to think of having your property violated and not having any way to recover it as 'petty.'"

"We regard property as expendable. That's what insurance is for," Kendra explained. "Of course, it's hard to put a dollar value on sentimental items. But that's not even really petty crime, that's just human nature at work, taking things."

"It's not your nature, is it?"

"Well, no," Kendra admitted. "But it's quite common for poor people."

"Not here," Rob observed. "But if that's not what you mean by petty crime, what do you mean?" he asked, leaning forward with his wine.

"Oh, basic assault, vehicle theft, rape, burglary, strong-arm robbery," Kendra said. "As long as you aren't seriously hurt, it's just like any other accident."

There was silence. She realized that some boundary had been crossed, but couldn't place it.

"Rape is a 'petty' crime?" Marta asked, looking very bothered.

"Well, it's painful and embarrassing short term," Kendra replied, "but not really debilitating. After the first couple, you get used to it, just like muggings."

The whole table was staring at her. She struggled with the horrified looks. Were they that naive about crime? Had none of them ever thought about what it was like? At all?

Kichan put her fork down, breathed deeply and stood. "If you'll all excuse me for a moment, please?" she said, and left the table. She was hurrying as she reached the hall.

Into the awkward silence, Rob and Marta both began to speak. He deferred to her.

"So, has anyone heard about Vermilion's new recording? I'm posing for the cover," she said.

Everyone, including Kendra, gratefully embraced the subject change. "Great!" her mother said. "Any details?"

"Not really, Mom. They are doing most of the background with both classic oil and electronic art, so it'll be a very surrealistic holo. Apparently it involves a dragon and some kind of alien creature. I'm spread out and writhing and having a really intense orgasm."

"Oh, that'll be good for business," her brother commented.

"Exactly," Marta nodded. "The rate was okay, but what I didn't get in percentage I'll more than get in advertising. Maybe even some outsystem orders for pics or some visiting muckymuck. Who knows? The art director loved it, said I looked delish, so I may even get some more orders that way, too."

Kendra nodded. She had found out that Mar also sold pictures, would do custom videos, modeled for several exoticwear manufacturers and did bit parts of acting. Rob had taken over as her agent and she had a net programmer on contract to keep her files from being hacked. She had a small sample site that could be accessed for free and would sell images gladly, but expected a fee for every viewing. She kept the code updated so they couldn't be downloaded or copied without approval and had filed several suits against secondary dealers who had swiped files.

Kichan returned, looking better, and the conversation drifted to camping, sports and eventually to Kendra's park work. No one seemed bothered by the earlier incident and they stayed quite late.

As they headed home, she asked her friends, "Okay, I'm confused. Crime is a taboo subject, but you can discuss your publicly displayed orgasms? I don't get it."

Rob and Mar exchanged glances and thoughtful looks. Finally, he spoke. "Crime is a violation of a person's self or property. Sex is a matter of human nature, and in this case, art."

I guess," she replied. "Back home, we talk about our attacks and how we managed. Sort of a release, I suppose. It's also kind of a bragging rights thing or just a story type of thing. Hard to explain. But sex is very private."

"I think," said Marta, "that sex in that context reveals too much of your feelings to strangers. It's a protective measure. The crime is superficial to you, so that's an okay subject."

"Which is exactly backwards," Rob said. "I don't know how you got into that mindset as a society, but it's guaranteed to destroy it."

"I think it's just another difference," Kendra insisted defensively. "I don't see Earth disappearing anywhere after all this time."

The others were silent. She joined them.

Chapter 14

"Democracy is based on the assumption that a million men are wiser than one man. How's that again? I missed something.

"Autocracy is based on the assumption that one man is wiser than a million men. Let's play that over again, too. Who decides?"
—Robert A. Heinlein, in *Time Enough for Love*

Kendra arrived home tired. It had been a hectic day, with a lot of planting and several rearrangements of spaces. Then she'd had to clear vehicles away. There'd actually been an election scheduled and the park was one of the prime meeting places in town, along with the Citizen's Council Building and two other large parks.

She hadn't thought any democratic process existed here. There was no provision for legislation in the Constitution and only the Citizens were allowed to make what few political decisions there were. She'd followed the news closely on this, just out of curiosity. She had assumed that as an immigrant, she was not eligible, then recalled that she was a paid Resident. She had as much voice as anyone born here.

It was a simple District matter. The starport wanted to expand and would have to destroy several existing roads to do so. Paying for them and construction of new ones, was a strictly private matter for the Jefferson Starport Corporation. She was still bemused by the notion of a private entity controlling traffic. It seemed dangerous, but there were two others competing with it. Usage rates were quite reasonable.

The question was, where should the relocated roads be routed? There were several farms and industries that had to be worked around. Three routes presented themselves as being easily exploited, but all three had their pros and cons. One would prevent expansion of an existing business park entity, which had the land but had not yet used it. They were willing to sell for the right price and instead stretch south rather than west. A second diverted far around existing land and would slow ground traffic from the suburbs growing out that way. The third would cut close to the bay, affecting Bay Park and several private beaches. For the time being the city had claimed all three routes and would not be releasing them until a decision was reached. A suit had been filed against the 'port and the city by investors, demanding release of land not being used for roads, as a constitutional violation. There was a petition from the suburbs not to use the circuitous middle route and another from civic groups not to use the seaside path. JSC had filed a demand that it be allowed to select the cheapest route, which was the one the suburbanites were opposed to.

Faced with a conflict that was bound to antagonize

everyone, the Citizens judging the suits had decided to put it to a popular vote in the District. They reserved the right to make the final decision, but had decided that a popular choice was necessary to that decision-making process.

The election was scheduled for six divs. Anyone was welcome to code a vote to Citizens' court, with residence number attached. Many did. Many others gathered in the parks and the Council building to hear final arguments. The lifter-elevated screen rippling in the breeze showed the discussions and a massive crowd formed, most arriving within a few segs of the voting time.

Cameras and aides were in place and the choices were read. "For the western route, through Parkfield Business Park, at the expense of JSC."

"*Aye!*" Kendra thought that best. The 'port would have to raise fees slightly or cut corners elsewhere, but it would be cheaper than distancing three towns' ground traffic.

"For the middle route, around the towns of Greenwood, Franklin and New Muncie."

"Aye!"

"For the eastern route, along the bay."

"Aye!" That last was clearly not popular and the few raised hands and voices were followed by good-natured chuckling, some of it from the voters who supported that lost cause.

"To be confirmed by review, the population votes for the western route."

That was it. Election over in ten seconds. Did these people do nothing at a slow, respectable pace?

She could determine why the park was used, anyway. Most of the voters stayed to socialize. She should have expected it. She had a soft drink and a sandwich from a vendor, watched a couple of performers and headed home.

There was a message waiting on her comm. Pulling off her boots, she sat back and cued it.

"Hi there," said a familiar redheaded woman. It was Jelsie Romar. "Told you I'd be home about now. It looks as if you're doing well. I'd like to stop by about six-fifty. Call me and let me know. Two nine nine nine three, two nine three seven five five. Bye."

Kendra said, "Place call to code from message."

"Dialing."

On the third flash, the call was answered. "Romar. Oh, hi. Glad you're there. You see, I have this body." She grinned.

Laughing, Kendra replied, "You're in luck. I work for Jefferson Parks, so I have a shovel."

Romar whooped in response. "You got my message I assume?" she asked.

"Sure. Come on over."

"Be there in twenty."

Jelsie hit it off with Marta as well as she had with Kendra. She was just very nice and sweet. She was also very religious, Kendra discovered. They were at Marta's place with Rob and Drew and were still talking and drinking as dark fell. "Oh, shoot!" Jelsie gasped, looking outside at the purple sky. "Full Gealach tonight! I'm supposed to do ritual!"

"We can do it here," Marta said. "My shrine is small, but you're welcome."

Breathing deeply, Jelsie said, "Thanks. You want to lead or should I?"

"You go ahead," Marta said. "This way."

Drew went along, partly for the service, partly to watch Jelsie. He had a thing for redheads. Rob went along to watch both women, and Kendra followed from curiosity.

Marta's shrine was all the way up in a loft, with windows facing in all directions and a skylight, too. It had soft lighting, a stone as an altar, and several bottles, bowls and bundles of incense. It was in earth tones throughout, with cushions and a low couch.

Jelsie and Marta stripped and donned robes. The others took seats on the cushions and waited. Romar selected an incense block from the abundant rack, placed it in a tray and set candles around the stone. She lit one, used it to light others and the block of incense and spoke the lights out. Then she took a goblet from the rack and poured wine.

Kendra had seen this ritual before, but Romar seemed to glow from within with passion. She added an invocation to Gealach before closing. She hugged and lightly kissed them all as she closed, then sat back, sweating lightly from the exertion.

"Oath of Blades?" Drew asked into the silence.

"Sure." "Yes." "Might as well." were the answers. Kendra didn't know what it was and kept silent.

Marta drew a sword from a rack on the wall and laid it in front of her. Drew and Jelsie pulled out their service knives and Rob produced his usual "utility" blade, all twenty-five centimeters of it. All lay on the altar, facing the center. Kendra looked askance at Rob, who gave her a very slight nod that she should just sit.

Jelsie blew smoke from the incense block gently across the blades, Marta sprinkled a drop of wine onto each from a finger. As one, they raised them vertically with both hands and dipped the tips toward the central candle flame. Drew sprinkled clove-scented oil onto a silk cloth and Rob took each blade in turn and wiped them clean. Again, the blades were presented toward the flame. The four intoned together, "Our blades, our bodies, our souls. For God, Goddess and the Freehold." They passed the blades flat across their palms and sheathed them. Kendra nodded in understanding. It was a ritual exclusive to the military. She knew many people who regarded military rituals as silly. She doubted any of those people were prepared to die for a cause. Once again she envied her friends their camaraderie.

They were shortly back downstairs again. "Thank you, Marta," Jelsie said. She sounded very relieved.

"Glad to," Mar replied.

They stayed all night. Marta made a polite hint to Jelsie, who declined. She considered Drew's offer for some time, then agreed to it. He looked delighted. Kendra shared a look with Rob, and they grinned, reading each other's thoughts. They glanced at Marta, who said, "Go ahead. I do sleep alone on occasion."

"Do you want to join us?" Kendra asked.

"Of course. But I don't want to impose."

"Oh, come on!" Kendra grinned. She loved getting attention and it was sensual to give. Marta's sexuality was a palpable thing, and very inspiring.

"If you're going to twist my arm . . ." Marta said and laughed, loudly.

Chapter 15

"Back to the Army again, sergeant,
  Back to the Army again.
  'Ow did I learn to do right-about-turn?
  I'm back to the Army again."
          —Rudyard Kipling, "Back to the Army Again"

"Could I see you, Kendra?" Hiroki asked quietly, looking rather upset.

"Cert," she agreed. "What goes?" She followed him into his office. He offered her a seat. She saw both Karen and Citizen Hernandez as she took it, and felt suddenly bothered.

"The city has had to cut our stipend totally," Hiroki said.

Hernandez continued, "Not by choice. But the economic crunch is hitting us. We have a duty to provide support to the military, and with trade reduced, our contributions from corporate sources have shrunk. There are several areas that can no longer be funded for the foreseeable future."

Hiroki picked up, "As I'm sure you've figured, Karen and I are the only permanent contractors. The others are hired as needed, and the labor pool are all court prisoners. We've cut into the budget for landscaping, raised the fees for rental, but what it finally comes down to is we have no work for you to do and no money to pay you. We are very regretfully going to have to terminate your contract." He flushed red at the admission and looked thoroughly ashamed. Kendra had learned that terminating an employee for other than disciplinary reasons was considered very discourteous, almost criminal.

She replied, "I understand, Hiroki. It's not your fault." After a moment's silence and a nod from him, she turned to Hernandez and asked, "My contract is being resold then? How much input do I get?"

"Your contract was paid by the park," Hernandez said, leaning back. "So it is terminated with no prejudice to you. It's the least we can do, since you are going to be out of work. Your debt is paid. I'll be happy to help you find something else. And possibly advance you funds for travel or such."

"Thank you, sir, but I have savings," she insisted. "And I'd like to explore my own resources first."

"Please come by to visit whenever you like," Karen said. She apparently had been there as emotional support for Hiroki. "And if something comes up, we'll let you know immediately."

"Thank you," Kendra said, her brain considering possibilities. She made awkward small talk that tapered off and finally said goodbye and left, retrieving her few possessions from her locker. She headed back for Marta's, having no other place to go at the moment.

❖   ❖   ❖

"Okay," Rob said after she told him, "So you are paid off less than halfway through your contract, unemployed and have savings. There are far worse situations."

"Oh, sure," she agreed, "but I'm still *unemployed* and have *limited* savings. And I don't think anyone wants a cultural assessment of Earth at this point." She smiled wryly.

Marta came through from the kitchen and said, "You can stay here as long as you want, love. You know that."

"Thanks," she said. "But I won't take charity. I'll pay for my board."

Marta started to object, but caught Rob's expression. She didn't understand it, but she held her comments.

Rob knew she felt out of place and why she couldn't take charity from friends. She might take it from a government, but there was no such here. The irony was amusing, since most Freeholders were diametrically opposed to her position, from the same motives.

"Come," Rob said with a gesture. "There's someone I want you to meet." He rose and headed for the vehicle bay. She followed him and strapped in.

He drove across town to a smaller business park, Park North. Like most, it actually was a privately owned, publicly accessible park with commercial and light industrial businesses surrounding it. He stopped near one edge, in what was technically a retail area. The sign above them said MILITARY RECRUITING STATION.

Kendra said, "But—" but he cut her off and led her inside.

By the end of the day, she was back in the military. She liked serving and being useful, and part of her homesickness had been for her military life. The Freehold forces impressed her and it hadn't taken much suggestion. The recruiter naturally was eager to meet his quota, but few slots were available. However, hearing of her prior service had made his job easier and he'd offered her the rank of corporal. She accepted, signed and was initially sworn in. In back, the old routine of placement tests and physical examination was almost comforting, despite its impersonality. The adminwork was as brief as she was coming to expect and they even had space in logistics. Part of her was nervous, but another part was thrilled at being part of a team again, of belonging to society. Rob had stressed that she needed placement soon and the recruiter scheduled her to leave a week hence. She cheerfully went home and sat down to a celebratory feast with her family, as she was coming to think of them, and slept soundly after gathering her possessions and making plans and lists.

The week was tense. She felt eagerness mixed with anxiety and took it out physically on Rob, who reciprocated even more passionately than usual. They spent a lot of time talking about nothing in particular, and some time talking about training, but always skirting the issue of departure and separation.

"I'm betting this is very different from the UNPF recruit training," he said to her one day at lunch. They were all staying at Marta's for the time being, and the pair of them were sitting at the heavy, carved bluemaple dining table.

"Why?" she asked, between sips of soup.

"Different philosophies," he said. "We're a nation of cooperative loners, doing what has to be done because it's reasonable. Earth for the most part is very social, everyone cooperating because they've been raised to do so. We think differently. And the UN officially regards force as undesirable, talks around the subject and always pretends it's using less than it is. They've got lots of money and personnel and don't have to be efficient. So they have a small operations force within a huge support structure, aimed at bringing strays back into the fold. Whereas we . . . well, what do we need a military for?"

That was something she'd wondered herself. "I'm not really sure."

"Neither are we," he said. "But being independent, we have to have our own. It's small, the ratio of operations to support is huge and the line between them blurred, and we can't expect to fight in nice urban settings, with all the water, power, roads and facilities we'd like."

He described training to her and she knew she should be listening, but it really wasn't what either of them wanted to talk about. She knew he wanted her to stay, she knew he understood why she had to do this, and they were both avoiding the issue.

At least they didn't fight.

Marta was less vocal about the military, more so about missing Kendra. The contrasts between the two women were small enough for them to be good friends, sufficient for Kendra to find interest in everything Marta suggested, even if she decided most of it wasn't to her taste. They spent the week hitting club after club at Mar's urging, building up socialization against the coming enforced weeks of spartan discipline.

Their goodbye was teary. Once again, Kendra was being uprooted from her home and dragged to a strange place to start anew. She'd thought it would be easier, having fewer possessions and family to worry about. It seemed that the dearth thereof made what she had that much more precious.

They all went to the port and sat around a café table, drinking chocolate and coffee, eating spiced snacks and plain quesadillas. "You're staring at me," Kendra said after a while.

"We're going to miss you," Rob said. He was staring at her face, her body, her face again. It was unnerving. Marta said nothing, just gripped her hand.

"I'll be back," she said, smiling. It was forced. Inside, she was nervous. Basic all over again. And what would it be like, with all her experience, to be a raw recruit again?

Soon enough, her flight was called. From habit, they walked briskly, then waited again at the departure lounge. It was still odd not to have any kind of security check. A token few employees stopped eager visitors from walking onto the planes and shuttles and that was it.

She was hugged from both sides, Rob and Marta seemingly determined to cling to her until the last moment. Then Marta kissed her. "Take care, be careful, and hurry back," she said.

Rob in turn gripped her tightly, pulled her close, firm muscles pressing against her from knee to shoulder, and kissed her hard and long. His hands held her at neck and waist. When they broke at last, he said, "Good luck. Love you."

"Love you," she agreed, her eyes damp.

The two hurried away, not looking back.

Kendra arrived in the town of Rockcliff in late afternoon and had to find her own way to the base. The taxi ride gave her the chance to look at the scenery of the western coastal range, much younger and sharper than the blurred edges of those near the capital. The landscape was vigorous, blue-green and yellow, with purple hazy peaks to the tallest mountains far off to the east.

Rockcliff was actually a considerable distance inland, despite being situated above the west coastal plain, and Mirror Lake was a perfect blue that blended into the sky. With few major roads and only a bare two centuries of development, the city seemed to well up out of the landscape. A modern, geometric corporate headquarters building grew like a massif out of the trees and she marveled again at the sheer, overwhelming sensuality of Grainne's scenery.

Dropped at the gate of the base, she was held until a student escort from training depot could come to get her, then dropped off at a huge barracks complex. She was led to a hundred-bed bay, stifling in the afternoon heat, and introduced to an instructor.

"Sergeant Carpender," her escort said, "Recruit Pacelli."

Carpender was tall, taller than she, and broad shouldered with a barrel chest. His hair was short and wavy brown and his face round and intense. He glanced at his comm and said, "A little early, aren't you?" His voice boomed.

"Transportation problems, sir," she said.

"What's the problem with being early? Never complain about that. You can help over here." He gestured.

Two recruits already in uniform were aligning beds and laying out fresh linen. She assisted by dragging the bedclothes from a truck outside and dropping a bundle on each bed. They were done shortly.

"You two are released back to your section," Carpender told them. "Pacelli, let's get dinner." She followed him across to a dining hall that was blowing out wonderful smells. She knew from more than a year of experience that Freeholders demanded excellent food, even at government facilities, and loaded her plate high after signing in. It wasn't dissimilar from UN facilities so she felt comfortable.

"So, can I ask about your accent?" Carpender inquired, sitting across from her. He'd filled his tray to capacity and then some, and dug in as he sat.

She explained her background in detail, since the recruiters had all the data anyway. He nodded periodically and asked some leading questions. He didn't seem to find her story problematic.

"I've heard all kinds of backgrounds here," he said. "Don't sweat it."

Then he asked, "Am I right that you are a bit below things as far as physical strength?" She agreed. "Okay," he nodded. "Then understand this: on the one hand, there aren't any allowances for that. On the other hand, we don't want you hurt. Keep me informed if there are any problems and we'll either get you supplemental training or, not likely, medical treatment if necessary. If anything has you confused or is outside your experience, ask. You have the right to know you are being treated within our safety requirements, and we need to know about any problems to do that."

She agreed politely and thankfully and returned to the barracks with him. Three other recruits arrived that evening. There were thumping and banging noises at night and when she awoke there were eleven of them. The main rush arrived by bus at 3 divs, bringing the total to fifty.

They were walked rather than marched to the training depot and had all their documentation from the recruiters redone for clarity. Some minor points were corrected and one person sent home on medical profile. He was directed to return in three months. Kendra never found out why.

Next, they were lined up for medical exams—very *complete* medical exams. Nanoprobes, electronic scans, and physical tests, including samples of blood, skin and hair. They were immunized with both nanos and a few hypodermics and given paper copies of the transaction as well as datachips. There were several briefings on training, procedures and other details. Kendra learned that there were Christian chaplains on base, including a Roman Catholic, although not a Catholic Reformed. Still, it was something. And she had a choice of local clock or Earth clock for worship. She decided that every ten local days was adequate, not being exceptionally devout. Besides, the idea of adapting every seven Earth days at twenty-four hours to the local schedule was bound to create waves and get her noticed.

"Strip," Carpender ordered. "Place your civilian clothes in the bag and line up here for haircuts. No talking, and keep your noses in your study manuals when not otherwise occupied." She was almost used to nudity with strangers, and peeled out of her unitard and slacks. She joined a cluster that was getting sorted into lines, and fell in.

They were lined up by height, which put Kendra near the front as the tallest woman by far, and the first one in. She could see ahead of her the men having their heads shaved. It was hard for her to believe that barbaric rituals like that were still part of a modern military. She pretended to keep her nose in her book, as ordered, but watched obliquely. Some of them were relaxed and expecting it, others nervous.

She was quickly at the front of the line and wondered how short they'd clip her. Collar? Neck? She stepped forward as a chair emptied, and a bib was slipped around her neck. "How short?" the . . . well, "barber" was the wrong word, but . . .

"Collar-length?" she half inquired.

"Back to the collar," he agreed sadistically, as the shears swept back from the center of her forehead. She gasped. They shaved women, too?? She quickly was despising the medieval thugs who had designed this course of training. What the hell were they thinking?

She was bald in seconds and urged out of the chair. She remembered her doccase through her daze, walked through the indicated door, and stifled her outrage. She fumed silently, afraid to touch her head and feel the stubble.

She joined the lines for uniforms and snuck a glance at the man currently on the pad. Light beams scanned him quickly, calculated sizes and reported it to a duty soldier. They still drew uniforms from the racks by hand! Why such a primitive approach? Automation existed for such minor details.

She stepped forward, ready to be scanned, when a firm grip on her arm pulled her aside. "Over here, recruit," a woman's voice ordered. She turned to see a sergeant and a private. "Legs spread and arms straight out. Eyes front," the sergeant continued. Turning to address the private, she said, "Around the neck—" and Kendra felt a band wrapped around her throat. It dropped away and the private yelled, "Thirty-four!"

The sergeant continued, "Chest and waist," and the private ordered, "Breathe in and hold, recruit." She complied. In seconds, she'd been measured by hand and sizes scribbled on a sheet. She was urged toward one of the troops drawing uniforms and as she handed her measurements over, heard the sergeant say, "Not bad. Try the next one." Apparently it was a training exercise. Well, it was good to know how to measure if the system was down. It would never happen on Earth, of course. Touching someone without a specific invite was grounds for criminal action. The detailed waivers doctors had their patients sign was proof of that.

She was handed a stack of uniforms and pointed at a painted square on the floor. "Get dressed and keep all gear inside the lines!" someone ordered. She'd give them this: they were very fast and efficient. And, she found out seconds later, they issued uniforms that fit. It took only segs to be back outside, carrying a duffle full of clothes.

The remainder of the day was all processing. Typical

military, but with little "hurry up and wait." No one
wasted any time and the recruits were processed fast.
They were fed, escorted back to the barracks and
bedded down.

The next morning, Carpender was an utterly different human being, if that was the term. He entered the
bay shouting, kicking and throwing things. If asked,
Kendra would have admitted she'd never dreamed such
language would be used in a civilized nation's military.

*"Dry those sticky fingers and hit the fucking decks,
you worthless worms! Three fucking seconds! I want
you outside in three fucking seconds! Did I say grab
any clothes? Move your saggy, no-load asses! Don't
talk! Don't think! When I want any shit out of you I'll
rip off your head and scoop it out!"*

Shocked senseless, Kendra swarmed outside with the
others. Few wore more than the shirt and underwear
she did, some were naked. It was cold outside. She
wrapped her arms around herself and wondered what
the hell was going on.

Suddenly, he was in front of her. *"Where the fuck
are you from, loser?"*

"Minneapolis . . . on Earth, sir."

*"I can't hear you! one would think with a chest like
that there'd be lungs underneath somewhere . . . Well?"*

Unbelievable! Sexual innuendoes? Kendra decided
she would not be the first to complain. But Rob's
warning seemed shallow in comparison to the reality.
Carpender was about to bellow again, so she inhaled
and shouted, *"Yes, sir!"*

" 'Yes, sir,' what??"

"I have lungs, sir!"

"Glad to hear it," he said and began pacing. *"Because
they are crucial to surviving recruit training and you
will exercise them regularly. Do you all understand?"*

There was a ragged chorus of "Yes, sir."

"*Bullshit! I want to hear balls and titties shaking when you answer! The commander is getting a little deaf, and can't hear you over there in his insulated office. If he can't hear you, he thinks I'm not doing my job. So you will sound off loud enough to reassure him and keep me gainfully employed shattering your wills. Do you understand?*"

"*Yes, sir!*" came the bellowed reply.

"Work on it," he advised, and strode back to Kendra.

"*Don't they have cold in mini-no-place?*" he bellowed, nose almost touching hers.

"*Yes, sir!*" she replied, loud enough to hurt her throat.

"*Then suck it up and take it, princess, because it is going to get colder and hotter than you can imagine!*"

"*Yes, sir!*" she shouted.

He addressed the whole formation again. "*There are footprints painted on the ground. Put your feet on them. Knees relaxed, backs straight. Arms straight down, thumbs along where your pants seams would be if you had any. This is the position of 'attention,' and it draws excess blood away from the brain, enabling miserable, vomitous, slimy little shitballs like yourselves to listen more clearly.*

"*I am Senior Sergeant Recruit Instructor Joseph P. Carpender, and you are worthless maggots. You will refer to anyone higher in rank than yourselves, which is anyone, by their rank and rating. Since you are all clearly too stupid to memorize 'Senior Sergeant Recruit Instructor Carpender' and since the war would be lost before you could say it . . . I'm not laughing, why are you, maggot? . . . You will address me as 'sir.' Can anyone spell 'sir?'*"

"*S-I-R?*" someone replied.

Without looking, he demanded, *"You will state your name when answering and address me properly. Try it again, assmunch!"*

"Asher Denson, Sir! Sir is spelled 's-i-r,' sir!"

He strode over and looked down at the recruit, who was in the younger-than-average category. *"Your first name is 'recruit,' maggot! Maybe someday you Will get a manly pair of balls and be allowed the honor of changing it to 'soldier!' Make your corrections."*

"Recruit Denson, sir! I'm sorry for the error, sir!"

"You're sorry, all right. Now apologize. Shut up!" he bellowed contradictorily as the kid tried to reply. He turned and paced again. *"For your information, 'sir' is spelled 'g-o-d.' I am god, and you will learn from me or be struck down."*

He was clearly reciting from rote as he continued, *"This is without a doubt the sorriest bunch of limp-dicked, banana-tittied, ass-breathed, masturbating, runny-nosed, slack-jawed, potbellied, macaroni-muscled, shit-sucking, gutless little trolls I have ever had the misfortune to have assigned to me! I do believe the commander is pissed off at me for being too gentle! Therefore, I will be harder! In the past, I have crushed the souls of some genuine ladies and men with my thespian talents. I feel my skills will be wasted reducing such a sorry bunch of nail-biting, pud-pounding, pussy-stretching, panty-wetting, jabbering yokels to tears and soggy pants!*

"But it is my duty, and I will do it.

"You do not have to, and will not, enjoy anything that happens here for the next eighty-six days. You will ache, you will cry, you will be humiliated and degraded, you will bleed. All this will do one of two things: either send you back to mama with your eyes bloodshot and teary or qualify you to become a proud

*member of the freehold military forces—the meanest,
baddest, most brutal bunch of professional* KILLERS
*who ever struck the fear of the god and goddess into
an enemy ten times their size.*

"*Learn now the first lesson,*" he said as he came
to attention and faced them. "*Anything you do can
get you killed. Doing nothing will get you killed. You
have all taken those psych tests where there are no
wrong answers. This is a test with no right answers.
War does not determine who is right. War determines
who is left.*

"*None of you are dressed as prescribed in the
recruit Training Manual. Since you have not yet been
read the relevant section, and since your literacy is
questionable, I will be lenient. You should each be
wearing nine articles of clothing minimum on this and
every day of your existences from now on. You will
each count how many articles you are wearing, sub-
tract it from nine, multiply the result by twenty. That
is how many pushups you will do as a reminder.
Don't even think of fucking with me by trying to do
less. You are not paid to think, and I can and will
multiple track you. Now drop and pump!*"

A hundred and forty pushups?? Kendra thought to
herself as she threw herself at the ground. *In this
gravity??* But Carpender was counting and she tried
grimly to keep up with the count. Then she fell behind.
She kept her own count as they progressed, until she
collapsed at forty-three. She hadn't thought she could
do that many.

"Problem, princess?" Carpender snapped from
above, almost gently.

"*My arms won't support me, sir,*" she grunted.

"Your arms will do anything your brain and guts
want them to. Get with it," he said, then moved

through the ranks to haze others. She forced her muscles to respond and shook through twelve more. The ranks were thinning as some finished and headed inside, but Kendra had plenty of miserable companions to keep her company.

Carpender came back. "That's ninety, isn't it, princess?"

"*I have only finished fifty-five, sir!*" she half howled, half whimpered.

"Well, there's no rest for the honest. You will stay here, with your tits freezing to the ground, until such time as you finish," he advised. "So suck it up and pump 'em out." He hoisted her aloft by her shirt collar, the fabric biting into her neck, and let go. She fell painfully down, banging her chin. "Take that one as a freebie," he said, walking off, "just for being honest."

Kendra was last to finish and struggled inside. Her arms were blessedly numb and most of her body was, also. She fumbled, shivering, into a uniform and back outside into formation.

Carpender flicked his eyes at her, but said nothing as she filled in the last slot. "Walk this way," he ordered.

They straggled along, not quite in step, and were passed by several platoons of more advanced trainees. Insulting cadences and jeers rang out, most of them familiar to Kendra, if blunter and ruder. She smiled inwardly. More roots she could recognize.

> "*Recruit, recruit, don't feel blue*
> *My recruiter fucked me too.*"

And

> "*Ain't no sense in looking down,*
> *Ain't no discharge on the ground . . .*"

They walked until they reached the issue depot again. Inside, they were tossed more gear, this time suspension vests and packs, body armor, tools, canteens . . . and rifles. They were issued their rifles once and expected to keep them for life. That shocked Kendra at first, but upon consideration, it made sense. A soldier who was honorably discharged was no different a person the next day, and no less trustworthy. Here, as in the UN, all veterans could be recalled to duty if needed. It did seem reasonable that they have their gear with them, rather than needing a reissue that would take days at best.

Back outside, Carpender went through excruciating detail on how to wear every item. "If you survive to become a soldier," he said, "you can wear it any way you wish. That is the privilege of the soldier. But as filthy little maggots, you will wear it in the fashion prescribed by the book. This is so the cadre can tell you haven't conveniently lost any items to try to wimp out on us.

"You will be armed at all times, on and off base, with at least a sidearm. It will be your duty to the Freehold to protect the Freehold and you cannot properly protect it unarmed."

He led them down several roads and into tall grass that had been beaten down by use.

"When soldiers walk, it is called marching. Before you can learn to walk, however, you must learn to crawl. We will spend the rest of the day learning to crawl. On your hands and knees."

They dropped quickly and gratefully. Then they realized that the gear was heavy and crawling hard work, especially when you weren't allowed to contact the ground with your torso.

Kendra was forced to her elbows, her arms not having enough strength to keep her upright. It had been a miserable morning, a boring lunch of field rations and an excruciating afternoon. The heat hit before noon and continued until well past the break for dinner. Sweat and grime mingled in a greasy film on everything.

After dinner, they walked back to the barracks and grounded all gear except rifles. They fell in outside again and Carpender took his usual position. "No-load," he said, using the moniker he'd attached to one recruit.

"Yes, sir!"

"Front and center. And Icebitch." After a few moments, he added, *"That's you, Pacelli. Are you waiting for an engraved fucking invitation? Did you decide this morning you were going to fuck up my schedule and my life?"*

"No, sir, no sir, and here, sir!" she shouted as she hit the line in front of him.

"Well, that's funny," he said as titters ran through the ranks. "Ever consider comedy?"

"No, sir!" she replied.

"Good. You'd starve. If you have energy for jokes, you have energy to give me twenty. *So does anyone who laughed. And anyone who groaned can make it thirty! And you, and you, and you, who don't have the integrity to admit to laughing can make it fifty!"*

Several segs later, they resumed. Kendra and No-load were back at attention in front of Carpender. "About, *hace!"* he ordered. Kendra swiveled on her heel.

"These two have prior service," he explained. "Not what anyone competent would properly call military service, but at least they learned how to march. At least, I *hope* you two know how to march, with your records," he said viciously, breathing over Kendra's shoulder, "because if you embarrass me, it will not bode well for the next eighty-six days."

"Split into three squads, here and here," he waved his hands to indicate. "Icebitch, take the left, No-load, take the right. I'll take the middle. If they can walk and turn corners without tripping before a div has passed, you won't have to give me fifty more."

Kendra waited a moment to see what Carpender did. He waved his group into a circle, so she followed suit.

She began the process of showing them attention again, facing movements, forward march, column right and left and left and right wheel. Then was the laborious time of getting a handful of people to learn left from right and remember that forward march commenced on the left foot. In exasperation, she handed several of them rocks to hold in their left hands. It actually did work.

A div later, Carpender came over and snapped orders. "Squad, by my command, Aten *shut!* Left *hace!* About, *hace!* Right, *hace!* About, *hace!* Forward, *harch!* Column left, *harch!* Column right, *harch!* Squad, *halt!* Adequate. At least they don't trip over their feet. You will be squad leader, and march them every night until they are competent. Say, 'Yes, sir.'"

"*Yes, sir!*"

"Shower, Shave, Shit and Sleep. Look for your names on the watch roster. Dismissed." He strode inside.

Kendra had never been more exhausted in her life. She couldn't lift her arms above mid-chest and could barely stand in the shower. It didn't help that the water was now cold; the heat had been turned off. She dried as best she could manage, drew on a shirt and underwear against the growing cold and straightened her bay area. She was too shocked by the day to lie down, so sat on her chair for a while. Open bay barracks, shaved scalps, screaming profanity and exercise as punishment. It was like something out of the Middle Ages. Rob had warned her that it would be harder than her UN training, but the magnitude of the difference was staggering. She ran a hand over her stubbly bald head again, and breathed deeply to avoid crying. She could hear

occasional sobs and restless movement from some of
the younger recruits. Some were barely sixteen Earth
years. How would they survive this?

Feeling cold, she finally dragged her aching body
into bed. Her head bristled on the pillow and someone was snoring to do justice to a shuttle landing. She
began griping in her head and was asleep before she
could frame three words.

As soon as she closed her eyes, it seemed,
Carpender was roaring for them to get up. She
snatched on her pants, stuffed her feet into her boots
and dragged the rest of it with her. The result of her
efforts was a mere fifty pushups for not being dressed
properly. Those who lacked clothing items did thirty
per item and fifty more. She decided to sleep dressed
from now on. Quickly finishing, her arms feeling
bruised from the abuse of the last two days, she waited
for orders. After a run that made her almost vomit,
they hit an obstacle course. She hated climbing up and
down the two artificial cliffs, even with the provided
ropes. She gritted her teeth as she clambered up a
cargo net into twenty meters of free space, then back
down. She slipped on a swinging rope and was soaked
in frigid water, then soaked again crossing a log bridge.
They didn't change, but went straight to breakfast.

She choked down food to keep her strength up,
and started to drink a bottle of liquid loaded with
protein and muscle-building nanos. These were issued
to all the women and some of the smaller men. The
physical standards of the FMF were very high and
were not adjusted for gender or disability as the
UNPF's were. There were few women recruits, she
noted, only about fifteen percent, and most of them
on the tall and rangy side, and even then they
needed the extra muscle builders to keep up with
the men. It had seemed degrading, but Carpender's

quick, pointed comment about the difference between men's and women's Olympic records drove the point home. Men average bigger and stronger than women, and the FMF took only the best physical specimens. Women and small men started with a physical disadvantage and had to work that much harder to meet the standards.

The glop was slimy and cold and she slurped it with distaste. Finishing, she dismally followed the others. As they were marched out to one of the many huge open fields, she pondered the next three years, drinking protein goo and working out at the gym daily to meet standards. It kept her morose as she stood in formation and waited. The usual confusing orders did little to shift her thoughts.

"Today, we begin unarmed combat training," Carpender said in his near-bellow. Kendra and her platoon mates stared across the grass at a more advanced class. They had disconcerting leers and grimaces on their faces. She shifted imperceptibly and uncomfortably. She was standing in what was called "horse riding stance," legs wide, body squatting low, until her thighs and calves burned with exertion. In seconds, Carpender was in front of her. "What's the matter, Pacelli? Too hot for you?"

"Weather is fine today, sir!" she shouted back. If "fine" was identified as somewhere north of 30 degrees, calm and dry at 3.5 divs, Io still with half the morning to rise and get hotter. The weather here in the Dragontooth Mountains was bizarre, frigid one day, scorching the next. The thinner atmosphere probably had something to do with it, but understanding it didn't make it enjoyable. Her clothes had dried from the morning run through a stream and the "confidence" course and were itching. Her breakfast was a greasy weight in her stomach.

Carpender turned and continued, "You will learn how to strike with hands and feet, how to grapple, how to avoid blows.

"Fingers locked behind your heads. Tense your abdominal muscles. Harder." Kendra stiffened as he ordered. "This is the basic position from which you will learn the first lesson today and every day.

"That lesson is how to *take* blows. Platoon two-seven-one-three, advance and strike."

With whoops and cheers, the other class charged them. One short kid who'd had his eye on Kendra the entire time closed and drew back. He punched her hard in the midriff.

The air wooshed out of her and she bent double. His second blow landed his knuckles in her ribs, the third squashed her right breast. Three more blows buffeted her shoulder, her jaw and her temple. As he retreated, she stood, fuming, stinging and gasping for breath. That was uncalled for and she intended to take it back with interest.

Then she recovered and steadied herself. It wasn't the kid's fault; he was just taking orders. Perhaps a bit too zealously, but anger wouldn't help the situation. Carpender's voice interrupted her thoughts.

"Do you feel that? *Do you?* Good! Controlled anger can be a useful tool. Uncontrolled anger will get you killed. So let us learn control. Attack again!"

Twice more she got thumped by upper students. The minor bruises on her face stung, but the blows to the guts and ribs were definitely debilitating. Just as she thought this, Carpender said, "Body blows cause injury. Face wounds are ugly and can be a psychological advantage, but body blows will take them out. Remember that." She made note of that. That phrase was hint they would see it on a test.

The first week was spent as a target for upper

students' pent-up resentfulness. They began learning to block the second day and had great incentive to learn to block well. She learned to block inside or outside with either hand, then her legs and gradually, to twist her body around the blows without losing her balance.

They added punches to their daily drill, then kicks. Sweeps, parries, counters, grapples, throws, headbutts and gymnastic contortions that bent an opponent's attack back on himself. They practiced with restrictions: hands only, feet only, blindfolded, shackled, doused with incapacitating agents, then combinations thereof. The drills increased her respect for Rob's and Marta's skill. She was beginning to realize how tremendously learned they were.

When it came their time to initiate recruits, Kendra had no trouble doing so. They needed incentive to learn and it was her duty to do it well. She hit them hard and reliably. The murderous glares in response only made her smile. She'd pulled her punches enough to avoid actual injury, but her victims looked at her with hatred.

Four weeks in, they began adding weapons. So-called "unarmed" combat made use of everything in the soldier's inventory except projectiles, from boots, sticks, entrenching tools and wire, to climbing spikes, helmets and even the rifle as a club. The simulators and dummies were revolting. Blood splashed, jaws and limbs separated, guts spilled and horrible screams brought home just how deadly a human can be when properly trained. More important than the physical skills, Kendra learned, was that it encouraged a willingness to engage the enemy and an attitude of capability. It required closing with an opponent and getting hurt and in that regard, she agreed it made for better troops than those who trained in sterile rooms with electronic aids. She slept poorly, bothered by the violence involved, but realized that it could be necessary to save her life. The sparring with dummy weapons was painful in blows taken and she could mark her progress in bruises from fresh bloodred to stale yellow. She had a tooth regenerated after one vigorous bout with a man twice her mass, all muscle. The lesson she learned from that was to *never* try to outbrute a larger, stronger opponent. Stealth and careful grappling were the tools of the small against the large, sheer force only for use against a smaller opponent.

They spent time on the weapons range every day, with their rifle/grenade launcher combination weapons and the school's machineguns, mortars, rockets and other ranged weapons. They practiced stripping and rebuilding weapons in the dark, while restrained and even behind their backs. She learned to separate actual components from bogus parts tossed in to confuse her and even to separate parts from unnamed weapons out, and assemble all the pieces into their appropriate forms. She could identify a weapon, strip it, clean it, assemble it, shoot it and clear malfunctions, whether it was Freeholder, UN, Ramadanian, Caledonian or from one of the smaller colonies.

The M-5 Weapon, Personal, Rifle/Grenade Launcher Combination, was a nasty piece of hardware. At five kilos plus, it wasn't very light, but it did everything. It fed the rifle from a solid clip of fifty rounds of ammunition, breaking off individual rounds at stressed seams. The cartridge was consumed in use for excellent thermal efficiency, leaving no empty case. It was suppressed to a loud coughing noise and had a two-stage trigger. Squeezing the trigger changed it to fire single shots, gripping the trigger back fired the weapon automatically. The grenade launcher fed from its own fifteen-round clip and the charges were programmable for proximity, impact, delay or delay-on-impact fusing.

The optical sight could see in infrared, low light, adjust for different gravity and instantaneous wind conditions and had a graduated reticle for range. The construction was solid and easy to maintain. The fit and finish was flawless to Kendra's eyes. She knew good machine work when she saw it.

They trained with the heavier support weapons, vehicles and comm gear. Everyone was given at least a passing familiarity with every ground combat weapon and most vehicle- and aircraft-mounted support weapons. The files of the training manual's text were in the tens of megabytes. She hadn't realized there was that much involved with basic military training.

Military training indeed. She now knew how woefully inadequate UN training was. The UN forces trained to oppress unarmed insurgents and civilians. The Freehold forces trained to fight any enemy, known or not, no matter how well armed. She was surprised when an alert was called on base and the instructors armed them with live ammunition, placed them in positions, then prepared themselves to engage an intruder. It was merely an exercise and over in segs, but they treated every one as if it were real, every time.

Orienteering, battlefield first aid, field sanitation, nutrition, military law and the laws of war, dealing with prisoners, riot control, firefighting, reconnaissance for unexploded ordnance, building emplacements and fighting positions, laying traps and explosives, more shooting—one hundred rounds a day, every day—swimming, climbing. The list went on. They rose with Io, started at "can," ate field rations, worked through twilight and stopped at "can't."

They had lessons in "space physics," the workings of the human body when away from gravity, the oxygen cycle and respiration and all the other text details of survival in space. Carpender and the others hammered into them that any mistakes in this block of instruction would cause them to wind up dead. They paid strict attention. Ship profiles and internal maps were provided for the twelve hull types and twenty-four variants currently in use in the Freehold, and various foreign military vessels they would be likely to encounter. Daily quizzes and drills were thrown at them and Kendra struggled to absorb the reams of data. She fell asleep at night to a mantra of "fleet carrier, cruiser, destroyer, stealth cruiser, gunboat, assault boat, factory ship, logistics ship, fighter, ELINT boat, missile frigate, rescue cutter, shuttle, ASP, ASP carrier, drop pod, satellite boat, fuel boat, yard boat, mine boat, intercept boat, cargo boat, jump point station, orbital intercept station, command and control station . . ."

The morning of the fifty-first day, they lined up to board a shuttle. Kendra had assumed they'd go to the starport for space training, but there was a strip at the base. They did a rough-field launch and were bound for orbit. The gees pressed them back into their cushions as the sky changed from brilliant blue to purple, then to black.

They would be in microgravity for nine days, with no breaks. As soon as they docked, they were rushed into the training ship, a cruiser. They were crammed into wartime troop quarters, six people bunked in a small cube, with three shifts on rotation. Their meager gear was stowed and they were immediately ordered to suit up for EVA.

There was a knot of total confusion at the airlock. Few of them had spaced, fewer been exposed to microgravity for any length of time. Some were sick. Kendra was thankful to not be bothered by it. Once outside, they snapped long tethers to the side of the ship and flopped around like fish, attempting to learn how to control their movements. The instructors let them play to acclimate for half a div, then shoved them into a formation and showed them the basics. They stayed out for another two divs, rehearsing basic maneuvers, eating and drinking from their helmet rations and getting exhausted.

Kendra would never have thought of microgravity as tiring, but it required constant attention to every muscle in the body, with no gravity to reference to. She swam in afterward feeling somewhat competent and decided she'd shower and sleep as soon as possible. She had a slight headache from excess blood flow to the brain and reminded herself to drink, even though she didn't feel thirsty.

No luck getting a shower. They stowed their gear after performing field maintenance on them, then ate a cold snack. They were given antiseptic wipes to help kill surface bacteria and wipe away grime, but no showers were available to them.

They rose early and were back outside practicing small arms in vacuum. They worked with basic shipboard repair gear, started learning first aid for vacuum, rescue procedures and survival. They spent all day practicing again. Suit maintenance again. No shower, again.

Day three, they began learning "boarder repel." She thought it most unlikely that anyone would actually board a modern ship, rather than just blasting it to shreds, but she learned what they taught her. Unarmed combat was very different with no gravity, requiring awareness of the surroundings to use as leverage. Weapons use called for pinpoint accuracy and the necessity of a suit and helmet, which made aiming awkward, despite the vid sights attached to the weapons. There was a minor casualty as someone misaimed and one kid screamed into his mike. The instructors cut away a section of his skintight suit, slapped a bandage over the wound and rushed him to the infirmary. He was back the next day, looking bedraggled and doped on painkillers, but working earnestly.

They started practice operations, swarming through and over the vessel, responding to an "attack" by instructors. They lost. They attacked the instructors. They lost again. They had no time to rest, but went straight to shipboard basic skills training after each drill. Some of them would be assigned shipboard duty immediately, the rest would almost certainly wind up in a habitat at some point. "As important as ground infantry tactics," the instructors insisted and ran them through more drills. Kendra got a quick shower on the fifth day. She was assigned to suit repair and was last in, so she was alone for four whole segs. Unbelievable luxury!

The sixtieth training day, they stayed aboard at tasks until dinnertime, when they were herded back into the shuttle as an abandon ship exercise and dropped to the surface. Trucks met them as the pods landed, rolled them across the base and delivered them back to their barracks, which had been kept manicured by lower recruits. They gratefully took cold showers and dropped back into their bunks, only to be awakened for a late-night exercise.

That morning, survival training, groundside. Very early, short of sleep, groggy. A heavy transport lifter, a VC-6 Bison, waited on the field. They boarded, along with three recruits recycled from failed exams, strapped in and were whisked north to the tundra of the Hinterlands district. Howling wind and snow awaited them and they clung together for three long days in tiny shelters, two people per for body heat. They built windbreaks of snow reinforced with tough grass, tried with little success to light fires and dug bugs, moss and small rodent analogs out of the matted surface. Kendra felt queasy at the thought of eating any of it, but did so. There was nothing else provided and the cold burned calories at an alarming rate.

The lifter returned, they boarded and were dropped on rafts into the East Sea, right at the iceberg line. They scavenged water from bergs at the instructor's direction, choosing the older and glacial ice that was low in salt, and managed to snag a few slimy fish to eat, raw. The moss from the tundra hit them then, causing screaming diarrhea. The little water they had went to prevent dehydration. Teeth chattering behind cracked lips, Kendra swore under her breath, keeping herself going with thoughts of what she'd like to do to the instructors, who had a heated, roofed raft-shelter to work from. The students weren't allowed within five hundred meters of it.

They gratefully scrambled aboard the vertol again two days later and flew southwest across the continent. They landed again, at 25 degrees latitude, in the middle of the Saltpan Desert. The temperature was over 35 degrees and the wind was their enemy once more. After the rafts, most of them were barely able to walk. They scavenged bitter alkali water from cacti and scrub in their solar stills, wrapped cloth around their faces to minimize the dust, and munched that dust with the meager rations they were issued, supplemented by a few more rodents dried in the scorching heat or cooked on stones that were hot enough to fry. They huddled in the shade of a few rocks and dozed fitfully in the heat.

Once again they were lifted and dragged farther south. Trucks met them at a rough forward base and drove them into the deep jungle. It was fascinating; a riot of green, yellow and orange hues, with multiple canopies and thick growth. Water was readily available, of course, bitter and slimy after decontamination with nanos, and she had no trouble shooting a bird-analog for food. The diarrhea persisted, but at least one could *wash* in a warm jungle. Biting flies were Freehold pests, not Terran, but the chemistry wasn't precisely compatible. Every bite raised a huge, hard welt that would sting for days.

Once trucked back aboard the lifters after that ordeal, the instructors handed out mugs of hot stew, chocolate and candy. Kendra hadn't thought she could be so hungry. She wolfed down everything offered, then was airsick, as were quite a few others. She wondered if the sadistic bastards planned that, too.

Then they underwent prisoner training, being stripped and searched, herded into cages, screamed at and prodded in a fashion that made their treatment so far seem positively pedestrian. They were blindfolded with stifling hoods for three days, denied food and given little water. They each had a code word the cadre tried to force them to reveal, with the promise of dire consequences if they did. No permanently injurious tactics were allowed, but they were exercised to collapse, forced to sleep on cold, damp floors with no blankets and glaring lights overhead, then woken before they could properly rest. The second day of it, Kendra was made to hold two buckets of sand at arm's length, muscles screaming, being rewarded with a stinging riot prod when her arms slipped. She'd heard rumors of the version of this used by Special Warfare troops, and shuddered. It could be worse, and that terrified her into dealing with it. She gritted her teeth, swore silently and stood it out.

Mercifully, the showers at the barracks were warm when they returned. They were allowed to sleep an extra half div the next morning, also. Once awake, they were told to pack their gear for their final exam. Eight days to go, then two days of processing. It was a tantalizing promise.

Kendra could tell a VC-6 by the sound of its engines, now. They were hauled back past the woods and landed in open, bumpy, rolling scrub. She was handed a compass and a map with destinations marked.

"Listen up!" Carpender bellowed. "This is a *solo* test until you reach your destination. Any maggot attempting to help or get help from another recruit will be recycled to the beginning of survival training." That announcement was greeted with silence.

"You will each take an emergency transponder and flare with you. Do not open the packets unless necessary, because there are no 'accidents.' You trigger it, you get pulled. You can also call on your comm. No 'accidents.' We hear your voice, you get pulled.

"Is there any maggot here who feels ill or otherwise unable to take this test?"

Silence.

"When next we meet, those of you who succeed will be *soldiers.*" Kendra felt a thrill at that, even though she knew it was all part of the mind game.

"Go." He turned away.

She bunched up with the others and leaned forward into her load. Despite the "solo" nature of it, the first leg was a route march, a brisk walk with all basic gear, of fifteen kilometers. They had one div to finish. Eleven minutes per kilometer might sound generous, but she knew better. There were blazes along the trail, but all she had to do was follow the pack. Her long legs lent her an advantage in walking speed, her background shackled her with a handicap in endurance. She kept a steady pace throughout, gasping and remembering to keep her water level up.

It was tiring, and she was soon panting for breath, her legs knotting into cramps before blissfully going numb from the pounding beat. Her thighs burned above her tingling, throbbing knees and her shoulders began to ache from the load. She wondered how far they had come, and sighted a blaze up ahead. She read it as the figures became visible and groaned. Four klicks. Damn. She checked the time on her comm, groaned again and increased her pace.

Stride stride stride stride . . . She slipped on a pebble, recovered and kept moving. It was unbelievable how far away that halfway point was. Fifteen klicks! In heavy clothes, on a rough road, with a basic combat load of more than twenty kilos. She took another swallow of water, which went down the wrong way. A coughing jag started and she staggered a few steps before recovering. When she fought her way upright again, she could see the halfway point ahead of her. An intermittent breeze was catching her. It felt revitalizing, but slowed her progress. She was sweaty and sticky in her uniform and wondered how much grungier she would get.

The platoon was strung out along several hundred meters by this point and she was surprised to find herself near the front of the main group. A quick glance behind showed several people having problems at the far back. She turned and slogged on. Endorphins were flooding her brain and she felt a bit dizzy. More water. Her galloping heart and rasping breath kept time as she walked and walked and walked. Another gust blew grit into her face and she snarled. Trying not to rub her eyes, she let them tear, flushing out most of the dust. A few persistent grains drove her nerves to distraction.

She could see people gathering up ahead of her and felt another blast of air. It cooled her heaving, sweating chest slightly, then chilled her ears, but it also slowed her pace further. She cursed, stretched out her stride and pumped out paces. Eyes on the ground in front, arms swinging for balance.

"Pacelli! Stop! You're done!" A voice called. She stumbled three more steps before she could turn around and look back. She was past the line. "Your time was point nine two, five nine," the evaluator informed her. She nodded and leaned forward, hands on her knees for balance. Breath sandpapered in her throat and she waved a hand at the medic nearby. The woman trotted over.

"What's wrong, recruit?" she asked.

"Dust . . . eyes," she hissed.

The medic sat her down and proceeded to flush them with water. She was better in seconds and had to reassure her friends that she was okay. The water ran down her back, mingling with sweat and cooling her. Then it oozed into her underwear.

She stood back up, her strength returning despite the loud drumming of her heart in her ears. She looked toward the evaluator, who was just clocking the last member of the platoon. It was little recruit Marissa Welker, not quite seventeen Earth years and barely 150 centimeters. She might mass fifty kilos, soaking wet in a snowsuit. "C'mon, Welker!" she shouted, adding encouragement to the other voices.

The girl stumbled across the mark and sprawled flat on her face. She dragged herself to her knees and threw up. Choking and gasping, she sucked down some water and looked up at the evaluator with scared eyes. He looked down at her and said, "point nine nine, nine two. You made it." There was a cheer all around. Hands helped her to her feet and over to a log to sit.

"Leg One, listen up!" the evaluator shouted. Kendra was part of Leg One. She turned and listened to the instructions. "You now will follow individual routes to the final rendezvous point. There will be tests given en route and you have four days from . . . right now. Move out, no talking and good luck."

Kendra flipped open the paper map and pulled up the compass. Her first point was . . . that way. Into the damned hills. 10,165 meters. She sighed and paced off, grabbing a string of black plastic beads to keep count. The grass was waist high, the ground full of dips, depressions and holes, and short, stunted trees blocked her every few steps. She'd taken a rough sight on a peak and simply headed toward it, figuring to calculate back azimuths once close. If there were no landmarks one would normally use satellite positioning. Only if it wasn't available was it necessary to use dead reckoning and, under those circumstances, she'd expect to *be* dead. That would indicate a lifeless desert or plain with no commo support.

The hill was bluff-covered and fairly steep and the trees got larger as she rose. Carefully guiding around them, she tried to calculate the distance off each pace that deviated from straight line while still keeping a bearing on her destination. Nine thousand. Not much longer. She scrambled up one of the bluffs in her way, slipping in the loose dirt that had fallen from it and looked back, estimating the horizontal distance involved. She made notes, flipped her beads and kept walking.

There was a clearing ahead, quite broad, and she entered it. A small tent was pitched and an evaluator sat in front of it, quite relaxed, heating chocolate over a field stove. He stood and nodded as she approached. "What's the drill, Evaluator?" she asked.

"I can't answer that until you find your mark," he replied.

She looked at him. Find my mark? She thought for a moment. This was the spot and the tent was right there . . . unless the tent was *not* on the exact mark and thereby giving away its location. She nodded and reached for her compass and what might have been a smile crossed his face. She found the mark on the map, sighted three peaks to orient to, and decided she should be farther west. Another fifty-three paces, then twelve south. And there was a metal disc set into the ground, invisible under the grass. She wrote down the number on it and came back to the tent. He signed off her arrival and time on his comm and hers and said, "Now you can test. Actually, as bad as this one seems, you'll probably thank me later for being first. You need to reduce your gear by six kilos."

Six kilos! That would make her walk lighter, but there wasn't much excess in her ruck. She sat and began fumbling. Ammo could be lightened a bit. . . and she could get rid of the spare uniform, as long as she could stay dry . . . better keep it . . . dammit! Nothing came to mind.

She pondered for a moment. Then asked, "From my total mass or from my gear?" Was this a transport mass question or just a weight question?

The evaluator recited again, "You need to reduce your gear by six kilos."

Only from her gear. She nodded and showed him a full canteen and a ration. "I'm going to eat and drink those. That's one point five," she explained and started munching while she sorted. She pulled spoons and other accessories from her remaining rations, and a few bulky components that didn't pack the calories of some others. He dropped the items on a scale and kept track. By carefully stuffing remaining ration components into as few packages as possible, along with excess ammo packaging and a few other items, she brought her total to 3.2. A good start, but not enough.

She dropped one magazine and a grenade, added her spare uniform and poured out another liter of water. She could refill it from a stream and save that bottle for emergencies. 5.2. She lost her spare undershirt and added the shoulder pads from her ruck. Socks could double as shoulder pads, but not vice versa. 5.9. Too bloated to drink more, she sloshed a bit of water out and he nodded. She finished the rations and because she was suspicious, asked, "Now that I've lightened it, can I pick the gear up again?"

"Only what you can swallow." He grinned. "But points for asking. I'll note that. You can go."

She thanked him and turned, comparing her map. Then she remembered that the mark was sixty meters away. He gave her a thumbs-up as she headed that way.

Her next mark was down a ravine and across a stream. Luckily, there was a downed log to keep her dry. When she was halfway across, a startling *bang!*, flash and whistle in front of her told her it had been boobytrapped. *Shit.* Since she was dead, she finished the crawl and stopped at the far side. "I flunked, right?" she said aloud, assuming the evaluator was nearby.

The evaluator dropped out of a tree a few meters away. "Yes, you did. The easy way is usually suspect," she said. She was a wiry, mean-looking woman with a hawk nose and gray eyes. She fished out another boobytrap from her gear and got to work setting it. "That's all for this one."

Kendra nodded and resumed looking for her mark. It was impossible to see landmarks inside the woods and she fought down panic. Pace count couldn't *possibly* work in terrain like this, so she must be missing something. There was the stream on the map . . . and she needed one other reference point . . . got it! She sighted Io through the trees, as well as she could, pulled up an ephemeris on her comm and compared the time. It should be . . . about there, and the stream was there, so the mark must be that way.

And there it was, at the base of a tree. She logged

it and had the evaluator, already finished setting her next trap, sign off.

The water was getting to her and she hurried off to find a tree in private. That done, she stomped deeper into the woods for her third mark. It was as tough as the previous one, as it was 1003 meters from a large outcropping clearly marked on the map and the only landmark nearby, but in trees deep enough to hide it. She very carefully measured her paces, chose her route to intersect as few trees as possible, and stopped. It should be in an arc along here.

She looked up, startled, as another recruit tromped into view. She didn't recognize him, but there were at least three platoons on the course.

"Hi," he said.

"Hi."

"I'm hopelessly lost," he said, cheerful and frustrated. "I think it's off to the left, but I can't see the outcropping and—"

"I can't help you," she warned him.

"Well, I know, but this one's a real virgin," he persisted. "If you—"

"I said I can't help you. Now please move away before you get us both disqualified." She was getting angry with this idiot.

"No prob, you pass," he said. "I'm the evaluator." He grinned at her.

Barely believing, she said, "That's nice. Now, where do I meet you, *after* I find the mark?"

"Right here," he laughed, realizing she wasn't going to trust him.

She walked along the arc her calculations suggested and then back. She had it narrowed down to a fifty-meter stretch, but for some reason she wasn't finding it. She was sure of the distance and checked the direction again, and again. The evaluator, if he was,

was still in her way in the same spot he'd last been
in. Then she figured it out.

"Please move your right foot," she asked him.

He stepped back laughing. "Damn! I get about nine
out of ten." He signed off and made another positive
note in her favor on his log.

She angled back toward the plain. Io was low when
she got there and she realized she'd covered thirty-
five kilometers, at a near run, in rough terrain and
without stopping. No wonder her feet suddenly felt
as if they were squeezing out of her boots. Well, she'd
camp on the plain. She had four days and had covered three marks today, which left three days for
seventeen others.

Which was an average of five a day, or almost six
a day for the remaining days. She'd figured on four
each of the next three days, but that left her five short.
She'd failed one and could fail two more. Four was
not an option.

So, rest now and rush later? But she knew that if
she stopped now, exhaustion would claim her. Push on
tonight, rest later. Assuming the evaluators were there.
If not, she'd camp out on the mark.

Glad she hadn't dumped her torch to save mass,
she flicked it on to get a better view of her map in
the fading dusk. Next one was almost eight more
kilometers, across the plain to the north. Well then,
slog on.

Bats and bat analogs fluttered by, spooking her. Not
good. She was reminded again that nights on Grainne
were *really* dark. Gealach was down and there were
no city lights glowing anywhere on the horizon. It was
creepy. Beautiful, but creepy. The stars were incredible, when she stopped to catch her breath. Then she
flopped her goggles down and dialed up the enhancement. She had to see where she was going. Every few

meters, she turned to look around, realizing it was illogical, but scared of the wilderness.

She dragged out her cloak to keep warm and fastened it down to her waist, leaving the bottom open for easier walking. When her breath started to mist she pulled her hood up. Keep your head warm to maintain body heat, she'd been drilled again and again.

Night vision enhancement was a tricky beast. It showed shadows, depressions and bottomless holes as dark areas. One had to either be very sure of the terrain or very careful or both to avoid injury. Her rate slowed considerably. She hadn't considered that, either.

Well, there was an evaluator's tent. Now to find the mark. She used the same trick as earlier, finding Vega and Sirius and referring to the ephemeris. Now, for some kind of landmark. The peaks were all but invisible, whether enhanced or not. Infrared showed little, as the mountains cooled quickly.

There was a fast, faint light to the west. Quickly turning, she confirmed it was a shuttle launch and zeroed the direction. Not exact, but close and you take luck when you find it. The city of Andrews was . . . there.

She found the mark in a few segs. It showed quite obviously on her goggles and she wrote the number down then approached the tent. The evaluator nodded and signed off. "What's to stop someone from waiting for another recruit and tracking them?" she asked.

"Me," he smiled. "Why, did you?"

"No!" she protested.

"I'm kidding," he assured her.

She finally noticed the other form hunched near the tent. "Breaktime?" she asked.

"If you like," he agreed. "Just don't talk any details."

The figure resolved up close as Welker. "Hey, how's it going?" She asked the girl. Well, legally woman, but seventeen Earth years would always be "girl" to Kendra.

"Flunking," was the reply, and the poor kid was straining to avoid crying.

"I thought so too, but you can make it," she said.

"I found two and failed both," Welker almost sobbed, cloak hugged around her skinny shoulders. "Then I got told I can't score this one, just because I arrived at it as another recruit did. If I hadn't had so much trouble getting close, I would have scored . . . but *he* says it was 'unintentional assistance.' I have to do seventeen more and not miss any."

Kendra whistled inside. That was tough. "Hey, you can do it!" she insisted. "Look at me. I didn't handle a weapon until I was seventeen, here. I come from lower gravity and thicker air." Leaning closer, she whispered loud enough the evaluator could be sure she wasn't cheating, "And this terrain, with no signs of civilization at all, is scaring the piss out of me."

Welker snickered softly. Kendra continued, "Rest up, sleep if you need to. Then go at it again." She stood and adjusted her ruck. "I'll see you at the rendezvous. I'm going out to wet my pants."

She strode off and could hear the evaluator chuckling and Welker giggling over her sobs.

The evening of the fourth day, Kendra felt pretty good. She'd forgotten that they had all night and early morning the *next* day to finish. She'd been tricked into thinking in day/night, rather than elapsed time. So she'd taken a full night's rest, along with her occasional naps, and had only two marks left, one of which was the rendezvous.

The tests had been grueling, but she'd passed so far, missing only the one the first day and one today.

One mark was set into the side of a cliff, requiring one to either climb a nearby tree and swing close, scale the cliff or hang far over the ledge. Several courses of fire were graded and there were no limits on rounds used. The trick was that many recruits tossed ammo to save weight at the first station she'd hit. Recruits had to make every shot count, hoard rounds and not waste ammo on targets one couldn't hit—some were beyond effective range or so hidden as to be beyond the accuracy specification of the weapon. But it was necessary to pass as many as possible and hope to fail only one for lack of ammo. By her calculations, if one kept every round, dropping food instead, and made every shot count, it was just possible to pass every course.

She had five rounds of ammo. That made her load lighter, but she would fail another range test. She figured that poor Welker would fail because of that, but she was sure the kid would bravely go through survival training again and do it one more time.

And she was out of food. Had she saved ammo insted of food, she'd be worse than hungry by now. "Not who is right, but who is left," she remembered Carpender bawling at them. There were no right answers on this test.

Her second to last mark should be just ahead. She took a back azimuth from a peak and measured Io and Gealach both. Right about here.

There were two discs in the ground, about a meter apart. She swore. Looking around, she found another one. Then three others. Everyone was getting a different one, but all in proximity.

It was too late to trudge back and try dead reckoning. She sat and thought, then decided she could miss this if she had to; the odds were good against another range fire. She took very careful measurements of Io as it set and shot Gealach again. She measured two peaks. All three lines converged and became a blob on the screen of her comm. If there wasn't enough detail there, there certainly wouldn't be on the paper map. She swore again and tried it one more time with just the last sliver of Io and Gealach. They were as close to point references as she'd get and far easier to measure than terrain features. She double-checked, sighed and moved over a few meters. There were three discs around her in a rough triangle.

Checking Gealach once more and using a peak in lieu of the now vanished Io, she narrowed it down to two. One seemed marginally closer, so she wrote it down.

The evaluator was almost two hundred meters away. She trudged over, handed him her log and he said, "Are you sure of this? You can't pick another one."

"Yes," she replied firmly, while inside, her brain said "no."

He signed off. "You made it."

"That was the test here, right?" she asked, gratefully exhaling a held breath.

"Mostly," he agreed. "You turn in your comm here and do the last leg on paper."

She opened her mouth then closed it. "I want a receipt," she said automatically, old habit from the UNPF, as she handed it over.

He raised his eyebrows. "Well. You're the first recruit to ask for one, this cycle." He turned, scrawled the serial number on a slip and handed it over. He had a pad of them ready to write. "Your mark will have directions to the rendezvous. Good luck."

Sighing, she looked at the directions and walked off.

Two divs later, she was groggy from lack of sleep, cold and hunger. The dark was slowing her down and spooking her again. Every time a critter made a sound or *stopped* making one, her pulse hammered and adrenaline flooded her body. It was damn tiring.

The mark should be about here. Gealach gave her enough light to measure from one snow-capped peak and she figured her direction and distance as close. Now to find the mark.

There it was! And all alone, not surrounded by fifty others. Relief washed over her and she bent over to find directions. There were none.

There was a board where they would have been clipped, but nothing there. She growled and shouted in exasperation. Great. Should she wait for some bozo to figure it out and run back? Call for help and hope they wouldn't recycle her? Wait for others to arrive and figure it out?

While she pondered, the sounds of a vehicle became audible. There was the bare buzz of a silenced engine, the bumps of suspension and occasional squeaks. A GUV rolled up nearby, and an evaluator hopped out. "Looking for this?" she asked.

"Yes, thank you," she said, relaxing several orders of magnitude.

"No prob. One very tired recruit thought it was his personally and dragged it with him. I'll stay nearby so it doesn't happen again," she explained.

Kendra read the directions, grinned and took off. The rendezvous was due north three thousand meters. The training site happened to be at five mils magnetic, so this would be easy.

She stopped in less than a seg, realized that it was five mils the *other* way and tried to backtrack.

The evaluator had moved. Then she realized she had run back without measuring. Fatigue. But excuses wouldn't do it. She'd run less than two hundred meters, so figure the five degrees and that would be close. The rendezvous couldn't be that small. It was just one last lesson she'd remember.

There were seven shelters pitched in the hollow that was the rendezvous. She made it eight, pitched her bag and crawled in, after reporting to the evaluator huddled next to a small fire. She was asleep almost before she could fasten the door.

She woke to voices and reluctantly crawled out, still short of sleep. There were over forty shelters now, and more people arriving on foot every few segs. Someone threw her a sealed ration pack that she dug into gratefully. She stowed her gear, and tried to work the kinks out of her legs. She had a huge blister, too, but it would have to wait. There was cheerful chat all around, realizing that the personal test aspect was over. The next four days of combat simulation would be sheer hell, but hard for an individual recruit to fail. It was experience for them, a test for the student NCOs and officers who would be running it.

Only segs before deadline, Welker limped over the edge, grinning hugely. Her ankle was bound for support, but she stumped forward and leaped up in triumph.

"I shot a perfect score!" she crowed.

"I knew you could do it!" Kendra lied as she drew near. A medic shoved them aside and pulled out a kit. "Now we can do a proper job on that," he told her. They would have to immobilize, inject fast-working nanos and do some therapy on the swelling and other tissue damage, but she'd be ready for the combat sim.

Two more recruits arrived in the last few moments and one dragged up the rear, past the deadline by less than ten seconds. He looked ready to kill when told he'd have to repeat from survival training forward. Kendra was transported out before the last stragglers arrived.

Chapter 16

"Both sides think they are about to lose. They are both correct."

—Old military proverb

The combat sim was more confusing than anything else. They had no time to recover, but went straight back to the field. They huddled on the flightline for most of a div, broiling between Io and fused surface until they were finally picked up by trucks. The trucks drove them along rutted tracks deep into the brush of a training range, where one truck was "killed" by a boobytrap. All aboard were pulled off, put onto an evaluator's truck and driven back to be re-inserted into the battle elsewhere.

Kendra was assigned to assist a mortar and dug a position while the gunner laid the weapon. At least she had a real shovel, rather than an entrenching tool. She was mostly done when a student from the NCO Leadership course came over and ordered her to get aboard another vehicle. This one dragged her to an artificial clearing, cut in the trees with explosives, where a lifter waited. The lifter took them over a cluster of buildings, dropped quickly at one edge and banged to the ground.

She bailed out with the others, took cover and advanced leapfrog. Fire lashed out from the compound and her helmet flashed and beeped. She was "dead."

After an interminable wait, during which it began to rain, she was herded into an open truck with other "casualties," and driven back to an entry point. Another squad leader took her and had her support an ambush on a convoy of supplies, still in the rain.

She crewed a vertol door gun, drove a truck, guarded combat engineers laying a bridge, shot, was shot at, acted as a training aid for the medics by screaming as if suffering pain and stress while trying to beat them senseless. That was fun until one of them slugged her to make her hold still, then trussed her to the stretcher. She was briefly pulled out and dressed in ill-fitting civilian clothes to storm the gate with a "protest group," then pulled back in and sent to support an ordnance disposal team. Then she guarded prisoners.

It came to her, halfway through a cold, miserable second day, with only one meal and her water running out, that she had no idea which side she was on, if she had been on the same side all along, how many sides there were or what the war was supposed to be about. Live artillery roared overhead on its way to an impact area that simulated a village somewhere in this madhouse. Aircraft buzzed, howled, roared or screamed, depending on type and conditions. They would drop flares at night, to illuminate various targets with assorted frequencies, and to blind others.

While she mused she was grabbed again and sent to run a target designator, painting incoming attack vertols with a laser.

The third one reacted by dodging and firing. Her helmet flashed again. Sighing, she dropped the designator and lay still, waiting for the medics to come for her body. She fell asleep.

Four days passed fairly quickly. Kendra was lucky, in that her time had been eventful if confusing. Some had been assigned to guard facilities or entry control points, had as little idea what was going on as she did and were bored stiff. She was hoarse, cold, aching, bruised, blistered, hungry and tired to the point of hallucinations, but felt good. They were *done!*

The "war" continued as they left. It ran all day, all night, all year, with new troops taking over as their classes rotated through. The "front" would gradually shift across the training range, allowing construction, maintenance and time for the poor abused plant life to recover.

"*Soldiers!* Listen up for assignments!" Carpender shouted. He read from his comm. "Aawil, Second Legion. Abel, Gate Control Command. Ago, FMS *Bolivar,* Cruiser. Ahern, Orbital Defense Command. Aires, Third Battalion, Seventh Brigade . . ." Kendra tuned it out as she pondered events. She felt far more military now than she ever had in the UNPF. She wondered what the future held. "Pacelli, Third Mobile Assault Regiment," she heard, snapping alert and grabbing the thrown datachip. That was Rob's unit! Had he arranged it? And Marta's. And Drew's. Well, that didn't sound too bad. She read the departure orders . . .

Which ordered her to stay here for forty-five more training days! She sighed in exasperation. Freeholders never relaxed.

❖   ❖   ❖

The next morning everyone was cheerful. Graduation! At long last. They checked each other's uniforms
for lint even more carefully than for inspection, waited
nervously for a div and a half then formed up to march.
Their cadences were elevating in the warm morning
air. It was promising to be a gentle day.

The sense of accomplishment was very real. All that
sweating, bleeding and training was an ordeal that most
people could not handle, she realized. As they marched
past the reviewing stand and turned eyes right, accepting salutes from the military people in the crowd, she
felt a stir that made her graduation from UNPF service school pale. That had been a summer camp by
comparison. There were cheers for her friends and
photos taken. Welker and Denson insisted on having
her in their photographs and contact codes were
swapped all around. Carpender came by and was polite
and gentle while he displayed a remarkable sense of
humor. It was an eventful morning. The afternoon
would be spent in packing.

Most of the platoon was boisterously stuffing gear
into bags and departing, with occasional teary eyes or
jokes, hugs and shoves. She shoved her kilos of property
into two heavy duffels and prepared to lug it across
the base to Mobile Assault Training Depot. The bright
spot was that Denson had orders for 1st Mobile, so
she'd at least have some company. A quick call to Rob
and Marta had gotten her congrats and assurance that
they'd fly out to meet her when she got a day free,
which they told her wasn't likely to be until the Equinox holiday, twenty-three days away.

She waited a few segs for Denson to get packed then
they shouldered their gear and started hiking. At least
they didn't have to do any formal marching and they

both were in civvies. But it was still a hot day and not a short walk with eighty kilos of gear on backs, shoulders and towed behind.

"You have friends in Third, Pacelli?" he asked. They'd been bunked near each other the entire time and frequently assigned as buddies.

"Uh . . . call me Kendra. Please. I'd like to have a real first name other than 'Icebitch,' 'Dumbshit,' or 'Recruit.' Yes. A sort-of manfriend, a sort-of ladyfriend and a friend."

"Oh," he replied. "Call me Asher. Two relationships?" he asked. "Or a tri?"

"Sort-of tri," she said, grinning. "My life is very sort-of right now." She shifted her second duffel, which was carried across the top of the one she wore.

He grinned back. "My brother got out of First about a year ago. I hope I don't have to meet some expectation."

"You will," she promised.

"Thanks. You're all friend," he replied in mock disgust. They walked in silence.

Kendra asked, "Do you have any idea what all we have to do for assault training?"

He whistled. "Um, amphibious planetside assault, ship and habitat, space, parachute and air and some miscellaneous stuff. We'll be busy."

"So much for unwinding," she complained. "I have to go to logistics intro course, then report in two days after I graduate, back where I fucking left from." It was getting easier to swear after practice. She shifted the damned bag again. It wouldn't stay in a comfortable spot.

"Well, we do have tonight free," he said cautiously. "I could spot you dinner . . ."

She turned her head. "Are you offering to spot me dinner?" she asked, "Or buy me dinner?" She glinted at him. He was embarrassed! This was sort-of fun.

"Uh, buy, I guess. If you don't mind," he sputtered. "Steak? And beer?"

Steak? From a cow? Yeah, what the hell. And an actual date, under local customs? Yeah, what the hell. They'd be busy enough and far enough apart it couldn't get too complex. And she did like the idea of some attention.

"Sure," she agreed. "Am I that hard to ask? Because of my age?" He was barely eighteen earth years, compared to her twenty-seven. It probably was a bit intimidating. "Or because I'm from Earth?"

"Um . . . some of each," he admitted. "I don't have much experience with women. And none in picking people up. And, well . . ."

"People from Earth are supposed to be prudes?" she supplied.

"Well, a lot of people say so," he defended.

"We do have sex on Earth," she smiled across at him. "And my ladyfriend is one of the highest paid escorts in the system. I know a few tricks."

That caused him to flush scarlet under his tan and she laughed silently. This was going to be fun.

The steak had been good, Kendra thought, and it hadn't bothered her too much that it was animal. And she'd been glad to get it. The depot had decided that they were prime candidates for cleaning and other chores. She'd finally had a few polite words with the duty corporal and explained that it didn't seem fair to get stuck with the duty when everyone transporting in or with family visiting was arriving in the morning. They'd both made plans to stay off-base, so why should the corporal be stuck camping there if he didn't have to be? He'd agreed that his own apartment or billeting would be more comfortable, and grinned a knowing grin as they left and he locked the door.

The beer was good, too and she'd had a bit more than she planned. Asher was definitely in for a shock if he was expecting her to be prudish. She smiled again. "Shall we walk dinner off?" she suggested.

Rockcliff was a beautiful town, with an utterly breathtaking view of the Dragontooth range and Mirror Lake. They walked along the second ring road, unconsciously fast from their daily training. The hotel was several blocks away; they'd found the restaurant by simply walking until they found one. She'd thought that very romantic and old-fashioned, even though she knew it wasn't uncommon here. The building was of rough stone, looking like a seventeenth century European factory and had real wooden beams inside. It did feel odd carrying a rifle each. But regulations insisted that military personnel be armed at all times and neither of them had a sidearm.

Asher had thoughtfully but needlessly spent some extra creds for a room that looked across the city to the lake. Well, thoughtfulness deserved a reward. She reached out and scritched the small of his back.

He squirmed, snapped, "Hey!" and dug back at her. They smiled a truce, moved alongside each other again and she poked for his ribs.

He turned and grabbed, missed her shoulder and got a handful of her left breast. "Really?" she said and stopped fighting. He looked as if he were about to apologize, even though his hand was still there. She saved him the embarrassment by leaning forward and kissing him.

She could feel his pulse and respiration go through the roof. She took his hand and said, "Let's go upstairs."

Kendra looked over at Asher, sleeping at last. Well, she couldn't complain. Endurance, creativity, strength and decent looks. Although she hadn't admitted it, it was her first date based purely on lust. And it hadn't been bad.

She'd had to be a bit demanding. He was very gentle and attentive, but she wasn't in the mood for gentle. She'd taken control and was surprised at her own energy. She realized she hadn't had time to even think about sex for the last ninety days. That must be it.

He'd commented once that she could be a professional and she'd had to remind herself that it was a compliment. She thanked him, said that it wasn't her thing, and he'd taken the hint.

Damn. They both had to be awake in about a div if they were to be on time. She called the desk for a wake-up call—a nice old-fashioned touch, she thought, as she arranged for it to be ten segs early. Perhaps a quickie before they left.

Chapter 17

"Parachute's not deployed
And ground's getting depressingly near.
Life, I love you so much
But you don't care for me, old bitch!"
—"Life, I Love You," a Russian skydivers' folk song

Assault training was run differently from recruit training. The instructors were no less forgiving, no less demanding, but they didn't act as condescendingly. They did require just as much effort.

Kendra signed in, comm chips and gear were thrown at her, a bunk assigned and a schedule laid out. A few segs later, they were boarding a shuttle for orbit again. They docked at a habitat and were stuffed into cubes, as before.

The training involved the specialized weapons and loads for fighting within a habitat. They learned to breach airlocks, override controls and to maneuver quickly in tight quarters. Emphasis was placed again on unarmed combat, since they were more likely in such confines to wind up in the midst of enemy forces. They ran exercises all day long and much of several nights. Then it was outside to rehearse assaults.

They trained with small assault pods for approaching and grappling quickly, pre-packaged explosive charges and plasma torches for cutting hulls, and learned to recognize and disable antennas and sensors. They used heavier weapons for those purposes and drilled again and again for precision and accuracy.

After nine days, they crammed rapidly into an assault pod and dropped through the atmosphere. They landed hard and deployed for attack. The instructors came around and berated them for sloppiness. After seeing the video of it, Kendra could agree. They took a ride into the stratosphere on a converted civilian ballistic craft and dropped again. Then again. They interspersed that with standard landings and "hot unloads" from the cargo bays, where they slid out the back on ACVs and parachute-retarded wheeled vehicles. Several vehicles took spills and there were minor casualties. They were reminded that in warfare those "minor" casualties would all be dead.

Anyone casualtied missed lunch the next day, regardless of whose fault it was. The purpose was to reinforce the risks involved and encourage attention to detail. It became a running joke about the "crash diet" they were all on. It lasted eleven more days, because the long flights into low orbit or the stratosphere made for tedious waiting for flights and flight-time. Kendra was only too glad to be done with it. She'd bruised all over from the impacts and decided that was not the most personnel-friendly way to fight.

That night, she took a few moments to call home. Rob answered and assured her he and Marta would be there the next evening. She asked if he needed directions and blushed when he replied with a smile, "I'm familiar with the base." Of course he was. She disconnected before she could say anything sappy. That could wait until they met. It felt odd to be talking to them. Unlike the UNPF, Freehold military training enforced separation from friends and family. She realized it had been some weeks since they'd last spoken.

Day twenty-one. They woke, were trotted to a hangar and drilled again through the basics of parachuting. They did several rehearsals on the ground before departing for the airfac. The traditional VC-6s were waiting and prepared to lift.

Instead of boarding, they shrugged into harnesses and clipped themselves to racks on the outside, reporting readiness through their helmet mikes. Kendra gulped in fear. She hated heights, and this was not the way she wanted to experience them. Before she could steady her nerves, the pilot lifted, straight up and fast.

She clung to her webbing and tried to lean back against the side of the craft as it jostled her. *Breathe*, she reminded herself as she gasped in a lungful of cold, fresh air. It helped. The ground expanded beneath them, features retreating as they drifted over the adjoining drop zone at five hundred meters. She listened to the pilot and instructor coordinating the drop and tried to unclench her knuckles. She had a dizzying view down through a cloud and looked quickly at the horizon as she'd been taught. It didn't help much.

"Stand by," her helmet advised. She prayed silently and closed her eyes briefly. Before she could finish, the voice said, "Go."

The snaps popped free and she dropped like the proverbial rock. As it registered, her stomach rose into her throat. Then she was yanked by the static line and gravity pulled her into the harness. "One," she counted, suddenly reminded of the procedure for emergencies, but the gear functioned flawlessly and the backup automatic system was unnecessary, as were the procedures she'd learned in the morning's drills. She counted two, twisted her head to check the canopy for inflation, then stared at it for emotional support. Those few kilos of fabric were keeping her from slamming into the ground. The count should have taken through five and she'd screwed it up, but at least her gear was working.

She grabbed her toggles and steered toward the target, watching for others. She was experiencing a rush and decided she could get used to this in time. Some were far more enthusiastic and two who had prior experience with parachutes were pulling stunts. She hoped they were soundly punished for the crime of enjoying themselves. Then she began to enjoy it herself. Io was shining, the sky was clear and the temperature was comfortably warm inside her jumpsuit. She kept looking up at her canopy for reassurance and back down at the closing ground.

She touched down near the target and rolled as she'd been taught. With the oversize, overstable gear the students were issued, it was unnecessary, but good practice. One should always get low in combat, she recalled.

They went up again immediately. Then a third time, jumping through a troop door in the side, then once more off the ramp at the rear. They were all aching from the harnesses tugging at them when they broke for the day.

They had the evening and next day free for Equinox and Kendra looked eagerly forward to Marta and Rob visiting. They were due about seven. She waited in the dayroom, not wanting to miss them by trying to anticipate their arrival at the gate.

"Bay, ten-shut!" someone bellowed and Kendra snapped to with the others. "Officer in the bay!" the speaker continued.

"As you were," a voice replied. She recognized it. Rob's. What the hell?

She turned to see him and Marta in undress greens. Marta looked as stunning as ever and Rob was wearing lieutenant's pips.

From habit, she snapped to attention again. "When did that happen, sir?" She asked, half joking.

"Geez, dear, relax," he laughed. "You don't have to call me 'sir,' my parents were married. I'm only dressed for dinner. Okura retired right on schedule and Bimi left for command school. That left a slot open, I'm ranking pilot, instructor qualified and have combat time, so I got Second Flight." He took a breath and added, "You look great."

She doubted that, with short hair and a uniform, but it was really good to see him. Marta turned slightly and gestured. "Are you ready, love?"

"Uh, let me get my rifle," she said. "And I invited Asher to come with us." She indicated him with her left hand. "Asher, Rob and Marta," she introduced awkwardly as she hurried to her bunk, self-consciously avoiding them.

Asher stood nearly at attention, trying to look relaxed, and greeted them, "Sir, Sergeant."

They were almost small-talking when she returned with her rifle. Asher was already armed, and they left. Rob told the recruit on guard not to call the bay to attention and they departed without fanfare, although Kendra could still feel numerous eyes staring in their direction, mostly at Marta.

They climbed into a rented aircar and strapped down. Marta promptly grabbed her and planted an eager kiss on her. She kissed back until oxygen deprivation cut in. Then it was Rob's turn.

While she recovered from the attention, Rob lifted and turned the car simultaneously. "Now that you've had some air time, I can fly like a real pilot," he joked as he rammed the throttle home. There were gasps and a giggle from Marta as gees shoved them into the seat. "Rob's a Hatchet pilot," she advised Asher over her shoulder.

Marta was next to him and added, "Yeah. And he got the CfC on Mtali. If his flying bothers you, just do what he does," she said as setup.

"What's that?" Asher asked, unsure and staring wide-eyed out the window.

"I close my eyes!" Rob shouted, laughing.

He slowed down and dropped into the local traffic pattern and in a few segs landed and roaded. "This the place you meant?" he asked Kendra.

"Yes. Asher brought me here two weeks ago." Was that all it was? It seemed years.

They walked across the road and into the hewn-stone building. There was a line waiting for service, but the Freehold operated differently from Earth. As soon as the staff saw the combat medals on Rob and Marta, they were ushered in and not a word of protest was spoken behind them. The manager personally delivered a bottle of wine, announcing it was with his compliments for anyone with a Citation for Courage. "Who do I have to kill for champagne?" Rob joked, then thanked him graciously.

The food was really good and Marta split her attention three ways with surprising ease. Then Kendra realized it shouldn't be surprising. Rob was polite and friendly with Asher and gave Marta occasional touches and conversation, but most of his attention was on Kendra. She reciprocated. She wondered how the evening was going to be, but Marta clearly had it under control and Kendra trusted her to handle it. She dug into her lemon-pepper roasted chicken and was dizzy-headed on wine in short order. It didn't take much.

"The short hair suits you," Marta said. She reached up and brushed the thick blond strands, now almost five centimeters long.

"Uh, sure," Kendra replied sarcastically. "You might have warned me about that."

"Why? Don't they do that in the UN?" Marta looked as surprised as Kendra had been when she got shorn.

Another gulf. She let the topic drop and got back into the conversation. "I think the second jump was scarier than the first," she said.

Asher nodded. "I wasn't going to admit it, but yes," he said.

"Was for me, too," Rob agreed. "The first one is an unknown. You'll learn to enjoy them."

"I do already," she purred and stroked his thigh. He laughed.

"Wait until you try free fall," Marta said. "The most fun you can have with your clothes on," she snickered.

After eating and drinking and chatting for a while, they stood and wandered out. Rob left a generous tip and thanked the manager. The service had been unobtrusively excellent.

Rob took her hand against slight resistance and commented, "This whole decorum thing in uniform takes some getting used to. You need to relax a little." She tried to do so and moved closer. On the other side, Marta undecorously mashed up against her and held out her other arm for Asher, who was looking a bit out of place. He brightened and took it.

The hotel Marta had booked was pricier than the one Asher had sprung for. She would have to let him know that Marta was loaded with cash and liked spending so he wouldn't feel too put upon.

The elevator was on the small side and they shifted

to fit. It wound up with Rob and Kendra standing together, Marta and Asher behind them. They walked down the hall that way and were still two couples when they entered the room.

Kendra pulled Rob against her inside the door and he grinned as he met her lips. He kissed along her chin and down her throat, making her arch in response. His hands on her hips and his weight against her were long-missed thrills.

Then Marta elbowed her way in. "Don't be greedy!" She smiled at Rob. Then she attacked with a ferocity Kendra had never felt before. Finally breaking, Kendra slumped against the wall, lust and alcohol making her giddy.

"I think you and Rob should burn off your mindless lust and we can play later. Meanwhile, Ash here can keep me entertained," Marta said. Asher had been feeling left out and looked it. He flushed red as Marta eyed him, clearly enjoying the idea.

After long, sweaty segs in a variety of positions, they broke apart. Rob sprawled back, gasping, and Kendra leaned to stretch out kinks. Mar ran questing fingers up her neck and began to massage the knots. She much preferred Rob's attention, but she had missed Marta just as much. She drew Mar into an embrace and let her hands and mouth drift across the flawless olive skin.

If it wasn't for her current heavy exercise program, she figured she'd have collapsed from exhaustion by now. Marta had been as energetic and demanding as always. She was about to beg for a break, but when she sat, catching her breath for a second, she saw the look in Ash's eyes. She pulled him close and spread atop him, feeling him inside her, aroused again and ready. He kissed her eagerly and she delighted in it.

She opened her eyes to find Mar kissing her and the men asleep. "Feeling okay?" Mar asked.

"Sure. Did I black out?" she asked.

"Not as such. You mumbled a few words about being ruined for regular sex, then fell asleep."

"Oh," she replied wittily.

"Speaking of which," Marta added as she began caressing her again. Kendra wondered if she was going to be allowed to sleep any more.

They spent the next day on a six-meter sailboat on Mirror Lake. She gratefully stripped naked and sunbathed as soon as the temperature permitted. It had been so long since she'd been outside without clothes that she felt odd about it again. She declined to join Marta in a dip over the side, however. The young woman resurfaced dripping and howling, her nipples crinkled from the cold and her lips taking on a blue cast for a few segs.

Rob pulled the tiller taut against the breeze, tacking them. He was experienced with sailing vessels too, and Kendra wondered again just how many skills were in his repertoire. She lazed on the deck while Marta teased Ash again. They munched a picnic lunch and headed back in the afternoon as Io began to bake them. There were hundreds of boats out by then, and Rob steered carefully. Kendra nodded at appreciative stares, still not used to them. Marta played to the audience and had a great time.

Mar was definitely amused by Asher. She was kissing and caressing him as they sat relaxing in the room. "You realize how lucky you are, I hope," Kendra grinned. "What would last night have cost him?" she asked Marta.

Considering, Marta said, "Sex with some variations, voyeurism, extended oral, about two divs worth . . . two thousand credits would cover it."

Asher looked suitably impressed. "Wow," he said. "Kendra said you were high priced, but wow."

"You don't think I'm worth it?" Marta asked with a cruel grin.

"Uh, yes!" he agreed quickly. Despite his minimal experience, he knew Marta was incredibly skilled and he'd be pondering the differences between her and Kendra, while trying hard not to rate them against each other. It was amusing, but Kendra was glad they weren't involved more than casually. It could get very confused and ugly if they were.

Marta dropped them at the barracks the next morning with twenty segs to spare. They changed and were ready for free-fall training, Kendra still a bit stiff from athletic sex.

After the daily exercise and shooting, they listened to the lecture again and ran through rehearsals one-on-one with the staff. Satisfied, they were herded back aboard the vertols, Kendra feeling well rested, and confident. There was just a twinge of nervousness inside and she looked around at the others. Some wore grins like Ash's and she wondered how many others had been trysting. She doubted any had had as athletic a time as she'd had.

They were quickly at altitude and Kendra was motioned to be first. Her stomach flopped, but she stepped forward. There was an interminable wait, then the ramp dropped, then there was more waiting as the landscape glided by. They were doing barely 150 kilometers, but it seemed faster. The jumpmaster walked casually out to the edge of the ramp and looked down while Kendra swallowed. He motioned her forward.

She stepped gingerly to the edge and stood there, buffeted by the slipstream as the instructor pointed down. "There's your target," he shouted over the roar. She could hear it live and in her headset in odd stereo.

She glanced down, nodding, not really seeing.

"No, lean over. Down there!" he repeated. She leaned, gripping the stanchion, and saw what might be a painted target. "Ready," he told her. She put her toes against the edge, waiting in the disconnected state she'd learned to associate with sensory or mental overload.

She heard a bellowed, *"Go!"*

Swallowing again, she dove off the edge and dropped, spread to catch the roaring wind. The air and gravity ripped at her, pulled her, tumbled her from headfirst to belly-down as she took a stiff *"Arch!"* while shouting instructions to remind and time herself. *"Look!"* she yelled and sighted her release handle near her right side. At *"Reach!"* she pulled her arms in toward her torso as she'd been taught and yanked the release while bellowing *"Pull!"*

It was supposed to be a five-second count. It had taken her barely one. But the gear worked as advertised and the canopy rippled and billowed over her. She checked it and could see other students deploying overhead. Adrenaline coursed through her and she whooped in delight. This was a rush.

The next trip was a ten-second delay from a faster craft, face-first in a rush toward the ground, rolling in the gale to a stable position. They did twenty seconds. They could go no further than thirty without oxygen and stopped there. Kendra would vividly remember that jump forever.

She leapt headfirst out the back, feet against her buttocks, arms extended to let the buffeting winds catch her. She flattened out in the sudden silence and heard the steadily increasing roar of the air past her ears. Occasional side-gusts caught her and there came a whuffing sound as she dropped through a wisp of cloud. Full gravity returned as she reached terminal velocity.

The world curved away from her in a vast panorama and she leaned sideways to turn for a full view. It was exhilarating and she grinned beneath her goggles. Remembering to check her altimeter, she was surprised to find it was only 185 meters and about five seconds into her flight. She had plenty of time. She turned back to the view.

She kept a steady eye on her altimeter. After a long time that was meditative and restful, she popped the canopy at five hundred meters as ordered. She found a rising thermal and managed extra hang time, in violation of regs. *It should cost to have this much fun,* she thought. She landed and reported in for dinner. They resumed afterward, doing a static jump and a free fall in darkness with night-vision gear.

The rest of the instruction block passed at a blur. They began jumping with gear and did more night jumps, into water, into thick woods with armor to prevent injury, then into mock urban settings. They practiced malfunctions, including releasing a "damaged" main and deploying the reserve. They used oxygen to go as high as seven thousand meters and practiced steering for their targets.

They were more than halfway through already. After Recruit Training, as busy as it had been, the breakneck pace here was staggering.

Up before Io again. Exercise, shooting range, classroom. They devoured the lecture and were driven to another training area. They jogged up stairs to the top of a one-hundred-meter training tower and donned harnesses.

Kendra snapped the rope through the links as taught and the instructor tugged it to inspect. "Okay," she said. "You can't fall as long as you grip the rope against your hip," she reiterated the lecture. "Try to hang on in front, you'll slip. Now, back to the edge." Kendra nodded, shuffled to the edge of the tower and leaned back. She felt fine so far.

She slipped one foot over, then the other, and gingerly edged down, feet against the building, slipping the rope through her fingers and snugging it against her hip. "Faster," she was ordered. "We don't have all day."

She quickened her pace, looking at the wall and not down and was quickly done. She was surprised at how easy it had been. She'd expected to be scared of the height. Free-fall training had put a stop to that.

She went up twice more for practice and prepared for the real training after lunch.

That was a different experience. She faced forward, standing at the edge. It looked like a long way down now. "Over you go," she was reminded.

She squatted and stepped over with her left, then her right. She stared straight down the tower to the packed ground below and paused. It was disorienting, and her hindbrain waited to plummet to her death. Gingerly, she stood out from the side, holding the rope taut in front of her. She stepped, then again, jerkily, shifting against the tower and hissing. Her adrenaline level was up again. If this continued, she'd be addicted to the stuff.

She continued jerking down the side. It was easier this way, once she was used to it. She could see where she was going and it was easier to control the rope. By evening, she was proficient and comfortable with the basics. They did one in darkness, then bedded down and rose early again.

They spent the day rappelling from vertols, finally leaping out the side and dropping fifty meters in five seconds using a friction lock to slow the descent at an increasing rate. They started in free fall down the rope, gravity building as they dropped and hitting the ground just hard enough to sting the feet a little. The friction heat could be felt right through the gloves.

By the end of it, she could drop, maneuver during descent, fire a weapon to clear a window and land inside it or hit a roof on the fly. She could reconnect to a trailing rope and lift, spreading to stay steady in the wind. She could drop from a moving craft, timing her descent to match the pendulum swing of the rope and land stationary at a selected position. They spent more effort on rappelling and roping than on any other task. Current doctrine held that this was the most useful technique for assault. It was a lot of fun to bounce across the landscape, once trained. Better than any amusement park ride she'd ever tried.

They spent what seemed now to be a very brief span on beach assault and additional land techniques. It was unlikely they'd ever be assaulting from water, but it was possible for a drop pod to land off-beacon. They practiced wading, swimming and using small boats. The two days were dawn to dusk affairs, but flew by quickly, although cold, wet and itchy. The last day of the block was spent frontally assaulting prepared positions. Kendra was reflective afterward. It finally hit her at gut level that she was learning to kill or be killed. A frontal assault would be suicide for most involved.

The final exercise was quick, brutally hard and messy. The students lined up at the beginning of the course, psyched and ready to graduate. From here, technical training for most, direct assignment to their new unit for others . . . and for some poor unfortunates, follow-up with Blazer training and perhaps Black Operations after that. Kendra shuddered to think about what could be worse than this.

She waited anxiously, a bit concerned about the test. She understood exactly what was involved, but the waiting was still unnerving. She approached the front of the line and killed time watching those ahead of her.

Her turn. "Pacelli, Kendra A." she recited to the evaluator.

"You ready, Private?" he asked her.

"Yes, Sergeant!" she replied. *Hell, no!*

"*Go!*"

She ran three steps and jumped into the trench, landing chest deep in frigid mud. Floating in it was assorted trash, refuse and rotten garbage. She held her breath and bent forward, slime rising over her face and into her ears and hair as she grasped the two sunken ammo cans left for her and grabbed the handles. As she stood, filth oozed down over her and into her clothes. She longed to wipe her face, but that would mean dropping one of the boxes, which would mean another dunking.

She waded forward, as close to a run as she could manage under the circumstances, feeling her boots squelching underneath as the mud forced its way in. The two cases, full of ammo and mud, were already heavy and dragged her arms behind her as she slogged onward.

She reached the end of the two-hundred-meter ditch exhausted, cold and aching. The handles had cut into her hands and she'd banged both shins, her knees and thighs with the sharp corners several times, front and back. She was only too happy to drop them. She wasn't happy with the high-pressure fire hose used to clean her off with even colder water, the spray blasting up her nose, into her mouth when she yelped and pouring liters of water into her clothes and down. The dousing added the burden of additional weight and she sprinted away as soon as she was clean. The hose chased her for a few seconds. Once out of range she coughed water out of her burning lungs and resumed at a slow pace.

There wasn't much point to the soaking, she thought, since she immediately had to dive face-first for cover in wet, limy sand that burned to the touch. The small arms fire blazing overhead was live, and while it was being held high enough to avoid injury, so she'd been told, it still made cracking sounds as it ripped by. She dragged herself along, cringing at the occasional low round. It actually was possible to flatten to half one's thickness, she decided, but the sand grains were a bit small for real concealment. She stretched her arms out again, scrabbled with her fingers, dug in her toes and crept under the first strands of razor wire.

She got snagged eventually and had to carefully snip the wire with her shears. The springy metal twanged along its length and bounced over, catching another trainee. He snapped, "Watch it, dickwad!" as an instructor poured a burst right over her head. Kendra flinched, and wasn't sure if the warm wetness she felt was lime and water or if she'd peed her pants. That had been close. Another bounding wire cut by someone else sliced across her hand. The sand rubbed in to create a fiery pain. She decided she could deal with it until she was clear, and crawled faster.

Once clear, it took her a few seconds to rinse the wound and spray sealer on it, then she ran for the target range. She found an open lane, punched her ID into the touchpad and unshouldered her weapon. She banged the grit from it, raised it and commenced fire at the pop-up targets. Once done, she slung it again and hit the track.

Unarmed combat test, and for evaluation, they meant unarmed. Someone could get killed from a clubbed rifle or shovel. The student was required to attack, and she took short steps toward her opponent. The man was smaller than she and her hunched posture caused him to misjudge her size. She straightened, raised her foot a full meter farther away than he expected, pivoted and kicked his ankle. He hopped back, changed stance and threw a fist toward her face. She rolled it aside with her right, circled her left hand down the other way to slow the parallel punch into her guts and tangled her left foot past his leading leg to kick the ankle she'd already abused. She grunted from the thump to her belly that he snuck in and breathed deeply and openmouthed as her diaphragm protested. Shoving his weight back onto the injured leg, she twisted her torso and he fell to his knees. She dropped her knee into the small of his back, stuck her extended left fingers into his throat and said, "Dead."

"Fine, get going," he said, clearly embarrassed by being taken down.

She stood and ran. Next was the cargo net, all thirty vertical meters of it. It no longer scared her, but her weapon tangled in the webbing and she was upside down by the time she unhooked it. She scrambled aright and finished the climb and descent.

There were twenty-two more obstacles, all sandy or muddy or wet or filthy or some combination of all of them. Her eyes were red and weeping from incapacitance gas before she was through, her lungs a frothy, syrupy burning mess. Once done with the ground test, she ran across a field-expedient airfac and boarded a vertol. As soon as it was full, the pilot lifted. They were taken to altitude and dropped, the target illuminated by laser and showing on their visors. Silently, they formed into squads and attacked a nearby position. From there, the orienteering course required precision navigation over short distances. Once graded on that, they boarded a shuttle.

Straight into orbit, they deployed in suits they donned en route and attacked a destroyer, cutting and blasting their way through the hull and seizing control. From there, they dropped in pods back into the combat sim for four more days of fun. It was raining again, and Kendra wondered if it was going to rain every time she went into the field. She was beyond exhausted from the level of activity and hadn't thought it possible to eat so much and not gain weight.

As Mobile Assault troops, she'd thought they'd see a higher complexity of battle. The local commanders, with absolute disregard for training, tossed them in anywhere they had shortages. It was a bit discouraging.

They cleaned up, slept and marched through another graduation, Rob and Marta in the stands, their own qualification badges proudly worn. She was dismissed, and went to spend the day with them. Ash had left, but said goodbye and kissed her and Mar as he departed. Then Rob had to make a contract appointment, leaving the two women alone. They went shopping, looking for exotic minerals and wood crafts, a love they shared. Kendra bought a green marble kitchen knife rack for Marta and had it shipped clandestinely. She had a bit of money now, which felt reassuring. She wasn't obsessed with the stuff, but it was impossible to live without, and a cushion let her sleep more easily.

Her hair had grown out to collar length, which made her less self-conscious in public. She also gradually became aware that she was totally unworried by any threat of crime. She knew she could instantly become a human chainsaw if attacked. She also no longer felt odd carrying a weapon. They were just tools to be used. It was a change in temperament she reflected on as they walked the cool, bright streets.

"One more stop," Marta insisted, and flew them a few kilometers to the outskirts of town. They stopped in front of a blocky building, thirty or so meters removed from its neighbors. A simple painted sign outside proclaimed CARDIFF CUTLERY. They went inside.

Rustic was perhaps the word. The back of the building, visible through an opening, was equipped with bay doors for loading equipment and material. Inside, it resembled an archaic smithy crossed with a machine shop. The front contained racks and displays of exotic cutlery. She'd never imagined so many varieties of edged weapons.

Mike Cardiff was about Marta's height, stripped to the waist and showing knotty biceps. He had a short, graying beard and mustache and a shaven head. "Well! Marta!" he said brightly in a resonant voice that belonged to a man twice his size. He grinned evilly and reached out his grimy hands.

She was still in uniform and squealed, "Don't even think it! Or I'll never kiss you again."

He wiped his hands off and held them at his sides while she leaned to kiss him chastely. "Who's your friend?" he asked as he leaned back. "Is she taken?" He leered comically at Kendra.

"Yes, by me and Rob. Mike, Kendra Pacelli. Kendra, Mike Cardiff," she introduced. Kendra took his hands and shook. He gave her a glance from head to toe that boosted her ego. His thoughts were obvious.

"You ladies look at the hardware, I have to check on one in the oven," he said and walked into the back again.

Kendra stared at the work. It was amazing. Some of the blades had grains and patterns like burled wood. She'd heard of pattern-welded and Damascus steel, but had only seen one small piece of Rob's. This was incredible.

Looking to Marta for assent, she lifted one from the rack. It was a standard kataghan pattern, chisel pointed, slightly S-curved, with a grip of nuggetwood set with silver pins. One nearby she didn't recognize by shape had a handle of malachite. She whistled in respect.

Cardiff returned with clean hands, wiping them on a rag and asked, "Any questions?"

"Not yet, but I am impressed," Kendra said. Marta was scrutinizing a small knife.

"Your accent is familiar. You're from Earth?" he asked.

"Yes," she agreed. "Minneapolis."

"Oho! Do I have a piece for you!" he said, guiding her by her elbow to another rack. He drew the blade from its slot and handed it over. She took it from him, curious, and stopped suddenly. The balance was amazing. It floated in her hand, seemingly ready to swing in any direction she willed without physical effort. She raised it and marveled at the artistry of it.

It was a wakizashi, she recognized. The blade was about fifty centimeters, patterned with interlocking curls of the constituent metal writhing like a snake along the length of it, treated with some chemical to reveal it in shades of gold and tan. It seemed to have a depth, hypnotizing the eye into staring into it. The sides curved slightly into an edge so fine there was no glint of reflected light. Just back from the edge, there was what she knew was a temper line. It was wavy, crisp near the edge and clouding into nothingness toward the back. The guard was a circle of carved black iron with gold hammered into it in the shape of a rosebud. The hilt behind it was a golden-hued wood that was tiger-stripe grained and had a depth of its own that shifted with the angle of the light. The scabbard Cardiff held was carved of the same wood.

"What *is* that wood? I've never seen it before," she asked, stunned by its beauty.

"That's actually quilted maple from Earth, salvaged from an old piece of furniture. I forged the blade from two damaged pieces. One was an old family blade that was too trashed to reuse as was. The other was an absolutely archaic Damascus shotgun barrel, also worthless in the condition it was in. You'll see the weld pattern change from Persian twist to waterfall along the shinogi, which is this line here, where the bevel starts." He indicated the break and she could see a faint line where the two patterns met. "So all the materials are from Earth. The surface is treated with titanium nitride for the gold tones," he finished.

Kendra wanted it. No, she lusted after it. She didn't dare look at the price tag. This was an entirely handcrafted work of art. She nodded and thanked Cardiff, putting it back on the rack. She turned to see Marta buying a small dagger, the grain of the blade twisted back on itself, hilted in Grainne amber and silver.

"Not getting it?" Marta asked.

"I want to, but I don't dare spend the money," she admitted.

"You need a sword for formal wear," Mar chided.

"But—"

"And it should be distinctive," she added.

"But—"

"And you'll never see that one again. Mike's stuff is magic that way. You come in and wait for one to call to you," she insisted.

"Marta, sto—"

"And you just finished your training, which calls for a special gift to yourself," she reasonably pointed out.

"Dammit, I—"

"And you want it," she finished.

Cardiff brought the sword over again and held out the tag. Sighing, she took it and read it. It listed the materials, the date finished and gave the name of the piece as "The Warbride." Below that was the price. Cr3500. It was more than reasonable for the work involved, but she flinched anyway. Even with the bonuses she received for hazardous duty, that was almost two months' pay. But she did want it. And another one like it would never exist.

She hesitated a moment longer until Cardiff said, "If you're a friend of Marta's and just graduated, then let's say three even. And I owe Rob."

"Let me guess, he saved your life on Mtali," she said. It was becoming a running joke.

"Nooo! I'm a civilian, thank you very much," he protested. "I just make the hardware for them. But he's referred a lot of people and does research for me."

She sighed and handed over her card. He scanned it and let the machine transact while he wiped the blade with a cloth and gave her a hardsheet of instructions. "Thank you!" she said, thrilled.

They left and Marta begged to handle it once. Kendra relented. She loved watching the light coruscate from the surfaces. She said so.

"That's all?" Marta replied. "It makes me wet to look at it."

"*Everything* makes you wet, dear," Kendra replied, laughing.

"Sure does. You want to?" Mar asked, running fingers down her shoulder.

"Umm . . . after lunch, you could probably talk me into it," Kendra agreed.

They parked at a downtown ramp and walked to a café. The sword thrust through Kendra's sash drew as many stares as the two women themselves did. It was a good afternoon.

Chapter 18

"My logisticians are a humorless lot . . . they know if my campaign fails, they are the first ones I will slay."

—Alexander of Macedonia

Logistics training was a forty-two-day course, but Kendra only had to attend the first week, since she'd tested proficient in all the software, accounting and technical matters. She was glad. These people never stopped training. So one more week would do it, then she'd finally be serving in the military again.

The first week was the combat logistics course. She wasn't sure what to expect. The barracks she was assigned to had small rooms of four trainees rather than bays, so she hoped it would be less intense than the previous courses. The hope didn't last, and she found the first day very confusing.

She and seven other "pipeline" trainees met outside, she wearing corporal's hashes and holding a sign with

their class number. Two older students who were
crosstraining came over, one a sergeant, who nodded
but let her keep authority for now. They cautiously
introduced themselves, wondering also at the new
environment. Kendra had learned that that was a fact
of military life and quickly identified with the crosstrainees. The other recruits weren't familiar to her or
each other at all, and formed their own clique. Well,
it meant she was fitting in, she hoped.

A woman almost as tall as Kendra, with a heavier,
lanky build as opposed to her angular one approached.
She wore senior sergeant stripes and was as immaculately made up as all instructors. Without preamble,
she read their names off her comm and made notes.
"I'm Senior Sergeant Logistics Instructor Joly. Senior
Joly is sufficient. We'll get introduced as we go. We
will leave for the firing range in ten segs, so grab
everything you need and let's go. I'll wait here," she
told them.

Kendra grabbed her weapon from her room; she'd
been carrying only a Merrill pistol. She added helmet, field harness and a cloak. It was fair so far, but
might rain later, and a cloak was handy to lie on for
prone fire. She was back downstairs and outside in
less than five segs to wait as the others trickled in.

Once everyone returned, Joly lead them on a run
toward the firing range. The pace was unhurried, just
fast enough to get the circulation going. The day was
hot, but a light, steady breeze kept them comfortable
and wafted the scent of mountain blossoms to them.
On the whole, Kendra enjoyed it, and running a few
kilometers was no longer a strain.

They neared the range, the din of small arms fire
increasing from subliminal pops to a steady crash as
they approached. There was a recruit battalion burning
off its daily crate of ammo, so they picked ten lanes

as far from them as possible. "Okay," Joly said, "let's fire a basic course of fifty and get to class."

The students nodded and stood waiting. "Yes?" Joly prompted.

"We need ammo, Senior," Kendra reminded.

"Why? You all plan to be in logistics, don't you? You were given the mission parameters, it's your job to provide the materials. I guess you better break into your basic loads and make it up later," she suggested.

Kendra and two others, including one of the crosstrainees, had left their basic loads in their rooms. They'd expected naturally that ammo would be supplied, as always. She flushed crimson, and burned more as she took a written reprimand for not being armed in accordance with regs. The class shared ammo from the open packs—basic load was one thousand rounds, so there was more than enough. Then Joly berated them for opening seven packs when one would have supplied everyone. "Wasting resources already. This is *not* the way we do things in the FMF!" she snapped. Then she dropped them for pushups. Technically, that wasn't done beyond initial recruit training, but no one felt inclined to argue with her. Fifty pushups was not the chore it had once been for Kendra, merely a reminder. She vowed to pay better attention to details.

Once done firing, Joly said, "We'll be doing a field exercise for the rest of the day. Pacelli, maybe you can redeem yourself by taking charge of logistics."

"Yes, Senior," she replied. "Where do I get supplies?"

"Training Depot Logistics, of course. Sign it out to this class number," she advised.

"Yes, Senior," she acknowledged, and headed off to gather everything.

She found the Logistics building, gave her class

number and requested ten basic loads of ammo; seven to replace the opened ones and three more for any firing they might do. She added marking pens, map chips of the area, ten field rations and some incidentals.

She lugged it all back in a crate, sweating, and distributed it to everybody. She'd gotten a pad of paper receipts and made everyone sign for everything she'd brought. Joly looked over and nodded. "Okay, we'll head out and see what you missed," she said, still with a faintly amused undertone to her serious countenance.

It was fifteen kilometers to the mark Joly made on the map. They were about three kilometers out when Joly commented, "This would've been easier with a couple of vehicles."

Kendra said, "I didn't realize we were allowed to."

"Allowed?" Joly replied. "We're logistics. If it isn't real property, which belongs to the engineers, it's logistics, and belongs to us. We don't ask. Everyone else asks us."

Kendra flushed again and slogged on. She'd remember that. Even without the snide comments from other students, who hadn't thought of it either, she'd remember.

Once at the mark, more or less, they sat and ate. Kendra handed out nine rations and Joly snagged the tenth, leaving her without one. Fuming, Kendra said nothing and grabbed a few crackers and pieces of candy from her gear. She'd been carrying them as emergency supplies. It was habit from recruit training and she made a note to never get rid if it.

They slogged back and Joly said to meet her at the club in half a div in civvies. They scattered to their rooms to clean up. At least, Kendra reflected, there was hot water here, and proper private facilities. Much like a hotel room, actually, and the staff gave them much more freedom . . . and much more responsibility.

At the club, Joly was quite charming. The class gathered around one large table and got acquainted. No one now seemed too bothered by Kendra's gaffe of not getting vehicles; it hadn't occurred to anyone else, either. Sergeant Carl Edwards, the student who ranked her, did suggest loudly but with a grin that she should buy a round. Shrugging, Kendra agreed. Joly politely refused, paying for her own. "Ethics," she said. No gifts from individual students.

The next day, more equipment was needed, and the students on the spot signed out kilograms of gear, forgetting items and being gigged. They learned to pin Joly down and figuratively beat details out of her. "Your commander knows what he wants," she said, "but you will need to make sure he gives you that information. Then add ten percent as a margin. Then stock anything you think somebody might ask for or has forgotten. And do it under budget and mass allowance." It didn't even sound simple. Kendra was somewhat familiar with the approach and offered advice the other students furiously entered as notes.

The last three days of the week was an exercise. They took vehicles, temps for sleeping, food, assorted field gear and extra fuel. There was a strict mass allowance, since they were being lifted out. It went quite well, except the student in charge of incidentals forgot toilet paper. There was much abuse heaped on him. Some had brought a little, others made do with the stuff from their field rations. Joly had apparently seen this before. She had a few rolls, which she sold at a stiff premium. All payments went to the Logistics Training Battalion unit fund.

Kendra packed her bags on Yewday night, waited for Marta to pick her up, and they flew back to

Jefferson. She would start at Heilbrun Base on Rowanday morning. "How you doing?" Marta asked as she drove across town to the civilian port.

Kendra was glad beyond words to be done with that nightmare and said so. "I'm exhausted. Mind if I sleep?" she asked as she reclined her couch after liftoff.

"Sure," Mar replied, to her already snoring form.

Marta's coupe was waiting at the Jefferson Starport and she lifted as soon as she cleared the safety zone around the facility. Kendra barely noticed. She was used to far stiffer maneuvers, now.

Rob greeted her at the door with a touch that indicated she'd soon be naked and sweaty if he had anything to say about it. She stalled him temporarily by showing him her sword.

"Great Goddess!" he exclaimed. "That's unreal." He examined it minutely, wiped the blade clean and dropped into stance. He made ten cuts in less than three seconds and whistled. Then he grinned what seemed a meter of teeth. "Wow," he finally whispered reverently. He read the enclosed certificate from Cardiff and looked up suddenly. "Riggs," he said.

"What?" Kendra asked. Marta looked over, too.

"Sergeant Lisa Riggs, squad leader of Seven Alpha Three. She and her squad died on Mtali, taking out the Shiitim air defense that was tearing our vertols out of the sky. Good friend of mine. The old blade Cardiff worked into this was hers," he explained, gazing deeply into the pattern on the sword as he spoke, as if looking for her there. Finally he scabbarded the blade, reversed it and passed it back and locked eyes with her.

"Time for you to participate in the Oath of Blades," he said.

Chapter 19

"Human nature is bad. Good is a human
product . . . A warped piece of wood must be
steamed and forced before it is made straight; a
metal blade must be put to the whetstone before it
becomes sharp. Since the nature of people is bad,
to become corrected they must be taught by
teachers and to be orderly they must acquire ritual
and moral principles."

—Sun Tzu

Once signed on-base, Kendra took a glance at the
list on her comm. It was a fairly familiar format of
inprocessing. She memorized the base map and got
cracking.

The commander's office was in a knock-down
building. The structures on base were either solid permanent fixtures or permanent-use "temporary" structures. This was a recent polymer shell on a fused
foundation. She entered what was clearly an orderly

room, saw a sign of light tubes that read "Assault Commander Alan D. Naumann, Regimental Commander."

She approached a desk, introduced herself and was told to head right in. She turned to the door and knocked twice.

"Enter," he said and rose as she walked in.

She saluted and said, "Corporal Kendra Pacelli reports to the commander."

He snapped his arm back and she beat him to lowering the salute. He looked at her with interest. "We've met before," he stated.

"Yes, sir," she agreed. He was just shorter than she, tanned and lean, brown hair cropped close. He had arrived at Mtali just as the UN was departing, and he'd swapped words with General Bruder in front of her. He was completely unintimidated then and completely in control now. "On Mtali," she confirmed. They'd met for about ten seconds, but he remembered her.

He walked slowly around her. "At ease," he said and she snapped down. "We are much more professional than the UN."

"Yes, Commander," she agreed.

"Familiarity is not tolerated on duty. I drive people hard. I expect performance with no excuses," he itemized, coming around in front again. He turned to face her, "And there is no embezzlement."

Before she could protest, he continued, "I know you were not involved. I want you to understand that that does not happen here. If you see anything inappropriate, you will address it to the chain of command or to me or to the IG, but it will not be unsettled. Say, 'Yes, sir.'"

"Yes, sir," she said. He was intimidating and she hoped he'd get done so she could get to her duties.

"You aren't wearing the Expeditionary Medal," he noted.

"But that's a UN medal, sir—" she said and was cut off.

"It is a combat decoration, is it not?"

"Yes, Sir," she confirmed.

"You're in logistics, arrange to have a few made up for yourself. Foreign combat decorations may be cleared for wear, as you should have learned in basic. And that one is certainly listed."

"Yes, sir," she agreed. That wasn't all bad, she thought. It would make her look more experienced.

"Now, your rank," he said, still standing. "Sorry, my manners first. Please sit and relax," he said, indicating the chair. He moved behind his desk and sat casually but straight. "The recruiters promised you corporal, so a corporal you are. The problem is, you have neither the training nor the experience. As soon as we can, we will send you to NCO Leadership School. In the meantime, you will have to manage. You are in a corporal's slot, so you will just have to do it. They should have bumped your pay and left you a private, but I don't know what they were thinking. If you can't manage to do the job, however, you will either be transferred or reduced. We do not carry people in Third Mob, unless they are casualties."

"Yes, sir," she said and swallowed. Already on the spot and not even here a day.

"There may be hassle from people, considering our current strained relations with Earth, and you having that accent. Let the chain of command know. I do not tolerate it. You are a professional and will be treated as such."

She was quickly introduced to the Executive Officer, Regimental Sergeant and orderly room staff and walked over to her section. Introductions all over again. It was becoming a habit. She entered and was met with stares.

"Corporal Pacelli?" someone finally asked.

"Yes," she agreed, and added, "Warrant," when she saw the speaker was a Warrant Leader. He looked to have Indonesian roots, and was of average height and lanky.

"Glad to have you. Where you transferring from?" he asked as he came out from behind a workstation and shook hands.

"Uh, pipeline," she replied, referring to the initial training course. "I'm a corporal because I have prior service. Sort of. UNPF. Mtali," she stuttered out.

He stared for a second only before saying, "Good, we need more combat vets. I'm Aman Sirkot. This is Sergeant Ron Davis," he introduced. Davis was clean-cut American looking and about eighteen local years. "You'll have the second NCO slot," he explained as she shook hands with Davis, "and this is Specialist Beker and Private Greer." Beker looked Russian and was about fifteen local years. She had tangled black hair in a thick growth on top. Greer was an unremarkable brunette, average features and height and was about twelve, Kendra guessed.

She was taken back to the warehouse where four more enlisted people were using a lift pod and brute force to shove containers around. "Everything the Third Mob needs to fight with, anywhere in space," Sirkot said proudly. "The rest of the warehouse squad is scattered about either accounting for gear or running errands." They watched for a few seconds until the other troops came over to be introduced. They all noted her accent, but no one commented. As far as they were concerned, if she'd made it through training and was a combat vet, she was acceptable.

❖   ❖   ❖

She had slight trouble fitting into the unit. She'd assumed it would run as her UN unit had. Show up, do the work, take an occasional class in a military subject, go home. There were many differences she'd never considered.

The Freehold forces had no civil service employees as support. They had occasional contractors, but only for specific tasks such as construction. All their regular operations were geared for war; there was no peacetime mission except training and support. The UN forces also assisted various government agencies, did charitable missions and other incidentals.

The Freehold forces started at a reasonable time, too, except during exercises. At 2:75 Rowanday they reported to the marshaling yard outside supply for a formation. They all signed in and received a briefing from Naumann. Some units did it by vid. Naumann insisted on a face-to-face. He said it reminded them they were soldiers.

From there, they all went to the range. The base firing range was huge, and they rotated from the precision short range, to precision long, pop-up target range, support weapon ranges—machineguns, automatic cannon, mortars, tactical rocket and missile—to foreign weapons, then a by-squad combat run through a course with surprise targets that changed every time.

After that, physical training, including unarmed combat practice. That was the end of a very busy day.

Mistday they took care of all administrative details and training vids, promotion tests, medical exams and any bookkeeping at the unit. The Logistics Company was kept busy handing out gear to new arrivals—including Kendra—inventorying tools, weapons, ammunition and other gear.

Ashday was parachute day, followed by PT and

unarmed combat. Oakday they did rappelling and assault, then maintenance of their gear. Yewday was vehicle operations and loading practice, then PT again. Sageday was a short field exercise in squads and occasionally platoons, involving orienteering, simulated raids, finding objectives, rescue and first aid and infiltration/exfiltration. They finished the week with Berday, which was a day for PT and optional sports or a monthly party for arrivals and departures. That was where she first had problems.

She'd thought she was fitting in well and had no reason to be concerned when Naumann stopped by Logistics at the end of the first month and asked to talk to her. She followed him to the dock area.

"This is unofficial and friendly and I apologize for skipping the chain of command," he began. "You aren't doing well in PT."

"I'm qualified, sir," she protested.

" 'Qualified' is marginal. We don't do marginal in Third Mob. One purpose of unarmed combat training is to get one used to violence, to be comfortable with the idea of pain. I want you to spend more time building muscle and fighting, and less time with the soft sports. And that means weight training, not stimulators," he ordered.

"Yes, sir," she confirmed.

"Second," he continued, "Social functions are optional, but you need to attend more of them. The correct phrasing is 'you may pass if other duty makes attendance impossible, otherwise appearance is mandatory.' It is important that NCOs set the example and be available for the other troops, and it is good for esprit de corps and unit cohesiveness to participate. And don't be afraid to drink at least socially. It loosens inhibitions and encourages talk, including that about problems. And an occasional drunken idiot is a challenge to keep things interesting and test our responses." He grinned as he said it.

She agreed to attend more functions. It would cut into more of her time.

"Also," he continued, less sternly, "I understand you have knowledge of machine tools."

"Yes, sir," she said. "Fixed and mobile robotic coordinate machines, mechanical, laser, electron beam and force beam," she said.

"How would you feel about qualifying as a machinist as a secondary war skill?" he asked. His phrasing made it clear she'd need a good excuse not to.

"How long is the school, sir?" she asked, sighing inside.

"No school," he said, shaking his head. "We'll have Warrant Chilton give you the end of course test. If he's happy, we'll document it for headquarters."

"Uh, sure. sir," she agreed. "If it'll help."

"It's impossible to have too many trained personnel," he replied. "And if you develop other skills or can act as a unit instructor, let Sirkot know. We'll keep you busy."

"Yes, sir," she acknowledged.

She took the test, impressing Warrant Leader Chilton and surprising herself. Then she found out that her pay would be bumped an additional five percent for each secondary skill she had. No wonder people competed for slots in the military, she thought. Free training in as many skills as one could manage and extra pay based on it. She'd already seen that employers preferred veterans. On Earth, she'd found out during her hitch that propaganda to the contrary, most employers regarded the military as a pool for losers.

The Freehold forces were paid far better than the UN. There were no taxes or other deductions, either, but there were additional expenses. One had to furnish housing, unless ordered to lodge on base, when duty required immediate availability. All meals had to be provided, except during exercises or combat. Kendra had planned on living with Rob and Marta and commuting, but the difference in their schedules made it awkward, as did traffic. From Marta's on the far south side of the metroplex to Heilbrun was about 150 kilometers, or 280 going around the bustle of downtown. It was just too far to commute twice a day with the heavy workload and no automated mass transit.

She paid the minimal amount of Cr5 a day to stay on base the first month and went home on weekends, then bought a small unicar. It was a ground-only; flight fees added up quickly. She still only made it home on weekends and a couple of days a week. She lived out of a duffel bag, kept her ready gear in the car and her battle gear at the unit.

Weekends were still fun and she appreciated the three-day format. She occasionally met one or both of her lovers at Rob's apartment for dinner or a tryst or both. Sometimes they'd travel up to see her. Still, she had less of a social life than she'd had on Earth. She wasn't unhappy; her work kept her busy and was productive. Rob invested her additional income in a variety of capital ventures and sent her regular reports on her assets. Her income was better than she'd had in the UNPF by a factor of three. Better than her father paid his technical employees, in fact.

She'd always been taught that pure capitalism was automatically evil. While not "pure," the Freehold system was as unregulated a system as had ever existed. Investors and shippers from all over space flocked to operate within its minimal restrictions and exported technology, labor requirements and sales. There was profit available for anyone willing to buy in. She took advantage of it with her pay and donated a monthly stipend toward an adoption center, deciding that was the local charity she wanted to sponsor.

Complicating social matters was the fact that about once a month the unit would deploy for anywhere from three days, in the case of a space assault exercise, to a week for ground exercises. She found out that they did longer ones twice a year. They were gearing up for an arctic exercise the next week. She shuddered at that thought. She hated working outside in the cold. Certainly, it got cold in Minneapolis, but people stayed inside; it was a modern, civilized town. People did not go out in subfreezing weather if they didn't have to.

The exercise that week was a surprise to her. She'd been in the military long enough to know how these things worked. They were woken early by comm and ordered to report in. She blinked awake, grabbed her gear and stumbled to the shop. She was second to report in and grabbed a cup of hot water and coffee powder from her bag. Freeholders might be chocoholics, but she preferred caffeine to theobromine as a stimulant. She slurped the warm, bitter brew.

What would happen next was they would wait around interminably while people staggered in, except for one or two incompetents who would claim to have slept late or that their comm wasn't working. She was surprised to find that everyone was present by the time she finished her first cup. *Good shop,* she thought. No, *great shop.*

Next would be almost a div of screwing around while they checked everybody's gear, made up shortages, listened to people whine that they couldn't keep their bags ready and make trips back to the barracks to get missing items. It would be worse, she thought, since many of them lived off base. While she was pondering this,

Sirkot directed her to detail a soldier to warm up her team's GUV. She sent Jackson to do it and wondered when they were planning on checking gear. She asked.

"What?" Sirkot replied, looking confused. "If they freeze, it's their own faults. Everyone knows the requirements for arctic deployment."

Which was exactly Kendra's thought. "No UN unit ever operates like that," she said. "A commander would be cashiered if a troop got injured in the field through any avoidable error."

"I've heard of that," he said. "It's called 'lack of discipline.' But thanks for double-checking; that's what NCOs are for."

They drove to the airfac, loaded into VC-6s, flew up to the tundra and began at once. It was an all-day trip, low and slow across the continent, endless kilometers of trees giving way to endless kilometers of prairie, then scrub, then frosted ground. Their first task as they deployed was to clear the area of a few boobytraps left by the aggressor forces, who were simulating the enemy. Then they pitched camp, including heating gear and set shifts and watches. The exercise proper commenced immediately. Aircraft flew, artillery launched and fired and infantry squads went out to raid and recon.

Kendra was given a data dump of tasks, including finding bodies for fighting positions, watch schedules, perimeter patrols, work details and normal logistics functions. She was partway through that when the "enemy" attacked on ACV skimmers. She dove outside to take cover and return fire, but couldn't find a fighting position. There was supposed to be one right outside the temp.

She burrowed into the snow in her mottled gray and white parka suit and prepared to engage any targets. None came near her position and all clear was called shortly. She rose, dusted off and went back inside. "Jackson!" she called.

"Yes, Corporal?" he responded, running in from the passage from the rear temp, which served as an ersatz loading bay.

"Where is my fighting position?"

"Um . . . I'm sorry, Corporal. I got distracted by some requisitions," he said, looking embarrassed.

"Well, please get undistracted and dig me one now. Unless you want me killed off in this exercise?" Red-faced, he grabbed a shovel and fuser from near the entrance and headed out.

That was about the only problem she encountered all week. She asked Sirkot about the problem and how to resolve it.

"You did, didn't you?" he asked.

"Well, yes, but doesn't it have to be written up?" she asked.

"What? For a basic mistake? Do they do that in the UN?" he asked.

"For every little detail," she confirmed.

"Bullshit," he said and sighed. "We must get you to leadership school. No, no, you're doing great. You are more than competent for a sergeant's slot, but you must learn the fine details. An error was made, an NCO corrected it, and that's as far as it goes. If it becomes a pattern, refer him to me, and if it doesn't stop then, *then* we'll write it up. How does the UN function with that much adminwork?"

"Uh, not as well as we do here," she admitted, and went back to work.

She still hated the vicious cold she encountered on her tasked infantry duty. The wind howled across the dunes of snow, which crunched under her snowshoes. Her visor polarized to cut the glare and cut the details, too, turning everything dull gray monochrome. She despised diving into the snow for cover and was only too glad to get back to the camp.

None of it was as bad as using a field latrine at -30 degrees. She apparently wasn't the only one with that opinion, because someone had taken a leak through the rear door of the shelter. She found the stained, melted snow, reported it, and thought Naumann was going to demand DNA analysis to identify the perpetrator. He ranted about sanitation and health and she was sure that the culprit was suitably scared. She was rather struck by his reaction herself.

Gealday morning, she again expected a disorganized mess, what was known in military parlance as a "clusterfuck." Again, it didn't happen.

The way it was supposed to work was that once marching orders were given, some few troops would proceed to try to get things done. Others would offer bad advice and get in the way. Still others would simply complain about how long it was taking and why couldn't everybody else hurry up? There'd be frayed tempers, all around incompetence and anger at "them" for not running a better operation.

Again, the Freehold forces declined to operate according to standard military procedures. The temp was being dismantled around Kendra as she stuffed her gear aboard the GUV. By the time she had all the equipment boxes she was signed for checked off and tagged for loading, she was standing on packed snow that had roughly the shape of the temp, outlined in banked snow where the walls had been. An engineer was dragging off their generator and heaters and the concealment netting was already crated with the admin squad's gear. The newest troops were filling in fighting positions and policing up trash. She began counting heads and realized most of them were already aboard the vertol. She was surprised and elated as she ran up the ramp. She dumped her data to Sirkot, who nodded and forwarded it, and within a seg, they lifted. The whole process had taken about sixty segs. Kendra fell asleep en route to catch up from the tiring schedule.

Once they were in the compound, before they had everything put away, Naumann's voice boomed through the air and the comms. "Listen up! After-action review tomorrow for all squad leaders and above. Overall, quite good, a few areas need some tweaking and tightening. *No more peeing in the snow!* Get the gear stowed and dismiss by squads. The unit will buy the first round at the club starting in one div. That is all."

There were a few cheers. Kendra decided she liked the way this military operated. She almost missed the morons and jerks who inevitably got in the way of real work. She was shortly educated to the fact that Freehold had them too.

Chapter 20

"Knavery and flattery are blood relations."
                                    —Abraham Lincoln

Sergeant Davis left the unit the following week. He had orders to the factory ship *Force*. Things were a bit hectic for the week after that, Kendra performing both his and her duties. Then his replacement arrived.

Her first impression of Sergeant Jim Wayland was a good one. He was outgoing, cheerful and imposingly big. He towered over her by a good ten centimeters. He shook hands and greeted everyone while cracking jokes.

"Kendra, glad to meet you," he said. "I'm looking forward to working with you."

"Jim," she said. He was brawny, with a craggy face and a goofy grin.

He immediately turned to Sirkot and didn't say another word to her. She figured he'd need some time to settle in and said nothing. He left shortly to finish inprocessing and she finished the workload for the day, although it took her an extra half-div.

Her perception changed as the week wore on. Jim seemed to find numerous excuses to miss appointments. He did good work, but only the bare minimum, leaving Kendra to pick up the slack. He missed PT completely on Ashday, claiming inprocessing incomplete. She sighed and ignored it. There was one in every shop.

Private Jackson did not get along well with him, either. Jackson was an arrogant twelve-year-old, but a damned good worker. He just had a bit more individualism than was good for him, a fairly common trait among Freeholders. It was still awkward to deal with in a military environment. She overheard one exchange.

"You don't understand, Jackson," Wayland was saying, condescension dripping from his voice. "You're a private, so you do the work. I'm an NCO, so I supervise."

"Sirkot told us both to do it," Jackson replied, "and it's a two person job. We'll be here all day if you sit on your ass."

"You'll bark like a dog if I tell you to," Wayland replied, laughing. It clearly wasn't intended to be derogatory, it was just a badly phrased attempt at humor. He seemed to need to make a joke of everything.

Shortly, Wayland left and was gone the rest of the day. He didn't inform anyone, and left invoices incomplete again. She exchanged looks with Sirkot.

The following week, Wayland loudly announced his intention to put in an application for an instructor slot at NCO Leadership School. Sirkot diplomatically replied, "While technically a sergeant can apply, no matter how good your fitreps are, you'll take second to any senior who applies."

Wayland nodded and acted as if he didn't hear. "It's all in who you blow. If they want someone, the rank doesn't matter."

"There is work you could do here, Jim," Kendra suggested.

"I'll get to it," he promised. He'd been promising that since he arrived. "Or I could make it worth your while to cover me, er, cover for me," he grinned, nodding with his whole upper body. Again, it clearly was intended as his necessary joke in every exchange. Kendra sighed and stared at her hand for a second.

"Please do not make sexual innuendoes, Sergeant," she said.

Nodding again, he replied, "Sorry." His face said he really wasn't. "Just think, though, if this works out I could be one of your instructors at NCOLS."

She didn't express her opinion of that idea.

They had a spaceside exercise the following week. Wayland actually did do all his prep work and the lift was smooth. Kendra hoped things were finally shaping up. An abrasive personality she could deal with, if the work was being done. She ignored his posturing and attempts at popularity as they lifted. It was going to be a long week.

The shuttle docked with a training ship. Rather than the usual cruiser, it was an antiquated frigate. The gangtube clanked into place and they swarmed across into the ugly, smelly little tub. They were crammed in like insects in a nest and were going to stay that way all week. The only good part was that she, Sirkot and Wayland were each on different shifts. Her fears had included being assigned under the loud jerk or sharing a battle station with him. His continued innuendoes had made her uncomfortable with the idea of being naked in front of him. She knew it was silly, but he brought out all her old hang-ups. "Naked" equaled "defenseless" in her mind.

They commenced combat simulations immediately, including an attempted boarding complete to a "blown" bulkhead. It was at shift change, and Kendra was quite close to the blast. She slapped her facemask against possible vacuum, grabbed a stanchion while snapping a quick-release line to it and shouldered her weapon. She braced a foot to prevent being twisted from recoil in the microgravity and waited.

It was only a harassing attack, designed to deprive one shift of sleep and make chow late. She recovered and headed back to her bunkroom. Wayland was just coming down the hall and nodded to her. He was talking enthusiastically to Warrant Leader Shemanski, the 3rd MAR's enlisted staffing chief. No doubt bucking for his leadership school slot that he wasn't going to get. And he wasn't wearing a secondary oxy bottle. Typical. That gave him five divs of breathing in the exercise bottle and no backup in case of a malfunction. He could be dead of suffocation before anyone could respond. That was a serious violation of the exercise rules, as well as lethally stupid.

At the end of her next shift, Jackson straggled into her cramped cubicle as she got ready to try to sleep. She found emgee disorienting and didn't enjoy it as some did. To make it worse, Wayland had come over from his bunkroom and was cracking loud jokes, trying to be the center of attention yet again. "Nice ass, Gorman," he snickered, flexing at the waist for his usual nodding accompaniment. "Wanna shower?"

She looked over, exasperated, as Gorman replied and Wayland retaliated again with, "But you get me hotter than a two-peckered billygoat!" She caught Jackson trying to catch her eye surreptitiously and nodded acknowledgment. She shimmied out of her sleeping bag and grabbed her mask and bottles. She was wearing nothing but a dull gray briefer and when Wayland saw the movement he shouted, "You look better in blue, Kendra. Maybe something lacy and tight?"

"Jim, just blow it out your ass," she snapped.

Looking offended, he replied, "Crap, lady, it's just a joke." His grin was condescending, as if he had no idea why she was offended. He probably didn't.

She swam into the passage behind Jackson and hunched into a corner to get some privacy. "What's up?" she prompted.

"It's Sergeant Wayland," he said.

She'd already figured that out and prompted him, "What now?"

"He is really bugging me with his gay humor, for one. His jokes cross the line from funny to . . . discomforting," he said. She nodded. While no one cared and private lives were kept strictly private, she'd figured out that Jackson was gay and shy about it. As unpleasant as she found the humor, he had to hate it worse.

"I'll mention it to Sirkot again and insist on counseling," she promised. "He's an utter creep. In your case, he's joking to annoy you. In my case, he wants me sexually." She shivered at the image, then shivered again. She hadn't realized it before, but it *was* a power game for him.

Jackson glanced around, clearly bothered, "But if you have him counseled, he'll take it out on me," he said.

Shrugging was awkward in emgee. "I don't know what else to do," she said. "He won't take hints. I've tried."

"Okay, Corporal," Jackson agreed. "And I want to change shifts. Please. He keeps plowing his work off on me and claiming he's 'supervising' while he licks the ass of the nearest officer. I almost dragged off and hit him yesterday," he admitted.

"Okay," she said, fingers rubbing her eyes, "if you get to that point again, *immediately* come and see me. If he asks, tell him you have an appointment with Sirkot. Apologize for forgetting and get out of there. I'll cover for you." This was bad. "I'll see if Beker can be persuaded to switch. She'll rip his head off if he says anything and with her father being a colonel, he won't do anything except complain," she offered.

"Thanks, Corporal," he sighed in relief. "I'll try to deal with one more shift."

Once back on the ground and at the compound, Naumann gave his usual postmortem. "Outstanding exercise," he yelled, looking impressed. "Tight, smooth and with all objectives accomplished, which gave battle staff the chance to improvise additional activity. See you at the club," he finished.

Kendra didn't feel enthused. Two of her six troops were on edge, since Beker had had a shouting match with Wayland. She'd dressed him down but good, too. Jackson was still a bundle of nerves and Kendra wanted to scream in frustration. Sirkot had noted her complaints and promised to get some action, but pointed out that not only was logistics a critical slot, but one of Naumann's areas of high demand, and there were very few NCOs available for the slot. There wasn't much to be done officially without making them all pay.

Then Sirkot dropped another bomb. "The commander noted some discrepancies on Jackson's final shift. He signed all boxes as inspected and three of them were not sealed. Two helmet modules were missing, but were turned in, fortunately. He wants a reprimand issued."

Sighing, Kendra said, "It wasn't Jackson. That had

to be Wayland goofing off again. He's great at impressing visiting officers, but no good at actually doing any work."

"I know," he agreed. "But we can't document it and Jackson signed for it." Wayland walked in at that moment.

"What's up with Jackson?" he asked, sounding genuinely concerned. After Sirkot explained, without mentioning Wayland's role, the man nodded. "I told him they were done, but I hadn't banded them. That was my fault," he admitted.

Kendra was confused by the man. If he'd stop acting so immaturely, he had definite potential. As it was, she didn't want to be in the same system with him.

"Alright, I'll straighten it out," Sirkot promised. He looked as tired as Kendra felt.

She went home to Marta's that night after a brief appearance at the party. Both her lovers were expecting her to be tired, but eagerly romantic. One look at her and Marta stripped her, dunked her into the hot tub and proceeded to massage her shoulders. "Goddess, love, you're as stiff as a board," Marta said. Rob handed her a drink and jumped in across from her. He began rubbing her calves.

After a few segs of relaxation, she described the situation to them. Marta sounded angry. Rob just nodded. "I've seen the type before," he said. "They tear a unit apart, generally drive about five people into resigning, then get sent elsewhere because no one can prove anything worthwhile. They suck too much cock to be properly nailed," he swore.

"So you're the officer, how do I handle it?" she asked.

"Keep on it. Of course, you may get sucked in yourself. He's good at passing the blame, I'll bet," he mused.

Marta complained, "Rob, you're making her tense again. Now I have to start over!"

"Sorry," he said.

Getting back on track, Kendra said, "*Nothing* sticks to him. He rides right on the edge of allowable behavior and never quite crosses it!"

"Which is more annoying than a bona fide insubordinate," Rob nodded agreement.

"Yes," she said and explained Wayland's admission of error and her surprise at it.

Rob looked thoughtful, "Well, that's not unusual. He doesn't mean to be an asshole, he's just insecure and sociopathic. He'd do well in Earth politics," he half joked. "Do you want me to talk to Naumann? As a reservist and an officer, I can say things you can't," he suggested.

"I don't want to pull favorites," she replied, "but thanks."

She was far too wound up to do anything romantic and lay in the bed in sleepless frustration, listening jealously to Mar moan and pant in impassioned fury through an allegedly soundproof wall. She waited for sleep to come.

Jackson managed to avoid trouble over the incident. Kendra found herself in Naumann's office with Sirkot, promising to counsel her troop to double-check anything handed to him.

"I apologize for having teams split across shifts," Sirkot said. "I was trying to balance experience levels. No harm was done and I don't want you feeling responsible for an error that wasn't under your control."

"Yes, sir, thank you," she said. "There's one more item I need to address," she added to Naumann.

She told him of Wayland's lack of an emergency oxy bottle. "I thought it was just an accident," she said, "but

he did it at least three times and also wasn't carrying
a basic load for his weapon. He said if he fired it, he'd
have to clean it."

Naumann ran his hand through his hair. "Right.
Warrant Sirkot? I'll take it from here, if you don't
mind?" he said rather than asked. Sirkot agreed, looking
grateful. Kendra saluted and left in a hurry.

Back at the shop, there was more trouble. Someone had posted a sign on the wall that read,

> **Why Jim Wayland is like a fart:**
> **He's loud**
> **He stinks**
> **He rose above his point of origin**
> **No one knows where he came from**
> **He won't go back there**
> **We never wanted him in the first place**
> **Any asshole could produce another one.**

It was obviously Jackson's work. Sirkot was over
talking to Naumann, which left Wayland in charge. He
was out back, berating Jackson quietly. As she
approached, he said, "Kendra, would you come here
please?"

She sighed and nodded. He continued, "This is
for the record." He turned back to Jackson, who
looked like a dog that had been kicked. "Private
Jackson, I don't like doing this, but I don't have any
choice. From now on, you will address me as 'Sergeant' at all times. You will not use any terms of
familiarity. You will not make any comments. You will
follow my orders to the letter and you will address
any concerns through the chain of command. Do you
understand?"

Eyes almost tearing, Jackson replied, "Yes, Sergeant
Wayland."

"Good," Wayland replied, sounding sad. "I'm sorry it's come down to this, but I don't have any choice. I've tried to be friendly and there's one or two people who just can't deal with it. So we'll just be formal and avoid any trouble."

Kendra was furious. She turned, looked up at him and said, "Then may I suggest, *Sergeant* Wayland, that you address issues with *my* troops through me or the squad leader. That is what the chain of command is for. And you can *immediately* cease any comments of a sexual nature, no matter how funny you think they might be, to either Private Jackson or myself, since we have asked you repeatedly to stop."

He looked stunned. Then he came back with, "I don't know how they do things in the UN, Pacelli, but this is the Freehold. You have to learn to joke. They aren't issued from the government here." He grinned the stupid grin she wanted to hit.

Jackson suddenly cut in. "Look, you conceited piece of shit," he shouted. A couple of the loading crew and drivers turned their heads at that. "If you can't take it, you better not dish it out in the first place. You're an obnoxious bigot, utterly incompetent and a disgrace to the uniform!"

Kendra hadn't known he had it in him. She applauded inside, while sighing. "Be sure of your language, Jackson," she said, knowing it was too late.

Wayland got an angry gleam in his eyes. "All right, asshole, if that's how you want to play it," he said. "I will be filing formal charges of insubordination. Since you seem to be the only person here who can't tell a joke when you hear one and can't seem to keep a military bearing, we'll just see where we go. First, you stand at attention when I am talking to you," he stormed. His voice was much louder. The loaders looked over again. Jackson tiredly stiffened to attention. Wayland strutted back and forth as he continued, "You haven't been able to act in a proper military fashion since the day I got here, you keep sneaking behind my back, trying to ignore my authority," he stopped pacing and stared down at the young troop, "trying to write up every little infraction you think you've found, posting insults in public . . ." He went on, but Kendra tuned him out. She'd flipped her comm to record and was letting it hear all this for later.

It was just then that Naumann appeared, Sirkot behind him. He silently approached, directly behind Wayland, and stopped to listen to the monologue.

"Attention," he said.

Wayland turned and threw a quick salute. "Oh, hello, Commander. Getting things ready for the rescue exercise?" The change in manner was instantaneous and amazing. His posture and body language immediately became open and friendly.

"I said 'attention,'" the commander repeated, raising his voice just barely, his expression blank.

Wayland slid into a belated brace and looked down at the far shorter officer. He looked confused and a bit worried. Almost as if discipline was a foreign concept to him. Well, it was.

Naumann paced around the trio as he said, "I spoke to Commander Lewis at First Legion. He warned me that you like to suck up."

He indicated Kendra and Jackson should back out of his way with a glance and walked through the space they'd occupied then turned around in front of Wayland again. Sirkot simply watched. "Not that I need such a warning. I've seen your type before. You crawl under the desk and try to blow the commander's ego."

He was behind Wayland now, who looked very

confused. It might be the first time he'd ever been dressed down publicly. Naumann leaned to speak up toward his ear. "I already have a big enough ego without your help," he said.

"I've given you several chances and I know Warrant Leader Sirkot has mentioned it to you. In fact, I have complaints from several sources, including at least two *outside* the unit. Also a few blind idiots who think you are the greatest leader since Napoleon. But they're all young and impressionable or layabouts going nowhere.

"So, we'll make this easy. You'll sign a resignation and get out. I understand they usually reassign you. I don't want to be embarrassed by passing you off on anyone else."

"Sir, if there's a misunderstanding, I—" Wayland said and was cut off.

"I may be the first commander you've had who actually has understood you," Naumann said. "You moved into a smooth unit and turned everything upside down. You're not even a BTB clown," he said, using the acronym for "by the book." "You use the regs to hurt anyone who won't kiss your hairy ass and ignore them when they get in your way. I won't argue with you. I'm just kicking you out."

"I'm not aware of any violations, sir. I think I'll have to insist on formal charges," Wayland replied. He sounded a lot meeker, his voice thinner and less sure.

Naumann spoke without looking up. "Pacelli."

"Sir."

"You can provide documentation of Sergeant Wayland's actions?" It wasn't really a question.

"Yes, sir!" she agreed. She was enjoying seeing him nail the jerk. A grin kept trying to cross her face.

Naumann continued to his victim, "I can easily support charges of conduct prejudicial to good order, conduct unbecoming an NCO, abuse of authority for personal gain, provocative speech or actions, sexual harassment . . ." He glanced at Kendra and Jackson. Yes, they'd been jokes, and the Freehold gave much more leeway along those lines, but the intent of them was to establish control. That made them technically actionable. Kendra wondered how he'd heard? Or was he assuming based on available evidence? " . . . Violation of safety regulations in a hazardous environment for your stunts in orbit and your platoon leader's report of your inability to accomplish assigned tasks in a timely manner."

Wayland opened his mouth, but Naumann continued, more loudly, "All of which are utter bullshit charges. Which is no reflection on the charges. It is a reflection on you. I prefer not to smear the unit with that kind of crap, which is why I want your resignation. I don't give a damn about you. You've abused my good graces."

Wayland's eyes were actually damp. Clearly he'd never been called out before. His whole mock-friendly manner and size intimidated people into giving him what he asked for or charmed then into willingly going along with his schemes. "Yes, sir," he whispered. He looked stunned.

Naumann flipped his comm open and said, "Security."

"Yes, Commander Naumann?" came the reply.

"Mister Wayland is to be escorted from the base. All his personal effects and he are to be out the gate by five. And I need an escort for him now."

"Yes, Commander," was the acknowledgment.

There was a pregnant silence for the long seconds until a private from security jogged over. Naumann said, "Escort Mister Wayland to the orderly room to resign. Observe but do not help as he gathers his personal gear and see him out the gate by five. And get him out of that uniform." He didn't bother to wait for acknowledgment.

Finally turning to the others, he said, "Private Jackson."

"Yes, sir!" Jackson snapped. He might be cocky, but Kendra had to admit he was earnest.

"Did you use inappropriate language to an NCO?" He stared levelly at the young man.

"Yes, sir," Jackson admitted.

"You will serve three divs extra duty this week. Since Corporal Pacelli has to cover additional work, you can do whatever grunt labor she has. In future, address complaints through your chain of command."

"Yes, sir," he agreed, obviously relieved.

Naumann continued, "Pacelli."

"Yes, sir?" she asked.

"We do not have another NCO lined up for that slot. You have been doing the NCO's work. I will be asking Warrant Sirkot to move you into that slot. That's an additional pay grade," he said.

"Yes, sir," she acknowledged. That was fast. She was now the number two person in the logistics front office.

"You will not be coming on the search exercise," he said. "I will be sending you to NCOLS. Don't screw up. I need you back here ASAP. We'll borrow a reservist or two for the time being."

"Yes, sir!" she agreed.

Chapter 21

"The more you sweat in peace, the less you bleed in war."

—old military proverb

The Freehold Military Forces Noncommissioned Officer Leadership School was known informally as "Tac Tech." Kendra had been surprised to find technical mathematics a prerequisite. She heard talk of "Tactical Calculus" around her unit and it had taken a while to realize it was an actual subject. Not only that, but it was heavily stressed for the entire four weeks of the course.

She caught a commercial flight on a ballistic shuttle. It was quick, jolting from high gees to emgee to maneuvers and landing. She was picked up by the base taxi and taken to billeting. This time, she had an NCO's room to herself, with standard hotel housekeeping service. She handed over the chip with her orders and her military credcard and checked in.

She arrived at class and was grateful to find coffee. Not instant, either. That boded well. Her class had barely ten students and they exchanged assessing looks. There was curiosity about her UN medal and questions for the lone soldier from Special Warfare, who looked far too meek to be a professional killer.

Seconds later, their instructor arrived.

"Communications is the key to modern warfare," Senior Sergeant Instructor Hugh Oleg announced as he strode into the room. "When I say, '*Room, ten shut!*' you all know what I mean. As you were," he said, releasing them from their instantaneous reactive brace. They resumed their seats.

"You'd probably understand it delivered in any language in this environment. If, however, I'd used, say, Russian to order everyone to stand on one foot, it's doubtful you'd understand it in this context."

He handed out three cards. Kendra got the second one. "Turn around and face the back wall," he ordered them. After they did, he said, "Mr. Langston, please stand at the board. You will be advised to draw the images the other students are holding. They will not be able to see your work for feedback. You may not speak. Ms Anderson, please begin."

Corporal Jenny Anderson hesitated only a moment then said, "This image is an equilateral right triangle, with sides at right and below as I look at them. The sides are approximately twelve centimeters long by estimation." Langston easily drew what she described.

It seemed simple enough to Kendra. Oleg was not satisfied. "What about this break in the line?" he asked her.

"I thought that was just a smudge. Sorry, sir."

"'Sorry' won't save lives. Every detail is important. Mr. Dubois, you're next."

Dubois began, "Langston, the image in front of me is a square constructed of translucent panels. We are going to rearrange them to form the shape of a capital T, sans serif," he said. There were a couple of snickers at the detail. "Place the red triangle at upper right. Immediately to its right, place the yellow triangle, below the corner and with the hypotenuses facing." There were giggles and chuckles at this point, because the instructions were not clear. "To the left place the blue rectangle, horizontal and aligned with the upper edge . . ." He went on and the laughs turned into hysterical guffaws.

After several segs, Oleg halted the proceedings. "Ms Pacelli, let's see if you can unravel this."

She turned her own card over and stared at it. It was the same problem, but the instructions Dubois had given made no sense. Then everything snapped into place. "Langston, ignore all colors. The large triangle goes at upper right, one side horizontal, hypotenuse to the right and underneath. The smaller triangle aligns hypotenuse to hypotenuse and at the right edge to create the right bight of the T's cross. The smaller of the two rectangles aligns with the figure so far and is horizontal to create the left bight . . ."

In seconds she was done and when she turned, Langston had it correct. He had one set of colors for his components, Dubois another and she a third. "Color blindness," she said aloud.

"That's one consideration," Oleg said. "Or the parts may actually be painted different colors from different generations of production. Each culture has its own assumptions regarding color, too. Lack of feedback can be due to either technical problems or because of assumptions that mean the mistake is overlooked until much later . . ."

It was a busy first morning. The afternoon was spent on tactical calculus. " 'It is impossible to predict all factors, but maximum accurate appraisal of the ones available will minimize errors.' That's what the book says. Now let's see where we go." It was fascinating, and there was a definite irony to reducing people to numbers for calculating battles. Kendra bogged down at first, but then caught on suddenly.

Oleg was flashing loads of data across their screens. "General terrain is represented by this algorithm and by entering grid coordinates of features here, their shapes and heights here, you can get a fair assessment of where to place your troops for a given objective. Then, plug in the relative numerical strengths of the units and enter any support weapons known. Now this is important," he paused to drive the point home. "You must *honestly* rate the estimated skill and training of the engaged units. If you lie to yourself about how great you are, you'll get killed that much faster. Too low and your attrition rate can suffer or you may fail the objective by not moving fast enough. Now, desired time to completion goes here . . ."

It did not, Kendra discovered, make command decisions any less complex. It created additional problems of finding the best data possible from all sources. They ran through numerous practice problems. They were reminded that this was simply introductory and that they'd be expected to practice further, with and without a comm, to improve their skills. "Wait until Senior NCO Academy," Oleg promised.

The day was a solid four divs long, eleven Earth hours, she thought, still converting occasionally. Kendra was exhausted, collapsed at once, and was barely conscious in time for the second day. As she sat moping into her coffee, Oleg strode into the room. "Logistics is the key to modern warfare," he said to begin the second lecture.

Communication, logistics, air power, intel, artillery, engineers, forward support, special warfare and other force multipliers. Every day another subject was thrown at them. Every evening, they read books from their required lists, while hyped on stims to improve their comprehension rate. It was a grueling, mind-numbing course and they had little time off even on the weekends. Twenty days of intense cramming was harder on the body than starvation and confinement. Kendra found herself eagerly looking forward to the mandatory exercise times, simply to work the knots out.

It was the second week that all the classes then in session, from first day to graduation, were gathered in the auditorium to hear a guest lecturer on strategy and politics. The lecturer was Naumann. He displayed an amazing breadth of knowledge of history and psychology, and Kendra was impressed by the sheer brilliance of his deductions and connection of such diverse subjects. She recorded and watched with interest as he finalized the talk with a summation of its relevancy to them.

"The basic flaw with the UN system is that it is based not on trust, but on force. Rather than a cooperative peace mission, it is an attempt to impose order from outside.

"Peace at the muzzle of a rifle is not peace, but imperialism and slavery. The UN points to its two hundred and sixty-three engagements as proof that the system is working, when in fact, it proves the opposite. From a military viewpoint, Sun Tzu teaches us that 'Hence to fight and conquer in all your battles is not supreme excellence; supreme excellence consists in breaking the enemy's resistance without fighting.'

"So obviously, the resident states of the UN are *not* sufficiently intimidated by the 'Peace' Force. They continue to rebel. The force is insufficient and unwelcome, yet they continue to attempt to impose it on each other.

"For comparison, the Freehold's government is a tiny fraction of a percentage. The residents are more numerous than and equivalently armed to the military. They are the defacto military. Power in a society lies with the military and who it will follow, rules. At any time, the residents could eliminate the government through revolution and demand or create a new one. The fact that they don't indicates a true willingness to make our system work. The basis of the system is maximum individual freedom and mutual trust between governors and governed. The UN is an authoritarian system, assuming ill intentions of all and holding the threat of punitive action as a means of control.

"This is why the UN *cannot* allow the existence of the Freehold. It is inevitable that some individuals will look to us as an example to aspire to or worse and more likely, with jealousy for our benefits. By not preventing it, the UN is giving tacit consent to our existence. Their governed will eventually ask 'why?' and there will not be a good answer the rulers can give. So they will inevitably attempt to destroy us.

"They have made diplomatic gestures of providing us with the 'systems' we lack, such as state-sponsored pensions and education. There is no way of bridging the difference in mindset, of explaining that any government-supported system is by definition government controlled and therefore authoritative and subject to abuse without possibility of objection. They cannot understand our rejection of what they perceive as generous offers.

"Their following offers were based on the assumption that such systems would need to be different, given the distance from Earth. They cannot see that our sociological assumption is that such systems must not be allowed to exist, no matter the real or perceived benefits. They are continuing to attempt to fix what we consider unfixable and have abandoned.

"Then force was applied, first politically and economically. With no restrictions on trade, our economy will—and has—shifted to other areas where necessary. The effect will be minor from a systemic viewpoint. Since there is no effective way for an authoritarian system to control the free market of a foreign power, we will suffer negligibly, while the member nations of the UN will find themselves losing essential luxuries that keep the population in check. We will be blamed for the loss. Once seen as offenders, it will be increasingly easy to use us as a scapegoat for *any* domestic problems, by inference and allegation. Such accusations will have the barest truth to them, but from such are the greatest lies knit.

"Physical force will ensue, probably after several engineered incidents to show us as oppressors of the individual. To an authoritarian, oppression of an individual translates as 'middle class oppressing the poor.' It is axiomatic that the ruling class truly cares for the peasants and is protecting the have-nots from the hated haves. The UN system is composed of 'equal' members, with some having the necessary inevitable privileges of the ruling class. To quote Orwell, 'All animals are equal, but some are more equal than others.'" Kendra had not until now been familiar with Orwell. His works, unavailable on Earth, were required reading for this school.

"It is important to note that members of ruling bodies usually fall in the upper point one percentile of individual wealth and wield power all out of proportion even to that extreme. When they talk of 'taxing the rich,' they are never referring to themselves. The laughingly called two-party system of the United States in the late twentieth and early twenty-first centuries consisted of two groups of predominantly inherited millionaires, one claiming to help the poor, one the middle class. In both cases, the taxes were disproportionately leveled on the lower and middle classes, not on the rich or themselves. Ironically, the party claiming most to care about the poor, whom we now refer to as neo-feudalists, had a thirty-percent higher ratio of millionaires than did its opponents.

"So the UN will attempt subversion of the Citizens, promising wealth and power under UN aegis, if they will help tax the 'rich' middle class to support the 'poor,' defined fluidly as anyone who can look and see others financially better off. In such a system, most of those 'poor' will wind up poorer, but because the 'rich' are being punished for the sin of being competent and successful, that injustice will be overlooked. The system is simply class warfare. A popular phrase from the late twentieth century US reads, 'Tax the rich to feed the poor, until there are no rich no more.' Stripped of its awkward grammar, this translates as destroying the wealthy who supposedly must support the poor. It was apparently forgotten that the original goal was to feed those poor.

"Such hatred is easy to foment, even in a system such as ours. Few people ever think of the differences in culture between themselves and those in other wealth brackets. It is always assumed that others lead essentially the same life, just with finer or poorer trappings associated with it. The extremely wealthy cannot visualize the relative expense of basics such as food to someone on a subsistence-level income and the poor view the rich as having more disposable income without any additional operating expenses, social obligations or risks.

"So the UN will attempt to create a class war here, then apply military force to 'abolish' the classes and set up its own governors, most of whom will be corrupt and sent to this 'remote' assignment as punishment. They will embezzle and defraud what they feel is due them for 'tolerating' the local population.

"The only question is 'when?'

"Official estimates range from four to twenty-five years. The Strategic Staff all agree that politico-diplomatic relations are heading that way. The UN Forces are changing their training to add more rural engagements. There have been several researchers and 'observers' from various technical and leadership branches of the UNPF here."

A soldier in back stood to attention and asked, "When do *you* believe it will be, Commander?"

Grinning slightly, Naumann replied, "I'm at variance with the Strategic Staff and I've been told not to express my opinion as a prediction. So my *opinion* is that we will engage here within the year."

Kendra sat up. Several others looked shocked, also. War within the year? With Earth? She had more reason than most to fear that. She'd been told her whole life on Earth that war was impossible. Her current training made her see the lie in that theory and her thoughts whirled. Where would she wind up?

The concept of war continued to bother her the entire way through school, but she managed a decently passing grade anyway. If Naumann was right, what would happen to her? They couldn't trust an expatriate from the future enemy. Her friends were loyal, but fiercely patriotic and dedicated and if they were forbidden contact she was sure they'd comply with the order, however reluctantly. She decided not to raise the issue with them. She'd rather not confirm her fears of what they'd do.

The combat sim was almost familiar by now. It differed in that Kendra was a fireteam leader. She took her fireteam out under the squad leader's direction and promptly got most of them, and herself, "killed." Then it happened again. She realized just how hard it was to coordinate six people at once in what was accurately called "the fog of war." At least she knew which side she was on now. The losing side. She recalled a comment Naumann had made, to the effect of "If your plan is working perfectly, you are about to lose." She smiled at the truism.

She took the entire weekend to relax after her return, spending lots of time soaking in the tub, being massaged and doing nothing. The strain had been awful. She was elated despite her worry, though. She was finally a fully-trained soldier and felt confident of her ability to handle anything.

The war started two weeks later.

Chapter 22

"Give me your tired, your poor,
  Your huddled masses yearning to breathe free,
  The wretched refuse of your teeming shore.
  Send these, the homeless, tempest-tost to me,
  I lift my lamp beside the golden door."
        —Emma Lazarus, "The New Colossus"

The watch at Station Ceileidh was usually a hectic but routine matter of shipping. Gigatons of material, data and people moved between Earth and Freehold daily.

That routine was suddenly broken when a traffic technician yelled, "Holy *shit*!"

"What is it, Sergeant?" asked the watch commander.

"Six ships, Lieutenant, and you'd better look at this," the technician said, gratefully handing the situation over.

The Citizen's Council held an emergency meeting by vid, those not present insystem represented by proxy.

Treasurer Griffiths had the most recent update on the station and explained the situation.

"We have six ships, barely functional, computer-piloted. Minimal support. They were loaded up on the Earth side of the point and sent through to us. Occupants are over one hundred thousand political deportees. We have to come to an immediate decision on what to do."

"Observer Naumann, military. Send them back."

"Griffiths speaking. Not possible. The drives need repair, the life support is failing. They were stuffed in and shipped. Several thousand are casualties already. They're here to stay."

"Naumann speaking. Scuttle the damned things and be done with it."

"Great Godde—Uddin speaking. Who let you in here, Naumann? Just murder a hundred thousand people out of convenience? And who are you to speak?"

"Dyson speaking. The commander is here at my request to provide a purely tactical input. I agree that the presence of these persons is intended as provocative. I recommend we find a way to get rid of them. Preferably alive."

"Uddin speaking. 'Preferably,' Marshal? If they're here, then we have to do what we can to help them. It's not their fault the UN is using them as pawns."

"Chinratana speaking. The problem I see is that these are malcontents and troublemakers. They are not psychologically suited to our system. They are predominantly untrained and the few who are trained will be reluctant to work. Their numbers are great enough to be a problem anywhere we settle them. I don't want to kill them, but we don't have the resources to support them, either."

It was agreed that the refugees not be killed. The wrangling on any further action took hours. Some

suggested forwarding them to another system or back
to Earth even if it was necessary to provide ships. "No
good," Griffiths advised. "The news in Sol System is
that we agreed to take them. They'll make a PR
slaughter out of this if any of them die."

"Uddin speaking. When did we agree to that?"

"Hernandez speaking. Apparently, they are claiming
it under the old Colonial Code."

"Uddin speaking. But we aren't a colony anymore."

"Hernandez speaking. I know that, Citizen, and you
know that—"

"Understood."

The final decision was to allow them in and disperse
then throughout the Freehold's cities and habitats. It
may have been the most humane decision possible. In
the long view, it was not the best.

The crowd was roaring and almost moblike. The
sergeant needed the amplifier to be heard. "Listen
up! . . . *Listen up!* . . . All right. We are about to start
processing everyone for admittance to the Freehold.
You will proceed through these doors," he indicated
them to either side of him, "and will be mediscanned.
You will then board shuttles and be transported to
various cities. Families will be kept together. If there
are any problems, please be sure to let someone know
and we will do what we can to help you."

The noise rose again and the crowd surged toward
the doors. The guards there found it necessary to use
minor force against the angry, demanding throng.

The processing would take several days and would
not be without its delays. The first of those came within
segs.

"Lady," the corporal medic insisted politely but
firmly, "in order to be allowed access to the Freehold, you and your children *must* be treated to assure

no diseases are admitted. We can make no exceptions."

"God does not allow his faithful to become ill, except as part of His Plan," she replied. "I refuse to let you interfere," she said, angry but with forced calm. "I have freedom of religious expression."

They argued for several segs, until finally the corporal called a superior. The problem was bumped up to a lieutenant before it could be resolved. He drew the corporal aside and said, "We'll check for contamination and quarantine her for two weeks. If it checks out, we'll admit her. But keep it quiet; we don't need several thousand idiots doing it just to avoid a nano."

The woman argued mightily against having blood, exhalation, urine or any other test. After multiple assurances that only observation would be performed and nothing given to her, she relented.

There were immediate problems as the malcontents were landed or docked in various cities. They'd all been shipped from Earth for various infractions, from multiple "petty" assaults and thefts, to rioting, looting and political offenses including protest and political rebellion.

Most were either unsuited for or utterly unwilling to work. This was not a problem that the Council would normally worry about. They'd either adapt or die and neither was an issue relevant to the minimal powers of the Freehold's government. What made it important was the foreign press, who were sure to publicize any "oppression" across space. There'd been a lot of wrangling, but the final decision was that any exception to the existing system, besides being unconstitutional and outside the legal bounds of the Council, was a bad precedent for the future. Integrity was decided, not without protest, as being more important than appeasement even on a galactic scale. Everyone held their breaths as the newcomers landed, demanded their "rights" and were told that the only right in the Freehold was to work or starve. Some laughed, others complained, most assumed the threat was a bluff. It was neither threat nor bluff, being merely a statement of fact.

Chapter 23

"Arms discourage and keep the invader and
plunderer in awe, and preserve order in the world
as well as property . . . Horrid mischief would
ensue were the law-abiding deprived of the use of
them."

—Thomas Paine

The three young men wandered into the bazaar and
separated slightly. They had long practice at being far
enough apart to deny involvement and close enough
for backup. They kept an eye on a table of jewelry. It
was not even cased, but lying out on a table. There
were no cops visible anywhere, the nearest had been
across the street at a restaurant. These people deserved
to be robbed. Two of them edged closer as the third
wandered away.

The first one idly pushed the second, who caught
himself on the edge of the table, surreptitiously sliding a necklace off. He regained his balance, snapping

at his accomplice and making a show of pushing back while pocketing the stones. They continued walking.

"Excuse me!" the table's owner, a small, slender woman shouted. "That's my necklace!"

The two gangers slipped easily into Plan B. The thief whirled, stepped toe-to-toe with her and screamed down at her. "Ya callin me a thief, snatch?"

The second one viciously pushed her into her table. It collapsed, spilling sparkling metal and stones across the grass. He drew back his foot to deliver a kick, only to notice the crowd moving closer. They should have been running or pointedly ignoring the scene, not interfering. He spun aside, dragged a cheap knife he'd found in the trash out of a pocket and held it out. His grip made it seem more of a talisman than an actual weapon. "Someone wanna *fuck* wid me?"

His wrist was suddenly clamped and bent into itself. The blade, still in his hand, punched into his kidney. Before the streak of pain properly registered, a massive weight crashed into his skull, behind the right ear.

The third one found a *whole table* full of guns! The array was bewildering, gadgets and mechanisms he didn't recognize at all. This place was heaven for a person trying to get what he deserved from life.

That one looked familiar and he picked it up. "Ya got pops for this?" he asked, grinning.

"Ammo?" the dealer queried. "Sure. You want ball, explosive, tracer . . . ?"

"Explosive! Hell yeah, man!" Unbelievable.

He took the offered box very carefully, put the gun down and loaded three into the magazine. "I'll take it," he said and made a show of reaching into a pocket. As the salesman nodded and reached for a box, he moved quickly, shoving the magazine home and cycling the slide. He jammed it forward toward the proprietor's chest, yanked the trigger, turned while snagging the box of shells and dug down to sprint.

Several reports, from suppressed pops to unadulterated roars sounded. He felt the freezing burn of bullets entering him and dropped convulsing.

"You okay, Gerry?" he heard a voice ask.

"I'm good, Shard." the gun dealer replied, coughing. "Damn moron shoulda used ball ammo against my vest. How's he?"

"Who cares?" was the response, hazily overhead. "He isn't moving, so he isn't a threat. I'll call City Safety."

"Thanks. Five years wearing this thing in case of an accidental discharge and some little fuck tries to murder me. What are the odds on that?"

The hood vaguely realized he was bleeding to death and wouldn't survive to see an ambulance.

There were hundreds of similar incidents across the system that week. They tapered off on a rapid curve, not because the perpetrators learned, but because they died. Human evolution had all but ended on Earth once man controlled his environment. But Darwinism still existed and those who couldn't adapt to massive changes in environment could still die.

Some who didn't adapt still managed to survive. That was not necessarily a positive outcome, either.

Chapter 24

"When constabulary duty's to be done
A policeman's lot is not a happy one."
—William S. Gilbert, *The Pirates of Penzance*

An annoying buzz woke Kendra. She was lodged on base again, being too busy to travel from what was sadly becoming less and less home. She grasped about, half blind, until she reached her comm. "Logistics Two, Pacelli," she answered.

"Automatic message. All personnel report to Third MAR Operations immediately. This is not an exercise. Say again, All personnel report to Regimental Operations. This is not an exercise. Automatic message . . ."

She was wide awake. Not an exercise. Her stomach flip-flopped as she dragged a uniform on, grabbed her field pack and ran. She sprinted outside and started walking for her car, but a carryall pulled up next to her. It was Lieutenant Smith from Engineering. "Climb on," he yelled and one of the mass of people in the bed reached an arm down to her. She heaved herself aboard and grabbed the side as he took off again. They were at the unit's compound in two segs.

As soon as she jumped down, she punched in a belated acknowledgment and reported present. She lined up behind Sirkot, counted to make sure her team was all present. Three were not, but the comm reported them en route. She reported Second Team accounted for and looked up in time to grab a visor extension that was tossed at her. *"Riot control, downtown,"* Naumann bellowed without need of amplification. His voice echoed through her comm as well, but he liked to shout orders. Old-fashioned, but good practice for comm failure, he claimed. She thought he just liked to shout. *"Load in paired squads, in order."*

That would put her squad on the third craft. Sirkot turned and said, "Grab a case of binders and an extra case of ammo. Make sure we have water."

"Yes, Warrant," she acknowledged. "Beker, report to me when Monahan and Lee get here. Jackson, come with me," she ordered in turn.

They sprinted the ten meters to their building. She coded the door and authorized issue on her comm. Jackson grabbed the ammo, she the binders, which were single-use polymer handcuffs, and added a case of field dressings. Sirkot had relayed his advisory on water and a line of troops appeared at the spigots by the door. She locked up, butted in line for water and headed back to the middle. Her comm showed Fourth Squad present and she handed the gear up to Sirkot, explaining about the field dressings.

"Good idea," he agreed.

The howl of vertols sounded and they moved back to allow space for landing. The first one filled and lifted in seconds, then the second. They swarmed aboard the third one and grasped the cargo netting as the pilot jumped into the sky. Wind buffeted them through the open side hatch as they tore straight toward downtown. It was a very brief flight, and rather than drift through the buildings, the pilot hovered above an intersection as they fast-roped down to save time. It would also be of tactical and psychological advantage over whoever they were to face.

Kendra was on the first drop, falling dizzyingly between the buildings to land in the middle of a crowd. Most of them had hastily drawn back as the ropes dropped, but some few tried to close with the squad. She reached out a hand to push people away and spoke in her best command voice, "Third Mobile Assault Regiment. Please stand clear." Most of the remaining residents backed up, but there were still three or four in the way. They were pushed back as the rest landed. The armory squad landed behind them and they secured the intersection against . . . shoppers.

They waited, wondering where the alleged riot was, getting amused and awed stares from the locals. It was a bit embarrassing, standing on a city street in full battle gear, waiting for orders concerning a riot that appeared not to exist. The traffic was awfully light, though and she could hear people discussing something in agitation. The words "riot" and "fires" and "damn aardvarks" reached her. She scowled. "Aardvark" was derogatory slang for anyone from Earth.

Her comm ordered, "Sirkot: Proceed three blocks south and hold at Bolivar and Meridian. Pacelli, form them up and wait for me." She tapped an acknowledgment and formed her fireteam into two ranks of three. The street was amazingly clear of traffic and they marched down the middle, the residents fleeing the now-apparent trouble and flowing around them. They could hear and see the fighting now and spread out to double arm's-width in two offset ranks. They reached their assigned intersection and waited.

Military and assorted civilian vehicles rolled up behind them seconds later. Two GUVs honked for clearance and rolled through the ranks, then turned sideways to block the street. Kendra nodded in approval. Naumann was good at command. She'd seen his brutal efficiency on Mtali, but it was good to have reinforcement of the concept. She turned back to the trouble ahead and saw rocks and Molotov cocktails flying, and heard occasional gunfire. She swallowed. This was real combat. That might be why the Reserves weren't handling it. It would take time for them to report to their arsenals and prep their gear, whereas the 3rd Mob had craft standing by around the clock. She shook her head and came back to the present. Second-guessing the political situation was not her concern. Keeping herself and her troops alive was.

Two other squads walked through their ranks and formed up ahead. This gave them eighty troops on this one street. Naumann was a firm believer in overwhelming force. Kendra felt confident. If the enemy had no doubt you'd win, they were less likely to resist much.

Assault Commander Naumann conferred with the city officials. He hated urban engagements and hated having so many innocent people mixed in with the troublemakers. He was vaguely aware that he was fortunate to be in the Freehold, where his options were very broad. Other systems' leaders would greatly limit his ability to operate from fear of losing votes. There were no votes here.

The Capital District Citizen's Council representative signed authority for the military to disperse the riot and Naumann looked at the info he had. It wasn't much, but little intelligence was better than none. His staff had links to the orbiting vertols now and had wired in the local news reports. A map was quickly building, showing where the trouble was. "MPs—prepare to disarm and disable fleeing rioters as they come through your area—break—local fire and safety assets, proceed down Capital and reinforce the MPs. Take your orders from Captain Cord—break—all units except MPs, advance in pairs, thirty meter separation, attempt to disperse and detain. Acknowledge."

Kendra stood in formation, scared as never before. The mob screamed and shouted and there came the sound of more smashing. The first squad moved forward to the "peaceful" protesters on the outside of the riot. Chanting what sounded like "No votes, no justice!" they had linked hands and were blocking the road.

A team leader—from the Reserves; there were some on scene—approached one, a chanting, shining-eyed young woman who appeared to be enjoying the fervor of the event. He stepped forward, grabbed her arm and said, "Lady, please come with me."

The woman pulled away, trying to break his grip.

He gripped her arm harder, applying pressure to a nerve with his baton. "Lady, it will hurt more until you come with me."

She grimaced, gasped and finally dropped, releasing her grip on the people to either side. She stood immediately, and commenced beating on his torso armor and helmet. He casually stunned her, shouldered her, and carried her away. His teammates closed in and began to apprehend her neighbors.

As one was led away, she struggled and then went limp, yelling at the soldier, *"Fuck you, you capitalist pig! You'll have to drag me!"*

Shrugging, the soldier released his grip, grabbed her ankle and proceeded to drag her—facedown. She screamed and cursed, trying to hold herself off the ground with her hands. The screams stopped when he reached the steps of the Civic Center. Her head bumped and tumbled down the steps, leaving a trail of blood and several teeth.

Most of the other protesters quickly decided their best approach was to go along peacefully. They were led away, each escorted by a soldier. Kendra watched in morbid fascination, her eyes constantly flicking back to the cavorting riot ahead. There was irregular gunfire from the street now and retaliatory fire from some of the shops.

"*Platoon!*" Sirkot ordered. "Forward! March!"

Kendra waited until he said, "Pacelli, take First Squad." Due to personnel shortages, he was both commander of the Logistics Platoon and First Squad Leader. Under these circumstances, it made sense for him to stay at platoon level and let her command the squad. It was still a burden on her mind. She relayed the order and stepped off with the others. "Arms at high port! Use minimum force, but whatever is necessary." She had a feeling that "minimum" would not be an accurate description of what was to follow.

Kendra gulped. The GUVs rolled aside and turned to flank her squad. Kendra found herself near the middle of the street and the edge of the crowd bellied out toward her. She extended her weapon, held firmly and strapped to her arm. One of the rioters turned, locked eyes with her and lunged.

"*Kill the pigs!*" he screamed, seizing her weapon and attempting to wrench it away.

She reacted with trained reflexes, twisting it back and swinging the butt as she kicked his ankle. The gun connected with his face, splitting the cheek. He staggered and collapsed. All across the street, the scene was repeated. The squad advanced at the order, stepping over the still forms. Behind them, the following squad slapped restraints on the down figures and moved forward to support Kendra and her squadmates, leaving the prisoners for another unit to worry about.

More rioters closed in. One raised a weapon. Kendra swung hers from trained reflex, the barrel aligned center of mass and she fired. The man seemed to explode as the high-energy slug tore through his body. As she felt adrenaline shock ripple through her, she heard loud fire from her left. She identified it as the machinegun aboard the GUV, firing a warning burst into the ground, and the crowd flowed across from left to right, anxious to avoid the heavy weapon. A rock caromed off her helmet, jarring her and making her head ring and she focused her attention forward again. Another man charged while swinging a pipe and she shot him. Her aim was low and the bullet tore his right hip apart in a splash of gore. He screamed, fell and screamed louder, a continuous agonized wail. As she stepped past him, he amazingly grabbed for her ankle and she kicked down. He howled as her boot slammed into his upper thigh. She hurried on, anxious to be done, away from all this. She gulped back bile.

"YOU ARE COMMANDED TO DROP YOUR WEAPONS AND PLACE YOUR HANDS ON YOUR HEADS. SURRENDER IN AN ORDERLY FASHION. ALL WHO CARRY WEAPONS WILL BE CONSIDERED TO HAVE INTENT TO USE."

There were mixed sounds from the mob, of outrage, pain, fear and confusion. Several people surrendered, others began shooting. Flames licked at buildings, the smoke drifting through the tortured streets, reluctant to rise in the humid air. Another squad, vehicle mounted, escorted a fire-suppresser into the area. More rescue equipment came up behind. Overhead, she could hear vertols delivering firefighters and more soldiers.

It took less than a div to split the riot into sections and crush most of the trouble. The rioters fled from the assault and ran through the gauntlet of military police who pinned them to the ground and shackled them with binders. A growing pile of stolen property and weapons showed their progress. That only left those sheltered in buildings or still looting and starting fires. Most building's alarms were sounding and smoke and chemical fire suppression agents drifted down and across the streets. They moved cautiously around parked or damaged vehicles, rooting out the occasional rioter or scared bystander.

The 3rd Blazer Regiment from Heilbrun had mobilized with them and was landing on building roofs. From there, they proceeded to systematically flush occupants down to the lobbies, where building security and local employers could identify who was authorized to be there. Kendra's squad was broken into teams, guarding the entrances to the FreeBank building she'd seen erected two years and a lifetime ago. They restrained a handful of fleeing rioters, then were released to document their activities for the courts. Kendra had to go over her actions and those of the rest of the squad, detailing some parts of the video record for use and certifying its accuracy. It was broad daylight again when she finished and work crews were still clearing rubble. The local residents were getting to work, trying to proceed as normal. There were additional reports as damage was found, but that was a civil matter, not for the military to worry about.

She growled in exasperation as her comm sounded. She flipped it open and read, *"Naumann—Regular duty day for Mistday is canceled."* That was a relief. She was too tired to track.

It finally dawned on her that she had shot and killed people last night. It was an odd feeling. Certainly they'd been trying to kill her, but she burned with remorse anyway. Why did they have to push so hard? Couldn't they see the futility? She hated the necessity and hated herself for feeling guilty.

She was silent the whole way back in a GUV. As they pulled into the compound, she checked off her people, brusquely reminded them to be in on time in the morning and to rest, and logged out. Then she left her gear except her rifle at the shop and walked the kilometer to the barracks. She collapsed fully dressed, sweaty, dusty and smoky, on the bed.

It was only a couple of divs until she was paged and ordered to report to the court as a witness. She rose achingly, dressed in her greens and grabbed her sword. She snapped the polymer combat fittings off, fitted the wooden ones for dress wear and caught a ride from the base taxi. There were a lot of people being called as witnesses.

She was still amazed at using her very expensive dress sword as a combat weapon. She'd protested loudly and Marta had replied almost in anguish, "You're going to take a soldier's weapon and *never use it*? That's insulting to the sword *and* to the maker."

The logic was inescapable, given the almost religious significance attached to weapons here. Or, in some cases, the blades *were* religious items. It was expected and Cardiff had promised to perform any repairs necessary due to combat damage.

Her reflection was interrupted as they arrived at the Council building. It was actually being used and several

Citizens had set up court in various halls. She was shuffled around to be cross-examined on her existing statements and to add details. Her first testimony was a whipsaw between prosecution and defense. She reported in to Hernandez's court, identified herself, confirmed her testimony and video from her display and was attacked by the defense.

"Corporal, would you describe your relationship with the Citizen, please?" the man asked. He clearly didn't like his clients, but was doing a viciously professional job of defending them.

"He was my sponsor when I first immigrated, Counselor," she replied.

"Yes, and what else?" the man pushed.

"Uh . . . he's father of one of my housemates," she admitted.

"'Housemate,'" the lawyer was pale and thin by local standards. He turned as if pondering and then swiveled back. "What type of housemate is this?" he asked.

"It's a sexual relationship. Do you have a point?" she snapped, exasperated.

"Order," Hernandez advised.

The defense said, "So, he advised and assisted you when you moved here, guided you through employment and is the father of your girlfriend, correct?" There were snickers from some of the Earth contingent, both defendants and witnesses. She blushed. Not at the question, but at their childish and rude reaction.

"Essentially correct, Counselor," she admitted.

"And you claim to be unbiased?" he asked.

"I don't remember saying that, but yes, I am. My video and report is correct and my answers have been truthful," she returned evenly.

He "hmphed" and turned her over to the prosecutor for cross-examination.

"Corporal Pacelli, where were you born?" the prosecutor asked.

"San Diego, California, North America, Earth," she replied.

"Where else have you lived?"

"Atlanta and Minneapolis areas, both on Earth, and Jefferson here."

"How did you wind up here?"

She turned and said, "Citizen, I can't answer that question." Please, no.

"Please summarize," he said.

Taking a breath, she said, "I left Earth under duress. I cannot give details for my personal safety."

"That's fine," the prosecutor replied. "Would it be correct to say that you have sympathies for Earth and its residents?"

"It would be," she agreed. "I still love my home planet."

"Has that affected your testimony? Specifically, has it caused you to treat the defendants, most of whom are from Earth and Sol System, in a harsher manner than was proper?"

"Absolutely not, Counselor." There were laughs from the locals now.

Most of the defendants were convicted, although enough were acquitted due to conflicting evidence to convince her the system was fair. One such was a man who had been detained wearing shorts and a shirt, no shoes and nothing else. He claimed to have been dragged along by the mob when he went outside to investigate. He was reported to have thrown rocks and was positively identified by witnesses, but no video corroborated the accusations. He had no stolen property and no injuries commensurate with vandalism. He didn't sound particularly pleasant, but detention and trial could explain that. Hernandez ordered him released.

Virtually none of the convicts had any assets. They were quickly sentenced to indentured labor. Kendra was a bit piqued that there were still jobs for them. Hers had ended due to economic problems. On the other hand, she recalled that hers had been paid in full.

Some of them refused or tried to. They were led away in chains and implanted. Some few were challenged by plaintiffs to duels they were unlikely to survive. Those would have to be appealed to the Council, but if the plaintiff refused to budge, a duel it would be. The outcome of those was almost certain; the defendant would be outclassed and die.

The two worst cases Kendra witnessed, while waiting to testify yet again, were a pair of rapists. They were positively identified on a store security file, by witnesses, by the plaintiff and by genetic evidence. The poor girl in question was nine local years old, fifteen Earth years, and barely able to speak her testimony. Chinratana was judging the case and was gently patient with her, as was the defense counselor. Judges had no power to clear a court of any except disruptive influences, but many spectators elected to leave from politeness and consideration. That left the relevant parties and anyone in official capacity for the day, including Kendra. The trial was in-depth, complete and seemed to Kendra to cover all details. At the conclusion and sentencing, the two were convicted and fined Cr2 million each.

The two were outraged and began yelling. "Man, this is boolshit!" one of them shouted. "A slottie walks out front, showing her punta, baring it *all* for us. You all know she was wanting it!"

Chinratana banged his gavel. "Prisoner, your case is closed. Your sentence has been set. You may pay it, work it off for the rest of your—in this court's opinion—worthless life, or you may appeal for a duel."

"Shit, *yeah*! I'll take a duel!" one of them replied. He pointed a suggestive finger at the young plaintiff, who quivered and began crying.

"Ms Ronson," Chinratana spoke, "your current circumstances make your fitness to duel questionable. Will you do me the honor of letting me serve on your behalf?"

"Y-yes, Citizen," she choked out.

"Thank you. Bailiff, arm the defendant."

The court guard drew her sidearm, cleared it, safed it and tossed it to the thug. As he fumbled with it, Chinratana whipped his own from its holster, cleared the bench and aimed in one effortless motion and shot him through the groin. The man screamed, thrashed to the ground and moaned briefly as he bled to death from massive hemorrhage.

"Citizen, on behalf of my client, I protest most strongly! I demand charges against you!"

Chinratana replied, "The duel was not handled according to protocol. If you have a power of attorney, you may charge me or his next of kin are free to. In the meantime, the court will recess for ten segs. Bailiff, detail a work party to remove this . . . *filth* from my floor and toss it in the nearest sewer."

"Does the surviving defendant wish to dispute the sentence?" he finished.

"No!" the kid snapped, his head shaking vigorously back and forth.

Kendra felt Chinratana had overstepped his bounds, but the case was rather grisly. She was glad to be released shortly and was drained almost to illness by the last two days. She had a nagging fear that it was not over yet.

Chapter 25

"An Ambassadore is a man of virtue sent to lie
abroad for his country, a news writer is a man of
no virtue who lies at home for himself."
                                        —Sir Henry Wotton

The press, particularly that from Earth, had a field
day with the events. Chinratana's shooting made the
headlines, as did the video of the military "brutally
beating and murdering" the "peaceful" protesters. No
mention was made of the fact that unarmed protesters, not blocking traffic, had been completely ignored
or that the actual number of casualties among the
rioters was about three percent. All focus was on a few
replayed scenes of rioters being subdued or shot by
soldiers, with their provocative assaults edited out, and
on protesters who were professionals at sobbing for the
camera eye.

The damage was done, however. The Freehold
government was portrayed as a fascist, plutocratic junta.

No mention was made of the superior standard of living, literacy rate and unparalleled individual freedom. Instead, focus was made on the "lack" of franchise and the "denial of basic rights" of state-sponsored medical care, public education and free access to entertainment.

There was nothing that could be done at the government level, although the issue was discussed at length. Chinratana was criticized for his outburst. "Morally right or not," Hernandez commented, "you were over the line and it's going to bite us badly. Even if I win the case for you, we lose."

"I know," he agreed. "The unrepentant little sod just made me want to flush him. I would have considered it a fair trade to be indentured for life to remove him from the gene pool."

Hernandez replied, "Which is exactly the purpose of the system we have, as we were taught in school. We as Citizens, however, have to be held to a higher standard.

"Anyway, it's done. The 'Lawful Citizen's Committee for Justice,' as his friends call themselves, has asked Uddin to be your judge. I'm sure he morally opposes your actions, but he'll try it fairly. I'll claim that the duel was requested and accepted and that the defendant's ignorance of the procedures was an intentional lack on his part, since he decided to accept without counsel. I think we're solid."

"If I could have done it again . . ." Chinratana began.

"Yes?" Hernandez prompted.

"I'd have shot him so he died slower."

"I agree."

Chinratana was acquitted of murder, the incident held to be a legal duel and it was mentioned once and ignored by the local press.

The UN press, on Earth especially, hailed it as

state-supported murder and demanded sanctions. Since sanctions were already in place and hurting the UN more than the Freehold, the shouts were meaningless. Behind the scenes, however, political gears were moving.

Chapter 26

" . . . the most expensive thing in the world is a second-best military establishment, good but not good enough to win."
—Robert A. Heinlein, "The Happy Days Ahead"
in *Expanded Universe*

Operation Swift was a total failure.

For simplicity, one small, well-stealthed carrier, the *Lyndon B. Johnson*, had been chosen. It spent several Earth weeks on a circuitous route to Freehold's Jump Point Four. The troops aboard pulled maintenance and exercise shifts until they were bored with them; the crew was bored from the onset. The crew knew the destination, but had no idea what the mission was to be. The troops knew what, but had no idea where. The enforced segregation between them kept the operation a secret. Very few on Earth, even, knew what was to happen.

Secrecy was not the stumbling point.

Contrary to entertainment vids, there are no pyrotechnics associated with interstellar jumps. "The Big Johnson," as she was affectionately and illegally called by her crew, slipped out of the jump point and drifted in free orbit past Faeroe Station. She had been deliberately lightened, emitted virtually no radiation, and so went unnoticed among the heavy, noisy traffic between Freehold and Novaja Rossia. She decelerated on a long, slow curve, plotted to direct her well away from any sensor platforms. Shortly, she was in an approach to Grainne.

The large vessel settled into a precisely planned orbit past the planet and back out of the system. Her mass was still masked and her dark hull went unseen. The ten assault boats she spewed out were encased in black, fuzzy clouds of polymer and used ultracompressed hydrogen to fall into a vector for entry. It would hide them until they entered the atmosphere.

That was when the battle plan made contact with the enemy. It didn't survive.

Ground Defense Station A-3:

"Warrant, I'm reading multiple craft on atmospheric approach. Orbital confirms my readings," the corporal on watch reported. The UN planners had relied on a few moments' confusion to get the boats lower. The Freehold military conducted regular exercises and had occasional smugglers who were considered fair game. Either way, standard operating procedure was to assume a hostile craft and prepare to launch. There were bonuses for effective response, whether during exercises or actual events. The corporal slapped the button that sent her data into missiles, intercept craft and Orbital Defense Command's parallel system, while her warrant attempted to communicate with the approaching craft.

"Unidentified vessels on approach to Jefferson Starport, vector four point seven five, this is Freehold Military Forces Ground Defense. Imperative you respond immediately or be destroyed. If unable to communicate, roll your craft or use flare. Say again . . ."

There was of course no answer and the multiple blips reinforced the probable military nature. The ground crew still did not know if it was a real attack or an exercise. It made no difference. They proceeded on a long-practiced routine.

"Corporal, there is no response on any frequency. Do you have visual evidence of maneuver or flare from any craft?"

"Negative."

"Orbital has not restricted launch."

"Do you restrict launch on your order, sir?"

"Negative. Launch on firing solution. Prepare to abort if necessary."

"Launching."

Tens of small missiles ripped out of their launchers and headed into the stratosphere with a suicidal scream. Six of the incoming craft were below safe engagement altitude, but the last four were high up in steep approaches, surrounded by nimbuses of incandescence from atmospheric friction. The missiles' circuitry calculated the probable location of the vehicles behind the glowing beacons and swarmed in in an orgy of death. All four craft were obliterated.

The first craft touched down hard and the pilot used thrust, wheel braking and multiple drogue chutes to achieve a quick stop near the military terminal. He punched the button that dropped the tail and the troops in back shed their harnesses and hit the ground. Behind him, the second boat prepared to land.

✧   ✧   ✧

A base engineer changing the processor on one of his maintenance bots watched the vehicles and running soldiers approach the terminal. The craft, he noted, had landed with total disregard for safety or procedures and wasn't a Freehold design. The uniforms were wrong, too, as were the trucks. He spoke quickly into his comm, slid for cover, drew his sidearm and waited. He saw the few flight techs on the ramp at this time of night scrambling for holes, also.

The UNPF 71st Special Unit lead elements pounded across the illuminated ovals the spotlights painted on the pavement. The sergeant in the lead raised his elbows and slammed the door wide, then jogged left and took the stairs two at a time toward what the map had indicated was flight control. There were supposed to be about twenty military and civilian technicians on duty and he anticipated total surprise and immediate surrender. Instead, he burst through the door at the top and took a fusillade of small arms fire. His armor stopped most of it, but some rounds took him in the thighs where it was thinner and a couple punched through his helmet visor. He was dead before he hit the ground in the high gravity. Those immediately behind him met the same fate and in seconds the force was backed up with Starport Security behind them and administrative personnel ahead, who, against all logic, were heavily armed and inhumanly accurate.

The tenets of logic were different in the Freehold.

As the third boat landed, Senior Pilot Albro Mayaguez was just flying his Hatchet into the area. He'd heard the call and hoped to get into the action. He saw the boat roll toward the maintenance hangars, anticipated there were more on the way and realized that his next move was childishly simple, if he acted quickly.

Yawing his craft hard and vectoring thrust, he slewed to a hover directly over the runway. Practiced hands dropped "Dewey's Revenge" into a hard landing or, more accurately, a controlled crash. He swiped his hand across two switches, covered but thoughtfully easy to reach and mounted side by side, then climbed out in a hurry and headed for the tall grass at a sprint.

Shortly thereafter, the fourth boat landed, tires chirping, and the pilot attempted unsuccessfully to guide his grounded projectile around the blockage in the center of the runway. The boat smashed into the wrecked vertol at better—or worse—than four hundred kph. The switches Mayaguez had thrown had bypassed all safeties and armed all munitions, which detonated on impact. The multiple explosions engulfed the shuttle and all occupants, killing most of them instantly and all in seconds.

The pilots of the fifth and sixth boats saw the explosion ahead and took what steps they could. For number five, just about to touch down, only the quickest and surest of pilots could have avoided the fireball. This pilot was neither and succeeded only in bouncing his craft off the surface, into a stall and almost directly down into the flames below. His remaining velocity dragged the maelstrom for several hundred more meters, ensuring the cleanup crew would be very unhappy with his charred corpse. Number Six's pilot had more time to respond and managed to abort his landing. Unfortunately, his craft had insufficient fuel for a departure, being loaded for fast assault. He made an admirable emergency landing in the grass of the Drifting Valley and he and his surviving passengers were "rescued" by a grinning squad of Freehold infantry reservists at dawn. The grins were not cheerful.

✦   ✦   ✦

The surviving troops of the second and third boats had been rolling across the port at high speed, heading for various secondary facilities to reinforce them. Three vehicles were destroyed by small surface missiles and four more by aircraft, at which time the major in charge decided to concentrate on a different target. He spoke orders and a small element departed in the direction of the main gate. The main body continued toward the maintenance and navigation sections.

Seeing the vehicles bouncing toward him, the guard first class at the gate made a tactical decision of his own. He keyed a command, called in a report on his comm and departed his shack at a sprint. He was clearly outnumbered and the gate should hold them long enough for support to arrive. Such support did, but not from the expected source.

Minutes later, one of the UN's most pessimistic sergeants had his appraisal of the situation confirmed. His squad was covering—more accurately, *cowering*—in a broad ditch while small arms fire came from the west. He had the grenadiers lob a few HEs in that direction and followed it with a few seconds of automatic fire, while screaming for backup into his comm. He was thankful for the lethal weaponry, which he'd tried to swap for standard nonlethal hardware at first. The idea of initiating killing he found distasteful. He'd been ordered to take the weapons anyway and didn't want to exchange them now. Three soldiers were down and their vehicle disabled. The comm was silent. The only response was more fire from the north. He risked a glance in that direction, switched to enhanced view in the moderate light provided by city lights and the local moon, then did a double take. He ducked back as a sustained burst chewed the edge of the slope. Four individuals with rifles were well covered and shooting very accurately and the two in the gully just outside the double fence were mounting a heavy machinegun on its tripod. He found that procedure totally bizarre and decided he never wanted to fight these people again. He elected to surrender at once.

The machinegunners were civilians.

"UNS *Lyndon B. Johnson*, this is Freehold Military Forces Gunboat Four Juliet Gamma One Seven. You are ordered to hold position and prepare to be boarded." The six-person crew of the gunboat waited anxiously for three segs, then sent again:

"*Lyndon Johnson*, this is Four Juliet Gamma One Seven. We know your comm is operational and you are receiving. We will be alongside in two point one hours. We will board your ship and seize it as contraband under the Geneva Conventions of twenty-one-sixty-three and sections of the Freehold of Grainne Constitution. You will respond immediately. If you do not, you will be destroyed."

This time there was a response. "Four Juliet Gamma One Seven, this is UNS *Lyndon Johnson*. You are ordered to surrender immediately. Your vessel will be seized under UN Code Title Five Hundred Seventy-Three regarding piracy. The only recognized authority in UN space."

"*Johnson*, I don't have time for legal games. You are within the Freehold of Grainne, de facto and de jure. You can surrender and be sent home or I'll nail you with a three gig warhead. Attempt to escape and you will be stopped before reaching any jump point, all of which are closed and guarded. The *George S. Patton* and *Robert E. Lee* are en route to take your crew off.

Personally, I'd rather blow the shit out of your cowardly ass, so please, crawl back to momma like a bawling child."

There was a pause, then a different voice said, "Four Juliet Gamma One Seven, please use radius point seven airlock, one hundred meters aft. You will be met by our marine detachment."

To his crew, the gunboat commander remarked, "Respond to an obvious psych ploy, then tell us you have nasties waiting. What an idiot! Well, at least he called our bluff." Raising his voice, he bellowed, "You ready, cargo?"

"Ready," replied the senior sergeant who was leading the squad from 4th Mobile Assault Regiment. They'd been hastily squeezed into the aft section as the gunboat left Orbital Defense Station Seven.

Nodding to himself, the pilot transmitted, "Understood, *Johnson*. We will dock in two hours."

The theory behind this operation was that the Freehold Forces would act as if nothing unusual had happened. An illegal landing had been stopped and the ship seized. The gunboat had handled the routine matter during its normal operations. It was another game in psychological dominance.

And it took incredible chutzpah.

The warrant leader pulled his boat alongside with a single, high-gee correction of thrust on manual. His orders were to spare no effort to overawe all UN personnel. He met the snaking gangtube, latched in, then reported that status to the *Johnson*. His crew immediately donned breathing gear.

The twenty-person squad from 4th Mob crawled through the tube, already in vac gear, and entered the *Johnson*. They were met by forty-three UN Marines in battledress, but not vac gear. No courtesies were exchanged and the two units stared warily at each other for several seconds. Finally, one of the marines spoke.

"I am Captain Lee Mihlbauer of the UN Marines. I am placing you under arrest. The charge is piracy. Lower your weapons."

Through his voicemitter, the sergeant's voice was tinny. "I don't think so, asshole." He made no move to either lower or raise his weapon. The units stared at each other for a few more seconds.

Then the captain raised her sidearm.

What followed was too fast to document later without video. The rearmost member of the squad, already clipped to the bulkhead, blew the gangtube. Emergency hatches slammed and pressure warnings shrieked, pitch dropping in the rapidly thinning atmosphere. The Freeholders swarmed through the marines. Those not killed by weapon fire expired from suffocation minutes later. Shortly, the Freeholders, minus one casualty who was dragging himself back to the gunboat, were gathered around the next hatch. They reported back to the pilot.

"*Johnson*, this is Four Juliet Gamma One Seven. There appears to have been an accident at the airlock. The structural integrity of your ship is breached. Suggest you immediately surrender so we can get a crew aboard to effect repairs."

"This is the *Johnson*. If you attempt to capture this ship, we will scuttle."

"Aw, don't risk your wheezing old heart, Captain. Say the word and I'll do it for you. They don't let me use any three-giggers on the practice range."

Within the div, the Freehold warrant leader and the Earth officer met face-to-face. The sergeant would receive a reprimand for his treatment of the *Johnson's* captain, but it would be filed with his commendation for capturing the ship.

Saluting, the Earther said, "I am Captain Denis Schwartz. Might I ask your name, Warrant Leader?"

"You may not. Thanks for the gift of a capital ship. I didn't believe my orders, but they were right. You didn't have the balls to scuttle to keep it out of enemy hands," the sergeant sneered. He spun in the microgravity, ignoring the captain's salute and added in a disgusted tone, "Gutless coward."

Marshal Dyson briefed his senior officers and a handful of unit commanders. "Their intent was to seize commo and declare a takeover, then stage elections that supported the protesters, bring in more troops and 'nationalize the assets of the junta.' The question I need input on," he said, "is what to do with the *Johnson*. We may or may not be able to squeeze funding for phase drive. If not, it would take a lot of refitting to be more than a marginal insystem ship for our purposes. The only civilian companies interested in a ship that size could afford better for not much more than the cost of refitting her."

Naumann spoke. "I assume, sir, that there aren't any foreign entities willing to risk the political repercussions of purchasing her?"

Nodding, the marshal said, "Correct, Commander. No colony wants the UN angry with them for using one of their captured ships. The few independent systems lack the resources to field such a craft. Although the Caledonian ambassador has made noises about taking it anyway, if there's a little more civilian support."

"The Brits always did have balls," Naumann replied. "If they'd stop counting noses and just tell the UN to drop dead—well, I don't think Earth could actually do anything about it.

"Have you considered just parting the damned thing out and letting Deep Space Salvage have the hulk?"

"That is one possibility. I would rather use or sell an intact ship, though."

"Right. A whole ship can always be broken up, but not vice versa. I'll consider it and give you any wild ideas." There were chuckles at that. Naumann was nothing if not creative.

Later, after the others had left, he approached his commander in chief. "As to my other wild suggestion, what do you think?"

"Commander, it is completely insane and sounds suicidal. Which I have come to expect of you. Have at it," the commander in chief said.

"Thank you, sir. I'll be on it today," Naumann replied. He was grinning as he left the office. It was time to ask Corporal Kendra Pacelli for information on a few subjects.

Chapter 22

"People in large masses may as well be sheep. Their collective intelligence drops to that of the weakest-minded member of the group. They bleat, they panic and are easily herded to safety, or to the slaughter."
—Alan Gunn

"We have orders," Captain Kenneth Chinran, Black Operations Team Seven, Freehold Military Forces announced. In seconds, the entire squad had gathered around. He waited until everyone was silent, staring at the eager grins and feeling the tension they projected. They'd been on Earth for months, waiting for instructions they might never get. Now they had a chance to do something.

"In about forty-six hours, we are to have staged a penetration of Langley Military Facility. I have a list of targets to be disabled, primarily commo and security. We will be remaining here afterwards, so we must plan for good concealment and evasion. Let's kick things together and get ready to roll," he said.

There were affirmations and cheerful hoots around the room. Finally, a chance to be soldiers again, rather than skulking nothings. "First order, no more drinking or drugs." He rode out the mock protests and continued, "Second, everybody get rested before we start. You all know this. Now, ladies and men, let's scheme." While rough plans had been in existence, they would have to be fitted to the timeframe and circumstances.

Two men and two women entered the club. The women were very attractive and just soft enough to emphasize their youth. The two men who sat with them were obviously friends, nothing more. They bantered a bit as the chairs filled. They already had neighbors on one side.

Within a few minutes, the women were dancing with two of their neighbors, clearly military men despite their civilian attire. They were somewhat older and were soon sweating to keep up with the energetic gyrations of their partners. Shortly, the civilian woman who was with the two soldiers, who'd been looking left out and a bit put upon, was dancing with one of the girls' male friends. She was enthusiastic about the attention and none of the three locals noticed the second man pawing through pouches and pockets for ID.

The four youths exchanged fake phone codes with the others, said goodbyes smothered in hugs and a couple of kisses and left. They'd also lifted available cash and credchits as cover and immediately scanned the cards for cash, then dumped them. Their real target had been the ID.

Behind them, Kenneth Chinran sat at the bar, watching and listening and recording as much as his scanner would allow. He was trying to confirm definite duty stations and names to go with them. Two more of his professional kleptomaniacs were outside, detaching ID placards from vehicles. Others were scattered at other popular spots, acquiring more intelligence and "locally procured assets."

Late the next night, the covert assault began. Three of the squad approached the farthest of the rear gates. It had originally had an access road that had long since succumbed to nature and been surrounded by hectares of swamp and brambles. They cut a link from the old-fashioned chain securing it and replaced it with a twisted piece of wire. Then they hid in the ditch inside the fence, cold and wet as it was. It was good, dark concealment.

Operative Cynthia Sanders, dressed to look older than her nineteen Earth years and driving a rental car with the ID disabled, drove up to the gate. She flashed her stolen picture ID, which the guard didn't even inspect in detail. She needn't have bothered dyeing her hair to match the photo, but better safe than sorry. She was waved through, waved back at the guard and turned along the perimeter road as soon as she cleared the gate. Her accomplice sat up in the back seat and said, "Nice job."

"Thanks," she acknowledged. "Let's get the guys." She followed the road, traffic becoming sparser as they swung away from the main buildings and adjusted her speed to give her a long safety zone ahead and behind. She neared the back gate, popped the trunk release and slowed to almost a stop. Even with her training and expectation, the only clue she had as to the procedure was the trunk lid raising, slamming, and a knock announcing success. She hadn't seen any of the three leave the ditch.

Chinran was a few minutes behind, dressed as a major. His car had the other stolen placard. He even stopped to chat with the guard for a moment, asking directions to a building he had no intention of going anywhere near.

The guard gave him directions and said, "You do realize it's not safe to be in uniform off base?"

"Yes, I do," he agreed. It took conscious effort not to say "sergeant," "soldier," or some other form of address, but that was just not done here. "I never left the vehicle and it hasn't been a long trip."

"Well, do be careful, okay?" the guard said with a sigh and a shake of his head. Officers.

Chinran agreed, thanked the guard and drove in. He was never asked for ID.

" 'Tight security' they call it," his passenger commented as they headed for billeting. He hadn't been asked for ID or his presence even questioned.

"Don't you feel safer already?" Chinran replied. They'd rehearsed their entry techniques against various Freehold military and civil facilities and even some friendly powers during joint exercises. UN security, such as it was, depended more on the public's assumption of its strength and fear of repercussions than on actual quality. It had been so long since an outside enemy had conducted an attack that the possibility barely registered as a risk in the minds of those tasked with it.

It wasn't long before the entire squad disguised as locals, trickled, by ones and twos, through back entrances into the base. Several met in a small four-room suite intended for senior officers. It had been rented to Chinran at cost to keep the facilities in use and paid for. Its relative spaciousness and distance from the bustle of the main base had decided him.

The squad went to work and it was bare minutes before Hell itself seemed to break loose, then go on a rampage.

0210 hours: Two people wandered into the open bay of Aircraft Munitions, snapped a few photos of open containers and planted some devices. All the shift personnel were out on the flightline and the building unsecured. They were well within a fenced and guarded perimeter, so what risk was it? They'd find out shortly.

0215 hours: The electronic lock to the base communication center was bypassed. Two "Safety Police" in uniform entered and no one reacted for several seconds. They had entered against regs and without authorization, but were in uniform, therefore assumed to be legitimate. That few seconds was long enough to take control, lash all the occupants into a human pretzel, ignore all the automatic message traffic systems and destroy the rest of the equipment. The base was now cut off from radio contact and most commnets. Any outside inquiries would be met with maintenance warnings. There was a slight risk of an emergency call, but even that would not elicit an immediate response from outside, they were sure.

0217 hours: Every fire alarm in the munitions building triggered.

0222 hours: Two "Safety Police" entered security headquarters with two "prisoners." In seconds, the building was locked down, the security staff trussed and the weapons vault opened by the simple expedient of pointing a gun at a woman contractor's head and demanding admission. The armorer inside at first refused, but upon orders from the ranking officer, opened the door. He'd hit the alarm button, but it had no effect, being routed through the comm center.

0223 hours: The base commander and his wife were awakened by black-clad figures sitting on their bed. They were quickly led away in shackles, to be stuffed with a growing number of hostages at the security office. The command post called Chinran to report that it was now under his control and its staff also subdued. Most of the base personnel were still asleep.

0225 hours: The base Vehicle Flight Control Center went down. No automatic flight would be possible overhead.

0230 hours: Automatic weapons fire raked rooftops in base housing. Calls to the Safety Police were unanswered. Those few on patrol streamed into the area to help and were pinned down. They called for assistance, but received none. Personal phones were put into use and the local civil police called for backup. The uncontrolled phone net was quickly ablaze with rumor, speculation, distortions and a few facts, some actually provided by the attackers. When the local police arrived at the gates, they found those gates locked and "guards" shooting at them when they attempted to force entry. One lifted his car and tried to fly over on manual. A shoulder-fired missile vaporized the vehicle. The rest decided to wait.

0233 hours: Craft on the flightline began exploding, as did cratering charges on the runway. A huge explosion took place in the Safety Office vehicle park. Unfortunately, the fire department was busy at the munitions building. Then calls came in of fires in base housing, in brush, trash containers and vacant units. There was a danger of spreading, but mission-essential equipment took priority. However, most of the firefighters lived in base housing and some elected to proceed there first. The department was scattered in minutes and unable to do anything useful.

0237 hours: The elevator to the Flightline Control Tower jammed, forcing the crew in the tower to stay there. Then a window was shot out. The crew cowered under their consoles and refused to move.

0315 hours: All the accessible gates had trucks full of explosives parked across them. The bombs were clearly visible, fuzed and blocking access. The local police knew that the base commander, civilians in housing and several important officers were all being held prisoner. They deferred to UN authority, which would not be able to issue coherent orders from its bureaucracy for hours. Approaching aircraft were being waved off and two shuttle landings were aborted to other ports.

0325 hours: Four people worked feverishly at comm terminals, downloading data onto flash chips and uploading other data from them. They hid all signs of their espionage and departed within the hour, just as the government was starting to draw up a plan. They slipped out the back gate on foot, wired it behind them and joined the rest of the team in their waiting vehicles beyond the marsh.

Explosions continued sporadically for the next day and a half. Attached to the front of the cell block in the security building was a neatly printed, well-lourished note that read, "It is our belief that this was what you were trying to accomplish in your recent efforts. Please let us know if we may be of assistance again. Best regards, your instructors." It and the prisoners were discovered about noon.

The Bureau of Defense was outraged and publicly embarrassed despite its best efforts to keep the story quiet. The investigators were even more incensed to find that not a single good photo or even witness description of the attackers existed. The headquarters base of the UN Military was a shambles and operations would be nonexistent until major repairs could be done to the launch facilities, recovery equipment, operations building and headquarters. The greatest anger was expressed at the wanton destruction of

Visiting Officers Quarters, which had been destroyed by the crude but direct method of activating the fire suppression systems—all of them. Water, foam and dry chemicals had doused the entire building, plastering every surface with gooey white paste.

There was no evidence to point to a source for the attack, so the Freehold was blamed. Ambassador Maartens denied all knowledge of it and insisted the Freehold was not at fault. To her knowledge, this was true. She'd received a coded message the day before that read, "If any excitement happens, it's not our fault." Since she had not been informed of any activities of which she should be aware, she could honestly deny any knowledge of the activities. She did, however, vow to herself under her sly smile to make some inquiries. Perhaps Warrant Leader McLaren would know who to ask, unofficially, about these alleged incidents.

Ambassador Maartens and her staff were ejected the next week. They were given twenty-four hours to evacuate, which was intended to create trouble for them. All embassy personnel had already shipped their personal effects and took most of the time allotted to destroy records, technology, and render the complex's buildings unusable. With three hours left, the handful remaining boarded a diplomatic VC-6 and departed. They landed at Dulles Starport and hopped a military transport. As the ambassador, her assistant, three technicians and one team of six guards lifted, the engines on the vertol they'd used slagged themselves and the craft caught fire. It was a useless hulk by the time the 'Port fire department arrived. There was a lesson to be learned from this, but the UN government was not paying attention.

Chapter 28

"You will not find it difficult to prove that battles,
campaigns, and even wars have been won or lost
primarily because of logistics."
                            —General Dwight D. Eisenhower

There was little official communication between the
two nations for the next half Earth year. Freehold registry ships were forbidden access to UN ports, which hurt
the UN as badly as it did the Freehold—many smaller
freighters used Freehold registry to reduce administrative costs. They diverted elsewhere and Caledonia,
Novaja Rossia, New Israel and Hirohito, among others,
found windfall profits in transferring the cargoes.

The additional shipping expenses, delays and shortages in the UN, were of course, blamed on the Freehold. The UN media, officially free but dependent upon
the government for licensing and most of its news, had
a field day roasting the Freehold as "evil capitalists"

who "oppressed the poor and workers" and "refused to compromise" from their "extremist" position. The pictures of the riots were broadcast yet again, enhanced and edited to show the Freehold Military as thugs. All shots carefully avoided showing the destruction and looting caused by the mobs, the attacks on the City Safety officers or the attacks on the armed troops of the 3rd MAR.

It was clear now that Naumann had been correct. The UN was trying to create a frenzy of blame, with the Freehold as the scapegoat. There was no legal way to evict the UN's reporters and observers from the system, although some of the worst were forcibly removed by subtle and not so subtle threats. The ones left behind, even the fair ones, could get little accurate information past the Bureau of Communications and that little was spun to foment even more trouble.

The Freehold Military responded by putting all personnel on alert, recalling and reequipping reservists and veterans and watching and waiting. Kendra was drained from long days issuing gear to veterans. She'd known intellectually that they kept their small arms after mustering out, but was still surprised when they began trickling in for spare parts, routine maintenance and ammunition.

The shooting ranges were also booked solid. When not in use by military units, they were open to off-duty personnel, reservists, veterans and the general public in priority order. There were also ranges for everything from spears and atl-atls to traditional bows to modern archery gear. Shooting was *the* sport in the Freehold and it was becoming a feverish event now.

Sales of emergency gear soared and the economy recovered most of its former slump. There were still plenty of exports, all shuffled around to reach Earth by other routes, and the need for ships, repairs and related support rose also. The sanctions appeared to have lost their effectiveness. Certain Freehold-specific products were now banned in UN space, but there was sufficient demand to create a black market. Since almost all Freehold registered ship captains hated bureaucracy and adminwork, that black market boomed. The intermediaries in other systems also benefited. Everyone, in fact, did quite well, except for the UN. Thousands of years of history failed to teach that there is no control over free trade in an open system and little effective control even in a closed system.

The only really negative effect was on specific goods that were now contraband to possess within UN space, but the operators in those industries were able to adapt into others. Kendra even got an embarrassed call from Hiroki, informing her that her job was available and she was entitled to first refusal. She first was angry, then amused, then grateful and finally thanked him graciously. She had a home she was familiar with. The war that she understood was coming was going to be a distant, political game and she got back to the business of logistics.

As weeks went by, the fears of conflict eased and the stress on logistics, the shooting ranges and other support facilities returned to near normal. She still had a regular workload of veterans stopping by for assistance and several new series of equipment came into issue. She and Sirkot advertised and ran an auction on the old gear, generating hundreds of thousands of credits of revenue for the unit. She was mildly shocked yet again. In the UN, extra money would have been spent to *destroy* the equipment, not sell it to civilians. She did a records check and found that fifty percent of the cost per unit of equipment was recouped by surplus sales. Whether it was guns or generators, target designators or drones, there was a market for second-generation gear and the military exploited it. Although to be fair, she was sure a few of the buyers from outsystem were mercenaries and terrorists, even if most were veterans, security firms, corporate operations and smaller foreign governments. But the lack of adminwork to determine the end user was yet another sore point between the Freehold and the UN.

Chapter 29

"An important difference between a military operation and a surgical operation is that the patient is not tied down. But it is a common fault of generalship to assume that he is."
—Captain Sir Basil H. Liddell Hart

The next sign of trouble was as sudden as the previous ones and not even Naumann had been able to accurately predict it. The first hint was Jump Point One losing communication. That was unusual and possibly bad, but didn't immediately register as a threat. When JP2 lost signal, it was obvious an attack was under way. Scramble signals went out, but massive amounts of UN firepower were moving insystem. JP3 was offline shortly thereafter, followed by several outer commercial stations. Research facilities in the outer Halo could not be reached, but often didn't maintain open carriers. By the time they could report either way, the trouble would be over.

The lightspeed lag gave several divs for fast-moving teams to overwhelm or destroy facilities in the system's outer fringes. Unknown to the military was that several carriers had already silently positioned themselves. With no emissions they weren't seen and the force was far too large to stop, especially when it took out communications as it headed insystem rather than attempting control from the inside out. The UN command staff had learned from its first mistake and had sufficient force for a real invasion now. The landing craft that deployed were too numerous to be taken out and escorted by aerospace support vehicles as well. Several died on their way down, but the rest landed, shattered the orbital and air defense systems and went after the host sites with a vengeance.

Kendra spun the wheel hard, cutting across the corner of a charge station. Angry yells and horns followed her. She floored the throttle, listening to the turbine howl, then backed off as she approached the gate. All she knew was that there was a general emergency recall. She'd been in town, picking up a purchase for the unit, when her comm had screamed. Whatever it was, it was not an exercise.

She had her ID in hand and announced, "Pacelli, Kendra A., Corporal, Logistics, Third Mob," as the guard waved a scanner at her. His partner and the dog took a quick walk around her vehicle. The animal handler nodded.

The guard tilted the muzzle of his weapon at the sky and said, "Report directly to the airfac, Corporal and don't worry about traffic. Most of 'em have already lifted."

She nodded, nailed the turbine again and cut across the parade field. She met a little traffic around the admin section, slowed slightly and picked up speed at Perimeter Road. Less than two segs later she rolled into the air facility.

There were no security troops on the line. It was a madhouse. Vehicles rolled around at high speed, way too close to the aircraft. People jumped between them and most weren't wearing line badges or safety gear. She jumped out, grabbing her comm, her rifle and her blade and caught the arm of the nearest person. "*Third mob?*" she yelled over the roar of equipment. It was barely audible.

"*Ahh . . . Over there!*" the tech bellowed back, indicating a row of vertols. She nodded and ran.

Approaching the idling craft, she saw a sergeant from base engineering. "*You take this one!*" he ordered, pointing. "*Flight engineer returning soon, lifting next!*"

She ran up the ramp, the noise diminishing slightly and heard a voice over the intercom ask, "Hido?"

"No, if that's your engineer, he's still out."

"Understood. Don't let anyone who arrives leave. We have a launch warning and an attack warning. We may lift without notice."

"Understood," she replied, grabbing a seat on the cargo web and buckling in, adjusting the helmet frequency to that of the intercom. She looped her sword across her chest, fastened her comm to her arm, locked her rifle into a slot and waited.

It was only about a seg later when the pilot announced, "Lifting!" The engine noise rose with that warning and the craft bounced slightly. The hatch closed and gees pushed Kendra down and back. The turbines boosted quickly to a painful howl and the vertol sought altitude, heading north.

"Whoever's in charge back there, report!"

"Pacelli, Corporal, Third Mob Logistics. Sole occupant," she replied, looking around.

"Great," the pilot replied, "You were supposed to be on the other side of the flightline. And they are already out of here."

"Sorry," Kendra replied. "Instructions got mixed up."

A brilliant light flashed through the ports and the pilot yelled, "Shock wave!" The tail pitched up and over, hanging Kendra momentarily upside down, blood rushing painfully to her head and sinuses. The craft tumbled, righted and yawed left. Kendra swallowed hard as it accelerated again and the pilot announced, "Clear."

"Nuke?" Kendra asked. She had a few bruises from the ride.

"Kinetic. Doesn't matter; the base is gone along with anyone still on the ground. It appears we are going to be friends for a while. I'm Nick, my friends call me 'Cowboy.'"

"Kendra."

"Pleased to meet you. Sort of. You'll find gear back there; grab a ruck, you'll need it.

"My instructions are to take this unit," he paused at the irony of the statement, "into Darkwood Hills and drop them there. You'll meet up with Resident Militia and any reservists you can find. Await orders or fight the war, as the case may be. You were supposed to be a squad of SpecWarfare folks."

"Sorry," Kendra replied, her guts roiling in fear and sadness for the tens or hundreds who'd died to get her and the others off the ground.

"So am I. We've got company coming, buckle down if you aren't. I hope violent maneuvers don't make you sick." It sounded like a challenge.

"I was a passenger with Rob McKay once," she returned.

"Rob—Well, I'd like to state for the record that I can fly rings around that maniac. But I'd be lying. I saw some of his airyobatics on Mtali."

"Can I inventory this ruck?" she asked.

"By touch. Keep it strapped," he warned.

"Understood." She rummaged in the harness and had to take several deep breaths to calm her nerves. She was shaking uncontrollably, and clenched her teeth to stop them from chattering. Sheer will gave her some outward semblance of control and she resumed her sorting. She found a full infantry load, extra medical supplies and explosives and extra ammo. There was a pack of field rations and a laser designator.

"Interceptors and hills," Cowboy advised as the maneuvers started. Kendra went into free fall as they came over a peak, was slammed down and to the left, banging her chin. She shook her head and was thankful her teeth were still clenched. She might have bitten her tongue otherwise. The craft decelerated, sliding her across the deck webbing, then the floor dropped out again as they reached a valley. She felt the craft pitch up, centripetal force pinning her against the floor as it became the wall. She could see trees through the port, then sky again as the craft finished its inversion. She stared down at the roof in fear as gees crushed her up against the floor. She was held in place as they pointed back into a gorge. Then the lifter rolled out. It wouldn't have been so scary if she could see, but except for an occasional shadow through the ports, there was nothing but shifting Iolight.

"Air superiority got one interceptor, orbital got a second. But we can't do this for long in a cargo lifter. You are getting out asap. Put on a rig, with a static line. You ever done what ess-double-yoo calls a 'suicide drop'?"

"No," Kendra said, wide-eyed as she pulled a parachute rig from the bulkhead. Another maneuver threw it hard against her. She clutched it and reached for a helmet. Long and repetitive training was all that let her run through the prep, as her brain was numb with fear. Again, she forced her knotting and trembling fingers to steady as they fumbled fasteners.

"Well, at least you've jumped. You'll be going out the side door. I'll drop into a valley, pull the nose up and yaw left. Inertia will pull you out. 'Chute drogues on the way up, you swing twice and hit the trees. Everything goes right, they'll never see you. Anything goes wrong . . . but it shouldn't."

Another violent maneuver caught her as she attempted to sling the ruck between her legs. She strapped her blade and rifle to her sides, clutched the static line and crawled toward the forward troop door, knees grating painfully on the corrugated deck.

She dragged herself up the frame, fastened the clip to the bar provided and said, "Ready!" She'd thought she was scared before. Now fear was starting to hit with a passion. Steely control of her breathing distracted her from the impending nightmare.

"Opening door. Sit and hang on tight, I may maneuver," he warned.

The door slid and latched open with a cold roar of slipstream, leaving her above a landscape tearing by in a blur.

"One last thing," he warned. "You don't have leg armor, so keep 'em crossed when you hit the trees or you risk tearing your femoral arteries. *Stand in the door!* Or sit, in this case."

"Cowboy!" she called.

"*Yo!*"

"For what it's worth, you can tell you friends that Rob McKay's ladyfriend says you give as sexy a ride as he does." She didn't feel as brave as she sounded, but a façade did help a little.

"Thanks, Lady," he replied. "Over this ridge and stand by . . ."

Free fall caught her again as they crested the hill, green and yellow trees below. Gees started to build as they arced out, then dropped away as the craft went ballistic. "On three," he warned and the craft began to yaw. *"One! Two! Three! Get the hell out of my airc—"*

She was ripped out the door by the violent rotation, arms trailing. A distant clang of the static line link striking the fuselage was drowned out by the turbines. Deceleration caught her as the 'chute grabbed air. Blue sky turned dizzyingly to bright green trees, to blinding Io, to trees again, and she closed her legs tightly as those trees came up hard.

Fortunately, she was swinging forward as she hit the treetops. A thin branch slapped across her like a whip. Her descent became more vertical, then back again and a heavy limb crunched against the harness. She gasped, air knocked out, and heard the sound of the interceptors screaming after Cowboy. Pain shot through her leg as her heel hit a bough hard, then the trees were ripping at her all over. She jerked to a stop.

Several ragged breaths were necessary before she could get oriented. She was about three meters above the ground, being poked by twigs and branches. She pulled the standard-issue hook knife from the rig, cut selected bits of webbing and succeeded in getting within two meters of the ground. She lowered the ruck, cut the last strap and landed.

She didn't scream, although the pain was searing. Biting her lip, she limped slightly away from the gear, caught a nearby bush and got untangled. She decided her first priority was to urinate desperately.

That taken care of, she examined her injuries. Bruised or fractured ribs below the left shoulderblade, sprained or broken right ankle, severe welt on right side of neck, shallow puncture wound in right outer

thigh and a nail torn completely off her left ring finger. Digging in the medical kit, she dropped antibiotic
and sealer into her thigh, took a general reconstruc-
tive nano for the rest of it, along with a light painkiller—she'd need her wits—and proceeded to sterilize
and dress her finger. She winced in pain, but got it
done. She sat back against a tree to rest for a moment.

She opened her eyes, confused. It was dark. *Great,*
she thought. *I'm supposed to be finding whatever local
authority there is, not napping.* She opened her comm
to report in and stopped, for the dim glowing screen
had a message waiting.

*"All personnel: Do not report. Remove transponder
from all comm equipment. Proceed as ordered. Additional information will follow."*

She stared for a second, then cleared the message.
A few taps gained her instructions on how to remove
the transponder block and she stuck the deactivated
component in a pocket of her ruck. It might be useful later. She couldn't think in what fashion, but it
might. She also knew now why the comm was a flat
block of hardware, rather than a flexible single mold-
ing. There was actually a small amount of maintenance
and modification that could be done to it.

Suddenly, fear caught up to her. The deep woods
of the Northern Border were no place for a person
raised in a modern city. Remembering her training, she
forced herself to get up and deal with it. Ignoring her
training, she turned on a torch.

In a few segs, she had a small fire going in a shallow
pit. It provided a little heat and a lot of comfort. She
set her shelter up near the base of the tree and crawled
in. Fuel was within arm's reach and so was the fire. She
chewed on a ration package while keeping the dim
flames going to build up enough coals to keep the fire

self-supporting. Once done, she snuggled back into her sleeping bag, rifle in one hand, thumb on safety and sword in the other, tip above her head.

Sleep didn't come. There were *sounds* in the forest and she was too terrified to move. She felt bladder pressure again, clamped down on it. Gingerly, she added another small stick to the fire, still clutching her rifle in the other hand. She felt all kinds of sensations and realized she was panicking.

This is stupid! she told herself. *You are a combat vet from Mtali. This is just a forest. You've killed a ripper that wanted you for lunch. There's nothing here as dangerous as you.* The words were logical and ineffective. She took to watching seconds pass on her comm. Tears welled up from accumulated shock, as she realized that friends were dead, her two home planets were killing each other, her worldview had just been destroyed for the third or maybe fourth time and that this night was subjectively going to last forever.

Eventually, she thought she could see some gray in the shadowy trees. She compared time to predicted sunrise and realized night was almost over. She huddled, twitching until the sky was faintly visible through the foliage, then jumped out to relieve herself again. The air was frigid, and she hurried back to her shelter, crawling in and finally falling deeply asleep.

She woke in filtered but bright Iolight and stirred slightly. Stretching, she was jarred awake at the sight of a rifle muzzle.

"Don't move," a rough male voice commanded. "Let's see your hands."

Sliding them cautiously overhead, she spoke firmly, "Corporal Kendra Pacelli, Third Mobile Assault Regiment."

"You got an aardvark accent there, lady."

Aardvark. *Earth pig.* She gritted her teeth at the

derogatory term and replied, "I'm an immigrant about three years back."

"Uh-*huh*. Where you been living?" The man asked. She saw he had friends. Three of them. Two other men and a young woman. Her old Earth habits found the woman's presence a reassurance.

"Jefferson, until they canceled my indent. I've been at Heilbrun Base since."

"Jefferson, huh? So which side of Liberty Park is the Council building?"

"Twelve blocks north."

"Name some good bars."

"Stanley's Surf n' Turf; good food, too. Level Three if you like dancing. Bellefontaine if you have a ton of money and like a good show—"

"All right, you'll do. And you move in richer circles than I ever did. You can get out now, Corporal."

"I dunno, Dak. I'd like to see some references," one of the others said.

"You heard of Citizen Humberto Hernandez? Friend of mine. Last year on Heritage Day we unveiled a new four-stage pyrotechnic shell that got everyone's attention. My sword comes from Mike Cardiff, if you've heard of him." She was angry now, although she understood their caution. She knew she was still in shock and was trying hard not to crack.

"Easy, lady. Corporal," Dak corrected himself. "I believe you." He offered a hand and helped her out of the small tent. She grimaced in pain and he gave her more support. "My sister-in-law is a nurse. We'll take you to where she is. Kyle, help with the gear," he ordered one of the three others. The young man nodded and shouldered her heavy ruck quite casually. The woman collapsed the shelter and gathered up the few other items. By the time they were done, the traces of fire were gone, as were those signs left by the shelter.

Not much was said on the way to the house. Kendra tried to remember the route, got lost immediately. She surmised they were near the north edge of the woods, as the trees thinned out slightly. Shortly, they entered marked fields and approached a small farmstead. She was glad to see it; her ankle was throbbing in pain. Her ribs, thigh and hand were tight aches that simply contrasted the pain in her ankle to an extreme.

As they neared the house, Kendra saw signs of others, also armed. Dak knocked for entrance and Kendra was quickly handed over to his sister-in-law Vikki for care. She was married to Kyle, Sandra was married to Dak and the younger man Brian was their son. The other two children were Eric, who looked about ten Earth years and Riga, a cheerfully bright-eyed two-year-old.

"You'll be fine. But that ankle is going to need lots of support. Keep it bandaged." Vikki Simonsen told her after a brief exam.

"Will do. So, Dak, what's the tactical situation here? And have you heard any news?"

"Only secondhand," he said. "They hit Maygida, Heilbrun and Merrill. Kinetic kills. Serious damage to the surrounding towns. They're landing a large number of troops. The cities are being occupied. I can't give you more than that at this time."

Nodding, she said, "Okay. What kind of force do we have here? I need a complete list."

"Well, we've . . . twenty-three adults in the surrounding farms. At least one rifle each. Several hundred rounds per. Some shotguns and pistols for defense at home. A few grenades—we picked them up cheap for blasting rocks. We have about a thousand kilos of commercial blasting agents, castable and plastic, no flake type. Usual night vision gear and we've got radios of course, some with scramble. Ten or so trucks, six cars and plenty of horses. Standard navigation gear for land management. There's plenty of food—we are a commercial producer, so no worries there."

Kendra frowned. "That's a very light squad. I hope we can find some support weapons." The UN organized its squads with eight soldiers: a leader, a squad weapon gunner and three buddy pairs with rifle/grenade launchers. The Freehold used twenty-troop squads, in three teams of six with a squad leader and assistant. The third team carried one each of an antitank launcher, heavy machinegun and a sniper rifle and was organized as pairs, one spotting and supporting, the other shooting. They put out a lot more fire than a UN squad, assuming one had the weapons.

"I'll check. What do you have planned?"

"Any veterans here?" she asked, stalling. She had no plans yet.

"No. My older brother is aboard the *Heinlein*," he said, "but no one here has experience otherwise."

"Okay," she said. "Then until I get more intelligence, we are going to limit activities to training only. I'll try to organize a program." She realized this was going to be a very difficult task.

"You stay off that ankle, Corporal," Vikki ordered her.

"Plan on it," she agreed.

Dak and his wife Sandra—the woman who'd been with him to pick her up—cleared a room for her. The house was a sprawling ranch and had plenty of space. It took Kendra the rest of the day to recover from the drop and half the next to convince them of the need to begin training. "If we are going to fight them, we have to be in shape. That means drilling." They finally relented, on condition she sit while they practiced under her guidance.

Kendra had cribbed as much information as she could from her comm the night before. The section on training insurgents was long, detailed and made a lot of sense. Most of it could not be used under her current circumstances. The book called for everyone, instructors and students, to exercise together, to lead by example and boost morale. She couldn't do that, currently. The risk of observation required that they practice at night, especially when cloudy, which was good training, since guerrilla warfare worked better when the enemy was handicapped by as many factors as possible. The daytime tasks of running a farm made that very tiring, annoying and stressful. This was good for practice also, but bad for morale among those who had never put the training to use and seen its benefits. There was insufficient ammunition for extended practice. "I can hit a human target five times out of six while running through heavy smoke," she explained, "but I shoot . . . shot . . . several hundred rounds weekly. We don't have that option."

Still, they took her advice earnestly and seriously, despite their complaints. Her ankle began to heal and she forced herself into hated exercise to restore the strength. She found her capacity waning without the amino boosters she was used to taking. She hadn't had a lifetime's exposure to higher gravity, a cultural emphasis on physical activity, nor the sheer upper body strength of the male physique. Every time she turned around, another handicap slapped her.

She gave regular pep talks to increase flagging morale, including her own, as the comm reported greater and greater "progress" of the UN's "development of the system." Two weeks went by and summer heat made their civil and military tasks more obnoxious.

One morning, Kyle burst into her room. She was sleeping naked above the covers and wasn't fazed, although her brain still took a moment to readapt to the local mores. "Corporal! Quickly! Urgent message!" he said, then turned and ran.

She rolled out, grabbed her rifle in one hand and clothes in the other and tracked Kyle's progress. She found him and the others gathered around the vidsat receptor. He was opening a toolkit.

Pulling on pants, she asked, "What goes?"

"Look at the reception meter," Dak said.

She looked. It was fluctuating wildly. "You can't fix it? Or is the satellite being captured?" she asked.

"No, no," he said, shaking his head. "This caused us to kick onto fault mode, but it is receiving. The control signal is acting oddly though, and is far too active."

"I noticed it," Kyle said to her quizzical stare. "I think it's a signal," he explained, as he attached two induction probes to the meter's base. His analyzer was plugged into a portable comm and after a few seconds translated words began to appear on its screen.

"—ural locations only. Further information will be sent daily at zero divs. Say again, this is Station Wye Wye Zed, transmitting to rural locations only. Further . . ."

She raced back to her room for her comm, sprinted back and queried it about Wye Wye Zed. She had to identify herself in intense detail to get the unit to admit it had heard of that designation. It was authenticated as real, but would not give more information than that. *Black Operations*, she mused. It had to be. Those cunning bastards. She smiled in admiration. Using the entertainment system control channels as binary data transmitters, while still sending the regular signals. That was just about undetectable.

"Plug mine in," she demanded and Kyle swapped leads. Immediately, her comm was able to pull out a second, encoded transmission. Everyone crowded around, heads in a gaggle, and stared intently at the screen.

Vikki shouted in triumph, as did Dak. Kyle shushed them and kept reading as they informed the others. Kendra grinned wider and wider. Those unbelievably resourceful bastards! They still had intel of some kind and were downloading the UN order of battle and movements. A table of frequencies, directions and an updated ephemeris for transmissions followed, with orders to bounce all signals off Syscom Sat 3. How her weak signal would reach that far, even through a dish antenna, or how they'd prevent the UN from retrieving those signals was beyond her. These people clearly had ways and every code checked out, including the hidden codes that were within existing documents. That and the details on UN forces that could be verified by at least some of the recipients. She wished for a means to double-check.

Was it too good to be true? She would be very cautious about logging in, but the risk was worth it to get intelligence for the fight. "Drive me out about twenty klicks and I'll report in tonight," she told Dak. "I'll need a dish antenna, too."

"We'll pull one of ours and keep it aside," he promised.

The response to her transmission was a load of troop positions and deployment schedules. However Intel or Black Ops or whoever was doing it, they clearly had good access to UN files. She decided the info was legit. If the enemy knew about her and wanted to show up and capture or kill her, they could have.

She sent a followup message the next night, transmitting back through the receiver following directions from the control station and hastily built by Kyle. She listed her force as "militia, small" without further details and was rewarded with a suggestion of targets and a promise of support weapons. She ceased wondering how it would be accomplished. These people redefined deviousness.

The targets were all forward units moving into the rural settlements to "liberate" them. She studied the list at length, ran calculations and picked one that was close by, small, and was suggested as having little combat experience. She wanted their first raid to be successful, and their second, and every raid after that. Then she chose an unorthodox target and method of attack.

"What?" was Dak's reply. "Why in the Goddess' name?"

"Trust me, Dak. I was in the UNPF, I know how they think. This will hurt them badly."

He shrugged and deferred. All they needed now was support weaponry. Kendra sent out a signal.

Said weaponry arrived the next day. A battered air truck flew in low and landed well clear of the house, letting its intentions be known. The body was ugly, but the engine sounded healthy. The pilot was a burly young farmer with full beard, dressed in timeless coveralls and natural-fabric shirt. "I'm Minstrel," he introduced himself. "We'll try to get you better stuff later, but this will have to do for now. Good hunting," he concluded, handing over the bundle, then was gone again. He never asked their names, and Kendra realized it was for security.

Chapter 30

"Molon labe!" ("Come and get them!")
—King Leonidas of Sparta,
when asked to lay down his force's arms.

Jefferson's residents were in shock as thousands of troops in powered armor and vehicles swarmed the streets. Shock turned to outrage, then to outright disgust and fighting commenced, disorganized at first, but still effective. Well-aimed shots from heavy rifles, grenade launchers and some rockets attacked the lighter vehicles and armor-clad troops. Rocks rained down on the grounded soldiers, along with rifle and shotgun fire. City Safety, most of them veterans, threw up roadblocks of cars to channel the attackers and dug out their old service weapons to make a brief stand before scattering.

As the downtown buildings were shattered and immolated, a handful of reserve and veteran combat engineers initiated "area denial." The first technique involved crashing a heavy ground freighter under a road bridge, blocking traffic. Several smaller buildings were demolished to seal streets. Then street signs and transponders were disabled or stolen, slowing down progress. It was still possible to use map and satellite, but that was not as fast as reading a street sign. Access covers to utilities were stolen and improvised mines scattered across the streets, with hundreds of decoys to slow the invaders down. If even one mine in fifty were real, every sighting must be treated as such. This slowed progress and left them open to attack. The other option was to drive through and risk losing vehicles and troops to that one of fifty. Sniper fire and lobbed grenades became constant and harassing.

The timetable for occupation and pacification was pushed back, but was still inevitable. Most of the residents tried to evacuate to the suburbs at least, the brush preferably. Even urbanites in the Freehold were well versed in rough living; the untamed wilderness was never more than a hundred or so kilometers away.

The UN already had the highways barricaded and forced most of the air traffic down. They wanted the civilians to remain, in the theory that it would reduce insurgency. Instead, it made the covert war that much more intense.

The town of Falling Rock, situated at the far western edge of South Coast District, was quite unremarkable. It had pretty but not spectacular scenery in the mountains above it. Its twenty-thousand-odd residents were typical industrial people, small farmers and commercial workers. Its youth either sought the city as they came of age, groused about their quiet town or worked in their families' businesses. The attack and invasion was seen on the news, as was the change from local sources to UN-approved news sources. They shrugged and prepared for the eventual visit from the bureaucrats.

It was a clear, quiet morning when many of the residents began to gather in the town square for the announced arrival of the UN delegation. It wasn't actually a square, but merely a wide spot on the main thoroughfare for cars to park. The courtroom, records office and meeting hall were each a single room of the town building, and the crowd gathered outside in the street. They huddled into their long coats and cloaks against the chill, nodded and shook hands in greeting and waited.

Shortly, three vertols circled and landed. The delegation debarked and walked around the crowd to the raised concrete platform that was common to all public offices planetwide. The three bureaucrats were immaculately dressed in expensive suits and were escorted by a platoon of soldiers in riot gear. They looked impressive, at least in their own minds. Stares were exchanged between the two groups. Had the UN representatives been better educated as to local culture, they would have known that a quiet crowd was an unhappy one.

"Greetings," the delegation leader spoke. "I'm Jacob McCormick. I'm sure there's been a lot of bad rumors as to our arrival, so let me assure you of our intentions. No one is in trouble, no one is to be detained. We are here to create some basic city services to improve conditions, provide administration for the town and we'll even employ some of you to help run the administration."

There was a loud mumble from one of the residents. "You have a question, sir?" McCormick prompted.

"I said," the resident said clearly, "that I wasn't aware our conditions needed improving."

"Well, it's not obvious without careful thought, but we really do have your best interests in mind. With our programs, no one will go without food, medical care or education. There'll be a minimum wage of twenty-two marks per div and an agent to assist those who can't find jobs."

"Son, I've lived in this town forty-eight of your years," his antagonist replied. "The lowest wage paid for farm work works out to thirty marks per div, and that's paid in credits, which are far more stable than marks, and untaxed. Everyone is fed and clothed who's willing to work and everyone is literate at least. After that they can teach themselves. Now, if your agents and bureaucrats need work so badly as to come here," there was scattered laughter, "I can find some sweeping for them to do. We don't need your meddling."

Some applause and jeers broke out. The UN soldiers stood impassively, but the officer commanding them looked around nervously.

McCormick waited for it to die and replied, "Okay, that may be true. If so, think how much better things will be when you have support to go with what you've accomplished—"

"That's circular logic. You presuppose you can do better," was the reply.

"Well, our studies show—"

He was cut off again. "Of course they do. *Your* studies show whatever you want them to show. But empirical data—"

This time, McCormick interrupted. "Yes, well that whole empirical thing is what we are here about. The days of empirical rule are over."

There was silence. It was becoming obvious to the crowd that McCormick had no idea what he was talking about and was reading from a script.

"Mr. McCormick, I think perhaps you should stay here to go to school with our kids, so that they can teach you basic math and logic."

"Who are you, sir?" McCormick asked frostily.

"Joe Worthington," was the unhesitant reply.

"And what do you do for a living, Mr. Worthington?"

"I'm a mechanic. Ground or air."

"Well, Mr. Worthington, why don't you stick to mechanics and let me stick to my field? I've been a political scientist for twenty-two years." He gave a smug look.

"I've seen your books, Mr. McCormick," Worthington replied.

"Then you recognize my expertise," McCormick nodded.

"I recognize that I've been jerking off longer than you've studied poli-sci. Probably got more satisfaction and accomplished more from it than you did from your pursuit and certainly hurt fewer people," Worthington replied amid gales of laughter.

The military officer spoke now. "Just shut your yap and let the man speak or I'll shut it for you."

"Free speech, Captain," Worthington replied, showing his knowledge of UN ranks.

McCormick replied, "Only as long as you aren't inciting riot, sir."

"Only when it's convenient to you, you mean." There were more shouts and voices.

Two soldiers moved through the crowd, shoving people aside and grabbing Worthington. He made no move to resist. "I thought you said no one was to be detained," he said as they took his arms and walked him back to their lines.

"Not unless they cause trouble," McCormick replied. He wore a look of satisfaction and distaste that was not at all pleasant to see.

"I believe Adolph Hitler said that, too—"

"That's enough!" McCormick shouted. *"You will treat me with the respect I deserve or be arrested right now!"*

"I *have* been treating you with the respect you deserve," was the reply. One guard thumped him in the gut with his rifle butt and he curled up.

Breathing hard, McCormick turned back to the crowd, who looked angry and more than a bit frightened. "Now, back to the business at hand. We will be conducting a census of the town. Each resident will need to give us their name, birthdate, race, occupation and income, marital status . . . and if you have multiple spouses you'll need to speak to a legal advisor to codify the relationship. Unfortunately, there will be no new multiple relationships. It reduces the number of residences and therefore affects property tax levels. We can't properly pay for schools if everyone won't do their fair share . . ." The crowd was getting louder, and the soldiers gripped their weapons. There'd been outbursts and even a few potshots in other towns. " . . . religion and dietary restrictions, and you'll each be assigned an identification number. That also helps businesses by helping them identify bad credit risks."

There were mutters and milling about. McCormick let it settle before he continued. "And you'll need to register any weapons you have. We won't be asking anyone to turn them in yet, since this is a frontier town, but as soon as we can provide police in the town and perimeter deterrents for the farms against animals—"

"*Rippers aren't deterred by sonics, you moron!*" someone shouted.

"*We will take care of it!*" McCormick shouted back. "*Must you people question everything?*"

The milling settled down and the crowd stared at him. The looks ranged from disgusted to murderous. "It is because of people like your Mr. Worthington that society needs rules like this. As soon as proper government is provided, you'll find you don't need to work so hard or be afraid of crime—"

"It's not crime that worries us! Freehold!" someone shouted.

Automatic weapons fire erupted, along with precise shots from marksmen. In seconds, four locals were dead and almost one hundred UN soldiers. The fifty Freehold veterans in the front rows were spreading out, coats flapping from where they'd drawn their weapons. A few more sporadic shots coughed out, then silence reigned.

Joe Worthington was alive and well. The two thugs flanking him both had neat holes through their foreheads, under the helmet lips. The backs of the helmets oozed. "Thank your boy for me, Fred," he said as a neighbor helped him up and dusted him off. "That was fine sniping."

There were eleven dazed or wounded UN soldiers left, along with McCormick. "Anyone want to ask them any questions?" asked a burly retired sergeant.

"Nothing he has to say is worth listening to. You need intelligence?" someone suggested.

"Military intelligence from a political scientist?" the sergeant asked sarcastically.

"You're right. Up to you, Carpender."

Senior Sergeant Carpender, FMF (retired) replied with a string of twelve shots. McCormick cringed and wept as the bullets approached, then howled and tried to get to his feet. The last bullet took him through the base of the skull.

"All right, Joe, are you fit to fly?" Carpender asked. Worthington nodded. "You and Daffyd and Toth get those vertols hidden. The rest of you, toss these bodies into the woods. We'll let the slashers take the evidence. Fire Chief, hose down from here to there," he pointed along the road, where splashes of blood were visible, "and use lots of water. We'll also need to patch those holes in the building and replace the façade completely as soon as possible. Distribute those weapons to anyone who doesn't have any."

Chapter 31

"He who is skilled in attack flashes forth from the topmost heights of heaven, making it impossible for the enemy to guard against him. This being so, the places that I shall attack are precisely those that the enemy cannot defend. . . . He who is skilled in defense hides in the most secret recesses of the earth, making it impossible for the enemy to estimate his whereabouts. This being so, the places that I shall hold are precisely those that the enemy cannot attack."

—Chang Yu (after Sun Tzu)

Kendra stared at the weapon she held. It was a marvel of modern engineering and desperate improvisation. It had cost less than Cr100 to build and could take out UN aircraft or light armor.

Manufactured from polymer plumbing pipe, it had an assembly at the rear to feed air and propellant into a lathe-turned combustion chamber. Propellant was a pressurized can of any of several industrial hydrocarbons that might be available, ether in this case. A piezoelectric trigger and a safety were mounted on the grip. The top had a relatively accurate set of sights. The magazine was manually pumped and gravity fed. The shells dropped into place and the propellant mix would shove them through the smooth barrel and downrange.

Those projectiles would then ignite a rocket engine and could reach decent distance and excellent velocity. Incendiary and high explosive were the only options, but she had a precious handful of fuses for them: proximity, laser-guided and infrared and magnetic distortion seeking.

The combination was cheap and effective, and the initial launch was relatively cool and harder to trace than pure rocket shells. It was produced by the technical branches of Special Warfare, and the craftsman responsible had added a quick engraving of 'Another fine product of Hell's Kitchen.' She smiled at that, then marveled again at the deadliness and simplicity of its design.

It was hot. Summer was brutal even at this slightly higher altitude and latitude and the humidity in the woods was reminiscent of her former home in North America. Glare from Io hurt her eyes, insects and dirt and twigs itched. She carefully wiped sweat away from her eyes and adjusted the sopping bandanna she wore. She could smell her unwashed body and feel her toes squelching in her boots in a mix of pondwater, sweat and grime. *No one ever claimed war was pleasant,* she thought. The towering cumulus clouds were pretty, though, as was the thick, tangled growth of the forest.

She looked back over the engagement area below. One of the UN support battalions had bivouacked in. For three days Dak and Kyle had observed their activities. The kitchen trailer would open and a line of troops would form, spaced five meters apart. The idea behind that was to minimize casualties.

But that kitchen trailer made a fine target, she decided, and killing the cooks, despite any jokes about the concept, would be disastrous to morale. No one wanted to eat nothing but field rations.

As the troops began to filter in and line up, she checked the foliage around her and took a good position for shooting. She would need to fire several rockets quickly, both for best effect on the target and to ensure the rest scattered for cover. That would give her enough time to retreat. The Simonsen's neighbor, Jack Connor, was to her left, ready to cover her retreat with a light machinegun that was a slightly modified ranch rifle. She could cover him in return and the four with rifles could provide suppressing fire. They'd appear to be a much larger force and too spread out for a counterattack to be effective. Hopefully, both for tactical effect and moral principles, they'd have no casualties of their own.

The first soldier entered the trailer to be served. She checked the mechanism, charged the chamber and began launching.

Thump! *Hishhh!* Pump the charging handle. Thump! *Hishhh!* Charge, thump! *Hishhh!* She fired all seven rockets, contact fused. She quickly opened the bulky magazine and commenced reloading. There were explosions, and a quick glance showed the trailer burning furiously, tilted from damage to one side. The metal was torn and distorted and she could see three still figures. The other two were likely at least wounded, as was the troop being served.

She finished reloading and held still, ready to launch again to support Kyle or use her rifle if anyone came her way. It appeared, however, that total confusion reigned below. She clicked her radio twice to indicate withdrawal and slithered slowly backward out of the blind.

They all met up one by one, a good distance away. Dak was last. "They're still clueless," he said. "That was a nice job."

"Thanks," she nodded. "Tomorrow, I'd like to hit the cooks between units, assuming they have replacements by then. If we can get the cooks to mutiny, morale will *really* suck."

"I'm curious," Kyle asked. "Why not hit the electronics or a support weapon?"

"Several reasons," she explained. "Taking out one piece of hardware will make no tactical difference. They have more resources than we do. Any stand-up fight, they'll kick our asses. Sorry, but it's true. Second, that's expected and not too intimidating. So we are confusing them by being unpredictable. Also, if they report bad morale because of food, the brass sitting in climate-managed comfort are likely to get upset with them, which will further reduce morale. I think if we hit the cooks every chance we get, we can destroy their fighting efficiency.

"It's also important that we run everything as quietly as possible—no war whoops, insults, graffiti, anything. That works fine in the city, with echo surfaces and lots of hard cover. Out here, silence is scarier. Most of the UN forces are city kids and those who aren't are from very different terrain. We'll keep them scared. I'm hoping they have cooks again by breakfast. If we take them out in the dark, it'll be that much more effective."

"No argument there," Kyle agreed. "Hell, I grew up here and these woods give me the creepies."

"Glad to hear it," she said, grinning. "I almost wet my pants after that bailout. Now let's hit the cave and get some rest. We'll be up all night."

❖   ❖   ❖

Very early in the morning, the six of them were quite close to one of the county roads. It was a hardpan surface, but in bad need of repair. Clicked code on the radio had told them that a replacement services detachment was in fact coming from one of the nearby units. They'd strung wire across the road in thick coils. Now they waited, several meters off the road, each covered in clothes and foliage to minimize infrared signature.

Shortly, the sound of vehicles was audible. Two vehicles. Presumably, one was an infantry escort. Not unexpected, but Kendra had hoped to avoid it. She shrugged and sat still.

The utility transport got tangled in the wire and stopped. The cooks in their vehicle stopped behind it. An infantryman, probably the ranking sergeant, jumped out of the first vehicle cursing.

"Back up you fucking morons! Can't you see they're trying to get us bunched up? Probably mortars over that ridge, with airborne recon! Back the fuck up!"

Kendra grinned at his assessment. This was not that technological a war, but she clicked a message to the others to wait. Once the entanglement was thought an accident, they would strike. Meanwhile, it was a very amusing scene. She was certainly glad not to be with the UN forces. Their common denominator was mediocrity and that was about to get more of them killed.

The driver of the second vehicle tried to reverse, but was panicky and inexperienced. He managed to jackknife the trailer into the ditch. The sergeant came back screaming again.

"Goddamn shit for brains! Are you trying to get us killed?" He turned toward one of the troops from the front. "Skaggs, go out to the right, Brunner, take a look out there, about a hundred meters," he said, indicating Kendra's general direction. She came instantly tense, ready to act.

"Yeah," Brunner agreed. He sauntered in her direction, got just into the trees and stopped. Shortly, there came a splashing sound. She laughed inwardly in relief. He wouldn't come looking for anything, she was sure. Her guess was borne out when he fastened his pants and leaned nervously against a tree, facing the vehicles. He was just deep enough in the trees not to be seen by his buddies.

The sergeant continued, "Everybody else, stay still and stay quiet. It doesn't look like an attack, but I don't want any problems. If you hear aircraft or arty, yell and take cover."

Nothing moved for several minutes. Brunner took an occasional nervous look to either side. After a bit, he sat carefully down, back to the tree. The troops on the road waited, twitching nervously. Eventually, the sergeant had them start work.

Two of the troops were untangling the wire, four pushing on the stuck trailer. The sergeant was still too loud, and too scared to realize how conspicuous he was because of it. Kendra decided to make an initial move. She stood slowly, careful not to brush any growth. Choosing her steps cautiously, she walked toward Brunner's position, drawing her knife. There was enough noise from the road to keep him from hearing her.

Shortly, she was behind his tree. Her left hand clamped over his mouth and chin and pulled his head back against the trunk while her right drove the point of her blade vertically into his shoulder. It scraped through the thick fabric of his armor and off bone and through rubbery flesh, then penetrated the subclavian artery. Brunner struggled, making the damage worse, and tried to yell. Cringing in distaste, she held

him firmly as his movements ceased. She wiped the
gory blade off on his shoulder.

Calculating the risks, hoping someone else would
follow her lead, she moved to the edge of the road.
Taking careful aim from the ditch, she squeezed the
trigger, felt the recoil kick her shoulder, clicked the
selector and squeezed again.

Her grenade slammed into the trailer, the explosion
shattering a good part of its rear quarter and tossing
two of the troops to the ground. She felt the blast slap
her as she triggered a series of bursts at the others.

Up at the front, there was fire, so someone had
apparently picked up on her move. She made sure all
four men and the woman at the rear were dead,
sprinted up front to see Kyle standing over two corpses
and hissed, "Down!"

The remaining soldier was still out to the right. Kyle
followed her order instantly and she dove into the
ditch. She eased her way up to the far edge and waited
as slimy water leaked into her boots.

Nothing happened for several segs. She stared into
the dark, sparingly using the night vision gear to conserve its batteries. Eventually, there was movement. She
ascertained that it was definitely a human shape, and
click-coded her radio. Shortly, she heard five clicks in
response. The figure in the trees did not take cover,
so he was not one of her squad. She took aim and
squeezed the trigger.

"Hey-" the UN soldier said, cut off by the cough
of her weapon. His head shattered and the body
slumped. Kendra grimaced. It had sounded as if he
had been about to surrender. Oh, well. They had no
way to take prisoners, anyway. This avoided a conflict between the laws of war and a successful
mission.

Quickly, they stripped all useful gear from the

troops, cannibalized parts from the vehicles and set incendiaries to destroy them. The bodies went into a hastily dug pit, covered with lime to keep animals away. The pit was distant enough from the road that she felt sure no UN troops would find it. That done, they ignited the incendiaries and departed.

The devices in question were remarkably low-tech. They consisted of blocks of sawdust that had been cast with melted wax. Once the fuse sections—glorified candles—burned into the body, they flared quickly and hot. Segs after they left, the vehicles were charred heaps of slagged polymer and distorted metal.

They returned to the farm, where they planned to rest for several days before making further assaults. Kendra typed a coded report of their activities, suggesting similar tactics be used elsewhere to disrupt morale. The div-ten upload transmitted the information as a burst. She wasn't sure who was receiving it, but supposedly it was fast enough and scrambled sufficiently that it would be hard to track. She was still nervous, but felt the information important enough to relay.

It had been a good start. They'd killed eleven enemy troops, disrupted two units, created morale problems and destroyed the kind of basic vehicles that were always in demand and always prioritized last for replacement. Killing was not the shock it had been the first time, she decided, although the last one had bothered her a bit. She just wished Rob or Marta were around so she could brag and celebrate. She tried to block off thoughts about them.

Late that night, Kyle woke her. She stumbled outside, wrapped in her cloak. "There," he said, pointing. He handed her binoculars.

"What is it?" she asked. There were flashes and streaks writhing through the air.

"Skywheel Three," he said.

She watched the metal and fiber vapor glow incandescent below the cold points of stars and considered. It didn't slow the arrival of landing craft—that was predicated on the number of landing sites. It did increase the expense. It also took away some of the predictability of the schedules. It seemed rather petty. There was no clear advantage to it, it was simply done to obliterate another part of the local society.

Or had it been done by the resistance to annoy the UN?

Chapter 32

"The limitation of tyrants is the endurance of those
they oppose."

—Frederick Douglass

Joren Lang was furious. Bad enough to have an
assignment like this, but the UN Senate was unsym-
pathetic and totally useless. He wanted to tell them
what to do with their "advice" from "committee."

"Create, implement and initiate procedures and
policies designed to provide basic governmental infrastructure for the Grainne Colony," his orders read. He
made a list.

1) There was nothing to work from. He'd have
   to start with a census.
2) He couldn't do a census while people shot at
   his forces.
3) The locals showed no desire to assist him. They
   cheerfully shot at anyone from the UN, in or
   out of uniform. They even shot at contractors,

civil service employees and other technical noncombatants. Of course, proving those attacks were deliberate for a war crimes tribunal would be almost impossible.

4) There were no records for income, no medical records, no safety standards, no central air traffic control, no standards on anything. No basic safety standards on toys. No public medical records, driving records, consumer standards. Nothing. Well, military records, seized. Many of those were scrambled and most of the military were dead. No help there.

5) There were no records on weapons. When he'd insisted that the ownership rate was well above the five percent estimated by the committee and that most of the weapons were not simple sidearms, he had been rudely ordered back to his task.

6) He couldn't even find building plans or property records for most areas.

7) There were no bureaus to run any of this. The assumption had been that he'd take over with force if necessary and that the workers would assist him because it was in their best interests. There were no workers and no one with any training insystem. He'd have to import clerks, techs, everybody. There were civilian specialists, certainly, but almost none had accepted the offer to be hired and learn governmental procedures.

8) It was so disorganized he couldn't even make a list that made sense.

The rebels' best weapon might be the total noncooperation he was getting. They didn't want any of the basic necessities of civilized life. Utter selfish savages, every one of them. He wished them all quick voyages to hell.

❖   ❖   ❖

The approach Kendra had suggested was enthusiastically embraced by a reserve Black Operations team in Jefferson. Lorin Neumeier, Kaelin Sudhir and Brent Rewers put it into effect immediately.

The three were dressed as joggers, and attractively so. Lorin wore a stretch top that emphasized her strongly built chest; the two men wore brief trunks and were lightly oiled to show their muscle tone. They ran along Commerce Boulevard, through territory the UN used as headquarters and billeting. It was fenced and walled for security and inaccessible to vehicles. Each entrance was watched by four guards outside, others inside at monitor stations.

They timed their approach to one entrance to coincide with intelligence from local observers. Seeing the moment they were waiting for, Neumeier increased her speed. Her teammates followed. As they closed on the target, she triggered the thought command that controlled "boost."

Boost, or Combat NeuroStimulant, was a combination of hormones, sugars and oxygen-releasing compounds. Each of them had an implant that generated and controlled the chemicals required and the appropriate thoughts triggered it. They shook slightly, vision blurring then becoming suddenly sharper. Combined with their training, they now could move considerably faster than an unenhanced human. They neared the gate, which had a staff car waiting for entrance.

Lorin shoved off on her left foot, met the first of the guards and kicked his near ankle. She seized his weapon, pointed it up and shattered his shoulder as she wrenched it around. He collapsed onto his ruined ankle, shrieking in agony. She turned to see Sudhir and Rewers tackling two other guards, and moved past them. She slung the first guard's weapon as she did so.

She collided with a fourth sentry and spun him around, sliding a hand under his chin, extending the neck and striking with her other fingers. He gurgled and fell, clutching at his throat. She turned, drawing a thin knife from the small of her back and felled a fifth. Her compatriots stepped around to the remaining troops and she closed on the car.

The window was closing, but she reached in and caught the driver, tangling him and punching the lock button. He was so slow, especially compared to her in her present state. She pinched a nerve, detached and slid back, opened the rear door. Inside was a very surprised-looking general. She hit his wrist, preventing him from attempting to point his drawn weapon and dragged him out by sheer brute strength. The others joined her and they carried him facedown at a brisk run. They wove through several streets and alleys, not stopping until they reached Liberty Park.

They stood him upright, seized his weapon and all ID and documents. While he stood dazed and confused, she pointed her commandeered rifle at his head. "I am a sergeant in the Freehold Military Forces. You are my prisoner."

"General Jacob Huff. UN Peace Force."

"I know," she said. "Strip."

"What?" he queried, confused.

"Take off your clothes," she repeated.

"Here?" he croaked.

In reply, she yanked the weapon's charging handle.

"Okay! Okay!" he agreed, taking his clothes off, dropping them. Sudhir gathered them up and left. She lowered the weapon, placed his hat back on his head and said, "You are released." She bounded sideways and disappeared.

Huff stood confused, then started to flush as he realized passersby were laughing at him. It wasn't his nudity they found worthy of hysterics, but his obvious discomfort. He removed his hat, unsure what to do with it but feeling silly wearing nothing else. Finally, he started walking in the direction he'd been brought.

Several hours later, one Binyamin Al-Jabr found himself assigned to guard duty, to replace David Morgern, who had been crippled and disarmed during the attack. He took his position at the gate. Twenty minutes later, someone shot him dead. Ballistics records later showed the bullet to have come from Morgern's weapon.

The war on Grainne had begun to get interesting.

In the Space Traffic Center at Novaja Rossia's Jump Point Two, Karl Borodin had been following the news of the war. He had friends in the Freehold and went about his task in tight-lipped silence. That work had doubled since a suicide squad had destroyed Freehold Jump Point One. Some lunatic physicist had flown a multihyper-capable ship into Earth space in phase drive, then entered the jump point from there, activating phase drive *inside* the point. The intersecting hyper waves had collapsed the point into itself, and incidentally taken a UN task force with it. Until a new point could be constructed, there would be no passage through that route.

So the additional traffic was taking the roundabout way through Novaja Rossia's system and then into the Freehold from there. Borodin arrived to find a huge schedule of tonnage to organize. He glanced over it and decided that being petty couldn't hurt and might help.

He started with a transport convoy and its escort from Earth. They might have military priority in Sol System, but this wasn't Sol System. They could wait. It was far more important that perishable goods, heavy equipment to support the colony effort on Shemya and medical research materials get through. Additionally, the three liners full of wealthy retirees would complain loudly if they were delayed. In fact, they already were. Better do something about that now.

By the time he was done gridding the schedule, the UN task force was in the queue three days back. He figured he could add another day to that through judicious shuffling. It might not help, but it couldn't hurt and it made him feel better. He also noted for the log that the liners' passengers had stopped complaining.

And if the UN didn't like it, they could take the additional ten days to cross the system to Jump Point Three . . . or go through Caledonian space and in through Freehold JP3. That added twelve days.

Chapter 33

"Our troops advanced today without losing a foot of ground."

—Alleged communique during the Spanish Civil War

Kendra got a brief personal note in one of her daily loads. It read, "Logistics to beat logistics. Brilliant. N." She assumed that was Naumann. So he at least was alive. That was hopeful. She missed her unit and wished for some way to rejoin them, but slogging on foot across several hundred kilometers of rough, hostile terrain did not appeal. She still had no word of Rob or Marta. Had they cleared the base? Or been vaporized?

She sighed, rubbed her eyes and ran more calculations. Where to hit next? It wouldn't do to create a pattern, so she decided to hit some more traditional targets. That posed risk, but so did everything, and this was a war after all.

The intelligence download and local observations showed another force moving to build a Forward Operating Location within reach of the north villages. The goal was clearly to cut off Delph' and Jefferson from any support and simply take them the old-fashioned way—by siege. She wondered why they simply didn't blockade traffic, then realized the answer: they couldn't. There was no air control, so there was no way to stop flights. Stopping every flight would stop the flow of food the UN itself was stealing. Well, buying with scrap paper that was worthless. Nor were there sufficient personnel to stop every flight. The UN couldn't just shoot them down.

It was really awkward trying to fight a war as a "liberator," when one depended on good press and the goodwill of the populace being liberated. The rebels had no such hindrance. Any good press was a win, bad press wasn't really a loss and they were free to maraud as they saw fit. Her mind buzzed with schemes and calculations. It was an exhilarating experience and she slept very little as she figured her strategy.

Near Jefferson Starport, which had been converted to a UN military launch facility, a reservist of the FMF lay in wait. He was in deep, cold mud, eaten by insects until welts covered his face and hands and very, very bored. None of this bothered him and little of it impinged on his higher thoughts. It was simply the environment he was in. All that mattered were the incoming targets. A flight of four fixed wings had lifted off more than a div earlier. They should be returning soon . . . and there they were.

The best time to hit enemy aircraft was while they returned from a mission, low on fuel and munitions, potentially damaged and with tired, cranky pilots likely to make fatal errors. Since they had no reason to expect trouble, the aircraft in question were following their normal approach vector.

Make that lesson number one, the soldier thought to himself. Never be predictable.

The craft were staggered out, clearly visible in his hooded binoculars, and the lead one was on approach to the abbreviated strip. Fixed wings needed more room than vertols to operate, but could carry heavier loads. It was a fair tradeoff, but in this case posed a risk as yet unconsidered by the invaders.

The soldier raised his weapon—a professional infantry missile launcher—sighted carefully and fired, reloaded and fired again in seconds. Without waiting to see if the missiles found their mark, he rose to a crouch and began wading closer to the flightline at an oblique angle.

The first missile locked on its target, the lead craft, which detected it, jinked and dropped. This placed it closer to the second missile, which had a far cooler exhaust and better ECM. It was the true warrior here, not its decoy cousin that had expended itself to draw attention away. The Sentinel's systems detected it, too, but were hampered by internal preprograms. It wouldn't evade closer to the launch point, couldn't drop lower and couldn't alter speed drastically without aborting the landing it was attempting. The cybernetic thoughts froze for a moment of machine time as it considered, then lit a warning in the pilot's environment.

The pilot saw the flicker at the edge of his vision, moved to take human control, but was slower than the artificial synapses of the machine and too late. The second missile passed overhead at high speed and detonated. Its self-forged warhead slammed down through the lighter armor of the top surface, shredding an engine. There were two engines and the craft would ordinarily have corrected immediately with more thrust to the other one, but it was on manual. The machine moved to retake control, the pilot hesitated in shock and the already stressed craft dropped slightly lower. It impacted the runoff, not hard, but hard enough to shatter the frame and injure the pilot. Warnings squawked and the other pilots aborted their approaches.

The terrain was not conducive to a ground search. ACVs would have trouble with the boulders and deep spots, wheeled vehicles would be mired and infantry was just not a concept the UN was currently embracing. A sensor sweep of the launch area found nothing and the decision was made that the rebel had departed. The craft resumed their approach.

The third missile was launched virtually at touchdown and the target in question couldn't dodge as it tried to land. The missile caught the target near the cockpit and the pilot's ejection seat kicked in automatically. He would survive, but the wreckage of his Sentinel, combined with that already clogging the runoff, made the surface a hazard.

At this point, bureaucracy became the enemy. The runway was technically unserviceable, but the Sentinels did not need its entire length by a wide margin. It would be safe to land beyond the damage, once the shooter was contained, but to do so would officially be a violation of safety procedures. If a craft was damaged due to wreckage, it would be blamed on whoever authorized a landing on the "unserviceable" surface. The officer in charge of flight ops called up the chain of command for a decision, the security officer called the external security unit for them to deal with the shooter, and the pilots waited, fuel diminishing rapidly.

The Freeholder was ready to escape, be captured or killed at this point. He'd had his two shots and was departing the area rapidly. He knew there was a margin of safety in his schedule, but also knew that luck was not a factor one could depend on. He slogged through the mire, getting closer to the river where a small punt waited, and hoped for the best.

It was true that troops in powered armor were the best means of dealing with the shooter. It was true also that not using a resource would cause fingers to be pointed after the fact. It was therefore decided, with all bureaucratic logic, to send a squad out to clear the area. This took about forty-five minutes, from call to suitup to actual deployment across the flightline with proper safety precautions and checklists. The soldier was gone by then, but his legacy lingered slightly longer.

The two remaining Sentinels were low on fuel. A ranking officer had to decide whether to try to divert to another facility, risk landing amid wreckage and response vehicles or attempt to refuel in air and wait. The wing commander made the logical decision to simply make a downwind landing from the runway's other end, with precautions for the wreckage, and gave the order to do so. It was too late.

Both craft ran out of fuel as they orbited around to make the landing and the pilots decided not to ride their crippled aerial steeds into the swamp. They ejected and were soon rescued by the squad of infantry returning from their no-joy search for the missileer. Their craft were destroyed, enmired and unsalvageable.

Several days later, the soldier crept back through the oily slime around the craft and removed their IFFs and a handful of useful circuitry for intelligence analysis. He shook his head in disbelief. If a Freehold craft was deemed unrecoverable, it was slagged to prevent precisely this type of intel gathering.

✧   ✧   ✧

Kendra's local insurgents roved around in small groups, leaving enough bodies to tend the farms. It took a few weeks for all of the adults to get a taste of combat and Kendra aged ten years inside. She was terrified of the possibility of an informer.

Kyle assured her that was impossible. "Not these people, not here. We're even more independent than the city dwellers. We hate even the suggestion of government meddling. And don't make the mistake of thinking of us as ignorant farmers. We've studied everything from the history of agriculture to business to chemistry. These people are solid," he said.

She believed him, but also knew enough mathematics to be certain there was at least one rat in the area. She hoped she was wrong.

She personally led most of the patrols until Dak convinced her that he, Sandra and Kyle had enough experience in the brush to avoid detection. The strain was wearing on her and was even worse when she *wasn't* leading the operation in question. Nothing she did helped her to relax and she wondered how long it would be before the stress caused her to crack.

The operations were getting harder, also. Every trick they used was, of course, quickly noted and defended against by the UN troops. Whether or not the bureaucracy allowed it, the people in question were not entirely stupid, those who survived a few missions were quite competent and the skills they'd used to bypass "the book" in peacetime were put to use in this new arena. Their motivation was the best available: survival.

Kendra led a harassment mission against the nearest firebase the UN was constructing. The end plan was to have a vertol contingent and a couple of artillery pieces placed in each of several overlapping circles to cover a large radius around every town. The insurgents were desperately working to keep the available support to a minimum for their own survival.

The firebase project was actually north of the farms and was in a broad prairie of tangled weeds and brush. There were no good enfilades or overlooks to use and no thick woods to hide from observation. Modern sensors would handily pick them up in the brush and it was doubtful they'd get close enough to do any real damage. A mortar would be of great use, but they had none. Her grenades lacked the range and were too valuable to waste on difficult targets. Their best option was to set traps along the ground route. Since the ground convoys were large and well protected, the most practical approach was to disable a vehicle and take a few potshots. The chance of inflicting serious casualties was slim, but it would slow things down and that by itself might prove useful.

Dak dug out some of his precious explosives, needed also for clearing boulders and trees on the farm, and Kendra called up diagrams of fuses and triggers. Kyle studied them briefly and assured her he could manufacture them. Once all components were ready came the task of setting the trap. It required stealth and deception, as well as painful labor.

Vikki drove them as close as was deemed safe and the three of them rolled out the back of the truck as it slowed for a bend. The UN was unlikely to observe a vehicle closely, but stopping in the middle of nowhere would attract attention if anyone was watching the area via satellite, aircraft or observation post. They bounced to the ground, Kendra bruising her pelvis painfully in the process, and shimmied into tall brush. Once safely in, they threw up camouflaged and heat-disrupting veils to sleep under and settled in to slap at bugs for the day.

That night, they spread out and began walking. The few fused roads out here were laid in approximate grid squares and they had a hike through rough terrain of five thousand meters. Using night vision of varying quality to find their way and keep their distance, they began slogging. They were unarmed, in case of discovery. Assuming they either finished or could ditch their deadly packages before capture, they would be in a much better position to deny involvement. Kendra doubted it would work, but to not do so would definitely cause problems in an emergency.

They meandered in the general direction of the target, doing their best to mimic animal movements. They stopped and started, cast about and moved in convoluted paths. Progress was tedious, frustrating, caused numerous aches, and they were quickly cold and wet as fog and dew rolled in. Prickly weeds, tangling bush and burrs and roots impeded progress. Near midnight, a springing sound of undergrowth caused Kendra to wheel about, drawing the machete she carried as her only weapon. She saw movement and felt a vicious tug at her calves and several sharp stings.

"Firethorns!" she whispered hoarsely to herself, then lay still, wincing in pain as the patch finished coiling. It dragged at her wounds, scratching across the fabric of her pants as she closed her eyes against tears of agony. Once she was sure it was done, she carefully drew out a folding tool and commenced cutting herself free.

She cursed as she did so, both in pain and because she could smell the dank, rotten stink of the decay beneath the patch where other, less fortunate creatures were slowly turning into fertilizer. Even in the chill night, insects buzzed about, feasting on the refuse. It was a stupid greenhorn mistake and she should have known better. The other two had skirted this area, but she'd cut across to avoid following an existing route and to save time.

Free at last, she sat back gingerly and began dumping anesthetic and disinfectant into the wounds. Her legs looked as if a large cat had shredded them, with scratches and seeping punctures all over. At least tetanus hadn't gotten much of a foothold here, although she was immunized. She wasn't sure when she was due for a booster. Maybe Vikki had some.

She rose painfully to her feet, feeling the wounds begin to inflame already. She pushed sorely on and hoped the swelling wouldn't impede her too much.

They did reach their objective before dawn and waited nervously for the first gray tinges across the broad coastal plain. She'd spent a long time convincing the others that UN doctrine would hold through almost anything—at dawn and dusk, everyone "stood to" and prepared for attack, that being the most likely time, according to doctrine. Dak had argued that one div, or 3 A.M. was most effective, since biorhythms were at their lowest. "Dak, you're arguing logic with tradition and bureaucracy. Trust me," she insisted. He shrugged and went along with her schedule.

They quickly dug a hole at the edge of the roadbed, buried the large bomb and ran the sensor wire across the road. Mud and dead weeds camouflaged the scar on the ground and they retreated as Io began to show. Now they had to get far enough away not to be detected when the device detonated.

The rest of the trip was anticlimactic. They hit the next road over, ten kilometers away, that night, spread out to wait for the truck that was their pickup and hoisted themselves into the bed. They were back at the farm, Kendra soaking her calves in saltwater to take the swelling down as the blast hit. They heard about it secondhand and from intel reports two days later. One truck had been destroyed, plus its cargo of a generator, and two casualties. The psychological effect would be greater. "Wish we could have watched that," Kyle commented. Kendra nodded, not really sharing the feeling.

"What should we come up with next?" she asked as she rubbed her burning, itching legs.

Adding to the UN's problems was a serious logistical error. During the first month of operations, twelve Guardian vertols had been shot down or blown up by "terrorists." Replacements were requested and the files were munched by the usual bureaucracy. Nine new ones were sent. In the meantime, three more had been destroyed. General Huff tried to order excess numbers to allow for projected losses and ran into a twofold brick wall of a bureaucracy that couldn't provide more than the current table of operations allowed, and soundly critiqued him for having a negative attitude toward operational capabilities. It was simply not politic to admit that any losses would occur. He gritted his teeth and requested fifteen, waited through four more losses for them to arrive . . . and was sent eleven. This was not the way to run a war, he decided, with bean counters tabulating the cost of ammunition versus body count and land area.

He demanded, and got, a visit from an oversight committee to discuss methods. This concept of nonlethal warfare was popular with the gutless types who were terrified of every vote and every tax mark in case it was held against their bureau at review time, but it was not how wars were won. His men and women were paying the price because, naturally and as always, the enemy saw no advantage to playing the same game. To them, the psychological advantage came from splashing as much UN blood as possible on as many news vids and Peacekeepers as possible. They'd even taken to mailing anatomical parts to comrades after battles. The only result of this would be a long, bloody war, and he sought a quick end from pragmatic and ethical considerations.

The committee that visited was the typical collection of stodgy types who saw admin as more important than people. He ensured they were driven through some of the messiest areas of conflict in Jefferson, where body parts and fresh blood made a queasy impression on them. A quick pass through the hospital with ad lib screams of pain added to the effect. Then he took them to a cold, dark hangar for his pieces de resistance.

Even before they arrived, they'd agreed to some of his demands, but they drew the line at initiation of lethal force. Under no circumstances would that be tolerated. He made a pro forma objection before springing his trap.

"You have the other concessions, General. You may operate as you would in any other disputed territory and use nonlethal bioweapons. But we can't condone deadly force initiatives based on hearsay reports of weapons that are more than likely nonexistent, nor can you shut down civilian power," the spokeswoman insisted.

"Let me display for you some of the 'hearsay' and 'nonexistent' weapons the locals have," Huff said, sarcasm dripping. He nodded and the escorting guards opened the hangar door.

He led the entourage into the dark cavern and stopped at a shape emerging from the shadows. "This is a twenty-year-old, but still combat effective Tee Dee Twenty-Three tank destroyer we confiscated from its civilian owner. Over here," he said as he walked, hammering his points home, "is a Vee Six Bison, civilian

model, retrofitted with six autocontrolled rotary cannon
for gunship operations. Here," he waved at a pile of
rifles, "are seventeen thousand and more *military* rifles
we confiscated from a town of less than one hundred and
fifty thousand residents. This is a pile of grenades made
from pipe fittings, publicly available commercial explosives and common hardware and fusing. They also had
these," he indicated a stack of rocket launchers, "these,"
a heap of machineguns, "and these."

He bent and retrieved one of the weapons in question. It was the same type of improv rocket launcher
that Kendra had. He explained the device's operation
and said, "Accuracy: terrible. Cost: about a day's local
wages in materials. Effectiveness: you can blame this
little terror for sixteen downed aircraft and forty-one
vehicles. Their expense was about nine thousand marks
in materials and eleven shooters. Our cost was one
point six billion in aircraft and vehicles, eight highly
trained pilots and fifty-six other personnel, plus morale
loss and reduced strategic advantage."

The delegation was appropriately silent. Had he
stripped naked and run screaming around the room he
could not have disturbed them more. "I want lethal
force," he said. "I cannot fight a war against these
animals unless I can use the same weapons they do,
which are all deadly."

It was necessary to defeat the military and the rebels
quickly, he repeated, so as to minimize resentment
among the civilians. Ironically, he'd learned this lesson
on Mtali, observing a Freehold commander, one
Naumann, doing exactly that to the factions there. There
was nothing pretty about war, except its conclusion.

There were murmurs exchanged, but the glances at
the captured weaponry assured him he had won at least
part of this battle. Now to fight the real one against
the rebels in the bush.

First, however, was the city. Rather than submit peacefully, the residents were fighting like cornered rats. The local gangs had plenty of weapons and were well trained. Despite any hype in the media, Earth gangs did not "outgun the police," nor did they have any real experience with their stolen weapons. The Freehold city gangs did. They would appear out of nowhere, through alleys and tunnels they knew well, swarm onto the surface level and hit a target, then retreat. In the sublevels, the UN had to maintain squad-sized patrols. Smaller groups had been tried and simply disappeared. It was one more stiff thorn in the side of the occupation. None of the usual methods would work against such tactics. Rationing, IDs or any other restrictions would only keep insurgents out, not control those inside who had them. A steady stream of criminal investigators tried without success to identify terrorists. Regular patrols helped minimize the activity, but at least once a week, a UN body would be found, usually violated in creative ways.

The patrols ran into less obvious problems. One such patrol was creeping through the depths of Commerce Court, night vision lenses in place, as all the tubes had been smashed. The shadows made it awkward to discern anything. Sweat poured off them in the dark confines, as they gingerly crept through the cluttered passage. It had been a busy, high-end commercial operation once. Now it was a rubble-strewn labyrinth. They were probing for enemy activity with the only bait that would work: themselves.

Eventually, they returned to the less shattered sections and their mood lightened along with the increase in illumination. It was no less dangerous, but the light made it seem far friendlier. They tilted their lenses back and spread out slightly.

There was movement, and they focused on it, weapons ready. The two in rear faced outward, ready for any envelopment.

"Hey," a soft female voice said. Two of them moved in closer.

The woman, girl really, was alone. She was thin and a bit disheveled but healthy. The lead soldier said, "ID."

She produced it carefully, and it matched her computer scan. "Says here you're a student in biology."

"I was," she admitted. "Maybe again when the war's over."

"What are you doing down here?" the field officer asked.

"Sleeping. Working," she said.

"What kind of work?"

In reply, she hiked up her short skirt. "What kind do you think? It's all I've got right now."

"Hmmm."

"So . . . you want some?"

There were comments and chuckles all around. "What about it, FO?" one of them asked. "Seems harmless enough. A little recreation."

Signaling for silence, the officer had the troops fan out and search the wreckage nearby, then the back passage to the shops. "All clear," she was told.

Grinning, she said, "Okay, guys, if you need to get off." There were whoops.

The girl smiled slightly. "Do you all for two hundred."

"Two hundred?" the ranking sergeant objected. "Tenner apiece. That's seventy." There were two women plus the officer in the unit of ten. That left seven men.

"Not me," one NCO objected. He'd been kidded before for his puritanical stance, but he'd made it clear it was a religious concern and the comments had stopped at once.

"Nor me," said the youngest and newest. He was still shy, but give him a few weeks.

"One and a half," she said, shaking her head.

"Seventy," the sergeant insisted. "For five, that's a deal."

Shrugging, she said, "Okay. Who wants it?" After a few jokes, one volunteered. The others argued over position and precedence.

The third troop said, "How about a switch? Something fresh." Obliging, the girl licked her lips.

Ten minutes of catcalls and rude jokes later, the squad prepared to leave. "What about you ladies?" she asked.

"I don't do women," one of them said.

"Nah," her buddy replied. "She'll do *you*."

"Be a thrill for me!" another said. "Just wish I had a camera so I could send a pic to your mom!"

There was shoving and teasing and one of the women agreed to at least pose. She yelped when touched and said, "Ooh! Not bad! Maybe I can live without men!"

"Come on, FO, you too!" someone said. She shook her head. Not in her position. It would be too familiar with the troops. Shrugging, the girl collected another twenty for the show, thanked them and waved as they wandered back to the surface, grinning and howling.

As soon as they were out of sight, she scrambled back into the darkness and entered a utility room. "Antidote!" she snapped as she opened the door. "And mouthwash. Goddess, those apes need to shower more often. *And* lose the body hair. Yuch."

Her assistant, a professor of biochemistry, slapped a tube against her arm and let the counter-virus seep into her skin. She had been contaminated with a short-lived, but fast-acting nano and was cutting her safety margin on infection close.

Above on the surface, the squad, field officer and observer made their way back to billets, secure behind a double perimeter. They were safe again, or so they thought. None of the six noticed any symptoms and were soon asleep, exhausted from the day's efforts.

Three days later, fourteen people were dead. The order to avoid local prostitutes was mostly unenforceable and did further damage to morale.

Chapter 34

"The real destroyer of the liberties of the people is
he who spreads among them bounties, donations
and benefits."

—Plutarch

The convoy was four vehicles with UN markings.
One was a Mk 17 Infantry Light Armored Wheeled
Assault Vehicle, the others simple multipurpose vehicles
with heavy weapons mounted. They stopped in front
of the farm and several people dismounted. They
approached the door and met Dak at the steps as he
came out.

"Yes?" he asked, bluntly and without any friend-
ship.

The one in civilian clothes spoke, "I am Lynet
Krishnamurti with the United Nations Readjustment
Task Force. I am here to give you an informational
package on the recent improvements we are imple-
menting."

"Thanks, but we don't need any improvements. I have the latest gear I can afford," Dak replied. He wanted them to leave quickly.

"Well, that's the point," Krishnamurti said. "One of the benefits the UN offers is investment capital to buy better equipment. We also guarantee reparations not covered by insurance, accident insurance . . . many benefits. This package is on hard copy and on datachip, compatible with most systems."

"And what does this cost me?" Dak asked, trying to sound like a suspicious bumpkin.

"It's free. The UN provides it as a service to all agribusiness operations."

"Well, if I need it, I'll call you. Thanks. Is that it?"

"I'm also here to assess your hectareage," Krishnamurti admitted.

"Not sure. Probably six or seven thousand." He knew to the millimeter what he planted, but he wasn't about to admit it. "Why?"

"We need an accurate measure to assess commercial property taxes. The package also contains information on tha—"

"Property tax?" Dak acted confused. "It's my property and a gift from the Lord. Why should I pay tax on it?"

Krishnamurti looked exasperated. Was every one of these peasants utterly ignorant of basic principles?

They wrangled for long segs, while the troops looked amused. They'd seen it all before.

"So let me get this straight," Dak was trying desperately but successfully to avoid hysterical laughter at his guest's discomfort. "In exchange for taxing the property the Lord gave me to clear and use and taking a whopping chunk of my income from said property, and dictating what I grow, how I grow it, what equipment to use, and how to wipe my nose most likely, you'll grant me a 'free' loan at interest to buy the equipment I wouldn't need without your regulations? And I'll have to spend an extra four divs a week, unpaid, doing bookkeeping to prove it to you?"

"Uh, put that way it sounds stupid," she said.

"Of course it's stupid!" Dak replied. "The only thing worth anything in any of that would be the accident insurance, if we didn't already have it and if my sister-in-law wasn't a nurse."

"Nurse?" Ms. Krishnamurti asked, making notes. "Is she licensed from an accredited school and is her license current?"

Dak paused for just a moment. Vikki had worked her way up in a major hospital, using the texts recommended by the physicians and attending classes as needed to maintain her proficiency. She was also a qualified veterinary surgeon and close to being qualified as a human surgeon. As far as "license," there were none this clown would recognize. The university had granted her a degree based on proficiency exams and an instructor's assessment in leiu of classes. How to explain it to this character who probably used a manual to have sex?

He didn't bother. "I want you off my property now," he said. "The Good Lord doesn't allow taxation of His workers and you must respect that." He made a solid attempt to sound like one of the Mennonite or Traveler sects.

"Religious objections, huh?" she replied, smirking. "I've heard that one before. If you are actually a Primitive Christian practitioner, you would be exempt . . . but I don't suppose you can name the Gospels?" That usually stopped them. There were almost no Christians at all out here, much less PC sects.

Dak snorted. He was educated and Kendra had briefed him also. "Matthew, Mark, Luke and John."

"Hmmmph," was the reply. "If you fill out the proper documentation and can prove preexisting membership in an approved sect, the board will consider your exemption."

"Fine," Dak replied. "Then please get off my property, and may the Good Lord bless you, ma'am. You need it."

"I thank you for your blessing, sir," she replied and turned, sighing. Every one of these hicks was going to be trouble.

One of the soldiers cut in, "If you will give us just a moment, sir, we need to take a census count of everyone resident here. We need to be able to provide proper protection and emergency services. And we need to give everyone a quick analysis." He held out a scanner comp.

"Devices like that are the work of the Adversary," Dak continued loudly, looking at it with contempt. "I will allow no violation of my body."

"It's completely nonintrusive, sir," the soldier assured him. "We simply scan your skin." And compare to seized military records to nab any reservists or veterans who were still at large. They were becoming a serious threat.

Some of the troops were doing a slow perimeter of the cleared ground around the house as the argument continued. Vikki stepped to the door and said, "It's all right, Dak. We'll trust the man." Kendra would be hidden, then. Dak nodded.

Dak, Sandra holding a bouncing, wiggling Riga, Eric and Brian their two teenage boys, and Vikki lined up. Kyle was out on patrol, but the intruders had no way of knowing that. The soldiers skipped Riga at first, saying there was no need to check a child. When Dak asked, "Don't children qualify for your help?" they made a show of giving her a quick scan. The omission was definite evidence that their concern was adults only. And that meant their concern was with rebellion. He shook inside at that confirmation.

The soldiers politely insisted on checking the area. Their search was laughable. They checked vehicle hatches, but not inside the equipment compartments where the weapons were hidden. They made a quick mag-scan of the immediate grounds, but didn't bother going out to the far shed where other gear was hidden. They didn't find the secondary crawlspace where Kendra hid in blackness among cobwebs, rats and snakes, trying desperately not to scream in disgust.

Finally they left to hassle the next farmstead. Dak wished them all an early death silently, while wishing God's Blessing on them publicly.

They waited to pull Kendra out for another half div. As she rose, Dak handed her a bottle of liquor and let her take several gulps before downing some himself.

"I'm alive," she thanked him, then shook. "Ewww."

Nodding, he replied, "I felt utterly dirty professing your religion as a hoax. It's obscene to have to hide behind something I don't believe."

"I'm sure God will forgive you," she said. Her religion, a comforting background against the world, was becoming more important to her as she faced daily capture and death. She'd put in a word personally when she next got a chance to pray. Say, as soon as she was sober. She followed them upstairs to clean up and change.

Chapter 35

"Mundus Vult Decipi."

—James Branch Cabell

Not all Freehold military personnel had been captured. There were always detachments and personnel in transit who slipped through any system. While not organized, these troops found bolt holes and tried to get messages through to someone, anyone with intelligence and command resources.

Commander Naumann had been one such, flying between installations when the attack hit. He sent such orders as he could to his exec, told her she was in charge and ordered his pilot down. He sheltered in a small town near the mountains and organized the forces at hand. There were quite a number of veterans, several reservists and a precious few active duty personnel. He began slipping them out clandestinely to bring in others.

One such catch arrived and Naumann, usually reticent, smiled broadly. His mind immediately began sorting through plans. "Sergeant Hernandez! Do I have ideas for you!"

"Professional, sir? Or military?" she joked. It was good to see familiar faces, especially since she had no idea if Rob or Kendra were alive. "Or personal?"

"All three," Naumann replied, laughing aloud. "Let me gather some other personnel and I'll tell you what I have in mind."

The local militia units were networking now, messengers relaying data. It was usually a few days old by the time it arrived, but it was intelligence. It wasn't as good as the no longer existent satellite feed, which had been destroyed after being located. Vid had been down for most of a month while that happened, as if to drive home the point, then brought back up to keep the propaganda flowing. Kendra mapped units, plotted and led and sent her farmers to harass them further. There was word that the UN headquarters in Jefferson was having a near mutiny. Apparently, guards were refusing to be stationed at the gates and were willing to be court-martialed and jailed over it.

A recent message indicated that a nearby militia squad wanted to meet with her, to discuss combining forces. She took Kyle, Dak and Sandra with her. She'd known them the longest and wasn't about to travel alone.

It was a long drive, almost two hours and one hundred kilometers, all along ragged country roads. They detoured several times to avoid UN roadblocks, warned by subtle signs tied to gates and fenceposts. She gritted her teeth, hoping none of the locals were turncoats. They might pass a roadblock . . . or be searched in depth or scanned. That would be the end of her operation and maybe her life. She could dress as a farmer's wife, but couldn't disguise her DNA. Nor were they about to travel unarmed. Stashed under junk and scrap in the back of their truck were rifles.

They should have just hopped in an airtruck, there being no really heavy cargo. But the UN was requiring notification of all air travel and unreported flights were all subject to forced landings and detailed examination. They lacked the personnel to check more than a few percent, but it still would draw unnecessary attention. They stuck to the ground.

It was dark, past curfew, when they finally arrived. The farm looked like any other and they swapped signals cautiously. Kendra hissed as they entered the house. Not him . . .

"Hello, Kendra," Jim Wayland said, smiling his trademark grin.

"Jim," she replied levelly, feeling her temperature and pulse shoot into the stratosphere. Jesus Christ! How did he wind up in charge and what did he want?

"So, you've been hurting them?" he asked.

He seemed earnest enough, so she nodded and detailed her efforts.

"That's it?" he replied. "We've taken out thirteen trucks, six generators, a radar and have at least twice that many kills."

"It's not the number of kills, though," she objected. "It's the effect of them."

"What, a few cooks?" He had a half-sneer on his face. "And you think that will beat them?"

She said, "We aren't going to beat them here, Jim. That's going to be done—" but he cut her off.

"It sounds like you don't have faith in your people . . . or in us. We're Freeholders, Kendra. Maybe the UN can't handle the task, but—"

"I am a Freehold NCO, Jim, unlike you, who are a civilian. I'm serving my nation the best way I know how and you have no right to suggest otherwise. I'm not a traitor."

"Look lady," Wayland said, exasperation in his voice. "I'm not saying you can't live here. I'm not even saying you can't be trusted. But it ought to be obvious that you have a weak spot for Earth. You have to admit that."

"Why? Because you don't agree with my targets?" she snarled. It was taking desperate effort to keep calm.

He snickered derisively. "What, a bunch of cooks?"

"Enemy activity in our area is almost nonexistent," she said.

"Of course!" he replied. "They don't think you're a threat. They've been at us nonstop."

"And you haven't done a damned thing except piss them off!" she shouted. "You can blow up all the generators you want, they'll build more. It's not what you destroy, it's the level of activity. Can't you see that?"

"Yeah," he smirked, "And we're getting more activity. *That's* what proves they're pissed off and hurt. If you'd been to Leadership School, you'd know that."

"I went, right after you left and was third in my class," she said. "Logistics is what they hammered into us every day, and you should know *that*."

"Wait a mo," one of his henchmen cut in. "This is the woman who got you booted?"

Kendra felt the world twist again. What?

Wayland nodded. "Yeah, this is her."

"Wayland, you got yourself thrown out by insulting people—"

"Insulting dorks and trying to make them grow up."

"*Insulting people* and violating safety regs. You were the one without a spare oxy bottle, remember?" She breathed hard, trying to maintain her composure and losing.

"Oh, yes, Ms Regulation herself. Real handy to get yourself promoted," he said. "Typical UN backstabbing. Perfect for petty details. Then when you get here, you completely ignore the Target Priority Table," he said, tapping the page up on his comm screen.

"That's for *conventional* warfare, which this is *not!*" she said. "And where the fuck did you get a controlled item?" she asked, pointing at the comm. It was a military standard model that he shouldn't have been able to keep after his effective dismissal.

"Right back to regs again," he said, shaking his head. "Typical."

She held her breath, trying to avoid a panic attack. *How did he do this?* she wondered. The man was a snake!

His troops were looking at her with mixed amusement and condescension, tinged with disgust. Kyle looked thoughtful. Dak was blank. She couldn't see Sandra.

"I think we should leave on this note," she said very levelly. "You run your ops, I'll run mine. Commander Naumann can reach me if he has a problem with my methods," she said.

"Naumann. Yeah, that's a little upstart who likes to swap casualties for headlines—"

"Goodbye, Jim. Folks, we're leaving," she said.

They followed her out silently.

She kept her eyes closed and feigned sleep while she collected her thoughts. Nothing good would come of this, she knew in her guts. Her musings were interrupted by Kyle asking, "Do you think there's anything to his theory about targets?"

"No." Her voice was automatic and curt.

"Good enough for me," he said.

"Guy's a manipulative asshole," Dak said through his beard. "He was hoping for a confrontation and is doing exactly what he accused you of: quoting regs for his own good."

"I just thought he was a scared geek, puffing himself up with brave words," Sandra said.

"Why can't they see that?" Kendra asked. "It was obvious to you guys."

"We're on the outside. People like that are persuasive," Dak said. "Life of the party, class clown, great to be around. Bet he disappears when there's dirty work to do."

She laughed. "Oh, you've met him before."

"His father, most likely."

Kyle added, "I take it we won't be working with him?"

"Not a chance in hell," Kendra said.

"Good."

Chapter 36

"All propaganda has to be popular and has to adapt its spiritual level to the perception of the least intelligent of those towards whom it intends to direct itself."

—Adolf Hitler

Kendra squirmed again in near agony. The latest nasty bioweapon had been sprayed as spores around one of their recent targets and they'd picked it up during an operation. It caused ulceration of the mucous membranes, and her eyelids were a weeping, gummy mass that left her near blind. Her nose felt as if it had been sanded with power tools and her tongue was swollen with jagged red wounds she could see despite her ruined vision. Her gums were so afflicted that her teeth were loose and she didn't relish her next trip to the bathroom. It was hard to drink enough fluid, but she forced another burning mouthful of lukewarm water down. Her nose was running, but she dared not touch it. In addition, the flaking, weeping wounds of severe dandruff were causing her scalp to bleed and shed hair in places. Whether it was a related effect or simply malnutrition and environmental in nature was unknown, but it itched and hurt as the skin came off in huge, fluffy flakes. Her hormone-balancing implant had expired and she found out what it was like to suffer menstruation. How did people survive in the Dark Ages?

Her squad was hiding in their farms, all gear well hidden against any routine scans, and they were simply waiting for a cure or for the infection to run its course. This attack was probably less lethal than the pneumonic one that had taken weeks to defeat and killed Dak's beautiful little girl in the process. Kendra could still see Riga smiling and trying to play as her breath bubbled through the liquid filling her lungs. Despite an around the clock watch, several local infants and toddlers had gone to sleep and strangled to death in their nightmares.

Perhaps in that regard, this was a more humane weapon. The people it left blind or toothless had an eventual hope of recovery. The children shrieked every time they tried to urinate. The psychological effect of that on a two-year-old was something she didn't want to consider. Some of them were looking a bit jaundiced. The official word was that all they had to do to get cured was to come and get an implant that would allow their positions to be monitored, for "the safety of society." DNA would be checked on all such persons and kept on file. It was completely voluntary. Only a terrorist would refuse, of course.

It was disgusting to see the Earth press still insisting that no violations of the Laws of War were taking place by the "liberators" of the UNPF and that the treatment they received as prisoners of the Freeholders was brutal. She recalled one such cast a few days before. They'd been gathered in the dark around a locally transmitted vid . . .

"This is Iakova Popovic with EBC News," the woman announced as the camera followed her along a fence. "As you can see, we are here in a rebel prison compound containing UNPF captives. They agreed to let us in here, far behind their line of resistance, to show us the conditions they maintain.

"You'll notice that the prisoners only have thin pads and a single light blanket for sleeping, many of which have been furnished by local civilians sympathetic to the cause. They are fed, but all of it is food from wild sources; none is professionally produced for human consumption. Meals are sporadic at best and no religious or philosophical dietary needs are being observed. There are rodents and other pests crawling through the site. Some of the captives are in need of medical care and all of them have been denied contact with their friends and families. The camp commander, a reserve captain in the former Grainne army, had this to say:"

The vid cut to an older man who looked very tired and worn. "—There can be no exchange of prisoners without UN cooperation, and the treatment they are getting is all they can expect—" he was cut off.

"EBC News has managed to acquire a list of prisoners from inside and we'll share that info on our access site with anyone who can identify a potential prisoner and their relationship with them. Contact the Red Cross or your nearest Bureau of Defense facility to make arrangements. The UNPF staff note that any attempt to attack the camp would lead to casualties, so they reluctantly must leave them in their current squalor for now."

The Freehold version, not available outsystem and not to most even on Grainne, was that the prisoners were being fed the same food as the guards and staff. The UN had been requested to arrange a swap and refused, probably fearing that actual testimony and reports from the field would ruin its various PR tracks. Nor would they take the badly injured. Every one that died or suffered in the competent but over-worked and underequipped hands of the Freehold-ers was further publicity. Some of the guards didn't have even the minimal clothing and shelter the pris-oners had. And all the prisoners had been allowed to send mail home. It had been delivered to the UN headquarters by a SpecWarfare team who had dropped it off at the front gate. The bag had been taken inside and never seen again. Their communi-cations had been "denied," yes, but by the UN, not the Freehold. There were even rumors that some UN prisoners had been returned and either disappeared or been badly abused by their own people to gen-erate publicity before being sent home. Kendra hoped it wasn't true, but was ready to believe almost any-thing about the enemy now. She shuddered again, sickened at what her home had turned into.

The camp commander's actual quote had been, "We've tried to exchange prisoners and been refused. There can be no exchange of prisoners without UN cooperation, and the treatment they are getting is all they can expect given our current state of affairs. My guards and perimeter patrols are no better fed or clothed. If you can at least get the list of detainees home to their families, you'll be doing us a great favor."

Kendra had flushed a crimson so bright it should have glowed as the propaganda from her home went on. She'd been glad for the darkness.

The "news" continued. "Further investigations by our team show the true threat the rebels pose to society. Out in the country, recruits as young as ten are arming themselves, brainwashed or scared into fighting by their extremist parents. In the cities, we spoke to several prostitutes who were under twelve years old . . ."

Of course, those were local years, not Earth years. The Freeholders didn't see the threat in that type of reporting, nor were they bothered by the "decadence" of prostitution. They were most annoyed by the people who were forced into it, rather than choosing it as a career. Kendra shuddered. The press was potentially a worse threat than the armed enemy and there was nothing she could do about them.

The good news was that patrols outside the cities had all but ceased. Certainly they were being reported to UN Command as normal, but most patrols were not actually being conducted. The few that were didn't stray very far, staying within artillery range usually and close-air support range definitely. They'd learned that to venture further brought quick death from the natives.

The bad part of that was that it was necessary to brave the support fire to damage the UN forces. That meant longer operations, reduced engagement time and higher casualties. No free lunch. It was getting harder to hurt the invaders and their position daily consolidated. The cities were de facto UN territory, the outlands de facto Freehold, but sparsely populated and ill-equipped. Those forces would never surrender, but would surely weaken with time. Short term: stalemate. Long term: loss by attrition.

The political news wasn't good, either. It appeared there was no General Assembly or colonial support for Freehold. There were occasional protests to the UN about its treatment of the "rebels," but no actual hard opposition. As hopeful and determined as the resistance was, Kendra had done a database search through her comm. There were no historical precedents for an oppressed people freeing themselves from an outside invader with such numerical advantage. The few cases there were all involved assistance from a third party. There was no such party. She wasn't going to share that bit of info.

It was three painful days later, almost a week after the affliction hit them, that the "wandering Minstrel" happened by. "I've got something you want," he said as he was let in. "Twelve doses of counternano to the runnies."

"Only twelve?" Dak asked. "There's forty people around here."

"All I can spare, friend, sorry. I have other people to supply. But if you draw blood in three days, anyone compatible can use it as a starter culture. These doses will take effect immediately, symptoms will heal naturally in a week, overnight with a reconstructor nano, and I have eighty doses of that you can have. The cultured version takes about two days to work fully, then another week for natural healing."

It was decided almost immediately that the children, Dak, Kendra, Sandra and Kyle would receive the first dose. That would be more humane for the children and allow best defensive capabilities. Everyone took reconstructors to at least alleviate the symptoms, and Vikki prepared supplies to treat the rest in three days. The other seven doses went to the neighbors.

Most of them were elated, but Kendra and Dak exchanged glances. What would the next bug be like?

Minstrel wandered over. "Dak," he said simply, "I'm sorry about Riga. If I could have done anything about it . . ."

Dak shook his hand back silently, gritted his teeth and squinted. The rage in him would only be appeased by death. Lots of death.

Chapter 32

"There is nothing more frightening than ignorance
in action."

—Johann Wolfgang von Goethe

"Fresh meat, Sarge," Corporal 1st Class Korkowsky
said. He waved the fresh-faced young kid into the
bunker. Sergeant Boli nodded while staring at him. *My
God, they get younger every rotation.* Or maybe he was
getting older. "Jacques Boli," he said.

"David Walking Sky," the kid replied. Give him this,
he was large. Tall, broad, muscular and very confident
looking. He stared levelly back at Boli and adjusted the
talisman around his neck. Well, that was good and bad.

Boli said, "You're new? No combat?"

"Uh, yes, Jacques," he replied.

"'Sergeant,'" Boli corrected him. "Forget that morale
lecture you got in training. Forget that Laws of War
crap. Forget the Doctrine of Reasonable Force. Forget all that shit. These fuckers exist to kill us, so we

exist to kill them. Discipline is necessary to match them, so discipline we have. I'm not your friend, I'm the sergeant who's gonna keep you alive long enough to get out of this shithole. Got it?"

"Uh, yes . . . Sergeant," the kid replied. He didn't hesitate too long and looked a bit scared. Good start. The cocky ones died first.

Walking Sky was initiated to combat that evening. It was more profound than losing his virginity had been, that was certain. There was a patrol planned, of a type called L&C—locate and clear. In a less sensitive time, it had been called "search and destroy." He helped load the vehicles with both lethal and nonlethal hardware and took a seat as directed. The squad gathered around where he sat, and Boli briefed them. "Okay, folks, here's the plan. We're being flown out fifty clicks along the road, checking for activity at this point," a dot glowed inside each soldier's visor, indicating, "and cutting across to here by eighteen hundred, which is about oh-two hundred local, and then returning. If we see any rebel activity, we will engage, circumstances permitting, and bring back prisoners. Any questions?" There were none. "Okay, we just have to wait for Field Officer Uberti."

A few minutes later, an officer approached. Boli nodded, grimacing, and said, "Good evening, FO Kirk."

"Good evening, Jacques. FO Uberti is otherwise occupied tonight. I will escort you," he said. Leaning closer, he added, "And this patrol will run by the book. Do we understand?"

Sighing, Boli replied, "We do, FO."

Walking Sky could feel the tension as they boarded the vertol. Kirk was not well liked, he could tell, but he wasn't sure why and knew it was not the time to ask. He busied himself with helping dog the vehicles down to the deck, then tried to lounge as casually as the others did on the rough benches and cargo netting that were the normal amenities aboard the craft.

It was a standard cargo version of the Lockheed 97 and easily carried the squad, both vehicles, the assorted weapons and its own crew. There were two gunners on each side, with stickywebs and machineguns. Aviation units had no problem being authorized for lethal force, with the need to keep their equipment secure. No one seemed to worry about either ground-based vehicles or the infantry who crewed them.

Walking Sky was glad for the ride, which hid his shakes in craft motion and turbulence. He craved a real gun in his hands, knew it was pure fear and tried to control it. Anyone he needed to stop would be stopped as well with a tangler or stunbag as they would with a bullet. Only critical encounters justified lethal force. That had been drilled into him from day one, but it seemed hollow and inadequate now.

FO Kirk's voice sounded in his helmet's headset. "Recon reports our LZ is clear. We are landing." It was shortly followed by a change in impeller pitch, presaging descent to the ground.

The landing was easy if a bit dusty and the air at ground level was thick and humid. *How different from the warm, dry coast, he thought.* Those mountains were a significant factor in the local climate. He stopped musing and assisted as the vehicles were released, fumbling in the dim red light that was used to minimize detection. Kirk and four of the squad, along with the Aviation Security Patrol team from the vertol, were outside making a perimeter. That patrol had a dangerous job, asset protection during deployment, but would then go back aboard and be relatively safe, at least until they dropped the next squad on its L&C.

Shortly they were aground and mounted the two vehicles. Boli pulled him gently by the shoulder and pointed to the lead truck. Walking Sky could barely see his gesture, despite long minutes to develop his night vision. It was the darkest he'd ever seen, and his pulse thrummed in his temples. It finally hit him in his guts that he was in a war zone, and people would try to kill him for leading them to civilization.

"I'll ride with you, Jacques," Kirk said to Boli as he climbed in the passenger side in front of Walking Sky. Boli sat behind the driver, one Sergeant Second Class Anita Chong, and above them on the foam dispenser was Senior Private Ellen Rish. Four others took the following vehicle.

"One other thing, Mr. Boli," Kirk advised. "If anyone loads or even handles a lethal weapon without authorization, I will have them court-martialed. Do you understand?"

Boli's hands stopped their silent fumbling with the weapon next to him and grabbed a tangler gun instead. "Understood, FO." He cursed silently, but Walking Sky could see the look on his face. This was going to be a scary mission.

As they rolled north, Walking Sky understood why everyone wanted so desperately to be armed. It was terrifyingly black, even more so than he'd thought. The amplifier visor helped a little, but there was nowhere on Earth that dark. Not a source of light anywhere ahead, no city glow, nothing. He also understood, he thought, Kirk's demand for obedience to the book. It would be too easy to shoot first.

He had no idea that with the field officer along, the mission was actually going to go as planned. Ordinarily, the squad would have stopped a bare kilometer or so away and hidden for several hours, cooking tea and coffee and improving camaraderie while keeping a firm watch with lethal weapons. This time, they drove along the unpaved road.

Walking Sky examined it as he could through his visor. It was hard-packed earth, fused somehow, whether physically or chemically, and surprisingly smooth. It wasn't that impressive visually, but was from a practical view. There was a lot of that here. He'd hoped to actually see, hear and taste some of the local society, understanding that civilians were policed but not oppressed. He'd had trouble finding anything out, but there was no local music on any net or frequency. There was no local-style food available in the base area. He saw no civilian activity near the gates of the bases as one would expect from vid and common sense, and little activity in town at all as they drove through. It wasn't as the vid had showed it and it was beginning to bother him.

There was no sign of activity anywhere along their route. Several times animals spooked but there was no sign of human presence at all. He stared for footprints, trash, anything that might betray a hint of people. Nothing. The air was incredibly fresh and sweet, despite being relatively close to the city. The contrast was profound. He couldn't know that the city air had been almost as fresh until the invaders and defenders had started blasting anything perceived as a threat. His eyes kept scanning as his thoughts idled.

Wait. There. "Mr. Kirk, I see something," he announced. Boli cursed next to him.

"Driver, stop. What is it, Mr. Walking Sky?" Kirk asked, turning.

"The grass here has beaten areas through it. And the vegetation over there looks disturbed."

"Yes, it does, doesn't it?" Kirk agreed, acting as if he saw it himself. Boli could tell he didn't. Damn kid! This was all they needed. Kirk cut into his thoughts. "You could learn something from this young man, Mr. Boli," he said. "He's attentive and follows the book."

Boli muttered something unheard, but Kirk was speaking again. "Mr. Walking Sky, why don't you show us your training further? You can lead Mr. Boli over to investigate. Ms Rish, cover them."

"You got it, FO," she rasped quietly.

Boli came around the back of the vehicle and pushed up alongside Walking Sky. "Nice job, asshole," he muttered. "Well, you heard the man. Go trip landmines." But the kid did do a good job; he squatted and began crawling carefully. Boli couldn't know that his people still stalked deer for spiritual practice and that the skills carried over.

The grass was indeed disturbed, and footprints of at least two types and sizes were visible. Boli was impressed with the kid's tracking. He might be all right after all, if they lived through another twelve hours of Kirk's by-the-book idiocy. He could hear the local insects abuzz and the occasional sound of bullfrogs and the amphibian-analog the locals called a lawyer. He liked that. Calling a noisy, inflated, annoying but useless animal a lawyer. He could get along with these people, he thought, if they weren't all having to kill one another.

They approached the woodline and the outline of a construction became clear. "It might be a hunting lodge," he whispered to the kid.

"Hunting?" He sounded confused.

"Yeah. The locals still kill animals to eat, and it's a sport," he explained.

"Wow." The kid didn't sound disgusted, but awed. Yeah, he might be all right once he adapted. Hopefully he'd live that long.

"But let's assume it's a trap. They may be in there or they may be a bit behind it, waiting for us. We aren't going in. It might be mined. We can go around slowly, kill a few minutes and tell His Highness that we looked inside."

"Do they actually mine some things?" the kid asked.

"No, son, they mine *everything*," he corrected. He keyed his mike and said, "Scan. Any IR or other indications?"

"None, Sarge," Chong replied. Her form of address was a compromise between real military discipline and the familiar terms the FOs encouraged for "morale."

Just then, there was a slight snapping sound. The forest chorus went silent. Boli said, "Shit!" and dropped flat.

His squad was good. Behind him, he heard incoming rifle fire punctuated by a pistol *crak!* He didn't know who had fired that, but it was definitely Kirk who was the target. Shame about that, but the man couldn't accept the way real war was and no one was willing to die in order for him to learn. Boli grabbed the kid's ankle and began shimmying backward. Then all hell broke loose.

Suppressed and full-volume weapons fire confirmed rebels, but they were on the far side of the road. The two gunners tried to swing around and their colleagues below scrambled for real weapons to reply with. In seconds, they were shooting back with a decent amount of firepower. Boli clicked his transmitter through to the fire support channel and called, "Rover Three, suppression, infantry in woods on my cursor, friendlies to immediate north on road." Air support and artillery would do no good this late in the game, but he had to go through the formality to prove he'd done all he could. Besides, they might hit one anyway.

Air Control replied, "Roger Rover Three. Standby . . . on the way."

Artillery followed with, "Roger Rover Three . . . shot."

Rounds continued to pop outward and Walking Sky thought he heard incoming fire, but couldn't be sure. He kept slithering.

It took them little time to make the short crawl to the vehicles and as they approached, the confirmation tone of aircraft sounded in their ears. The craft were high overhead, but their precision munitions rained down on the last known and estimated positions of the rebels. The two used that diversion to sprint back toward the vehicles and dove into the cold, sandy grit at the road's edge for cover.

Nothing more happened for long seconds and Walking Sky held his breath. Fire continued sporadically, the squad now out of the vehicles and in the dirt, moving to avoid being easy targets, avoiding clumping together, calling out directions to each other and insults and epithets to the enemy. It didn't seem to Walking Sky that there was much, if any, fire still coming in. While he mused, Artillery spoke in his ears, "Impact."

He hunkered lower, mouth open to equalize pressure as he'd been taught. There came the loud popping sound of bursting charges, followed by the popcorn crackling of antipersonnel munitions. White flashes in the trees ruined his night vision, as he'd forgotten to turn away or set his visor to polarize. Through the dazzle, he could see twigs and leaves showering off the branches.

"*Cease fire!*" Boli shouted into his comm. The shooting tapered off.

The rebels were gone. Just one more harassing attack to add casualties to the bill. Bastards. Green, driving the second vehicle, had been shot through the side of the head. The mess inside the cab was impressive. Nura, in back, was wounded through the shoulder, but the others and the medicomm were dealing with it. He'd be fine until they got back. There were a handful of creases on the vehicle surface from near misses.

The lead vehicle had two casualties. Kirk was dead, of course. Chong was tucking a rebel-built pistol back under her body armor. She and Boli exchanged glances and looked measuredly at Walking Sky. He said nothing. They nodded and continued.

Poor Senior Private Rish had never known what hit her. One high-power round had taken her right through the turret armor and breastbone, barely above the foamgun's receiver. The second one had gone through her throat, in the line between helmet and body armor. Her head was resting on but no longer connected to her shoulders. Walking Sky helped retrieve her body, then walked between the vehicles and threw up. He was beginning to understand the way things worked around here. He decided he didn't like it at all. He nervously kept his finger on the trigger of the rifle Boli had handed him as two of the squad examined the ambush site.

"We're probably safe here," Boli declared. "That rebel fireteam is likely ten clicks away by now. And visibility isn't bad. We'll camp here until evac arrives. Keep your eyes and ears sharp," he directed.

"Yes, Sergeant," was the reply all around. Walking Sky echoed it himself, just barely later than the others. He'd loaded his rifle and planned to keep it that way. Rish would've had a chance if she hadn't been trying to change from foam to projectiles when the attack came.

"Call the meat wagon," Boli ordered.

"On the way, Sarge," Chong confirmed.

"Want to guess how many that was?" Boli asked Walking Sky.

It took him several seconds to realize it was addressed to him, calm his nerves and reply, "Oh, a squad or two." Similar power seemed reasonable.

"Now pay attention, son," Boli said and ran the vid back. It started streaming, and the attack happened all over again in slow motion. Gauges spiked on screen, indicating movement heard by the detectors, and heavy mass indicating weapons appearing through the trees.

The rebels seemed simply to flow out of the trunks and rise from the ground. They swung around with no wasted motion at all, fired a volley, then two more before disappearing back into the landscape. Seconds later, the streaks of the squad's outgoing fire lit and tore at the trees. "Four," Walking Sky corrected himself, incredulously. Sarge was right; they weren't human. Less than twenty shots, three casualties with four rounds and the rest near misses. No stray fire at all.

"We average several thousand rounds a casualty," Boli said. "They average about fifty, because they hold their fire until they are ready, then fire and leave. Ours shoot anything that moves or spooks them and call in support fire at the slightest excuse. Which is as it should be. We have more ammo than them. Any questions?"

"No questions, Sarge." The kid replied. He'd shoot anything that moved and piss on the nonlethal force crap. He wanted to get home alive. "Well, one," he added.

"Go," Boli prompted.

"Why do we patrol like this when we have vertols and aircraft? Can't we just bomb them from a distance?"

"Bomb who?" Boli asked.

"The rebels," Walking Sky replied again.

"What does a rebel look like?" he asked rhetorically. "They have no fixed bases, no area we can pin them down to. They are farmers, shopkeepers, business people out of work. They don't want us here and they are willing to die to stop us, and we can't tell them from the locals who support them or from the neutral ones or from the few who support us. We patrol on the ground so we can draw fire and hopefully get a few here and there. And so they can see that we aren't going away. We can always send more."

The evac vertol arrived a few moments later and lifted off again with Nura and the bodies. The eerie false quiet returned to the woods. Airborne help or artillery were only a few seconds away even out here, but that few seconds was all it took to die.

"We need more personnel," Walking Sky assessed.

"That we do, son," Boli agreed. "But we don't have it, they won't let us have it and they deny it's necessary for 'a few rebels.' Assholes."

It had been an eventful first day on-planet.

Boli made him watch as he filed his report and accounted for the casualties. As reported, they had received fire while investigating the anomaly, tried nonlethal weapons unsuccessfully and had to resort to lethal force in self-defense. FO Kirk had died in the firefight, so Senior Master Sergeant Boli had made the decision to use deadly weapons. They counted rounds fired, turned in the remainder and their weapons and returned to the bunker/barracks.

Walking Sky was unable to sleep. He'd drift halfway out, see Rish's shredded body and Nura's pulped head and jolt awake.

It had been a rough day, and Kendra dropped aching into her bed. Rough, but worthwhile. They had kills to add to their total and she felt good about it. She just wished they could have arrived sooner.

They'd tromped the four kilometers back to the woods and had been setting up an observation point when noise alerted them. They dove into the growth, waited quietly, and realized it was farther in. Carefully, Kyle had crept off to identify the noise, then clicked an urgent warning.

They converged through the trees, cutting across a curve in the road by going over a hill. This road predated the use of orbital missiles to cut straight routes and wound through the hummocky forest. Kendra joined him on one side, Vikki on the other. Brian and Eric were with them, leaving Sandra to watch the baby and the farm. They glanced through the heavy growth.

Below was a terrifying sight. A civilian vehicle had been stopped by a squad of soldiers. The soldiers were clearly harassing the occupants just for fun. Their definition of fun was on the grotesque side.

The car's male occupant was on his knees. His lips were bleeding from the obligatory slapping around and while they watched he took another punch to the guts. He made retching sounds and convulsed.

"Shit, Kyle, you and Brian get over to the other side for a three-way ambush. Dak, you and Vikki take the north, I'll cover this point," she whispered. They slid off into the bush, leaving her a lone spectator.

Naturally, they dragged the woman out and stripped her across the hood of the car. *"What is it about aardvarks and rape?"* Dak had asked once. Marta probably could give him a sociological explanation, she thought. Rob would discuss the history of atrocities in warfare. Truthfully, Kendra didn't know. It happened here all the time, it had happened on Mtali and it had happened in every war in history.

Dak clicked ready. She acknowledged and waited for the others to get in position. *Soon*, she hoped.

There were noises from the back of the vehicle. *Dear God, not kids!* she thought. Dak clicked again and she acknowledged, willing him not to do anything too soon. She hunkered in and got a good aim below.

While the rape commenced, the male victim was shot in the groin at point blank range with a stun bag.

He curled into a ball and twitched more. There were jeers and laughs at the handiwork. Then someone shot him in the face with stickyweb.

As he scratched at his face, trying desperately to tear a hole through which he would still not be able to draw a breath until his diaphragm and groin muscles became unparalyzed anyway, Kyle clicked ready. Kendra squelched a long and a short on her transmitter, then curled around her rifle and fired.

On the outside of the curve, Kyle and Brian had the south, Vikki and Dak had the north and Kendra was across from and between them. They'd practiced this regularly on paper, often in rehearsal and not at all live. She hoped it would work anyway. The five of them should be sufficient for the nine in the squad below.

Her bullet caught one soldier between his body armor and helmet. He thrashed and dropped. Rapid fire caught two others, against their armor and exposed arms. Either Dak or Vikki got a clean shot through both legs of the current rapist, who screamed and fell.

The other five scattered into the brush, shouting. Kendra slid back and moved several meters north, not wanting to stay in a location that might have been sighted. She heard fire coming from a couple of points that would be troops below. Lousy fire discipline, since they couldn't possibly see anything to shoot at.

Kendra crept forward a few centimeters at a time, rifle over her arms and ready. She stretched out her ears and eyes to locate a target. There was a buzzing feel to her brain and she felt an excitement that was not fear. Movement caught her eye, barely, and she twisted her rifle up and shot. She knew she'd missed and shifted again as he returned fire. Move, shoot. There was one, still twitching. She ran forward and swung her weapon, putting a bullet through his neck.

They were all quiet now. The victims could be heard slightly, down below.

She knew about where another was and thought about a grenade, but the rifles were suppressed. The noise of a grenade explosion would carry a long way, even through the trees. Better not to risk it. She fired a burst, then again, and was rewarded with a yelp. Then fire came from both sides. She threw herself flat.

Stupid! Stupid! She had run down into the kill zone and her teammates saw movement. Being camouflaged, they couldn't tell who was who and were shooting at anything in that zone. Damn. Four nasties still loose and she couldn't move.

Nothing to do but wait and shoot anything that came close. There was rustling and a patch of leaves moved aside. The figure rising was not wearing hunting camo, and was wearing UN woodland material. She made a shot into the hip, just below the armor, and was rewarded with a scream. It stopped quickly, as massive hemorrhage from the hypervelocity slug ended any woes.

After several more seconds of sporadic fire, she clicked out an advisory and stood. There were two bodies below her, leaving two. Where the hell were they?

There! By the car. She swung her rifle up and shot one as he tried to aim at her. The other gave her a defiant look and started shooting. He fired into the car, then shot the woman whimpering on the hood, then the slightly twitching figure on the ground. She got him, but too late.

In seconds, everyone was gathered around the scene. "Oh, shit, no!" Vikki said. "It's the Thompsons!"

Dak was furious, gently covering up the woman's body, weeping aloud. The child in back was a girl about six local, dead of course. There was nothing to do but drag the bodies into the woods for the slashers and swipe all the weapons and ammunition. There was little intelligence on the enemy bodies, but then, they'd shown little intelligence, being this far out and unescorted. The vehicle had a machinegun, which they dismounted and took, and the rest of the equipment was quickly torched. There was no point in recovering commo gear; the coms were all coded individually and no one in their group knew how to crack it. They had several put aside for when they did find someone trained in that art.

They were silent on the way back. Obviously, the Thompsons were friends of Dak and Vikki, but they didn't offer information and she wasn't going to ask. She just wished they'd been sooner. Maybe it would have helped. Maybe not.

Chapter 38

"Laws are silent in time of war."

—Cicero

If summer operations were bad, winter was even worse. True, there were no bugs and no grimy sweat. On the other hand, it was harder to hide footprints in snow and harder to move. There was the constant risk of cold injuries, and Kendra was peeling dead skin off a frostbitten ear. It was superficial, but hurt. The cold led to flaking, itchy skin and painful dandruff, clogged noses and bleeding sinuses. It was painful to excrete, as it took several segs to get undressed and then was hellishly cold. Then there was the way they glowed on infrared. She thought about suspending operations for better weather, but it would allow the UN to solidify its position. She decided to press on.

The tempo was slower, the immediate risk higher. It balanced out. That was Kendra's thought as she lay under a thick bush, swathed in heavy clothing. She wore a thermal undersuit, quilted liners, pants and shirt, a parka with another quilted liner and her cloak on top with the winter camouflage section out. Her outer clothing was also covered in sewn white fabric mottled with gray paint. Vacuum-insulated boots, elbow-length shooting mittens, scarf, balaclava and hood completed the outfit. She could barely move, and it was still brutally cold on her face. She wished for a true arctic assault suit, but realized she had to make do with what she had.

She became alert as the convoy below came to a halt. It appeared to be engine trouble on the part of the first truck. The crews of the other two came forward. Sloppy to bunch up like that, sloppy to send so few vehicles and sloppy to assume the rebels wouldn't operate in the cold. She wasn't going to complain about that sloppiness, however; one took one's targets of opportunity as they presented themselves.

She coded a burst and moved closer. They were oblivious to her team, even as they came out of the snow and the trees. As near as she could tell, only two of them had lethal weapons. They weren't wearing night vision, having relied on the vehicle displays while driving and not anticipating an attack.

She raised her weapon and fired twice. The two with rifles dropped. The others tried to scatter, but were rounded up by her team. Someone had misunderstood and another soldier was shot as he came around the vehicle. Or maybe not misunderstood. It was hard to quickly tell who was armed with what and Dak still had a tally. She shrugged inwardly and rounded the survivors up.

"Into the back of the truck," she ordered and they obeyed in a hurry. It was almost sad the way they refused to fight. She shook her head. She should be grateful.

They didn't drive them to the farm out of security considerations. They went instead to a hunting lodge on the edge of the wood. It was a simple wooden building, not far from the road, and the falling snow promised to hide the tire marks and any sound.

At rifle point, they were prodded into the shack. Dak and Kyle lined them up while Sandra and Kendra kept them covered. The prisoners were searched by the foolproof method of stripping them bare. They struggled and received a few bruises, but were shortly naked against the wall. "Who are you?" Dak demanded.

There was some foot shuffling. "Who are you?" he repeated. "Speak up and you can have your clothes." Wind blew a trace of snow through a chink between the planks.

One protested, "Man, that's boolshit! We got a right to—"

"You have the right to have your balls shot off if you don't answer me," Dak informed him, kneeing him in the testicles. He collapsed, squealing, and curled up.

"Who the fuck are you?" he asked again.

The three standing looked at each other. Finally, one spoke. "Ash, Gerald B. Master Sergeant Second Class, UNPF service number—"

"That's fine," Dak cut him off sharply. "And you?" he said, facing a second.

"Minar, Vashon D. Sergeant."

The others identified themselves in short order. Nine of them, all under thirty-five Earth years, ranging from specialist to master sergeant second, three of them women.

Dak tossed over their underwear. "Now, what post are you from?"

"I protest!" Ash said. "We've told you who we are and you have to treat us—"

"After the things I've seen you animals do," Dak rasped, "you should be glad you're alive. Now, what post? Give me some answers or it's going to be chilly."

Shouted refusals echoed in the small building and nothing happened for several segs. "You're bluffing," one of them said finally and reached for a parka.

Sandra shot a round into the dirt floor bare centimeters from his reaching hand.

"We're not bluffing, punky," Kendra said without thinking.

They gaped at her. Her accent had come out thickly in the presence of other Earthers.

"*Jeezus!*" Ash said. "You're a fucking human, not a rebel?"

His words hung in the air and the antagonists stared at each other. Dak finally broke it by saying, "Aardvark, I asked you your unit."

Shouting began again. Kendra heard "aardvark" tossed around, "rebel cocksucker," and a few other epithets. Into a pause she said, "Quiet."

She was obeyed. That of itself stunned her for a moment. "I'm from Minneapolis years ago, I live here now and I'd like some answers. All we need is data to confirm a few things."

"Fuck you, whore," Ash said. "This procedure is bullshit, your rebellion is bullshit and you're a fucking traitor." The noise picked back up. One of the younger ones tried to get in her face and managed to spit on her.

She punched him, hard enough to hurt through her glove and he went down, face split. "You rebel cocksucking punta! You—" and another shouting match broke out.

This was not good. They had so little respect for authority and so little training in real military matters that they were acting as if it were all a vid show.

Thrown dirt and snow splattered her, and it was frozen hard enough to hurt. It was the same kid.

Kendra was revulsed. Had she actually been part of this? This undisciplined? This stupid? She wanted to deny it, but she remembered her own contempt of authority. Nothing obvious, but she had rarely ever used honorifics like "sir" in the UNPF. She'd thought it was casualness, now she realized it was lack of respect for both people and the system.

She snapped back to alertness as she heard the kid snarl, "Just like one a them Midwest *slutas*. I've *fucked* puntas like you a thousand times since we landed. When we get found, you'll get dragged. Ah'll be looking, snatch. I jest hope you like havin' yo ass slammed. You beg nice and we might use a little axle grease—"

Kendra whirled, dragged him off the ground and jammed a stiff hand into his solar plexus. As he curled up, she kneed him several times in the face, feeling his nose shatter against her knee. Her own pain was a welcome focus and she yelled incoherently. She drew back slightly, chambered her foot and snapped the armored toe of her boot into the ruin. His head bounced back and the body began to collapse. A quick draw, a release of strength like an uncoiling spring and her sword sheared the head cleanly off. She chopped it on the ground and hacked the body a few times, then leaned on her knees, panting for breath, pulse thundering and throbbing in her temples as blood dripped from the Warbride. Finally raising her head, she asked, "Dak, do we have any way to process prisoners?" Her voice was bereft of emotion.

"No," he replied and raised his rifle. Eight coughs of the muzzle were unheard under the meaty slap of rounds hitting flesh. Three of the faces carried their expressions of horror and disbelief into death. The others had died too soon to comprehend.

Rage burned inside her, her body hot and itching. She wiped off the sword, sheathed it and turned away from the grisly scene. "Close up here. Can we burn it behind us?" she asked.

"We'd better. What if they find the bodies like this?" Kyle replied.

For an answer, Kendra turned and disemboweled two of the dead, poked out the eyes on a third and made two savage chops into the groin of a fourth. She jabbed the headless body a few times and said, "Fuck them."

She turned and walked out into the snow.

Well, that was obviously an overreaction, she told herself later, lying in bed. Certainly they'd had to die, but mutilation would not help. Although, she admitted, it might scare a few of the UN newbies into the arms of a therapist and off our planet.

Sleep wouldn't come and she knew why: tension. Her body was taut, alert and wired with chemicals. She'd enjoyed it, because of the damned attitude the punks had thrown. Idly she realized that abusing the enemy would not win friends and might scare them into extreme measures. It was still a deep, buried thought and barely reached the surface.

Meanwhile, she needed some way to relax, and her hands were brushing her nipples and thighs. It didn't take long to forget everything else, her brain embracing pleasure over pain. She fell into an exhausted stupor, her body racked by cold, pain, adrenaline and endorphins.

Chapter 39

"The enemy of my friend, he is my enemy. The friend of my enemy, he is my enemy. But the enemy of my enemy, he is my friend."

—Arab proverb

General Huff was near the entry point being used by recruited locals to enter the new administration center. It had once been a bank building and was quite new, if a bit worse for wear. An imposing structure, even. The locals made up for any social lack with their technological development. There was potential for them, he thought, if he could get them to see that there was no need to fight.

It wasn't too chilly in the Sun, but quite cold in shadow. *Very much like a desert climate on Earth,* he thought. Winter had been long and spring would be longer. He was curious to see how the local life developed as it thawed, and how the war would progress. He liked to get out and look around whenever possible.

Other ranking officers preferred to stay detached and he understood their rationale. He thought it was better to associate with the locals and get feedback from them. The more one knew, the better the dealings.

The locals who had been hired were in three categories. First were those who didn't care and took any job offered by anyone. They were mostly unskilled or only marginally so. Second were the schemers who were trying to bilk the UN system. They were expected, even useful, but he did not trust them. Some were a security risk, others simply whores who could be bought. The last group clearly hated the UN, but had families to feed. Those he trusted for their honesty and tried to get along with. He'd prefer not to use any local workers for the risks of espionage and terrorism they posed, but the General Assembly didn't want to send more overpaid government employees. They were overpaid because of laws passed by the General Assembly under pressure from their unions. Those same unions had it written into their contracts that the employees couldn't actually be sent anywhere useful, as it presented a risk to those overpaid employees. Instead, they produced yoctobyte after yoctobyte of adminwork. Hell of a way to run a war, Huff thought.

A voice behind him spoke, "Sir? You're an officer?" He turned and froze.

She was totally out of place, in a conservative business suit and scarf. She was poised, slightly sad looking and incredibly beautiful. "Yes, why?" he asked.

"I need work, sir. I'm very capable, but no one will talk to me."

He nodded to his guards, who let her through. They kept her briefcase, after she opened it to prove it was not a bomb. At least the rebels didn't run to suicide missions. Not very often, anyway.

"What type of work?" he asked.

"I'm trained as a social worker. I can be very useful here," she said. "But I missed the deadline for ID and no one will make any exceptions."

Typical bureaucrats, he thought. Not one of them could do any original thinking. Lang was the worst of the bunch. He was so bent on ramming adminwork down these people's throats that he didn't see the real potential.

"Come with me and we'll see what can be done, Ms—"

"Erte. Bonita Erte."

"Come then, Ms Erte."

She followed him toward the office block, looking a bit relieved. He wasn't sure, but he thought there was a deepness to her eyes that he found enticing. She stayed closer to him than his guards, obviously nervous about the hassle within, and brushed him in the elevator. He felt a ripple and reminded himself to be professional.

Lang saw reason quickly enough and promised to find her a slot she could serve in. He looked a bit put upon, but not badly. "We'll have to do a DNA comparison at once, of course," he said.

"I understand," she said, smiling softly. "Security and all that." She went with the clerk who handled her application personally and smiled at him as she did. They entered a small cubicle at the end of a row, and a medic reached for a sealed lancet.

"Um," she said, "do you mind if I do it myself? I'm really a wimp about pain."

"Well . . ." he said.

"Please," she said, dark eyes staring into his. He nodded and she beamed a smile that warmed him to his toes. She took the package, tore it and turned slightly, broad sleeves flopping. She hissed slightly and turned back, offering him the card smeared with blood. She clenched her finger in a napkin and dropped the lancet in a disposal receptacle.

Twenty minutes later by Earth time, she had a job counseling. She wasn't told who or why they'd need counseling, but it was a job. She breathed a sigh as she left the building, clutching her new ID. The borrowed blood specimen in the bag taped to her wrist had almost coagulated by the time she got in. That had been close. Now to avoid any issues that would bring her into question. Subtle surgery combined with makeup and hairdo changed her face quite a bit. She should be safe, especially with her assumed body language. It would have to be enough.

She approached the gate again. "I'd like to thank you again, General is it?" she looked at his shoulders queryingly.

"Huff. Jacob Huff," he replied, taking her hand. She winced slightly as he caught her "pierced" finger. Good. That should clinch it in everyone's mind.

"I'm grateful, sir," she said. "And I have some funds, still. Is there somewhere we could get a cup of chocolate?"

He took a deep breath. Well. "Let me show you to the officers' club."

"Thank you."

Guerrilla warfare in spring brought its own problems. There was the mud, the shifting weather and vicious wind, the mud again and other, unpredictable threats. Kendra was quickly learning a fatalistic approach to enemy fire. She'd been wounded once, a "mere nick" that had burned and stung for days. Sooner or later, one would get her. She was more worried, to the point of occasional nightmares, of the risk of capture. She could expect harsh, punitive treatment from the UNPF if caught. Besides the existing charges of alleged embezzlement, of murder of her friends, of fleeing pursuit and the provable charge of desertion, there were the potential charges of transferring classified information, aiding the enemy and fighting under a foreign flag.

She tried to ignore all that. She knew the truth and where her allegiance lay if no one else did. She was taking tremendous risks, but she was accomplishing much. That thought brought her back to the present.

It was an ambush again. They were tracking another pacification team as they went from farm to farm, registering people, seizing anything deemed a threat and anything the team took a fancy to. Her opinion of her former service was still sinking into the depths.

She also had a battle going on within herself. The incident in the winter with the prisoners was by far the worst atrocity she'd been involved in, but it was not the only one. On several occasions she'd shot prisoners and she'd beaten several brutally for intelligence. Justifying it as "necessary" didn't help either legally or ethically and it was getting harder to determine right from wrong in this war. International law called for humane treatment of prisoners and their release if facilities were not available. Practicality dictated that anyone who knew details of her insurgents had to die. As far as intelligence, she needed the information to keep herself and her people alive. She was willing to torture to do that. She shook her head fractionally and brought herself back to the present yet again.

It was a surprisingly gentle day and, being early spring, the insects were not yet out in force. The ground was still damp, cold and frosty in spots. She itched from twigs and rocks poking her and wished again she'd taken the time to clear the area. Visibility and hearing were good and she had both audio and optical sensor gear borrowed from Dak. It was lighter and less restrictive than her helmet's ensemble, if not as well armored. She decided the tradeoff was worth it.

The Peacekeepers were now taking heavy automated weapons on all convoys and more personnel and vehicles. It was getting far harder to surprise and disable them. Kendra expected that trend to continue and heavier vehicles to be included shortly. Without support weapons, the odds would keep stacking against her people until they were all dead or gave up the task as hopeless. She supposed at that point she'd have to decide between a suicidal lone war, as her military oath seemed to require, or a life as a farm woman on a UN colony, dreading discovery for her past. Neither appealed much.

This operation was being done slightly differently, because of the increased enemy capabilities. Instead of trying to overwhelm the force, deliberate hints of insurgent activity were being placed. That would hopefully get the soldiers out of their vehicles and into a good position. Of course, they were all using lethal weapons out here now. Whether or not they were authorized, Kendra hadn't been able to find out, but they'd abandoned the restraining weapons for rifles and grenades.

Kyle had set up a false ambush below them, complete to a shooting blind. It had been occupied long enough to leave evidence for the sensors. Now he, Kendra and their neighbors the Goranas were situated above and around that site. Dak and Sandra were across the road to take care of stragglers. Kendra supposed that soon the forces would become too large for her unit to face profitably. The first invaders had been units of five to ten personnel. Before winter, it had increased to ten to fifteen. This one numbered three squads—twenty-four.

She gratefully dropped the ration she'd been munching. Vikki had cooked them up and they were basically a large sugar cookie-bar with nuts and chocolate within, blended with extra protein and nutrients. They tasted great at first, were boring within days and were sickening now. She wondered if she'd ever eat chocolate again once—if—this was over.

There was movement below and she tensed slightly, prepared to dump four of her precious grenades and a couple of clips of ammo into the area. Minstrel had brought more, but had cautioned her that supplies were limited. All the regular armories had been seized early on and what they had came from private sources and theft. She steeled herself to fire every shot as if it were her last.

She heard an NCO below say, quite softly, "They're here. I can feel them." His voice traveled farther than he would have liked due to the still air and she could hear it clearly. A twig snapped below her and she tried to place the troop who had just blown cover. The leader said, "Further up there. Got to be. Probably four or five of them."

She stiffened. He was experienced and that was bad. She shifted imperceptibly, in order to take him out first, then heard another sound.

It was a low growl. It didn't register at first, then her mind sorted through memories. It *was* familiar, but what was it? She heard it again and it fell into place. Ripper. It had broken the twig, not them.

Oh, shit, she thought. That was bad.

It slunk into view, clearly prowling and sniffing. She froze, willing it to trace the scent to the false ambush site and not her. Holding her breath to keep as still as she could, she waited. Which would it be? Get ripped? Or shoot and be discovered? She could still hear the Peacekeepers muttering below.

She saw the animal now. Long, low, sinuous and rippling with muscle. It had heavy jaws and huge retractable claws and looked more vicious than even the stories told about them, even more vicious than the ghost of a memory of years before. Without seven million years of coexistence, they had virtually no concerns about humans and had been known to kill military-trained hunting leopards. They were impressive, no doubt about it. Something about them inspired fear on an instinctive level and she whimpered inaudibly.

Now, *it* saw *her*. Their eyes locked. The predatory gleam in its gaze was more than intelligent and her body decided it would shoot if attacked, her brain not working properly at the moment. It took two careful, padding steps, dropped down into a catlike crouch.

It sprang. She raised her rifle, then hesitated. It was moving sideways. She adjusted her aim, then realized she was not the target. Not for now, anyway.

A gurgling scream snapped her awake. The UNPF NCO was the new target, and the wet sound was his throat being ripped out. The beast rolled through the brush below and there came the sound of small arms fire. Shouts of fear and confusion added to the din and someone acting quickly but incorrectly blew up the shooting blind.

Kendra clicked a code. *Wait. Close up.* They'd take their allies where they found them and clean up the damage afterward. Besides, she was shaking too badly to be of any use. Fusillades of fire and sporadic explosions from heavier weapons indicated the direction of the battle and she rose, carefully moving lower and closer. She kept her weapon up, safety off, in case the animal came back her way.

The noise was localized and she presumed it was now surrounded. That was dangerous for both it and its former prey and she kept alert. "What the fuck is that?" she heard.

"Beats the shit outta me, but it killed Boli," someone replied.

Behind them, another voice spoke into a radio. "Cancel that artillery and air support. Attacker appears to be a local animal." The voice sounded relieved and disgusted.

"Well, kill it before it comes after us," was the reply to the first speaker, followed by weapons fire. The ripper screamed a metallic reply.

"Assmunch, all you did was wound it."

"Well, why not? I bet I can get the other knee this time."

"Look, let's just get out of here and consider ourselves lucky not to have a firefight."

Another speaker said, "The other knee? You're on."

Another report. Another scream. "I win."

"Bullshit. That's a back leg, not the knee."

"It's got four knees."

"You said 'the other knee.' That means the front one."

"Guys, let's just go," insisted the bright one.

"I didn't say that. But if you insist," the shooter argued and fired again. "Geez, Walking Sky, try to have a little fun, huh? Besides, you're not in charge, Chong is."

"She's down at the vehicles, which is where we should be," was the reply.

"Yeah, so Frank's in charge up here."

Walking Sky persisted. "Frank, you're new. I know what I'm talking about."

"Oh, can it, kid," Frank replied. "This'll only take a minute. Try for the tail, Freddo."

This was truly revolting, Kendra thought. Just kill the poor creature and be done with it. Laughs, animal screams of pain and more shots assaulted the air. She heard a click code confirming her orders and an extra signal at the end informing her it was the second attempt. She'd missed the first one while listening to the cruelty below.

She coded back as she rose and found a good position, then signaled to attack.

The enemy was gathered around the makeshift arena, except for one driver and one gunner who showed good sense and professionalism by staying with the vehicles. They were applauded for their efforts with bullets to the neck by Sandra and Dak. The rest were in a rocky gully, surrounded and with their backs to the Freeholders. No sense of chivalry interfered and they were disposed of without ceremony. A couple of wounded were dispatched with shots to the head, and Kendra approached the ripper while the others looted the bodies. In theory, personal effects should be returned, military equipment reused or sent for disposal. All the latter would be distributed across the plain to farmers and resisters. The personal property would be destroyed, unless it had intrinsic value. If caught storing it, they'd be charged with looting anyway, and there was no way to return it. Besides, the psychological effect was better. The rebels rarely allowed escapees and frequently made all evidence disappear. It was hard on families back home, but that of itself was of use in convincing the invaders to leave. It was logical, and Kendra hated it.

She stayed several meters back from the twitching, crippled beast and stared for a moment. Proud in motion, it looked quite pathetic with its shattered rag doll legs. The pain was obvious in its face and moans. She'd never heard a wounded one, and it sounded like a cross between a cougar and a bear. It jerked and shuddered as it turned to look at her, then seemed to shy away. It met her eyes again, almost seeming to beg. As she raised the rifle, it leaned back as if accepting its fate. She fired once through the brain and ended its misery.

"Thanks, friend," she said softly.

They set incendiaries on the vehicles and left in a hurry, before support arrived.

Calan entered the headquarters and waited for the guards to identify him. They shortly nodded and sent him into Lang's office. Lang didn't waste any time playing the politics of waiting. He knew how valuable Calan was to them and met him immediately. "Welcome, Mr. Calan," he said, smiling. "Thanks for your information on that rebel mole, Hernandez. We're still looking, but with a picture, I'm sure we can narrow down the suspects soon. I understand you have some more information for us?"

Lang was easier to deal with than the soldier types. They regarded him as a *traitor*, just because he could see the outcome and desired to keep his position through the chaos. Lang understood the practicality of it and gratefully accepted all his help.

"I have a name for you. A name that will be very useful in demoralizing the rebels. All you have to do is say the name," he said, cryptically.

"A rebel leader?" Lang asked.

"First, let's discuss my terms," Calan said, approaching it cautiously. A name wasn't data that could be leaked a bit at a time. It had taken research and money to find out this jewel, and it was only serendipity that allowed him to recognize its value. "I want a share equal to the reward when you find them."

"Reward?" Lang asked. "I don't understand."

Smiling, Calan said, "This is a fugitive from Earth who moved here and became a traitor. This person now belongs to the rebel military and is guiding them against you using knowledge of UN tactics. There's already a reward. I want it matched."

Attentive now, Lang said, "Agreed. And I think I understand. We advertise that we want this person, offer a reward and let them argue amongst themselves." He nodded appreciatively. "Tell me, then."

Calan keyed a code, handed over his comm, which now showed Kendra's pic and bio. Lang looked confused, entered her name on his system and scanned the response.

"But she was exonerated. Robinson was convicted of embezzling, misappropriation and foreign favors. But he tried to blame lots of other people. At most, she'll be tried for AWOL, and probably not be punished much under the circumstances."

"She's assisting the rebels, now. And since you never publicly rescinded the reward, it still stands. Someone will turn her in for the money. And they'll fight over it." Lang nodded. "I don't know what we'd do without your expertise, Mr. Calan."

Calan smiled. It was good to be recognized for his ability at last.

Chapter 40

"Killing the enemy's courage is as vital as killing his troops."

—Carl von Clausewitz

The spring continued with sporadic attacks and ambushes while the UN consolidated its hold. They were actually paying little attention to the farmers, because they eventually would have to knuckle under. After the initial scan to round up reservists and veterans, they'd stayed increasingly away. Kendra had no illusions that it was simply to avoid bad morale and that they would be back in force once the cities were pacified. The cities were more secure every day, and not because the locals were afraid to shoot at the UN, but because they feared repercussions against civilians.

It appeared that the local commanders were not conducting the patrols and raids they were supposed to, because of the effect of the resulting casualty counts on morale. Their reports still indicated such was the case, according to the intel that trickled through. That was good, but was only a temporary reprieve. Kendra continued her war because her orders were to do so, she had nothing else to do and because it might stay the inevitable long enough for there to be political interference. She wasn't betting on it, and it was a struggle to maintain a positive image for her followers.

Occasionally, a message would appear with useful information on targets, current events and even comments on outsystem politics. The latter usually contradicted the UN position and were good for morale. Also, whoever was producing the casts had a sense of humor. The jokes, biting and brutal, were the best thing for morale short of a high bodycount.

She accepted one such message, requesting support to the southeast, at the town of Fall Creek. They were asking for both personnel and cargo vertols, preferably from larger farms. Those were not easy to move clandestinely, but it could be done. She treated the request as suspiciously as she did all of them and dug into her comm to confirm.

The message was from an Engineer Lieutenant Sheila Chon, who checked out. As long as the intelligence network hadn't been compromised yet, it was a legitimate order. So far they'd been lucky in that regard. The satellite network had been taken out, but hard ground-based intel still came in, if slower. It took several routes, including through Minstrel, but was still useful and valid and updated about monthly. Kendra decided to accept the orders.

They were going to be awfully close to Delph', however. Fall Creek was barely fifty kilometers away from the town, and she knew there was a sizeable amount of firepower present near Delph'. They'd have to do whatever they were going to do fast to avoid taking losses. That was easily within aircraft range, even within light artillery range. She decided to follow up cautiously before committing her troops.

That evening, she caught the UN news and her blood froze. EBC had a full segment on her. None of it was untrue. The press had centuries of practice telling the truth the way they wanted it told. They stated that she'd been accused of embezzling, true. Accused of killing two people to escape, true. Accused of fleeing justice, true. Accused of helping the rebels, true. All absolutely true. All utterly misleading and wrong. She closed her eyes, fuming quietly. She wanted to be left *alone*! Why couldn't everyone just go away?

Shit, this was bad. Now the reward was up again, here. And they knew she was near the capital. How long before some oppressed farmer decided it was worth it to turn her in for the money? Perhaps right now?

Dak watched silently nearby. He was convinced it was utterly untrue in *any* detail. Kendra was perhaps the bravest woman he'd ever met. If the damned aardvarks were *all* of her caliber, there would never have been a war. He saw the offered reward and snickered. As far as he was concerned, she was worth ten times that as a friend, never mind as a soldier. The rest of the locals would agree with him, he knew. They had never heard of her or seen her if anyone were to ask.

The next day, an unfamiliar vehicle rolled up in front of the farm. Kendra ducked into her snake pit to hide and Dak went out to parley.

Wayland was there with three of his team. "Hi, Dak," he said. "Just came by to see Kendra."

"She's not here anymore," Dak replied cautiously. "Just came by" seemed most unlikely.

"Oh, come on! I know she's here. We've been watching."

"Why?"

The question hung there. Why was obvious.

Kendra stepped out of the house, brushing at cobwebs. "It's okay, Dak. Let's see what he wants." She nodded cautiously.

Wayland returned it. "There's some people I need to take you to," he said.

"Who?"

"I can't discuss it here," he said. He glanced behind her.

"Sure you can," she said. It was obvious where this was going. Waves of heat swept across her from worry.

"Well . . ." he said. "Under the circumstances, it's obvious that you aren't a friend of the UN." He stopped.

"Was that ever a concern?" Dak asked.

"Look," he said, exasperated again. "Under the circumstances," he realized he was repeating himself. "I think we all agree we'd be safer without her."

There was more uncomfortable silence. "I think you're right," Dak said. Kendra stood wide-eyed.

"Good," Wayland said, letting out a breath. "I know a quiet place she can hide and we can get on with the war."

"You're assuming I'm worried about being safe, though," Dak said.

Wayland's troops were suddenly aiming rifles. "No," he said. "We aren't going to shoot our own people. But I really think Kendra should come with us." The rifles lowered.

"Where?" Dak probed again.

"Dak, be rational. The UN wants her. If we let them have her, it draws attention away from us. We could get better intel and do more to them."

"You think they'll trust a turncoat?" he snorted, mustache waving.

"No," Wayland agreed. "But that's the beauty of it. She's not really one of us." He obviously missed Dak's point.

Kyle, Vikki, Sandra, Brian, Eric and two neighbors were suddenly on the porch, armed.

"Okay, forget it," Wayland said, looking around. "But don't say I didn't warn you. And don't try to contact us again. She's a danger, and we don't want to be anywhere nearby when she gets hit."

Dak stared at him. They hadn't contacted Wayland in the first place. "I don't think that will be a problem. Now get the fuck out of here."

Wayland turned. Kendra had a sudden insight. Gritting her teeth, she reached into her coat, drew her Merrill and shot Wayland in the back.

Rifles swung at her. Rifles swung back the other way. Standoff.

She stood unmoving, staring at the crumpled corpse. Dak looked back and forth and addressed the other three, "If he'd sell anyone out, he couldn't be trusted. I don't think there's a do with you guys—" he stared at Kendra, who shook her head, eyes squinted, "—so go back and fight your war. But don't even think of talking to the enemy. Because we'll make sure everyone knows. And you'll be the ones who suffer. From both sides."

They nodded, boarded the truck silently and drove off.

Kendra slumped against Dak and sobbed. Sandra patted her shoulder then guided her inside. "It's okay, hon. It had to be done," she said.

Kendra couldn't sleep. God*damn* them! Wouldn't they be happy until she was dead? She crawled out of her cot, pulled on a cloak for warmth and sat fuming. She didn't notice the first beep from her comm. The second one registered and was a welcome distraction. Then she paused. Was it possible for it to be good news?

She activated it and punched to decode the message. More war orders. Fine. She momentarily decided killing would be good, then forced her civilized self through the haze. The message descrambled and she began reading. It took a few seconds further to unscramble in her brain.

"You need help. Arrangements made. Transfer to my headquarters. Details follow. Naumann. Authentication Cowboy, Mckay, Urquidez."

Naumann! He'd do that for her? But that was dangerous! She could stay hidden . . . then she broke into sobs. She'd follow that man to ground zero if he asked. Idly, she realized that he knew it. And that that criterion was part of his professional calculations . . . and never entered his personal thoughts at all.

Dak hugged her goodbye. "Vikki says she's sorry she couldn't make it. You take care and we'll see you after this is finished. You have our coordinates?"

"Yes," she agreed. "I'm hoping we can be done in a few more months," she lied, not wanting to tell him it was all pointless. There would always be more attackers. Nothing else to say, she waved, turned and sprinted for the vehicle. The driver was someone she recognized from 3rd Mob and she was gladdened that at least some survived. As far as she'd known, everyone still on base had been killed by the kinetic weapon.

He was a senior sergeant. She was surprised to get a driver of that rank. "By the way, Corporal," he said grinning as they bumped away, "you are now a sergeant."

"Really?" she asked. "Thanks, I guess."

"Don't thank me. You'll probably be higher shortly. Naumann is keeping the chain of command filled. He's a colonel now, too."

"It sounds like he's going to go down fighting," she replied.

"Going down? You've really been out of the loop here, haven't you?" he asked, surprised. "We've got them out of the Halo, except for mopping up, and they'll be off the surface in a couple of weeks, tops. The habitats are sort of holding; no one wants to use the force necessary to win because of the risk of destroying them, so they'll surrender once they have no support. That leaves the gates, which we can blow if necessary. Actually, JayPee One is already blown."

Kendra was shocked. It was impossible! "We're winning?" she asked, wanting to hear it again.

"Not winning. We'll still be a mess, but they'll be gone. Best we can manage under the circumstances."

A small airtruck rolled from cover. They squeezed into the cramped rear compartment and waited as it vibrated jarringly and lifted. It was a typical craft for farms to use to resupply from the cities and the UN tried desperately to keep track of them, but couldn't ground them without providing support to the farms that fed them and the Freeholders. The fact that they couldn't provide that support was indicative of the trouble they were having.

Still, the pilot kept them barely above the trees and wound through the low areas of the hills. There was always the risk of being intercepted or shot from orbit. It was a long, loud, painful flight; the noise suppression equipment was damaged and it would not be good for the cover story for it to be well maintained. It worked, that was all.

They flew west, following the edge of the forest. Another craft rose from the tree line, just barely in front of them and they flew in tight formation for a few segs, then the other craft continued while they landed. "Let's just hope they weren't looking too closely at high rez," the pilot shouted. "But they should be too busy scoping the city for insurgents, trying to figure out what we're doing. That, and there's a *lot* of activity in space to keep them busy."

The plane was stowed under the trees again, and Kendra wiggled painfully out. They were not far from Delph', she figured, and there was a lot of bustle visible under cover of the trees. She was directed to a cave in the bluff and scrambled up to it. There were black curtains a few meters in, overlapped for light discipline.

It was cut deeper than appeared from the outside, and all by hand. Shoring timbers supported the expansions and equipment was stacked inside, all of it light-weight tactical field gear. There was Naumann, surrounded by staff as usual, directing and plotting.

He nodded and motioned for her to stay as he continued with his briefing. He finished shortly and came over. "Sergeant Pacelli," he greeted. "You were actually promoted quite a while ago, but we decided not to tell you. If captured, corporal was safer for you. I'm afraid the TO&E has been a bit of a mess. And you aren't a sergeant anymore."

"I figured it was only a field expedient," she replied. "Thanks for getting me."

"You are far more useful to us than them. If I could have, I would've doubled the reward for anyone who'd kill potential captors." His grin was not pleasant. "You will revert to permanent rank of senior sergeant—" she gulped in surprise at that. Bumped two grades in one day. "—and assist here. I need competent staff for the upcoming project."

She nodded. Naumann went on, "Bare details that you need to know: we attacked a sizable force near here and pinned them down. All the activity in your area was not directed at you, as you thought, but were units attempting to reinforce the ones here. The city underground has been sabotaging their logistics and knocking out transport. We've been keeping them under light harassing fire everywhere in the district except here. I pulled all available professional troops from the other cities and ordered what units I could to remain passive. They think they've neutralized us. They are gathering all their planetside force right here and have been pounding Delph'. Tactically, that's fine; there are few assets in Delph'. It's very hard on the locals, but I have to use them as cover. The UNPF thinks we are cornered, nearly defeated, and are concentrating force around us. If the press weren't crawling through the area, they'd just nuke Delph'. See how valuable the enemy press can be?" He grinned the cruel smirk again.

"We are about to crush them totally. You'll get such details as you need. And you'll stay here."

"But how?" she asked. "Insurgents have never defeated an invader without outside—"

"Eighteen percent higher gravity. Twenty percent lower partial pressure of oh two. Local support. Armed residents. Time and distance from the decision-making command. Lesser independent authority to their commanders. Bad logistics. Poorly trained, poorly disciplined troops in lousy physical condition. Commanders more concerned with politics than fighting. Commanders untrained for battle. Commanders unwilling to risk mistakes or expose troops to fire. Troops who are chosen to be 'representative of the society' and not as prime physical and mental specimens. Troops not allowed any errors and therefore unwilling to do more than the bare minimum. Morale, bad to start with, smashed into nothing by you and your devotees." He smiled at this part and she blushed. "No moral or political support from the rear. No good commanders, as they all pulled strings to avoid being sent here. Dependence on our trade for their own system. Unwillingness to commit full resources or efforts. Inferior transportation. Lack of an intelligence gap. Should I continue?"

She stared for several seconds. "I never added all those up," she admitted.

"Neither have they," he replied.

She was shown a billet farther up the hill. It was a bunker dug under the trees, covered and sodded and all but invisible. The trees would hinder air-based sensors from finding such a small hole and to approach on the ground was tactically impossible. She lifted the leaf- and debris-covered door, noting which tree it was near and looking down to get an idea of its overall location. She remembered that she should take a different route in each time, to avoid treading down a trail.

Inside wasn't bad. A few rays of light came in through side slits and her eyes adjusted. There were two shelves with sleeping gear and one empty one, which she took. They could use light during the day, battery supplies permitting, but not at night. It would show on a scan. She decided to put her cloak on top of her sleeping bag for extra warmth. Nights would be chill. With luck, this would be home for a week. Without, it might be a grave.

The reservists and militia down in Delph' had no idea how much firepower was being brought in for their support. The sound of weapons crackled up into the hills sporadically, as one group or another engaged enemy patrols. Naumann called in other units from time to time, throwing them into the fray to die, be captured or escape. The UN must be convinced that the "heavy" resistance was a sign of desperation, while massive force snuck into the hills above and positioned around Jefferson. Elsewhere in the system, the few professional forces left accepted orders that looked suicidal, trusting to Naumann to know what had to be done.

That night, Kendra helped drag an artillery piece in. It had arrived in a very heavily stealthed cargo lifter and was in pieces for easier transport. "Easier" was relative; it was being moved by human strength. The pilot jumped out to help them. He was a short, skinny, geeky-looking kid, with an amazingly deep, resonant voice. He took a grip alongside hers on the cargo net and heaved.

"How's things, Cowboy?" someone asked. This was the Cowboy who'd flown her?

"Not bad. Staying low, staying hid," he replied. Yes, the voice matched.

"Cowboy, I'm Kendra Pacelli," she said. "Thanks for the ride, way back when."

"Hey!" he replied, smiling. "Glad you made it! Rob's still alive, in case you didn't know."

"Thanks!" she sighed in relief. She'd been avoiding that subject. "I didn't. Tell him I'm here if you get a chance."

"Will do," he agreed with a nod.

They were done, and he disappeared in the vertol, she back to the cave.

Naumann confirmed that Marta was still alive also, and assigned elsewhere. Kendra felt much better and sat down to her console. The first order of business for the day was to update the logistics files for Naumann's strategic calculations. It only took a few segs, but the files were numerous. They had current issue gear, captured UN gear of three production generations, old Freehold gear that some retired reserves had brought, personal hardware from collectors that spanned several systems and years and farmers with ranch rifles in three main calibers and several oddballs. Probably more ranch rifles than military issue. They'd be the main infantry force, led by professionals.

She then switched to the main task, plotting coordinates for the support weapons they had, using an algorithm that calculated range of weapon, rate of fire, hardness of target, distance, and direction. The comm gobbled the data and spit out graduated zones where the weapons would have their best chances to hit targets. The battle staff would decide from there where best to site them. It was a complicated process and she added the new intelligence data that had been brought in. *The UN had a lot of stuff down there,* she thought, and wondered again what Naumann had planned.

She found out why they were so secure in the bluffs: iron. The hills were rich in iron ore, giving a tang to the water. It also distorted magnetic and mass sensor readings. Since the bluffs were quiet and unremarkable, the UN patrols had stayed out of them for the most part. Only the occasional patrol came anywhere near, and none deeply into the woods. Several days previously, one team had gotten close enough to encounter the Freehold forces. It had been destroyed, the soldiers killed and the vehicles moved several kilometers away to be found. An in-depth check of the satellite recon and communication record would give the lie to the location where the wreckage was found, but no one was interested in doing the necessary work. It was written off as a random attack and forgotten about. After all, the rebels only had minimal forces making sporadic attacks, so why waste effort?

❖   ❖   ❖

General Jacob Huff panted hard from exertion, gasping. He reached down and dug his hands into the thick hair of his lover. Her hands were all over his hips, thighs and scrotum. Her lips were massaging him and he felt his muscles tightening. He spasmed, feeling her tongue enthusiastically work him. After a few moments of silent ecstasy, he felt her moving higher. Shortly, she was snuggled under his arm. "My God, Bonita, you amaze me every time."

She laughed lightly. "Liked that?" She kissed the side of his jaw, fingers tracing patterns on his chest.

"You're going to kill me," he said.

"Not too soon, I hope," she said. "You still have a war to fight."

"Yes, but I'd rather resolve it peacefully. Why can't most of your people see that?"

"We've been struggling to tame this system," she replied, fingers moving up to his chin. "It'll take a while to get used to being settled. I'm sure most people will come around once things get organized." She leaned on one elbow and stared at him.

"I'm glad to hear you say it. It's so frustrating to try to help people who fight every effort." He stared back at her liquid eyes. How did he find a woman this sexy and intelligent? Perhaps she'd be agreeable to returning to Earth with him. Linda was gone, and Bonita was so exotic and mannerly. He still had trouble believing her background. She might be trained as a social worker, but that wasn't how she earned a living.

"How did you happen to become a prostitute?" he asked.

"I told you before," she said, shoving him and grinning.

"I still have trouble believing it," he replied.

"You also get turned on hearing about it," she said, grinning.

Her perception was astounding. He watched her sit up next to him, her hands still caressing his body. She never stopped doing that when they were together.

"I learned massage and just drifted from there. A friend of mine advised me on how to set up, and I started. There's more money in sex than just massage, and more in either than social work."

"Didn't it bother you?"

"Sometimes," she admitted. "I refused clients now and then. But the money is good."

Her attitude was a bit mercenary for him, but it seemed to be normal here. More of the evils of uncontrolled capitalism. He wasn't sure how she would take a suggestion to go to Earth, and she certainly couldn't be a prostitute. But what legal skills did she have? Plenty, but how could she use them? She had no license for social work.

"Just how far are you willing to go for money?" he asked.

"How much money?" she asked. "Or are you asking what I'll do for you?" She grinned and kissed him.

"That's it," he agreed, feeling arousal again. He reached down for her smooth mound and found her already caressing herself. He became instantly ready and said, "Show me something we haven't done yet."

"That covers a lot," she laughed. So cheerful. "But I have an idea . . ."

Thirty minutes later he sagged against the pillow, drenched in sweat. God, she was amazing. "I have to report in," he told her, moving to get up. "That was wild."

"Never done that before?" she asked, heavy-lidded. She wiggled suggestively.

He laughed and said, "No. Not what I expected at all. Join me in the shower?"

"I'm sorry, love. I need to sleep," she said, snuggling deep into the covers.

"All right. I'll see you in the morning," he said, slightly let down. He kissed her and left the room.

She quickly bounced out of bed and flipped the combination on his doccase. It was a simple lock and wasn't even coded to show the times of entry. In less than a seg, she had photographed every document whether a duplicate or not, just to be thorough, downloaded his comm into a vampire module—it didn't analyze or decode information; it merely read the matrix as it was—and had relocked it. The tiny camera and module disappeared again. She'd pass things along shortly. Not that the memories were close to full, but much of the info must be time sensitive. Grinning wryly, she calculated. Based on her hourly rate and the intelligence she was getting, he was actually getting a fair price as a double agent, without even knowing it. The only inequitable part was going to be when she inevitably killed him.

Marta wasn't looking forward to that, but orders were orders.

Chapter 41

"When strong, display weakness; when weak, feign strength. If your target is nearby, make it appear to be distant. Only thus will you achieve your objectives."

—Sun Tzu

Programming continued at a frantic pace, constantly changing as new equipment was smuggled in. It was frustrating, endless revision, removing useless outdated blocks but not erasing them in case things changed yet again. The troops not involved griped nonstop, but relocated equipment as ordered. Most of the battle was being fought now, in detailed deployments and plans. The actual engagement would be of less relevance. While no battle ever went according to plan, proper preparation enabled a disciplined army to make the most of actual conditions.

"Kendra," Naumann said quietly behind her.

She turned and said "Yes, sir?"

"I want you on the ridgeline when we start. You'll have a platoon and your own squad. Considering the lack of trained personnel, you'll have to take a lot of control at fireteam level due to all these rank amateurs. Can you handle that?"

"I guess I have to, don't I?" she replied.

He nodded. "I need all the experience I can there. This isn't raiding, sniping or ambush. This is going to be face-to-face, brutal warfare. If anyone breaks, we all die."

"Yes, sir, I understand."

"You'll have tac commo, all the ammo we can spare and some tactical support weapons. We don't have enough body armor to spare; what we have is needed for the assault troops. You will have explosives and emplaced weapons. Can you hold there, even if they come face-to-face? Even if your troops try to rout?"

She breathed deeply. "Yes, sir."

"I'm asking you because I trust you to understand what's at stake and not flinch," he said.

You're asking me to die. "Yes, sir," she nodded, breathing again. "I'll do it."

He squeezed her shoulder and left. She turned back to the program at hand and realized she couldn't work further on it now. She closed, secured and stood. The actual engagement would be of less relevance, except to those who fought it.

Outside was warm and dry, thoroughly black to her vision. As her eyes adapted, she saw a few stubborn dapples from Gealeach pattering through the heavy cover. From the south came the muffled rumbles of fighting in Delph', as it was slowly being shredded into rubble. South of there, Jefferson was being systematically looted and raped, triaged as lost to the enemy . . . for now.

So here's where it ends, she thought. I've made my decision on my home and I'll die trying to save it. Can he really pull this off? Or is it just a defiant gesture?

She sat there a long time, pondering what the future held. Until recently, she thought they'd lost already. Now she found that Naumann had cobbled together a regiment from the dregs available and the local farmers and intended to fight an army over a hundred times his size. There was no way he could use infantry and light support against such odds, and the UN had support craft in space and more they could call. Every calculation she ran showed their task to be suicide, but he clearly had a plan. It hit her suddenly that she trusted her commander with her life, or her death and wasn't at all afraid of not being able to follow his orders. She would do as he said and believe he knew what he was doing.

What did he have planned, though? His comments about the force comparison made sense—the Freehold forces were the better trained army, even with militia recruits. They had morale, the home territory advantage and all the basic advantages of shelter, food and other resources. The UN had massive superior firepower and logistics, however.

Naumann's current exec was a retired captain of intelligence. She'd had some field experience and had briefly worked with Naumann some years before—a fortuitous occurrence due to the small size of the Freehold military. She met with him after Kendra left. They discussed equipment and personnel assignments. "One question I have to ask, Colonel," she prompted.

"Yes, Karen?" he asked.

"How reliable is Pacelli? She seems earnest enough . . . but I do have to question her background. It's not her honesty. But is she cold-blooded enough to kill her former nationals?"

"Yes," he said without hesitation.

"Will you bet your life on it?" she persisted.

"I just did."

A grunt told him she accepted that answer.

Later that day, troops began trickling through in small groups. Personal equipment was swapped around and Kendra knew what was happening and why. Everyone tasked with infantry work on the ridge was being equipped as well as could be, with tac helmets, weapons and full ammo loads, extra batteries and additional intel gear. They had light tactical support weapons, including mortars and a few missiles and some nasties Special Projects had come up with. *Those bastards are scary,* she thought. *They all must have grown up building bombs in their bathtubs, considering the devious little gadgets they devise.*

The engineers were lugging explosives, incendiaries and mines by the ton, by hand, and she knew what that was for, also. The weather had turned decidedly blustery, wet and nasty for the season, with a cold front, the type the locals called a "howler," blasting down from the north. Naumann loved bad weather for tactical advantage.

So, this is it, she thought yet again. Another nervous check of her gear indicated everything was still ready. Her only question was if she was. As it became dark, runners began taking messages and Naumann nodded when she caught his eye. He looked calm, but very sober.

"This is it," he finally said, echoing her thoughts. Total silence descended in the bunker, and Kendra could feel sparks of electricity in the air. All eyes were on him and he commenced giving prearranged orders. People disappeared to slip into positions and all unnecessary equipment was quietly removed if small, disabled so it could be reused later if not. None would be left useable for the enemy.

"Everyone rest for the next div, then I'll call you as I need to," he ordered.

Kendra obediently pulled her cloak around her and tried to nap, but her anxiety made sleep a futile goal. She stayed quiet, tried to meditate and discovered she was fondling her sword, running fingers along the length of its spine.

After what felt like years of waiting, someone tapped her shoulder. She realized she had napped. Adrenaline purged her body of fatigue and she turned to face Naumann.

His voice was firm and loud. *"It's us against the universe. When do we attack?"*

Smiling in spite of herself, she muttered, "Now." She could hear similar mumbles from other 3rd Mob troops. It was a common joke in the unit.

"When?" he demanded.

"NOW!" came the ragged chorus.

"That's better," he replied, nodding. "We'll turn the rest of you into mobsters yet. Senior Sergeant Pacelli."

"Yes, sir?" she replied.

"Please recite our unofficial motto for us."

She inhaled, and enunciated, "Outnumbered, always; outgunned, usually; outclassed, never."

"Thank you," he acknowledged. Turning back to the group, he said, "Keep that in mind. Attitude is half the battle, and that is the attitude I order you to have." There were a few very quiet snickers, but levity did not seem to fit the occasion and they tapered off.

He continued, "I haven't given anyone more than bare details and their own specific orders. Thank you for trusting me with the little you had to go on. Here's the quick and dirty synopsis. You won't have much time to share it with your troops, but they'll be able to sense your confidence and that will do a lot.

"We have a large proportion of their military command and control right here. The scattered rest is facing only unorganized civilian resistance at this point, and expects that trend to continue. They rely on quick-response reinforcements if they can't handle a local situation. In a few short divs, there will be no UN military chain of command in this system to lend that support. The troops left behind will be handled by the civilians. Our job is to take out the infrastructure so the locals can protect their own homes, because *they outnumber the invaders tens to one!* The fact that the enemy wears uniforms doesn't make them more than human. They are outnumbered, facing equal weaponry and will lose. All we have to do is destroy their support structure, all of which is in this valley and the capital—"

"And in space," someone added from the rear.

Naumann nodded. "In a few divs, the assets in space will not be an issue. The assets here will be ours and the forces in Jefferson will have to do things our way or starve to death. *We* will be besieging *them.*"

"What about Jefferson HQ and the base there?" someone else asked.

Naumann replied, "We have a Black Ops team, what about them?" There were cheers and chuckles at the sheer arrogant gall of that response.

He continued, "As of now, the space assets are handled. In a few segs, the Drifting River is going to burst through its levees and flood the plain. With river to the west, flood to the north, there's only two ways the UN can move. The south will be an utter dead zone of artillery and close air support that they won't dare fight. The east is Braided Bluff, which will be protected by our infantry, reinforced with all the explosives we can spare.

"Infantry," he said, picking out Kendra and several others by eye, "you are the anvil on which we are going to grind them to powder. No matter what happens, *you must not break*. I expect many of you to die, I won't lie to you. But we will stop them right here and that will be the end of it. If you don't hold, then we all die and there's no backup plan."

Sober looks greeted that. Grim determination followed.

"I don't believe in luck," he finished. "But if anyone has any prayers in any faith or any lucky charms or rituals, now would be the time to call them in, with all favors." He sat silently for a moment and Kendra threw a quick prayer in. They had precisely one chance to win and keep their system. There was no margin for error built in. Very few mistakes would be needed to destroy any hope of the future.

With nothing more to do there, Kendra slipped out the back and headed for her bunker. She had a perimeter of mines and emplaced weapons to control and a platoon of sixty troops to support it. There were thirteen veterans, reservists and active soldiers, the other forty-seven being militia. Most of them, at least, were by now experienced guerrillas. There were a total of seven platoons on the ridge, with all the supporting munitions that could be emplaced. She wasn't optimistic about their chances. She trudged out, following the assigned route on her comm into the dark. There were several kilometers to cover on foot to the ridge and the last section would be all sneaking and lizard-crawling through weeds.

Chapter 42

"Our archers are so numerous," said the envoy,
"that the flight of their arrows darkens the Sun."
"So much the better," replied Leonidas, "for we
shall fight them in the shade."

—Simonides

Jacob Huff was lying back, "Bonita" astride him,
playing with him and with herself. "I love how you feel
inside me . . ." she was moaning. It had been trouble
justifying a civilian escorting him to Jump Station
Three, but a little abuse of the system had been worth
it for the results. Besides, the shuttle had to lift anyway, full or not.

Everyone they met guessed at once why she was
along. And they were wrong. *I think I'm falling in love
with her*, he admitted. He was neither the only one
nor the first to get involved with a native. Not even

515

the first in this conflict. It was still a shock to experience it.

He shook, close to orgasm, and grabbed her breasts, trying to pull her down.

His comm sounded a general alarm, destroying the mood. "Shit!" he snarled, trying to untangle. Bonita cursed also, but held him in place with her thighs. "I've got to go," he protested, pushing her. He rose, reached his comm and was about to reply when she said, "Jacob?"

He turned to her, just in time to feel the thrust into his throat. He thought at first it was a weapon, then his eyes saw her hand draw back and repeat the blow to his solar plexus. Fingers! My God, she was inhumanly strong! As he tried to breathe, she shoved him effortlessly against the wall. Her long legs moved elegantly, trapped him and a hand clamped on his throat. He tried to wrestle, but her other hand jabbed into his left shoulder, immobilizing the arm. She grabbed his right arm, twisted and held it. He was starting to see black splotches swimming in front of his eyes and knew finally that she was killing him. "Why?" he strangled out, almost inaudibly.

She leaned closer and whispered, "Because you want to destroy my home."

Her eyes were still deep and beautiful.

"Now," Naumann ordered. He had retreated to a bunker behind the ridge on Torpenhow Hill, but still within easy vehicle reach of the front. A command car waited nearby, engine idle. The battle staff burst into furious activity, coding and transmitting. There came the muffled *whump!* of artillery and the sound of people and equipment moving through the trees. But the unheard aspects were at least as important.

Drifting far overhead, in the total silence and serenity of orbit, was one of many intelligence satellites. This one was of UN origin, but there were others of local manufacture, recoded and in use to betray their owners. IS3-17, as it was known, was providing data on the firebase and its perimeter. It showed the lazy flow of the river, traffic on the roads and a few anomalies that would be investigated by armed reconnaissance teams. A well-placed charge punched through its casing, shattered the delicate instruments inside and damaged its orbit. Within seconds, others flashed into death. Farther out, a manned relay station had already been breached. The crew had hurried into vacsuits as a second charge damaged its solar array. More charges demolished the antennas. It would be a struggle to stay alive and relaying data suddenly became irrelevant to them. Even had they still been functional, they would have seen a mass of sheer noise from sophisticated interference and hacking. Throughout the Halo, various craft and stations were under attack.

So far, the pattern was not obvious, for there were decoys and feints along with the more harmful assaults. All attention was focused on the disruption and the UN officers reacted to it as best they could. None had yet deduced that the attack was focused on communication and control paths.

Nor was anyone making the observation that the majority of the enemy was located on the planet, not out in the depths of interplanetary space. So far, this had been fought as a technological war, with the ground troops supported by massive artillery, air power and orbital strikes, all controlled from satellite and space-based assets.

Below on Grainne, along the Drifting River, several dikes rumbled as deeply placed charges damaged the structure. Previously compacted dirt, now loosened, collapsed and was swept away by the current. The berms heeled over into the water, slumping until waves spilled over the top. Trickles became streams, then raging torrents.

The artillery shells had been launched precisely; high angle for the first shot, sequentially decreasing charges and angles for the subsequent ones. There were few tubes, but they tossed a huge salvo upward in a few seconds.

Three vertols lifted out of the hills. They'd been hidden in caves, and slipped out of the trees unseen for now. Accelerating brutally, they angled toward the beginning carnage. One of the three was actually a cargo lifter with hastily improvised launch racks and munitions. It dragged slightly behind the other two, engines straining. It dropped lower for cover as the two Hatchets rose for tactical advantage.

"What the hell?" The UN satellite commo tech jerked upright from his slouch. The data on-screen made no sense. He shoved his coffee and food aside and began pulling data.

"What do you have, Will?" Colonel Upper Grade Andropos asked from across the aisle as he snatched a headset and comm to get into the loop.

"Nothing," Will answered. "Something's screwed up. Give me a few moments."

"What's nothing?" Andropos probed again.

"Just vej and fucking wait, okay? This doesn't make sense."

A disciplined soldier would have reported the inconsistency immediately. A disciplined soldier would not have spoken to an officer in that fashion. But the commo tech was very protective of what he considered proprietary information. It was seconds later when he finally and reluctantly admitted his findings.

"I've lost satellite feed, that's all. Gotta be something fucked up somewhere."

Andropos spun and asked, "*All* the feeds?" He punched through channels and confirmed that as correct.

"Yeah. Damn piece of shit system," Will groused.

The ground rumbled and shook slightly. There was the sound of distant thunder and a flicker of power.

"They've killed the satellites!" Andropos shouted, suddenly aware of the danger.

"It's just a system glitch, okay?" Will replied, turning. "I'll fix the fucking thing if you just back the fuck off!"

A salvo of shells landed within milliseconds of each other. The concussions from the explosions shattered equipment, slapped the technicians into the sides of the vehicle and destroyed gear. There came the howl of low-flying aircraft and the rattle of small arms.

Andropos tried to access tactical data, map data, any kind of data. His technological tools had been obliterated and his command technology had taken a dive almost five hundred years backward, to when line-of-sight radios and observers provided intelligence. He had no observers in place and a garbled roar came through his speakers. He was effectively blind. A second salvo slammed into the ground and he rode the shock wave, unable to regain his feet. He waited impatiently for the shakes to stop, then struggled upright. A small but close explosion tore the door off the hinges and heavy bootsteps clunked through.

"FREEHOLD MILITARY FORCES. SURRENDER OR DIE!"

Up on the ridge, the snipers and support weapon crews unloaded ordnance at a furious rate. Their targets were across the river, but were still within range. The snipers were focusing on crews for the weapons below, the hardened projectiles from their long, heavy fifteen millimeter rifles punching through bodies and armor and destroying gear. The shooters had literally been buried alive over the past three days, scanty rations at hand, lying silently in carefully dug positions or where necessary, camouflaged on the surface and waiting in their own filth, barely breathing. The strain would have been visible on their faces, were anyone close enough to see. It did not affect their marksmanship. Every time a UN soldier tried to mount a piece of equipment, that soldier died. The machinegun and missile crews jumped into preplanned position and aimed at only the few crewed vehicles and massed troops. Mortar crews sighted in on defiladed positions. To the south, Blazer teams crept forward from the river and the trees.

The Combat Air Control team called coordinates to the two Hatchets and scouts drew further artillery down on selected equipment. Their first priority was the UN armor. No armor could stand against modern firepower, but it was virtually unstoppable by lightly armed civilians. Tanks were great tools of oppression. Also a threat were the particle beam guns that could claw artillery shells from the sky. They could not be allowed to start shooting.

The cargo lifter dropped into the melee and furious supporting fire stirred the ground around it. Rob brought his Hatchet down in a twisting, rolling dive and chewed the area around it to plowed mud, every shell in a ten-meter-wide band, ten meters out from the vertol. He pulled into an Immelman and dusted an antiaircraft crew as he powered away. The fire lifted as the aircraft did, leaving more Blazers and Mobile Assault troops behind. Peeling off in twos and threes, they got behind the enemy and cut them down. A handful of lunatics drove combat buggies across the bottom of the ridge Kendra and the other infantry were to hold. Their light vehicles were loaded with deployable mines that spread across the ground to make an additional obstacle. Kendra and her unit had already set several thousand kilograms of explosives in the trees.

The UN headquarters was in utter disarray. All feeds were down and all wavelengths jammed so even coded and scrambled signals were garbled. There were fragmentary reports from nearby observers, but the reports did not make sense.

General Meyer, the UN 7th Division commander, spent several minutes assembling marginal data into some semblance of order and by then it was too late. He concluded it was an attack, but surely the rebels didn't have enough force to take his divisional position?

"Where the hell is that water coming from?" he demanded.

"The levees upriver have been destroyed, General," an operator told him, drawing in data.

"That's ridiculous," he objected. Or was it? Higher ground was to the east and the water couldn't rise fast enough to be a credible threat. And there were regular patrols through the bluffs. There was no way the enemy had more than a squad or two of observers up there.

"Have all sensitive equipment moved above the flood line. Then come back for everything else. Send three platoons up to Beta Five, and Seventh Squadron. That should hold against any rebel harassment. Send out an extra sweep of this area—" he indicated on the map "—and double all perimeter watches until we get the feed back. Looks like they're trying to scare us. We're going to get a bit of excitement," he concluded.

"Two Sentinels orbiting to the south," someone reported.

"That's odd. Why would the Jefferson AO be in our airspace?"

"Don't know. They're heading this way, though," was the shrugged response.

"Ask them for a data dump and have them wait. We might need the air support." The Sentinel was not an ideal close-support platform, but it would do.

"Change targets, change targets," Naumann ordered. There had been minimal casualties so far, but that was about to change. His command vehicle was loaded and he hopped in. Strapping down, he plugged into the comm and ordered his driver to advance.

The UN was retreating above the high-water line and his support weapons would hit from the south. There was no retreat north, with the river arcing in a huge bend and now flooding, which left the bluffs to the east, unless they simply rolled over him. They could, and he wouldn't be able to stop them. Hopefully, it would not occur to them as possible.

Cowboy landed in a hurry, unstrapped and sprinted to the waiting UN Guardian, nodding at the replacement pilot for the cargo lifter. The Guardian was not as well armed as a Hatchet, but it had excellent flight characteristics. And it was what was available. The Blazers already had it idling for him and set the stolen UN IFF transponder. "Coded," the sergeant in charge advised him as she saluted with a grin and sprinted for the cargo craft.

Eight Guardians had been captured intact and flight capable, with munitions for ground support already loaded. Some of the instruments were out—victims of smash-and-replace programming to override security protocols. He bypassed as much as possible, did a quick battlefield check and lifted. Rob McKay was orbiting waiting, and he joined him. The rest of their merry band was aloft in moments and they headed north, low and slow. The two "Sentinels" were simply stolen IFF transponders mounted on Hatchets. Had anyone bothered to look beyond the signal, they would have noticed that the flight characteristics were wrong. Rob and his wing had been sweating about that, but Naumann had been correct again; the enemy was generally incapable of thinking beyond the expected. It would be almost impossible for any UN automatic system to target them now. Manual weapons, of course, were still a threat.

The artillery salvo that hit near UNHQ was larger, if less precise and uniform than the initial shoot. The Freehold tubes had been joined by captured UN pieces and some undriveable but shootable armor. More than three hundred shells dropped howling from the stratosphere and without satellite support, local counterbattery fire only accounted for a fifth of them. A second salvo landed slightly farther north, then a third. It turned into a moving swath of death, driving the UN troops ahead of it.

Naumann didn't like what he saw. There weren't nearly as many artillery rounds available as he had predicted. Only eight Guardians had been captured, rather than the twelve he'd expected—one of the missile teams had gotten a bit too enthusiastic. He pulled the seven less experienced pilots out and sent them to threat assessment. The eight pilots he did use were perhaps the best close-support pilots in the FMF. That would help. "Cut half the tubes on the next five volleys, advance as planned, then cut to thirty-five percent fire after that. Keep them rotating to save force and make every fifth tube counterbattery. How is CAC coming?"

"CAC reports they will be designating targets in six segs," support control reported.

"Understood. Take care of the arty and armor first, then get them on the bluff," he ordered. He keyed his mike and said, "Infantry. Naumann. Air support will be there soonest. Hold position."

General Meyer was having problems of his own. The rebels couldn't have enough explosives and auto systems to keep this up for long, but he was taking serious casualties. There was nowhere to retreat, with the river on two sides and artillery rolling up from the south. He couldn't fight artillery without air support or modern counterfire. He *could* fight the rebel ground forces. But how many casualties would it take? He kept pushing his troops, trying to sound confident. Would they hold long enough to fight their way through? There was no contact of any kind with Jefferson, so he had to assume the airbase had its own problems. He ordered his remaining light mortars and vehicle cannon to target the hillside from the bottom. That should clear a hole through the mines and hopefully take out the troops behind them, too. He sent a wave of drones up, risking their loss to get intelligence. He had to know what was up there. He demanded intel from every unit, camera and vehicle, and tried to lay out a counterattack.

Buried in her hasty position, Kendra heard Naumann's advisory. *Hold how long?* she thought. There were a *lot* of UN troops down there, with a lot of vehicles. Most of those had served weapons. It would turn into a bloodbath if it became supported infantry attacking a numerically inferior force of grunt infantry.

She watched from her position. It was a hollow dug in the earth, a web of netting and twigs over a woven polymer mat and a layer of sandbags as rests and cover. The tiny portable monitors showed the automatic weapons arming. The first echelon detonated, sending out hypervelocity shrapnel in an arc like a circular saw. Bodies cut in half collapsed in heaps, some wriggling in brief agony before finally dying. The UN forces momentarily stopped, then spread out to flow around her. "Station Three, this is One. Data sent," she advised as she dumped the video into the net. Incoming intelligence from other stations showed a huge force massing. There were far more enemy than anyone had anticipated and they had no air or arty support yet. She frowned and overrode automatic for the second echelon. She triggered the mines from outside in, to channel the dismounted troops for greater casualties. Gouts of mud erupted skyward and UN soldiers ran to avoid the carnage. Her reinforcing squad took aim at any vehicle and she ordered them to choose targets toward the outside first. "This is One. Engage automatics from the outside, say again, engage toward the middle of your position. Cut them into as many bits as possible," she ordered her other two squads. This was going to be unbelievably bloody.

She chose now to launch her three drones, laying a bisected V across the zone. The drones dropped sensor mines that armed on impact and split the approaching force into two pinned groups and two small groups of stragglers. She directed automatic fire and the drones over them. The drones sought movement and targeted. When they exhausted, they detonated, adding more bodies to the toll.

The forward elements hit her first perimeter, well up the slope and in the trees, and the M-67 Hellstorm system tore them to pieces. Fragmentation mines, direction-seeking concussion, and anti-armor mines blasted across the landscape in a dark gray pall of mindless death. On one of her monitors she saw an Octopus mine trigger, leaping through the air, sensacles waving until it brushed a horrified, retreating soldier and detonated. The screen went blank as the camera was destroyed by the blast. It cut to the second perimeter camera. "Left support, drop your loads and retreat to Line Two," she ordered. There was a flicker of confirming indicators and of charges arming, then her attention swung back. "Reserves reinforce the right," she ordered as she switched frequencies and continued. "This is One. Go to manual and do as much damage as you can, then switch back to automatic. Prepare to engage on ground. Hold positions as long as you can. We will retreat toward the east and south as necessary."

Her screens turned to static. Someone in the UN had finally taken control and found some of the frequencies she was using. She had two wired feeds left. Quickly sketching in her mind her last recollection of the scene, she scramble transmitted, "Right, retreat on your own authority. Give me data soonest. All units ground and cover." She paused five seconds, then detonated the entire remaining first echelon, setting the second one to individual automatic. It was not as effective as sequenced groups, but would last slightly longer. She was rapidly running out of explosives and still needed to hold as long as possible.

She swore as one of her remaining feeds died, hit by a stray shot. Right informed her they were retreating. She ordered left to pull back as soon as they thought it advisable. This was not good. Any hole in the line would mean huge casualties and probable loss of the battle. One echelon of mines left.

The last feed died. She set everything to automatic and grabbed her gear. With nothing left to do here, she might as well head out. That meant almost certain death, unless a miracle happened. It didn't occur to her to run and abandon her troops.

The bunker had tendrils of smoke, but outside was a scene from hell itself. Dark night sky, pounding rain, howling wind through the trees. There was the steady cacophony of small arms, the occasional slam of explosives and distant, barely audible screams. A stench of blood, scorched meat, ozone, chemical residue and fresh earth assaulted her nostrils. "All elements retreat to second perimeter," she ordered over the noise. Flashes from weapons and illumination threw ghostly, cavorting shadows through the trees.

There was the scream of a light shell, probably mortar, she thought. She flattened and was grateful that it detonated in the treetops. She praised the thick forest and hoped it would hold. Then there was the basso chatter of cannon fire chewing into the ground. It wasn't well aimed; the weather and lack of intelligence forced the gunners to resort to eyeballs, but it was still potentially lethal. The *crakcrakcrak* sound set her ears to ringing. She cursed and ducked.

Meyer grinned in triumph. The mines had dropped off to almost nothing. The opposition was sporadic now. If he could punch through the few remaining elements, he could throw the entire front into disarray. That would make it a matter of force versus force and the UN had a far larger army. Now to drive the nails into the coffin. There couldn't be more than a few squads opposing them in Sector 2. He urged the troops to attack. He understood reluctance, but hesitation would be lethal. They *must* attack quickly. That damned enemy artillery was good, and it was chewing his support to pieces.

Kendra slipped cautiously forward toward the battle, her tac giving her details of the horror below. The last echelon of mines, reinforced with a few hastily thrown scatterpacks, was detonating at the bottom of the slope. "All elements cover in the trees at one-ought-ought meters, line abreast," she ordered and picked a spot near a stout bluemaple. Rain trickled down her back and between her buttocks, cold and shivery. She stuffed her clips into pockets and pouches, readily accessible. This was going to be ugly.

The trees were thick enough and heavy enough to prevent even armor from entering, so the smaller vehicles wouldn't be a problem. Most of the heavy vehicles had been captured or destroyed, all but eliminating that threat, but there were undoubtedly more mortars and rockets available. Her squad had three M-41 Dragonbreaths and a small mortar, two squad weapons and one last trap. That and Naumann's belief that they could hold until the UN broke and surrendered.

She heard an advisory from her left neighbor, whom she knew only as "Second Platoon," nodded to herself and ordered, "Inverted V position, elements at twenty-meter intervals, stand by on tubes." With the squads in V formation, she could have them retreat as they took casualties—and they *were* going to take casualties—and still have a line abreast formation with decent defense. It also gave better crossfire opportunities. She moved back ten meters behind the line she'd set. Thank God they all had modern helmets with tac and comm, if they could use them properly. She got a row of green acknowledgment lights and hunkered down to wait. Wet dead leaves plastered against her as the wind gusted past. She noted that the friendly artillery was decreasing. Either ammo was running low or they were taking casualties.

It wasn't a long wait. A probe in force moved quickly toward the ridge, one soldier carrying a sensor suite. "Squad leaders engage at will—break—First squad fire on my command," she ordered. Just a bit closer . . .

"Fire," she snapped. Three rounds took the bearer, four more the pack he carried. A volley dropped the rest of the probe, some covering, most dead. Sporadic fire returned and one light winked on her helmet. Casualty. Lethal. It was not someone she knew personally, just a name: Lowe.

There was a large, seething mass approaching, vehicles crawling to the edge of the woodline with ground troops among them. She could pick out darting figures on her visor and the signs of others behind them. They were waiting to determine where her troops were, then they'd rush. She had the one last area weapon left. She warned, "Fire in the hole," and coded for ignition, then closed her eyes and felt the actinic brightness against her face, right through the polarized visor. The improvised weapon was a string of white phosphorus and magburn canisters along the edge of the trees. It hurled white-hot flame into the troops dismounting from their vehicles, creating more disorder and casualties and a roaring fire to damage night vision and sensors.

There was a pause, then the rest of the UN troops swarmed forward as the initial flash died, desperately seeking cover in the same trees that protected the defenders. She raised her weapon and fired a string of fifteen grenades along the approaching front, the recoil hammering into her shoulder. There'd be bruises there tomorrow. She reloaded quickly as the second wave hit the dense cover of the trees. Her squad was taking shots at the attackers and she could see them falling. There were six directly ahead of her, less than one hundred meters away and closing at a run. Her rifle pointed almost of its own accord and she commenced careful, rapid single shots as they appeared through gaps between the boles. Six rounds, six hits, then three more as others appeared. Another light winked on her visor. "Eighteen, Two, fall back and fill in," she shouted to hear herself. "And fire the tubes!" Her own weapon was relatively quiet, but the simple mass of fire brought the volume up. There were explosions among the trees that threw sparks and debris across her vision and added to the din. She moved farther to her left, the south, where the shooting was heavier. She scrolled through her vision options, but found nothing obvious to shoot at. A glance at the other two squads she commanded didn't offer much. On the other hand, the reservists leading them seemed to have their heads on straight. They were following her lead and keeping order.

The shrieking hiss of the Dragonbreaths startled her, even though she expected it. Three tongues of flame lashed into the approaching mob, the flash ruining night vision and momentarily blinding sensors. Men and women screamed as the chemical fire reacted with their skin to burn hotter still. They thrashed in agony as their squadmates recoiled in horror. The weapon was intended for bunkers, not open terrain. Temporarily stunned and illuminated, they dropped by the tens from desperately accurate rebel rifle fire from Kendra's platoon and the flanking units.

Movement. It was too high to be ground troops and too small and low to be an aircraft. It was a recon drone, hovering quietly on its impeller, guided through the trees by its robotic mind. She took careful aim, letting the grenade read the image, then squeezed the trigger. The small hyperexplosive charge smashed the pod, its turbine shattering at high revs, the pieces tearing chunks from nearby limbs.

Becoming resolute again as the incendiary brightness faded, the enemy advanced en masse. Kendra shot dry, reloaded quickly and tried to shoot back to her previous line of aim, now covered with incoming troops crashing through the underbrush. There was a brief pause and she switched to a fresh clip. She had two full clips of one hundred left and one of thirty-seven. After that, hand to hand. After that, she didn't want to consider. The war was lost, that was all.

Another casualty, only two spaces from her. "Fourteen, fall back and fill in," she ordered again and retreated one tree during a lull. It had a boulder next to it she could use as a better defensive position. She had barely reached it when another salvo of mortar bombs detonated. Before the firecracker pops of antipersonnel rounds finished, a second one of standard high-explosive hit, booming echoes through the trees. Illumination flares were glaring overhead, but the shadows confused what vision the light gave. She hoped that was true for the enemy, also. The occasional canopy fire they ignited was quickly doused by the rain, but hot cinders of twigs blew down here and there. She slapped at her neck and brushed off a glowing ember.

She could hear fire from the sides, indicating that the other sectors were still holding to some degree. How much longer? She wiped droplets from her sight screen. Water was running into her boots now and her pants were soaked and cold. Her breasts were tingling from the chill as they had in basic training, a lifetime ago. Branches fell from the trees as cannon fire shattered them. The occasional trunk exploded in a shower of wooden needles. The forest was just one more casualty of the battle.

The enemy was well into the trees, crawling and darting through the weeds toward her position and shouting. She leaned across the rock, breathed and commenced firing. Pops and louder bangs sounded all around her and more of the enemy collapsed, some screaming for help, some silent and some wiggling closer.

She set her grenades for minimum range, airburst, and fired three down the center. She had two hand grenades, but hoped it wouldn't get that close. She knew better.

The enemy was covering and creeping nearer. She sighted one figure as he shimmied forward and put a bullet through the top of his head. That earned her a torrent of return fire from his comrades, rock chips slashing and stinging across her face as she ducked. Time to move.

"Elements retreat twenty meters by leapfrog. Provide cover," she ordered her whole force. Then she slid low and lizard-crawled backward, rifle over her arms in case she needed it in a hurry. Another light blinked. Dead. An explosion shattered the ground next to her, spraying her with mud and stinging like a hard slap. Whatever it was, it was a thankfully small charge and the soft wet ground had tamped it just enough to expend its force upward. Her hearing dropped a level despite the helmet cushioning and a ringing sound drowned out much of what she could hear.

She hoped they retreated in an organized fashion. They were doing admirably well for predominantly untrained amateurs; only nine of sixty were veterans of active duty. Most had some experience, but guerrilla fighting was different from a stand-up battle. None of the guerrillas had ever used tac helmets, and she worried that the wealth of intelligence displayed would distract them.

As she slithered farther, her hand brushed a mate to the bomb that had just missed her. This one was sunk into the dirt but had not hit hard enough to explode. Perhaps it had ricocheted off a tree. No matter, it was still live and she shied from it and worked her way around.

Clicking in her ears indicated a scrambled and burst

message being decoded. "Pacelli, retreat at once to Zeta Three. Report when clear," Naumann's voice was barely audible in her ears. She boosted the gain.

Retreat? At once? How the hell do I do that? she thought. If we cover, they'll kill us as they roll over us. If we run, we get shot in the back. If we retreat piecemeal, we get cut to shreds. The only thing that came to mind was to let them roll through and attempt to surrender, then hope to survive whatever Naumann planned. That was suicidal, too. Zeta Three was the grid mark south of them along the ridge. So what was happening up north?

She forced herself to think. "Forward elements, fall back forty meters soonest. Report when done." Leap-frog them back a few meters at a time, covering each other as they did so? What would conserve troops and be effective? A click signaled another message.

"Pacelli. Retreat to Zeta Three immediately. We're—" it chopped off.

Her helmet was dead. More jamming. The sights on her weapon and the grenade controls were frozen, too. Directional EMP.

She realized now why the fire was so heavy—it was all concentrated at her position in an attempt to break through. Naumann was going to blow holy hell out of the area. If her troops were there, they'd be hamburger.

The problem was that the platoon on her right flank was no longer capable of holding. There was fire coming from that direction, indicating that they were either being forced to retreat or had been subdued. If she pulled back from the right flank, the UN troops would simply follow her. Some would die, but they'd be inside the perimeter. Naumann certainly had the temperament to kill his own troops to get them, but not enough soldiers to waste. If she retreated, they would be swarmed. If she held, they'd be under whatever Naumann was about to throw. Either way, her troops were dead. And she had no commo or night vision.

She stood and sprinted, tossing her helmet aside. Fire spattered the ground around her feet as she dodged trees. She counted paces through her rasping breath and angled downslope. She was working on eyeballs alone, assisted by flarelight, hindered by smoke and dark. A sharp pain burned across her left arm as a branch snagged her, but she kept running.

The end troop, whose name she didn't know, turned at her approach and fired. He yanked the weapon aside as he identified her, and missed. *"Incoming!"* she shrieked, gasping for breath. *"Move out Now!"*

He stood and ran, taking a supporting position behind a tree and waiting for her.

"Go now!" she screamed and pointed. *"Twenty meters, then right and keep going!"*

A hum alerted her. She spun and saw another recon drone, hovering and scanning. She swung her weapon up and fired a grenade. It arced away, struck a limb and detonated. She cursed. Her weapon had been set to minimum airburst when the EMP hit them, but it had defaulted to contact fusing. It couldn't accept proximity fusing, as the sensors and controls were damaged. She took careful aim and fired again at the small pod. She missed as it easily evaded, and fired at it again. This time she hit and it exploded, metal and fiber confetti drifting out of the smoky cloud.

The damage was already done. The incoming fire was intensifying and seeker projos swarmed down. She ran back upslope obliquely, hearing them *zizzzzz!* behind her as they sought human body temperature. The enemy knew what line they were on now.

She had a repeat of her first warning, as the second woman in line almost wasted her, too. *"Incoming! Run!"* she repeated and staggered past. She ordered the next one to get the message to the other side and pull them back, then alert the next unit. He nodded and ran.

She ducked past a tree and another drone sat a bare two meters from her, drinking in data. She fired bullets at it as it tried to dodge. It thrust up then over and down again. Finally, a few shots grazed it and she caught the main probe panel with a lucky shot. It drifted away, weaving as it did and she downed it with two more shots. A distant series of thumps indicated another salvo of canisters full of seekers on the way from small mortars.

The squad was peeling back slowly, which was still dangerous, but might let some of the others survive. They'd have to clear a safe distance, then hold it against anything that came. If she could get a runner to the next platoon for support, they could keep the UN where it was until the artillery arrived. Seekers swarmed through the woods like angry hornets, seeking warmth to bury themselves in. The cold wetness of the trees made it easy for them to find the blazing heat of the defenders' bodies, but also interfered with their flights. Kendra heard a *zizzzzz!* and a meaty thunk as one caught her in the calf.

She stumbled, rolled upright and kept limping, shrieking under her breath in tortured agony. It felt exactly as she'd been told it would to get shot—a freezing, burning, electric cramp through the muscles.

She reached the second man from her position, whose leg was shattered. He'd tied a tourniquet and stopped the bleeding, but couldn't possibly walk. He was barely conscious. She slung her rifle, pulled at his arm and began dragging him, fire lancing up her leg.

Waving her left arm, she stumbled toward the last troop in line. He came running to help. "*No!*" she shouted. "*Retreat!*"

Through the roaring confusion she somehow detected death approaching from all sides. She spun and walked a burst of automatic fire into a disorganized gaggle of UN soldiers just coming through the trees, shooting offhand with her left hand, the weapon a heavy, kicking weight on her wrist, an ache in her arm. Sighting movement in the dying flicker of a flare, she lobbed three more grenades, still set to contact fuse, into an approaching knot from the right flank. The enemy were spilling through the gap to her right, pounding for the summit to hold the position and fight an attrition battle that they would surely win. She fired to her left again, then to the right, while backing away with her burden.

Her good ankle twisted on a branch, spilling her to the ground. She stifled a scream as her casualty groaned, still alive, and she forced herself to her knees and up under him. She muscled him into a rescue carry, more painful but faster. After nearly three hundred meters of sprinting through rough terrain, with a burden for the last fifty, she was seeing black spots. A hidden tactical part of her brain made her reach for, arm and throw her two hand grenades to keep the enemy's head down. They were small charges, but even with the cover of the trees they were close enough after her feeble throws that the blasts ripped at her. She ate up one clip and let the weapon hang from its sling so she could reload with her single available hand, falling uphill and to the right.

Her last right-flank troop had either not heard her or ignored her. He dropped two clips at her feet, took the limp form from her shoulder and hefted it easily across his brawny back. "You have the rifle, you cover me! Back soon!" he shouted and took off at a sprint.

Kendra grabbed the clips and turned, throat too dry to talk or swallow, and pumped out her last nine grenades. There were figures darting all around her now and she wasn't sure if any were friendlies. There wasn't time to decide. She leaned against a tree for support, raised her rifle and used the iron sights. She had no idea how many she killed, but the barrel was hot enough to burn her hand by the time she finished the next clip. She reached for another as she retreated. Then her unconscious kicked in again. She threw herself flat.

Rob threw his craft over the ridgeline inverted. That allowed maximum gees and better control. He grunted as the strain hit his guts and legs, and triggered the cannon. *I hope the friendlies are clear, because I'm killing everything,* he thought. He raked the fire straight down, rolling around his point of aim to right the craft. That was as close as he dared get to the reported Freehold line, not wanting to perpetuate the oxymoron of "friendly fire." As he leveled across the plain, he unloaded incendiary and HE bomblets and a canister of butterfly mines. They were nasty little things, basically two razor blades and a detonating cap. They'd cripple anyone who stepped on one.

He Immelmanned back on his course, straining the engines and the airframe, and locked missiles and rockets back along the route he'd come. He designated two points on the top of the ridge and tossed HE that way, then tore to his right along the treeline. He dumped the racks on what looked like an entire regiment of dismounted infantry, their vehicles parked and useless. He lit a few tanks, just because he could, and any ADA, because he had to and to keep them too

busy to worry about the friendlies, and headed south.
He'd swing between the chain of hills and come back
to the aviation position that way. He hugged the earth
for safety as he went, driving the speed up past 2500
kpd. "Target tank, target ayda priority, target, one, two,
thermal, selsee, three retar antarm, target target four
five, reset dez, target one, target mortar two, eecee
flare, left cannon target three, target four thermal, mass
target five cannon . . ." He controlled his craft with the
surety of years of practice, straining the system to the
edge of its envelope with the mass of targeting data.

He punched through a large, low cloud of smoke,
lifting slightly, just in case. Sensors didn't show anything in it, but he wasn't taking chances.

Pain!! Shock. Heat. Cold. Electromagnetic pulse
directed at his craft was powerful enough to overload the shielding capacity of his craft's frame and
hit his implant. The controls flickered in his sight,
resumed chaotically with figures that made no sense.
He scanned, still stunned, head throbbing and eyes
blurring. He'd dropped dangerously low while recovering.

WARNING! flashed in his environment. He scanned
the telltales and saw nothing, and felt no touches at
his temples. Control link gone or implant module
damaged. Vision began to fade. He swore and slowed.
At least he was clear of the UN lines. Now what?

Control was failing. The ground was coming up fast.
He pulled and nothing happened. Boosting throttles
didn't help.

Shit.

What the hell was up there? Meyer wondered. He'd
saturated the area with what support weapons he had
and the drones showed only a few infantry. The squad
leaders were still reporting heavy small arms fire and

the casualty count confirmed it. Could they all be in dug-in positions? But sonar and seismograph showed no major holes. Individual positions shouldn't be hard to overrun . . . unless there were a *lot* of them. That many should show some kind of thermal reading, sound or *something* the drones could measure. Nothing. The rebels had just plowed the area with close support, so it had to be clear now. He relayed that advice and ordered them to push harder. This should do it. If they could break through now, the enemy would have to surrender or be slaughtered and he could call for reinforcements.

The sky filled with the basso fabric-ripping sound of high-speed cannons. Hatchets made that sound, and nothing else. Wet splinters showered Kendra as the swath of death moved within meters of her and downslope. She stood quickly, surprising a Peacekeeper about to step on her. He staggered, confused and staring blankly and she kicked his kneecap, wondering why her calf no longer hurt. As he stumbled, she brought her leg up, knee in his face, and crashed her rifle on the back of his neck. She jerked a half step, knee searing, and shot again. The buddy of the last assailant appeared next to her, pointing the muzzle of his weapon into her face. She stared down the black hole for only a microsecond, then parried it and smashed him in the face with her muzzle as she shot. She swung around and fired at another trio stumbling into view. Her clip ran out and she reached for another. She had none. She buttstroked another soldier as he charged blindly past, kicked his ankle from under him and circled her foot over to crush this throat, feeling the gristly crunch up her leg. She grinned unconsciously. This was it. Time to die. A ripple ran up her spine.

Slinging the weapon and drawing her sword, she turned and ran uphill. Another drone sat in the crotch of a tree, trying to be inconspicuous. She jabbed the blade into the nacelle and the turbine shredded, throwing needlelike shards into her hand. They didn't do much damage, but her hand blazed with white-hot pain. As she ran past, the sky was ripped again, level with her, as a pilot gunned along the bottom of the hill. Ahead of her, two UN troops were braced against a tree, shooting at someone from her squad. She slashed across the spine of one and thrust into the kidney of the second. The first one screamed and thrashed to the ground, half paralyzed. The second simply collapsed. The keen blade had sliced through fabric designed to resist impact, not cutting.

Sheathing her sticky, gory blade, she grabbed the weapon and magazines from the dead one as she rolled for cover, bullets cracking past her. It was familiar from practice years past and Freehold training, and she retreated backward, shooting at anything that moved, starting with the one she'd wounded with her sword. The targets were backlit by the roiling fires below and she picked them out and picked them off. Fire. Aim. Fire. Aim. A round cracked past her ear, ignored in her current frame of mind. Shoot. Shoot again. Reload.

She saw movement, aimed toward it, then realized in the shifting light that the clothing of the figure on the ground was local hunting camouflage and the person wearing it was not in anything resembling cover. He was still moving, though. She fired three bursts to keep heads down and ran downslope. Her calf cramped with every jarring heelbeat and she winced, biting her lip. A few rounds made her flinch and she ducked lower, running hunched over.

The casualty was one of hers, but she had forgotten his name. Again she slung her weapon, heaved him up and around and over her shoulder and backed away, firing with her half aching, half tingling-numb left arm. Her bursts were fired for directional effect, not with any real hope of hitting anything. She stopped shooting as incoming rounds replied, aiming where her weapon had been when she fired. A part of her brain realized that meant that the UN helmets were nonfunctional, also. The pilot must have emped them as he tore overhead.

She chose her aim carefully and walked a series of bursts into the area in question. No further fire came from that one, but tens of others whipped past, cracking as they did. She stumbled, recovered and carefully lowered her burden behind a shattered stump. She crouched, rested her arm on her knee, and recalled where the last flashes had been. Returning to single shots to conserve ammo, she returned fire as fast as she could aim and squeeze. The enemy approaching seemed simply to materialize out of the flickering light and she swung back and forth, stopping the closest, taking any targets of opportunity between them. It was a losing proposition and she knew it. Fire. Fire again. Click! Curse and reload with one partial magazine. She quickly checked for her sword, realizing she would need it again soon.

Her shots spaced longer apart, then stopped. She could see UN troops throwing their weapons, scuttling behind trees and waving their arms. Cries of "Surrender!" and "Medic!" sounded all around, mingled with curses and screams.

The hillside was eerily quiet behind the voices, bereft of weapons fire. Smoke and steam drifted past in a nightmarish illusion of reality. She could hear ringing in her ears and wondered if she were deaf. There was smoky fire below and to her right.

Running fingers through her hair, she waited for any sign of movement. Nothing. She crawled behind the tree, dragged her second casualty over her shoulder, turned and trudged, alert for danger, watching for her people. There they were. Eight of them and one wounded, anyway. And more fires behind them. She and her casualty made it eleven out of twenty.

Her hair was sticky, she thought. In a moment, she realized it was her hand. Blood. Probably from the victim she'd carried. Then she remembered the shower of shrapnel from the drone. Then she noticed the neat gouge in her arm, where she thought a branch had caught her. It was a bullet wound and suddenly hurt like hell. Her arm cramped up and she winced. Blood was running freely. Her leg turned rubbery, then tensed up, dropping her sideways.

She collapsed as hands reached for her.

General Meyer stood as the rebel commander entered. A man, quite young and shorter than he, saluted and said, "I am Colonel Alan Naumann, General. I accept your surrender. Please order all your assets to cease fire and prepare for internment."

He saluted back. "I already have, Colonel. My congratulations on a brilliant mission. I wouldn't have thought it possible . . ." he tapered off, realizing that his career and perhaps his life were over. Outside, his headquarters company marched by, hands on heads, escorted by Freeholders. The prisoners looked stunned and occasionally sent awed glances toward the outnumbered enemy that had simply refused to yield to reality.

"Congratulate my troops. I just led," Naumann said. He looked distracted. "We will take you to the capital and arrange for your return. This battle is won, but there is still a war to finish."

"Thank you, Colonel. I'm amazed at your total destruction of our satellites," he hinted.

"Yes?"

"I understood you had no local space assets. How did you destroy them?" he asked.

Staring levelly, Naumann said, "That was the Special Warfare Regiments and a few remaining boats."

"To *all* the stations? But how did they get through the sensor fields?"

"That I cannot tell you." The sensors were programmed to ignore vacsuited individuals to make maintenance easier. Typical bureaucratic laziness. Naumann had no intention of revealing that at this time.

"But how long did that take? How much oxygen do they have?" Meyer asked. That wasn't possible!

"Not enough," Naumann confirmed.

"But . . . I'll ask our ships to search for survivors," he offered. Mother of God!

"Thank you for your offer. That won't be necessary. They had no way to evacuate from the structures anyway," Naumann said. He looked very tired and hurt.

Meyer stood silently, eyes locked with Naumann for about a minute. His mouth worked silently, finally rasping, "I would consider it an honor to attend that memorial, sir."

"Granted," Naumann nodded. Turning his face away, he said, "The guards will escort you to our headquarters."

Kendra sat at a UN medic's tent, now run by Freeholders. They'd patched her arm and leg and the flesh wound in her other leg she hadn't noticed and told her to wait for a scanner to become free. The surgeon in charge expressed the opinion that she'd lost thirty-five percent of her hearing, but that would have to wait for better facilities.

She sat silently, tired and sick and emotionless. Someone had told her she was a hero, and her force had held the brunt of the attack. The four-hundred-odd Freehold regulars and militia along the ridge had held against almost seven *thousand* UN infantry troops with weapons and vehicles. She nodded, uncomprehending, and tried to ignore her ringing ears.

Reports were coming in across the system. The UN fleet had been captured or destroyed, mostly by converted mining craft and ore carriers using mining charges and beam weapons. Once command and control was lost, the UN forces had muddled about helplessly, individual commanders untrained and unwilling to take charge and give orders. The casualties had been horrifying on both sides. The SpecWar Regiments had captured or destroyed every fixed station that mattered and two cruisers at a cost of ninty percent casualties.

And there'd been biochemical attacks south of Kendra's position, an act of desperation by an artillery commander who had hoped to save his troops. There were tens of casualties, alive but raving from the vicious neural toxin.

Cowboy was dead, brought down by ADA fire. Rob was reported missing in action, which meant dead. Kendra supposed she should be crying for his loss, but couldn't track enough to hurt. It occurred to her she was one of the lucky ones; alive, mostly intact and not screaming crazy from nanowar. She didn't feel lucky.

"In here!" a voice called. Marta snapped alert. Freehold or UN? Risk a fight? Or surrender? Was it over? She was still asking herself questions as the door was pried open with a bar. She waited to see how it developed.

UN troops swarmed into the room. "Here's the general. Dead," one said.

"Are you okay, ma'am?" one asked.

Before she could answer, the first shouted, "Fucking sure she's okay! Someone fucking strangled him!" He leaped over to her, raised his hand and punched her. She blocked it, stepped aside and disarmed him. As she raised his weapon, a massive blow crashed into her head. She staggered back into the wall, her face in agony, sinuses already stopped with blood. She tried to get into a defensive stance, but the shock and suddenness had her totally disoriented. She felt several more blows and mercifully passed out.

Chapter 43

"All warfare is based on deception."

—Sun Tzu

Not all the UN's satellites were down. A spare handful existed, varying in status from "functional" to "deadlined for overhaul." The UN battle staff aboard the flagship and the captured Sheppard Military Station brought up data and sensors bit by bit, acquiring what minimal data they could. Numbed shock ran through the staff as they realized just how badly their equipment had fared. Controlled fear could be smelled as they searched frantically for a marauding fleet. It was hours before they stood down from that alert and most of the crew immediately had to supplement the personnel attempting to get data of any kind from the surface.

Trickles of intelligence filled in a few gaps, but most of the map was a huge black zone, marked "Status undetermined." The fear created a trembling tension that threatened to break out into panic at any moment.

The command staff knew in detail what forces the Freeholders had started with. They knew fairly accurately what they had destroyed or captured. They had estimates of what force was left in both military and civilian hands. That intelligence flew in the face of the more than decimated UN strength that could be accounted for. Something had smashed the ground forces into powder, but what? Something had brutally crippled their space-based Command and Control network, but what?

Little rebel activity was visible, but the flood plain around Delph' was a scarred graveyard of armor, artillery, close-support craft and materiel. No response came from any command unit and only garbled, terrified demands for help from a few soldiers and platoons cut off from their headquarters and hiding. The base at Jefferson Starport wasn't responding, even though it looked only lightly damaged.

It was a day later that an assault boat rose from the planet and neared the station. It sat, well within range of the defensive batteries and defiantly challenged them. "You are commanded to surrender to the Freehold Military Forces within three minutes or be destroyed," came the only transmission.

The three ranking officers stared at each other, shook their heads in utter hopelessness and complied. The boarding party were all Freehold regulars, in spotless armor and gear. That appearance was the final crushing blow and the prisoners offered no resistance. The Freeholders had to hide their triumphant grins. The prisoners didn't need to know that this was the only boarding crew and boat left in the planet's vicinity. Not yet, anyway. Nor that it had three trained professionals and seventeen experienced militia dressed accordingly and looking as professional as possible. The senior sergeant in charge reported back, "Station Sheppard secure."

"Acknowledged, Three Juliet Two Zero," the ground controller replied. Behind her the battle staff waited, stock still and silent. Turning, she reported to Naumann, "Sir, the system is secure."

The cheer that exploded in response could probably have been measured on the Richter Scale.

Chapter 44

"When you have secured an area, don't forget to
tell the enemy."
                                    —Ancient military proverb

The war continued despite the victory at the bluff.
While the head had been destroyed, the thrashing body
of the behemoth was still a grave threat. It was a manageable threat, but still to be taken seriously.

The Freeholders were helped by a huge set of
cultural assumptions. No matter General Huff's
assessment, the UN staff and soldiers still clutched
at the belief that "high number of privately owned
weapons" meant five percent or so, and most of
those in the agricultural areas. They visualized a few
hunting rifles or shotguns and had not been dis-
abused of that notion. Those battles in the major
cities were easy to chalk up to captured weapons.
Most Freeholders had refused to fight when the
odds were suicidal and had instead waited. Any

number of signals would have ended that wait, and this was more than sufficient.

Weapons came out of closets, out of barns, up from the ground and in from the woods. Fully seventy percent of households were armed, most multiply so. There were still enough weapons for every adult and most juveniles and they were not all hunting gear.

Most surviving veterans still had their military rifles, some, machineguns. Even with the captured and casualties, the weapons were often recovered by other rebels. And military weapons were reliable, sturdy, and cheap as surplus, thus were very common. Target shooting was one of the most popular sports, whether it was with pistols rapid fired at ten meters or large bore rifles at two thousand. Support weapons were less common, but grenade launchers, machineguns, small cannon and howitzers were not unheard of. Along with readily bought and readily hidden explosives, plenty of aircraft and the willingness to use it all, the Freeholders were a credible, competent militia, with a military heritage nurtured from the time of the old English fyrd.

Certainly, most rifles were used for pest control on farms, but a self-loading military rifle was a cheap and convenient means of doing so. Shotguns were excellent for hunting, had been little changed, only refined, over the last five hundred years, and were still as deadly in close-range and urban combat as the military and police had found them centuries before. Pistols were readily concealed under coats and Freeholders had adopted more Earthlike dress for that reason.

Without the support of air superiority, artillery, a credible threat of space-based retaliation and a large staff, the tactical odds evened tremendously. Logistically, the locals now had better access to materiel, and half a million scattered UNPF troops suddenly found

themselves outnumbered, even with the massive inflic-
tion of rebel casualties, by 300:1. It wasn't quite that
bad on an engagement basis, as they tended to be
clustered in urban areas with only small patrols
detached elsewhere and protected by the threat of massive retaliation. But that threat was now gone and those
who were dug in could only listen helplessly as the cries
for help of those comrades were snuffed out one by
one, and wonder where the command structure was.
They awaited their own turn and hoped that succor
from above was to be forthcoming.

Kendra led her friends cautiously into Delph'. Dak
and Kyle were now with them, as were several others she knew at least peripherally. They'd been flown
in with as many other volunteers as could be located.
The basic force structure was one FMF member, any
rank and specialty, as squad leader, and nineteen locals
as the remainder of the squad. Some very few squads
had half their troops equipped with RGL weapons or
seized UN weapons or missiles or snipers. Kendra was
not so lucky. At least she had a working comm and the
commnet was up. Most of her squad had seen action.
She didn't envy those who had neither in their squads.
    Sighing, she led them forward, on foot, into the
south edge of Delph'. The town was mostly intact, but
that wasn't likely to last. The remaining UN troops,
perhaps four thousand, were dug in and panicked.
Getting them out was necessary, as they could be
reinforced with a drop if any assets were still insystem.
And they had some support weapons. And there were
still civilians trapped here. They couldn't be starved out.
    It was eerily quiet the first div, as they checked
houses one at a time. Some few civilians met them and
reported what they knew. A map was gradually being
built and it would help, but distressingly large areas

of it were black. All such civilians had their residences searched, in case they were under duress. Some were. Usually their faces showed it.

She would have thought anyone rational would have surrendered by now. There were reports of single UN troops fighting squads. She couldn't understand panic on that level.

They hit an industrial zone and began digging through the buildings for pockets of resistance. She expected a fight and was not pleasantly surprised. Massive small arms fire erupted from several sources and they scattered for cover behind a flowerbed that was still manicured despite the destruction. One of her new kids dropped in a heap and she cursed as she ran a search for sources. There and there. "Dak, to our front left, third floor, second window from the right, and to our right, rooftop, one third of the way south," she advised. He acknowledged with a yell and began sending troops out. She lobbed a grenade toward the roof, fused for altitude, and ducked as more fire came from the left. She was exposed and the only cover was bad cover. Then the enemy came running out, right in front of her, and something crashed into her helmet. She shot the first soldier automatically and swung for the second, noting the third was flanking her. She stepped sideways to close with number two and shot offhand at number three who flinched. Kendra finished her turn and buttstroked number two under the jaw, feeling bones splinter. The third one was raising her weapon and Kendra spun, shooting twice. The girl grimaced momentarily and stared at her with deep eyes until Kendra's rising weapon smashed up under her visor, just to make sure. It wasn't disgusting or horrible anymore, Kendra thought. It was just a job. "I'm going to check inside this building," she said over her helmet's comm. "Team One with me, Two around the back, Weapons stand by for support," she ordered.

After a quick look through the door showed no obvious threats, she darted inside to get out of the rubble-strewn street. Inside, she looked around for signs of life, information, anything. Her vision faded. Malfunction! She unsnapped her helmet and shrugged it off, swearing to herself. She turned to the left and saw movement too late. A heavy weight crashed into her head.

She felt and heard a rush like water and her eyes swirled from blotches to colors. She was aware of returning to consciousness. Momentary nausea passed, the world spun and she looked up at figures in UN uniforms. She suddenly was aware of her pants being yanked down. A hand clamped her mouth shut and covered it. She could smell earth and scorched polymer on the rough skin as her briefer was ripped open.

"Another baldie!" a voice from her ankles hollered in triumph. It was tinny in her ears.

"I think all these bitches are bald!" one behind her added, then laughed at his alliteration. He thought it quite clever.

Kendra fought down panic as her legs were forced open. Her brain tried to relax, fighting her instinctive impulse to clamp tight. She tried concentrating on a bit of rubble stabbing her in the back. Another wave of tension hit her as fingers fumbled inside her, then she felt his weight drop carelessly on her hips. She grunted.

"Oh, yeah! Take it, bitch!" her attacker crowed. He drew back and shouted, "Little girl, Daddy's *home!*" and thrust painfully into her. She felt something tear and the pain of friction.

Amazing, she thought. *I'm not panicking. Relax until he's done, then . . .* The unarmed combat techniques for shackled feet flashed through her brain. *Never thought I'd need those,* she realized, *but pants around the ankles are effectively shackles. Strong kick as he pulls back, probably to his lower ribs unless his chin becomes available. Bend over backward in a ... well, not a scorpion kick, but what would you call it? Doesn't matter. Then roll sideways and take a snake or leopard strike to number three's throat or groin.* She figured that the radio in her helmet had failed before the vision circuit, since none of her people were present. Likely from that impact. Had it been a shot? Stupid to assume, stupid to run ahead, stupid, stupid, stupid!

"Make it quick, Cody, I got seconds!" the man holding her mouth said.

"My turn! You had seconds last time!" she heard from near the door.

"You're the new kid. You do her last and we'll get out of here. If it bothers you, try her back door. And get back over there and keep an eye out."

"We're fine, they all ran off," the shrill young voice insisted.

"Good. After they pass, we'll head back to the south. Teach these hicks."

She felt his thrusts intensifying and a sudden thought did scare her. *Oh, shit, I'm fertile! I don't want to be pregnant! How would I deal with that?* Her Catholic upbringing made her very uncomfortable with aborting a pregnancy, but she knew she wouldn't want to be forced into motherhood. Her muscles clamped down.

"That's it! *Ride* me, baby!" the rapist said and laughed. She looked up in time to see his head shatter. A thin red mist settled over her as the muffled shot hit her ears and registered. Two more shots heralded the deaths of the others. Sudden relief was replaced by sudden nausea—the rapist's sphincters cut loose as nervous control was lost.

The body was yanked off her, leaving a pool of blood soaking into her uniform. Dak looked down, then at her face, then everywhere *but* her face. It would almost have been amusing had it not been so embarrassing. "Lad . . . Ma'a . . . Corp . . . Sergeant, are you all right?" he asked, flushing red in embarrassment.

"I need a dressing," she said immediately.

He yanked one from his gear and said, "Where?"

"Not for a wound, just to clean up," she replied. He handed it over and leapt back, averting his eyes. She used his dressing and two of her own to gingerly clean the assorted blood and filth from her skin, then jammed a clean one down as a bandage, fastened her half-torn briefer and got her pants back in place. She tore a shirt off one of the bodies and used it sop up the excess liquid covering her. Poor Dak looked terrible—ashamed, disgusted and ashamed at being disgusted. He unconsciously backed away as she stepped forward, and she saw a look of murder under the other emotions.

"Thanks, Dak," she said. "I'll be with you in just a moment." She was amazed at the calm in her voice as she turned, dropped to her knees and spewed vomit. She coughed twice, stood up slowly and snagged a drink. The warm water made her throat feel slightly better, at least. "Let's go," she ordered and headed for the door, limping and stiff. He followed, but stopped at the door. She waited and stood back while he heaved his own guts. He nodded vaguely and followed.

They regrouped with the others at the next building north, and determined that Kendra's helmet had been hit hard enough to damage the battery pack. "What kept you?" Kyle asked. He had equipped three of the newer recruits with UN weapons. He stared through the blood from her two head wounds, trying to discern any injuries. "You all right?"

"Had to stop for a drink," Kendra said, gasping from exertion as she looked at her damaged helmet. Her head was hammering and throbbing. "And three nasties. Dak got them all."

"Adding to your total, huh?"

Dak shook his head. "These were bonuses," he replied, eyes finally meeting Kendra's. She nodded in response and took the lead.

"My helmet's out," she said. "So we'll go at it carefully. Keep alert." If anyone noticed her awkward gait, they didn't mention it.

It took twelve days to clear Delph'. Kendra personally went into The Coracle and cleared it. It was a shambled ruin and she wondered if the owners were still alive. The arena was also demolished, hit by artillery. They cautiously advanced building by building, most of them rubble before they were done. The UN troops were trapped, terrified and cut off from any chain of command. About a third surrendered immediately, looking dead as they marched past. The rest were too afraid to give up or expected eventual succor from overwhelming force that would never come. They fought to the death and took the town with them. Mass bombing would have been more humane and quicker, but the politics of warfare made that impossible; they had to be given every opportunity to yield, if for no other reason than to minimize civilian deaths.

The UN had superior numbers. The Freeholders had far better training, morale, logistics and knowledge of the area. It was still costly in casualties. It reminded Kendra of the continual wargames, as they shifted tactics and personnel around in mass confusion, losing troops, getting garbled orders and being badly supplied and supported. It was classic urban warfare and she hated it within segs, despised it within divs.

Approach a building, scan it. If nothing showed clearly, blow the door and stand back, toss in a flashbang if available, a grenade if not. Charge in and shoot anything that moved, including rats and occasional curtains. Check to make sure it was clear and leave one person as guard until the line advanced or a counterattack hit. If it was occupied, demand surrender. When they refused, about half the time, call for air power. Level the building. Note it on the comm. Repeat.

The formula never became routine. As she entered a house the first day, gunfire shattered the doorframe around her. She hosed the attacker as she dove for cover and shook for most of a seg before continuing. Dak had thought her shot.

One panicked little kid hit her with a stun bag. She woke, nauseous and dizzy, to see his brains and guts splashed across the wall behind him. He'd had no lethal weaponry and had stupidly made a stand with the stunner.

On the third day, a sniper's bullet from a second-floor office slammed into her chest from the left. She collapsed and tried in vain to breathe. Splotches marred her vision and she was sure she was dead.

"Kendra! Listen to me!" She became aware that Dak had been shouting at her and that she'd been dragged to cover. "You're not hit bad, but we have to get your armor off!"

She nodded, again close to vomiting; that was just the way she lived now. Dak tugged gently at her armor and she winced in pain, then bit her cheek against a shriek and tasted blood. Everything looked gray.

No, everything *was* gray. Shattered stone, brick, polymer, dust and haze. That was normal. The ripping sound was her briefer being cut away. She realized she was in shock. Then Dak raised a bottle.

Disinfectant splashed under her left breast and she fainted from the pain.

Awake in seconds, she didn't throw up yet again. There was fire stabbing icy and electrically through her chest and it hurt to breathe, but at least she could breathe. Then the painkiller hit her and everything turned blissful and blurry. Then the augmentation nano snapped her back to alertness. She grabbed the offered canteen and gulped water. She heard him say, "It's mostly pressure trauma, with some superficial lacerations from the armor splinters. You'll be fine."

The great thing about modern battlefield medicine, she thought, was that you didn't care that your chest felt as if it had been run over by a truck. It still felt that way, you just didn't care. She knew she'd be ravenous in a few segs as her drugged body demanded energy, and reached for an emergency ration to beat the rush. She told Dak to take over until he thought she was tracking properly and followed him back toward their op point to meet up with survivors from other squads to bring theirs back up to full strength. She couldn't name the half-trained but brave militia fighters who'd died in the last three days. Nor could she remember sleeping. That's right, she hadn't.

That night, still without a functional tac helmet, dependent on intermittent audio, she made the tactical decision to rest. They pulled back into a cleared area that was mostly rubble, set watches of four, each commanded by one of the old hands and crewed by one of the fresh new troops and two others, and designated a latrine area. They were visible, but not near any immediate threat. It was too dangerous to fight at night if they didn't have to, since most of them, including Kendra now, had no night vision gear. Sleep was necessary if they were to be effective, so she gave the orders. No one objected.

She was awakened at three, groggy from too little sleep, but she felt marginally better. *On with the show,* she thought. Under orders from some Reserve lieutenant whom she didn't know, she went in to see the medics again. Her squad came along, acquired replacements for their evacuated casualties and got some rest. She passed out while awaiting treatment.

The medics must know her file by heart now, Kendra thought. She'd declined to discuss the massive bruising and trauma to her groin. They knew what had happened anyway and offered counseling she didn't want. *Just leave me the hell alone, all of you!* she thought. They gave her a topical nano for STDs. The sudden demand for that aspect of medical technology revolted the local surgeons. They were professional but cold with the prisoners, staring at them as they would parasites. They treated her trauma, the numerous cuts and abrasions, her chest, checked her arm and leg, gave her a pregnancy inhibitor—they didn't ask; it was standard policy—and ran another scan on her hearing. They couldn't tell her much. Therapy later, and she might regain some of it.

"We have to act now," Naumann urged the remnants of the Council. "Earth will send another force as soon as they can put one together, and we *cannot* fight another campaign. We have one chance to nail them and we will never, *ever* get another."

"But you are talking about the murder of six *billion* human beings!" Uddin said in outraged shock.

"So what do you suggest?" Naumann shouted. "That we let them destroy us?"

"Our total population is less than four percent of the *death* count you suggest!"

"And who argued against the philosophy of might makes right?" Naumann asked.

"Listen to—"

"*No! You* listen!" Naumann shouted, rising to his feet. "We are *beaten.* We can't fight another planetary engagement. We have no fleet. If—*when* they send another force, they will annihilate our troops, enslave our residents and we will never rise above it."

Chinratana protested, "But the Colonial Alliance—"

"Is *powerless!*" Naumann trod over his comment. "They have no military, they have no economic force. They dance to the tune of the UN General Assembly. Without outside force, we will be as helpless as they. And. There. Is. No. Outside. Force," he finished. There was silence.

"You want us to authorize the murder of six billion Terrans, who are not responsible for the actions of their government," the elderly man protested again.

"There are thirty billion people on Earth," Naumann said. "They can stop their government any time they wish, simply through brute force or civil disobedience. No tyrant ever rules without the consent of the ruled. They are *guilty* by their inaction.

"And if not them," he finished, "you condemn our people to rape, torture, murder and economic slavery. You've seen how they treat us, you must know it won't change. This will be the dumping ground for every incompetent, troublemaker or sociopath who can't hold office, and there will be no protection against it." Naumann was breathing hard, anger straining his voice.

The Citizens looked guiltily around at each other. Most of them had been protected from the worst, but they had seen it take place. Their own future was decidedly short if the UN gained political control, but most of them were courageous enough to put that risk second to the safety of others. Now they had to consider if they had the right to place the entire Freehold in their own position.

"I call for the question," Griffiths said tiredly.

"Second," Hernandez said. How the two of them would vote was certain.

There were thirty Citizens present, from both District and Freehold councils, with proxies for eighty-three more. Each name was called aloud, no computer system being available. The tally rose in jumps, some in favor, some opposed. Griffiths kept the list and recounted it when done.

"The resolution is to authorize the Provisional Military Forces to engage the infrastructure and civilian population of Sol System as military targets. One hundred thirteen votes present, no abstentions," he paused to let that last be noted. No one had shied from the responsibility inherent in the vote. "In favor, eighty-two. Opposed, thirty-one. The motion carries." There was a collective gasp of relief and shock, even though everyone had known how it must end.

Hernandez turned to Naumann and said, "Colonel, carry out your operation as described."

"Yes, sir," Naumann agreed and stood. His firm exterior had returned.

"Colonel Naumann," Uddin said.

He turned to the speaker, "Yes, Citizen?"

"Good luck, Colonel. And may your God forgive you."

"Understood, sir," he acknowledged with a nod.

By the end of day five, Kendra was bandaged in other places from burns and nicks. Her ribs were stiff and her left arm wouldn't raise above halfway from the cumulative effect of its wound and the tautness of her ribs. Her legs ached with every step and cramped up when she held still. She trudged on.

There were bodies in the street, mostly UN, some Freehold militia and occasional civilians. Then the odd ones, like the six-year-old boy still clutching a rifle and the body of a two-year-old girl that looked as if she were simply sleeping. She tried to stop Dak from seeing that one, but he saw and began shaking with rage. She noted he hadn't taken any captives or wounded anyone. He wasn't deliberately murdering would-be prisoners, but he was doing his best to not give them the opportunity. She found she no longer was bothered by it. Eventually, the few remaining UN troops surrendered or suicidally attacked. The morning of the twelfth day, they simply appeared in the streets, hands and weapons held high and let themselves be taken. Some few arrived firing mindlessly, until they ran out of ammo or were cut down. The battle was over for most of them and the Freehold was secure for the time being.

Marta swam awake through a nightmare, gasping through her mouth. *I'm hyperventilating,* she realized. She was lashed down and felt touches she couldn't be sure were real or dreams. Unbidden, an ugly scream erupted from her throat and she snapped a foot out, contacting something. An answering howl indicated she'd caused some damage.

"Fucking *cunt!*" someone said, and a huge weight smashed into her wounded face. She felt teeth splinter, pain lanced through her jaw and she blacked out again. Her last thought was that it was real.

She woke again, feeling tumbling vertigo. She was completely restrained and wet. Vague memories surfaced. She'd been doused with a bucket of water. She was still alive, despite contusions, lacerations, massive trauma and the damage to her face. As she took stock of things, there was more violence. *Not again*, she wished, *Goddess, not again. I seek peace in the storm— this can't be happening—this—in the storm. Sun strengthen my spirit, oceans wash me clean, winds . . . oceans . . . winds . . .* Her prayer evaporated in another scream of utter terror and hopelessness.

Chapter 45

"It is easier to do one's duty to others than to one's self. If you do your duty to others, you are considered reliable. If you do your duty to yourself, you are considered selfish."

—Thomas Szasz

Naumann stormed into the new command center, hurriedly being wired and set. He stopped against a bulkhead and oriented himself with everyone else. It still looked like a converted freighter, but it would place the battle staff closer to the operation. "We do it," he said simply. Everyone present turned silently to their systems and went to work.

There was a target that Naumann found controversial, but could not drop from the list. He sighed, realizing this was going to be a painful operation, and paged Kendra Pacelli.

While he waited for her, he took up another issue.

"Ops, what do you have on that rescue mission?" he asked.

The operations officer replied, "Nothing yet, sir. We think she's in Jump Point Three, but it's a big facility. Despite the surrender order, we're still digging aardvarks out of there."

"Get to it. I want her back," he snapped.

"As soon as we can, sir," was the confident reply.

"Sorry," Naumann apologized. "Strain. Hernandez is a first-class troop and I want her back alive. We owe her."

Kendra had no idea what Naumann wanted. She was busily scheduling loading and docking sequences, with far too few docks and far too much materiel. In between times, she was coding information for the targeting instruments the weapons would carry. That was not properly a logistics task, but then, much of what she'd done the last several months hadn't been logistics, either. She ended a plot of fuel schedules and saved to hard memory. Then she dragged herself through the crowded tube to the rear cargo bay, now command post.

"You paged me, Colonel?" she asked. He looked drained and sad. He was flanked, as always now, by four Black Ops people with no sense of humor. She thought assassination was an extremely unlikely step for the UN to attempt, but Naumann was taking no chances with his safety. It wasn't cowardice; he was more than capable of protecting himself, but there were no other officers of his level available. He kept the bodyguards, even when they got in the way.

He nodded to her. "Let's find a corner," he motioned and twisted around, swimming for a gap between instruments. She followed and somersaulted between them, yawing to the same orientation as Naumann. His wall of henchmen kept a discreet distance, but were close enough to swarm her or him if necessary. Considering that he'd recently sent most of them to their deaths, she was amazed at their dedication. Utter emotionless professionalism. Scary.

"The target list is out," he told her. "There are some cities locked in and others that are tentative."

"Do you want me to help prioritize them, Colonel?" she asked.

He winced. He hadn't even thought of that. This was definitely going to hurt. He blurted out, "Minneapolis is on the final list."

Kendra was stunned silent. It hadn't occurred to her that she'd be intimately familiar with any targets. She stared emptily, her head whirling and not from free fall.

"There are . . . assets in place that could warn your family," he said, and before the hint of relief in her face could become a false hope he finished, "but I cannot compromise security by doing so. Because I believe your parents to be as honorable as you, I'd expect them to try to warn the government. They'd probably be ignored, but I cannot take that risk."

Kendra felt near to fainting. She had sudden flashbacks to a team of "civilians" she had briefed in detail on central North America and another debriefing she'd had several months before and gulped back bile. After gathering her composure, she said simply, "I understand, Colonel."

"I'll have the chaplain meet you in your quarters," he hinted rather than ordered.

Kendra shook her head. "If it's all the same to you, I'd rather stay. It'll keep me occupied. And I don't want to see it done half-assed."

It took three tense, nervous days of preparation to finalize the massive operation. Naumann barely slept and his temper was frayed. There were so many details and this was properly work for someone who had been to war college and held a rank at least two grades higher. Strategic weapons properly required a huge staff and on-site presence. Since he was the only one available, he saw the futility of complaining, not to mention the damage to morale. He worked furiously, driving himself over any doubts or remorse, and tried to sit calmly during the rare moments when nothing was pending.

Kendra saw the tired intensity of his determination. She had no idea how he maintained the pace. He jumped from analyzing the continued recovery of the planet and dictating orders for it, to directing the tattered remains of the fleet and the volunteer reserves to strategically important positions, to planning a massive counterattack against Earth. He demanded absolute perfection of data from his sources and got it. He spent divs staring at screens and making minor adjustments. Somehow, he had scraped up enough phase drives to outfit marginally enough weapons for what he had planned. Brandt StarDriveSystems had a few in preparation and storage facilities in the outer Halo and Meacham Hyper had finally paralleled the Brandt work, just before hostilities erupted. Naumann clearly wasn't happy with the numbers available, but he assured his staff it would be sufficient.

From her viewpoint, he was a strategic genius. The sheer numbers they faced had convinced her even a stalemate was impossible, but he was driving toward a win. Unbelievable. She dozed when she could, programmed data as it came in and kept her emotions clamped tightly. If her friends could suffer the massive losses they had already, she could accept the risk to her family and home. She didn't have to like it.

Finally, they were finished. All craft were loaded, all weapons set, everything sealed and ready. They would stay here and the task would be handled at Earth by automatic systems and a few control personnel. Intelligence reported a UN task force in the Caledonia system, ready to transit and attack. There was no margin for error. If this didn't work, they could all expect life in prison if they were lucky, brainwiping or death if not. She tried not to think about how she would be regarded if captured, as it made sleeping impossible.

Chapter 46

"In peace there's nothing so becomes a man
   As modest stillness and humility:
   But when the blast of war blows in our ears,
   Then imitate the action of the tiger;
   Stiffen the sinews, summon up the blood,
   Disguise fair nature with hard-favour'd rage . . ."
            —William Shakespeare, *King Henry V*

It was Monday morning rush hour in Minneapolis' zone +6 and traffic was as bad as it always was. Pedestrians and floaters and vehicles all fought for space. The crowd at the corner were mostly familiar to one another and stared around as they waited for transportation or crossing signals. A white van pulled over to a curb and set out a warning beacon. It broadcast its signal to traffic control and flashed an alert to the controls of any vehicle in the area.

One man got out, levered up a ground panel and reached inside. A subtle *snick!* indicated success and traffic suddenly halted as the grid control was destroyed. The self-control functions on the vehicles kicked in and began feeding them one at a time, very gingerly, across the intersection. Traffic instantly snarled for blocks around and a second *snick!* ensured the damage would not be easy to fix. He continued inside, dumping data from cubes into various lines to other parts of the grid. No one paid any attention to the van; it was background.

"What the hell are you doing?" a cop snarled. The terrorist did not recognize his specific uniform, but the thuggish attitude was unmistakable. He stepped forward while smiling and raised a hand to gesture. The gesture turned into a vicious attack that dropped the cop to the pavement and the man departed.

Nearby, a woman dressed as a visiting professional walked into a construction site. She had a protective hat and shield and a comm. She strode through the site, watched occasionally for her young prettiness, but unbothered by questions as to her purpose. It was a matter of seconds to get the attention of the force crane operator, approach and disable him and board his equipment.

There was a girder in the beam and she took advantage of its mass. It made a satisfying hole in the side of a nearby building and dropped lethally onto the frantically gesturing site boss. She slid out while panic reigned and dropped her hat and shield as she left the fence. A quick turn took her inside another office block. She found the maintenance access and a few seconds fiddling with a coder let her inside. A swipe of a deadly toy scrambled tens of data lines, and another access a few meters away crippled the elevators and drop tubes. She turned and left, pulling a manual fire alarm as she did so. Outside, a car swerved across traffic, inexplicably on manual, and bumped another. That one stopped, but the manual operation confused the already snarled local grid. It attempted to correct, failed, and a third vehicle rear-ended the second.

She slipped into the first car, which turned in traffic and fled. The route had been chosen to keep them on the outside of the growing circle of chaos. There was little outgoing traffic this time of the morning and the driver wove rapidly through it, terrifying other operators.

Several bomb threats were called in and two police cars had been set on fire, along with two fire protection units, which were trapped in their garages and roaring with explosive-induced flame. A few real bombs detonated high in skyscrapers, killing workers within and showering the crowds below with rubble and glass. Every building began evacuation to the streets. Illegal firearms were in use, shooting out windows in the finance district. A power transformer went offline, disrupting business in the city building. Toward the outskirts, a substation caught fire. The resulting shift in power flow at a critical time caused fluctuations across the grid, creating numerous secondary problems. Faulty software caused a series of pressure waves to rupture water mains. Fire alarms were sounding in tens of locations. The local police had experience with riots, but not in preventing them. They watched helplessly as the city ground to a halt, one problem after another dominoing into madness. It might be days before order was restored. They would have been shocked to know that four people were responsible for all the mayhem.

The pattern was repeated in Chicago, Milwaukee, Saint Louis and elsewhere, with poison gases, bombs, system failures and attacks. The undersea city of Baja Pacifica had its dome shattered by a tiny nuclear device. Europe and Asia received their own share of abuse.

Several well-designed worms and windows created gaps in the comm-nets, bouncing through electronic space like manic grasshoppers. But while politicians at hastily arranged conferences sweated, a far worse danger was brewing, minutes and infinite distance away.

A silent swarm of death snapped into existence near Earth. There was localized interference due to gravitational distortion. Blurred ripples surrounded each dropout, damping almost immediately. The sight would have been fascinating and eerie to any observers, but there were none to see it. Shortly, however, there would be billions of witnesses.

The first wave, oriented, fired powerful retros to position themselves, then triggered. They immediately reentered phase drive in a precisely planned manner. With no destination, their mass converted to pure energy, still within the normal space-time reference. Googolwatt levels of photons streamed forward, only to smash into the obstacles ahead—the cities of Earth. Detroit felt the lead sting by nanoseconds, being directly underneath the first. The wave front vaporized much of the northern industrial sector and the ground beneath it. The shock wave tore outward, shattering everything as far as Windsor and Pontiac. The overpressure could still be felt to slap structures as far away as the Toledo suburb.

Other weapons burned Yokohama, Dallas, Madras, Kuwait, Rio de Janeiro and Djakarta. The carnage was terrifying and from orbit could be seen the incandescent ruins left as signatures. They would glow for days.

The second wave rocketed forward on chemical engines at extreme acceleration. Only seconds after the first wave they detonated in low orbit, blowing clouds of ions and dust in a screen against any possible detection. Some few of them continued down, to hit hardened military targets. These were dirty explosions, designed to trap the occupants until heavy rescue equipment could arrive.

The third wave were large blocks of foamed polymer to confuse sensors. Inside them, precise charges detonated and the warheads within stopped dead in orbit. Another charge accelerated them vertically at over eight thousand meters per second. They dropped over their targets, glowing red as they passed through the atmosphere in seconds.

The warheads in question were mere bars of metal with simple guidance packages—the weapon Kendra had seen used to cut a pass for a road. They steered straight down for any large mass. At that brutal velocity, they vaporized on impact, blasting holes into buildings. Polymer, concrete and glass rained down in their target cities. Fires erupted, buildings began to slowly topple from structural damage, traffic ground to a halt and deep holes punched into buildings made evacuation awkward.

The dust settling in the atmosphere contained tailored nanos that sought crops in fields and hydroponics factories. They were coded for specific crops. It had been standard practice on Earth for centuries to tailor specific seed and fertilizers, both to improve yield and to ensure "customer loyalty," since the same manufacturer provided both the seed and the necessary nutrients for it. This policy had not changed when those producers were nationalized; the yield was better from such plants than from natural ones.

The nanos infiltrating that artificial biome were coded to block some of those catalyzing nutrients. Within days, several important species of grain would wither and die. A percentage of the vat-grown meats would also suffer. If casualties on Earth were as predicted, the shortage would not be too severe, merely enough to keep the industrial base busy feeding the survivors.

If casualties were lighter than expected, this supplemental attack could be thought of as "Plan B."

Earth's and Sol System's defensive net snapped awake. It looked for targets and found none. This was partly due to the scarcity of such targets—a mere twelve small ships scattered throughout the system's volume—partly due to their stealthiness and partly due to a third attack, or second backup. Naumann was known for his thoroughness.

During the raid on Langley Facility, several software agents had been infiltrated into the local net. Each had been individually crafted by experts, all of whom were unaware of their colleagues' efforts. Human skill from Freehold had made them all but undetectable. Human laziness on Earth had salvaged most of the network, rather than building a new one. Those agents had attached themselves, byte by byte, block by block, to any convenient transmission. They were cunningly crafted and deeply hidden and had slumbered silently until certain sequences of code awakened them. They woke now.

Angrily and triumphantly, they tore into the software that had carried and fed them. Various parts of the networks were swamped with alerts, rendered blind or had their information doctored only subtly. With no basis for comparison, the artificial intelligence had to start from nothing, compiling data and attempting to determine what was wrong where. The agents danced maniacally from system to system, occasionally defeated, but more often steps ahead of attempted fixes. It would take days to correct all the errors to an acceptable level for combat and days more to check the results. The system would never regain full efficiency and would eventually have to be abandoned.

None of the attacks were indefensible against. None were particularly state of the art, although the phase drive engines used as directional energy weapons were a new twist. It had simply been thought unthinkable to attack in such a fashion, laying waste to civilian territory so callously. And it would have been unthinkable had not the UN attacked Freehold first with nukes and kinetics and had not "Madman" Naumann been in control of the Freehold military.

Few cities are equipped to handle more than a few hundred deaths per ten million population in any given day. The combination of attack, induced riots and the predictable panic reactions of millions of terrified inhabitants brought the death tolls into the thousands, then the tens of thousands. It became impossible for emergency services to get into the cities. Panic spread even to cities not attacked, rumors of impending doom creating wild disturbances and attempts at evacuation. The UN and regional governments tried to squelch news stories, but the necessities of modern communication made it all but impossible. Those attempts created further panic that either the government had lost control, had been subverted by one of many conspiracy theories floating around or was attempting to eliminate what civil rights were left. All government forces were tied up preventing the trouble from spreading; none could assist the shattered cities. Without power and water, they began to die, rapidly.

With only bare hours of food available in the stores and no water, the fighting escalated to food riots. Young parents gladly killed the elderly to ensure food for their children. Street toughs and organized crime saw profit, as did some storekeepers, until they realized they were trapped themselves. With a virtual ban on any modern weapon, it quickly devolved to contests of sheer brute force with improvised weapons. Fearing the gangs, families grouped together and attacked any gathering of youths preemptively.

Fires, started for heat and light, ignited buildings with poor or substandard attention to codes. Thousands of building custodians who had paid off inspectors began to realize the error of their ways, as apartments and offices became roiling torches to careless desperation. The death toll kept rising. Heat and cold added their own numbers to the count. In the sublevels, ventilation and lights failed. Those trapped below turned into howling beasts, tearing each other apart with their last breaths.

Automated repair equipment swarmed through the tunnels and streets, blocked in every direction. Mindlessly, the machines tried route after route until their power ran out or response circuits overloaded. A few, stressed far beyond the point where a human controller should take over, malfunctioned into orgies of destruction.

Hospitals, denied power, lost all patients in supportive care and most in surgery. Drugs and nanos quickly decayed without refrigeration. In terror, the hospitals locked their doors to keep out the masses of casualties they couldn't care for. Police stations and government offices also barricaded the mob out.

Shortly, the legions of dead would begin to rot. There were no facilities to process them, no transport or handlers. Rats and other vermin would run rampant.

It would be weeks before any semblance of control returned. Even then, the deaths would continue until the infrastructure could be restored. Earth no longer had any resources available for war.

Chapter 47

"War does not determine who is right, but who is left."

—old military proverb

Caledonia Jump Point One Traffic Control suddenly found itself swamped. The message that came through from Earth on a priority drone was panicked and inconsistent, but made it clear that all UN registered merchant and military vessels were needed at their home ports at once. It requested emergency humanitarian aid from all planets and asked that a cease-fire with Freehold be negotiated immediately. It advised that an envoy would arrive shortly. The message repeated.

All Earth merchant ships immediately requested traffic plans back to Earth and incoming messages from other systems indicated that large numbers of vessels were all traveling that way in the next few days. The fleet bound for Freehold that had been held up for the last six days also reversed course, abandoning its obvious assault.

The controllers didn't know what stunt Freehold had pulled, but the veterans who'd met Freehold forces provided plenty of rumors. Most were close in spirit, but wide of the mark. Later that day, a drone arrived with a message from the Freehold, ending debate.

"This is Colonel Alan Naumann, commanding the Provisional Freehold Military Forces. I read a statement from the Citizen's Council of the Freehold of Grainne.

"Earlier today, elements of our military attacked the infrastructure of the United Nations of Earth. This resulted in the deaths of many innocent civilians. We regret that necessity.

"The survival of our system, our people and our way of life depended on ending the UN's assault on our system. Their attack was unprovoked, unjustified and a political attempt to gain power and profit at the expense of our residents. Our requests to be left alone, our historical documentation and guarantee that we are a neutral nation, no threat to Earth or any other sovereign system and our requests for political resolution to the dispute were ignored. It was made clear to our Citizen's Council that only unconditional surrender and acceptance of a lifestyle we choose not to embrace would appease our invaders.

"Our cities were bombed with weapons of mass destruction, our civilian shipping seized, our military personnel and civilians were tortured, raped and abused in violation of all laws of war and all human decency. Our residents were left without power, without representation and without food in a black parody of a medieval siege, attacked by biological agents that indiscriminately killed and maimed noncombatants, and our legitimate, self-selected government representatives were imprisoned or forced to assist these would-be conquerors.

"Faced with the destruction of our society, we took all civilized and reasonable steps, from negotiation, appeal to all human societies in space and to limited military engagement. We drove the invaders from our system, to be faced with further brutality en route to us. Lacking any credible forces for limited engagement, having exhausted all peaceful and rational means to maintain our sovereignty and our very lives, we were forced to resort to limited major war to render the UN incapable of continuing this outrage.

"Details of our counterattack are included in this transmission, describing where damage was done and where aid will be needed most. We regret the impossibility of providing aid ourselves, since our system has been reduced from its previous wealth to abject poverty. We urge all nations to provide aid to the UN and guarantee safe passage through our jump points to humanitarian craft. We ask only that you remember our needs for aid also and recall that we were their victims.

"There will be no further attacks on the UN, its registered ships, citizens or interests, provided no further attacks take place against ours. We reserve the right to retaliate to any attack at a time and place of our choosing. All UN-based commercial interests are encouraged to resume trade immediately with their Freehold counterparts.

"Should the UN or any other nation, state or party attack our society or its interests, our current state of affairs dictates our only viable response to be a similar attack against a second echelon of Earth cities or any other attacker's infrastructure. What forces we have are dispersed for this eventuality, but no attacks will be initiated without provocation.

"Patrick Chinratana, speaker for the Citizen's Council of the Freehold of Grainne."

✧   ✧   ✧

The message and attached images and reports of the UN attack shocked human space into silence. Shortly, that silence exploded into debate. Fear, disgust and hatred all mixed freely, with the obvious jockeying for political power underneath. The UN's current state left a huge power vacuum and there were those determined to fill it. Some pushed for occupation of Freehold; the images convinced them that the threat was not idle.

Humanitarian aid did flow, and quickly. Gigatons of food, medical supplies, generators and personnel arrived from every system save the Freehold. It sent minimal materials as could be spared, but no personnel; the risk of mob violence was too great.

Chinratana and Naumann accepted an invitation to Triton in Sol System to discuss terms and reparations. Caledonia agreed to arbitrate.

Chinratana was unsure what to make of Naumann. The man was a gentleman in every sense of the word and compassionate to a fault. But he was also the most absolutely ruthless bastard he'd ever met. He'd spend out of his own pocket to help cure a civilian from another culture, who was victim of a third nation's hostility during the Mtali conflict, but would willingly exterminate six billion people in warfare. He wondered how the man slept at night.

After spending long hours of the trip formulating a debate strategy for their goals, he wondered if the man *did* sleep.

Chapter 48

"It doesn't require a majority to prevail, but rather
an irate, tireless minority keen to set brush fires to
people's minds."

—Samuel Adams

Naumann was escorted by his usual team of Black
Ops bodyguards, backed up by Kendra. He had
asked for her as an intelligence asset, to help decode
cultural assumptions. She'd agreed, reluctantly, but
was fascinated by the proceedings. There was also
a squad to protect Chinratana and a well-crewed
light cruiser, the *FMS Puckett. The* light cruiser,
currently. No others could be accounted for, although
one or two might still exist. Chinratana had protested, but Naumann was firm; the UN was not to
be trusted, even under a white flag. The politician
had deferred to military expertise, greeted his bodyguards politely and graciously and made no mention
of them.

The ten-day trip to Jump Point Two was boring for Kendra. She spent her waking time answering questions about Earth customs, gestures and language, and her off hours, unable to concentrate, sleeping poorly. Once in the Caledonia system, it was a mere five more days of mind-numbing tedium to its Jump Point One and then only three days of anxiety to Triton.

They were settled into quarters in pairs and Naumann assigned a female operative from Black Ops to stay with Kendra, as a precaution against any attacks. "I'm sure I'm being paranoid," he said. "And we'll do it anyway." The woman was polite enough but distant and Kendra went straight to sleep to recover from the stress of the trip.

The negotiations began the next "morning," by Earth clock. Kendra was seated in the front row of observers, wearing major's rank to justify that proximity, and keep her as unobtrusive as possible. She wore sufficient makeup to change her basic appearance and had changed enough over the years to be hard to recognize anyway, it was hoped.

Naumann and Chinratana stalled and delayed until they were seated facing her. She'd been told to make a surreptitious signal if she noticed anything, either a confusing cultural assumption or a deliberate ploy to outflank them in debate.

On one side, a brilliant blue UN flag was placed in a shiny frame. Everyone stood to polite attention for the brief ceremony. Then Naumann dropped his first bomb.

Instead of new cloth, the Freehold flag was a torn rag. It was an infantry unit's headquarters flag and it was scorched, wrinkled, faded and weathered. Holes and tears dotted it and the mounting grommets had pulled loose. Kendra heard a couple of UN public affairs people cursing the brilliance of the move. One side looked like the victim and it wasn't theirs.

"Our position is simple," Chinratana began, looking along the table at real people rather than images. "The United Nations of Earth are to remove all military and political personnel and materiel from our system, return all our personnel and materiel and agree to end hostilities. They are to pay compensation to all those they displaced, benefits to all survivors of casualties, the cost of rebuilding three cities and make no further incursions into our space except for trade and diplomatic purposes."

"We'll pay for your three cities when you *butchers* pay for our fifty," the senior UN delegate, Genevieve Rouen replied. "There's only six major industrial cities you didn't destroy!" she spat, eyes hard as flint.

"They survived from pity," Naumann replied. "It was a pity I didn't have more bombs."

Rouen came out of her seat. "Listen to me you—"

"NO! *You* listen to *me!*" Naumann bellowed. The force of his words threw the delegate back into her chair. "You attacked us with weapons of mass destruction, with no threat to your people involved. Our actions were to stop that intrusion and *your* genocide."

There was a lull and Chinratana said evenly, "Had you accepted our requests for peaceful negotiation, it would not have been necessary."

The senior arbitrator, Prime Minister MacRae of Caledonia, said, "I do think there must be some kind of mutual compensation . . . but I don't believe Grainne is obligated to pay for all damage done."

Naumann interrupted with, "Very generous of you, Mr. Prime Minister, seeing as our requests to *your* government for aid were met with a cowardly reply of 'We can't interfere.' " Had you put pressure on Earth earlier, the way your foreign affairs department is now, looking for a slice of their pie, I would be able to sleep at night. You think I *enjoyed* sentencing millions upon millions of children to death because their parents couldn't act like adults?"

"Very well," MacRae said, trying to regain order. "We appear to have a cease-fire and agreement to return prisoners, property and assets. We shall table for now the reparations on either side. Let us discuss disarmament and monitoring of the combatants. Our committee has calculations for your review. The gist of it is that Brandt StarDriveSystems and Meacham Hyperdrive are to be directly monitored by the government of the Freehold and a neutral party. No drives are to be sold other than to approved end-users and all technological developments are to be shared with the Committee on Peaceful Space Development. The UN is to be limited to fifty military star drive vessels, which is two per jump point and member planet. The Freehold will be limited to eight—that allows two per jump point and two expeditionary against piracy or other activities. Insystem forces are to be held at a level not to exceed one percent of population and reservists are to be included—you seem to have had an army a good ten times the size you officially reported, Citizen Chinratana." His smile was somewhat wry.

"The existing UN colonial members and the Colonial Systems' Alliance have arranged for political infrastructure support—education, public aid, law enforcement, agricultural oversight and all other basic functions. When your own governments are ready to resume those tasks, we can arrange for step-by-step withdrawal."

The UN contingent were nodding. Kendra watched Chinratana, who was watching Naumann. Naumann was pacing. He had the lead for now. The man had a *very* powerful personality.

"I don't think you ladies and men understand," he began. "These statist, imperialistic, cowardly little baboons started a war with a nation less than one percent their size, purely as an exercise in propaganda to draw attention from their own little Orwellian charade. Their stated intent in *their own internal memos* was to mundicidically exterminate our leadership, industry and social fabric bit by bit, creating us as a race of scapegoats for every problem their bloated bureaucracy failed to address. They used bioweapons, nukes and kinetics to preemptively cripple our civilian industries and prevent argument. They systematically tortured, raped and murdered 'war criminals' who were merely defending their homes, as provided for in the Geneva, Hague and Mars conventions and you gutless worms did nothing but write 'stern notes' of protest while our people died of starvation and cold!" The expression on his face as he stared at them made it appear he'd found maggots in his food. The diplomats stared in shocked silence.

"Now you want to disarm us, realizing that we won't play your petty games. That makes us a threat to your status quo, much like we were to the UN, so you want to saddle us with the same failed bureaucracy that has been tried for the last *thousand fucking years* and *failed every single time!* much like the UN did.

"Well, ladies and men, you better have your bombs ready, because mine are." He sat down, drew his sword and commenced wiping the satiny surface with a cloth, staring directly into the eyes of the man across from him, Fouk al-Visr of the Ramadanian contingent. The man shifted his eyes cautiously around, finally looking into his comm.

Chinratana broke into the nervous, embarrassed silence with, "We do appreciate your offer of political support. I know few of you believe we actually know what we are doing or that our residents are happy that way, but it *is* an internal affair and we are quite happy to deal with our own wounds our way. All we require is a guarantee that the UN will not again be allowed to attack us. We were, and remain, absolutely neutral to any engagements and have no imperial goals of any kind."

There were protests, reconciliations, deals offered. Chinratana and Naumann refused to budge. "I could insist on and enforce an unconditional surrender. All we want is to be left alone and for them to pay damages. Nothing else is required and nothing else will suffice," Chinratana said simply.

Realizing the futility of the issue, the other parties agreed to the resolution. It was clear they were not happy and would build their own militaries up to face the potential threat of either nation. Terms were agreed and signed and there was a break for food. It had been a very tense day. Most were surprised at that; they'd expected a week of posturing to get results. Once again, the Freeholders showed their knack for streamlining procedures to the bare bones. They skipped the peripherals and went straight to the point, or the throat.

Chinratana was received cautiously, Naumann treated with distant courtesy inspired by fear. He didn't seem bothered by it. When they resumed discussions that evening, he cut right to the heart again.

"The UN prisoners we have are in detainment, accounted for and awaiting transport home. As provided for by international law, all are as healthy as permits and have had regular *attempts* at correspondence. Any MIAs you may have I will attempt to document. I'm sure there are a few, seeing as our planetary defense was at least as efficient as our . . . recent efforts.

"When can I get a list of detainees from you and when will they be ready to travel?"

Rouen shifted uncomfortably. "Well, it's not as easy as that. They were dispersed through the system for safety—"

"To your labs and prisons for entertainment, you mean," Naumann cut in emotionlessly.

"—for *safety*," Rouen insisted, "both from retribution and to avoid escape."

"Retribution from who and for what?" Chinratana prodded. "Since you attacked us, why should they be in any danger of retribution?"

Rouen squirmed again, "Well, anyway, records are quite destroyed due to your recent attack. I'm not sure how many or where they might be. It will take some time to put together a list and arrange transport. If you could help finance the effort, then of course . . ." she faded off.

Instead of taking the bait, Naumann asked, "Can your agents, soldiers and department heads follow orders?"

"Yes . . . ?" Rouen replied.

"Then tell them I want my people accounted for and on ships tomorrow. Any MIA better have *very* convincing documentation or I'll just have to start a second echelon of cities," he said as he reached for his comm.

"You'll do no such thing!" MacRae cut in. "It may take some time."

Naumann replied, "Time when my people can be made to disappear, sustain injuries that prevent them from talking or otherwise be hurt more than they already have been. The Freehold Military Forces does not leave mistakes uncorrected or abandon personnel for political reasons. I guaranteed them I would not leave them behind and I'm not leaving Sol System without them. I want them back now, I will not be extorted, and if that is a problem, I believe I have a Black Operations team near Sydney, if you'd care to see a city die the way London did."

"You'd destroy a city over your MIAs?" MacRae strangled out.

"Since that statement implies that you also regard

soldiers as less than human, you are invited to try me," Naumann replied flatly.

Chinratana interrupted, "Colonel Naumann, that's enough. Thank you for your efforts. Please return to our suite and I will finish negotiations."

Naumann stood, saluted stiffly and marched out. His henches followed without expression. Kendra rose, looking pale, and joined the entourage. Her escort took the opportunity to turn to the assembly and make a throat-slicing gesture with her finger.

Naumann heard a knock on his door and carefully put down the book he was reading. It was a real bound book and almost irreplaceable. The copy of Kipling's verse had followed him around for fifteen years of military service. He sprang to his feet, one moment at rest, the next upright and quivering.

It was Chinratana. "Good evening, Colonel. I hope I didn't embarrass you with my request that you leave?"

"Embarrass me? By doing your job? How go the talks?"

"Finalized," he said, with an exhaled breath. He'd been holding it for some time. "I admit I hadn't expected them to accept your threats, but you bluff like no one I've ever met. We must play poker . . . just for fun, of course."

"I wasn't bluffing, Citizen," Naumann replied with a shake of his head.

"I know," Chinratana said. "And that was obvious to them. They clearly fear what abilities we have left." There were barely enough forces available to conduct a hull inspection and both knew it. It would not be admitted anywhere outside Freehold System. "But I am glad your threats don't need to be followed through."

"So am I, Citizen. So am I."

Chapter 49

"If it were possible to heal sorrow by weeping and
to raise the dead with tears, gold were less prized
than Grief."

—Sophocles

Kendra was in Rob's apartment. She wasn't sure what
the legal issue was or what would be done with his will
after he was declared legally dead. She wasn't actually
sure how a legal declaration of death was done here. All
she wanted was somewhere familiar to be alone. She'd
wangled enough fuel to spend every other night there
and had access to a vehicle. It was considered acceptable use as long as she could justify it and she shuttled
other soldiers around and watched for looters as she
went. She'd actually chased two from Ms. Styplwchak's
flat. They were more deportees from Earth and had tried
to threaten her, until she pointed a rifle at them and they
became very polite, leaving the bag of loot behind. She
hadn't seen them in the area since.

George the cat had survived, she discovered. He mewed one morning and sat remote from her, sniffing the air. Finally satisfied, he approached cautiously, then began rubbing her ankles. He was emaciated, his fur matted and shabby looking in his old age, but his presence cheered her slightly. She'd have to find some food for him. Luckily, he ate almost anything, she recalled, and he was unlikely to be finicky under these circumstances.

Her phone sounded, answering the question of when limited service would be available. It would make it easier than having to relay through her comm. She answered on the first beep and took a moment to recognize the caller.

"Marta! Hi!" she said, surprised. *I thought you were dead,* went unsaid.

Marta was a wreck. Her normally perfect features were bandaged, sutured and glued. Underneath she looked disheveled, tired and lined. "I need to see you," she said. Her speech was slurred around orthodontal splints. With her damaged hearing Kendra barely understood her.

"Sure," she agreed, masking her concern. "Where are you?"

"My house. Can you come over now?"

Kendra looked her over again, decided it was urgent and said, "On my way."

"On my way" turned into a half div. The traffic was terrible. Pedestrians, repair vehicles, regular traffic, military traffic and others all battled for space. Kendra drove as aggressively as she dared in a borrowed military vehicle and was shaking when she pulled into the parking ramp, although not on the scale of whatever was bothering Marta. She jogged up the steps and held her hand over the sensor. Nothing happened, so she knocked.

"Who's there?"

"Kendra."

Marta opened the door, standing well back. She held a military pistol in one hand. Kendra walked around her and watched as she closed and locked the door. Seconds later, she had to brace to hold herself upright as Marta grabbed her in a bone-breaking hug. Sobs began to emanate from the heavy fall of black hair. They held the pose for segs.

Marta finally sat, wincing in pain. Her shoulder bore surgery marks and her posture indicated her ribs did too. There were scars around her left knee and both wrists and ankles. She said, "I'm glad you're alive. Any word from Rob?"

"Not yet," Kendra shook her head and looked around. "Cleared this place, didn't they?" Many of the furnishings were damaged or missing.

"They took the Reck," Marta agreed, "and what they did to the Lubov . . ." She indicated with her head. Kendra looked at the classic oil, the nude figure grafittied with crude sexual additions. "I almost wish they'd burned it. I'll have to," Marta added bitterly.

Kendra waited, sensing the young woman was nerving herself to broach a painful subject. The pistol on the table and her hesitance at the door clearly indicated a problem, considering Marta's usual self-confidence. She decided to be patient. When Marta blurted, "Let me get us some wine," she nodded assent as her friend rushed to the kitchen. There were more sobs, and it was many seconds before she returned with glasses and an opened bottle. One glass had clearly been used already. The air carried a tang of liquor, not wine. Kendra bit back an inquiry and stayed quiet.

"I assassinated General Huff," Marta said to her glass. "I was in place as his lover."

Kendra was mildly shocked. She said nothing, not wanting to interrupt.

"He wasn't evil. He genuinely wanted to help us, in his own way, and did stop a lot of atrocities. I liked him. Then I had to distract him with sex and kill him. Do you know how hard it is to make yourself passionately hate someone for a moment, long enough to get your hands on his throat, then stop all emotion and kill him coldly?"

"No," Kendra softly said. She felt a sudden surge of emotion and her mind momentarily flooded with images from her own private hell.

"That was just as everything hit for Two Bricks," Marta continued. "I didn't know the name of the mission, of course.

"I killed him and tried to leave. I must have missed the tick by seconds. Every hatch slammed shut and locked when the alarm sounded. I didn't have any tools, so I had to wait to be released. It was . . . *them*," she said, murderous vehemence emphasizing the last word.

"The UN?" Kendra asked.

Face screwed tight, hugging herself tightly, Marta shook, tensed and shattered the wineglass in her hand. She jerked upright, staring confusedly for a moment. Then her training took over and she wrapped a towel around her lacerated hand. "That needs treatment," Kendra suggested.

"*It can wait!*" Marta hissed through her teeth. She said nothing for several moments, then said, "There were seven of them. I counted. I'm not sure how many times I counted, but there were definitely seven of them. I was there for thirteen days, wondering when they'd stop hating me enough to kill me."

"My God!" Kendra muttered. She reached for words, but found nothing.

Whirling close and gripping Kendra's collar, Marta shrieked, *"How can you call that a 'minor' crime?? What kind of sick fucks are you??"* as blood trickled and seeped into the fabric of Kendra's uniform.

Stunned motionless, afraid for her life, Kendra said, "Marta, you're scaring me." The grip lessened slightly. Breathing deeply, she continued, "I'm not Terran anymore. And I didn't do it." She reached up to detach Marta's hands, one slick with running blood.

"There's a difference between simple rape and torture," she finished.

"Not to me," Marta said, eyes still blank and lifeless. "I would kill every one of them slowly. But they have to be tried by a war crimes tribunal back on Earth. I'm told they'll be severely punished, perhaps even jailed." She burst into gales of laughter, then tucked her head in her hands and sobbed.

"Let's see to your hand," Kendra suggested again and pulled it gingerly down to the table.

"Surgical kit, closet by the door," Marta said, muffled through her fingers. Kendra ran to get it.

It was a field kit, with no regeneration gear. Simple sutures and glue would have to do. It was not the worst laceration she'd seen, but it was one of the hardest she'd dealt with. The tension level in the room was palpable, and not knowing how her friend would react was unnerving. The conversation didn't help.

"That happened to you twice?" Marta asked.

"Uh . . . yes," she agreed, deciding not to mention recent happenings.

"And it was no big deal to you?"

"Not afterwards," she admitted truthfully.

"You bitch!" Marta snarled.

Kendra took it silently. Anger was probably healthy. There was still a huge gulf between their worldviews. She treated and dressed the injury, then sat back. "I'll do anything I can, love," she said, "but you need to see a professional therapist."

Marta grimaced in anger. "There are very few . . . *rape* counselors in this system. It wasn't a problem we had much of until Earth decided to save us," she rasped bitterly. Unconsciously, her legs crossed tightly and she hugged herself again. Her head bowed and she cried loudly.

"Stay here," Kendra said. "I'm going to make a call." She patted Marta's hand, tensed as it jerked away, and withdrew quietly to the spare bedroom. It, too, had been vandalized and looted.

Three spoken call attempts failed to register. It might have been system problems. It might have been the anger in her voice. She punched in the number, stabbing with a finger. The call was answered immediately.

"Naumann, oh hi, Kendra," he answered.

"I'm at Marta's," she said without preamble. "What the hell is being done about this?"

He replied immediately. "Doctor Wuu is en route from Green Door on a Class J courier. She should be there in three days. She's the best there is, and we'll figure out payment later. I wanted Hern . . . Marta in the clinic here, but she refused. I am pulling every string I can to get the assailants tried for war crimes here or in Caledonia, rather than Earth. She's on paid medical status until I decide otherwise. And I've already got the adminwork in progress for a VSM." The look on his face indicated that if he didn't get what he wanted that someone would be dead where he stood. It was chilling enough that Kendra was stunned into silence for several seconds.

"Wh-what can I do here to help?" she finally replied.

"Anything you think will help. You're on compassionate leave too," he added.

It was impossible to feel ill toward the man.

"You may talk to Doctor Wu if you wish, also," he said supplementally.

"Why would I—?" she began. He interrupted her with a word:

"Delph'."

He knows. She paused for a moment. "I'll be fine, sir, but thank you."

"If you are fine, where's my incident report? I plan to crucify every single one of them." His voice was very controlled, with steel underneath.

She garbled incoherently for only a second, then said firmly, "You'll have it tomorrow, sir."

"Fine. Then see the doctor. It will also help you deal with Marta."

She agreed and disconnected.

Back in the common room, Marta was sobbing still and had gone through a good part of the bottle. Approaching gently, but loud enough to be heard, Kendra softly said, "Hey."

Marta looked up and her face was again a shock. More surgery would be necessary before it reverted to physically pretty. As for that inner smoldering beauty, it might never resurface. "What?"

"Naumann says there's an expert on the way. In the meantime, you'll have to make do with me. And I'm not leaving until she gets here," she insisted firmly. "I'll do what I can to help."

"Thanks, love." Marta nodded aside. "Not that there's much you can do, unless you can arrange a quiet cabin where I can torture people to death."

That statement triggered an old memory. Trying to direct the conversation slightly, Kendra said, "Then you can help me. I was raped last month in Delph' as we retook it."

She expected Marta to be compassionate or shocked. Instead, a look of rage welled up again.

"Makes *you* feel right at home, doesn't it? Not a problem at a-all."

"It's . . . different," Kendra insisted. *The dirty, sticky feeling. The feeling of being an object and not a person. The pain and embarrassment. The disgust. The nightmares.* "We had classes on coping in school. And there are plenty of counselors. And it does hurt for a while."

Without warning, Marta slapped her burningly across the face. Then her weight landed. Kendra was reminded again that Marta was not small and was lethally strong. Fortunately for Kendra, she was not in her best condition and was incoherent. Despite that, she was managing to cause serious pain and some injury.

"*Senior Sergeant Hernandez!*" she snapped. Marta stiffened, then collapsed across her, moaning. "If you want me to stay and help, you will control yourself. I'm not willing to be a punching bag without some kind of rules and padding. And I won't accept excuses."

Marta leaned back, then sat heavily on the worn rug. Her eyes were puffy and residual sobs broke through periodically. She nodded, then her lips moved silently. "I'm sorry," they mouthed.

Climbing to her feet, Kendra began giving orders. "First, put the bottle away. It won't help. Then case, holster or unload the weapon until you are sober. Is the bathroom intact?"

Marta nodded assent as she gathered up the shards of glass and the bottle.

"Good," Kendra continued. "Then put that away and come upstairs." She turned and hurried ahead.

She undressed and started the water in the shower. Marta was only moments behind. Her pistol was holstered.

Kendra kept the firmness in her voice, still nervous about further outbursts. "Lock the door and code it. Put your pistol there, where you can reach it. Then get undressed and get in." She stepped in and waited.

Marta joined her shortly. Her posture was no longer proud and defiant. She was still slumped and meek. "I showered earlier," she said, "and the swelling is down enough that the soreness is fading."

"This is psychological cleansing," Kendra explained. "Wash off every contact you remember. If you need to turn away for privacy, that's fine. We'll stay here until you feel clean."

"There isn't that much water," Marta said with a weak grin.

Both women scrubbed thoroughly, periodically turning away in embarrassment at some particular indignity. It was nearly a div later when they got out to dry off. It took most of a bottle of moisturizer to unwrinkle their skin.

The floor was flooded, as Marta had insisted on leaving the door open for visibility and the air curtain was broken. Hopefully enough of the house's systems remained to take care of it, but Kendra decided it was a minor irritation.

Once dry, she ushered Marta into the bedroom and told her to sit. Marta complied, knees folded rather than crosslegged. "Now listen to me," she said. "You are a soldier. You were captured. You were tortured and abused as a prisoner. What you have are injuries and wounds. The physical nature of them *is not important!*" She waited while Marta locked eyes with her, then glanced away again.

"They were trying to break you," she said. "You are still here, alive and have most of your home. You completed your mission. It was an almost impossible mission and required an exceptional soldier to accomplish it. Now, this is important," she said, pausing. Marta looked back up.

"You won."

She waited for that to sink in for long moments. "You won and we won. You survived. Even after being abused as a prisoner, you survived and won again. And nothing can *ever* take that victory away from you." Her own eyes were damp and Marta was crying openly. But her posture was straighter.

"And they lost," she finished. "Now, shall we toast *that*?

Kendra woke to feel Marta moving in her sleep, uttering nonsense words and flailing at remembered demons. "Marta," she whispered. "Wake up, dear." She kept a comforting hand on her lover, but was careful not to restrain her. There was a sudden intake of breath and Marta was awake.

Kendra eased carefully into a hug, then tightened it as Mar clung to her tightly. She stayed rock still, suddenly phobic from her own memories. "Lights minimum," she whispered. The glow helped drive the fear a slight distance away.

Being unable to sleep further, Kendra rose and put on a robe. She retrieved her own sidearm and carried it with her. Marta's fear was suddenly contagious and the house no longer felt friendly. It would need a thorough cleansing. The thought of a Druidic ritual as a philosophical necessity made her uncomfortable again. *Dammit, I'm a Christian!* she thought to herself.

She sought a comm and was relieved to find one intact upstairs. It had been shoved into Marta's private shrine, which had apparently served as a local residence for a UN officer. All her religious items were destroyed or gone. Mindless ignorance seemed worse than deliberate hatred. She sat and composed her thoughts, wanting to finish this quickly. She took a breath and began:

"Recording. Pacelli, Kendra A., Senior Sergeant, Logistics, Third Mobile Assault Regiment, service number three one seven eight eight two three zero two two, date twenty-seven May, two hundred and eleven.

"To: Naumann, Alan D., Colonel Commanding, Provisional Ground Forces, Freehold Military Forces.

"Subject: battlefield incident report, pursuant to claims of violation of Geneva, Hague and Triton Conventions relevant to treatment of prisoners of war by the UN Peace Force. Reference date thirty-six April, two hundred and eleven." She paused for breath. The stilted, formal language she used helped distance things slightly, but it still wasn't pleasant.

"During Operation Counter, while commanding a squad of reservists and local militia in the town of Delphtonopolisburg, River District, my squad was disrupted by an unknown number of UN infantry at point S on the map." She highlighted the location and referenced it.

"Upon being separated, I fought a close-order engagement with three enemy personnel at point E. I count three casualties by small arms fire and hand-to-hand combat. Immediately afterwards, I entered the building where the attacking force had deployed from, indicated by point 'R.'

"Inside this building, my preliminary scan indicated no personnel, large animals or tactical threats. That assessment was in error. Available evidence indicates my tac was malfunctioning. Its visual system degraded at that time. A post-mission report was filed with Regimental Maintenance.

"Tactically blind, I proceeded to remove my helmet and tac. I was attacked during this procedure by three UN personnel, all male. I cannot identify them, but post-battle analysis may be able to. Their intent seems to have been to capture a live prisoner, as they subdued me by brute force, stunning me and forcing me to the ground.

"Upon awakening, one named 'Cody' was in the process of preparing to rape me. He had lowered my pants and the others, names unknown, were holding me down. I attempted to fight, but was too weak and restrained to do so. Upon undressing me, a second one made comments that indicated they had raped other female prisoners; specifically, he noted that most Freehold women remove their pubic hair.

"My legs were forced apart, he dropped his pants and proceeded to forcibly penetrate me. Neither of the other two made any physical or verbal attempt to stop him. They argued over who would rape me next, before they left to attempt to rejoin their own forces. I stopped struggling at this point and prepared to fight once released, since their weapons were put aside. I felt certain my strength and training would have been sufficient for an effective engagement.

"At that time, five divs, sixty-seven segs, thirteen seconds by comm, militia Corporal Dak Simonsen entered the building and shot all three attackers. I redressed and we regrouped with the surviving members of my squad.

"Sworn under my own oath—break—system, time and date this damn thing." Her voice cracked as she spoke.

"Command not understood."

"System, time, date, transmit," she repeated, turning away. Rape was handled on Earth with privacy. Here it had to be splashed across the system. She understood the rationale, but that didn't make it pleasant to describe intensely personal indignities.

"Accepted. Done," the machine acknowledged.

"Fine. Fuck you."

"Command not understood."

Not everything had been looted from the house. When built, it had a small vault hidden in the foundation. Normally open, a friend of Marta's had put their swords, jewelry, civilian weapons and other valuables inside and locked it, then placed the panel back. It had not been found. It eased the anger that the two women felt, reinforced the loss of the unprotected property and made Rob's loss even worse.

Naumann called later that morning with some helpful news. "They found Rob McKay," he said without introduction.

Kendra said nothing for seconds. Finally, daring to hope, she asked, "Alive?"

"Yes, but in bad shape. You are as close as next of kin as there is. Get over and see what you can do."

"Yes, Colonel," she agreed. It wasn't an order she would need repeated.

She identified herself at the clinic and the hushed tones in response scared her. Was he in pieces in a regen tank? Missing limbs or organs? Gruesomely disfigured?

A slim doctor with major's insignia came out. "Senior Pacelli, Kendra if I may? I'm Lou Rostov."

"How is he, Sir?" she asked.

"Physically, fine. Minor abrasions and contusions, but few permanent marks." Kendra exhaled at the news.

"But he was hit by a vicious nanovirus we are still tracking," Rostov said. "He's not rational."

"What are you doing?" she asked.

"Nothing yet. We just got him this morning. I'm not even sure exactly what the intended effect is," he admitted.

"Can I see him?" she asked agitatedly.

"Certainly, but you need to be aware of a few things," he cautioned, taking her arm and steering her down a corridor. He explained as they walked.

Rob was alternating rapidly between apparent rationality and violent emotion. He would switch from normal speech to gibberish and appeared to be hallucinating. "Whatever they used was tailored for total mental incapacitation and is unique enough there's nothing on file even approximating it. And *our* records made it through the war completely intact. We have several tens of casualties and most are responding to standard counters. He isn't, for some reason."

They stopped at a door. "A few more things," Rostov advised. "He was found by some steaders who recognized him as ours, but had to lock him in a shed for safety. He was locked up for six weeks. I'm reluctant to restrain him for fear of causing more trauma and don't want to trank him, both for fear of interaction and because I need to study the symptoms. You can see him, but I'll be scanning everything."

Kendra nodded, "That's fine. Let me see him." She was impatiently eager.

Rostov opened the door for her.

Rob sat in the corner of a sterile-looking room. He didn't notice her at first, so she glanced around. The room was much like a cell and had a bed, a toilet and little else. It would be hard for a disturbed patient to damage himself.

"Rob?" she said.

He looked up, grinned and jumped to his feet. "Kendra!" he shouted, walking quickly over. He gathered her in a hug, then kissed her passionately. *Seems fine to me, Doc*, she thought. Rob drew back, still holding her around the waist and seemed to freeze. He was motionless for several seconds, then started to laugh.

"What's so funny?" she asked.

"I'm sorry," he said. "You have fomombyse curling out of your hair."

"What?" she asked. He ignored her, slapped at something overhead and pushed past her. He felt along the wall for a seg or more, seemingly tracing cracks. Then he turned.

"Oh, there you are," he said. "Let's go." He took her hand and led her around the room.

"Go where?" she asked, nervous. Irrational behavior was scarier than violence.

"Home," he said. "I've got some supwervosid to take care of. You can help."

"What is a supwervosid?" she asked.

"I don't know. What origin is the word?" he returned. "*Oh, shit!*" he snapped and threw her down. She rolled, wondering if there was a real threat this time. There was not. "Give me your gun," he demanded.

"I'm not armed," she said.

"That's fine, give it to me," he insisted.

"I don't have one," she said again.

"Dumb ass!" he said and leapt over her. He attacked the wall, which was designed to give enough to prevent injury. She rose and made the mistake of trying to pull him away.

He turned and rocketed a fist at her face. She blocked it, started to slip sideways, then felt the other hand catch her right under the ribs, low on her right side. Breath knocked out, diaphragm too paralyzed even for chi breathing to help, she staggered backward and collapsed.

Her vision and breath returned, to see four burly orderlies holding him down. Another assisted her out the door.

"Are you okay?" Rostov asked.

"Will be," she nodded. "I should know better than to let a parallel punch get me."

"He's a friend. You couldn't expect it."

"Sorry I stirred him up," she apologized. She was nearing tears at seeing Rob so helpless.

"Don't be," Rostov said. "I'll need to review it further, but it appears that unusual occurrences, like your arrival, allow him to focus better. He responded more to you than to our staff."

"Does that help?" she asked.

"Everything helps at this point," Rostov admitted.

She went back the next day. Rob was responsive, but the intermittent laughter and shakes were unnerving. Halfway through lunch, he suddenly heaved his plate across the room. "Yucch!" he said, recoiling.

"What?" she asked.

"Worms? Dozer slugs? I'm not eating that," he protested.

"That was a sandwich," she said. "What you saw was part of a dream."

"I know," he agreed. He stood and approached the wall. "Check this out," he said, pointing.

"What is it?" she asked. The wall was featureless.

"This here," he indicated an imaginary vertical axis, "is your arrival time. The horizontal is the duration of your stay."

"Yes," she prompted.

"It shows the date!" he said. "Don't you get it?"

"No, Rob, I don't. It's another hallucination," she said.

"No, no! I'm serious about this. I can calculate the date!" he insisted.

"Why?" she asked.

"To find the exit," he said. "I've figured it out. Come on!" He took her hand and led her on a circuitous route again. She remembered him mentioning, in the distant past before the war, that his dreams frequently involved long, labyrinthine travels. It seemed to have carried over to his current affliction. She made a note to tell Rostov of it.

"You have news?" Kendra asked during her visit the next day.

"Yes," Rostov agreed. "First of all, his module was damaged by EMP. We'll need to replace it afterwards, but that's merely symptomatic. What we have is a nano that . . . well, stripped of the medical jargon, creates a permanent dream state. It is nonlethal and only affects *most* of the higher functions, so the claim of 'harmless' toxin is accurate, from a legal standpoint."

"He's *dreaming*?" she asked incredulously.

"Hallucinating, dreaming," Rostov said. "Whatever you call it, it is all controlled by the same area of the brain. This nano embeds itself and starts producing chemicals to stimulate such thoughts. All we have to do now is figure out why he's different from the others and how to counteract it. So far, we have nothing to base it on. The UN claims the lab that created it was destroyed.

"That's why I wanted to see you," he continued. "I gather the two of you are close?"

"Lovers."

"Good. We need someone close for moral support and familiar enough to not be considered a threat. It also helps to have personal information that will tell us if we are getting side effects that damage the personality. This will be a risky procedure.

"Then, of course, there's the not minor consideration of legal guardianship until we are done," he said.

"Marta and I are as close as he has to family," she said. "But we will support anything that might help."

Nodding, he said, "I'd hoped so. We'd like you to be here during most of his conscious periods to help. But I have to warn you that it will be intensely personal and embarrassing. The higher functions will be stripped away and the baser instincts—anger, lust, fear—will come out much stronger. And we will have to monitor for safety, analysis and research." He reddened slightly as he explained.

Kendra agreed and left with the news. She wasn't sure why she hadn't told Marta yet, except that it didn't seem like a good idea.

Marta was cooking when she got home; she could smell it as she entered. "I'm home!" she shouted loudly as a precaution and headed up the ramp. Marta was waiting, hand on pistol. She nodded, dropped her guard and kissed her lightly.

"Hi," she said. Marta replied and headed back to the stove.

"We've found Rob," she said, and Marta froze for a moment.

"Alive?" she asked. It was an ordinary question these days.

"Physically fine," Kendra assured her. "Affected by some tailored nano that creates hallucinations. They've been working on it."

"Can we see him?" Marta asked, anxiously.

"I've been in, but you shouldn't," she advised. "He's not coherent."

"I can handle it if you can," Marta insisted, serving up a bed of fried noodles with chicken. It was in small pieces because Marta couldn't chew properly anymore. Kendra decided to table the argument.

The food was good. Marta seemed to be on edge again. Then Kendra remembered that her therapy was to start the next day. She decided not to mention it unless Marta brought it up first.

They lit a fire after dinner and sat together. Marta drank less than her recent habitual amount, Kendra noted. She consented to being massaged and stiffened only occasionally as Kendra brushed some spot that triggered terrifying memories.

Marta was tense all night, tossing restlessly and lashing out twice. Kendra finally headed for the spare room.

Marta's first session was that morning. Doctor Wu arrived late enough for them to sleep in, had they been able to. Kendra greeted her, shaking hands. She was a small oriental, tanned almost black from living in the inner Halo. Her face looked fragile and young, but the muscles indicated heavy orbital work.

"Pleased to meet you, Kendra," she acknowledged. "I'm told you may wish to talk to me also?"

"'Directed' would be closer," she smiled wryly, "but I guess I should."

"I would appreciate it," Wuu said, nodding in an almost bow. "I like to interview people from other cultures, to study the different perceptions of . . . incidents like this."

At Wu's request, Kendra disappeared into the yard for a div. She tried to recover some of the manicured landscaping with only a few hand tools but it was a futile task and she knew it. Still, it gave her something to do besides worry. The dirt and grime felt good. She threw herself into pulling weeds and straightening bricks and didn't notice the passage of time until Doctor Wuu called for her. She rose, aching from exertion, and went inside to wash her hands and get a glass of water. Wuu was waiting for her in the living room, seated relaxed and comfortably in the chair across from the couch. She'd pulled it a bit closer.

"Where's Marta?" she asked.

"Upstairs meditating. It went well, for a first session. She's very strong and I think she'll be fine. It also helps that she's military. For most survivors, we let them take control of the situation and make them feel secure. For military personnel, it sometimes, and in this case is, easier and faster to put them back into a disciplined system. The structure reassures them that order still exists and helps them deal with the attack as a failure of the system; anarchy, if you will.

"A large part of her problem is the cultural perception, that somehow she has been grievously hurt by this. The physical injuries from the rape were actually not bad, compared to say, the damage to her face and left knee. The psychological injury shouldn't be that bad—she was unconscious for most of it, although there is still sensory input while unconscious.

"Her greatest trauma comes from having not put up a fight. She's a rated master in unarmed combat and this made her feel totally helpless and insecure. That we can deal with. And it ties in to the cultural perception again—you may have noticed that most people here have trouble using the word 'rape.' Which is not to say that it is wrong for it to be considered a disgusting crime, but there is a lot of emotion attached to just using it."

Kendra asked, "So what about the attitude I grew up with? That you accept that it happens, but doesn't demean you? That the real loser is the attacker?"

Wuu ran a hand through her thick silver-black hair. "Not being demeaned by it is healthy. Realizing that the attacker is lashing out against his own insecurities is healthy. But I have a fundamental problem with accepting that it happens. It *is* a terrible thing.

"The problem between the two of you is that she rightly perceives it as an act thoroughly insulting and degrading in intent. Her attackers were telling her that she was merely a thing to vent frustration on, in a very intimate fashion. You perceive it as revealing their helplessness and rage at the situation. You are both correct. But you both need to see the other side of the equation."

She continued, "I'm not suggesting you should feel as violated by your attack as she does by hers. You obviously are coping better in that regard. But you should consider that the *motive* of the attackers was to degrade you thoroughly, to show contempt for you.

"Now, legally, rape is awkward in the Freehold. Without an actual criminal code, it is hard to quantify the damage done in financial terms, as with robbery, arson or even murder. The victim is left alive, frequently with only minor physical injury. What is the loss? This runs into collision with the moral outrage at the concept. It happens rarely here, because this *is* a more civilized society. Its rarity and the higher standards of personal responsibility make it far more offensive. So we juggle the minor legal issue with the huge moral issue.

"As far as the two of you," Wuu said, "Marta sees that you are coping better, ignoring that her circumstances were far different, from her perspective, than yours. She knows you have been through this before with very minor post trauma. She finds this offensive— it indicates unconsciously to her that she is not coping, that you are stronger and that she is even less in control because of that. It would be easier if you couldn't sympathize, because then she wouldn't have to see you dealing with it.

"Now, shall we talk about your feelings?" she asked, folding her hands in her lap.

Chapter 50

"Oh, that way madness lies; let me shun that."
—William Shakespeare, *King Lear*

"I'm coming with you today," Marta announced the next morning. Kendra was drained from the therapy session and felt sure Marta was also.

Surprised by the comment, Kendra warily said, "Rob's not really in shape for guests."

"Why not?" Marta asked. "He knows me better than he knows you."

"Yes, but . . ." Kendra began. "He's very confused. I'm not sure we should do this. Especially since he has no control over himself. It could be bad for you."

"I'm a battlefield trauma medic. I've seen some thoroughly disgusting things. If he's merely having tracking problems, I can handle it. Really," she insisted. "Are you trying to keep me away?" she asked, a bit accusatorily.

"No," Kendra replied. *But I don't want to see you get hurt.* This was not good. She couldn't tell Marta why without bringing up her recent gang rape, which she didn't want to do. Nor did she want to keep her away. But there was no way to hint at the reason. She spent the rest of the trip hoping for some convenient way to call Doctor Rostov and warn him. There didn't seem to be a way.

As soon as they arrived, she insisted on checking in with Rostov. She explained in a very few sentences as she led him out for introductions. "This is Marta," she said. "She wants to visit Rob today." She hoped he'd get the hint, having heard some of Marta's story.

Frowning, Rostov shook his head and said, "I have to advise against it." He looked at Kendra and she shrugged back. Marta said, "What's the problem here? I'm as close as Kendra and I want to see him. If he's not comfortable, I'll leave. As far as me being uncomfortable, I'm a professional. Now can we stop wasting time?"

Rostov reluctantly agreed and Marta headed for the ward. Kendra followed, noting that he made a quick call for help. She met Marta at the door and said, "Let me go in first."

"Sure."

Rob greeted Kendra as she entered. "Hi!" He hugged her and kissed her as usual. His eyes still had that vacant look. She turned him away from the door as Marta slipped in.

"Feeling better?" she asked, gripping his wrists.

"Mostly. Except for a fight with a weolk a few segs ago. That is an hallushination, right?" he asked, concentrating and looking unsure. He rubbed his eyes.

"As far as I know," she agreed. She'd kept his attention focused on her as much as possible and felt a sinking feeling as she said, "I brought someone else," and pointed.

Rob turned, paused for only a second and shouted, "Mar!" He gathered her in a hug, wrapped a hand in her hair and kissed her deeply. She stiffened momentarily then made herself relax. As he pulled back, she looked happily at Kendra.

Rob was moving, urging her back against the wall. She looked concerned at first, then increasingly scared as he pinned her against it and began kissing her neck. He pulled at her pants and she convulsed in panic, grabbing for his hands as he reached in to fondle her.

Her terrified scream staggered him back. He hopped around, confused and crying, and Kendra caught him. She helped him sit on the floor, then turned to Marta, who was curled in a fetal position, whimpering. Medics swarmed into the room and moved to assist.

"I *told* her it was a bad idea!" she insisted to Lou Rostov. "Why wouldn't she listen?" Tears ran as he took her hand and guided her out. "No," she protested. "I've got to help them!"

"We'll help them," he assured her. "Right now you need some support yourself." He steered her to an empty office and into a seat.

"Listen," he said. "Right now, she's trying to pretend that everything is normal. His reaction is within the parameters of the condition and she knows that, technically. But she saw it from a personal viewpoint, not her professional one."

"I should have stopped her," Kendra said, breathing deeply to calm herself.

"I doubt it would have helped," he said. "Had you brought up her . . . assault, it would simply have made her determined to prove you wrong."

Nodding, she asked, "And what about Rob?"

"He'll bounce right past it. Remember: nothing is real to him right now. It's all part of a dream." She nodded in understanding.

"Speaking of which," he said, "we are ready to try some treatment. We have a tailored enzyme which should attack the nano, and a nano of our own to normalize the chemical levels in the brain."

"Wow. What did that cost to concoct?" she asked.

"We haven't figured that out yet," he admitted. "But the military is covering it and there are other victims of the same agent. And it wouldn't be an issue; our veterans get treated no matter the cost."

"When do we start?" she asked, nervous.

"Tomorrow morning at three. Bring a book or something," he advised. "Hopefully, most of it will be boring. Bring spare clothes—it may get messy."

Kendra took several segs to recover her calm. Despite any words of reassurance, she felt responsible for Marta's collapse. And the next day wasn't going to be pleasant.

Rob was sitting on the bed and kissed her as she arrived. "Hi, sexy," he said, grinning. He brushed a hand across her left breast, sending momentary shivers through her. She squirmed slightly and redirected his hand.

"We're here to work today," she reminded him.

Rostov cut in with, "Lieutenant McKay, do you understand what we are about to do?"

Turning to face him slowly, Rob stared through him, seeing something besides the psychiatrist. "You're going to try to treat me with a tailored nano."

"Good," Rostov agreed. "And you consent to this treatment and to Kendra being here for support?"

"Shure," Rob slurred, grinning. "Gotta be better than adrigamij with a petrowheeler."

Nodding as if understanding, Rostov directed, "Hold out your arm."

Rob made no response as the cold liquid carrier

dissolved through his skin, taking the submicroscopic devices with it. Rostov left, and he and Kendra talked as it gradually took effect.

Rob suddenly strangled and retched. Kendra gripped his shoulders, hoping it would be a short incident. He recovered and sat slowly back up. "That . . . was not pleasant," he said.

"What was it?" she asked.

"You ever suck snot out of a goat's nose?"

Kendra's throat clenched tight. A sudden mental connection made her recoil in horror. She forced herself to regain control and swallow. "My God, dear, is that what you're seeing right now?"

"No, not seeing it," he replied. "I was doing it. Or thought so. It was the lumpy bits. . ."

She tuned him out and pretended to be listening. He suddenly clutched at her and pulled her tightly to him. He whimpered and gasped, eyes closed, seeing some inner demon. Then she felt a warm wetness seeping through to her thigh. *Oh, trif,* she thought. *Well, that's why I brought extra clothes.*

She stayed with him for three days. He slept little, she less. His reactions indicated hallucinations affecting every sense and strange realities that only he was privy to. She napped in a chair when she could and subsisted on cold leftovers and water, the food she'd brought completely forgotten. She hoped it was less draining for him, as she took a moment to stare at her red, gritty eyes and sagging face in the metal mirror. A quick rinse with water didn't help much. She moved back to comfort him, as he twitched in his sleep.

Finally, Rostov came in and motioned her to follow. He closed the door behind her and said, "Go get some rest. We aren't having the results we wanted."

"Can you tell why?" she asked, sinking lower at the news.

Shaking his head, he replied, "It should have had some effect by now. We are missing something. I'll let you know."

She wandered home, driving aimlessly to clear her thoughts. Then she spent a long time soaking in a hot spray. She dressed in loose clothes and went downstairs, where Marta was cooking. When Marta hugged her, she reciprocated and accepted a light kiss.

"How is he?" Marta asked, serving up some stew.

"Not better," Kendra admitted, feeling tired again. "They're running some more tests." She began crying. "I *hate* seeing him like this! He's trapped underneath, but can't get out."

Marta pulled her closer and said, "They'll manage, I'm sure. It just takes a while."

Kendra looked up. "How are you doing?"

Nodding, Marta admitted, "Better. It isn't a torture session to talk about it with Carla—Doctor Wuu— anymore. She seems to think that my training and background make it easier for me to disassociate it."

"Glad to hear it," Kendra said.

"Are, uh, you up for anything this evening?" Marta asked nervously, gripping Kendra's shoulder.

It took a moment for the words to register. "You mean . . . romantically?" Kendra asked.

"If you're comfortable with it," Marta said hastily. "I feel bad about this, but I'm glad Rob isn't here. I couldn't handle a man right now. But if you . . ."

I am not the slightest bit interested in sex with anyone right now. And I would far prefer a man. "Sure."

Marta grabbed her and kissed her hard and deep, surprising her with the strength of the response. She kissed back, allowing sensuality to control it.

Marta poured a drink—wine only, and stopped after the one drink. Kendra took that as a good sign. She leaned back and accepted a leg massage while studying Marta for signs of distress.

"What?" Marta asked when she caught her.

"Just seeing how you're healing," she said, not quite a lie. The scars on her face were rapidly fading and the swelling retreating. There was still some bruising and discoloration, and it would be weeks before Marta's teeth regrew from the forms placed in her mouth. Her leg, ribs and shoulder were gradually regaining muscle tone. From the outside, Marta looked better. Her eyes were still furtive and lacked the intensity and brightness they'd had. Hopefully, that would return in time.

Upstairs, Marta undressed. She'd taken to wearing clothes for sleeping since her attack and rarely was nude at all anymore. Her figure was still spectacular, even with her meek body language. She slipped into bed and waited for Kendra.

Kendra followed suit, wanting her to be at ease. She snuggled up alongside and accepted another kiss with a bit more enthusiasm. "What would you like, dear?" she asked, leery of doing anything to upset her.

"I just want your presence," Marta said. She was running her fingers over Kendra's throat, shoulders and breasts. Kendra nodded, closed her eyes, and enjoyed the touch. She concentrated on the gliding caresses, and felt her skin tingling. Lips brushed hers again, very gently, and she felt her mouth melt into another kiss. It grew in intensity, and she let her own tongue glide over the exposed skin of Marta's throat. She reached out a hand.

Marta tensed then relaxed, but she took Kendra's hand firmly in her own. She carefully drew it around behind her, and tugged to indicate it should stay there. Kendra tried not to tense herself.

She felt Marta's fingers drifting over her ribs and down her belly, and moved her legs slightly. The questing hand sought her thighs, then slipped between them. She stiffened and Marta simultaneously relaxed, flowing against her. Marta's fingers gently teased her, and they locked lips under a fall of heavy black hair. Nothing was said for long segs.

Finally, Marta stretched and turned. "You were faking," she said factually.

"I was very close. I'm glad you enjoyed it," Kendra replied.

"I did. I guess you've got a lot of things stressing you. I'm not imposing, am I?" Marta asked, fingers tracing down Kendra's ribs again.

"You can't impose, dear," Kendra assured her. "If you need me, I'm here."

"I know," Marta said, but she sounded reassured. "Thanks for faking."

Flushing, Kendra said, "I'm sorry—"

"Don't be!" Marta insisted. "Can you even guess how many times I faked it for someone else's pleasure? As long as you don't lie about it, there's nothing wrong with it."

They snuggled in close and drifted asleep. Kendra felt relaxed for the first time in weeks, and slept well.

She spoke to Dr. Wuu again the next day. She felt affronted as the counselor dragged information out of her about the battle in Delph'. It hurt more to discuss it than leave it lie, she thought, but she went along with the program.

"This isn't really what's bothering you, is it?" Wuu asked, sipping apple juice. She always looked utterly relaxed as she dissected someone's soul. "You keep trying to justify their actions as understandable, even acceptable. So tell me about your experiences generally, about why you feel responsible."

Kendra grimaced and growled. She was frustrated enough to want to scream. "It's just war. We murdered and crippled people daily," she said.

"And you feel that justifies them raping and torturing prisoners, just because of frustration? There are accepted rules of engagement, you know," Wuu replied.

"Goddammit, I know!" Kendra shouted. "But murder was a part of it, so why not rape and torture?" she panted, pulse throbbing. "I gapped a few people who were trying to surrender, because there was no way to drag them along. Technically, that was an atrocity. I shot people at several hundred meters, who had even less idea what was happening and had no chance to surrender, but that's legally okay. So is planting bombs. Roughing up prisoners for intel is wrong, leaving them shrieking in agony as you retreat is okay. Why is any of it considered acceptable? Where do we draw the line? Why is murder acceptable?"

"'Murder' is a specific crime of wrongful killing. It legally and morally does not apply to self defense, defense of another or killing in battle. We must keep our terms precise. The semantics define how we think," Wuu said.

"*What I did*—" Kendra shouted, and stopped.

"Yes?" Wuu prodded.

Kendra said nothing, looking down at her hands. She felt a wall crumble inside. That wasn't what was bothering her. She knew what was and she could never, ever admit it.

"Did you like killing, Kendra? Is that why you think of it as murder?" Wuu asked.

No answer.

"Did you enjoy watching them die? Hearing them scream? Was it a thrill to shoot them, crush them, stab them?" she probed in a monotone.

No answer.

"Did it excite you?" she asked. Again no response. Her voice dropped to a whisper as she asked, "Did it make you wet?"

"Fuck. You. You. Bitch." The words ground out from between clenched teeth in a hoarse whisper. Kendra shook in a rage she'd never before felt.

In a light conversational tone, Wuu asked, "Is that why you try to defend them? As mortification of the flesh for your sins committed?"

Kendra stood, whirled and swung her arm hard enough to pull muscles. Her glass shattered in the fireplace, throwing shards for meters. She stood panting, wide-eyed.

Wuu said nothing, just sat and waited patiently. She gave no indication of distress from the outburst, nor when Kendra stormed into the kitchen and grabbed a bottle. Several gulps of liquor burned down her throat and set her stomach afire. She gripped the counter, knuckles white and stared with watering eyes at nothing. Finally sighing, she returned to the common room.

"I suppose you're going to tell me that's a natural reaction?" she said, tears and sarcasm dripping.

"You're a human being. Anything you do is natural. It may be rarer in some than others, depending on the reaction, but they are all natural," Wuu said.

"I enjoyed killing them," Kendra admitted. "It might be 'normal' if they were vicious animals or brutal thugs, but they were just here to do a job," she said.

"And it was your job to stop them. Were you good at it?" Wuu asked.

"Of course I was good. I'm alive, aren't I?" she retorted.

"Is that bad?"

"No . . . but . . . they . . ." Kendra began. She stopped.

"They were from your society," Wuu finished. Kendra nodded.

"Killing is a brutal, vicious, dangerous job," Wuu said. "Empathy for the enemy delays your reactions and gets you killed. It is *necessary* to think of them as nonhuman, as 'krauts,' 'gooks,' or 'aardvarks,' to enable you to shut off the civilized part of your brain and revert to the killer mentality. By thinking of your own culture as nonhuman, you degraded yourself. You took justifiable delight in being good at an almost impossible task, made tougher by your relationship to the enemy, and succeeding. By enjoying death, you violated your moral principles. By feeling the typical hormonal response that provokes the same reaction as sexual excitement, you felt dirty. This was reinforced by your religious training, which taught you that sex is a private, holy matter. Your church's cultural concept of penance makes you feel that you deserve a sexual punishment for a sexual sin. The odds of war brought one to you. You feel ashamed and violated by your attack, but also feel you deserved it, so you feel ashamed at feeling that shame. Intellectually, you realize a conflict, but cannot describe it," Wuu said. It was the longest speech she'd made.

She continued, "Warfare is hard to accept for many people. It is easier for those raised here, because we maintain a martial aspect to our culture that most do not. Can you name for me one act of yours that violated the Conventions?"

"I shot prisoners," she said.

"Prisoners you couldn't take charge of, whose release would have compromised your unit. Their deaths were tactically necessary to your mission. Was it against the Conventions? Yes. Was it murder? No, it was warfare.

Did you allow or participate in any torture or rape? Deliberately harm civilians?"

"I smacked prisoners around for intel," Kendra said. "I needed to find out where they were based. We killed a lot we found doing . . . things. Then we started killing them whether they surrendered or not. And we smashed a few, outright murder just for belonging to the other side. And there were some I . . . hacked to pieces in frustration," she admitted, eyes closed in pain and shame.

"Most of that treatment of prisoners was to protect the civilians supporting your rebels, correct?" Wuu asked, and Kendra nodded. "Technically a crime, but you were protecting civilians, which they should have helped you to do. It gets very hazy in war as to who is combatant and who is not. The days of 'name, rank and service number' are gone, if they ever existed in real life. That's why troops are never told more than they need to know. You were gathering information to protect your home from invaders. As far as the outright killing, it happens in *every* war. About thirty percent of all combatants violate the conventions. Many of them enjoy it. They often feel guilty when they get home, because they are thrown back into polite company where theoretical ideals overcome practicality. Revenge is not legally recognized, but is very common and a very human emotion. I have some bad news for you, Kendra," Wuu said. Kendra looked up to meet her eyes.

"You're civilized."

The irony of it caused Kendra to laugh herself into more tears.

Wuu smiled back and said, "You applied your talents to being the best killer you could be, did it well, never let your feelings get in the way of that killing. You did attack some simply for being the enemy, but the provocation offered makes it understandable if not right. And you now feel remorse over your actions, indicating an intact moral sense. You had a bizarre environment to deal with and you did deal."

"So why do I feel so bad about it?" Kendra asked.

"I don't know. You tell me," Wuu said, reverting to her questioning self.

It was more anxious days before a conclusion was reached about Rob. Rostov called and she hurried in for a conference. He seemed relaxed when she rushed in and she took that as a good sign. "You have news?" she asked breathlessly.

"We do," he nodded. "There's a second tier effect to the nano that was not obvious at first. The hallucinations are deliberate damage by the first routine. The second routine is attacking his flight-control implant and generating images and inputs there, which are highly confusing, since they can't be referenced to a cockpit environment. Then, as the devices fail, they are attaching themselves to the module and creating control problems. The design on this bastard—" it was the first time Kendra had heard him be anything other than dispassionate "—is the work of a truly sick genius. This team is the best in the system, and it took us weeks to figure it out.

"Additionally, as our counter attacked the infection, it built up more plaque on the module and created more, but subtly different, hallucinations. And it is self-replicating. It degrades with time, of course, but it will keep regenerating toxic levels. And there's a standard biovirus that is symbiotic with it that keeps it fed with the enzymes it needs. We're trying to kill that first. It looks like they feed each other to perpetuate the effect and when they find a module they generate the second effect to disable that, too. It's worse for pilots and interface programmers than for anyone else. We can't prove that was a deliberate design, but I'll put money on it.

"Your efforts here may have saved not only Rob, but the seven others who either have no next of kin or whose we cannot contact and are harder to interact with. We owe you."

"No you don't. It's my duty as a soldier and as his friend." She wanted nothing to do with this disgusting weapon, even as part of the cure. She continued, "I'm guessing you have another counter-agent?"

Rostov ran his fingers through his hair. "Well, actually, no," he said. "The existing therapy is sound and the side effects of additional nano-loading would be very unpleasant. And this agent is *very* pervasive. We aren't likely to get it all, and the combined effect would manifest again. So the bad news is that he can never fly again, no matter what happens."

Kendra took that in in a cold shock. "That'll kill him," she said, trembling. "Do you know how important flying is to him?"

Rostov nodded. "From his spoken dreams and flight record, I can guess. But the damage is not repairable with current technology. I'm sorry." He seemed very embarrassed by the limits of his capabilities.

"Well, then," she sighed. "I guess you do what you have to."

Kendra sat waiting, impatient but still. Rob had come through the removal of his implant in fine shape. A created virus destroyed its structure and the residue of both flushed out in the bloodstream. He was kept lightly sedated as the counter-virus was readministered and then allowed to wake. He stirred and Kendra became alert. His eyes opened.

"Morning," she said simply.

"Hi," he replied. "Raging hangover."

"It will get worse," she assured him. "The counter-virus is working this time."

"Huh?" he muttered. "To counter what?"

"The hallucinogen you picked up at Braided Bluff," she explained. Rostov had said there might be minor confusion and memory damage. She held her breath for an answer.

"Oh. Right," he said. "It worked this time?" He suddenly sat up, leaned over and vomited hard. She stood and ran to help him.

"It's working," she said when he stopped. "But you will still be experiencing hallucinations as it flushes out."

He gagged again momentarily. "How bad?" he asked raggedly.

"Worse than before," she admitted. He sat and was still, staring into space. Then he chuckled.

"Well," he said, "I may as well enjoy the good bits while they last." He laughed out loud, pointing at something only he could see. He calmed again in a few moments. "This must be hard on you," he thought aloud.

"You have no idea," she said, feeling scared, nauseous, protective, disgusted. A spectrum of emotions tumbled through her and she tried hard to suppress them.

He interrupted her meditation. "How's Marta?"

"Better," she admitted. "She was scared, that's all."

"Why?" he asked.

"Just things that happened."

He gripped her wrist hard and gave her a stern look. "Don't lie to me. Being sick makes me neither stupid nor incompetent. What happened?"

She was in a panic as to whether it was safe to tell him or not. She decided to go ahead. "She was captured during a clandestine mission and tortured and gang-raped."

He nodded, brow furrowed in thought. "That's disgusting," he said. "Tell me all of it."

She spun the details out for him, all the way through Marta's reaction to him. He interrupted her several times to go through some severe reaction or another. He had another fit of vomiting a few segs later, then began scratching itches. They increased maddeningly until he dragged himself across the ground, trying to abrade his tortured nerves. After lucidly absorbing more details, he leapt across the room, snatching a blanket from the bed and hiding beneath it, quaking in terror. He was unable to eat lunch, and lay on the floor whimpering. Kendra attempted to help him up, but he gave every indication of more nausea so she helped him back down. He sucked water from a bottle, face pressed against the smooth polymer, dripping cold, stale sweat. "Cooler," he begged, and she ordered the floor coils down five degrees. Segs later, he began twitching again.

It took three more days of waiting, sleeplessness and pain. She watched tearfully as he thrashed, vomited, rolled around on the floor from nerves driven to distraction, held his ears against sounds only he could hear and couldn't shut out and clawed at his face.

Not all his visions were negative. At one point, he began seducing her, very tenderly. She was shy of the blatant cameras, but agreed to his advances. She soon forgot about the environment and enjoyed his attentions. His brain was still very much alive underneath and stayed in control through their mutual excitement. He collapsed shortly afterward, exhausted from all his activities. She tucked a blanket around him and napped in the chair.

He woke lucid. He was worn and beaten looking and very hungry. He ate and kept the food down and suffered only an occasional flash of hallucination. "I hope that's it," he said tiredly, rubbing his eyes.

Rostov came in with an assistant and watched while Rob's responses were tested. He gave no expression either good or bad and left shortly. Rob was experiencing somewhat lesser effects now, and slept deeply and uninterrupted, snoring loudly. Accepting a risk, Kendra wrapped an arm around him and slept with him. She cried herself to sleep. How long would it be before things were normal? And what would constitute "normal"?

Rob was pronounced fit the next week. Kendra drove him to Marta's, he not being allowed to operate equipment yet. He kept the vent open for fresh air and looked queasy by the time they arrived. That was expected. His brain had adapted to the control module and lacked balance of its own now. That should improve, they'd been told, but not completely.

He greeted Marta very gently, utterly platonic and friendly. They exchanged stares, each reading the other's thoughts but not able to speak. They simply hugged, then sat apart while Kendra took over as hostess. It would take a long time to get used to each other again.

She traveled into duty every day, feeling better with both of her friends to watch each other. She still called to check on them several times during the three divs she worked. She tried not to sound as if she was checking on her dysfunctional children and neither of them ever mentioned it, but it obviously bothered them. She tapered the calls down to two, then to one at lunch. They did seem to be making progress.

Rob needed a lot of physical attention and his sex drive was normal. Marta's was not back to normal, but improving. Since Marta couldn't deal with Rob yet, and he realized his control was still lacking, Kendra found herself busier than she'd ever been, as exclusive lover for each of them. She was okay with Rob, leery around Marta, and still not entirely comfortable making love to a woman without a man present. It was aesthetic and sensual, only rarely orgasmic. She had to work at it to stay interested and interesting to Marta.

Rob was shortly able to run the house and as the net came up he resumed work. There was plenty for him, but no one could pay much; the economy was a shambles. Marta received a letter from the bank informing her that they were waiving accumulated interest on the mortgage, but payments must resume within five months. Most of her investment assets had disappeared and her military pay would just cover the house, but nothing else. Kendra's covered the basic essentials of food, power and water. Rob was working tirelessly to bring in enough to handle repairs, vehicles and incidental expenses. He cut his tenants a deal of two months free rent with at least quarter payments after that, no rent for the war months and up to a year to resume full payments and make up any shortages due for partials. There wasn't much money there, either.

He gradually got details from Marta, and realizing Kendra was rather cool sexually, talked her into revealing her experiences. He was quiet and perceptive and made fewer and gentler requests for her in bed. She found it both helpful and painful. She wanted to give him all the attention he desired, but just couldn't relax yet.

Rob spent three days buried in his comm, digging through UN files. She wasn't sure how he hacked into their system, but she did overhear him make a call to military intelligence. He pulled in a favor or two and made notes, then crawled back into the net.

Chapter 51

"Home is not where you live, but where they understand you."

—Christian Morgenstern

"Call for Kendra . . . Call for Kendra . . . Call . . ." the comm announced. She stared at it for a moment. Rob and Marta were here and Naumann would use her military comm. Who could it be?

"Answer call Pacelli," she said.

"Ms Kendra Pacelli?" the caller asked. It was a woman with a European English accent, blond, dressed in current business fashion.

"Yes?" she replied. What was this about?

"I'm Monique Sten, with the UN delegation. Would it be possible to meet with you?" she asked.

"About what?" Kendra asked, trying not to sound suspicious.

"We wish to apologize for the way you were treated regarding the logistics thefts. While it became apparent you were not a guilty party, that information was badly handled. Can we meet this afternoon?" Sten asked. She looked somewhat anxious.

"I can be there at five-thi—er, one o'clock," Kendra agreed. "I'll have an injured friend with me," she said. She was taking Rob for backup. She couldn't explain why, but it seemed a wise precaution.

"We'll see you then. Thank you," Sten smiled and cut off.

Rob agreed to go. He hid Marta's smaller gun under his clothes, strapped the Merrill on his hip and climbed in next to Kendra. She drove gently to avoid distressing his sense of balance, and headed for the UN office, near the spaceport. The 'port was functioning again at a reduced level and massive construction was going on to restore it to full operation.

As expected, they were stopped at the door and required to check their weapons. There was a delay while the UN located a female guard to pat Kendra down. She suggested the male guards just go ahead and search, not being bothered by the idea. The guards were bothered, blushed and stammered negatives. Kendra wasn't too surprised when Rob managed to sneak the second weapon in, despite and due to, a laughably inexpert search.

They were led right in to Sten's office and seated. She introduced Rob in passing, and Ms Sten offered refreshments. She took a soft drink. Rob took water and sat silently. He betrayed a very slight tension that indicated he was ready to fight if necessary, but would start nothing. It was doubtful anyone save Kendra could see it, even if, as she assumed, they were being recorded.

"First of all, Ms Pacelli," she began, "we wish to extend a formal and very sincere apology. Your attempted detention was a mistake by an overzealous security detail. We understand completely your fear, which was only reinforced by their unlawful treatment of your friends."

"What happened to Janie and Tom?" she asked.

"They were held for a few weeks, but were released. They were not badly hurt, but were treated unprofessionally and we compensated them for their trouble. Naturally, it didn't make the news. There was a risk of it creating a disturbance," Sten explained.

Kendra had to think back to remind herself that the UN could do that. There was no possible way to keep it silent here. But then, it couldn't happen here.

"You must understand," Sten said, standing and looking out the window, "that there were numerous incidents over a period of years that were similar. While they do happen occasionally, they are *not* condoned and we do stop them when we find them. Several ranking inspectors from UNPF Department of Special Investigations and the Bureau of Security Interior Investigation Office were made to retire. An oversight committee will be watching for similar incidents in the future."

Kendra waited. What was the point of this?

"The charges against you were dropped, but it was believed you were dead and since no one likes to admit to errors like that, it was never publicized. You know how the press is." Kendra did indeed.

"The bounty recently was simply a military attempt for psychological warfare purposes. It was not sanctioned by any civil charges. Again, I'm sorry you were treated in such a fashion and stuck in the middle." Sten looked quite embarrassed at having to concede all this. Kendra gathered heads had rolled.

"So, with all that said, all charges dropped and your military service obligation completed for the record, I'm happy to offer you a free transit home. We'll work with you to find you a home and employment," she finished, looking more relaxed and cheerful. Her smile was honest and open.

Kendra was too surprised to speak. She pondered the implications for a bit, then said, "I served in an active capacity with the Freehold Military."

"We will not hold that against you," Sten assured her. "We also know you were involved in the incident at Langley. Believe me, we understand what it means to take orders and we know you weren't willingly fighting your own people. The war is over and this is just one of the situations we have to resolve. It's actually lucky the bounty was offered on you or we would not have been aware that you were here and wouldn't be able to make reparations. Which reminds me; your accumulated pay for the UNPF, plus leave time, is to be paid. And as I said, we'll be glad to help you get placed in employment."

Kendra understood, although she doubted Rob did. It was an embarrassment to the system and had to be corrected to make these people feel at peace.

Home? Her parents were dead. Her brother could be anywhere. The planet was a shambles. There'd be a lot of work to do. Constructive, peaceful work. Her thoughts whirled. "I can't give you an answer yet," she said. "I have to think about it."

"Please," Sten said, nodding. "Contact me when you have decided."

They left unhurriedly and said nothing until they were in the car and traveling.

"Well?" she asked Rob.

"I think she's honest. The question is, do you want to go back where 'mistakes' like that can happen?" he asked.

"I don't know. But it still is my home," she said. "I have a lot here, but . . ." She tapered off.

Rob nodded. She'd been caught between both sides and seen a lot of violence up close. He still missed his parents after ten years. How must she feel? "It's your call," he said. "I imagine it's a tough one to make. But you'll always be welcome here, no matter what you decide. And Mar and I will front you the return transit fee, if necessary." He hoped she'd stay. "And I do love you," he added. He wanted to shout about the stupidity of trusting a system that could fuck up to that level and cavalierly offer cash as compensation, while the idiots responsible got a pension instead of sued into indentured hard labor. He knew she'd get defensive, and it wasn't fair to try to influence her. He kept silent. She was too wrapped up in her thoughts to notice.

That evening, they all sat around and avoided the issue. Kendra was very introspective, wondering what would happen to her parents' assets, whether or not enough relatives survived to make memorial arrangements. She'd never been particularly close with her cousins.

Marta refused to give any input, simply saying, "I'll support you either way, love. It wouldn't be fair of me to judge a system I've never been to."

She sat thinking, alone. Rob and Marta had gone upstairs, leaving her in the dark comfort of the common room. She stared at the dimly lit cases of minerals and other decorations. The Lubov painting had been restored. Rob knew experts in the field and had refused to tell Marta what it had cost. It was a striking piece. And it was from Earth. Almost five hundred years old.

She came back to the present. As beautiful and amazing as the Freehold was, she was still an outsider. People heard her accent and gave her curious or angry glances. She would forever be a stranger here. And despite all the complaints about the UN, her family was well enough placed that there weren't any real problems. They were honest business people and she'd be fine.

She fell asleep on the velvet warmth of the couch.

Chapter 52

"Revenge is like a margarita: salty, with a twist of lime."

—Leon Jester

"Mr. Calan!" a voice greeted him as he left through the back.

"Yes?" he replied. The man was well dressed, but Calan didn't recognize him. "Do I know you?"

"We have mutual acquaintances," the stranger said. He stepped closer. "Kendra Pacelli and Marta Hernandez."

Calan stiffened at the names as Rob grabbed him. He slammed Calan into the wall, turned him around and jammed his hand onto the sensor. The door opened. Rob shoved him through into the silent office and let the door close behind them.

"You hurt a lot of people, Mr. Calan," Rob said, sounding coldly angry and disappointed.

Calan stood shivering, trying to remember the basic

martial arts he'd studied so many years ago in school, as he backed behind the imported cherrywood desk. But his opponent was clearly a master, younger, in better shape and mean. "I did what I thought was right," he tried to explain. "I was sure we would lose and I thought—"

"Horseshit," Rob replied as he approached. "You were looking for credits and trying to hurt Kendra because she wouldn't let you *pimp* her." The word was a gross insult in the Freehold.

Calan said nothing. Rob stepped forward, holding him against the wall with one hand. He shifted slightly and began.

Calan gulped and turned purple as the first blow paralyzed his diaphragm. He tried to scream as his elbow was shattered, but the pain reinforced his inability to breathe. More blows followed, until he passed out.

He snapped awake from the whiff of an inhaler under his nose and tried to scream, but there was tape across his mouth. He snorted air through his nose, until the inhaler was stuffed against his nostrils again. He gagged, eyes watering, and rolled his head. His entire body was on fire, from toes throbbing from being crushed, to shoulders stabbing in pain from fractured collarbones. His brain somersaulted and he tried to vomit, choking when it couldn't escape, and swallowed as much of the sour, bitter fluid as hadn't burned his lungs into a paroxysm of coughing. He was barely conscious from oxygen deprivation again, and the inhaler was a mixed blessing as it scorched his nostrils.

"My first thought was to leave you alive," Rob said. "But you can afford regeneration, and even that pain isn't enough for shit like you." He pulled out a long, slim, deeply hollow-ground dagger. It was the work of a true artist in metal. Calan snorted for breath and stared in paralyzed fear at the glinting steel. "Then I decided to cut you, let you bleed to death slowly, thrashing around in pain. But you might live until morning and then we'd have the same problem—your survival." The blade twirled through Rob's fingers idly. He'd spent so many divs handling knives that it was unconscious. "So I've decided to tweak your pains a bit at a time, until you pass out. Then I'm going to wake you. Then I'm going to kill you." The look on his face was utterly emotionless.

Kendra saw the news that morning. Calan had died in a particularly grisly fashion. His family had hired an investigator, but very diplomatically admitted there were tens of people who might want him dead. The cost of a detailed forensic investigation wasn't really warranted, since none of his inheritors had accused any other. It was assumed to be dealings from the war that had gotten him killed, or perhaps some data he held from his association with the UN had been covered up. If nothing obvious turned up, it would be dropped shortly. Just chalk it up to the war.

Rob came downstairs then, looking tired but cheerful. "Calan is dead," she said to him, gauging his reaction.

"Oh?" Rob replied, looking genuinely surprised. "I assume that's okay? You aren't bothered by his loss?"

"Rob!" she said, demanding.

Rob shrugged. "I didn't want him sliming out of things. It would be hard to quantify damage and he'd probably try to claim it was all a ploy to discredit him. The evidence is too slim."

"That was murder, Rob," she said.

"I killed an enemy agent who was still a threat. Do you deny he was?"

"Dammit, that's not the point!" she shouted, beginning to cry. "I've seen enough suffering to last several lifetimes. Whether he deserved it or not, it was *my* choice as to how to punish him."

Rob looked a bit guilty. Just a bit.

"Do you need more therapy?" she asked, half as a threat.

"I'll never fly again, partly because of data that shitball *gave* to the enemy as a bargaining chip. You were put in a position where you were hunted like a dog, then thrown into a vicious battle. And Marta . . . and this bottom feeder was *profiting* from it! I think it was *excellent* therapy," he finished. They stared at each other for long seconds.

Marta opened her door and came down to see the tableau. "Hey, what's up? I just heard that someone sliced Calan to pieces. I guess you weren't the only one with a grudge, huh?" she said to Kendra.

Kendra sat still for a few measured seconds, then replied, "I guess so." She looked at Rob as Marta eased by him. Then she looked away.

Marta swung past Rob as she headed for the kitchen. Unseen by Kendra, she winked at him, a grin flashing for just a second and then gone. She hummed softly in the kitchen. "So, who wants eggs?"

Chapter 53

"The exquisite gut-wrenching beautiful painful
joyful sorrow I feel when I look at the ways of my
people makes me want to soar like an eagle, or kill
myself, depending upon what day it is."

—Michael James

"Senior Sergeant Pacelli reports," Kendra said, with a sharp salute and a brisk snap to attention.

"Kendra," Naumann acknowledged with a nod. "Relax. Why so formal?"

"Well, Comman—uh, Colonel," she stammered slightly, "this is important, so I want to make sure it's done right."

"Very well. What can I help you with?"

"I want to resign," she said quickly, gulping.

"I see," he replied. "Well, ordinarily, I'd say 'no' out of hand; we are desperately short of good personnel and you've been one of the best. But what are the circumstances?"

"I've killed more than my share of people. Been wounded and hurt. Hated by people on both sides. I don't even know which side is mine anymore. My family is dead," she started crying, "partly because of my actions. I've done my duty and plenty more. I've taken more than anyone has a right to expect."

Nodding, Naumann said, "I can't begin to empathize. But can I ask the favor of you taking leave for a month or two and then reconsidering? I really need good people and I hate to lose you. At least stay until we demob at the end of the year."

Shaking her head and blinking tears, she snapped, "No. It won't change my mind. There's another thing. I've been offered a chance to return home."

"You can't," Naumann said. At her confused look, he explained, "Oh, you can return to Earth. But do you think anyone will accept you after you've served here?"

"I wasn't planning on telling anyone."

"I see," he said. His face was a mask. "So one of the bravest, most honorable careers in the Forces is going to be buried like a mistake . . ."

"*Stop it!*" she snapped, loudly. "I've earned my way home. You can keep me here . . . but I want to go. Please."

"Sorry," he said. "I have my own feelings and shouldn't have dug at you." He shuffled and keyed as he spoke. "I'll grant a release, on conflict of interest. Effective today. And an account for expenses until we get the snarl of the finance system cleared up." He scrawled a signature and handed the documents over.

"Thank you, sir," she saluted again. She accepted the package and his return of her salute, then turned and left quickly.

Sitting once again in Liberty Park, which was gradually being restored to something that might eventually approach its previous splendor, she took stock. First, she'd need lodging. Then, she'd need to say her goodbyes. The last scheduled UN returnee flight was in six days, after that, the traffic schedule got hazy. It would be best to lift then. She'd need to pack her still meager possessions and arrange to transfer her funds. Her sword she'd leave to Marta, her other hardware to Rob. Her uniforms she'd burned. Not out of disgust, merely as a symbolic breaking of ties. Realizing the Druidic symbology of such an act, she clenched her eyes and sat motionless for a few minutes. Calm again, she shuffled through her documents.

An honorable discharge. A chit for Cr5000. A Citation for Courage, a service medal, six battle stars and three Purple Hearts. She mused as she walked. From the corner of her eye, she saw one of the old Earth oaks, now graffiti-scarred and with broken limbs. Somehow, that bothered her more than the shattered buildings across the street.

"Wine cooler, Kendra?"

She looked up, startled, and realized her feet had taken her to Stanley's. Some of it was boarded up and the sidewalk was a mess, but he was doing his best to get his business restored. "Thanks, please," she agreed.

"And is there a promotion in the works for you? It seems everyone else is getting bumped a number or two." He slid a drink to her.

"Not likely, Rupe," she grinned sadly. "I just resigned. I can't take any more of not knowing whose side I'm on."

"Oh!" he said, shocked. "I always figured you were on the side you morally supported. Even if that side was only you."

"I'm sorry, Rupe, I don't want to be rude, but I don't want to talk about it and I don't want people feeling sorry for me. This is what I need."

"No offense," he agreed. He drifted into the background, but maintained his usual courteous customer contact.

This is it, Kendra thought, as the alarm woke her. *Lift in two divs. Or should it be five and a half hours?*

Marta had been polite, understanding and turned cool. She clearly felt Kendra was running out on them, but did not voice her feelings. Rob had finally given in and argued, pleaded, been logical, all to no avail. She still didn't fit in here. She loved the planet and wanted to, but it was not her society.

As she gathered her few personal belongings and packed them, her phone rang. She reached for it, then decided to let it record. She'd be dumping it at the port, anyway. Earth used different frequencies and a different system. Then she reached for it anyway.

"Pacelli."

It was a recorded message from Naumann. She let it play.

"Wanted to catch you before you left," he said. "This is from two years ago at the commanding officers' dining-in. The campaigns have changed and the pace certainly quickened in two and a half millennia, or even the six centuries since this was written, but I think it is still appropriate. Keep it in mind when you get home."

The scene cut to a podium. Naumann stood there, dressed in mess dress, only wearing commander's rank. He stepped in front of the podium, stood firmly to attention and began to recite:

Legate, I had the news last night—my cohort ordered home
By ships to Portus Itius and thence by road to Rome.

I've marched the companies aboard, the arms are
    stowed below:
Now let another take my sword. Command me
    not to go!

I've served in Britain forty years, from Vectis to
    the Wall.
I have none other home than this, nor any life
    at all.
Last night, I did not understand, but, now the
    hour draws near
That calls me to my native land, I feel that land
    is here.

Here where men say my name was made, here
    where my work was done;
Here where my dearest dead are laid—my wife—
    my wife and son;
Here where time, custom, grief and toil, age,
    memory, service, love,
Have rooted me in British soil. Ah, how can I
    remove?

For me this land, that sea, these airs, those folk
    and fields suffice.
What purple Southern pomp can match our
    changeful northern skies,
Black with December snows unshed or pearled
    with August haze—
The clanging arch of steel-grey March, or June's
    long-lighted days?

You'll follow widening Rhodanus till vine and olive
    lean
Aslant before the sunny breeze that sweeps
    Nemausus clean

To Arelate's triple gate; but let me linger on,
Here where our stiff-necked British oaks confront
  Euroclydon!

You'll take the old Aurelian Road through shore-
  descending pines
Where, blue as any peacock's neck, the Tyrrhene
  Ocean shines.
You'll go where laurel crowns are won, but—will
  you e'er forget
The scent of hawthorn in the sun, or bracken in
  the wet?

Let me work here for Britain's sake—at any task
  you will—
A marsh to drain, a road to make or native troops
  to drill.
Some Western camp (I know the Pict) or granite
  Border keep,
Mid seas of heather derelict, where our old
  messmates sleep.

Legate, I come to you in tears—My cohort
  ordered home!
I've served in Britain forty years. What should I
  do in Rome?
Here is my heart, my soul, my mind—the only
  life I know.
I cannot leave it all behind. Command me not
  to go!"

The image faded. Kendra looked off into the brilliant sky. "You *bastard*," she muttered. She didn't recognize Kipling's "The Roman Centurion's Song," but
it reached inside her. Blinking at tears, she saw a
sudden kaleidoscope of images. The gate closing behind

her at Langley. Jelsie's weapon pointed at her. Rob and Marta The mountains, ocean, riverside and hectic cities they'd shown her. The life-changing challenge of recruit training. The assorted residents and militia who'd looked suspicious upon hearing her accent. Rupe, Ms Gatons and Dak and the others who'd accepted her as she was.

So where is my home? she asked herself. She fretted for several segs, then shook her head. Resuming her pace, she headed to the tran station.

Arriving at Jefferson Starport, she walked calmly up to the InterTrans desk. "I need to postpone my departure," she said, sliding her credchit across.

"Certainly Ms Pacelli. There is a cancellation fee at this late time, I'm afraid."

"I understand."

She'd left her bag in storage at the 'port. She'd walked here, to Laguna Park. Five divs, she'd sat in silence. Io had set, the sunset brilliant behind her. She stared at the darkening violet of the east as the kittiwakes circled and dove for fish. The breeze increased slightly and gusted, and she played the message again. Clouds tumbled and swirled and she stared at Gealach as it rose, a lopsided, angry orange ovoid, taking shape and brightening, riding above the clouds in three-quarter phase, bluish and bright, though smaller than the Moon seen from Earth. The waves crashed on the rocks to the north and hissed on the sand below. The beach was still unblemished by "improvements," and she marveled at the vital smell of salt air.

She was still sitting there as the flashes of false dawn gave way to gray-blue and eventually dull orange as dew dripped coldly off her clothes. Io finally appeared, a sliver of gold fire that widened and grew. She stood but stared still, mesmerized by the slow, majestic sunrise, unlike anything visible on Earth. She played Naumann's message once more and mumbled along with it.

Finally, she made her way back to the base. Only seven kilometers. She smiled at the concept of anyone on Earth walking more than a hundred meters or so. Her new decision was *right*, she was sure. Life would be a bit less complex; it would certainly not be easier.

At the gate to Heilbrun, she had to get clearance to enter. Then she had her bag searched. She tolerated it knowingly, wondering how many Freehold civilians would see it as an invasive act. She walked to headquarters, entered and found Naumann in his outer office, dealing with subordinates.

"Get that done, and quickly, please," he said to one, dismissing him. "Well, Ms Pacelli, how can I help you?" he asked, formal and correct as usual. He ushered her into his office.

"I thought your message was a slimy trick, Naumann," she said.

"You're here. It had an effect of some kind apparently," he observed.

"So what message where you trying to send?"

"Just that we all wish to return to the past, but it never happens. I wanted you to think about where your accomplishments have been, there or here, and then make an informed decision."

"I'm staying," she said.

He nodded. "I think that's the right choice. But you had to decide," he agreed.

"But you aren't above some prodding in the direction you think best."

"No."

She expected more, but he left it there. "I'd like to resume my duties," she said.

"Can't. Sorry," he said with a shake of his head. "I filled your slot immediately. I can't have holes in a vital area like logistics."

"Then I'll take whatever you have open. 'A marsh to drain, A road to make,' I believe the quote is? I never was a civilian, I see that now. I'll go wherever you need me," she said, feeling a ripple of adrenaline again. Would he actually refuse? She *had* made a big issue of leaving when he clearly needed her.

"I can use you. You can't be a senior," he said with a slight grin.

"That's fine," she agreed, relieved. She belonged again and it didn't matter where she was from.

He raised his hand and she hers. He recited the oath and she responded back. He coded in a document authorizing issue of basic gear. She explained about her uniforms and he grinned. "No prob. It comes out of your pay. Will Senior Hernandez be willing to part with your old sword?"

"That I don't know. I hope so. I couldn't have taken it to Earth, with the laws there."

"See, that would have stopped me right there," he commented. "Well, you'll be active until the end of the year, then you revert to reserve, unless something picks up. Let's both hope it doesn't."

"Agreed," she said. She took the proffered sheet, "Logistics. Thanks. I can work back up to . . ." her voice trailed off. *"Warrant leader?"* she asked in a small voice.

"The senior sergeant slot is filled by Beker. Sirkot was promoted and sent to Legion Logistics. They need all the experience they can get. I wasn't sure who would take his slot, now I am. You'll need to go to Advanced Leadership School, of course."

"Uh, yes," she agreed. Then, trying to avoid crying until she left, she said a very sincere "Thank you."

Chapter 54

"Go Stranger,
and to the Spartans tell,
that here obedient
to their laws
we fell."

—Simonides

It was rather enjoyable to be in formation, Kendra thought. Usually she'd hated them, but the Freehold forces had no field officers to make boring speeches and the line officers seemed to understand the need to be brief. Of course, they were all former enlisted, weren't they? The geometric precision was pleasing to the eye, and now knowing the history of military formations, it was an interesting ritual. This one was a formal one for the news and only a handful of medals were being presented. Literally thousands of awards were being made to the surviving soldiers.

Almost without exception, they'd fought like demons and without regard for personal safety.

Most of the medals and other awards had simply been handed out. There were too many to count, like her three Purple Hearts, for example. Naumann half jokingly referred to them as "medals of stupidity." He should talk. He now had six.

Unlike the UN, the FMF presented awards in ascending order. She thought that was better. It stopped the lower awardees from feeling like afterthoughts, since they were awarded first. On the other hand, they were overshadowed by the higher awards. It still seemed the better approach. They were currently dealing with four Valorous Service Medals, including Marta's. Hers was diplomatically phrased as "For exceptional service while serving alone in a deep covert operation, succeeding in her objective of neutralizing the enemy commander, and surviving capture and torture administered as a direct result of her mission." Probably most of those present had heard a few details of her treatment and Mar winced slightly at the wording. They also awarded her a Purple Heart and a Prisoner's Service Medal.

"You okay, dear?" Kendra asked as Marta resumed her slot next to her. The formation was theoretically by unit, but her friends had managed to squeeze together in Headquarters Company, 3rd MAR with her.

"I will be. I don't think I'll hang this on the wall for a while, though," Mar said, shivering slightly. It took a moment for the words to register. Kendra's hearing implant was still a new toy and rather flat sounding. They said her hearing would improve with regen therapy, but this would have to do for now. There were other awards being given, but the two women weren't listening. Kendra did take another glance at Marshal Dyson. He still looked rather ragged after his "trial" by the International Criminal Court and the two Earth years of his "life" sentence for "war crimes" he'd served before Naumann had forced his release.

Kendra was about to say something about it to Marta when her ears caught, "Logistics Warrant Leader Kendra Anne Pacelli," and she started. A guilty part of her thought she was about to be berated for rudeness to others. Then she heard "Front and center!"

She automatically stepped back out of rank and marched the long walk toward the stand. What could they want with her? A VSM?

She climbed the stairs, reported and saluted the marshal and he whispered, "Right face." She pivoted to face the formation.

Behind her, the adjutant's soprano intoned the familiar, "Attention to orders! To all whom these presents come, greeting."

She paused, then read, "Citation to accompany the award of the Citizen's Medal—"

Kendra felt the blood drain from her face. Her lips silently mouthed, *What?*

No. Not possible. Her knees felt weak. Her ears started working again and she heard, "Then Senior Sergeant Pacelli distinguished herself on thirty-four April, two hundred and eleven, at the Battle of Braided Bluff. Sergeant Pacelli was leading a platoon of reservists and militia and also acting as squad leader for the platoon's first squad, tasked with holding the ridge against the final UNPF occupation forces.

"Air support was unavailable, leaving the infantry to hold against seventeen-to-one odds. Sergeant Pacelli carefully and expertly employed all her position's automated, emplaced and support weapons, then ordered her own squad to engage with small arms.

"Massively outnumbered, Sergeant Pacelli retreated only as far as necessary to allow her platoon to continue engaging with superior position. Her unit held without support or fighting positions for more than two divs while taking small arms, mortar, rocket and direct-fire artillery fire, guided by enemy intelligence drones.

"Her position bore the brunt of the UNPF counterattack, and the platoon at her right flank was destroyed. Sergeant Pacelli received orders to retreat to clear the way for close air support. At that point, communications failed.

"Heedless of her own safety, Sergeant Pacelli ran more than two hundred meters through enemy fire, becoming wounded in the left arm in the process, and ordered her squad individually to withdraw as she returned, destroying three reconnaissance drones en route. Finding Militia Private Adam Warren injured and immobile, she carried him from the area, still engaging the enemy with her weapon. While doing so, she was wounded in the left leg.

"Finally able to relinquish her casualty to Reserve Corporal Drake, she turned and reengaged the enemy with rifle fire and grenades, accounting for an estimated twelve casualties, ensuring the safe retreat of her squad and keeping the enemy in the target area. She had no cover and was surrounded on all sides by enemy troops."

Well, yes, she thought. *But I wasn't trying to be brave. There was nothing else to do. And it sounds like I was a one-woman army, the way they say it.*

The adjutant was still reciting: "At that time, close air support attacked the enemy on her right flank, delivering ordnance within ten meters of her unprotected position. Immediately the craft was clear, she again engaged the enemy. Out of ammunition, she fought hand to hand and secured an enemy weapon.

She resumed shooting, accounting for an estimated sixteen more casualties. During the course of the battle, she was wounded a third time and injured by a drone that she destroyed.

"She held her position as six squads approached, then charged forward through their fire to retrieve a second casualty, Militia Private Daniel DaSoto. Shouldering him, she retreated to the cover of a downed tree and defended the position and Private DaSoto for the remainder of the battle, accounting for another nineteen estimated casualties. Unable to advance through her fire and that of her squad, the enemy finally broke and surrendered. Her captured weapon held three remaining rounds.

"Sergeant Pacelli's actions led directly to the success of the battle, saved the remaining lives of her platoon and of more than two hundred and fifty other soldiers on the ridge, who, without her selfless efforts, would have been engaged at close range and overwhelmed. It is certain that without her actions, the battle would have been lost and the war's rapid end not achieved without much greater combat and loss of life.

"The courage, honor and devotion to duty and to her unit and nation displayed by Senior Sergeant Kendra Anne Pacelli, above and beyond that normally expected of soldiers of the Freehold in the face of battle, reflect great credit upon herself and the Freehold Military Forces and set the standard by which others will be judged."

"Signed under my hand, this nineteen September, two hundred and eleven, Citizen Patrick Chinratana, Speaker for the Citizen's Council, by unanimous vote."

The so far silent crowd let loose a few gasps at that revelation.

Kendra was still stunned and weak-kneed as the marshal draped the ribbon over her head. She remembered almost too late to lower her head to help. She straightened to thousands of camera eyes fixing her. She waited for a few seconds, knowing they had to have their invasion of her privacy, then made hurriedly to leave, remembered the marshal and turned back. He reached out and shook hands very sincerely. "It is an honor to serve with you, Warrant Leader," he said and saluted. *Oops!* she thought. *I missed the salute.* They'll forgive me, I hope. She snapped her best response and waited for him. "Thank you, sir," she said, unable to manage more.

After several seconds, the adjutant behind her coughed slightly. She suddenly recalled that this decoration, by regulation and tradition, meant anyone of any rank had to salute *her*. She dropped it quickly and the marshal dropped his. She turned to leave and as she descended the steps heard above her, *"Forces!"*

Shouted orders rippled across the field from subordinate echelons, army down to battalion, with gaps due to casualties. It ended with a flurry of shouted, *"Company!"*

"By my command, pre-sent . . . arms!"

Flustered and overwhelmed, she popped her arm up quickly, then resumed her march back to her slot. Thunderous applause surrounded her, going on enthusiastically for long seconds.

Rob and Marta steadied her. "Brace up, girl," Rob said.

"I'm about to cry," she whispered. She was bursting with sweat, tingling and shaking, and everything sounded even more distant than her implant already made things. Another speaker was adding some words that she knew she should listen to politely. She was too distracted.

"You're allowed," Rob said. "No one doubts your courage."

"You knew about this, didn't you?" she asked.

"Yes," he admitted. "I had to help reconstruct my run, as well as I remember. Which isn't much."

"Bastard!" she said, smiling. Tears were running, but she was happy.

"Love, regardless of what you think, you were suicidally brave. Anyone else would have turned and run," Marta told her.

"Call me stupid," she said. "It never occurred to me . . . because I thought we were already dead."

Rob didn't tell her that Naumann had consulted with him as to whether or not she'd accept the medal. Additional merit was added because she was an expatriate from the enemy side. They weren't sure how she'd feel about that so it wasn't mentioned. He didn't tell her either that she'd been put in for a commendation for her work on the attack on Earth. He knew she wouldn't want any reminders of that.

"You are very much alive," he told her, as they applauded the speech. None of them had heard it. Few others had, either. "And are going to stay that way."

"*Attention to orders. To all whom these presents come, greeting,*" the adjutant shouted, without amplification. They all braced and became silent. "*Posthumous citation to accompany the award of the Citizen's Medal. Private Aaron, David J. Corporal Abraham, Lois L. Private Allan, Nicolas M. Lieutenant Andries, Jack C. Senior Sergeant Atama, Mvumbu K. Sergeant Babbage, Charles A. Operative Benitez, Rojero G. Captain Botan, Vera L. Operative By The, Jade S . . .*" The list went on for long segs to absolute silence from the crowd. Over two hundred names were read. The adjutant was crying openly, but her voice was firm. " *. . . Costlow, Derek L . . .*" made Rob hiss and close his eyes. Kendra twitched as she heard " *. . . Senior Sergeant Romar, Jelsie C . . .*" She briefly closed her eyes and prayed. For Jelsie, she made it a Druidic prayer. *"The above named members of First, Second, Third and Fourth Special Warfare Regiments distinguished themselves by unsurpassed courage and valor during the system battle of thirty-four April, two hundred and eleven. These men and women voluntarily infiltrated the UN and UN held stations and space facilities throughout the system, armed with explosives, and destroyed the intelligence and support infrastructure of the occupation forces. All accepted this assignment knowing it meant their deaths. Their sacrifice allowed the planetside forces to engage a superior enemy force with greatly reduced intelligence and strategic threats. Without their unwavering loyalty, the war would have been lost.*

"The courage, honor and devotion to duty and nation displayed by these soldiers, above and beyond that normally expected of soldiers of the Freehold in the face of battle, reflect the highest credit upon themselves and the Freehold Military Forces and set the standard by which others will be judged."

"Signed under my hand, this nineteen September, two hundred and eleven, Citizen Patrick Chinratana, speaker for the Citizen's Council, by unanimous vote."

There was absolute silence for seconds that dragged on seemingly forever. Finally, shouted orders in the distance broke it and the skirl of bagpipes drowned out the twitters of birds. Kendra was just glad she wasn't the only person almost blind with tears. Besides the pipes, there were volleys of rifle salutes, and five Hatchets screamed low overhead, one pitching up and roaring vertically out of sight in an ages-old tribute. She could see Rob staring wistfully at the craft he'd never fly again.

Then she had to stay for the reception in the awardees honor. Everyone immediately joined the line that filed slowly past the slabs of malachite and black marble that bore the names of the two hundred and six soldiers whose deaths had made it possible for her to even fight. There was palpable silence, the visitors keeping quiet in awed respect as they stared through the monument into their own thoughts.

There was Jelsie. She ran her fingers across the incised letters, then bent to kiss them. She would find out what information was available about Jelsie's mission. She was sure she'd been enthusiastic and willing, even knowing the cost.

Naumann stood at the far end and nodded to her as she approached. He saluted her, which embarrassed her, and she returned it. Then he introduced the man with him, who was in UN uniform. "Kendra, this is General Meyer, the UN commander from the ridge."

Meyer threw a sharp UN salute, which she returned in kind. "An honor to meet you, Warrant Leader," he said. "I'm grateful that at least some of the bravest survived. I just wish we'd been able to have more people of your caliber on our side." His tone was ironic, rather than angry at her circumstances.

"Thank you, sir," she replied. They stared awkwardly for a few seconds and she turned her attention back to Naumann. "I appreciate the thought, but I don't think I deserve this, sir," she said, indicating her medal. "All I did was what I had to."

He looked at her with what she thought was the most gentle expression she'd ever seen from him. "Kendra, the after-action review showed three clear divisions of force on the bluff: air support down one line and across the base, a similar line where the explosives got them and a location just above that where the casualty density was simply appalling and they couldn't move past it. They ran into the proverbial brick wall. All witnesses agree—there was one squad there, and one lone soldier with a rifle out in front. You. We probably would have won without you, but you saved hundreds of lives."

A sudden wave of realization swept through her. She'd *saved* lives. All her thoughts had been on those she killed directly, but there were several times as many who'd survived because of it. That take on things improved her spirit immensely. She tried to stifle a grin, realized how silly it must look, grinned anyway and nodded. "Thank you, sir," she said and saluted. Then she caught herself again—*he* had to salute *her.* It didn't seem proper.

Rob and Marta were joined by Drew and the three kept her covered from assault from the rear. She still had hordes of people in front, wanting to shake her hand, beg autographs, thank her for saving them or a family member, asking if she knew so-and-so.

"Well done, Warrant Leader," someone said. She returned a salute, nodded and took the hand. The booming voice was familiar. Then it registered.

"Sergeant Carpender!" she said, surprised. Her old instructor.

"Warrant Leader Carpender now, but yes. Thank you for honoring me by setting such an amazing example," he said.

"No, sir," she argued. "Thank you for your training. I'd be dead without it."

He joined the entourage and they sought some semblance of privacy, Rob rounding up security personnel from 3rd Mob to help keep the crowd back.

"I'd just retired," Carpender told her, "and suddenly was back in action. I skulked around Falling Rock and kept them busy." Kendra nodded. She'd heard about Falling Rock and his description seemed to be too mild.

They chatted for a few segs, the crowd slowly dissipating. Finally, Kendra said, "I need to get out of here. It's embarrassing. But you are always welcome to visit us."

"Yes," Marta agreed. "We'd be honored."

Carpender grinned and said, "I can't refuse an honored invitation from this family. Thanks, I will."

They said goodbye and her bodyguards whisked her to a staff car, thoughtfully provided by Naumann. They gave the pilot directions and headed home.

They were again made aware of the injuries they'd all suffered by Rob getting airsick. He was highly embarrassed. No one else mentioned it. Just one more reminder of the horrors now behind them.

Epilogue

"It is well that war is so terrible, or we should get too fond of it."

—General Robert E. Lee

It was good to be together with her lovers again, Kendra thought. Or maybe "at last" was more accurate. She found she was comfortable with Marta now. They were together in Marta's huge bed, gasping and sweating from electric exertions. In the bare few seconds between sex and conversation, she reflected on the events of the last few segs.

Marta had tensed as Rob entered her, but seemed to relax immediately. Her muscles and sinews had stood out clearly as she screamed in pleasure and that was a clear indication that her emotional scars were healing. Nor had Kendra protested when Mar dragged her into a scorching embrace. Mingled scents, tastes, the feathery touches of hair and questing lips and fingers that she used to find sensuous were now orgasmic in intensity and she neither knew nor cared which of them was exciting her.

Eventually words were spoken, interrupting her thoughts, along with long kisses and stretching. "Thank you, love," Marta said to her, hugging her close. "I feel a lot better."

"I'm glad," she replied.

Rob gathered them both in and held them. "That was better than I remembered . . . but my memory is a bit shaky. Better remind me often," he grinned at the dark humor.

Marginally uncomfortable, Kendra asked, "So, what are you planning? You mentioned something?"

"I got a contract with Lawjin Orbital. They need a system installation monitored and renovation of the surviving equipment. I'll be supervising the other contractors," he explained. "It's a start and I'm sure there'll be repair work to be done. I was going to apply for a pilot slot with Higgins Recovery, but . . ." He tapered off. He'd never fly again. He had no implant for high-performance craft and was subject to occasional disorientation. He could perhaps fly a private craft over empty wilderness, if he felt suicidal.

Marta said, "And I got lucky. Bellefontaine is back in business. They agreed to take me on a month-to-month contract. I'll be hostessing and doing guest escort. As soon as the nets are completely back, I've got an ad in place. I lowered my rates to start with, but I'll boost them again as soon as possible. There'll still be a market for my pictorial work, although outsystem is harder to collect on."

"Are you okay with Bellefontaine?" Kendra asked, gripping her hand.

"I'm fine, love," Marta assured her. "Really. Occasional nightmares," she admitted, "but no conscious problems. How about you?"

"I'm okay," Kendra agreed. Mostly because she'd seen what happened to Marta and realized the difference in scale. And one did get used to pain with practice, but she wasn't going to say that. "I'm glad the UN did pay my back pay, but considering how much hassle it was to get that out of them when I said I wasn't going back, I'm really glad I didn't. It's a decent chunk of cash. I'm on orders through the end of the year. After that, I don't know.

"Maybe I'll take up gardening."

Military Glossary

Airfac: Air facility. Aviation depot on an FMF base.

Antarm: Pilot shorthand for "Antiarmor." Used to voice activate weapons.

Avatar: UN air superiority aircraft.

Ayda: Pilot shorthand for ADA, or Air Defense Artillery. Used to voice designate a threat or a target in the combat environment.

AO: Area of operations. Delineates a geographic region of military responsibility.

Black Operations: The elite FMF clandestine special warfare units. Trained to acquire intelligence, construct improvised munitions and disrupt enemy operations behind the lines or even in enemy home territory. Also conducts active espionage and counter-terrorist operations.

Blazer: The elite FMF special warfare tactical units or soldiers assigned to them. Units consist of, among others, Combat Air Control, Combat Rescue, Roving Reconnaissance, Insurgency Instruction and Combat Pioneer.

Break: Call word used to indicate the end of one transmission and the beginning of another.

Bro: Pilot shorthand for "broadcast," used to instruct the system to transmit to all units.

Butterfly: An antipersonnel bomblet shaped roughly like a butterfly, with explosives in the body. It creates incapacitating minor wounds, typically to the feet.

CAP: Acronym for Combat air patrol. Aircraft aloft, armed and patrolling for potential threats over a military position.

Charlie: Rearmost unit in an operation, from "Tail-end Charlie."

Citation for Courage: (CfC) Third highest FMF combat decoration. Awarded for "Conspicuous courage under enemy fire."

Citizen's Medal: (CM) Highest FMF combat decoration. Awarded for "Outstanding selfless bravery and personal sacrifice in battle." Usually awarded posthumously.

Dez: Pilot shorthand for "designation."

Dragonbreath: See M-41

Eecee: Pilot shorthand for "electronic countermeasures."

ELINT: Electronic intelligence boat. Command and Control and intelligence gathering spacecraft of the FMF.

Emp: An Electromagnetic pulse weapon.

Envi: Pilot shorthand for "Environment." Refers to the sensory input received through the helmet and cockpit controls.

Fitrep: Fitness report. Necessary approval for promotion or retention.

Flashbang: Stun grenade that generates high-intensity light and loud report, but minimal blast. Casualties are still possible.

FMF: Freehold Military Forces. The unified defense structure of the Freehold of Grainne. Consists of ground, air, orbital, space and support units.

Guardian: UNPF close support vertol, maneuverable, well armored, adequately armed but not as well as the Hatchet.

GUV: General utility vehicle. Carries a six-person infantry team. Can be rigged as an ambulance, gun platform, mortar, missile or other support weapon platform, repair or recovery vehicle or for cargo.

Hatchet: FMF close support vertol, very maneuverable and heavily armed but slower than a Guardian.

HE: High explosive. Standard bomb or shell for area effect or equipment.

Hellstorm: See M-67

IFF: Identification, friend or foe. A transponder that lets intelligence systems determine which aircraft are friendly.

IG: Inspector General. Military office charged with enforcing regulations and eliminating corruption.

M-5: The basic infantry weapon of the FMF. Consists of a 15mm grenade launcher and a 4mm carbine, both fed by unitized ammunition clips. Capacity of fifteen grenades and fifty rounds of 4mm. Computerized sights for low light, infrared, laser designated (for grenades) and adjustable for local gravity and air pressure. Loaded mass 5.2 Kg.

M-41: FMF antibunker and incendiary projector. Fires hypergolic liquid and flammable metal powder. Named the "Dragonbreath."

M-67: FMF combination mine system. Mixes antiarmor and antipersonnel mines to slow an enemy. Named the "Hellstorm."

Mass target: A formation of personnel, as opposed to vehicles or structures.

Mils: The circle is divided into 1000 mils for purposes of orienteering.

Mob: Slang term for a mobile assault unit. The members are colloquially known as "Mobsters."

Mobile Assault: FMF rapid-deployment infantry units, self-contained with light artillery and close air support. Typically deployed as regiments.

Octopus: A sensor-activated mine with spring-loaded "sensacles." Upon being triggered, it launches itself toward the target and detonates when any part of the sensacles make contact.

Overwatch: To hold position and provide cover as another unit advances.

PARSON: Primary Aerial Reconnaissance and Satellite Observation Network. The Freehold Military Forces eye-in-the-sky intelligence gathering system.

Projo: Slang for "projectile."

Retar: Pilot shorthand for "retard," a parachute equipped or finned weapon designed to slow after being dropped.

RGL: Rifle/grenade launcher. See M-5.

Seev: Pilot shorthand for CEV, or combat engineer vehicle. Used to voice designate targets.

Selsee: Pilot shorthand for self-seeking. Used to voice program and/or activate weapons.

Sentinel: UNPF fixed-wing air superiority aircraft.

Special Projects: Laboratory of the FMF Special
  Warfare branch. Manufactures drugs, espionage
  gear and weapons for specialized purposes and
  tests new equipment and captured enemy gear.

Spec War: Acronym for FMF Special Warfare units
  or personnel. Includes Blazers, Black Operations
  and Special Projects.

Tac: Slang term for the tactical environment display
  in an infantry helmet.

Vertol: Vertical take off and landing. An aircraft
  lifted by thrust rather than airfoil effect.
  Typically used for close support and battlefield
  transport and evacuation.

Valorous Service Medal: (VSM) Second highest FMF
  combat decoration. Awarded for "conspicuous
  bravery and risk of self in battle."

Viff: Vector in forward flight. A trick used by vertol
  pilots and drones to maneuver or evade fire by
  using engine thrust at odd angles.

Horology: Freehold of Grainne

revolution: 504.2103 local days, 592.52291 Earth
  days
rotation: 28 hours, 12 minutes, 12.9888 seconds
calendar: 5 weeks per month, 10 months per year,
  4 festival days plus leap year every 5 years, no
  leap year in years divisible by 50

clock: day: 10 divs
div: 2 hours, 49 minutes, 13.2988 seconds Earth,
    100 segs local
seg: 1 minute, 41.5329 seconds Earth, 100 secs
    local
second: 1.0153 seconds Earth

Environmental notes, planet of Grainne

gravity: 1.18 Earth normal
diameter: 13 092.433 km
density: 1.1443 Earth 6320.25 kg/m^3
axial tilt: 20 degrees
orbital distance: 1.50362 AU
orbital eccentricity: 3%
climactic details: 77% ocean
partial pressure O$_2$: 82% Earth normal
barometric pressure at sea level: 73 kPa

DAVID WEBER

<u>The Honor Harrington series:</u> *(cont.)*

Field of Dishonor

Honor goes home to Manticore—and fights for her life on a battlefield she never trained for, in a private war that offers just two choices: death—or a "victory" that can end only in dishonor and the loss of all she loves. . . .

Flag in Exile

Hounded into retirement and disgrace by political enemies, Honor Harrington has retreated to planet Grayson, where powerful men plot to reverse the changes she has brought to their world. And for their plans to succeed, Honor Harrington must die!

Honor Among Enemies

Offered a chance to end her exile and again command a ship, Honor Harrington must use a crew drawn from the dregs of the service to stop pirates who are plundering commerce. Her enemies have chosen the mission carefully, thinking that either she will stop the raiders or they will kill her . . . and either way, her enemies will win. . . .

In Enemy Hands

After being ambushed, Honor finds herself aboard an enemy cruiser, bound for her scheduled execution. But one lesson Honor has never learned is how to give up!

Echoes of Honor

"Brilliant! Brilliant! Brilliant!"—*Anne McCaffrey*

continued 🖘

PRAISE FOR
LOIS McMASTER BUJOLD

What the critics say:

The Warrior's Apprentice: "Now here's a fun romp through the spaceways—not so much a space opera as space ballet.... it has all the 'right stuff.' A lot of thought and thoughtfulness stand behind the all-too-human characters. Enjoy this one, and look forward to the next."   —Dean Lambe, *SF Reviews*

"The pace is breathless, the characterization thoughtful and emotionally powerful, and the author's narrative technique and command of language compelling. Highly recommended."
—*Booklist*

Brothers in Arms: "...she gives it a genuine depth of character, while reveling in the wild turnings of her tale.... Bujold is as audacious as her favorite hero, and as brilliantly (if sneakily) successful."   —*Locus*

"Miles Vorkosigan is such a great character that I'll read anything Lois wants to write about him.... a book to re-read on cold rainy days." —Robert Coulson, *Comic Buyer's Guide*

Borders of Infinity: "Bujold's series hero Miles Vorkosigan may be a lord by birth and an admiral by rank, but a bone disease that has left him hobbled and in frequent pain has sensitized him to the suffering of outcasts in his very hierarchical era.... Playing off Miles's reserve and cleverness, Bujold draws outrageous and outlandish foils to color her high-minded adventures."   —*Publishers Weekly*

Falling Free: "In *Falling Free* Lois McMaster Bujold has written her fourth straight superb novel.... How to break down a talent like Bujold's into analyzable components? Best not to try. Best to say: 'Read, or you will be missing something extraordinary.'"   —Roland Green, *Chicago Sun-Times*

The Vor Game: "The chronicles of Miles Vorkosigan are far too witty to be literary junk food, but they rouse the kind of craving that makes popcorn magically vanish during a double feature."   —Faren Miller, *Locus*

MORE PRAISE FOR
LOIS McMASTER BUJOLD

What the readers say:

"My copy of *Shards of Honor* is falling apart I've reread it so often. . . . I'll read whatever you write. You've certainly proved yourself a grand storyteller."
—Lisa Kolbe, Colorado Springs, CO

"I experience the stories of Miles Vorkosigan as almost viscerally uplifting. . . . But certainly, even the weightiest theme would have less impact than a cinder on snow were it not for a rousing good story, and good story-telling with it. This is the second thing I want to thank you for. . . . I suppose if you boiled down all I've said to its simplest expression, it would be that I immensely enjoy and admire your work. I submit that, as literature, your work raises the overall level of the science fiction genre, and spiritually, your work cannot avoid positively influencing all who read it."
—Glen Stonebraker, Gaithersburg, MD

" 'The Mountains of Mourning' [in *Borders of Infinity*] was one of the best-crafted, and simply best, works I'd ever read. When I finished it, I immediately turned back to the beginning and read it again, and I can't remember the last time I did that."
—Betsy Bizot, Lisle, IL

"I can only hope that you will continue to write, so that I can continue to read (and of course buy) your books, for they make me laugh and cry and think . . . rare indeed."
—Steven Knott, Major, USAF

What Do *You* Say?

DAVID DRAKE RULES!

Hammer's Slammers:

The Tank Lords	87794-1 ◆ $6.99	☐
Caught in the Crossfire	87882-4 ◆ $6.99	☐
The Butcher's Bill	57773-5 ◆ $6.99	☐
The Sharp End	87632-5 ◆ $7.99	☐
Cross the Stars	57821-9 ◆ $6.99	☐
Paying the Piper (HC)	7434-3547-8 ◆$24.00	☐

RCN series:

With the Lightnings	57818-9 ◆ $6.99	☐
Lt. Leary, Commanding (HC)	57875-8 ◆$24.00	☐
Lt. Leary, Commanding (PB)	31992-2 ◆ $7.99	☐

The Belisarius series with Eric Flint:

An Oblique Approach	87865-4 ◆ $6.99	☐
In the Heart of Darkness	87885-9 ◆ $6.99	☐
Destiny's Shield	57872-3 ◆ $6.99	☐
Fortune's Stroke (HC)	57871-5 ◆$24.00	☐
The Tide of Victory (HC)	31996-5 ◆$22.00	☐
The Tide of Victory (PB)	7434-3565-6 ◆ $7.99	☐

The General series with S.M. Stirling:

The Forge	72037-6 ◆ $5.99	☐
The Chosen	87724-0 ◆ $6.99	☐
The Reformer	57860-X ◆ $6.99	☐
The Tyrant	0-7434-7150-4 ◆ $7.99	☐

Independent Novels and Collections:

The Dragon Lord (fantasy)	87890-5 ◆ $6.99	☐
Birds of Prey	57790-5 ◆ $6.99	☐